BOOKBURNERS

BOOK BURNERS

SEASON 1

CREATED BY
MAX GLADSTONE

WRITTEN BY
**MAX GLADSTONE MARGARET DUNLAP
MUR LAFFERTY BRIAN FRANCIS SLATTERY**

ILLUSTRATED BY MARK WEAVER AND JEFFREY VEREGGE

SAGA PRESS

LONDON SYDNEY **NEW YORK** TORONTO NEW DELHI

SERIAL
BOX

SAGA PRESS

AN IMPRINT OF SIMON & SCHUSTER, INC.

1230 AVENUE OF THE AMERICAS, NEW YORK, NEW YORK 10020

SAGA PRESS and colophon are trademarks of Simon & Schuster, Inc.
For information about special discounts for bulk purchases, please contact Simon & Schuster Special Sales at 1-866-506-1949 or business@simonandschuster.com.
The Simon & Schuster Speakers Bureau can bring authors to your live event. For more information or to book an event, contact the Simon & Schuster Speakers Bureau at 1-866-248-3049 or visit our website at www.simonspeakers.com.
Also available in a Saga Press paperback edition
The text for this book was set in ITC Berkeley Oldstyle.
The illustrations for this book were rendered digitally.
Manufactured in the United States of America
First Saga Press hardcover edition January 2017
2 4 6 8 10 9 7 5 3 1
ISBN 978-1-4814-8557-9 (hardcover)
ISBN 978-1-4814-8556-2 (paperback)

TO MY PARENTS, FOR EVERYTHING
—*MARGARET*

TO MY FAMILY, FOR PUTTING UP WITH ALL OF IT
—*BRIAN*

TO MY SISTER, SHELLEY THORNTON
—*MUR*

TO LIBRARIANS EVERYWHERE. WITH APOLOGIES.
—*MAX*

CONTENTS

EPISODE
1

BADGE, BOOK, AND CANDLE

MAX GLADSTONE

1.

Sal Brooks would have described herself in a police report as early thirties, female, brown hair, five nine, exhausted, borderline breakdown case, shaking hands, haunted eyes. Then she'd have deleted everything after "nine" and continued with the details of the incident. In this case: *Forensic analysis of the museum theft yielded an Astoria address. Arriving on the scene with warrant in hand, Detective Collins and I were fired upon from the window by a white male, late forties. After a brief exchange of fire, Detective Collins forced the door. Behind the door—*

Sal set her badge and gun on her bureau and gripped the first two fingers of her left hand. Her stomach ran a floor routine even the Russian judge would give full marks.

She'd seen blood before, and bodies. The severed fingers in the ashtray on the coffee table in Astoria that afternoon . . . those were worse.

They'd yield prints, at least. Which would not help her sleep tonight.

Her cell phone rang. Perry. She didn't pick up. The ringing

stopped before the call forwarded to voice mail, then started again. Still him.

"Perry, this isn't a good time" was what she started to say, but she didn't get halfway through her brother's name before Hurricane Perry struck shore.

"Sal, thank you, thank you, thank you for picking up. I'm so glad, it's wonderful to hear your voice, I missed you, how're things, how long has it been, anyway, can I come over, like, now?"

"It's been a month." She thumbed a gap in her blinds. The sidewalk under her window was bare, and the street almost empty. Red Toyota pickup, Honda Civic, garbage, two young guys staggering home after drinking off a Thursday night. Thank God. The last time she'd heard Perry talk like this, he was on the run from some crazy scenester drama and hadn't waited for her permission to come over, just called her from the sidewalk in the rain and looked up, dripping, with that hangdog John Cusack look she knew he practiced in the mirror. "Since the last time you were in trouble."

"It's nothing big, Sal, I promise, nothing you should worry about, just, you know, Internet stuff, and then I started arguing with my roommates and you know people can get crazy sometimes, like, crazy. It's not the same thing as last month, I swear, I just need a place to be, you know. I'd get a hotel if I could." If he had money for a hotel.

She peeked out her corner window just to be sure. He wasn't down there, either. "I've had a very long day, Perry."

"I know, I know, every day's a long day for you, I'm so sorry, but I just kind of need a place to rest for a little while, and I *did* apologize for last month, and I sent you flowers."

"David still isn't returning my calls."

"You deserve better than a guy like that, a guy who doesn't understand the importance of family."

"David has a huge family. He's a good guy. He just doesn't like being kicked out of bed because my kid brother's locked himself out of his apartment. That was a good thing, emphasis on the 'was.' And the flowers you sent were fake."

"Better that way; they don't die, right? And it wasn't just that I locked myself out. And anyway, I'm improving, I mean, you don't have anyone over now. Do you?"

Her eyes narrowed. She glanced out each window again. "Where are you?"

"What do you mean?"

She realized she could hear his voice twice: once through the phone, and once from the hall.

Sal marched from her bedroom past kitchen and living room to the door. She unbolted the bolt, unchained the chain, and pulled the door open.

Perry was less wet than she'd last seen him, at least. One hand pressed an oversized Star Trek phone to his ear. He wore a dirty tan trench coat, open, over a ratty black T-shirt with three pixelated hearts on the front and a fourth half-full, and jeans torn at the knee—from his nervous habit of clawing them while he worked on his computer, rather than from wear. His other hand held a large rectangular parcel wrapped in more T-shirts and duct tape, which he waved at her, then stuck under his arm, and waved again with an empty hand.

He deployed John Cusack version 1.2.

She clicked her phone shut.

He started warming up John Cusack version 1.7.

She sighed, and smiled, and hugged him. "Come in, doofus."

He set up in the living room, and she put water in the kettle. "Do I want to know why you're here?"

"Thank you so, so, so much." He set the parcel on her living room table and undid the duct tape. "It's not dangerous, I mean, I'd tell you if it were, you know, but I got into a fight with the roomies over a project we're working on together, sort of, and I want to make sure I'm right before I go home. Just need some time to work on this thing myself. Bunch of poseurs. Don't know Altaic from Aramaic." He unwrapped the T-shirts layer by layer, each silk-screened video game reference worse than the last.

"I get that one," she said. "It's the, what, the game with the dysentery. Why all the T-shirts?"

"Sal, do you have any idea how old this thing is?" He folded a Mario shirt back to reveal a thick tome bound in pale leather, with gold wire on the spine. The pages' ragged edges were dyed blood red. Sal remembered severed fingers in an Astoria ashtray, and her stomach made a second pass at the floor routine.

"No?"

"Old, and I mean *old*. I shouldn't be handling it without gloves."

The kettle cried, and Sal followed its protest to the kitchen. "You should get new roommates. You fight more with those guys than I ever have with an ex. Even Jeremy." She returned with two mugs of coffee.

"It's just professional differences, I mean, we're working on big problems, borderline intractable, arguments get heated. There are different strategies about how to approach the artifact. Aiden, you know, roommate Aiden with the crush on you, he wants to scan the whole thing for word frequency analysis, which just seems patently silly, the codex form factor suggests it's supposed to be read, like by people, and anyway, Aiden's security protocols are hella lax, which matters when you're under surveillance." He took a sip, made a face. "Is this instant?"

"Wait. Surveillance?"

"Todd says it's the Bookburners, that's why they wanted the book out of the house, which is just so dumb—if the Bookburners were after me, how would I have even made it here?"

He set his hand on the book's cover. Sal hadn't noticed before how the leather was discolored: Most of it matched Perry's skin, but a crimson bloom spread beneath his fingers. She heard a sound she couldn't name: a footfall, maybe, or a whisper, very soft. Goose bumps chased goose bumps up her arms.

"Perry, who are the Bookburners? Do you think someone's following you?"

"I thought you didn't want to know."

She leaned over the couch, over his shoulder, and checked through the blinds. Street still bare. Red Toyota pickup. Honda Civic. Garbage. E-Z Carpet Cleaner van.

"Please, Sal. They would have nabbed me on the way. They did not. Ergo, I wasn't followed."

"What the hell is going on?"

Someone knocked on her door.

"Shit," Perry said.

"Jesus Christ, Perry." She grabbed her phone off the living room table. "Who is that?"

"Aiden. Probably."

"Mr. Brooks?" The man on the other side of the door was unquestionably not Aiden—too old, too sure, too calm. An accent Sal couldn't place twined through his words. "Mr. Brooks, we're not here to hurt you. We want to talk."

"Shit," Perry repeated, for emphasis.

Sal ran to her bedroom and returned with her gun. "Who are you?"

"I'm looking for Mr. Brooks. I know he's in there."

"If he is, I doubt he'd want to see you."

"I must talk with him."

"Sir, I'm a police officer, and I'm armed. Please step away from the door."

"Has he opened the book?"

"What?" She looked into the living room. Perry was standing now, holding the book, fingers clenched around the cover like she'd seen men at bay clutch the handles of knives. "Sir, please leave. I'm calling nine-one-one now." She pressed the autodial. The line clicked.

"Stop him from opening the book," the man said. "Please. If he means anything to you, stop him."

"Hello. This is Detective Sally Brooks," and she rattled off her badge number and address. "I have a man outside my apartment who is refusing to leave—"

Something heavy struck the door. Doorjamb timbers splintered. Sally stumbled back, dropped the phone, both hands on the pistol. She took aim.

The door burst free of the jamb and struck the wall. A human wind blew through.

Later, Sal remembered slivers: a stinging blow to her wrist, her gun knocked back against the wall. A woman's face—Chinese, she thought. Bob haircut. Her knee slammed into Sal's solar plexus, and she fell, gasping, to the splinter-strewn carpet. The woman turned, in slow motion almost, to the living room, where Perry stood.

He held the open book.

His eyes wept tears of blood, and his smile bared sharp teeth.

He spoke a word that was too big for her mind. She heard the woman roar and glass break. Then darkness closed around her like a mouth.

Summer sun baked her skin. Sal lay, fourteen years old, on a raft atop the pond out back of her grandparents' Carolina homestead, while Perry read aloud on shore. Her hand trailed into the still water. The water *was* still, but moving, too; the raft rocked her head back and forth, and her body wasn't fourteen anymore, and dammit she was dreaming, wasn't she?

If she strained, she could hear voices on the other side of the dream.

"You lost him." A man's voice, lilting, close—a different voice from before. "How did that happen?"

"He opened the book, is how." A woman's voice. "Do you need a picture?"

"I have crayons in the truck if you'd like to draw one."

"He tried to hit me," she replied. "Got her instead. I pulled her out, but he made the window before I could catch him."

"So the boy's off grid with a rider in his head, in a city of eight million people. *Wonderful*, I think we'll call that. A-double-plus effort."

Sirens.

"Christ," the man said, "they answer calls quickly here. Come on. Is she—"

"Fine."

"Are you sure?"

Don't open your eyes when lying on your back. Bad for them. You'll see too much of the sun.

She forced them open. The man kneeling over her was red haired and beautiful. "Sorry. Have to run. Have a nice rest. You'll feel better in the morning."

He pulled away, and the ceiling grew new shadows, which fell to crush her again.

2.

al, in the department clinic, with whatever she had to hand, was how the Clue solution would read if someone didn't start making sense soon. She glared over the doctor's head at Collins, her partner, who leaned against the wall, arms crossed, looking like he'd rather be anywhere but here, carrying anything but the news he carried. Her head swam. "I've told you four times," she said. "My brother came to my apartment. Three people followed him. I gave you their descriptions. They broke down my door. There was a fight, and I woke up when the officers arrived. It's not that complicated a story."

"You're sure you saw your brother?"

"Of course I'm sure. It was Perry. He had some kind of fight with his roommates."

"Breathe," the doctor said.

She breathed. The stethoscope chilled her skin. "So what's the problem?"

Collins shifted, but if he'd been trying to get comfortable, his expression suggested that he'd failed. "Who says there's a problem?"

"Come on, Collins."

"Here." He passed her a tablet. "Hit play."

Security camera footage rendered her apartment building hallway in ghoulish greens and whites. She saw herself open her door and peer out into the hall, smile, step back, swing the door wide, and close it again. "This is the wrong footage."

"It's not, though. Check the time stamp."

"Perry's not there."

Collins lowered his chin toward his chest. It didn't touch due to the extra chin in the way. "Scratch one theory."

"You thought I was seeing things."

"Who knows? We got your testimony; we got a living room with broken glass and two cups of instant coffee; we got a tape that doesn't match your story and falls apart ten minutes later."

"Stare up at the ceiling," the doctor said, "just with your eyes. Keep them wide, please."

The doctor's flashlight burned the world. Sal forced herself not to blink. "So you don't have the intruders, either."

"Tape falls apart, like I said."

"Shit."

"Sal, come on. Chinese woman, white guy with red hair, unnamed third guy with—quote—old, accented—unquote—voice, doesn't give us a lot to go on."

"Irish," she said. "The white guy had an Irish accent."

"Great, Sal. In New York, that sure narrows it down."

"Someone must have doctored the tapes."

"First responders pulled them. If someone messed with the footage, they did it fast."

The doctor released her eyelid, and she blinked pink blood-webbed blotches from her vision. "The other eye, please." And again the world was light.

"They planned this," Sal said. "Whoever they were. It couldn't have been random. They were after Perry. They hacked into building security."

"Which would make sense—I mean, it'd be possible, if paranoid—except those cameras don't talk to the Internet. They're not even digital. There's an actual, honest-to-God tape system in the building basement, looks like it was installed back when I was hunting *Playboys* under my big brother's mattress."

"Gross, Collins."

"There was a rat nest on top of the cabinet. Good thing we still have a VCR. Nobody got to that tape before our boys did, trust me. And you should find a new landlord. That building's a dump."

"My brother's out there. Somewhere. I saw him."

The doctor finished with the flashlight and stepped back. "She's good to go. If anything's wrong, I can't see it." Sal squeezed both her eyes shut until the pink went away.

"Thanks, Doc. Can you give us a minute?"

When the door closed and left them alone, Collins sank into the doctor's chair with a long hiss, as if he was under such pressure he had to let out steam to bend. He looked at the back of his knuckles rather than at her.

"You know none of this makes sense," he said.

"I know what I saw."

"And the more you say that, the weirder it sounds. Nothing on the cameras. I mean, nothing. No blood."

"What, do people think I just snapped, imagined my brother being kidnapped, beat myself up, broke my own damn living room window?"

"You were upset when you left yesterday."

"Of course I was upset. We found fingers in an ashtray! I freaked out, but that doesn't mean I'm nuts."

"We went to your brother's apartment. His roommates say they saw him this morning."

"Did you see him?" she asked. Collins shook his head. "Then they're lying. Or he escaped. Either way, he's into something big. He needs help."

"We told the boys to call us when he shows up again. For now, you should take a day or two, calm down, rest."

"And if I don't?"

He shifted his weight back on the chair, which creaked. "The lieutenant asked me to tell you all this, so it doesn't have to get formal."

"I have to find my brother."

"Sal—"

She pushed herself off the table and grabbed her jacket from the hook by the door. "If you won't do it, someone has to."

"I'll pretend I didn't hear that," he said. "Stay out of trouble, okay?"

She laughed, opened the door, and walked fast until she hit the street.

Theories were for people with more patience than Sal Brooks, but the Brooklyn-bound Q train stopped over the Manhattan Bridge, so she had time to make up a few. "I'm crazy," the nuclear option, didn't compel. The doctor said she was fine, physically. People snapped all the time, zero to nuts in sixty seconds, but this kind of snap didn't match her experience. If she were cracking, her story would make more sense, or less, or both. She'd met people on this very train who told her with overwhelming conviction that they were the product of genetic experimentation by the United States government using alien DNA, and they'd built a prototype trans-port beam to take them home, which they'd show her if she visited the compound in Jersey they shared with their four lovers chosen to embody the classical Chinese elements. As if she'd trust some-one who asked her to go to Jersey.

So far she wasn't ranting about conspiracies or screaming obsceni-ties at passersby. Count crazy out, for now, though crazy people probably did that too. Once you reject the possibility you're mad, anything you do, no matter how strange, must be sane. Keep going in that direction and you're one step away from the creep with the chopped-off index fingers in his ashtray.

The train crossed the river.

But assume you're not crazy, she thought. *Perry didn't come to you because of an argument with his roommates; he didn't drop by to say hello. He was afraid. Maybe he thought they wouldn't follow him into someone else's apartment. Or maybe he knew he could escape somehow, if he just had time to—*

Read that book. Which made no sense.

She rose out of the subway onto a long, wide Brooklyn street with three-story brick houses on both sides, blank dark windows, Italian bakery, convenience store. Newly opened coffee shops indicated these blocks were a hairsbreadth from hip. When the neighborhood crossed over, Perry and his friends would have to move. Providing, of course, whatever mudhole they'd stumbled into didn't swallow them first.

Perry's roommates knew *something.* If they had seen him this morning, they could tell her how he looked, where he said he was going when he left. If not, they had lied to cops, which gave her leverage.

Not that she'd need much with Aiden and Todd. The boys scared easy.

She took a quick turn around the block. Dead for ten o'clock in the morning, most of the locals at work somewhere else. Cold November air tossed a *Sun* front page down the sidewalk, and Sal shouldered deeper into her jacket. She walked past the boys' townhouse, which was the only one on the block still decorated for Halloween. A big, rain-soaked, felt-and-wire spider clung crookedly outside Perry's window.

Parked cars lined the street, mostly foreign made. One finned pink Cadillac belonged in a Mary Kay reward brochure or a museum. And an E-Z Carpet Cleaner van.

Every instinct in her screamed, *Keep walking.* Call backup at least. Only idiots and martyrs throw themselves into situations they don't understand without cavalry waiting.

She didn't know it was the same van. She was already on shaky ground back at the office. And the people who'd broken into her house seemed to have no personal feelings about their intrusion. If she remembered correctly the conversation she'd overheard, they even thought they had saved her from—*something.*

Still, though.

If Sal really wanted to rule out any chance she was crazy, she shouldn't have walked straight to the van, drawn her gun, thrown open the rear doors, and told the two monitor-lit figures inside, "Hands where I can see them."

The Chinese woman rolled her eyes and then raised her hands to the level of her shoulders. "I told you we should have switched vans."

The redhead backed away from the keyboard and swiveled in his chair. "She was out cold. How was I supposed to know—"

"Where the hell is my brother?"

"That's an interesting philosophical question, really," the guy said. Nice accent. That was the concussion talking. Focus.

The Chinese woman shifted forward in her chair.

"Don't move!" Sal shouted.

"Excuse me, Detective Brooks," said a voice from the sidewalk behind her—a man's, deep, older, and studiously calm. The voice from the door. Sal drew back from the van and turned to include him in her field of vision. "I think there's been a misunderstanding."

He was tall, Hispanic, and wore a priest's black shirt and collar. He held a tray with three coffees in one hand, but the other was raised, palm up, between blessing and surrender.

"Who are you? What the hell is going on here?"

"I'm Father Arturo Menchú"—accent on the second syllable— "and as for your other question: I can explain, if you'll let me."

They stood on the sidewalk beside the van. Menchú had wanted to talk inside, but Sal gave him a what-kind-of-idiot-do-you-take-me-for look, which ended that line of conversation fast. Red looked uncomfortable out in the open—he kept shifting from foot to foot and glancing over his shoulder, hands deep in his pockets. The woman just watched, arms crossed. A lot of lean muscle hid beneath her black jacket. Sal liked her. After a confusing day, straightforward hostility felt refreshing.

"You're priests," Sal said, skeptical.

The woman laughed, once.

"I'm a priest," Menchú said. "Grace, of course, is not. Liam's a lay brother."

"Why did you break into my apartment last night?" She considered adding "how," in reference to everything: the broken door, the book, the corrupted tape. Decided against it. One problem at a time.

Menchú set the tray of coffees atop the van. "Your brother's in possession of a rare manuscript that does not belong to him. It used to belong to the people we work for. It was stolen seventy years ago. Turns out the volume spent the last seven decades in the Metropolitan Museum's sealed collection. Two weeks ago, someone broke into that collection and made off with a number of books, including this one."

"You're saying Perry was part of the museum heist." She remembered Astoria, yesterday: severed fingers and an ashtray full of blood. White male, mid-forties. Shots fired. Hope of recovering—Christ—fingerprints. "No way."

"Not directly. Your brother and his friends were one of many parties looking to buy the stolen texts." Father Menchú kept his voice calm, maintained eye contact, presented himself to her at an angle. He was good at seeming nonthreatening; part of the job, Sal guessed. Her attention drifted back to Grace, who grinned, baring teeth. "There were others, willing to pay more. Your brother stole the book from the original thief, and left a copy in its place. We reached out to your brother, hoping to resolve the issue without violence, but he ran to you. And then he ran from you. The book is valuable, if only to a collector, and the people he stole it from don't like to lose. We can keep him safe, if he works with us."

The fingers had been wedged into the gaps in the ashtray meant to hold cigarettes. Their nails pointed out: sunrays of flesh and bone.

"He should go to the police."

"We are the police," Menchú said.

"Bullshit."

"We're special consultants to the police department on this matter. If you'll permit me." He reached, slowly, for his breast pocket. She nodded. From within he produced a business card with a cell phone number Sal recognized. "This is Chief Gallagher's card. She'll confirm my story. We were overzealous last night, for which I offer my apologies. Perry is in great danger."

And there it was, beneath the professional polish, beneath the professional assurance Sal had heard too many times from priests and lawyers—Menchú cared.

"I'm sorry," he continued. "I know this has been a huge shock. I know you're worried about your brother. So are we. We need to find him."

"One man," Liam said, "off the grid, in a city like this. Paying with cash. No problem. Anyone else you'd like me to find while I'm at it? Elvis? Amelia Earhart?"

Father Menchú ignored him. "It's possible his friends know something. But they're scared. They won't talk to anyone they don't know."

"We're wasting time," Grace said. "We should just knock down the door."

Liam nodded. "Great idea. Worked so well last night."

There were a thousand procedural reasons Sal should leave. But Perry was in danger, and if these people had the chief's blessing, she could help them without breaking orders. Technically. "I can help."

"No," Menchú said. "I'm sorry. We can't involve you."

"I'm involved already. This is my brother we're talking about. Every second counts. If you go in there without me, you'll learn less than the cops did this morning."

"We know what we're doing."

"So do I."

Menchú's eyes were deep and sad.

Liam cleared his throat. "Let her in, Father. We're shorthanded, anyway."

The priest sighed. "Very well."

"One question," Sal said as she climbed into the van. "You said you're consultants. Where from?"

The old man raised one finger to his collar. "Isn't it obvious?"

3.

esus Christ," Sal said when Liam handed her the bug. It was barely visible against the cosmetic tape. When she set it against her skin, she didn't feel the slightest chill of metal. "This is good gear."

"My specialty. And this one." Liam offered her a thin silver cross on a chain.

"What's this for?"

"Stuff," he said. "Just put it on, okay?"

"I don't believe in God."

"He believes in you." He laughed as if he'd made a joke. "Think of it as a temporary deputization."

Grace checked her watch. "We could have been inside twenty minutes ago."

"Talk normally," Liam said. "And we'll hear. If there's trouble, use the cross."

"Panic button?"

"More like a mood ring, only in reverse. If you see something strange, try touching it with the cross. There are"—he wiggled his fingers—"circuits and stuff."

"You're joking."

"Oh ye of little faith."

"Thanks," she said, and left the van.

A skull knocker stared out at Sal from the boys' front door, a half inch left of center. Drill holes covered with duct tape pocked the door to either side of the knocker—they'd tried to screw the knocker in three times without measuring the door's actual midpoint, and after the third attempt agreed to celebrate their success.

The mailman had given up on the overstuffed mailbox, its contents congealed by rain into a sodden block of pulp and ink. Layers of junk mail formed a newsprint marsh on the front step, sporting an impressive array of greenish molds.

Sal stared into the skull's glass-chip eyes, squeezed her own eyes closed, opened them again, and reached for the hinged lower jaw.

Before she could touch it, the door jerked open to reveal Aiden, tall and gangly, wearing pajama bottoms and a dirty flannel shirt. He stopped the door with his foot, but he was too skinny to quite fill the small gap. "Sal, this is a really bad time."

She shoved the door. He stumbled back, upsetting a pile of mud-caked boots, and she pushed through into the narrow musty hall. The door slammed behind her. "Where's Perry? What the hell have you gotten him into?"

"Perry's fine, Sal. Come on. This is, like, illegal search or whatever. I know my rights."

"I don't give a shit about the weed you have in your desk, Aiden. Perry's in trouble. True or false?"

"Perry's, um . . ." Aiden spread his arms to span the hall and block her path, between a rack of mud-splattered coats and a cross-stitch Perry'd made of Darth Vader's mask. "Perry's fine. We're fine. We had, a, you know, small disagreement last night, but we've taken care of everything. Maybe we could go out for coffee and talk about it?"

"Let's talk here. Unless there's something you're trying to hide."

"Hide? No, of course not. What would we try to hide from you?"

She jerked forward as if to duck under his left arm; when he braced to grab her, she jagged right, and he fell into the coats while she swept past into the living room, a sea of pizza boxes and USB cables. A rust-dotted Ren-faire sword hung on the wall. Something green bubbled in a beaker on a Bunsen burner atop a claw-foot table she'd rescued from curbside recycling for them. Stairs rose from the mess to the second floor, where the boys slept, when they slept at all. Todd—black, older than Perry and Aiden, though he didn't act it—sat at the couch flanked by two monitors, with a heavy leather-bound book open on a stand on the coffee table. He looked up and blinked at Sal through goggles. Aiden's coat-muffled cursing from the hall mixed with music from upstairs, or something like music: a stream of bleeps and blips she remembered from sitting cross-legged on the carpet, eight years old, playing Nintendo.

"Sally! Great to see you. Didn't expect you to drop by. Perry didn't say anything." The prescription goggles warped Todd's eyes to silver-dollar size. "But this is a really bad time."

"Aiden said. The bad time wouldn't happen to have anything to do with my brother's disappearance, would it? Or the museum theft?"

Todd let go of the book, too fast. His blue latex gloves left a trace of powder on the brown leather, which was embossed with a vine-and-knot pattern. Or were those vines after all? "I really don't know what you're talking about, Sal. Like we told the cops, Perry came by this morning. He was fine. He looked scared, but that's it." He swallowed hard. "Theft, though? You think Perry was mixed up in something—"

"I haven't seen that book around here before, Todd."

"Look." He raised his hands, fingers spread. "Perry's the one who gets the books. We analyze, translate. Upload. It's all aboveboard, as far as I know. Maybe Perry got himself in deep with the wrong people, but I don't know who or why."

"You just read the books."

"That's it," he said.

"So if I came back here with a warrant, what would I find?"

"You don't want to do that, Sal. I mean, really."

"I want to know where my brother is."

"He doesn't want to see you."

"He came to my house last night, terrified. Nothing's changed between now and then."

Behind her, in the hall, Aiden recovered.

"Sal." Sweat ran down Todd's temple to his cheek. "Maybe we can talk this over somewhere outside?" His eyes jerked up and left.

She turned. Three bedroom doors upstairs—one for Aiden, one for Todd, one for Perry. Perry's, the one with the Japanese cartoon scroll, was slightly ajar. "That sounds like a good idea," she said, then ran up the stairs and burst through the door into Perry's room.

Monitors illuminated the unmade bed, the bare bookshelves, the piled clothing. There should have been sunlight, but the Halloween-store spider hanging outside Perry's window blocked the sun.

And Perry himself sat in ripped jeans and bloodstained shirt, curled like a shrimp over his keyboard, unblinking eyes inches from his central monitor. Barefoot. Hair tousled. One day's growth of beard. Jaw muscles snaked, relaxed, snaked again as he rocked in his chair, typing.

"Perry!"

Except.

Detective Brooks, a lawyer might ask someday, *how did you know the person sitting in the chair was not your brother?*

And she'd open her mouth before the courtroom, but no words would come out. An audience would stare at her. The judge would drum her fingers. The lawyer would lean forward. *Any time, Detective Brooks.*

The clothes were Perry's, the body language ditto.

But still, when she said, "Perry?" the second time, her voice was uncertain.

He stopped typing, uncurled himself vertebra by vertebra from the keyboard, and turned to her. His eyes focused on the wall behind her. He smiled woodenly. "Sal. Sister. I'm sorry you had to come here."

"Perry." She'd imagined hugging him when she saw him again, imagined hitting him too. Neither seemed possible now. "Perry, you're here." As if saying that would make it true.

"I am. And you should go, Sal." What a reasonable suggestion. "I have work to finish, if you don't mind."

She didn't. But her not minding was strange. Wasn't it? "Perry, what happened last night?"

"Nothing," he said. "I was pushed, you see. The Bookburners chased me, and I took help where I could find it. I'm perfectly fine. Better than I've been in a long, long while. You're a . . . police officer," he said, as if he'd just looked the fact up in a fine-print list. His words didn't match the movements of his mouth. She focused through the fear—and why fear? He was her brother.

But maybe he wasn't, right now.

His mouth was not moving in time with his words, because

the words he spoke were not English, even though that was the language she heard. "It must feel like this when you solve a case. When the whole world makes sense at once. I've been working on a puzzle for a long time, and I just needed the right push."

He reached for her.

There seemed to be a great deal of space between them all of a sudden, but his arm grew longer to bridge the gap. A finger of ice pressed against her skin above her heart, so cold it burned. As the hand approached, it no longer looked like a hand at all, not like a hand of flesh. Torn corrugated tin twisted around paper-and-woven-plastic bones, forming fingers. Black oil dripped from ragged joints. The arm was a length of rebar wound with trash bags and shredded cloth. Bottle-glass eyes reflected the monitors' blue glow. Thin lips parted to reveal metal teeth, wet with more oil.

But some traitor impulse still insisted this was Perry, her brother, there was no reason to pull back from him, there was no reason to run, she should let this thing touch her, that the oil on its metal skin was not oil in fact but a whisper, a voice that might help her if it only got inside—

The cold fire against her chest was real. Her skin seared, froze, cracked. She followed the pain back to her body and retreated, unsteady, as if her legs belonged to someone else. She staggered out into the hall. The arm stretched toward her, impossibly long.

She slammed the door shut on the thing's hand.

The Perry-thing didn't seem to care. It kicked the door open. Mangled fingers clicked back into place. Its smile split as it widened. It didn't need a face anymore. Just teeth.

From the bedroom she heard a window shatter.

Bottle-glass eyes widened. A black blur knocked the thing that was not her brother into the wall. Sal blinked, and the blur resolved into Grace. Slivers of window glinted from the insteps of her boots. She raised one of Perry's monitors overhead and slammed it into the fallen creature's face.

Sally thought, *Help.* Her hand went to her shoulder holster, but Grace and the creature were too close, moving too fast. It threw Grace back, wriggled to its feet without concern for any principles of anatomy, and ran at her. Grace jumped back onto the bed, out of reach, dodged a tin claw, then pounced onto the creature before it could recover, toppled it to the ground, and struck it in the face four times with her forehead. A ceramic plate on the thing's face broke—Grace clawed inside it for something Sal couldn't see.

"Take it easy! That's my brother!"

"It's not," Grace said. "It never was." The creature threw her into the desk. Grace roared, dodged left; a claw shattered one of the remaining monitors. Grace grabbed the broken flat-panel from the floor and hit the arm, which snapped.

"Grace, get back! Give me a shot."

"I have this. You worry about the guys downstairs."

"What?"

"Go!"

She went. Behind her more screaming, more broken glass. Downstairs, Todd sat in front of the book. His blue-gloved hands stroked its paper. He looked up and over at her.

"Todd, Jesus Christ, there's something up there."

But his goggle-swollen eyes were black from pupil out to edge. He turned a page of his book.

The sword on the wall was missing.

Footsteps in the hall beside her. Sal ducked back onto the staircase. The sword rang off the wall—no edge on that blade, which made it marginally less dangerous, but a four-foot-long steel bar would break her bones just fine. The sword tore a deep gouge in wallpaper and drywall and fell from Aiden's hand. Before he could recover, Sal kicked the back of his knee, hit him a few times in the face, and he fell.

Todd still sat, watching her, turning pages.

Like Perry last night, staring at her as if from the bottom of a deep well.

A heavy weight struck the front door, and the latch groaned. A man swore—Liam's voice—and Aiden's body began to move, more like a marionette than a person, a structure manipulated by contracting individual muscles.

"Todd, close the book."

He blinked, slowly.

She reached for the cover, thought better of touching the leather with her bare hands, and tried with the sword instead. When its tip touched, an electric shock seized her. The apartment squeezed around her like a fist, and again the cold fire flared against her breastbone. She opened her eyes—she'd fallen back onto the stairs, and Aiden was crawling toward her. She kicked him back and pushed herself upright. Unclenched her hand from the sword.

Crashing sounds from upstairs—a cry of pain, a frustrated roar.

If there's trouble, use the cross. . . . Like a mood ring, only in reverse.

Dammit. None of this made sense. But—connections—the cross had burned her free of the Perry-thing's influence. It hurt her, and she followed that pain back to her own mind. Maybe it could protect her from the book.

She undid her top shirt button. The cross lay heavy against her skin, as if stuck by magnets. She pried it free; it left a red welt. *Think about that later. Think about all this later. Just do.* The closer she brought the cross to the book, the heavier it seemed. Her arm shook.

What the hell were all those gym hours good for, if not for this?

She hooked the book's cover with the cross and swung it closed.

Sometimes in the winter, after twenty minutes' walk down long avenues against a vicious wind, she'd take shelter in a subway stop and feel her body expand without anything to fight against. She felt like that now. Silence unfurled. The closed book vibrated like a plucked string. The cross had lost its sheen—all tarnished save where her fingers touched the silver.

Aiden lay still, breathing heavy. Todd collapsed, trembling, to the sofa.

She shook him by his shoulders. Pinched him. Struck him across the face. Tried the cross. The tarnished bit yielded no reaction. When she touched the part that was still shiny to his cheek, she heard a hiss. His eyes snapped open, and he screamed at a higher pitch than she'd thought his voice could make.

"Todd. Dammit, Todd, are you okay?"

"Sally," he said. "Sorry."

"What the hell's going on? Where's Perry? What was that thing?"

"Came this morning. Got into our heads. Left the dummy in his room, and the book—the pages talked to us. Told us what to do."

"It's done. I closed the book."

"It got inside." He touched his chest. "Still there. Whispers."

"Where's Perry? The real Perry?"

"Storage." He coughed. "Took the other books, told us to stay here, distract people. He's—"

Black tendrils wormed across Todd's eyes, through sclera and iris toward the pupil. Cords of muscle stood out on his throat.

"Shit." She tried the cross again, but he didn't react. Covered in tarnish. She looked around, unsure. Maybe something here could help. But the house was a mess, except for the claw-foot table where the burner was no longer burning. She heard a hiss and smelled—

The door burst open. She was already halfway down the hall, pulling Todd by the collar of his shirt. Dude weighed like a billion pounds, not to mention Aiden, who was at least out too cold to fight. Her back hurt like hell, and her legs were rubber, were jelly, were really fucking tired. Liam stood in the door, blinking like an idiot. "Gas!" she shouted, and saw him wince—earpiece, linked to her mic. "Help me!"

He ran up the hall and grabbed Aiden. They left a wet trail through pulped newspapers and fallen leaves. Sal looked back and saw Grace slip out Perry's bedroom window to the fire escape. She made it to the neighboring building before a hammer of air struck Sal in the chest and she fell.

Fire painted Liam's face orange and green. Sirens wailed, too close for comfort. Grace dropped from fire escape to sidewalk. Sal stood; Aiden and Todd sprawled, unconscious but breathing, at her feet. "We have to get out of here," Liam said.

Understatement of the millennium, candidate number one. And yet.

"What the hell was that?" She was shouting again, and she didn't care. "Any of that? No single piece of anything that just happened makes sense."

"Unless you want to be an accessory to arson," Grace said, "can we talk about this later?"

"Why am I an accessory to anything? I went in to help my brother and his friends. Now their house is on fire, they're I don't even know what—"

"Unconscious," Liam supplied.

"Hypnotized, or something!"

"That too." The sirens were close now. An old man in a bathrobe stood a short distance up the street, staring. A crowd gathered in front of a coffee shop to watch the smoke. "Look, can we have this conversation anywhere else?"

"I'm not leaving without an answer."

Liam stuffed his hands in his pockets. "I don't— There's no— It's fucking complicated, okay?"

"Then uncomplicate it!"

An iron cuff closed around Sal's arm, only it wasn't a cuff at all, but Grace's hand. There was blood on the woman's face, but no open wounds Sal could see—a few cuts, which, dammit, could not be scabbing over already. Could they? Grace's eyes were stars around which the world wheeled.

"Magic," Grace said.

"Magic?"

"Magic."

"Grace," Liam said, "she's a civilian. I mean, are you really sure we should be talking about—"

"You want to waste time keeping her out of the loop, waste your own." Grace hadn't turned from Sal. "We deal with magic. Okay?"

"Okay," she said. "Magic. Christ."

"We can tell you more. Not here."

4.

tart with that thing in my brother's room," Sal said when they stopped the van near Prospect Park. "What was it? Is Perry dead? What did it do with him?"

"Homunculus," Father Menchú said. He sat on an upended milk crate in the back of the van, working his key chain like a rosary. "He's not dead, and the homunculus didn't do anything with him— Perry was driving it from a distance."

"Homunculus?"

"They're not so bad once you get to know them," Liam said. He was running a property records search, half paying attention, as if this whole damn situation was normal, which made Sal even angrier. "Well, no, scratch that. They stay bad. Just an understandable kind of bad. You get used to it."

"You do this all the time."

"I wouldn't go so far as to say *all* the time." He swore at the monitor.

Menchú offered coffee. "Grace didn't drink hers."

Sal glared at him over the cup, and he withdrew it. "Tell me everything."

"Get out of here," Grace said. "You've done enough."

"You tell me magic's real, and then you want to kick me out?"

"You were frozen on that sidewalk. Bad place to talk. You can leave now. I would."

"But you didn't," Sal said, "obviously."

Grace's eyes were sharp as broken glass.

Sal spoke fast to cover her discomfort. "Perry was not controlling that thing. Whatever spoke to me, it was not my brother. I want the truth."

"I didn't lie to you," Menchú said. "Not as such."

"You said my brother was in trouble because he stole a book. You didn't mention magic or homunculuses or whatever."

"I said your brother was in possession of a stolen book."

She blinked. "Oh."

"This isn't easy for anyone to hear the first time. The three of us are . . ." Menchú hesitated, searching for the right word.

"Monster hunters?"

"Archivists."

"Okay," Sal said. "Now I'm confused."

"The three of us are part of a society responsible for stocking and tending the Vatican's Black Archives."

Sal frowned. "I saw a Discovery Channel thing about that. Forbidden books. Heresies."

"That's what people know," Menchú said.

Grace stood, squeezed past the priest into the van's passenger seat, pulled a dog-eared copy of *Pride and Prejudice* from the glove compartment, kicked her feet up on the dash, and started reading.

"The world's bigger than most people know," Menchú said. "Imagine we live on an island in an ocean full of monsters. Most of the time we're safe from the monsters. But sometimes the tide rises.

Sometimes the monsters cause big waves. Sometimes people dig channels that run out into the deep ocean, and hungry things come in. Sometimes they mean to; more often it's an accident. These channels take the form of . . . artifacts. Books, often. Anything that connects one mind to another. For the last two thousand years, artifacts in Europe and the Americas have wound up in the Vatican's Black Archives. The book your brother brought to your apartment is the *Liber Manus*, the *Book of the Hand*, which we assume is the name for the monster the book contains, a charismatic world-eater type with a taste for human minds. It surfaced for the first time in the nineteenth century, in London, shipped for America on the *Titanic*, and arrived in the care of a half-drowned baronet. The *Liber Manus* was unharmed by the crash, of course. If it could be damaged by such conventional means, we'd be out of a job. Before the book could do serious damage in the States, local officials killed its bearer and locked the volume away. The book's been quiet for generations, and the warnings became department gossip. Precautions slipped. Traces of the *Liber Manus*'s existence reached the Internet, and your brother found them."

"So Perry's, what? He's been taken over by a sea monster?"

Grace, in the passenger seat, turned a page loudly. "He opened the book," she called back. "The Hand jumped into his mind."

Liam clicked his mouse, swore, clicked again.

"Demons," Sal said. "You're talking about demons."

"It's not clear what they are, theologically speaking," Menchú said. "Some present themselves as fallen angels, but they may be lying. Some don't speak with us. Some can't."

"Demons," Grace said, and turned a page.

"How did Perry even get this book?"

"There are communities—" Menchú said.

"Idiots," Liam added.

"—loose associations of amateur scholars and technical experts who believe information wants to be free," Menchú continued. "Your brother and his friends belong to one. He and his friends, and their friends, know enough of the picture I've just outlined to believe the metaphor is literal. They're mostly harmless, but your brother found a book with real power. He stole the merchandise from the initial thieves, who then turned on one another."

Fingers in an ashtray. Sal shuddered.

"He brought the book home. His friends kicked him out because they were afraid of reprisals from the surviving criminals."

"And us," Grace said.

"So he went to your apartment. When we followed him there, the book offered him escape. He opened it. Ordinarily the, ah, demon's control over your brother would have been limited in its first hours. We underestimated the depth of his study. He had the necessary languages, the right frame of mind, and no tools to resist possession. The Hand jumped into him. He must have left the homunculus at his apartment to keep watch, and to retrieve needed materials and information. He controlled it through the book in the townhouse."

"Was that the, whatsit, the *Liber Manus*? Did I close it?"

"Hardly," Liam said. "The book you closed back there was just a chump text."

"What?"

"A poor copy," Menchú explained. "The Hand recorded a piece of its name there, and projected its power through the name. That book will have burned up in the fire—unlike a true work, an imperfect copy has no special properties beyond its content. Find Perry, and we find the *Liber Manus*."

"Which is turning out to be terrifically easy, just for the record," Liam said. "Perry's cell phone's dead. No property records on file. Traffic cameras follow him from the house at nine this morning, but lose him in a tunnel."

"And now the demon is free, riding your brother's mind, somewhere in New York. It will cement its control, and once that's done, it will gather acolytes."

"Cement," Sal said. "So you can still save him."

"If we're lucky, we can close the book without hurting him. Cut off the demon's control."

"And if you're not lucky?"

Menchú's lips pressed together. He returned the van keys to his pocket. They rang like bells. "When we close the book, he might be too far gone to come back. Your brother's friends, in the house—they were, let's say, wading in the surf. Perry's swimming in a riptide."

"No."

"You don't know what these things do when they get out of hand."

"How bad can it be? I've never seen a demon attack on the news."

"People disappear all the time. All over the world."

"Murders. Accidents. Shit happens."

"And sometimes the world swallows people, and those left behind forget. A corner of an island falls into the sea. How can you tell it was ever there? Not even bones remain. If you know how to look, you can see the cracks where land once was. Lost legions. Lost cities. Have you ever heard of the town of Colebridge, New York?"

"No."

"Exactly."

"That's impossible. A whole town can't just disappear."

"Information decays. Paper lasts, but people are good at

disbelieving evidence. Those who don't know how to feel around the edges of a gap might never notice gaps at all. The mind closes to cover even the largest wound. When was the last time you thought about the place where you were born?"

"You're saying it might eat New York."

"The more time we spend here, the longer the demon in your brother has to shore up its control. If you know how to find him, you could save lives. Including his."

"If I know anything, and I tell you, you'll go in there, guns out, and hurt him."

"We want to close that book. We want to save these people."

"Go to the cops, if he's so dangerous."

"What would you tell them? How could you explain the situation so they would intervene knowing what they faced?"

"The chief—"

"Knows us. She calls us when your people are out of their depth."

"We could show them evidence."

"By the time the fire department's done, the homunculus will be a pile of melted garbage. Magic leaves no traces for forensics."

"You guys can't be it. It's just the three of you in a rented van?"

"Hey," Liam said. "I like this van."

"This is a job for the government. The Men in Black. Some, like, I don't know, some Library of Congress thing. The CIA."

"The problem," Menchú said, "is older than your government. Its solutions are older too."

Liam leaned back in his chair and looked at her upside down. "Besides, if you think we're low-budget, imagine the team a library would field."

"This is what we do. These are the calls we make."

"Not today," Sal said. "Not if I go after him myself."

Before Menchú could respond, she burst from the van into the cold gray morning and ran through the hedge into the park.

Rain soaked through her sneakers and the ankles of her jeans. She smelled ripe mulch and pulping leaves. Bare branches clawed the sky. Hands forced deep in pockets, head down, she marched through the park. Once she was out the other side she could hail a cab south, reach Perry's storage unit before Menchú and his team. If they were telling the truth.

Of course they were, or thought they were. She'd seen that garbage thing wearing her brother's face—or had she seen it after all?

She had. But—

The mind closes to cover even the largest wound.

If she kept walking, would she forget her brother? Or was this just the usual serving of post-traumatic stress, as memory chopped weird meat into chewable chunks? There had been a lot of weird in that house.

Either way, she had to get to Newark, fast.

"Detective Brooks!"

Liam's voice.

"Sal," he said, closer, desperate.

Keep walking, she told herself. But she'd never been good at listening to herself, especially when she made sense.

His arms were out, palms down, his eyes wide. He looked paler than usual.

"You want to tell me to trust Menchú," she said. "That you guys know what you're doing. You're talking about my brother's life."

"I know how it feels," he said. "I've been there."

She had a good few sentences of tirade left, but that stopped her.

"I walked his road. I was a punk. I knew the truth was out there. I looked. And what I found, Sal, it got inside my head." He took a step toward her. She didn't retreat. Gray clouds shifted against a backdrop of gray clouds. "I lost two years to a baby version of the thing that's in your brother now. One minute it's February 2011, I'm using a three-year-old library management system exploit to get a sealed manuscript out of the vaults at Trinity, and then it's October 2013, I've missed the World Cup, and Grace and Father M. wake me in a warehouse basement in Prague. There's blood all over the walls, and I have wires coming out of my arms." He pushed up the sleeve of his Windbreaker and the flannel beneath. Red scars pierced his corded muscle and textured his tattoos. "I don't know what I was doing for those two years. Nobody knows. But Grace and the father found me, and brought me back."

She reached for his forearm, for the scars. He pushed his sleeve back down before she could touch him.

"We care. We know what we're doing. And your brother is in danger. If you know where he is—dealing with this yourself is crazy. Give us the information. We'll help him. I'll help him. But, trust me, it's a bad idea to tackle this world alone."

His eyes were blue, and very bright.

"He's my brother," she said. "I'll save him. You can help, if you want. But he's mine."

"We can work with that."

"Let's go, then. We have a drive ahead of us."

5.

ewark," Liam said, without further comment, as they crossed
the Goethals Bridge.

"Perry and his friends needed cheap storage. They go through
a lot of equipment, buy books by the foot at estate sales, on eBay. I
didn't know why," Sal said, "until now."

"You never wondered why your kid brother was laying in a life-
time supply of dead men's books?"

"He's done weird shit since he was a kid. Before this it was five
years of collecting old gears and selling them at steampunk conven-
tions, which was, you know, also a weird way to use his history
degree. I have my life and he has his. Or did, I guess." She counted
the rounds she had left, checked that her weapon hadn't been
damaged in the fight in the house. She didn't plan to fire it, but
then, she never went in planning to fire. If she did, she'd have to.

"See, Grace? We never would have found him without her help."

Grace shrugged and turned a page.

Menchú passed Sal a manila envelope containing another
silver cross.

"I have one of those already."

"They don't work when they're tarnished. Swap it out. Drop the used one in the envelope."

She pulled the chain over her head. It felt much heavier than when she'd put it on. "It's the cross that matters?"

"The cross guides us in our faith," Menchú said.

"But the silver's the pertinent bit," Liam added. "Worked silver, the older the better. It soaks up magic, which is where the tarnish comes from. We're still working on the why. Stings like a— Well, it stings, but that's better than letting some bastard root around in your skull. And the Church has a lot of crosses lying around, turns out. Seal the envelope."

The glue tasted of wood pulp and horse hooves. "Any of that coffee left?" It was cold, and never had been any good, but at least it tasted like coffee. The new cross hurt when it touched the seared skin on her chest, but it felt lighter than the old one.

"Thank you for coming with us," Menchú said. "Grace speaks highly of your courage."

"Does she? Thanks."

Grace didn't look up from her book. "Just don't get us all killed."

"Not my plan," Sal said. "Take the next exit."

The storage locker complex sprawled over asphalt acres, and still they drove past it on the first try. "He's turning us away," Menchú said.

"At least we know he's here." Liam pulled a U-turn.

Sal's cross burned. She saw, with her mind's eye as much as with her physical ones, the WE-STOR-IT sign, remembered driving Perry here the first time, before he and the boys got their beater Olds. *Those who don't know how to feel around the edges of a gap might never notice gaps at all.* "Now. Left." Liam yanked the wheel, and they slid down a driveway into an empty storage parking lot.

Liam parked at the end of a row of vacant spaces, and they hit pavement. Easier to say what wasn't different about this space than what was. The character of light hadn't changed. The colors weren't dimmer or more vibrant. There wasn't much noise of any sort save their footsteps, but she could still hear trucks roll down the highway in the middle distance. Nor was there any of that spatial oddness she remembered from the boys' house. The storage units lay in long rows, all right angles and closed garage doors.

It just felt . . . less, somehow. She'd heard that cats and dogs freaked out before earthquakes and tidal waves, before sinkholes opened to swallow houses. They knew when the ground was going wrong. Maybe people had the same sense, less keen—maybe they only felt this way when the collapse was bigger, deeper, more fundamental. The world, Menchú had said, was an island eaten by an ocean from beneath.

Maybe he was wrong.

It didn't feel that way.

This was bigger than she felt, walking away from the E-Z Carpet Cleaner van in the storage parking lot beside three people she barely knew. This was bigger than any of them, but it was damn sure bigger than Detective Sally Brooks. Something that could eat the world like this—she couldn't fight it; she couldn't arrest it. Liam, Grace, Menchú, they all seemed to have some kind of angle on—magic. Call it by name. She'd brought them here. She could stay in the van, tell them the locker number, let them take it from here. Stay safe.

Sal laughed.

They looked at her, uncertain. Menchú especially. "Detective Brooks. If you want to wait—"

"Can't you feel it?" she said.

He shook his head.

"Perry, or whatever's inside him. It's strutting. Putting on a front. Trying to scare us off. Me in particular."

"The Hand is dangerous," he said. "It will eat us if we give it a chance."

"Yeah. But now, more than anything, it wants us to leave." She bared her teeth. "Third row, fifth locker on the left. Let's go."

Menchú, on the approach, didn't share her optimism. "Its hold on your brother lasts as long as the book's open. Close it—"

"With the cross. I know."

"Don't use the cross if it's tarnished, and don't touch the book with your bare hands. I'll try first. Grace and Liam will deal with any guards."

"It's been awake in our world for less than a day. You think it has goons?"

"It may have turned people, like the boys in the townhouse. There must have been others here when it arrived."

She looked back at Grace and Liam. Grace's novel had vanished into a pocket; Liam pulled a fingerless glove onto his left hand and snapped it closed at his wrist. Grace rolled her eyes at the sound, at the glove, at Liam in general.

"Cross," Sal said. "Don't touch the book. Anything else?"

"It may tempt you, as you get closer, offering bargains. Don't trust it."

"I figured. I mean, it's a demon."

The door to Perry's storage locker door was rolled down, its padlock locked. She glanced back for ideas.

Grace struck the padlock with a cinderblock, and it broke. She shrugged.

Liam closed the snap on his second glove.

Then someone tackled him from the right.

"Shit!" A large man lay on top of him, meaty fingers pushing toward his throat. Before Sal could react, Grace was there—she grabbed the man's We-Stor-It uniform polo shirt and threw him back with a twist of her hips. The uniformed puppet pushed himself upright—eyes wide and black from edge to edge—a foot taller than Grace, easy. She kicked him in the knee, struck him in the temple with an elbow, and he went down. Black tears left dark lines down his cheeks.

"Shit," Sal said in a different tone of voice than Liam had used.

Other figures emerged from the alleys between the storage units—men and women in uniform, a family of three with the daughter in pigtails. Sal felt that she should have seen them approaching. Of course, Liam should have seen the driveway before it was time to turn. Grace spun, trying to face all directions at once. Liam pushed himself to his feet.

Menchú turned to her. "Still think it's scared?"

Sal could have answered. Instead, she opened the door.

Candlelight flickered behind layers of fake Victorian furniture and chemical glassware, disused futons and piles of books—leather bindings and paperbacks, journals and diaries and dime-store lesbian detective novels. And there, at the far end of a narrow path through junky cast-off dreams of mystic grandeur, behind a semi-circle of open books, stood Perry.

Well. Not stood. Floated.

"Sal," he said, or the thing inside him said, and smiled, and his teeth were points, and there was no tongue in the pit of his mouth. "An unexpected pleasure."

She should have waited for Menchú. He'd done this before. But this was her brother. So she ran into the locker.

Which turned out to be for the best, because when a puppet jumped her from a gap between the boxes, Menchú was there to pull it (*her*, she corrected herself, these things could wake up, probably) off her back. Of course the puppet then grabbed a chair and struck him in the head, but he seemed more staggered than hurt.

Sal marched toward the thing that wore her brother. "I bet," she said. "That's why you tried to keep me away. Perry, if you're still in there, I'm trying to help you."

That smile didn't waver. The books' pages turned of their own accord. He raised one hand, and a shadowy headwind blasted her. The soles of her shoes left black streaks on the concrete floor. "What did they tell you, Sal? That this wasn't me? Is that the lie they spun?"

"My brother wouldn't do this."

"Are you sure? If your brother had the power we have now—"

"'We'?" she said.

"Oh, fine. Spoil my fun. How can you tell the difference, anyway?"

"My brother has a tongue."

"I can make a tongue, if you'd rather." Fire licked his teeth. "This is your brother's body, and I have his brain right here—who's to say I'm not him, just with the power he always wanted? I can rifle through his memories, every dirty thought, desire, each terror and suppressed impulse. Delicious and nutritious. Would you like to know how many times he wanted to kill you? How many times he hated you?" He turned ten pages of the leftmost book forward, then flipped three pages back, an unpracticed chef working an unfamiliar recipe.

She forced herself toward him, step by step. The cross froze and tore her skin. Burn victims flashed through her memory: charcoaled edges of flesh and white bone showing. "He didn't do any of that. Those thoughts don't matter."

"But they do! You feared an unjust world, and so you became a cop. That's what he thinks. He feared being powerless, so he sought power, which led him to me. That's your lovely little weakness, you humans—you're so blissfully susceptible to destiny."

The shadow-wind reached gale force. Somewhere behind her Grace and Liam and Father Menchú fought for their lives, for her, for Perry.

"What do you want with this?"

"What does anyone want?" Perry said. "A future. Futures taste grand. And you people have built so many of them for yourselves, like ice cream flavors. A hundred years back you expected more of the same forever, until maybe some god scooped his favorites off to play in a cut-rate heaven. Bland. Tasteless. But now—starscapes and apocalypses, gray goo and futuristic despotism, oil crises and pandemic collapses, floods and robots and monsters, oh my! Fresh universes of fear. Your brother's spinning them by the billions inside me. You could join him. Suffer through a few million hells for me, and I'll give you a paradise none can match."

"Perry," she said. So close now, but with every step the wind grew twice as strong. And she heard whispers, too, whispers that were colors, voices like claws in her belly. The cross wormed into her; the cross pierced her; the cross wriggled into her heart. "Perry, wake up. This thing needs you afraid. Listen to me. It's your sister; it's Sal; I'm outside your fucking door and I need you and you better open up right now or so help me God—"

Perry's eyes opened. The real ones, the brown that matched her own. John Cusack version 1.7. Real tears ran down his cheeks. Then he crumpled, clutching his face. The voice that wasn't his screamed words she couldn't hear. The shadow-wind stopped. She knelt before the books, before the Book, the *Liber Manus*. Seconds, maybe, no more. She pulled the cross from around her neck. She'd lifted bodies that weighed less. Her arms trembled.

The cross was black. A smooth tarnish covered every surface, even the chain. She scraped it frantically with her fingernail but couldn't mar the matte.

Fuck.

No silver around. Nothing *like* silver. Battered paperbacks, that was all.

And Perry was recovering. No. She recognized that body language—the straighter shoulders, the deeper breathing, that was the Hand reasserting control.

Behind her, Menchú fell.

It took the Hand time to learn her brother. If it jumped into her, Menchú and Grace and Liam—and hell, Perry—would have a few critical seconds to close the book. And if it jumped into her, it would let Perry go.

Perry wanted to kill her, the Hand had said. Well, fine. She'd wanted to kill him, too.

What else were siblings for?

The Hand-in-Perry straightened and smiled its sharp-toothed smile with the tongue of flame behind. She tackled the *Liber Manus*, slammed it shut, and flung it from her like a poisonous snake she'd caught by the neck.

The sinkhole feeling, the brink of catastrophe, the incipient collapse—stopped.

The world blinked.

Sal was still Sal. She was so shocked she almost didn't notice when Perry began to fall.

She caught him before he hit the floor. "Perry. Come on, Perry, wake up."

No answer. He breathed deep, and his teeth were back to normal, and there was a tongue in his mouth again, but his eyes were closed. She slapped him. No answer. Shook him. "Perry!" Nothing.

Menchú set his hand on her shoulder. He looked blurred. She blinked, and he grew edges.

"It's okay," she said. "We won."

6.

Emotions take up space, which is why all priests, from bearskin-kilted Wotanites down to modern Xenuphiles, make such a fuss over architecture. Rooms shape the feelings within. Parallax crushes impressions of size: high ceilings and pointed arches hold more heaven than the sky itself. Close chambers fit cozy emotions, or stifling ones. A dense nest will accommodate sweaty sex and a mushroom-assisted voyage to the outer spheres. But don't whisper to your lover in a cathedral. Don't look for Wotan in a closet.

Don't hope to feel any way but forlorn by a hospital bed.

Sal stood by Perry's side and listened to heartbeat beeps through a cruddy speaker.

"This is the first time I've seen him in anything but a T-shirt," she said. "The first time since we were kids."

"I'm sorry," Menchú said from the door.

She turned from the bedside. She hadn't when she'd heard him approach. Only knew it was him from reflections. "He could wake up any day."

"Yes."

"Or the Hand might have dragged him along with it. Back out there. Into the ocean."

"Maybe."

"We could open the book."

"And the Hand would come out again. Now we have the *Liber Manus* in custody, we can keep it closed. Keep the world safe. That storage locker was a treasure trove—Perry and his friends had collected several copies of dangerous texts. We have those, too, now. And the world's safe for the moment. That's what winning looks like."

"We can't fight these things at all?"

"We can keep them out," Menchú said. "But there are more all the time. More this year than last. More this century than the one before."

"Are all of them that bad?"

"Not all that . . . hungry. We found a pair of wings that would let you fly if you put them on. A well that answers questions."

"Have you found one that brings back souls?"

"Not yet," he said. "Before you ask—"

"You don't know what I'm going to say yet."

He looked at her over the rims of his glasses.

"Fine," she said. "Go ahead."

"It gets worse. You wanted to keep your brother safe. Look what happened."

"I'll save him. These sea monsters of yours—I want to learn their names. And you need me. Liam has the tech side down, and Grace can fight, and you know the secrets. But none of you are cops."

"You wouldn't be either," he said, "if you join us. Not in practice. You'd keep your badge—technically you'd be seconded to the Vatican—but we don't work like cops work. I've seen men and women end up like Perry. I have friends the world forgot, as if they were never born. When I was your age, I thought I could get to the bottom of all this. But there's no bottom. It just keeps going down."

"I'm ready for that."

He laughed. "You have no idea what you're saying." But he held out his hand, and she took it. "Welcome to the team."

EPISODE
2

ANYWHERE BUT HERE

BRIAN FRANCIS SLATTERY

1.

The door was simply a wooden door, made from three wide planks. Sal had just walked through the broad rooms and long hallways of the Vatican Library, with their marble and their frescoes and their saints in a million colors, the kind of stuff that hit you over the head with the knowledge that you were most definitely not in America anymore. Old Europe. Old money. Old secrets. Secrets within secrets. Compared to all that, this door looked like it was going to lead to a broom closet.

Except there was Father Menchú, his hands behind his back, waiting for her.

And there was a seven-pointed star on the door.

"Looks a little satanic for around here, doesn't it?" Sal said.

"Everyone says that the first time they see it," Menchú said. "It's an old symbol of protection. The Society's entire library is shaped like that star. Ready to see it?"

Sal nodded.

"You sure you're all right?" Menchú said.

"I'm fine," Sal said. "Let's go."

Menchú opened the door. They found themselves in a little room with no apparent purpose—bad architecture, which, considering it was the Vatican, was a little surprising. *If this were in America, there would be vending machines here,* Sal thought. *Vending machines and trash cans.* But it was just the top of a staircase, a twisting, black metal staircase.

"It's wrought iron," Menchú said.

"More like overwrought," Sal said.

Menchú laughed. "You haven't even seen all of it yet."

The stairs corkscrewed below them for at least four stories. The middle column was a rod of iron. The outside was a lattice of metalwork that Sal thought at first was covered in barbs, until she saw that the barbs were animals and trees, figures of people in the act of various gestures. The wonders of the natural world. It was beautiful. It was like being inside a birdcage.

The ceiling above them vaulted away from the staircase and down in seven separate vertical segments, like frozen waves, like outstretched wings. *We're in the center of the star,* Sal thought. There was light below them. Sal looked down.

She was looking at a city. A city made of books. Books were stacked into skyscrapers, piled into neighborhoods. They seemed to cover the entire floor, from the walls to the bottom step of the staircase. As she got closer, Sal could see narrow pathways through the towers. Someone had started off with a system, bookcases in neat columns across the room. The bookcases were all still there. But the project had gotten out of hand, and now the cases were jammed, and there were stacks of books on top of them. Though, off to the left, there was a place that looked like a clearing, a source of light.

"Asanti?" Menchú said.

"Yes?" a voice called from the clearing. Sal couldn't say why, but she liked whoever was talking already.

"Is everyone here?"

"Yes," Asanti answered. Sal could just about hear her smiling.

A different voice, then—Grace's. "You're late. By eight minutes."

"I'm sorry," Menchú said.

He really means that, Sal thought. *What does that mean?*

"I'll meet you at the bottom of the stairs," Asanti said. "I've moved a few things around, so it's not as easy to get through."

Asanti was tall, a good three inches taller than Sal, and her long dreadlocks, piled and twisted into a colorful scarf, made her seem taller still. But there was nothing imposing about her. Only a quick smile, eyes that seemed to spark.

"So you're the new recruit Menchú thinks so highly of." She extended a hand. "I'm Archivist Asanti."

"Sal."

They shook hands.

"Welcome to the Black Archives of the Societas Librorum Occultorum. Come in. The others are waiting."

Asanti guided Sal and Menchú through the towers of books, talking as she went.

"The library was built in the 1400s—the architecture gives that away, don't you think?—when the Society's collection grew a little too large and a little too dangerous to have in broad daylight, or just sitting in some monastery. Take a left. No, the other left. That's it. We are now in the only central chamber of the library. There are seven chambers radiating off of this one. Each one has a small antechamber, with the larger rooms beyond that. Just in case something gets out in the library, you understand, and we need to seal it in."

Sal glanced back at the staircase. Now it looked like a strand of DNA, ascending into the gloom until it disappeared in the middle of the ceiling.

"Let me guess," Sal said. "The antechambers are really small, awkward spaces."

"That's right," Asanti said.

"Like the room at the top of the stairs."

"Exactly," Asanti said.

"The idea being that at least some of the things that get out of the books, if they get out, are too big to fit in those spaces."

Asanti looked back at Menchú. "I see why you brought her on," she said.

"How often do they get out?" Sal asked.

Asanti and Menchú looked at each other.

"It hasn't happened yet, on our watch," Menchú said.

"And before that?" Sal said.

"The last one was centuries ago," Asanti said. "We've learned to take far more precautions now."

They came to the clearing Sal had seen from the stairs. There was a wide Oriental rug on the stone floor. Liam was sitting on a couch. He gave Sal a quick, friendly smile. Grace stood by a coffee table, her arms folded. An easy chair next to the coffee table was empty. Lamps balanced on stacks of books, which functioned as end tables. At the far end of the rug was a desk, with another wooden chair behind it.

On the desk—besides still more books and a phone that looked about fifty years old with a compact switchboard attached to it, and a small lamp—was a faintly glowing orb, housed in a glass case, hooked up to a contraption of wires, gears, and screens.

"What's that?" Sal asked.

"Cuts to the chase, doesn't she?" Liam said.

Grace nodded with approval.

"This," Asanti said, "is how we get our assignments."

"What, do you shake it up?" Sal said. "Like a Magic 8 Ball?"

"Unbelievable that I never thought of that before," Liam said.

Grace and Menchú both looked at Liam.

"What is she talking about?" Grace said.

"It's this . . ." Liam mimed shaking an 8 Ball.

"What, like a cantaloupe?" Grace said.

"No," Liam said. "You ask it questions, like you're using it to tell fortunes."

"You use a cantaloupe to tell people's fortunes?" Menchú said.

"No, it's . . ."

"Can we move on, please?" Grace said. Sal nodded. *This woman is speaking my language.*

"Yes, let's," Asanti said. "We just call it the Orb. It alerts us when a new magical force appears in the world."

"I don't follow," Sal said.

"It could be that some magical event has occurred. It could be that some sort of creature has . . . emerged from wherever they emerge from. Or that someone has cast a powerful spell. Or it could be as simple as someone opening a magic book."

"Opening a book where?" Sal said.

"Anywhere," Asanti said. "Anywhere in the world."

"It looks old," Sal said.

"The Society has had the Orb for centuries," Asanti said.

"But some of those parts look a little newer than that," Sal said.

"Over the centuries, as the Society's work has broadened and become more precise, we've been able to make some modifications."

"You figured out how magic works?" Sal said.

Asanti looked at Menchú again.

"Not exactly," Asanti said.

Sal's brow furrowed. She turned to Menchú. "The Society uses magic?" she said. Accusing. Hurt.

"It did," Menchú said. "In the past. It doesn't anymore. Not like that."

Asanti sighed.

"That's not much of an answer," Sal said.

"Well, it's the best one you're going to get right now, Detective," Grace said. "I'm guessing that, as a former law enforcement officer, you're smart enough to know that the Society's relationship to magic is complicated even though its stated mission is to lock magic away forever. Yes?"

"Yes," Sal said.

"Great," Grace said. "So you're okay?"

"I'm fine," Sal said. She took a deep breath. "Please just continue."

Grace turned to Asanti. "You were saying."

"All right," Asanti said. She pointed to a small display of flip-clock numbers. "Thanks to the modifications, when the Orb detects a magical anomaly, it's able to tell us where it happened. Latitudinal and longitudinal coordinates. Right down to the second."

"Well . . . ," Liam said. "That machine's a bit"—he waved one hand in the air equivocally—"dodgy."

"It's close," Menchú said.

"Yes," Liam said. "Close enough to buy plane tickets. Then it's my job to start really narrowing it down. I check with my network. Antiquarians. Curio collectors. Parish priests. Magic hunters."

"Magic hunters," Sal said.

"Yeah, you know, like tornado hunters, except magic," Liam said.

"So those ghost-hunter cable TV shows are real?"

"Oh, no, those are fake. If they were real, the cameras wouldn't work around the ghosts."

"We're getting off topic," Grace said. "Again."

"Right," Liam said. "I also read the papers. I listen in on police chatter. Check blogs, even. Status updates. Like I do all the time, except in a more focused way. Looking for anything weird."

"You're looking all the time?" Sal said.

"Well, yes, because it turns out even the Orb doesn't catch everything."

"It catches most things," Menchú said.

"*Some* things," Liam said.

"I imagine you find plenty on your own, anyway," Sal asked, and looked at Grace. Grace smiled back at her. *Thank you for keeping these boys in line.*

"Absolutely," Liam said. "Even when the Orb goes off, and I'm narrowing it down, I find a lot of things not related to what we're looking for. But eventually—usually by the time we absolutely need it—I've narrowed it down so we can bag it and tag it."

"Bag it?" Sal said.

Menchú produced a shroud from his pocket.

"If it's a book, or some other artifact that we can carry, we wrap it in this. Keeps the magic contained until we can bring it back here."

"Let me guess," Sal said. "That shroud is magic too."

Menchú shrugged helplessly. "The mission couldn't be clearer," he said. "Find the magic and lock it up."

Lock it up. He said it, Sal thought, as if he was passing along a mantra. Something he repeated to himself to keep his focus.

"So you collect all these books and magic wands and amulets, bring them here, and then what happens?" Sal said. Then she looked around. "These aren't all magic books around us, are they?"

"Oh, no. That would be dangerous," Asanti said. "These are just reference books. The real magic books, I catalog and then lock away in one of the seven chambers connected to this room."

"And no one ever looks at them again," Sal said.

"Well," Liam said, "that's the idea, anyway."

"Why don't you just destroy them?"

"Someone tried that about seven hundred years ago," Liam said. "Turns out we don't know how to destroy a magic artifact without unleashing the magic that the artifact contains. Thankfully they had the good sense to try it on something relatively benign."

"Relatively," Menchú said. "The artifact turned water into wine."

"That doesn't sound so bad," Sal said.

"The reports of the aftermath are sketchy," Menchú said, "but it seems that there was a flash as the artifact exploded, and it affected all the water within a half mile of here. Including the water in the people."

"Oh," Sal said.

"Yes," Menchú said. "We don't know if all artifacts react so violently when destroyed, but we're not eager to experiment."

"So what happens now?" Sal said.

"Now?" Menchú said. He looked at the Orb. "We wait."

"We have a little downtime, then?"

"Yes. Until we get our assignment."

"Then I want to see my brother."

Menchú nodded. "Let's go," he said.

Sal was already lost. They were in another part of the Vatican Library, another underground hallway, though this one was ornate as could be—more ornate, even, than the places in the Library aboveground, where tourists gawked and took pictures. It meant something for a secret part of the building to look like this, Sal figured. Someone, at some point, had amassed a lot of wealth, a lot of power, for part of the organization. And with those things, a lot of impunity. And they wanted whoever visited them to know it.

Got it, Sal thought. *Loud and clear.*

"We're not keeping my brother in the hospital?" Sal said.

"We moved him here because we thought this would be safer," Menchú said.

Not for him, Sal thought. *For everyone else.*

Menchú gestured to a row of four carved wooden doors, painted and embossed with gold. They looked like stained-glass windows.

"These are the offices of the monsignors for the Society," he said. "One for each team. Team One was and is a full-combat team. Team Two became diplomacy and public relations. You could think of Team Three—that's us—as acquisitions and storage."

Sal nodded toward the fourth door. "What does Team Four do?" Sal said.

"There is no Team Four," Menchú said.

Sal raised an eyebrow. *Please go on.* Menchú caught it.

"There used to be a Team Four," he said. "Just as there used to be a lot more magic in the world. The Society originally developed four teams to deal with the magic."

"What was Team Four's job?"

Menchú paused, looking for the phrase. "Research and development," he said at last.

"They tried to use magic," Sal said.

"As I said," Menchú said, "there is no Team Four anymore. The Society—and especially the fighters on Team One—are very grateful for what Team Four accomplished. But there came a time when the risks were not worth the gains."

They passed by a large space that looked like a courtroom. Natural light streamed in from above. The ceiling was several stories above them, and all glass.

So that's how far below ground we are right now, Sal thought.

"This is where we all meet, when we need to," Menchú said. "The team leaders, the monsignors, and the cardinal."

"So the cardinal sits behind the bench?"

"When he's officiating, yes," Menchú said.

"To pass judgment."

"Sometimes to appear impartial," Menchú said. "Or simply to understand what happened in a complicated case." But Sal could tell she'd struck a nerve. Menchú didn't like the hierarchy any more than she did. Maybe he liked it less. *What the hell,* Sal thought. *Let's poke that nerve.*

"You've been here awhile," she said.

"Yes," Menchú said.

"Ever thought about having the cardinal's job?"

"I've thought about it," Menchú said.

"Didn't want to pursue it?"

"It was offered to me once. I didn't take it."

"Desk job's not for you?"

"It's complicated," Menchú said.

Two men wearing vestments passed them in the hallway. They both, Sal noticed, had unusually shaped heads. One of them was very round; Sal imagined his skull looking like a volleyball. His face was packed into the center of the front of it. His tiny ears seemed glued to the side. And his hair didn't know what to do; there was no place to lie flat. The other man had a very long face, a towering forehead. It was as though his head was made of taffy. Sometime during his childhood, someone had pulled on it, and it hadn't gone back to normal.

Balloon and Stretch, Sal thought. She took a mental picture.

Menchú nodded at them. They nodded back. Then, in unison, they gave Sal a very scrutinizing glance, a once-over. Sizing her up. Cold. Calculating. Sal got the distinct impression that they didn't like what they saw.

The two men kept walking. Sal waited until they were out of earshot.

"Who are they?"

"Desmet and De Vos," Menchú said. "Part of Team Two."

"Those guys are part of diplomacy and public relations?" Sal said.

"Also exorcisms," Menchú said.

Sal almost laughed.

"They're good at their job," Menchú said. "That's what matters." But Sal could still hear a little twinge in his voice. There had been a reason he didn't introduce her to them, and it hadn't been just because she didn't speak Italian.

"Come on," Menchú said.

The hallway turned and turned again until they reached another carved door, not as ornate as the others. Unpainted.

"Here," Menchú said.

The room had paneled walls, a plaster ceiling with a chandelier, a woven rug on a deep red wooden floor. But other than that, it was a hospital room. Perry lay on a bed with a thick mattress and a metal frame, surrounded by machines. Wires ran from his scalp. An IV ran from one arm.

Sal went to his side and put a hand on his chest.

"He's breathing on his own, at least," she said, putting the bravest words she could find on what she was seeing. "He looks good."

Menchú kept a respectful distance. "He's receiving the best care he could get anywhere," he said. "We're looking after him physically and spiritually."

"Supernaturally, you mean," Sal said.

"Holistically," Menchú said. It was a gentle correction. "Your brother isn't in prison or quarantine. If he woke up and he was . . ."

"Himself?" Sal said.

"Yes, himself," Menchú said, "he would be free to go. We wouldn't keep him."

Sal swallowed.

"I know we've talked about this already," she said. "I know you can't say what the chances are of getting that . . . demon . . ."

"The Hand," Menchú said.

"Yes, the Hand—I know you can't say what the chances are of getting it out of him, or if there's anything else we could be doing to wake him up. I understand that it's all a big question mark. But he's still in there, right? Or has he been taken somewhere?"

"We think he's still in there," Menchú said.

"And he's not brain-dead," Sal said.

"No," Menchú said. "Not physically, no."

She moved her hand from Perry's chest to his forehead.

"What's it like for him in there?" she said.

There was a long pause. She could tell Menchú was searching for an answer.

"God only knows," he said at last.

"God and Perry," she said. Then, "Just Perry."

How do we reach him? He's all by himself in there, Sal thought. *Out there. All alone.*

Then she had another, much worse, thought: *Except that he isn't alone. Not at all.*

Right then, the chances of finding the cure, finding the right book, seemed so remote. Impossible. The tiniest sliver of a needle in a universe of haystacks. They'd found a pair of wings, Menchú had told her. A well that answered questions. Wondrous and useless, totally useless. Where was the book that would bring her brother back? And who in the world was going to find it?

2.

G abriel lived by himself in Madrid, in the apartment where he was raised, a ramshackle string of rooms off a long hallway that smelled vaguely of mildew, though he could never find the source. His parents had both died, his father years ago, his mother not long after, and he lived among the things they had left behind. The wallpaper was starting to peel off the walls; his parents had put it up when they moved in. That was their double bed in the biggest bedroom, their bedspread. Gabriel ate at the dining room table they had bought when they were first married. The curtains he drew over the windows were the ones his mother had made.

Gabriel's only regular visitors were two sisters from upstairs, Elena and Victoria, who came over every few days when they needed to escape their own parents, their own smaller apartment. They thought of Gabriel's place as their secret castle. To them, its rooms were vast and unending, and they spent hours exploring them. The remnants of his parents' lives were souvenirs from distant places. Elena and Victoria loved the collection of figurines, of angels and animals, that Gabriel's mother had kept. They took them out and played with them on the dining room table while Gabriel made them a snack. Gabriel liked the girls, appreciated the company.

Gabriel kept the apartment, just barely, through a series of small jobs. He had been an office clerk. Then he was a cashier at a pharmacy. Then he became the manager of a movie theater. It was his favorite of the jobs he'd had, even though he knew there was no way it was going to last. The theater was falling apart around him— it was in worse shape than his apartment—while the street bustled with pedestrians outside. Almost none of them ever came inside.

But he loved the movies. The owner had a taste for the surreal, which suited Gabriel fine. They played *The Spirit of the Beehive* once a month. They ran Buñuel. They ran Jodorowsky. Gabriel sat in the back, behind the three or four other people in the theater, and let those movies take him away. He knew they were supposed to be unsettling. They were designed to worm their way into your brain and lay eggs. Change you. But they didn't unsettle Gabriel. He found them soothing. They were an escape.

At last, the theater's owner decided to close down the theater for good and asked Gabriel to help him and some kids he'd hired off the street to clean the place out. The kids were from somewhere in North Africa. Gabriel didn't ask where because it seemed rude. They spoke very little Spanish and worked hard. Gabriel gave them a couple of hammers, screwdrivers, and a crowbar, and got them on the job of removing all the theater's fixtures—the counter, the lights, the carpeting—all of which the owner was hoping to sell. Gabriel went down to the basement to clear out the film canisters that hadn't been touched in years. He was sure the film inside was ruined. It had to be. As much as the owner loved movies, he hadn't taken care of the stock. So it was just a question of clearing everything out. Which was how Gabriel found the book.

It was on an upper shelf in a closet along with some old canisters and a rusty wrench. Gabriel had no idea how long it had been there. He slid it off the shelf and held it in his hands. It was big, big enough that he had to cradle it like a baby. A heavy baby. The cover's thick leather was so wrinkled and textured that it looked like a mountain range seen from a plane. Gabriel brought it under the light of the naked bulb above him. There was the faint outline of a title. It had been legible once, maybe even gilded. But the gold was long gone, the lines that formed the letters worn away. As he was running his hand over it, he noticed that the book was warm.

He had the strong sense that he had discovered something he shouldn't have. But he wanted it, anyway. He left the book in the basement when he dismissed the boys for the day so they wouldn't see it. After everyone had left, he waited until the street was a little quieter. Then he carried the book home that night in his arms.

He had left the windows open in his apartment, and it was cold. He put the book down on the dining room table. The windows rattled as he closed them. The floorboards creaked beneath his feet. As he moved from room to room, he was, more than ever, aware of the bleakness of his surroundings. There was the threadbare couch he could remember from his childhood. It was long past used up. There was the braided rug on the floor, worn and faded. There was the chair he'd found on the street and dragged to his apartment. It took him two hours to do it, and he almost never sat in it. The dim, tiny kitchen; the bathroom with the chipped tub. All the photographs on the walls were pictures other people had taken; almost none of them included him.

He picked up the book. It still felt warm in his arms, even warmer than before. It occurred to Gabriel that he couldn't remember the last time he'd had anybody over, besides Elena and Victoria. He didn't know the girls' parents at all, beyond the barest friendly acquaintance. And he knew no one else in the building. The apartments had all turned over since he was a kid, and he hadn't met any of the newcomers.

He couldn't remember the last time he'd been out, either, with other people. He wasn't sure when he'd stopped calling his friends or returning their calls. They must have stopped trying to reach him after a while, but he couldn't pinpoint the precise moment it happened. At the time, he felt like he was making tiny decisions. He'd receive a message, a voice mail, a text, something. Then he'd think, *I'd just rather stay in tonight.* But now he saw how all those decisions added up. He'd walked out of the crowd, step by step, over the years, and kept walking, and now he was alone.

He regretted all of that.

If I could be anyone else now, he thought, *anywhere else, I'd be happier.*

His bedroom was at the end of the long hallway. He went in and sat at the desk at the window. He put the book in front of him on the desk and opened it. It was written in a language he didn't recognize, with letters he'd never seen before. Were they even letters? Was it some kind of code? It was impossible to tell. He started leafing through the book, thinking there might be some diagrams or pictures, something to tell him what the book was about. There weren't. It was just page after page of indecipherable characters.

Then, under his fingers, the book got even warmer. The ink on the pages wriggled. The lines moved, rearranged themselves into words Gabriel knew, sentences he understood. He was in the middle of a story, a vast one, full of characters and action, too much to comprehend at once, too compelling to ignore. He flipped back to the beginning of the book, the first chapter, and read the first sentence.

"Gabriel," said a voice close by.

His mother was standing right behind him. She put her hand on his shoulder. His father stood on his other side, smiling, hands in his pockets.

"How are you here?" Gabriel said.

"Just keep reading," his father said.

The walls of the room began to glow, as if they were made of paper and there was a warm light behind them. They wavered. A ripple passed through them. The floorboards heaved and settled, heaved and settled. Gabriel could hear more people behind him, friendly voices and laughter. He looked up at his father. His father wasn't his father anymore. He was someone Gabriel didn't recognize but knew was a friend, a good friend. His mother had changed too, into someone else, someone Gabriel felt he had known for years. They had traveled the world together.

He looked up, into the darkened window. It was a mirror now. It was a vertical pool of water, still and unbroken. It carried his reflection. And he could see that he was not himself.

He had changed into a younger man, tired after a long trip but satisfied with what he had done. No. He was an older woman, flooded with memories of decades spent with her partner, two women living on the edge of a knife. She wouldn't take any of it back. Now he was an artist at the end of his life. He'd made a series of paintings that he already knew would outlast him. Two hundred years from now, they would fill people with awe. Now he was a girl, with all her life in front of her, nothing but possibility. She was surrounded by crowds—family, friends, people who would soon change her life.

The water on the wall became a waterfall, and it unfurled into a river that flowed between his feet. The walls gave way, and the ceiling opened up. The floor broke apart into a rich soil. Trees shot from the ground, climbed into the night sky, and spread their limbs above Gabriel's head until they covered the stars. Gabriel looked down at the book on the desk, the open page. The ink was moving faster and faster, words flashing by, sentences shooting across the paper like arrows. He knew it was all going more quickly than he could read, but somehow he understood it all. He was ecstatic, breathless. So carried away that he didn't notice at first that his fingers had sunk into the book itself. His hands had melted into the paper, until it was impossible to say where he ended and the book began.

3.

The Orb lit up, as though some ember smoldering inside it had finally caught fire. Asanti didn't notice. She was amid her books with a headlamp, looking for *Instances of Magick and Other Queer Occurrences in Clackmannanshire*, written and privately printed by a Scottish city councilman in 1841. She'd read it years ago, but something about Perry's case rang a bell. Something that made her think that Perry should be transferred to a more secure facility. He needed constant watching. Maybe they all needed watching. But she had to know more to be sure. She still hadn't found the book when she heard the numbers clacking on the machine. She ran to her desk, picked up the phone, and hit a switch.

Sal was in her new apartment, a tidy little unit in a nondescript building in a nondescript part of Rome. Someone in the Vatican—she would never know who—had arranged it for her. It was ready for her when she got there. White walls. A double bed under a fluorescent lamp. A small wooden dresser, a little table with two chairs. A shaded balcony that looked out over the alley behind the building, where cars went into and out of the parking garage underneath.

It would do.

Her phone pinged. She didn't know she had an international plan. Someone must have arranged that, too.

She got Asanti's message and hurried across town. Into the Library. Through the wooden door. Down the stairs.

"You're the last one here," Grace said to her. She was standing in almost exactly the same spot she had been before. *Did she even move?* Sal thought.

Liam was on the couch, tapping away at a laptop. As soon as Grace was done talking, he raised his eyebrows and shook his head.

"I heard that," Grace said.

"Where are we going?" Sal said.

"Madrid, it appears," Asanti said. She was poring over a stack of papers at her desk.

"Though where exactly is unclear," Liam said.

"We have the coordinates."

"Yes," Liam said sarcastically. "We have the coordinates."

Menchú nodded. "Good." He turned to Asanti. "Any idea what we might be facing?"

Asanti didn't look up from her papers. "Madrid has been officially purged of magic for more than five hundred years." She gave a sad chuckle.

"The Inquisition?" Sal asked.

"Oh, no," Asanti said. "The Inquisition was just a witch hunt, and not of real witches. Nothing to do with magic at all." She turned a page. "But even so, Madrid seems dry. There was a brief flurry of magical activity during the Spanish Civil War, and the usual spotty records of underground societies during the Franco years and after. But they seem like dabblers. There's no indication that any of them got hold of anything truly magical. No books or artifacts or anything else that I'm aware of."

"So whatever we're dealing with, it's rogue," Grace said.

"That's right. Possibly predating the Inquisition, when they declared the place clean."

"Arabic?" Liam said.

"Could be," Asanti said. "But that's a guess. Not even a hunch."

"So we don't know what we're facing," Grace said. "At all."

"Afraid so," Asanti said.

"This isn't going to be like Eyjafjallajökull, is it?" Grace said.

Asanti looked up at last, slightly irritated. "No, this is not going to be like Eyjafjallajökull," she said.

"The volcano in Iceland?" Sal said to Liam.

"Yep," Liam said. "You know those eruptions in 2010? No one could fly in Europe for days? Apparently not entirely the result of natural forces."

Grace interrupted. "There was a dragon. Seven stories high. Living under the volcano. Which had been there for over a thousand years, and was the subject of several local legends. But were we told any of this when we got on the plane?"

"My Icelandic was rusty," Asanti said. "It won't happen again. It's certainly not going to happen in Madrid." She said it with a sudden authority that made Sal believe her. Grace did too. She backed down.

"Well, whatever is happening in Madrid," Liam said, "I haven't heard anyone call the police about it yet."

"Thank God," Menchú said.

"What happens if the police get involved?" Sal said.

"You're a cop," Liam said. "You should know. Things get a little messy. Let's just say the sooner we get there, the better." He sighed.

"Why can't they just take the books out to a barn up the back ass of nowhere and open them up there? Everything would be so much easier."

"How's your Spanish?" Grace said.

"I can order at a Mexican restaurant," Sal said. "That's about it."

Grace shook her head. "Americans," she said under her breath.

They headed out to the airport.

4.

The family living downstairs from Gabriel heard noises above them and thought it must be the building. In the apartment upstairs, where Elena and Victoria lived, the family heard their floorboards creaking when they weren't walking on them. Something was going on below their feet.

"Go down and see how Gabriel is doing," the parents told their daughters. They knew he lived alone, and even if they didn't know him well, they were worried about him.

So the daughters skipped down the stairs to Gabriel's door. They knocked. There was no answer. They knocked again.

They felt a rush of air around their ankles, first toward the door, then away from it. Like a long, sighing breath.

Then the door opened, all by itself. And great hands, strong yet soft, scooped them up and took them in.

The girls didn't get a chance to see what the apartment really looked like now. For Elena and Victoria, Gabriel's apartment disappeared. Their own selves disappeared. They became wizard queens, floating in the air and creating kingdoms all around themselves with waves of their wands. They sprouted transparent wings from their backs and became pirate fairies, raiding ships and islands that floated in the sky. They were swooping dragons in a world where the only land was a sheer and never-ending cliff that disappeared into the clouds above and below them, and cities like gigantic mushrooms grew from trees that clung to the rocks. At last they were sea creatures they couldn't have described to themselves, even as they were described in the book. They were slim beings with fins and gills, long, flowing tentacles, braids in their hair. They swam in a pink ocean among eight-eyed leviathans and a web of towns that drifted in the current together like a school of jellyfish.

They didn't know where they really were or what was really happening to them.

It took the girls' parents a few hours to realize something was wrong. The sisters' visits with Gabriel were never short. But the kids were always home before dinner.

"How long have they been down there?" their mother said.

The father looked up from his phone. He hadn't realized how late it had gotten.

"I'll go get them," he said. He headed downstairs to the landing in front of Gabriel's door. He could hear what he thought were voices. He could hear something, anyway.

"Elena? Victoria?" he called. They didn't answer.

He put his hand to the door. It was warm, warmer than it should have been.

There's a fire in there, he thought.

He called out his daughters' names again. There was still no answer. He ran down the stairs to the superintendent, and they both came back up to Gabriel's landing.

"Gabriel?" the superintendent called. "Are you in there? Are those girls with you?"

The superintendent tried his key. It turned, but it didn't unlock the door. Then it stuck, as if held there. As if something had reached into the lock from the other side, something with very powerful fingers, and had latched hold of it.

The superintendent jiggled the key.

"I can't even get it out," he said.

"My girls are in there," the father said.

"Gabriel!" the superintendent yelled. "If you don't open this door in thirty seconds, I'm calling the police."

They waited. It was quiet on the landing.

Then they felt the air move, all around them, from up and down the stairs, as if it were being drawn under the door to Gabriel's apartment. They watched as the door flexed outward in its frame. It was inhaling. It was as obvious as it was impossible. They felt the wind rush around their ankles, first toward the door as it ballooned, then away, back into the stairwell, as the door smoothed and flattened again.

They looked at each other. Each one confirmed to himself that the other had seen it.

"Call the police," the father said.

5.

They were on an Alitalia flight. At first Sal was a little disappointed that an outfit like this didn't have its own airplane. Then, when—at a wave of some papers from Menchú—they got the next four seats to Madrid and were escorted through security at once, she got a little more respect for the whole operation. Maybe they didn't have a plane. But they did have about a thousand years of favors to call in, and they didn't mind doing it whenever they needed to. Or even when it just made their lives a little easier.

The pilot told the cabin and crew to prepare for landing in Madrid. Menchú was still sleeping, his mouth slightly open. Grace, sitting next to him, had finished *Persuasion* and was just starting *Northanger Abbey*. Sal watched her for a minute. Grace turned a page every twelve seconds or so. Sal timed it.

How could anyone read that fast? Sal thought. *Why would anyone want to?*

Then Grace caught her watching, and Sal looked away.

"Are you all right?" Liam asked from the seat next to her.

"Why does everyone keep asking me that?" Sal said.

"Well, right now you look a little green."

"I don't like flying very much," she said.

"Really?" Liam said. "You might have picked the wrong job."

"I think the problem is that I've chosen the wrong state of consciousness." She nodded toward Menchú.

"You could be right. But then you'd miss this delicious snack."

He'd been doing this since they left the Vatican, trying to chat with her. She would say *chatting her up*, but if that's what was going on, he wasn't very good at it, or at least not very good at getting to the point. But he kept doing it, whatever it was. In the car on the highway out to the airport. While boarding the plane. And now here, on the plane, for two hours. Forcing conversations that they didn't need to have, forcing jokes that she didn't think were all that funny. Exercising his wit just a little too often, but not hard enough. And he talked about *nothing*, nothing that mattered, nothing worth a damn. It was setting off all her personal alarms. It was like he was trying to hide something behind this thick verbal smokescreen he was kicking up. But what was he hiding? It was getting on her nerves.

"Liam?" Sal said.

"Yeah?"

"Whatever you're trying to do here, I think you might be trying a little too hard."

Liam sighed. "I'm sorry."

"It's okay."

"I'm talking too much."

"Yes. But it's okay."

"It's just that . . . Grace and Menchú, they're not talkers. And we spend too much time in planes and cars not to talk."

"Was the person before me a talker?"

"Yeah."

"Why'd he leave?"

"She was a she. And I don't think I'm entirely at liberty to say."

"You're not giving me a lot of faith in this organization."

"Good one," Liam said.

"I'm serious, Liam."

"Sorry."

He took a pretzel out of the bag on the tray in front of him and chewed it more slowly than most people chew pretzels.

He was still being annoying, Sal decided. Then chided herself for being harsh.

He just apologized and backed off when you told him how you felt, she thought. *He's not trying to screw you or screw you over. He's just trying to make a friend. Don't fault him just because he's terrible at the preliminaries.*

But then, she argued back to herself, *you give him an opening and you'll never hear the end of it.* She took a breath. *Oh, what the hell,* she thought.

"So," she said, "about Eye . . . Eh-ya . . . the volcano in Iceland."

"Eyjafjallajökull?" Liam said.

"Yeah, that," Sal said. "What was it like?"

"I don't know," Liam said. "It was just before my time here. That was when I was . . ." He put his hands together as if he was about to pray, then tilted them, lay his head on them, and closed his eyes.

"I see," Sal said.

"Though I doubt I did much sleeping."

"Has anyone ever figured out what happened to you?"

"Asanti's been over the case a few times," Liam said. "She has some guesses, but nothing concrete. We don't know what possessed me. Aside from Grace hitting it in the face over and over again—well, probably that means hitting *me* in the face—we don't know exactly why it let me go, either. Or, for that matter, if it really did. For all I know, it's still in here." He tapped his temple with a finger. "For all I know, I'm going to wake up tomorrow and try to kill all of you, then take over the world."

Sal thought of her brother. Again. She forced him out of her mind and took a sip of her drink.

"That was a little awkward," Liam said.

"It's okay," Sal said.

"No, it's not okay. Not with your brother the way he is."

Sal narrowed her eyes and looked at him again. He was more observant than she'd given him credit for, after all.

Liam lowered his voice. "Look. You may have noticed I'm in suspiciously good shape for a man who sits in front of a computer all day. It's not just so I look good in a suit. It's part of a strict regimen I've kept for myself. Of exercise. Of diet. Of sleep. I've got everything down to the rep, the heart rate, the calories, the minute. I do it because I want to make sure I don't slip. I want trip wires all over my life so if the demon's still in there, I can tell if it starts taking over, and so you can tell, too. You catch me eating a piece of cake and it's not someone's birthday, you lock me away. Yeah?"

"Yeah," Sal said.

"That goes for all of us on this plane. I know we seem flippant. I know it looks like we don't get along. Maybe we don't even like each other very much. Sometimes I don't know if we do. But the mission unites us, you understand? Each of us has lost too much to magic to take it as anything but dead serious. I can't promise that in two years you'll have your brother back. I can't. I can promise you, though, that we won't stop trying. We'll go the world over, wave every magic wand we can. And with every step, we'll make sure we save as many people as possible from the same fate."

His face, for the first time since Sal had met him, was completely earnest. He wasn't being nice, or trying to get something out of her, or keeping secrets. He was just telling the truth.

"We're doing everything we can," he said. "*I* am doing everything *I* can."

"Thanks," Sal said. *Maybe he's not so bad,* she thought. "I'm glad you're here," she said.

He patted her hand twice. She didn't move it.

6.

The officer who showed up at the apartment building was a burly man with a friendly, mustachioed face. On him, the police uniform—the brightly colored shoulders, the checkered band on the hat—looked almost clownish. The superintendent looked at him and felt afraid for him.

"Which apartment is it?" the policeman said.

"I'll show you," the superintendent said. Halfway up the stairs, he said, "There's something about the door."

"What?" the policeman said.

"You'll see."

A nervous man was waiting on the landing.

"You're the girls' father?" the policeman said.

"Yes," the father said.

"So tell me what's happening here," the policeman said.

"You should just look. At the door."

"That's the key jammed in the lock?"

"Yes. But that's not what you need to see," the superintendent said. "It's that the door is breathing."

"Breathing?" the policeman said.

"Watch."

The policeman watched. The superintendent was right. The door *was* breathing, without question. There was no other way to think of it. The policeman stared at it for a minute.

"How long has it been doing this?" the policeman said.

"A couple hours."

"My girls are in there," the father said. "I'm sure of it."

"What's the tenant's name again?" the policeman said.

"Gabriel Medem," the superintendent said.

The policeman knocked on the door. "Mr. Medem?"

There was no answer.

"This is the police, Mr. Medem. I understand you have two little girls with you. I'm concerned for your safety and theirs. Please open the door."

The door seemed to sigh.

"Mr. Medem, open the door if you can."

The door inhaled.

"Mr. Medem?"

The door held its breath. The policeman saw it. He looked at the father and superintendent and put out his hand. *Step back, okay?*

The policeman cleared his throat. "Mr. Medem, if you don't open this door—"

It happened so fast that the father and the superintendent didn't really see it. But the policeman saw it all. The door flew open and slammed against the inside wall, and a giant, spidery hand of wood and bone snatched him up and pulled him inside. It wasn't soft or gentle this time.

The door slammed shut behind him, and a layer of twigs and hair grew over it.

The hand dragged the policeman down the hallway. The floor-boards were half gone, the holes covered with grass, with bark, with skin, with what seemed to be a sheet of fingernail. He passed the door to the living room. There were the two girls. They were floating off the floor, their arms and legs out, their hair splayed around their heads, as if the room were filled with water. No. They were suspended from the ceiling, pushed up off the floor, by a swarm of threads that kept breaking and rebuilding, breaking and rebuilding, every second. The rug teemed with them. It was a dark meadow. The lamp had twisted forward and grown eyes and bony limbs, stretching toward the floor. The couch had a thick pelt of fur, six squat, hairy legs that ended in clawed feet, and a mouth full of irregular teeth. It was climbing up the wall.

Everything was growing. Growing something.

The policeman kept getting dragged, first to the far end of the hallway, then into the room with Gabriel and his book.

The man was still at the desk. The book was still in front of him. But it was hard to tell how much of him was left. Gabriel's arms had fused with the book up to the elbows. His head was down, on the book, on the desk. The policeman couldn't see anything of his face. Just his ears at the level of the pages. Gabriel's feet had melted into the floor. And from his back, it was as though he had tried to grow wings, seven wings of skin and cloth, but they were too big for the room and had melded with the ceiling instead. The walls of the room were hair and plaster. No. Splinters and sinew. No. The policeman didn't know what the walls were. And, within a breath, it didn't matter anymore. Things that felt like fingers, or snakes, rose out of the floor and coiled around him, curled into his mouth. Then the policeman was somewhere else. He was a winged serpent in a crystal cave. He was a gargantuan snail with a thousand colonies of sentient insects anchored to his shell. He was a huge, many-legged thing nestled inside a silver egg. When he hatched and spread his wings across the sky, the world would shudder with wonder.

Outside the apartment, the father and the superintendent looked at each other, then back at the door.

"Officer?" the superintendent yelled. "Officer?"

"What do we do now?" the father said. "Do we call the police?"

"That *was* the police," the superintendent said.

"I mean call them again," the father said. "My girls are still in there. They're still there; do you hear me? We have to do something!"

"What do I tell them?"

"I have no idea," the father said.

7.

Team Three's van was caught behind an idling taxi. Grace, behind the wheel, cursed under her breath.

"Take the next left," Liam said.

"How much time do you think we have?" Grace said.

"The police were called just before we landed," Liam said. "Something strange in the neighborhood. An officer arrived at the scene. Nothing else yet."

"All right, then," Menchú said. "The usual plan. Grace, you take point. Liam, you're right behind her. Sal, I want you to get the artifact, whatever it is. Okay?"

"Okay," Sal said.

Menchú looked at Sal—her eyes sharp, her jaw set.

"Are you all right?" he said.

"Yeah, I'm fine," Sal said. "Why?"

"You look worried."

"This?" Sal said, pointing at her face. "This is my game face."

Liam laughed.

"Game face?" Menchú said.

"You all must have game faces," Sal said. "Everyone has a game face."

"I . . . ," Menchú said.

"Oh, you have a game face, all right," Liam said to Menchú. "It looks like this." He narrowed his face and scrunched up his nose.

"I do not look like that," Menchú said.

"If we could get a camera to work around here," Liam said, "you would know just how wrong you are."

"I don't have a game face," Grace said.

"You don't ever *not* have a game face," Liam said. "Take the next right."

They turned the corner onto a wider street. There was a police car parked in front of an apartment building.

"At last," Grace said. She stopped the van behind the car. They all started getting out.

"You're sure you're okay?" Menchú said to Sal.

"Yeah," Sal said, a trace of irritation in her voice. *Everyone stop asking.* "Let's do this."

The door to the apartment building was open.

"The call was to the second-floor apartment," Liam said. "The super said two girls from another apartment are trapped in there."

They bounded up the stairs. At the landing they met the super-intendent and the father.

"Who are you?" the superintendent said.

"You called the police," Menchú said.

The superintendent and father looked at each other.

"The police already arrived," the father said.

"We're backup," Menchú said. "Where's the officer?"

The superintendent pointed at the door. "You might want to wait just a moment," he said. "Until it does it again."

"Does what again?" Menchú said.

The door sighed. Bulged outward and flattened again.

"I see," Menchú said.

"What's going on?" the superintendent said.

"Don't worry," Menchú said. "We've seen this before."

"I've been a super for twenty-three years, and I've never seen anything like it."

"Which is a testament to the fine job you're doing keeping up the building," Menchú said. "I see this all the time."

He nodded to Grace, Liam, and Sal. Grace positioned herself on point, right in front of the door. Liam and Sal were right behind her.

Menchú turned to the father and superintendent. "Better get back," he said. "Up. At least three steps." He reconsidered. "You know, better if you just go all the way up to the next landing."

"My two daughters are in there," the father said. "Are they in danger?"

"Not for much longer," Menchú said. "Now please give us some space to work."

The father and superintendent hesitated.

"*Go,*" Menchú said. This time they moved. They retreated to the landing above.

Menchú looked at Grace and nodded.

"Whenever you're ready," he said.

The apartment door flew open before they could move, and this time, four tentacles of muscle and hair rushed out, snapping, flailing. But Grace was too fast. She was inside the door before the tentacles could catch her. They turned back inward and snaked in the air toward her. She dodged them, caught them herself, and ripped them in half.

Another tentacle reached for the door. Liam jumped and blocked it from closing, so Sal got a nice view of what had become of Gabriel's apartment.

There was no apartment there anymore. It was a pulsing tangle of bone and hair, wood and teeth. Sal could see shapes lurching in the gloom. And Grace was fighting her way in. Something bellowed. Something else screeched.

"Need some help, maybe," Grace called.

A vine slithered across the floor to Liam's foot, grew a three-fingered hand, and wrapped itself around Liam's ankle. It started to tug.

"Oh no you don't," Liam said, and braced himself in the door-frame.

Sal raised a questioning eyebrow at Menchú, caught his eye. He nodded and handed her the shroud he'd had in the library. He pointed toward the door.

"Go," he said. "Get it. Whatever it is."

Sal leaped over Liam. Her feet landed on something soft. She looked down. It was a carpet, except that now there were tufts of hair growing out of it. It growled and writhed, tried to fold itself up over her legs and trap her. She kicked it off and kept moving down the hallway. The carpet slithered after her. The walls were closing in; the floor began to buckle. The air itself seemed to be thickening, filling with something. It was hard to run, way too hard. She was moving too slowly, like in a bad dream.

There was light, greenish light, coming from somewhere. To her left, out of the corner of her eye, she could see into what used to be the living room. Something was happening in there. There were two girls suspended in the air. They looked like they were floating in jelly. The floor was a heaving landscape of moss and spikes of wood, outcroppings of bone. A long, distended creature was curling around them in a corkscrew from the floor to the ceiling. A four-legged creature that used to be an end table but now had fur and spikes along its spine was crawling across the ceiling toward them. It was carrying something in its mouth. Sal couldn't tell what.

It was all too much, too much at once. For a moment it threatened to break her open. If she let it, it would put her on the floor, laughing or screaming or crying, or all three. But then her police officer's mind kicked in, the one that had seen murder victims and traffic accidents and suicides and just dealt with it, just gotten down to work. She took what she was seeing and put it away.

Later, later, she told herself. *Keep moving. Keep moving. End the threat now.*

She made it halfway down the hallway. And saw at last what Grace was fighting.

There were two of them, like spiders or crabs, things with bulbous bodies and spindly limbs. Things that were made of other things—tufts of hair, spurs of bone, thin muscles wrapped in papery skin. They both had huge, panting mouths, lined all the way around with sharp wooden teeth, and they made staggering lunges toward Grace, trying to catch her in their limbs. They would eat her alive if they did.

But Grace was too fast. Way too fast.

And Sal saw now why one of the things was moving slower than the other. Grace had pulled off three of its legs. The separated limbs lay in the muck on the floor. In the time Sal glanced down and glanced back up again, Grace ducked under the creature's body and took two more legs in her hands. As Sal watched, she pulled. The legs came out, and the creature, with only one leg left, toppled over. Grace jumped in the air and landed on the body with both feet. It caved in beneath the soles of her boots with a squelching *pop*. Its skin cracked and an orange-brown porridge leaked out of it. The other creature let out a long, angry wail.

"Go," Grace said. "I got this." She was wet and spattered, but her face was flush, her eyes alive.

She loves this part of her job, Sal thought. *Loves it.*

Sal kept going. The doorway at the end of the hall was closed. Sal put her shoulder to it and busted it open.

The first thing she saw was the policeman, lying face up. He was held down by a rug of long, thin fingers that looked like they were made of fat. They were growing from the floor, and they curled all around his body, into his mouth. The walls expanded and collapsed, expanded and collapsed, like a dying lung, panicking. The window at the far end of the room was coated in a translucent layer of skin. There was greenish-yellow light coming through the ceiling, through the walls, through the floor. And there, sitting at the desk at the other end of the room, a giant web of hair-pocked skin stretching from the ceiling to the floor and into his back, was a man, his head buried in a book.

It looked at first like he had fallen asleep. Like he'd been studying too hard. Then Sal noticed that she couldn't tell where his hands were. His hands, his arms—his *face*—were somehow inside the pages. As though the book had turned to water, and the man had dived right in, but then the book had solidified again when he was halfway inside.

There's no way he's alive, Sal thought. But he was. His chest rose and fell, rose and fell. In time with the walls.

It's the book, Sal thought. *Get the book.*

It was only a few feet to the desk.

But she couldn't run. She felt fingers grasping from the floor.

They were enveloping her feet; they were climbing up her legs. She wrenched one leg free and took a step closer to Gabriel. The fingers came at her faster. She pulled the other leg free, took another step. One more step and she'd be able to do what she needed to. But the fingers were skittering up to her waist now, across her chest and back, over her shoulders. They felt their way over the back of her head and onto her face. She shot her arm out, grasping wildly for the man at the desk. She couldn't reach him.

The fingers crawled over her eyes, over her nose, over her chin. She felt them, then, slipping between her teeth, wriggling down her throat. Her feet left the floor, and she was being dragged down.

Who would come for her? Grace? Menchú? Who would save those girls?

Those girls.

Sal opened her eyes.

The fingers were gone. The room, the apartment, the entire city of Madrid.

She was standing on the gentle, dark green slope of a soft hill under a pink sky, near the crescent shore of an orange sea. At the top of the slope was a low line of full trees. She could hear birds calling from far away in the darkness of the branches.

But around her, it was quiet. It was bliss.

Then she heard voices coming from the woods, instruments reedy and brassy, rattling percussion. A parade emerged from the shadows, heading down toward the ocean. There were dozens, no, hundreds of creatures in the throng, all knobby heads and spindly legs, and the music was frantic and joyful, full of expectation. The parade got thicker and thicker, and at last the trees parted and

Sal saw that maybe twenty of the creatures were carrying a platform on which sat a huge, six-armed goblin with serene eyes and a benevolent smile. The goblin laughed, deep and echoing, and the creatures cheered in reply.

The parade was heading down the hill. And Sal was in the way. She stood her ground.

Where else was she going to go?

The first of the creatures, a big drum strapped to its belly, got within just a couple of steps of her before it seemed to notice her and stopped. It let out a long whistle, and the parade came to a shambling, wheezing halt. The giant goblin's eyes, which had been fixed to the sky, looked down at Sal.

"You're interrupting," the goblin said. He spoke English, or he spoke Spanish and Sal heard English, or it was all magic and the language didn't matter.

Sal took a deep breath. She put the pink sky and the orange water out of her head and focused on the voice.

"You see that all is well," the goblin said. "What are you doing here?"

The man in the book, Sal thought. *This is him. Or I might as well assume it is until I have a better idea.*

"You're in danger," Sal said.

The goblin smiled. "I am right where I belong," it said. "This is the Anywhere that I want to be." The smile, friendly and peaceful, grew wider. "Would you like to join me here?" the goblin said.

"I'm already here," Sal said. "In fact, I'm not sure you gave me a choice."

"But it's beautiful here, isn't it?"

"Yes," Sal agreed. "It is. But I don't think I want to stay." She thought of what was happening back in the apartment. She knew she didn't have a lot of time. She took a chance.

"I guess I just wish you'd asked first," she said.

The goblin, for the first time, stopped smiling, and Sal saw an opening. *Whether the sky is pink or blue or plaid,* she thought, *it doesn't change the fact that this is, in the end, just another hostage negotiation.*

She looked through the goblin's enormous entourage and found them, quick: two pale little figures with thin limbs and heavy-lidded eyes. *Those are the girls,* she thought. *They have to be.*

She made a leap that she hoped would work.

"More important," she said, "I wish you'd asked *them.*"

The goblin's eyes shifted downward to look at the girls.

"They're happy here," it said.

"Are they?" Sal said. "Did you ask them?"

"They come over all the time, and beg me to let them stay. And I hear how they play. The things they imagine! They have the most creative minds." The goblin's smile returned. "In fact, everything you see around you now, from the trees to the hill to the sea—even to me—is from their heads. Did you know," it said, gesturing with three of its arms at its own body, "that this is the way they see me?"

Now all six arms spread out wide.

"And this is the world they want."

"For a while, I bet they do," Sal said. "But they live right upstairs from you, don't they?"

"Yes," the goblin said.

"So maybe they love all of this, just like you say. But only to visit. At the end of the day, they go home, don't they? Their father or mother gets them and they go home."

"That's right."

"Well," Sal said. "Their father is waiting outside right now, and he's really worried about them."

"He's a good man," the goblin said, "but they don't want to go yet."

"How do you know that?" Sal said.

"Because we're so happy."

"Because you don't see what's really happening. What you're doing to yourself, and to your apartment, and to those girls. Back there. In the world."

"Everything is fine back there," the goblin said.

"No," Sal said. "It isn't. Look for yourself. You can see back there, can't you?"

"Yes."

"Then look."

The goblin's eyes rolled skyward and kept rolling. They rolled all the way around, looking inward, into its skull. The goblin's mouth opened. It gasped.

"Oh God," it said, and shuddered.

Sal expected to feel some sense of victory, but it wouldn't come.

The eyes rolled back again and looked at Sal. Now the goblin's huge face was pleading.

"I didn't know," it said. "You have to believe I didn't."

Sal nodded. "I believe you. Can you fix it?"

"I can let them go, and everything else," the goblin said. "But I can't get myself out."

"If you let me go, I can do it," Sal said.

The goblin nodded. "Do it," it said. "Though I don't know how much of me will be left when you do." It set its jaw. It had made its decision. "I'm sorry I caused all of this," it said. "I didn't mean to."

"I can't imagine you did," Sal said. "You're Gabriel, right?"

"Yes."

"You're a good man too, Gabriel."

The goblin didn't answer.

"Now let us go," Sal said. "Please let us go."

The goblin closed its eyes. The sky, the sea, the forest, the parade—they all winked out.

With a long shout, Sal pulled herself free. She was back in the room, back in the apartment. The fingers were gone. But the whole place was shaking around her, on the verge of collapse. Gabriel, the man in the book, was twitching and writhing. The walls were coming down.

Sal stood up and took that final step, the last one she needed. She was close enough now. She fought her way through the sheets of skin around her, put one hand on the desk and the other hand on Gabriel's shoulder, and pulled.

He came free from of the book a lot more easily than she expected. There was a sound like a sheaf of wet paper being torn in half, and he just slid out, like a foal being born, bringing fat wads and strings of matter with him. She didn't have time to see if he still had hands, or arms, or a face. In that moment, she didn't care. It was the book. She slammed it shut, picked it up, took the shroud out of her jacket pocket, and wrapped the book in it.

There was a loud gasp, a choking sound. The walls stopped breathing. The skin across the window dried out, cracked, and split open. Sal expected something awful to come out of the tear, but nothing did. The skin just hung from the wall now, brittle, flapping, letting in light. The fingers holding the policeman to the floor had already withered into twigs. They looked like they would break as soon as he moved. The mud, the moss, the vines, all dried out in an instant, leaving only dust and scraps.

There was light from the hallway, natural light. Sal heard something in the hallway thump and clatter to the floor. Someone said, *"Whew!"*

Grace.

"I'm guessing you got it?" Grace called from the hallway. "Whatever it was?"

"Yeah, got it," Sal said.

"All clear," Grace yelled.

Menchú was there in seconds. He saw Sal crouched on the floor. The book, wrapped in the shroud, was on the floor next to her. She was checking the policeman's pulse.

"He's okay," she said.

"Great work," he said. "Really fine."

"Not fine enough for him, though," Sal said.

Gabriel lay on the floor, panting. At first Sal thought that he was just covered in something; something was on him. Then she saw what it was. He had aged. A lot. He was old, older than he was ever meant to be. He was a thousand years old and withered away. His eyes had sunk into their sockets. He turned his head from side to side, and the last wisps of his white hair fell away from his cracked scalp. His white tongue moved behind his shriveled lips.

"*¿Lo vieron?*" he said.

"What's he saying?" Sal said.

"He's asking us a question," Menchú said. "He is asking if we saw it."

Menchú knelt down beside Gabriel, put a hand on his chest.

"He's dying," Menchú said.

"*¿Lo vio?*" Gabriel said again.

"*Sí,*" Menchú said. "*Sí.*" It was a kindness, Sal realized. Menchú didn't know what Gabriel was talking about. But Sal did.

"*Sí,*" she said.

Gabriel cackled. A flood of slurred words rushed out of him. Menchú smiled, said words that had to be of consolation, of comfort, though Sal didn't understand them.

Gabriel coughed. The words slowed. He coughed again, twice. He tried to say something else, but he couldn't. A long, slow breath came out of him. Another one didn't follow. Menchú said a quick prayer and closed Gabriel's eyes.

"What was he saying?"

"He was telling me everything he saw," Menchú said. "Beautiful, exquisite things. The most wonderful things he had ever seen in his life." He looked back toward the hallway.

"That's not what we saw here," he said.

Sal didn't say anything.

The policeman opened his eyes and shifted on the floor, as if he was waking from a long nap. There was dust all over him, all that was left of the fingers holding him down. He opened his eyes and blinked. The first person he saw was Menchú.

"*¿Qué pasó?*" he said.

"*¿Saber?*" Menchú said.

It was as though there had been an explosion in the apartment two hundred years ago and then it had been left to rot. The ceiling was falling in. The floorboards were split, breaking up. The walls were losing their plaster. The furniture was toppled, overturned, broken, shredded. And everything was covered with dust and cobwebs. They hung from above. They lay in the corners and along the floor. The superintendent was walking through it in shock, shaking his head, moving from room to room—taking in the rusted oven, the shattered bathtub—in despair. Grace was in the hallway, dusting herself off. Liam already waited on the landing.

"Come on," he said. "Time to move."

The policeman was on his phone, calling for backup. He motioned for them to stay put. Grace already had her back to him and was halfway out of the place. Menchú was right behind her.

"Come on," he said to Sal. "This is the part where, right now, you're more criminal than police."

Before Sal left, she got a glimpse of the two girls. They were standing amid the wreckage of the living room, not a wrinkle on their clothes, not a hair out of place, huge smiles on their faces, their voices bright and cheerful. They were telling their father everything. They had seen wonderful things, amazing things. They had been to impossible places. They had to tell their father all about it. And he was there, on his knees, first hugging one, then the other. Just thankful that they were alive. Two siblings, side by side.

One of them recognized Sal and waved.

Perry, Sal thought. She realized she'd managed to keep him out of her thoughts for a couple of hours. The mission, its details and its danger, had pushed him to the side. But now there he was again, front and center. Unmoving in his hospital bed in the wood-paneled room. No, worse: the way he was just before he went under. Sal tried to dredge up an old memory to replace that—a day at the lake when they were kids, a fight in the backseat of the car, the stupid face he made at her when she graduated college. Anything. But she couldn't do it. What the Hand had done to Perry was in her head now for good, and there was nothing she could do to get rid of it.

8.

Sal felt the crash from the adrenaline high as soon as they were headed out to the airport. They watched a police van fly past them in the opposite direction, sirens blaring. She wondered if it was the team dispatched to investigate whatever had happened in Gabriel's apartment. She wondered what kind of sense the police would be able to make of it. They'd take a lot of pictures, do a lot of measurements, collect evidence. They'd get some vague sense of what had gone down by interviewing the superintendent and the father. There'd be some sketchy descriptions of everyone on Team Three, but not enough to incriminate anyone. And it would be clear that whatever had happened to the entire apartment, and to the poor guy with the book, couldn't have been done by four human beings in five minutes. Team Three would be just one more anomaly in a mountain of anomalies in the police report. The only facts in the case would be the damage to the apartment, that two girls and a police officer were still alive, and the man who lived in the place was dead. Of unknown causes.

Sal was a good cop—she knew that—but she wouldn't have been

able to put the case together with what the police had to work with. They didn't cover magic and demonology in forensics training.

Sal felt, then, an almost overbearing weight of all the cases she hadn't been able to close, all the loose ends she'd never tied up. The bodies with no names. The things she'd never quite managed to explain. How many of them were the tattered leftovers of some magical event? If she were to go looking, how many of those unsolved cases would she find in the files of the Black Archives?

Was this what Menchú had meant when he said that there was more magic coming into the world than ever? And would that just keep manifesting itself as a series of open cases, unexplainable phenomena, until there was so much magic in the world that it was too late to deny it?

We're not prepared for that, Sal thought as they got on the plane. *We have no idea how to live with it.*

She was asleep five minutes later.

She didn't feel much better when she woke up in Rome. There was a debriefing with Asanti in the Black Archives. It went by in a haze. Sal reported what needed reporting—what she saw and what she did—but couldn't offer much in the way of clarifying thoughts or analysis. Someone else was going to have to do the thinking right now. What she needed was sleep. About twenty hours of it.

She was still on the couch when the others got up to leave. First Grace, followed by Menchú. Liam lingered, as if he wanted to talk to her. Sal didn't have the energy so just closed her eyes for a moment. When she opened them again, Liam was already starting up the stairs. She got up at last.

"First mission," Asanti said. "How does it feel?"

Sal bristled for a second. That did it: Now everyone on the whole damn team wanted to know how she felt. But something in

Asanti's voice made her let down her guard. Asanti wasn't worried. She was just curious.

"How did it feel when you first got here?" Sal said.

Asanti smiled. "For me? I was excited. But I had already seen a bit of what magic could do, and that glimpse was not nearly as terrifying as what you saw. Or as personal."

"What did you see?" Sal said.

"That all of these things that we're locking away down here are part of our world. As much part of God's creation as the clouds in the air. Sometimes I suspect that if we understood it better, we would see that magic isn't so much a part of our world as it is that *we* are a part of *its* world."

"Magic is God, huh?" Sal said.

Asanti laughed. "I wouldn't go that far."

"You don't sound like you believe in the mission very much."

"Oh, I do," Asanti said. "I just don't believe magic is evil. What I believe is that most people should not be using it."

"Who should?" Sal said.

"Officially speaking?" Asanti said. "No one." Her smile faded at last. "I'm sorry about your brother."

"Thanks."

Sal was expecting another speech about how the Society was going to do everything it could to save him. But Asanti didn't say anything. She was just sorry. It was all that needed to be said about it. The silence in the conversation opened a door. Sal walked through.

"Asanti?" Sal said. "Are all the missions like that?"

"No," Asanti said. "Some of them are worse. Much worse. But you will see things no one else has seen. Things that, I think, will put you beyond faith. Faith asks you to believe that miracles can happen. You will know that miracles happen because you will have seen them with your own eyes. That's worth something, I think. Worth the hardship. Though I don't think it's worth losing a brother."

Sal knew the answer to her next question already, but she wanted to ask it. She wanted companionship.

"Will we be able to save him?" she said.

Asanti shook her head. "I don't know," she said. "But your best chance is here."

That was when it all caught up to her. Perry. She'd wanted to tell him to get lost, when he'd needed her help more than he ever had.

Grace. Tears of blood. Wrong smiles. The coma.

Fingers tangling around her legs. An apartment that looked like it'd been dropped from the top of a building and crashed into the street. A man turned into a husk with a wretched, euphoric smile on its face. *Did you see it? Did you see it?*

She saw it, all right.

She found herself crying, harder than she'd cried in a long time.

Asanti didn't say anything. Didn't ask any questions or offer cheap consolation. She just walked over from behind her desk and gave Sal a long hug, until the sobs stopped and her breathing steadied again.

"I just want my brother back," Sal said.

Asanti nodded.

Sal's phone pinged.

"What the hell?" Sal said.

"Who is it?" Asanti said.

Sal looked at her phone. "It's my parents."

"What are you going to tell them?" Asanti said. The phone was still pinging.

I am fighting monsters for the Catholic Church so I can save your son from a demon that possessed him after he opened a magic book. It was so ridiculous when she thought of it that way that she almost laughed. But what *was* she going to say?

Sal looked up at Asanti.

"I have no idea," she said.

EPISODE
3

FAIR WEATHER

MARGARET DUNLAP

1.

Sal's footsteps seemed unnaturally loud in the empty corridor. She stopped. No traffic noises from outside. No thrum of an ancient ventilation system. No voices from any of the rooms she had passed. In fact, no sign of another living soul in the last . . .

Sal sighed, checked her watch. Assuming time hadn't become completely unhinged—and what did it say about her life that *that* was now a necessary mental caveat?—she had been wandering, lost, in the back halls of the Vatican for nearly twenty minutes. Which meant she was late. And above and beyond Grace's strange fixation with punctuality, Sal hated being late.

Unfortunately, she also hated asking for directions. Throughout her career it had always been important to her to be the one who helped other people when they got lost, not the clueless rookie who had to get on the radio when she couldn't find her way through the South Bronx.

Not that she had ever done that.

Although, Sal thought, *if I'm getting nostalgic for my days in the four-two, living in Rome must really be getting to me.* As if that much hadn't been obvious the night before, when she'd caught herself watching MSNBC International just to hear familiar accents.

Sal looked around the immaculate corridor, filled with hundreds of years of art and artifacts. There was no sign that anyone used the corridor for anything, but still—not a speck of dust or dead roach to be seen. Clearly, it was time to get her head around the fact that—at least until she was able to bring her brother out of his demon-induced coma—she was really not in New York anymore.

There was nothing to be done about it.

It was time to ask for directions.

If only there was someone to ask.

Anyone at all.

Where is Tom Hanks when you need him? Hell, she'd reached the point where she'd have settled for a homicidal albino monk.

"You probably took a wrong turn at the Old Gallery of the Late Crusades," said a man behind her. "It's an easy mistake to make, looks almost exactly like the New Gallery of the Early Crusades."

Sal whirled, reaching (for the hundredth time) for the gun she no longer carried. Although in this case, being unarmed was probably just as well, since the man who had spoken turned out to be outfitted in full tactical gear with what looked like a bolt-action rifle hanging easily at his side. Getting into a shoot-out in the back halls of the Vatican would be even more embarrassing than getting lost.

"Who are you?" Sal demanded. Then after a moment to reflect she added, "And how did you know I spoke English?"

The man answered her second question first. "I knew you spoke English because you're clearly the new recruit for Team Three, Sal Brooks, formerly of the NYPD," he said. "As for me, I'm Christophe Bouchard, currently leader of Team One, formerly of the Canadian Rangers, Quebec region." Bouchard grinned at her. "It's too bad we didn't get called in on the New York job. I would have snapped you up before Menchú got the chance to recruit you for the Black Hole."

"Black Hole?"

"Team Three. Books go in; nothing comes out." He turned and gestured down the hall. "Here, let me walk you out of the maze, or Asanti will think I've stolen you."

Sal decided, since he had volunteered, that this didn't count as asking for directions. Falling into step beside him, she asked, "So, if you know all about me, why didn't you come say hi earlier?"

"Team One and Team Three have historically not had the best of relations."

"Why not? Antique firearms aside, you're the most normal person I've met in weeks."

"Antique?"

"Were you afraid a semiauto would freeze in the harsh Roman winters?"

"You were police. How often were people happy to see you show up?"

Sal shot him a look. "You want to see my badge? I still am police. Just on loan to the Vatican." *Technically, anyway.*

Bouchard let it go. "We're the guys with the guns who get called in when there's something the Black Hole can't suck up. And Menchú and Asanti don't like admitting they need help."

They rounded a corner, and a familiar voice added, "Also, Team One are a bunch of trigger-happy loons who never found a problem they didn't think an arseload of C-4 couldn't solve."

Liam. Sal wasn't sure if he wasn't happy to see her, wasn't happy to see Bouchard, or wasn't happy to see her *with* Bouchard.

Bouchard shrugged. "I don't hear a lot of complaints."

"You might if you left anyone alive behind you."

Sal could practically feel the tension vibrating between them. "Okay, then. If the territory has been sufficiently pissed on, Liam is no doubt here to remind me how late I am, and I'm sure you have to go load your blunderbuss or something."

Bouchard gave her a wounded look. "You really aren't going to let this gun thing go, are you?"

"Not anytime soon, no."

Shaking his head, Bouchard offered Sal an ironic salute, and with a nod to Liam, left them.

Liam scowled as he watched the other man's departing figure vanish around a corner. "We should get back. Asanti's got something for us."

"Glowy Magic 8 Ball acting up again?"

"Signs point to yes."

As it turned out, the Orb was sitting quietly in its apparatus. But that didn't seem to make Asanti any less nervous.

"The shopkeeper said he thought he had a book for me, a really old one, in Greek. But when I went to see him this morning, it was gone."

"The book?" Sal asked.

"The bookshop."

A pause.

"Well," said Father Menchú, "that's rarely good."

The priest-turned-demonic-book-finder heaved himself to his feet and reached for his coat as he turned to Liam. "Take fifteen minutes to dig up whatever history you can on the address, then head for the van. I'll get Grace and meet you there."

"Fifteen minutes isn't much time," said Liam.

Asanti was already headed toward her reference stacks. "I'll keep working from here. I'll call you if I find anything, or if the Orb spikes."

Menchú nodded and turned for the spiral stairs leading up out of the Archives. Sal called after him, "What about me?"

He paused, clearly having forgotten that Sal was in the room. Sal quashed a spike of resentment. The rest of the team had been working together for years. It would take more than a few weeks for her to find her niche. But Menchú had recruited her, and it stung to be overlooked.

He reached into his pocket and tossed an item he found there to Sal.

"Go warm up the car."

Sal looked at the van keys in her hand. She was about to object that that wasn't exactly what she'd had in mind, but there was no one left to object to. Sal sighed. She really hoped she didn't get lost on the way to the Vatican garage.

Of course, even though Sal had successfully found, checked over, and started the team's ancient white panel van without getting lost even once, Grace still insisted on driving. Given her experience with Italian drivers, Sal didn't put up much of a fight. Traffic was at least a relatively nonviolent outlet for Grace's more aggressive tendencies.

On the way, Liam briefed the team.

"Turns out, Asanti has been cultivating her own connections with the antiquarian booksellers of Rome for the last fifteen years. Which would have saved me the trouble of setting up my own if she'd bothered to mention it earlier. Anyway, her hope was that if someone came across an artifact, they'd tip her off and for once we could get to the book before anyone managed to open the damn thing."

"How's that working out?" asked Grace.

"Since this is the first we've heard of it, obviously, they didn't find anything that needed to be bagged. Until now, I guess. But she says it has netted some obscure esoterica for the reference library." Liam paused. "And also for her personal collection of diaries written by French travelers in West Africa during the colonial period. Which is another thing I didn't know she had, but is apparently one of the most extensive in the world."

"Everyone needs a hobby," Sal mused.

Grace frowned. "I thought Asanti collected sketches by the early modernists."

"Everyone needs . . . many hobbies?"

Menchú cleared his throat. "Does this particular bookseller have a history of interesting finds?"

Liam shook his head. "Average, at best. But he keeps good biscotti in the shop, so she visits regularly, anyway. And before you ask, I checked the address against our records. No history of possessions, unsolved crimes, or even strange traffic patterns in the area. If something weird happened, it probably came into the shop from outside, rather than tunneling up from underneath."

"Does tunneling happen a lot?" Sal asked.

"Iceland," Grace reminded her as she pulled across three lanes of traffic and threw the van into park.

Menchú caught Sal's expression and put a reassuring hand on her shoulder. "It's rarely volcanoes. Sinkholes, sometimes, but like Liam said, that doesn't seem likely in this case."

Sal was not reassured. "I would feel a lot better if I thought you were just trying to haze the new guy," she said, and slid open her door.

Unfortunately, she was pretty sure they weren't.

✦　✦　✦

When Asanti had said that the shop was gone, she hadn't been exaggerating. What had once been an antiquarian bookshop, tucked away on a side street between a jewelry store and an art gallery, was now a pile of rubble. The city police had put up tape across the entrance, but there was no other sign of an official presence on the scene.

"Just as well," Menchú said. "Okay, everyone, let's find out what happened."

Menchú went over to talk to a small group of onlookers clustered on the sidewalk about half a block away. Liam pulled out his laptop.

Grace considered the ruins of the bookshop, the undisturbed buildings on either side, and the complete lack of an obvious demon or other bad guy for her to start hitting, and plopped herself down on the bumper of the van with a copy of *Cold Comfort Farm*.

Sal, not sure what else to do, joined Grace by the van.

"Tired of Jane Austen?"

"Finished."

"Finished?"

"She only wrote six novels."

"You know, if you ever want a break from reading all of English literature, maybe we could—"

"Can't."

Sal blinked. "You don't know what I was going to ask."

"You were going to suggest we grab a drink after work."

"Or coffee. It could have been coffee."

"I don't have time."

Well, Sal could certainly recognize a brush-off when she heard it. Especially when it was delivered with a sledgehammer. She went over to join Liam instead. He was squatting near the wreckage with his laptop balanced on one muscular arm and didn't look up at her approach. "I'm not getting much interference. That's a good sign: If the book *was* one of ours, at least no one opened it."

"Do all demons wreck electronics?" Sal asked.

Liam shuddered. "Not *all*. Just most."

"So maybe this was one of those?"

"Let's hope not," said Liam, "but if I'm playing *CSI* for this little party, I'll take a working computer for as long as I can get it."

Sal couldn't argue with that.

The procedure should have been familiar to Sal. Show up at the scene, talk to witnesses, start putting together a narrative to explain the events that had turned an average day into an extraordinary one, at least for this small segment of the population. The problem was that while Sal had the experience and the training for this situation, she didn't know enough Italian to be useful. Besides, between a naturally warm demeanor and his clerical collar, Menchú was ridiculously good at getting the locals to talk to him, so even if she had been able to do more than stumble through a dinner order in a mixture of Italian and cop Spanish, it wasn't as though he actually *needed* her help.

So here she was, finally in a situation that she actually had the skills for, and she still had nothing to do.

And then Sal spotted it.

Across the street was a narrow doorway, labeled with a small plaque that read HOTEL TRANQUILLO and adorned with five flag stickers that advertised the languages spoken within. One of the stickers was the Union Jack. Bingo.

Inside, the hotel was certainly *tranquillo*. In fact, it was deserted. Behind an unattended desk in the front foyer was a slightly open door, and beyond it, Sal could hear voices speaking English. Since no one was there to stop her, Sal invited herself in.

The door led to a courtyard filled with four tourist couples and their guide. Or, at least, Sal assumed that the odd man out was their guide, since he didn't have a partner with a matching Windbreaker. Also, he was a good twenty years younger than the median age for the group, and carried a clipboard.

Sal tapped the man on the shoulder. "Excuse me?"

"Sorry to disturb the tranquility. We'll be out of your way in just a few minutes." Then he turned, saw Sal, and blinked. "You're not Sophia."

"No."

"Well, we'll be out of the courtyard soon. Is that what you needed?"

Sal raised an eyebrow and gave him her best *Are you kidding me?* expression. "No."

The man blinked again. He had very nice brown eyes, actually, almost honey colored. "Ah. Yes, I'll stop anticipating. Bad habit of mine. Sorry. Ask your question."

"My name is Sal Brooks. I'm a detective."

The man took this in. "Aaron Smith, pleased to meet you."

"Did your group stay here last night?"

"Yes."

"Mind if I ask them a few questions?"

"Not at all."

Unfortunately, the tourists all proved to be singularly unhelpful:

"Slept like a log."

"Didn't hear a thing."

"So jet-lagged, didn't move all night."

"Only thing I felt was Bruce snoring next to me."

Sal was about to thank the group for their time and leave empty-handed when the guide pulled her aside.

"The building that went down. The old bookshop?"

"Yes. Do you know it?"

"Actually, I was there yesterday."

Sal raised an eyebrow. "Oh?"

"A lot of my groups stay at this hotel, and I sometimes go over to the bookshop to chat with the owner if flights run late and I have a little time to kill," he said, then added, "He kept really good biscotti in the shop."

"That's the rumor."

"Anyway, I don't know if this is important, but when I stopped in, he was having a discussion with another customer. It seemed like it was getting heated."

"What were they arguing about?"

"I didn't exactly linger, but from what I could tell, the young woman was there to pick up a book. Apparently, the owner had inadvertently promised it to two different customers and didn't want to sell to her anymore."

"Do you remember anything about this woman?"

"I think she was in her twenties? Blond, tanned, like she spent a lot of time outside."

"Italian?"

"Australian, I think, from the accent. She was wearing deck shoes and a polo shirt, like a uniform, if that helps."

"Did you notice a logo? Name tag?"

"Sorry."

"That's okay. Thank you for your help."

Sal turned to go, but the guide's voice stopped her.

"Is he all right?"

"Who?" Sal asked.

"The shopkeeper. Did he get out of the store before it collapsed?"

Sal paused. She had no idea. And she realized that this tour guide was the first person that day who had even asked. It hadn't even occurred to *her* to ask, which wasn't exactly a comfortable thought, since protecting people was kind of baked into her job description.

The guide sensed her unease. "Sorry. None of my business."

Sal nodded and quickly left him and his tour group behind her.

Katie returned to the boat later than she had planned—she'd hoped to get back the previous night—but she wasn't surprised to find Paul, the first mate, waiting up for her.

"Skip making you stand watch while we're in port now?"

Paul drew her into his lap, and Katie put up only token resistance. "Just wanted to make sure you got home safe."

"And here I am, safe. . . . Or do you want to check for yourself?"

She expected him to take that as his cue to let his hands begin a slow migration down from her waist, but instead, Paul reached for the plastic bag she still carried. "Is that it?"

"Yes."

"Lemme see."

Katie tugged it away. "Since when do you care about Mr. Norse's books?"

"We sail all over the world chasing these things, and this is the first time you've ever brought one back."

"We do not sail all over the world looking for books."

"Don't we? When was the last time we were in port and there wasn't some bookshop for you to check out?"

Katie had never particularly thought about it. "Okay, so he likes books. So what?"

"Did you tell him you had this one?"

"Of course. I called from the train."

"Then why haven't we gotten word to go meet him? Or that he's coming here? I've been on the bridge all night. Nothing. He finally finds what he's looking for, and now he doesn't even want to see it?"

"Could be about the chase."

Paul snorted at this. "If he doesn't want to see it, I do."

"There's nothing to see. It's just an old book."

"Maybe I want to read it. I'm a man of letters."

Katie swatted him with her free hand. "I've been to Athens with you—you don't read Greek. Besides, I have strict instructions. This thing goes straight into the safe."

"Fine," he said, and let her go.

Katie pushed herself up off Paul's lap, taking the bag, book, and herself out of reach. His voice caught her at the threshold.

"Don't you wonder, Katie?"

"No," she said, and slipped away.

It was true, Katie thought as she tucked the book into the owner's private safe. She didn't wonder. She had seen enough when the book-seller had shown it to her in the shop.

Whatever this book was, she wanted no part of it.

"Ostia," Grace said without looking up from her book.

Father Menchú nodded in agreement.

"'Ostia'?" Sal echoed.

Liam took pity and explained. "Small suburb not far from here, on the coast. It's got an ancient silted-up harbor that rivals Pompeii.

You should check it out sometime when we're not on duty."

"Thank you, department of tourism. Why Ostia? Are Australian expats really into silted harbors?"

Grace finished her book, rose from the sidewalk, and started for the van. "Tell her on the way," she said. "Daylight's burning."

Father Menchú shot Grace a look that Sal had difficulty reading—impatience? Guilt?—before turning back to answer Sal's question. "Ostia is the closest place to Rome where you can berth a yacht."

2.

Twenty minutes of Grace's maniacal driving later, they were in Ostia: home of commuting Romans, ancient harbors, and a crapton of yachts.

Sal looked out at the marina. What she knew about boats began and ended with the Staten Island Ferry and reruns of *The Love Boat* that she had watched with her college roommates in a fog of cheap booze and insomnia.

Liam was on the phone with Asanti. Grace—still lacking someone to kick in the face—was reading a new book. Menchú stared out at the yachts, frowning. Sal approached him.

"It doesn't look like all the crews wear polo shirts. If you're right about where our girl came from, that narrows it down a little bit, at least."

Menchú made a noncommittal *hmm* noise.

"I could wander down, see if I can pick up some gossip," she offered.

Menchú's eyes were still fixed on the docks. After a long pause, he finally said, "I don't think that will be necessary."

"Look," said Sal. "I think I just proved I can be useful. Let me do my job."

Menchú turned to her in surprise. "Of course you can be useful. That's why I wanted you on the team. But I believe there's a simpler way to find the boat we're looking for."

"And what is that?" Sal couldn't keep the edge of impatience out of her voice.

Menchú pointed to a vessel docked at the end of the marina. "Does that yacht look . . . blurry to you?"

Sal looked. Squinted. Looked again. Damn him. It did.

The view got less and less blurry as they approached the boat, which according to the writing on the transom was called the *Fair Weather.* Menchú took point, and Sal was curious to finally see an alleged cover story in action. So far, every cover she'd seen the team use basically went: "Look at the weird shit going on right in front of you. We are here to deal with it. Do you want to deal with it yourself? No, we didn't think so. Thank you for your cooperation."

Captain Childress, however, was proving skeptical.

"I am sorry," Menchú said, managing to sound both apologetic and puzzled without giving an inch to the resolute captain. "We were told the vessel was for sale."

"That's correct," said the captain, "but if you want a tour, you're going to have to go through the sales broker or speak directly to Mr. Norse, the owner, before I can let you aboard."

Apparently, the team didn't look like people about to drop multiple millions on a boat. Which, in fairness, was an accurate impression. The Catholic Church probably had deep pockets, but

Sal got the feeling that buying a yacht wasn't an expense request Asanti would be able to get approved.

As Menchú went in for another attempt, Sal heard a familiar voice talking to someone in the next slip. She looked over to check. Yes. It was Aaron, the guide from the Hotel Tranquillo. Frowning, Sal went to investigate.

"Fancy meeting you here."

The guide seemed unruffled by her sudden appearance. "Hello again," he said.

The deckhand he'd been talking to shot Sal a smile. "Hey, I'm Nick."

Sal ignored him and kept her attention on Aaron. "What brings you to Ostia?" she asked.

"I handed my group over to an archaeological expert for a tour of the old harbor. It's impressive. Like Pompeii without the crowds."

"So I hear. If it's that good, why aren't you with them?"

"It's only impressive the first seventy times. After that, it goes downhill fast. And I try to keep up with the crews that come through. Sometimes their guests are looking for a private tour."

Sal nodded to Childress and the *Fair Weather* behind them. "Ever talk to him?"

At this, Nick let out a short laugh. "If you're looking for work over there, don't bother. The *Fair Weather* doesn't charter, and never takes extra hands."

"Close crew?" Sal asked.

"Paranoid owner."

"What's he got to be paranoid about?"

"Who knows? Mafia ties? Drug money? Cult leader? Whatever it is, it made him enough money to buy his boat, so I guess he's pretty good at it." Nick made this sound lascivious, although Sal had no idea how he managed to pull off the effect. Everyone had their talents, she supposed.

"Well, thanks, Nick, and . . . Aaron, was it?" She turned back to the guide.

He stuck out a hand. "Yes. And you're quite welcome."

Sal shook it. His hand was warm and dry. Grip was good. Which was faintly surprising for a man who apologized as frequently and easily as Aaron did, but Sal tried not to read into that. As she let go of his hand, Liam appeared at her elbow, and Sal let the Irishman draw her aside.

"At your old job, how did you get into places people didn't want to let you in?"

"With a battering ram."

"Subtly?"

"With a warrant?"

Liam gave her a withering look. Sal answered with an apologetic shrug.

"I was a beat cop; then I was a detective. I wasn't doing weird undercover shit. Except once on a RICO thing . . ." Sal trailed off. *Actually, if the owner of the* Fair Weather *does have mob ties, that might come in handy.*

"Hey," she said, turning back to Nick and Aaron, but Nick had, thank goodness, returned to work, and Aaron was nowhere to be seen. Must have gone back to get his tour group.

"Hey what?" asked Liam.

"Do you think captains of yachts with shady, paranoid owners are as nervous as low-level fences?"

"I have no idea what you're talking about."

"It's okay. If I'm wrong, at least Grace will probably get to hit something."

"That should put her in a better mood."

"Win-win, then."

Putting on her best own-the-street swagger, Sal walked back to where Menchú and Captain Childress were still talking. Or rather, Menchú was talking. Childress was rapidly losing patience. It would have been nice to have a little more information to really sell this, but ultimately, the key was confidence, not evidence. Fortunately for her.

As they walked, Sal whispered to Liam, "Stand behind me, don't say anything, and look like a badass."

"You want Grace to play heavy, too?"

"I need someone who looks like a badass. Grace looks about as threatening as a wet cat."

"Clearly you've never tried to bathe a cat."

"Not the point. Can you handle not smiling for two minutes?"

"I'll do my best."

"Good."

And then there wasn't time to say anything else because Sal was at Menchú's side. She tapped him on the shoulder. "Look, we don't have time for this. You may as well tell him that we're here for the book."

"Sal—?"

"What book?" the captain broke in.

Sal turned to him. "The book that was supposed to be collateral."

And there was the hook. Sal maintained her blandest expression and willed the captain's mind to fill in the blanks with appropriately terrifying details.

The captain hesitated. Shit. He wasn't going to go for it.

And then Menchú effortlessly picked up Sal's thread, as though they had done this a hundred times before. "Perhaps," he suggested gently, "we should discuss this somewhere more private."

Sal sensed Liam shifting his weight behind her and pictured him squeezing a heavily tattooed fist. Unfortunately, it would have ruined the effect to turn and look.

Captain Childress swallowed, then sighed. "Whatever dispute you've got with the owner, there's no need to take it out on my crew. I promise you, they're just here to run the boat."

Father Menchú gave him a reassuring nod. "I swear to you, we have no desire to hurt anyone."

The captain eyed Liam nervously. "Even him?"

"Especially him."

With a last furtive look up and down the dock, the captain moved aside, and Sal and the others stepped onto the yacht.

As they followed the captain through the boat, Father Menchú touched Sal's elbow, wordlessly directing her to fall in beside him and let Liam and Grace pass.

"What made you think that would work?" he asked.

Sal shrugged in what she hoped was a nonchalant manner. "Gut feeling."

"Your new friend on Team One didn't tell you about any of this?" asked Menchú.

Sal blinked in genuine surprise. "No. Why would he be involved? I thought Liam didn't find any indications of magic at the scene."

"He didn't. But something caused that bookshop to collapse." Father Menchú let that sit between them for a moment, then asked, "Any other gut feelings I should be aware of?"

"Not so far." Sensing that Father Menchú wasn't quite satisfied, Sal added, "Nothing concrete. I'll give you a full debrief once we get back to HQ."

Father Menchú smiled. "I never doubted you would." And with that, he quickened his pace to catch up to the others.

Frowning, Sal followed him to a small lounge area. What she saw stopped her in her tracks. The blur effect that Menchú had noticed on the boat had transferred. While the ship around them appeared perfectly solid and sharply focused, the rest of the world, visible through the lounge's floor-to-ceiling windows, now seemed shrouded in a filmy mist. Sal looked to the other members of the team and saw that they had seen it as well. The captain, however, appeared oblivious.

Sal shuddered. Whatever was going on, they needed to find—and close—the book that was causing it. Quickly.

"What's this about?" the captain asked.

"The book belongs to the Catholic Church—" But that was as far as Menchú got before a second man came in from the deck.

"Who are they?" he asked the captain.

"Associates of Mr. Norse."

The other man made a skeptical noise to express his opinion of associates of the owner, but otherwise did not dignify that with a coherent response.

"This is my first mate," the captain explained.

"What do they want with the book?" the first mate asked.

There was a pause, and Menchú asked, very calmly, "What do you know about the book?"

He glared. "Nothing. It's just some old book Katie said she was picking up for Mr. Norse."

The first mate's eyes were locked on Menchú, but his hand was reaching for the pocket of his khaki trousers. Sal's training kicked in instantly. "DO. NOT. MOVE." Her hands went to her holster.

Except, dammit, she *still* did not carry a gun. That realization slowed Sal for a fraction of a second. And in that fraction of a second, a lot of things happened. Very quickly.

The first mate reached into his pocket and came out holding the wooden grip of a small but viciously curved knife. As he swung it through the air toward Father Menchú's throat, the light caught it and the blade shimmered, wickedly sharp.

Sal grabbed Father Menchú by the arm and dragged him away from the first mate, as the captain reached out at the same moment and attempted to knock his officer's arm aside. Their elbows caught, and with a snarl, the first mate tightened the arc of his swing, bringing his arm back around to try to stab the captain.

And then, suddenly, Grace was in the middle of the fray.

Sal wasn't even sure how the other woman had gotten across the room. One moment she was holding up a wall with her shoulder, and the next she was standing between the captain and the first mate.

Correction: Grace had hurled herself bodily right at the first mate's descending right arm, pinning it between his body and hers, while she wrapped her legs around his waist and used every ounce of her mass like a cannonball. And while Grace's mass wasn't all that much, it was enough to throw off the first mate's center of gravity.

That's a hell of a move, Sal thought, *if you aren't worried about breaking your fall on the way down.*

Sure enough, when the first mate toppled, Grace fell right along with him, tumbling over his head, and Sal could have sworn that she could hear the crack of two skulls against the floor. But either

Sal misheard, or Grace simply didn't care. An instant later Grace was back on her feet with her heel planted against the fallen first mate's windpipe.

"Do you need him able to speak for questioning?" she asked Father Menchú. Then added, "Decide quickly. The fall will only stun him for a couple of seconds."

"Please," Menchú said.

The captain gaped. "What are you talking about? You can't just—"

The first mate lunged up, and Grace calmly kicked him in the temple. He fell back to the floor, barely conscious. Sal pulled out her handcuffs—which she did still carry, thank you very much—and was about to ask Grace if she wanted her to step in when the man wrenched himself to one side. He still had the knife, and his hand was already in motion.

This time, the blade struck home.

Before even Grace had time to react, the first mate buried the knife in his own heart. The wet *thunk* of impact was followed by a fountain of steaming arterial spray, hot and coppery in the air. Sal moved to cover the wound, apply pressure, do something, but Liam stopped her. Grace was already blocking the captain.

"Don't touch the body," Liam said. "Until we know what was in him, we don't know about possible contamination."

Sal fell back, remembering Perry, and the thing that was not-quite-Perry, and the way he had turned his former roommates into puppets.

"He's not a body," the captain objected. "His name is Paul. I've worked with him for ten years—"

The captain abruptly stopped talking. The body, or Paul, or whatever it had been, caved in around the stab wound in its chest.

Flesh and bones collapsed, melting into a rancid black ooze that smoked against the yacht's immaculate taupe carpet.

As Sal watched, the rib cage gave way with a wet squelch and a fresh gush of steam. The captain was right about one thing. It wasn't a body.

Not anymore.

3.

"We should get out of here," Grace said.

"Out of this room? Or off the boat?" Sal wasn't really expecting an answer, but Grace supplied one.

"The room, now. The boat, eventually."

"What about that?" Menchú indicated the expanding puddle of black goo.

Liam knelt by the body, poking at it with a silver-plated pen he'd found somewhere. "It's an exothermic reaction. That's where all the steam is coming from. But it doesn't look corrosive. What the owner is going to do about the carpet is another problem entirely—"

Behind Sal, the door opened. "Hey, Skip, are you in here—?" The voice, and its pleasant Australian accent, cut off abruptly. A young woman wearing a uniform polo shirt stood in the doorway. Sal supposed she should have expected her to show up sooner or later.

The woman, however, was clearly not expecting to see a group of strangers in the lounge. Then she spotted the remains of the first mate and let out a terrified, wordless scream.

Even as Sal helped maneuver the woman back out of the room, she felt just a little bit jealous.

She could have used a good scream too.

The door to the lounge had barely slammed shut behind them before Grace was bracing the woman—who couldn't have been older than twenty-five—against a wall.

"What did you do with the book?"

"The book?"

"The one you bought last night," Father Menchú clarified, escorting the captain out into the lounge, "from the little shop in Rome."

"I . . . What?" She looked helplessly to Captain Childress for guidance.

"It's okay, Katie," he said. "Just tell them."

"What happened to Paul?"

"The book," Grace said.

"I put it in Mr. Norse's safe."

"Take us there. Now."

Skip said it was okay, so Katie led the strangers through the owner's suite and into the closet where his personal safe was secured. She hoped like hell the book was still where she had left it. She hated to think what these people would do if they thought she had lied to them.

They wouldn't even let her open the safe herself. Just demanded the combination, and Katie decided not to argue. Not after what they'd done to Paul.

While the strangers were distracted with the safe, Captain Childress stepped up behind her, speaking low in her ear. "Whatever they want, Katie, just give it to them. Keep them busy. If I see a chance, I'm going for the radio."

Katie nodded and wondered if his first call would be to the police or to Mr. Norse. Katie had heard the rumors about the *Fair Weather* before she signed on, but the promotion to chief steward and purser was too good to pass up. So what if the owner was interested in rare books? She'd met plenty of rich people with much stranger hobbies. And the weirder rumors, the whispers of strange and evil things, were too wild to be credible. Besides, the crew had seemed nice, the lack of charters meant lower tips but also lower aggravation, and ultimately, in the sixteen months she'd been aboard, she hadn't regretted her decision once.

Until she picked up that damn book.

The big guy with the tattoos finally finished checking the safe for . . . whatever he was checking it for. Was he smudging the room with sage? Anyway, he finally got the safe open, and then the one dressed like a priest used what looked like an old pillowcase to pick up the book.

He frowned and looked at her. "Did you open it?" he asked.

Katie shook her head.

"It's okay if you did," he pressed. "We just need to know."

"I didn't," Katie said. "It was creepy."

"If it was so creepy, why did you argue with the bookseller when he didn't want to sell it?" asked the brunette woman who hadn't slammed Katie up against a wall.

"Because Mr. Norse had arranged to buy it."

"Do you know why he wanted it?"

"No."

"You didn't ask?"

"I'm the head steward. If the owner wants something, I get it for him. I don't ask why he wants it, and even if he had told me, I wouldn't tell you."

"So he did tell you," said the Asian woman, who *had* slammed her up against the wall.

Katie gave her a withering glare, but did not answer.

"Guys, bigger problem here?" said the big tattooed guy. "If she didn't open it, what happened to the first mate? I'm going to guess that he didn't generally go around trying to stab people, not to mention the whole melting-into-black-goo routine."

"Maybe he opened it. Or touched it, or was susceptible for some reason. I don't think that's really our number one problem right now," said the brunette.

"We have a bigger problem than a dead first mate turning to goo on the carpet?"

"Yes," the brunette said. "Normally, once we've bagged the book, it's problem solved, right?"

"In general."

"Then why is the view out the window still blurred?"

Katie turned. The closet was too small to accommodate more than one person at a time, so most of the group was gathered in Mr. Norse's stateroom, which had a set of glass doors that led out onto a private balcony.

The view looked fine. Katie was about to let it go when she remembered the captain's request for a distraction. Well, she'd see what she could do.

"Blurred? Are you all high or something?"

"Ignore her," said the Asian woman.

"No." Katie pointed emphatically at the brunette. "She said the view was blurry, and it's clearly not. I've been cooperating, but if you're all just a bunch of junkies . . ."

She could see them exchanging looks as she continued to rant. Well, that was fine. As long as they weren't looking at Skip, they could roll their eyes about her all they wanted.

Katie yelped and jumped as she felt something cold at the back of her neck. A chain. The brunette had dropped a half-tarnished silver crucifix over her head. *They* are *all high,* she thought. *Even the priest.*

Then she looked outside again, and for some reason, she couldn't make her eyes focus. She had time to think: *What have they done to me?* And: *Is Skip seeing this?* Then her stomach flipped, and she fainted.

"Generally," Father Menchú said to Sal, not upset, but still chiding, "we try to be a little more gentle when introducing civilians to the reality of the nonmundane."

Sal winced as she heard another round of retching from the bathroom. "Sorry." Then she went back to her original question. "But if we've bagged the book, why is everything outside still in blur-o-vision?"

"Could be something else on the boat," Menchú suggested. "If this Mr. Norse is a collector, he could have all kinds of artifacts aboard."

"Great," said Grace.

Liam, still examining the book through the shroud, shook his head. "Or, the more likely explanation: the binding has been damaged."

"Binding, like a spell?" asked Sal.

Menchú shot her a look. "What do you know about binding spells?"

"My brother played a lot of Dungeons and Dragons when we were kids. Still does. Did. Dammit."

"Actually," said Liam, "I meant, literally, the binding." He pointed to where the back cover had separated from the spine along two-thirds of its length, barely connected to the rest of the book at all. "Even when the book isn't open, it still isn't closed."

"I really wish that didn't almost make sense," said Sal.

Grace swore. "You mean that thing has been . . . leaking?"

"The shroud should still contain it," said Menchú, thoughtful.

"That's great for keeping it from getting worse," said Liam, "but it doesn't look like it's helping it get any better."

Grace frowned. "Wasn't there a case in China like this?"

"Back in the twenties?" Menchú asked.

"No, later," Grace said. "I read about it. A book got damaged, then started oozing something that spread like a contagion."

"What happened?" Liam asked.

"It became the Asian flu pandemic of 1957. Estimated worldwide death toll between one and two million before a team finally found the book."

"How did they stop it?"

"Buried the book, the monastery where it was housed, and everyone inside it under a landslide."

In the pause that followed, the door to the small bathroom opened, revealing a very wan ship's steward who had finally managed to regain her feet.

Grace frowned. "Wasn't the captain in there with you?"

Katie shook her head.

"Then where the hell is he?"

Childress had to hand it to Katie, that fainting spell had been a stroke of genius. If they lived through this, he was going to make sure she got a raise.

Once he had slipped away, his first stop had been the bridge and the ship's radio, but someone had sabotaged every comm system on the ship. No Internet, no sat phone, nothing. He wasted more time than he should have, checking over the ship's systems, trying to find out what had been done to them. But when he noticed his old magnetic compass spinning crazily on its bearings, he gave up hope that this was something he could remedy with a quick fix.

If he was going to get help, he needed to get off the boat. He felt a twinge of regret, leaving Katie behind, but his best chance to help her was to get the owner on the horn. It wasn't like they were in the middle of the Atlantic. The marina office was just at the end of the dock. *She'll be fine,* he told himself, and made for the aft deck.

Thanks to her longer stride, Sal was able to catch Grace, even with the other woman's head start.

"Do we have a plan?"

"Find the captain. Keep him on the boat."

"That's an objective. Not a plan."

"That's a big word for a dumb cop."

"Hey," said Sal, "I read too, you know."

At that, Grace cracked a smile. It only lasted a fraction of a second, but Sal was sure it had been there. And then, just as quickly, it was gone. "We're probably too late, anyway. Unless the captain's an idiot, he'll have gotten as far from this boat as possible."

"And he's not an idiot."

"No." Grace scowled, as though this were a personal insult.

They were coming up on the doors to the aft deck now. Frosted glass. Sal's stomach clenched. If the captain was out there, the glass meant he'd be able to see the movement of their approach against the static background of the hallway, but they were effectively blind.

Grace must have had a similar thought. She paused and indicated for Sal to fall in behind her. "I'll take the door. If one of us is going to get shot, better it isn't you."

And before Sal could open her mouth to ask what the hell *that* was supposed to mean, Grace popped the door and barreled through onto the deck. Sal—never one to leave her partner without backup—charged through right behind her.

The captain wasn't waiting for them in ambush.

But he was waiting for them. Hanging in midair. Stuck like a gnat on a drying snot bubble to the blurry field surrounding the yacht.

They were all on the deck now, staring up at the captain. Against Sal's better judgment, "all" included Katie. She had expected another bout of vomiting and unconsciousness when the woman saw what had happened to her boss, but all she did was quietly breathe, "Oh, Skip," and fall silent.

The sun was setting, sky glowing pink behind the trapped man. The sight of Katie seemed to rouse him back to coherence.

"Sorry, Katie."

"For what?"

"I was going to leave you here."

"You would have sent help. You take care of us."

Whether it was the sun or some effect of the field he was trapped in, the captain's lips were dry, and they split when he tried to smile at her. "Not well enough."

A drop of blood oozed up from his lip and fell to the deck below. Sal stepped forward to draw Katie back from him, then froze.

The drop on the ground wasn't red. It was black.

Sal half expected the deck to begin smoking—it seemed

only appropriate if people were going to suddenly start bleeding black ooze—but just like when the first officer had killed himself, the drop didn't seem to be reacting with the wooden surface. Except . . . Sal blinked.

It was just one drop of blood, but it was . . .

"It's spreading."

Grace stopped in the middle of whatever she had been saying to Liam and turned to Sal. "It's what?"

"Spreading."

In a few seconds the single drop had grown in size from the diameter of a dime to a half-dollar, and Sal was running out of currency large enough for comparison.

"Was it doing that when the first mate . . . ?" Liam asked.

"I assumed he was just bleeding out."

"Shit."

A quick check confirmed that what had once been the floor of the boat's forward lounge was now a lake of black ooze. At least it didn't seem to be throwing off heat anymore, now that the body was completely gone. Although, as silver linings went, that was a pretty thin one.

"What's below this?" Father Menchú asked.

"Crew quarters, then the hull."

Father Menchú took this in with more calm than Sal was currently feeling—what with being trapped on a boat slowly filling with demonic black ooze—but she supposed part of his job was to keep a calm face on things. Either that, or he had a good plan for getting them out of this mess. She really hoped it was the latter.

Menchú let Katie lead the way to the deck below but stopped her from entering the room directly beneath the lounge. Carefully he opened the door.

What had once been a crew cabin was now filled with oily tendrils dripping down from the ceiling vents like tar from a sieve.

"Was anyone in there?" he asked.

Katie shook her head.

"Where's the rest of the crew?"

"For the trip to Miami, we just have two more. But they aren't aboard. Sarah went into the city to meet one of her chef friends and get some fresh groceries while we were in port. Luc was picking up supplies."

"When are you expecting them back?"

"Sarah will come back sometime this evening, late—she made it clear we were on our own for dinner. Luc will be back later than that probably, or tomorrow morning if he meets someone."

Father Menchú let out a long breath. "Were they on the boat last night?"

Katie nodded. "Sure. Like I said, we live here. . . . Are they going to . . . What happened to Paul and Skip, is it . . . is it going to happen to them? To me?"

"No. The silver in the cross is protecting you. You'll be fine."

There was a long pause.

"Are you just telling me that so I won't freak out and try to run?"

Grace shrugged. "You're welcome to run if you want. But if you do, you'll just end up stuck beside the captain."

Katie blanched.

Since looking at the goo didn't seem to be doing them any good, Father Menchú led a general retreat to the aft deck, where they could at least warn off anyone trying to board the boat.

Liam found, to his disgust, that his laptop was just as out of commission as the team's phones and the ship's radio and, grumbling, broke out paper, a mechanical stopwatch, and a slide rule. After timing the spread of the goo under the captain, he worked out that they had about an hour before it got deep enough to swamp the boat.

"And once it hits the water, we'll all be in it. Literally *and* figuratively."

"Unless the field around the boat keeps it contained," Sal pointed out.

"You want to bet the Mediterranean on that?" asked Liam.

"Okay, so we have somewhat less than an hour to figure out what's going on and stop it."

Sal looked over to where Katie stood by the captain, holding up a glass of water with a straw so that he could drink. She didn't seem to be listening, but Sal lowered her voice, anyway.

"Was I lying to her earlier? Is she going to be okay?"

"Unless Team One gets wind of what's going on and decides to solve this little problem with a tactical nuke."

"They have tactical nukes?"

"No."

"Well, that's a relief."

"They do have a whole lot of napalm though."

Father Menchú gestured for their attention. "This is all academic. Phones are out, and we can't leave this ship. We couldn't call for Team One even if they were the only option we had left." He leveled his stare at his team, and Sal felt her spine stiffen reflexively. "But we still have a little time, and I have faith that this group will come up with a better solution."

Sal hoped like hell that he was right.

4.

F orty minutes later Father Menchú's faith in the team's problem-solving abilities wasn't looking especially well-placed.

"As far as I can tell," Liam explained as he ran a hand through his short red burr in exasperation, "what we've got is every part of a demon infestation except the actual demon: hallucinations, psychosis, evil goo, the works. What we don't have is a demon at the center of it all."

"How do we get rid of all of that normally?" asked Sal.

"It goes away when we banish the demon or close the book."

"So, why can't we close the book now?"

"It's already closed. Just leaking."

"But what if we opened it, then closed it again? That could act like a kind of reset button, right?"

Liam looked at Sal like she was the product of a demon-induced hallucination. "Are you implying that this situation would be helped by adding an *actual* demon to it?"

"No, but remember Madrid? We didn't have to shove all the weird crap going on in that apartment back through the book. As soon as we took care of the center of the infestation, the whole accessory pack got sucked back in with it. The problem here is that we've got all of the extras, but no main guy to tell them it's time to go home. If we open the book, it gives the goo something to attach to. Then we close it again, banish the demon to the other side, and the goo goes away along with it. As long as we get it into the shroud immediately, it all stays contained, right?"

"Doing what with a what now?"

"More important," Sal forged ahead, "if we open the book, it might trigger the Orb, and then Asanti will know that we need backup."

"Napalm kind of backup?"

"I'm not saying I want to die a fiery death, but it's probably better than millions dead of the demonic flu."

Liam opened his mouth to object. Then closed it again. Sal guessed it was the best she was going to get.

"Great. I'm going to do it."

She turned on her heel and took off. That spurred Liam into action.

"Wait! You can't just—"

"Not talking about it, just doing it."

"But Father Menchú—"

"Will be able to honestly say he had no idea what I was planning if this all goes horribly wrong."

Behind her, Sal could barely hear a muttered "If this goes horribly wrong, we're all going to be dead."

Unfortunately for Sal's grand plans, Liam also had long legs, and so was only seconds behind her when she arrived on the aft deck. The instant he had Father Menchú in sight, he started yelling about

Sal's "harebrained scheme," and since her scheme didn't actually take that long to explain, Father Menchú was fully briefed by the time Sal reached book-snatching distance.

Menchú gave Sal a look. "Is that what you were planning?"

"Well, 'unleash bloody demon hell' wasn't *actually* part of the plan, but I suppose Liam's right that it's a possibility."

Menchú took this in, then nodded. "All right."

"All right?!?" said Liam.

"It makes sense, I don't have another suggestion, and we're rapidly running out of boat."

Grace shrugged, as though unconcerned about the prospect of being consumed by evil demon goo.

Liam was not mollified. "You can't be serious. Us ending up dead is the best possible end this plan could have."

Father Menchú put his hand on the taller man's shoulder. "Is the bridge still accessible?"

"Last I checked."

"Then let's see if we can move out of port. Just in case."

Katie cut the final line securing the ship to the dock. As the last member of the crew aboard who was still standing, she felt like it was her place. She and the priest had finally gotten Skip down to the deck, and she'd managed to give him a little more water, but he had lost consciousness a few minutes a later.

Katie felt the engine sputter beneath her feet. They were limping, but it was enough. She looked over at the brunette, who stood nearby. The silence felt heavy between them. Katie had worked for foreign princes, venture capitalists, and movie stars. She had never before been at a loss for something to say.

When she'd taken her first training course, her instructor had said that if they ever didn't know how to deal with a guest, they should ask if they could help. Most people were hard-pressed to take offense at someone who was trying to assist them. She'd quipped, "If you get taken over by Somali pirates, just ask if they need something. You're not the captain. You don't have to be a hero, you just have to survive."

Katie felt a puff of laughter escape her lips.

"What is it?" the woman asked.

"Just something I learned in training."

"You trained for this?"

Katie shrugged. "I work for billionaires. They taught us to be prepared for anything." She looked over the deck, one half of which was now covered in a thick lake of goo. "Never covered anything like this, though."

The other woman nodded.

Katie wanted to ask again if they were going to be okay, but held her tongue. She didn't want to sound like she didn't trust these strangers. Even though she didn't. Quite.

"You're going to get through this," the woman said, as if she sensed her doubts. "I know this is scary, but these people are very good at their jobs."

"Did you train for this?"

"I trained to be a cop. That means that anything that tries to take you down has to go through me first."

Sal told herself there was nothing to worry about. The plan was simple, just like she'd outlined it to Liam. Open the book, trigger the Orb, release a demon onto a yacht that was quickly being covered in evil goo. Close the book, get it back into the shroud, and all of their problems would be solved.

Sal carefully set the book on the floor and unwrapped it using a pair of silver serving tongs Katie had produced from the boat's kitchen supplies. Not as good as a three-hundred-year-old crucifix, maybe, but better than trying to use her bare hands. Father Menchú had underlined that quite strongly. She'd gotten lucky in Perry's storage unit; she couldn't count on escaping direct contact with a demon unscathed again.

Sal was in the owner's cabin, which was, for the moment, relatively goo free. The boat's silverware—solid silver, not plate, some people really did have more money than sense—was laid out in a circle around her, and a circle of salt poured inside it just for good measure. Katie had brought a box of it from the galley when she'd gone for the silver, and no one had the heart to tell her that salt wasn't actually a thing for keeping out demons. And what the hell, it couldn't hurt, right?

Sal could barely see out the cabin windows—just enough to tell they were in open water. She gripped the fresh silver cross Liam had given her. Her previous one had gone to Katie, and besides, it was already half covered in tarnish. Sal hadn't even noticed when that happened. How quickly had the supernatural become normal that she didn't even *notice* the effects the silver was protecting her from? She appreciated that Liam, in spite of his doubts, was giving her stupid plan the best chance of success that he could.

Of course, it wasn't like they had any better options.

"Drive it or park it."

That was Grace. Standing behind her with a long-handled broom. Ready to knock her away from the book and move in herself if Sal failed.

And if Grace failed too? Or if the demon didn't clean up his mess after him? In that case . . . Sal put that thought firmly out of her mind. If this didn't work, whatever happened next would almost certainly be someone else's problem.

Sal placed the book on the floor and leaned in to flip open the cover. The plan was sound. Everything would be fine. Just like she'd promised Katie. And if it wasn't . . . that's why Katie was with Father Menchú and Liam in a salted silver circle of their own on the foredeck, as far from the goo as they could get. If Katie didn't live through this, she would at least be the last one to go down.

Sal wrapped the cross's silver chain around her hand. This was what she had signed up for. First with the NYPD, and again with the Black Archives. No matter how weird things got, that hadn't changed.

Sal opened the book.

There was a rush of light. Sal had always thought demons lived in the dark. But it was light. Everywhere. And a smell of salt and kelp, and the tug of a current against her hands, as though she could feel the rip in the world that the damaged book had created, and all the things that were rushing through it. In both directions. The pull wanted her. To fill the hole or to feed the stream, Sal wasn't sure. There was just the current and the burn in her hand where she held the cross, hot against her skin. Too hot to hold. Must hold. Must . . . She was gasping for air, she was . . .

Sal was on the floor. Looking up at Grace, who had dropped the broom and was shoving the shroud-wrapped book into a bag filled with assorted silverware. Just for good measure.

"Did it work?" Sal asked.

"If by 'Did it work?' you mean 'Did a giant river of goo nearly suck me back into the book along with it?' then yes, it worked."

"Am I okay?"

Grace squinted at her. "You're an idiot. But a living idiot."

Sal decided that was good enough and went back to being unconscious.

5.

al discovered that a side benefit of her stupid plan was that the powers that be let her go straight home instead of debriefing at the Vatican with the rest of the team. Once the monsignor was satisfied Sal wasn't actually possessed, of course. But determining that was a process Sal remembered only dimly, and since it involved more chanting and incense than needle sticks and intimate scrubbing, she decided it was far more pleasant than doing decon after an anthrax scare.

When some of her mind came back, she managed to rouse herself enough to ask Father Menchú a question.

"The captain?"

"Didn't make it."

"Katie? Is she okay?"

"She's fine. She's with the rest of the *Fair Weather*'s crew, at a hotel."

Sal thought Father Menchú said something else, something encouraging, before leaving her apartment and closing the door behind him, but she might have already been asleep and imagined it.

The pleasant haze of sleep was shattered by a phone call.

Sal groped for her cell, finally locating it in the pocket of her crumpled pants, and brought it to her ear.

"You need to go back to Ostia. Now."

Instantly awake to the tone of the words if not their meaning, Sal sat up. Her feet hit the cold tile floor, sending a shock of adrenaline through her system. Then her mind caught up with the rest of her.

"What? Who is this?"

"It's Aaron."

"The tour guide? How did you get this number?"

"Just come back to the marina. Now."

Sal was about to hang up. She knew she should call Father Menchú. She certainly should not be following the instructions of a strange man who had called her in the middle of the night on a phone he never should have been able to reach.

And then she heard the faint sound of sirens on the other end of the line.

"I'll be right there."

The cab had to drop her nearly five blocks away from the water, due to the firemen and emergency vehicles thwarting even her Roman taxi driver from getting closer. Once she was on foot, Sal used a combination of body language and judicious flashes of her badge to force her way through the cordon to the gatehouse at the edge of the marina. A security guard was shouting at the top of his lungs in Italian, his meaning plain even to a monoglot like Sal. At the end of the dock, orange and green flames leaped over the heads of the gathered firefighters, reaching up to paint sky.

The *Fair Weather* was burning like a Viking funeral.

Twenty feet away, Aaron stood in the shadows. Very calmly, Sal walked over to him and grabbed him by the shoulders. "Who did this? Was this you?"

He shook his head. "No. This was you."

Sal let go of him, pulling her hands back in shock. "What? No. I didn't— We didn't—" Understanding dawned. "This was to cover up the death of the captain."

"In part."

"What's the other part?" Sal asked, already dreading his answer.

"To eliminate any possible vectors of contagion. You and your team they can watch over. But the Society can't give a job to everyone contaminated by the touch of magic."

Sal felt the pit of her stomach drop out. *Katie.*

Katie hadn't told the others much, just that the *Fair Weather* had been secured as a crime scene following the disappearance of its captain and first mate. She and Sarah had gone to the hotel bar to mourn, speculate, and drink, until the hour and the vodka had finally borne the other woman off to bed.

Katie stayed at the bar, telling herself that she was waiting for Luc, making sure that he got in all right, even though she knew he was almost certainly finding comfort in the arms of a handsome young Italian man and would not return until morning.

Eventually, Katie returned to her room, where she found she was not drunk enough to banish the scenes that played across her mind whenever she closed her eyes. She called room service.

Ordered another drink. The priest had said the bill would be covered. He'd told her not to worry. Easy for him to say. He had also said that something from the book had infected Paul and Skip. The same book she had carried from Rome to Ostia.

She remembered how the tarlike wave had surged at the end, rising up as though to swamp the boat before suddenly receding into Mr. Norse's cabin, like blood washing down a drain. She fingered the cross that still hung around her neck. Was she infected too? If she nicked herself in the shower, would her body collapse like Paul's? Would her black blood fill the pipes, spill out into the streets, until the world was covered in a black tide?

A knock. Room service. Just as her hand reached the knob, the door burst in, followed by a man in black who reeked of smoke. He pressed a cloth against her face. Katie inhaled to scream, and the smoke smell was replaced by something sweet and rotten.

Everything went black.

Sal called Liam, then Menchú, who told them where the crew had been put up for the night. The three of them arrived at the hotel just as the coroners were bringing out a draped body on a stretcher. Menchú approached them and spoke quietly.

Of course, if Padre would like to say a prayer over the body, the attendants would be happy to wait a moment. The signorina was in no hurry.

When Menchú lifted the sheet, Katie's lips were pale blue against her skin and the white cotton.

"They didn't give her one to the head?" Sal murmured to Liam.

"They wouldn't have wanted her to bleed."

Sal felt sick.

Asanti was livid. The team was gathered near her desk, where she was loudly arguing with the monsignor in charge of their little division of the Black Archives.

"There was no sign that young woman was infected."

"There was no sign she wasn't, and she had more contact with the book than anyone. Our superiors decided they couldn't take the risk."

"Your job is to talk them out of stupid ideas. To remind them that burning the innocent and guilty together and letting God sort it out went out of fashion with the Inquisition."

The monsignor took a long breath. When he continued, his voice was very low, and very calm. It made the hairs on the back of Sal's neck stand up. "You don't know how close they were to ordering the death of everyone who set foot on that boat. You still have a team. You're welcome."

He turned to leave. Asanti called after him. "What about the bookshop? Did Team One take that down too?"

The monsignor paused. "Of course not," he said. "We didn't know the book had been damaged then. There was no need to purify the bookshop until later."

Sal sat by Perry's bedside. *I promise,* she told him silently. *I will get you out of here. I will keep you safe. Somehow.*

A footstep behind her. Liam. "Hey."

"Hey."

"It's okay, you know. They're not going to hurt Perry."

"How can you be sure? He was possessed. Contaminated. How do I know that someday some cardinal won't—"

"Because I'm still alive."

Sal had forgotten that Liam had once been possessed himself.

"Every case is different, and whatever went south on this one, he was nowhere near it."

Sal nodded but didn't move. And then Liam's hand was on her elbow, gently guiding her to her feet. "Come on," he said. "I'll walk you home."

They walked through the Old Gallery of the Late Crusades on their way out. Sal caught a whiff of acrid smoke, the kind that came from burning treated lumber, lingering in the air as they passed.

Once out of the Vatican complex and onto the streets of Rome, Sal took her arm back. Liam was content to walk side by side.

"Every time I think I have this job figured out, what's going on, what's expected of me, something like this comes and slaps me in the face. I mean, I knew the work was dangerous. I'm okay with dangerous. I'm not okay with my superiors not having my back."

"We have your back."

"The team does. But Menchú and Asanti don't have the codes to the nukes."

"I told you. There aren't any nukes."

She didn't laugh.

They walked in silence.

"The worst thing is, I catch myself wondering if they were right. One life for four million is pretty easy math, and if we have a demonic possession detector, no one's told me about it. What if she wasn't clean? What if *we* aren't clean?"

Liam sighed. "I worry about that every day. All we can do is the best we can."

"It doesn't seem like enough."

"On the bad days, I worry about that too."

Sal searched Liam's face. "This was a bad day, right? Tell me this isn't fair to average. I need this day to be one of the bad ones."

"It was pretty bad," Liam said. "Could have been worse, though."

They were almost at her building. Sal noticed that her hand had fallen back against Liam's arm without her noticing. He didn't seem to mind.

Well, what of it? Wanting companionship after a close call with death was a psychologically proven phenomenon. Or at least a baby-boom-nine-months-after-9/11 proven phenomenon.

Then she remembered something else Liam had told her. She hastily took her hand back. Liam looked at her, confused.

"Something wrong?"

"Aren't you a monk?"

Liam shook his head. "No, I just live with monks."

Her eyes narrowed. "You're not just saying that to get into my pants?"

Liam blinked. "Is that . . . ? I hadn't thought you wanted . . ." He pulled himself together. "I swear to you. I am not a monk."

Sal took a moment to think about that.

"So, no vows?"

A slow grin spread across Liam's face. "Not that kind."

Sal couldn't help her own smile in return. When his lips met hers, they were just as hungry. She kissed him as she fumbled for her keys to the building. He kissed her back as they went inside, and they kissed each other as they stumbled up the stairs and into her apartment. Finally, she forced a break. "Wait."

"What is it?"

Sal felt her face heating. She couldn't believe she was about to say this. "Do men who live with monks carry condoms?"

Liam threw his head back and laughed until Sal had no choice but to force him to shut up with more kissing.

The answer, as it turned out, was yes.

It took some doing, but after a week of walking the streets and asking questions in her rapidly improving Italian, Sal found Aaron the tour guide. She was almost sorry when she did; the search had been such a comfortingly familiar activity. But in the end, she didn't need comfort. She needed answers.

Aaron didn't seem surprised to see Sal walking up to the terrace of the small sidewalk café where he was installed with a newspaper and an espresso. He rose as she neared and gestured for her to sit down. Almost as soon as she did, a waiter was at her elbow, depositing an espresso and two small paper tubes of sugar. Sal wondered if Aaron had been expecting her. If she had only found him because he allowed her to.

Sal was waiting for the waiter to get safely out of earshot before speaking, but Aaron beat her to it.

"No backup?"

Sal shook her head.

"Why not?"

"Because you helped me. And you seem like a nice guy who doesn't deserve to be set on fire. Then again, you also tracked down my phone number, which I never gave you; you seem to know who I work for, which is more than I've told my own family; and, frankly, you have been entirely too convenient throughout this entire goddamned mess. My turn."

"Haven't I helped you enough?"

Sal ignored this. "Who are you with? Interpol? One of the local agencies?"

"I'm not with the police."

"Then who are you with? And why are you allowed to know about what's going on—which you clearly do—and live, while poor Katie ends up chloroformed?"

Aaron sighed. "Information is like a contagion. It spreads. Your employers do an admirable job controlling that, but they aren't the only players in the game. As much as they might want to eliminate the knowledge and use of magic completely, not every vector can be silenced as quietly as a young ship's steward. The world is vast, Sally Brooks, and not even the Vatican can see the entire picture."

Leaving a few euros on the table, Aaron got up, tucking his umbrella and newspaper under one arm. Sal caught his elbow. "I'm going to tell my team about this conversation."

"Of course you will," he said. "You already promised the priest you would. Don't worry about me. As it happens, my superiors and yours are on very close terms."

Sal could have let it go at that, but she had one last question.

"The collapsed bookshop. Was that you?"

Aaron smiled.

And then Sal wasn't holding his elbow anymore. His eyes grew in her field of vision until all Sal could see was white. A white so bright it burned. She felt a rush of air and the brush of feathers against her skin.

By the time she managed to blink past the afterimages left on her retinas, Aaron was gone.

EPISODE
4

A SORCERER'S APPRENTICE

MUR LAFFERTY

1.

Browsing Asanti's library by herself was Sal's new favorite hobby. She had never seen a place like this, though it reminded her most of a moldy old library relatives had shown her in Savannah, Georgia, with humidity-damaged first editions of *The Adventures of Tom Sawyer* and *Gone With the Wind* and *A Christmas Carol.*

Her team kept suggesting she should relax between missions. She really didn't need to be at headquarters sitting around, they said; why didn't she enjoy Rome when she had the chance? But in a city where she didn't speak the language and had few—all right, the number was closer to zero—friends, Sal had nothing to do. There was only so long she could read, listen to music, and lie over Skype to friends in America about her life in Rome. At least here in the library she could learn something, or maybe run into a team member and have a real conversation.

Sal used to think stakeouts were bad. Lots of sitting in cars that reeked of cigarettes, lots of shitty coffee, lots of fattening foods. Five minutes of action. Then more sitting.

This job thankfully didn't involve sitting around in cars, but waiting for demon attacks made stakeouts feel like bird-watching—which, to be fair, Sal also hated.

And the waiting. The waiting made her as tense as a guitar string—Sal would definitely be an E string, her spine taut and tingly, ready to spring into action. But when there was no action, the tension became exhausting.

Griping about boredom did, however, allow her to pointedly not think about Liam.

Her stormy emotions after their night together had nearly been overwhelming. Liam left quietly in the night, much to Sal's relief. The sex had been phenomenal, no doubt about that. Both times. But had she been with him just because he was the only person on the team she could relate to? And had he been drawn to her for the same reason? He clearly had some issues with Grace, the only other member of the team close to his age that he could maybe have something in common with.

Then there was the question of his faith. Liam was no priest, and they'd never talked much about faith beyond his jokes and the job's requirements, but in the dark bedroom she'd seen his body covered with ecclesiastical tattoos, saints and knots and thorns and blood. What did that mean? Could the man who'd marked himself like that walk away from casual sex with healthy feelings? Sal did not look forward to that conversation. Or any conversation, really. Perhaps if she pretended nothing had happened, he would too.

Sal browsed Asanti's books, careful to keep to the open area of the library and not edge into the locked rooms where the seriously dangerous books were held. She couldn't help but think it would be fascinating to go into the forbidden rooms, but she had enough to keep her busy in the allowed section.

She thought of them as Asanti's books, which seemed odd. They definitely didn't belong to the archivist; if anything they were closer to her prisoners than her children. But Asanti seemed to have a different view of the books than the others. As far as Sal was concerned, there was only one way to look at these horror-movie props that had complicated, ruined, and taken so many lives.

Wandering the library, Sal tried to determine what ancient language the books were written in. Then she would try to figure out Asanti's cataloging system. Sometimes books with the same languages were shelved together. One section consisted entirely of green books of the same shape, like an ancient encyclopedia set. Another had one shelf holding books, and then the shelf underneath was empty, and then the third shelf had books again, and the next shelf was empty.

Not all the books were shelved, either. Stacks of books, some of them eight feet high, created labyrinthine walkways, making Sal feel very young and lost. She wished Asanti would give her some hints as to what these books were, but as much as the team encouraged her to relax in the off hours, they each seemed pretty busy with their own things all the time.

Asanti seemed to be in the library whenever Sal was in there. Despite telling anecdotes of her large family, she didn't appear to see them much. Surely she had her own place, but Sal had never heard about it. Menchú was always bustling about looking very busy on his way to or from something. Grace was simply Not There; Sal only saw her when they had a mission or a meeting. Liam constantly seemed to be searching for one thing or another online. Busy people. And then there was Sal.

As if she heard Sal's lonely thinking, Asanti entered the library, swearing loudly in French. Sal assumed it was swearing, based on the vehemence and the stomping. Asanti began to rummage through her desk drawers, fishing out a dull pencil and making notes on a scrap of paper.

"I can't understand French, but I have the feeling I should be offended," Sal said mildly as she emerged from the stacks. "Is everything all right?"

"Everything is fine, it's always fine, we chase the demons, we get the books, we shelve the books, we save the day. Every day is sunny here," Asanti snapped. She finished writing and stared at what she had written, her dark face going ashen.

"I may be making a jump here, but you seem very not fine," Sal said. "What's going on? Do you want to talk about it?"

"*Non,*" Asanti said, tossing the paper onto her desk. "I'm going away for a few days. Menchú has the care of the library."

"Where are you going?" Sal asked, edging closer as if Asanti were a bomb that Sal had to defuse. She had never seen the archivist this agitated. She reached her hand out to pull a tissue from Asanti's desk.

Asanti looked up, her cheeks glistening with tears. "You ask a lot of questions."

Sal nodded unapologetically. "It's my job. Hard to turn off." She waited.

Asanti sighed. "An old friend has died. I'm going to his funeral."

Sal handed Asanti the tissue without speaking, and the archivist took it with a word of thanks. When she wiped her eyes, Sal glanced at what she had been scribbling. They looked like the coordinates that Asanti received from the Orb when it alerted her to demonic activity.

"How long will you be gone?" Sal asked.

Asanti sniffled, then folded the tissue into a square and stuck it into a pocket in her black pants. "A few days at most. Travel, the funeral, and I have to help his niece get his affairs in order." Asanti was looking down at her desk. Then she sighed and looked Sal in the eyes. "You may as well know, the old friend is my mentor, the man who recruited me to this job so many years ago. He retired to Glasgow. His name is—was—Father Seamus Hunter. We remained close after he left."

"I'm so sorry," Sal said. "Can I do anything while you're gone?"

"I'm sure you can," Asanti said absently as she tidied her desk, sliding a magazine over the scrap of paper with the coordinates. "Thank you for listening. I must go pack now."

She turned, the corner of her purple tunic catching some papers on her desk, spilling them to the floor.

"I got it; don't worry about it," Sal said, putting her hands on Asanti's shoulder to keep her from bending down to clean up the mess.

Asanti gave her a grateful smile and swept from the library.

Sal bent and began gathering the papers. Most of them were in Italian or French, but the coordinates were in numbers, and those Sal could read. Chewing on her lip, she thought for a moment, then folded the paper and stuck it in her back pocket.

Grateful that Liam wasn't in his computer lab, Sal booted up the laptop and logged on as RIVAL DOG.

Liam had set up the guest partition on his computer when the others complained that they needed to use his machine sometimes. The Society had computers, but they were quite old. Liam's personal laptop was portable, and he was always tinkering with it to improve it. The guest login had limited abilities, but at least Sal could get online. The username convention had been Grace's idea, Sal had learned, in poking fun at Liam's desire to mark and guard his territory.

Sal searched for the coordinates and Glasgow came up, not surprising her at all, though apparently the Orb hadn't been feeling cooperative enough to provide a street address. Time to play Liam. A search on Glasgow produced millions of links, with the top hit being a Yelp review of a restaurant: Thistle on the Moor. She tapped a pen on the table, trying to figure out why Asanti got incoming information from the Orb but felt the need to lie to her—and, presumably, the team. A lie of omission, but still. Asanti had been with the organization longer than anyone; she was the last person Sal would think would betray them. Sure, she had her differences with Menchú, but so did they all.

Menchú had not been pleased when Sal had finally gotten him aside long enough to explain about the mysterious Aaron. Sal did not have a lot of room to point fingers at Asanti for withholding information, she realized, but she was still burning with curiosity.

She'd made it this far trusting her gut. And her gut was telling her to find out what Asanti was hiding.

And anyway, she didn't know for sure that Asanti hadn't told the rest of the team the truth. Sal could easily have been left in the dark simply because she was the newest. It could be a matter of Asanti not trusting Sal, not of the rest of the team not being able to trust Asanti.

Sal left the browser open and the paper with the coordinates stuck underneath the laptop. She took a deep breath and stood. She needed to talk to her teammates, and she needed to deal with the most uncomfortable first.

Sal sent a text to Liam, asking to meet him at a coffee bar near her apartment.

Sure thing. Gimme 45, came the immediate response.

Forty-five minutes was enough time to see Menchú in the interim.

＊ ＊ ＊

"Come in," Menchú called from his room after Sal knocked.

Sal had seen his door when she'd been given the tour but had never been inside. Menchú lived in spartan quarters that seemed to better fit poverty-focused Franciscans than the wealth on display at the Vatican. He had a simple single bed against the far wall, a bedside table with a lamp and a notepad, a dresser, and a desk. At the foot of the bed was a wooden trunk with a large lock. Beside the desk was a bookcase, packed tightly with both dusty old books and a few newer tomes on religion and mythology. Lying atop the bookshelf, as if it didn't belong, was a current mystery novel by an author whose name Sal recognized.

"One moment," Menchú said, hunched over a book. He gestured to the room vaguely. "Make yourself at home."

On the dresser were many pictures of the team through the years. Younger Menchú and Asanti with some older people Sal didn't recognize. Newer pictures of Liam and Grace, looking as if they—well, at least Liam—had just come from a workout or a rough assignment, Liam with a swelling bruise on his jaw and his hair mussed, and Grace pristine as ever. One photo of Asanti, Grace, and Menchú caught Sal's eye, near the edge of the dresser. They stood in front of a pyramid in what looked like South America, the sun rising over their shoulders. Asanti and Menchú looked much younger, but Grace looked the same.

"Where was this taken?" she asked, picking up the frame.

"Peru," he said, not looking up. "Two years ago," he added as if anticipating her question. "Liam showed us the amazing wonders of Photoshop to erase some of the years' wear and tear."

Sal quirked an eyebrow. Menchú was giving an awful lot of

information that she hadn't asked for. She wondered if he were protesting too much. Oh well. One mystery at a time.

The team leader looked up from reading his hefty tome and smiled. "What can I do for you?"

"I heard about Asanti's mentor," she said, figuring it was best to stick with the truth as she tried to pull information from him.

"Ah, Father Hunter." He closed the book, marking his page with a red velvet ribbon. "Yes, she's quite broken up about it. They were very close."

"Closer than the two of you?" Sal asked. "I mean, you two seem united against the world."

Menchú chuckled, a slight tone of bitterness touching his tone. "Oh yes. He recruited her. Unlike everyone else currently on the team, Asanti was not conscripted after a violent or frightening incident, manufacturing intense loss. She was eager to learn about the wonders of magic, and he took her under his wing."

He rubbed his face and thought for a moment. "Father Hunter retired some time back, and I took over the team. I don't think Asanti has ever forgiven me for not being him."

Sal frowned. "That doesn't make sense. He retired—someone had to take his place. That's not your fault."

"Most emotions aren't logical," he said. "We get along fine now, but she took some time to acclimate to my position."

Sal chose her words carefully. She picked up the picture of Asanti and Menchú on his dresser. "Asanti's been on the team longer than any of you."

Menchú paused. "You could say that," he finally said.

"So it's safe to say that she loves this organization," Sal continued.

Menchú chuckled again. "I'd go so far as to say she probably loves it too much," he said.

Sal put down the frame and faced Menchú. "What do you mean?"

"Surely you've noticed. Her view of magic isn't the same as ours. Our jobs here are to find, neutralize, and contain magic. But once we contain and shelve it and we are officially done with the job, Asanti's curiosity can get the better of her, and she continues research. It's within the safety of the Archives, which is heavily protected, but she still approaches our horrors with interest and wonder. She insists knowledge is vital to understanding, but she doesn't have enough caution."

"So she's not as scared as the rest of you," Sal said.

"As you say."

"But you trust her?" she asked finally.

"Of course I do," he said, frowning and tilting his head at her. "We risk our lives for this job. When we don't trust each other, people die."

Sal nodded. "When will she be back from the funeral?"

"I gave her three days, tops. I'm keeping an eye on the Orb in the meantime in case the world decides to catch fire," he said, glancing at his huge tome. "In fact, if you'll excuse me, I need to finish my reading here and then get to her desk."

"Thanks for your time," Sal said. "Do you know if Grace is around? I wanted to ask her something while I was down here."

Menchú didn't look at her, instead focusing on his book again. "I don't recommend it. She's resting, and doesn't like being inter-rupted during her private time."

Sal checked her watch. "It's almost noon," she said.

"Grace is a bit of an introvert. She doesn't spend a lot of her down-time with the team. Ask her whatever you like when next you see her, but don't seek her out when she doesn't want to be found."

The voice was still friendly, but Sal could hear the commanding undertone.

"Don't mess with Grace. Got it," she said to herself as she shut the door behind her.

That left Liam, meeting her in half an hour.

Drinking two espressos was a bad idea. Sal didn't know why she felt the need to drink coffee when she was nervous, but that's what happened.

When we don't trust each other, people die.

The underlying message was clear: Don't hide things like Aaron from the team again, Sal. She didn't regret hiding it, but she did regret the effect it had had on Menchú's trust of her.

The impending talk with Liam wasn't helping her nerves, and she was about to order a third espresso when he showed up two minutes early.

Her hands trembled slightly as he sat down. He held himself stiffly, sitting upright in his chair.

"How are you, Sal?" he asked, sounding painfully formal. The guy needed something to put his mind at ease.

"I'm good. Are you all right? You look a little . . . rigid. Bruised rib?"

Liam relaxed a fraction. "I worked out with Grace last night. It was more rigorous than our sparring bouts tend to be. My ribs will remember it."

Sal felt odd thinking of Grace and Liam together, sparring, sweating. She rooted around in her backpack and pulled out some painkillers, putting them on the table between them. Liam took the bottle without comment and shook out two tablets, then handed it back to her.

"Thank you."

Casually pushing aside the giant elephant in the room, Sal said, "Did you hear Asanti's mentor died?"

Liam's eyebrows shot up, shock evident on his face. "Ah, no, I hadn't heard that. They were quite close. Is she terribly broken up about it?"

"Yeah, actually," Sal said. "It worried me. I couldn't ask her about it—it felt too personal—so I wanted to ask you if you knew anything about him."

Liam smiled, a lopsided grin. "You couldn't ask her, but you don't mind nosing around behind her back?"

Sal shrugged, not feeling guilty. "I'm a detective. Sniffing out information is something I can't very well stop doing. I don't think I should be ashamed for wanting to spare her feelings—but I still want to understand my new team."

"Asanti and her mentor were thick as thieves, as people say," Liam said, finally relaxing a little. He met her eyes in little flicks, not avoiding her, but not holding her gaze for too long. "They were a pair who actually enjoyed the work here, not in a righteous evil-fighting way—"

"Which is the way you enjoy it," Sal interrupted.

"Too true," he said. "Most of us, I would say. But they saw each mission as a sort of exciting treasure hunt. Asanti has never respected what we do as having the danger that it does. She's her own worst enemy, I'm sure. One of these days she will be more interested in studying a book than containing it, and that could be the end."

"Of what?"

"Her. Us. Everything. Take your pick."

The waiter came to their table; Sal ordered a decaf coffee, and Liam ordered an espresso. She mulled this new information over. "You sound like you don't trust her."

Liam frowned and sat back, crossing his arms. A moment passed before he said, "I worry about her passion for the dangers we unearth. She sometimes seems like a curious child poking a stick at a snake. But—no, I do trust her. She's served the team longer than any of us. If she was going to screw up, she would have done it by now. We just see things differently." He looked around the bar, uncomfortable and tense again. "I think fear is good. It keeps you sharp, keeps you on the lookout for the nasty things that can kill you. I just wish she were more afraid."

Sal nodded slowly. Their drinks arrived, and they sipped them in silence.

Sal put some money on the table, frowned at it, counted in her head, and then put a little more down. Liam smiled at her. "You'll get the hang of it."

"I hope so. I think I tipped the waiter one hundred percent the other night. And you guys don't even tip here, let alone that much. I think he thought I was inviting him home with me." Liam colored, and Sal fought to keep herself from rolling her eyes. This boy was too sensitive. She cleared her throat. "Anyway, I hope nothing happens while Asanti's gone. It's pretty clear we need her, whether incautious or not."

Liam sat up straighter and looked at her expectantly.

"I'll see you around. I have some things I have to look into," she said, and got up, smiling weakly.

"Right," he said, looking at his half-empty cup. "Thanks for the coffee. See you around."

That hadn't been awkward *at all*. Sal gritted her teeth as she walked back to her apartment. The discomfort with Liam had to be put aside for now. Something had lodged in her brain, something from her web search, and she had to figure out what it was.

Back in her apartment, she turned on her computer and opened a browser. She put "Glasgow" into Google and swore when the results came up.

The top hit was a restaurant review. Who would search for Glasgow restaurants over searching for the city itself? The second top hit, a review. Third, a restaurant review—same restaurant every time. The Wikipedia entry for the city didn't even show up until page two. The Glasgow city government website came up on the third page.

Now it was officially weird.

Sal chewed on her lip a moment, then checked flights to Glasgow. She sent a quick text to Liam; then she called for a car to take her to the airport.

2.

al didn't like traveling without her gun.

She would never admit it, but dealing with the fact that monsters and magic were real was a little bit easier than dealing with the fact that few people in Europe carried firearms. Not even the police in some countries. And since she wasn't officially police, anyway, she couldn't get away with it. She certainly couldn't travel internationally with a gun.

Her toothbrush, though, they couldn't take that from her. And she could fashion that into a shiv if she absolutely needed to. If the demons would give her just a few minutes to shave it down. And time to find something to shave it with.

As her taxi pulled up to the terminal, she thought back to her days in college working at West Park's EXTREME Cuisine at the foot of the Slippery Bunny ski slope in Vermont. It served fancy fusion cuisine for a clientele of hungry skiers who would rather spend fifteen dollars on a burger than twenty dollars on salmon fillet with dill sauce. She worked only during ski season, but Sal had learned more about crowd control from her few months as hostess there than in her time at the police academy. Restaurants were weird. And it was *very* weird to see one dominating searches for Glasgow.

Distracted by her thoughts, Sal didn't notice Asanti waving at her until she was nearly past the woman, who waited in the ticket line.

"You took much longer than I expected," Asanti said, frowning.

"Well, the traffic was . . . Wait," Sal said, blinking at her. "You're not surprised to see me?"

"You have an intense desire to learn the truth, do you not?"

Sal felt like she had been caught doing something naughty. "Well, yes."

"I knew you would follow to find out more. You're not the only one who is skilled at reading people," Asanti said. She handed Sal a boarding pass. "Here's your ticket. Let's go."

Asanti's mood was on much more solid ground now, and she seemed her old, stoic self. "I'm glad you're nosy and can't leave anything alone," she said as they walked toward their flight.

Sal grinned at the backhanded compliment. "You deliberately manipulated me into coming. That's impressive."

"Yes," Asanti said. "My face isn't always in those books."

"I'll have to be more careful around you," Sal said, only half joking.

The tickets were for first class, and Sal soon found herself in an unfamiliarly cushy seat with a vodka tonic pressed into her hand.

"I need backup," Asanti said after they took off, speaking softly. "I couldn't ask the others. No one else would understand."

"Understand what?"

Asanti spread her hands over her tray table, as if the answers were written on her wrinkled dark skin. "Father Hunter didn't retire, as most people consider retirement. He and the Society agreed mutually on his departure. He'd had enough of the politics and the rules, and they'd had enough of his—as they said—'cavalier attitude' toward his work. As if it were a sin to enjoy your calling."

This fit with what Sal had been told, but the retirement issue was new. "So he quit and moved back home?"

Asanti nodded. "His sister had died a few months before, and her young daughter had no other family. So it worked out. He went back to Scotland to raise her. He adored his niece."

"You're not going there just for the funeral," Sal guessed.

Asanti looked out the window at the rapidly retreating city. "Magic—everything we do in the Society—was amazing to him. He saw it as God's greatest gift to us, and it was our duty to God to learn as much as we could about it. Father Hunter even saw it as our next evolution. If we or our children or our grandchildren could learn as much as we could about this wonder, we would be evolving, be closer to God."

"That's a . . . *different* perspective from any I've heard since I joined this happy family," Sal said.

Asanti smiled sadly. "He was the only one who saw it that way. He taught me to see it through his eyes, and I did for some time. But I have seen a lot of horrible things as well, and never became as idealistic as he is. Was."

Sal thought back to the few horrors she had seen thus far, and of Perry sleeping away in the bowels of the Vatican.

"Father Hunter never saw it as evil? Never? From what I've seen, magic hurts a lot of people."

Asanti turned back to her, looking more energetic. "He saw power as a tool. A hammer or a scalpel is useful in the hands of a carpenter or surgeon. But if you give a toddler either of those, it will almost always end in disaster. We are the toddlers and magic is the tool, but Father Hunter wanted us to eventually become the carpenters and surgeons."

Sal dropped her tray table to accept another vodka from the flight attendant. "I want to believe you, and it sounds great, but I just keep thinking about Perry. That shit was not good magic."

"I said Father Hunter's view was idealistic. What he could never figure out was how to make us grow from toddlers to adults without ending the world. We don't have someone experienced to show us how to use these tools. That's what we need."

"Then maybe we're focusing on the wrong thing," Sal said.

Asanti regarded her. "That's a good point. The only problem is, we're usually too busy cleaning up messes to actually learn much. We only hear about them after they cause damage."

Sal took the opening. "That's the other reason we're going to Glasgow, isn't it? I saw the coordinates you got from the Orb, Asanti. What else is going on?"

Asanti put her hand on Sal's. "What I'm about to tell you could cause a great deal of harm. It could get me fired; it could get Father Hunter posthumously excommunicated. It's the reason I chose to deal with this without the whole team. Can I trust you not to tell the others?"

Sal nodded. "All right. I can't promise anything. If things are truly terrible, the team needs to know. But if I can, I will keep it between us."

"When Seamus left the Society, he took a . . . keepsake. A book."

Sal shook her head as if she hadn't heard correctly. "He took *what*?"

"His position was a sort of combination of my own and Menchú's, both team leader and archivist. He would contain the books and shelve them. Sometimes he would read them. One day we had a mission to recover a book that he swore was good. It was an easy mission, one of the easiest I can remember. No one got hurt; no one fought. The book did no harm, but we took it in, anyway. He knew the book hadn't hurt anyone, and so Father Hunter wanted to study it. He assured me it held benevolent magic. When he left, he didn't want his studies to end because he was no longer part of the Society, so he took the most passive book he knew of. He kept me apprised of his use of the book, and what he learned, and I kept his secret and covered up the missing book by doctoring the files."

"How do you know he was telling the truth?" Sal's voice was hard and rushed as she tried to avoid raising it on the plane. "He could have been possessed and lying."

Asanti looked at her coldly. "He was my mentor, Sally. I know."

Sal rubbed her face and sat back and sighed. "All right, someone who may or may not have been a toddler was running around with a scalpel. Then the toddler died. What happened then?"

Asanti took a sip of her tomato juice. "That's where the details get fuzzy. He was supposed to will the book to me; the plan was for me to come to his funeral and bring it back to the Society."

"But the Orb fired after he died. Someone's using his book instead of packing it away for you," Sal guessed.

Asanti nodded. "Something must have gone wrong. So I have to retrieve it."

"What did it do?"

"He never would tell me. We talked about things on a larger scale, how he had managed to contain the magic within to focus it on a good cause. He was so excited about it, and it was such a nice change to talk to someone who wasn't absolutely convinced that magic is one hundred percent evil."

"God, Asanti. I can't believe you put yourself in this position," Sal said, looking up at the flight attendant button and contemplating another drink.

"As I said, the other options are excommunication and termination—of employment, if I'm lucky," Asanti said, and winced. "Can I count on you?"

Sal closed her eyes. "If you're not the one holding the book right now, we have to look to the next closest person to him. I guess we're going to start with this niece of his."

"He lived with her above her business in Glasgow. I have the address."

"Then we head there," Sal said.

"Reason for visiting Scotland?" the customs official asked. She was a pale, bored-looking woman of about sixty.

"Funeral of an old friend," Asanti said, presenting her passport.

"Same," offered Sal. "And nothing to declare," she said, wishing again there was a way to take her gun easily from country to country.

The lady smiled suddenly and said, as if she hadn't heard the word "funeral," "I hope you enjoy your stay. If you have a chance, check out the restaurant scene. Thistle on the Moor is the best restaurant in the city."

"Country," interjected the customs official next to her, a young woman with a severe bun and small gold earrings.

"Probably the world," their customs official agreed.

"All right, then," Sal said, feeling oddly uncomfortable with this sudden endorsement.

They walked out of the customs area and into the terminal.

"Do we have a sense of what we will be dealing with?" Sal asked as they walked.

"I'm starting to think I do. Father Hunter was convinced it was benevolent magic. The Orb wasn't clear on the perceived threat, which is one reason I wanted to deal with this as independently as possible. If we can just shut it down before the team finds out, that would be best."

"You're saying we don't really have a plan?"

"That is what I am saying," Asanti said, hefting her bag higher on her shoulder.

"We should have at least brought Grace," Sal said. "I don't have any weapons."

"If it's good magic, then you shouldn't need weapons," Asanti said.

They stepped out into the cool Glasgow afternoon and looked for the taxi line. Each cab sat idling, each of them advertising the same restaurant on their doors. Purple, lavender, and black letters welcomed visitors to Glasgow and suggested they try Thistle on the Moor restaurant.

"This Thistle place is kind of prominent," Sal said. Asanti pursed her lips and nodded.

They got into the lead cab, and Asanti gave the cabbie the cross streets.

"That's a popular part of the city," the cabbie said. "Got the best restaurant there."

"Thistle on the Moor?" Sal asked, taking a shot in the dark.

"Oh, you've heard of it?" He turned in his seat, causing the cab to swerve slightly. "The food is legendary. I'd suggest that you go, but you need to book a few months ahead of time if you want a table. I got the missus a reservation for our anniversary. Thirty years next November!" he said proudly, turning back to face the road.

"That's great, congratulations," Sal said, looking out the window. They passed a bus, upon which an ad for Thistle on the Moor beckoned her to visit.

"Be careful, though. The reservation system isn't respected by everyone, and people line up every night hoping to grab themselves a table. The line usually ends up in a fight," the cabbie said, cutting off the bus and causing the bus driver to blow her horn.

"Every night? A fight in front of this restaurant?" Sal asked, turning back to him.

"Pretty much, yeah," he said.

"And this isn't a big deal? Where are the police?"

"That time of night? They're usually in line for Thistle on the Moor."

Sal sighed and looked at Asanti. "I'm going to take a wild guess here and say that Father Hunter's niece is a chef? And that the 'business' she lives above is a restaurant. And that the restaurant is Thistle on the Moor. And now we know where the 'beneficial' magic is going."

Asanti nodded grimly. "Your assumptions are correct. I had hoped it was simply a good restaurant. But now I am thinking otherwise."

"A good restaurant with limitless marketing funds? Come on, Asanti! When I searched for Glasgow online, Yelp reviews for Thistle on the Moor were the top hits! There's some serious manipulation to pull people into this restaurant, and it's getting bigger. It's going global now. Nightly fights? The more people that come to this restaurant, the more violent it's going to get."

"The sorcerer's apprentice," Asanti whispered. "It's wonderful when magic can be used to drum up business, but no restaurant can handle feeding the world when it tries to knock the door down."

"Scalpel in a toddler's hands," Sal said, truly understanding the meaning.

Now that her hypothesis was set, Sal could see the influence of the magic everywhere. People wore primarily shades of purple, lavender, and black, and any public advertising space was for Thistle on the Moor, except for a Glenfiddich billboard currently being covered by a Thistle on the Moor ad.

"You're in luck; it's not open yet so the street isn't closed," the cabbie said, pulling up to the curb on a corner where a line had begun forming. "The traffic usually starts locking up about an hour before the restaurant opens, and driving through there is a nightmare. Good luck, and try not to get caught in the riots."

"Riots? Don't the cops do anything? I'd think they would close the restaurant if it's causing that many problems," Sal said in disbelief.

"Shut it down? It's the best restaurant in the country!" the cabbie said, acting as if she had suggested canceling Christmas.

He retrieved their bags and put them on the curb. "Have a lovely visit, ladies, and do try Thistle on the Moor if you can. It's a nice part of the city, if very busy. I don't come to this part of the city unless I'm trying to get into the restaurant."

"And how often is that?" Asanti asked.

"Oh, about every other night," he said. He tipped his cap and pointed at a healing scratch over his eye. "Got that the other night after the fights started. But one person with reservations got sent to hospital, and I got his table." His eyes gleamed with excitement.

"That's great," Sal said with forced enthusiasm. "Thanks for the advice." She paid the cabbie, who grinned widely at her, gallantly tipping his hat again.

Sal grabbed both of their bags from the sidewalk and put one over each shoulder.

"I'm glad you thought to exchange some money at the airport," Sal said. "I didn't know some cabbies don't take plastic."

"I think we're a block away from the restaurant and Father Hunter's apartment." Asanti led the way across the street so they didn't have to push through the hungry crowd.

The crowds were indeed getting thicker on the sidewalk. One block down from where they had come in, police were in the process of cutting off the street entirely because the sidewalk foot traffic had begun to spill into the streets. Their cab had only just been able to squeeze in before cops put up barriers.

"Looks like we got here right in time," Sal said. "That guy wasn't kidding."

"Nor about the popularity of the restaurant," Asanti said, pointing across the street.

Thistle on the Moor was a tiny restaurant, with glass windows facing the street on two floors. Thistles had been painted on the glass, but they were starting to wear in some places from people touching the windows and leaning to get a better look inside. It was on the corner of a block of shops, but every other shop around was closed. An alley ran along the right side of the building.

"You'd think they would close down for a death in the family," Sal said. "If Father Hunter was as close to his niece as you say he was, shouldn't she be in mourning or something?"

"Not if the magic is driving her to keep it open," Asanti said. "And it's pretty tiny for so many advertisements. This is starting to make sense."

Sal and Asanti stood on the side of the crowded street opposite the restaurant. Sal shook her head at the throng of excited people. "Having worldwide ads for a tiny restaurant is beneficial magic?" she asked. "This is beneficial like eating cake for every meal is beneficial." Her opinion of Asanti's mentor was falling rapidly, but she wasn't going to talk to Asanti about that right now.

Asanti pulled out her phone. "I'll give his niece a call to see if she's there or taking time off."

Sal wondered what a harried hostess would do if the chef demanded that she juggle the reservations to accommodate a family friend.

Asanti smiled when she heard the voice at the other end of the phone. It made her voice sound friendlier even though her eyes grew cold. "Hello, Mary Alice? It's Asanti, yes, lovely to talk to you too, dear. . . . Yes, in fact, I just got into the country for the funeral. Will you be having a wake?"

She paused and allowed the woman on the other end to talk. "The funeral for your uncle. Father Hunter?" Sal looked at Asanti, startled. Mary Alice had forgotten about her uncle's death?

"I see," Asanti continued. "And your restaurant remains open? Don't you think you need time to mourn? You should really take some days off."

Sal could hear sobs coming from the other end, but couldn't make out any words.

"Of course this is what he would have wanted; I completely understand. But since you're not closing, and I'm in town, would you happen to have a table open for two? I've heard wonderful things about your restaurant and would love to visit. You can find some room for me and my friend, can't you? . . . At the bar? Tomorrow night? That would be just fine, thank you so much."

Asanti put the phone back into her large purse. Her smile had faded completely. "Yes, she's been possessed. We must figure out what's going on before we move on her."

"Let's get to the hotel before this crowd gets bigger," suggested Sal. "We can get some rest and deal with this tomorrow."

3.

Don't you think we should have called for backup?" hissed Sal as she followed Asanti across the street to the front of the line. Perhaps it was because they were closer, but the gathered crowd looked larger than the previous day.

"Not yet. We need to see what we're up against," Asanti said. "You can handle yourself in a fight, can't you?"

"Yes," Sal said. "Although I haven't gone up against a full riot on my own before."

"You'll make do," Asanti said. She didn't make eye contact with the people in the line as she stepped up and knocked smartly on the glass door.

A wide-eyed young man in a white apron unlocked it and stuck his head out. Sal noticed he kept his booted foot at the bottom of the door, propped to stop the group from pushing it open.

"Good evening, sir," Asanti said, smiling again. "We are special guests of Chef Hunter. Yesterday she assured me she would find room for me at the bar tonight."

The busboy opened his mouth, looking as if he were about to

protest, but then shut the door in their faces and locked it quickly. He turned his back to the door.

"That didn't go well," Sal said. "What now?"

Asanti shook her head and pointed at the busboy, who was clearly listening to something from the kitchen. He turned and opened the door again, looking quite pale. "Of course, ladies. Won't you come in? I'll get the bartender and some menus."

They entered, with howls of protest sounding behind them.

The interior was, well, wrong. Sal couldn't put her finger on it. The decorating was lovely, with black and purple flowers on every table. Sal quickly counted at least fifteen tables downstairs, with a few two-top tables around the bar. Each table also held small candles, already lit and flickering.

The hostess met the busboy with the menus, shooting Sal and Asanti a frightened look. Her black hair was twisted into a bun atop her head, some strands coming free, and her dark skin was pale as she looked at them briefly, then back at the busboy. He whispered urgently, pointing at the kitchen and then back at them.

"We've made an impact already, wonderful," Sal said.

"That was done even earlier, look," Asanti said, gesturing behind Sal to the window facing the street. Their early entrance hadn't gone unnoticed, and people had begun hammering their fists on the glass, then started hammering their fists into one another.

"It's early tonight, goodness," said the hostess, approaching them. She wore a sharp black suit and limped on her right leg slightly. "It is the price of fame, I fear. Chef Hunter has instructed me to bring you some smoked trout as an appetizer, and the bartender will be here soon to take your drink orders. Can I get you anything else?"

"Glass of water?" Sal asked hopefully. The woman nodded.

The bartender, a short man of about twenty, arrived, tying his apron around his waist and looking at them as if he wished he could throw them out. "Ladies, what can I tempt you with?" he asked, forcing a smile.

Asanti ordered a Dark Island Reserve beer, but the bartender said they were out. She ordered a white wine instead. Sal stuck with soda water. Best to stay sober if she were suddenly playing Grace's role with the fighting. Especially since she didn't know what she was fighting.

Sal's water arrived, and she saw a small lipstick smudge on the glass. She snapped her fingers and looked around the room again. The flowers in the vases were slightly droopy. Not dead, but clearly not fresh. The candles burned low. The tablecloths were stained here and there, and one table had crumbs on the tablecloth when the restaurant hadn't even opened yet.

The bar looked to be out of gin in addition to Dark Island Reserve beer, a local favorite according to the signs behind the bar, which seemed odd for the beginning of the night.

"This restaurant looks as if it's midshift," Sal whispered to Asanti as the bartender searched for a corkscrew for Asanti's wine.

"What do you mean?" Asanti asked.

"The restaurant hasn't opened yet," Sal said. "But the place looks like it's been open for hours. They're out of a Scottish beer and gin, and the place is dirty."

Asanti looked around with fresh eyes, slowly nodding as she saw what Sal saw. "It's like they have too much going on. They can't hold the basics together."

The hostess opened the door and chaos flowed in.

Once the customers came in, they changed. All of them were eager, some of them sporting injuries from brawls outside, but they all smoothed their clothes and calmly followed the hostess to their seats, where each person whispered to a lover or a spouse, or entertained a small group. The waitstaff came forward, looking, like the restaurant, as if they were at the middle or end of the night, not the beginning. The bar filled with people waiting for their tables, and the place was like any other nice restaurant bar Sal had ever been to. People discussed football and politics and news and told work anecdotes. Beside them, a woman was breaking up with her boyfriend and he was trying not to cry. Across the bar, two men were arguing about whose turn it was to buy the football tickets. Nothing turned violent or frightening, not like outside, where people still fought to get in.

Drinks began to flow, and Sal and Asanti paused to eat their appetizer.

Sal frowned as she chewed. "Something else is weird."

Asanti raised an eyebrow.

"The food is good, but not amazing," Sal said, leaning in to whisper. "It's not worth fighting over."

Asanti opened her mouth as if to protest, but Sal stopped her, holding up her hand. "I'm not putting the place down, but I figured the food had to be an orgasm on a plate to cause this kind of fuss. I was even a little worried we might fall under the spell if we ate it. But it's just standard nice restaurant food. Where does the magic come in? Is it all marketing magic?"

Asanti considered what she had said, chewing slowly. "We need to talk to Mary Alice," she said. "I just wanted more information before confronting the poor girl."

The "poor girl" looked to be orchestrating a slave-driving restaurant with a worldwide reach, but Sal allowed Asanti her fluffy illusions. "I agree, we need to see the back of the house. They aren't likely going to allow us to go straight back. I think we'll need to access it through the alley."

"Let's go," said Asanti.

Asanti covered the drinks and appetizer, leaving a tip for the bartender.

"I thought you don't tip in Europe?" Sal asked as they left, side-stepping a guy kneeling on the sidewalk, holding his stomach where it looked like he had just been punched.

"I think that boy needed it," Asanti said. Sal couldn't disagree.

The line had gotten more or less structured after the restaurant had opened. Police at either end of the block halfheartedly tried to control the crowd. Sal looked back inside; the hostess dealt with the crowd in a harried way but still worked efficiently. Her eyes flicked frequently to the line out the door, as if she were expecting something.

The bar was now packed, as was every table. Each person who bypassed the line dressed in the restaurant's purple and black. They each had a purple thistle pinned to their breasts—just like everyone who ate at the tables. People with reservations must get these, Sal figured. She frowned. She was still hungry. It was an insistent hunger, one that usually led to unwise food decisions, like when she went too long without lunch and would settle for the closest fast food she could get to.

The line's order then dissolved in an instant. The crowd was buzzing like a hive, watching those with reservations with envious eyes. But one person, a man of about fifty with salt-and-pepper thinning hair, looking wealthy and important in a gray suit (but still in the walk-ins line), reached out for a woman's arm with one hand, and his other hand went for the thistle pinned to her dress.

The crowd acted as if it were a stick of dynamite just looking for a spark. The woman cried out and punched the man immediately, and her partner leaped at him, knocking him to the ground. The line broke, some people rushing for the door, others trying to stop them. Fists flew; kicks lashed out; angry voices rose.

Instinctively, Sal looked to the police. They were already present—she figured the situation would be calmed instantly. But the bored-looking officers were now wading into the fray, adding to the chaos, looking for their opportunity to get in the front door.

In Sal's experience, people reacted in one of two ways to riots. They either ran into it, the energy of the crowd pushing them on, or they ran away in fear. This riot had only the first kind. The gender, age, or race of the people involved didn't matter—everyone on the block seemed to be running forward to fight for a table at the restaurant.

Asanti remained calm. "Why haven't we been affected by this mad desire?" she asked. "By all rules of magic, we should be running back in there as well."

Sal shrugged, figuring the question was rhetorical but answering anyway. "That's your area. I'm more interested in finding the back door and getting away from this nuthouse." She grabbed Asanti's hand and started to skirt around the fights to access the alley. She had to dodge a fist here, a pair of grabbing hands there, and a rather frightening face, lips peeled back, preparing to bite her hand that held Asanti's arm. Sal kicked that person in the knee and he fell, howling. Sal and Asanti hurried to the alley, which was remarkably empty.

"Why aren't they trying the back door?" Asanti wondered.

"No one goes into a restaurant by the back door except for

staff. People don't even consider it. I'm betting very few people are dining and dashing, either. They want the full experience. And, by the way, the magic is working, I think. I'm feeling very odd coming back here. We're not supposed to be here."

"The magic has soaked into Glasgow gradually," Asanti said, her voice barely audible over the crowd. "That's why we're not affected very much right now. It's permeated the city slowly, without anyone noticing. That's also why the Orb's information was so sporadic. If we stayed longer, I bet we would feel it. "

"It's not slow anymore. I'm getting hungrier. I can feel the draw," Sal replied, and hurried forward.

The side door to Thistle on the Moor was propped open, with two busboys and a waitress smoking outside. The busboys wore white shirts with lavender aprons, streaked liberally with blood. One busboy, a burly lad who looked like he'd missed his calling as a bouncer, smoked his cigarette with a shaking, red hand. His face was pale with two bright red spots on his cheeks.

"I can't do it anymore," he said, his voice high and shaking. "I'm so fucking tired." He broke down and began heaving with exhausted sobs. It was like watching a mountain cry. The other two watched him impassively—not unsympathetic, but not surprised either.

"You gotta pull it together, Mac," said the waitress. "The fights started early tonight." She peered down the alley and caught sight of Sal and Asanti. "Hey, you can't be back here. All customers go in the front door."

Sal sent Asanti a meaningful look. "We're not customers," she began.

"What?" asked the crying busboy, standing on the concrete steps and trying to hiccup his sobs back. "Everyone is a customer. Even we're customers on our days off."

"Really?" asked Sal. "When was your last day off? You look like you haven't had one in a while."

He looked confused for a moment. "I—I don't remember rightly." He looked to the other two for help.

A face appeared at the door, a young woman in a chef's uniform. She didn't look as exhausted or harried as the others, but the staff froze when they saw her. "Break is over," she said pleasantly.

They jumped up as if shocked and made to go inside, but the weeping man pointed at Sal and Asanti.

"Chef, there are customers in the alley. They're not supposed to be here."

"Hello, Mary Alice," Asanti said.

Confusion crossed the young woman's face, and she opened her mouth briefly, then closed it. Her eyes flared a purplish red, and Sal took an involuntary step back.

"Customers aren't allowed back here," Mary Alice said, her voice growing deeper. "Take care of them," she told her employees, and turned to go back inside.

While these people were clearly under the influence of whatever magic was at work, they were not in top physical shape, and Sal felt guilty fighting them. The waitress, she now saw, had wrist braces on both arms, and the busboy who wasn't crying walked on thin legs with a limp. But each of them approached with the energy of another world, an energy Sal was unfortunately getting used to.

Asanti stepped forward, startling Sal, and met the waitress, reaching out her arm and clotheslining her. She went down into a heap, her head hitting the pavement.

"You're full of surprises today," Sal said. The thin busboy was on her then, his hands reaching for her throat. She sliced inward with both forearms, trapping his arms between hers and squeezing, the pressure forcing him to loosen his grip. She stomped on his bad foot and was about to break free when Asanti slammed into her. Sal had been unable to see what the bigger busboy was doing to her friend, but clearly he wasn't as easy to put down as the waitress.

Sal ended up in a pile of garbage bags with the big busboy on top of her, his hands tightening around her throat. She struggled, but the lack of solid ground beneath her made it difficult, and the world started to go gray. Then she heard a clang, and the busboy slumped over her.

It was over by the time Sal had struggled out from underneath the boy and regained her footing. The three people who had attacked them were unconscious, slumped against the wall where Asanti was trying to position them. Grace stood in the middle of the alley, the bodies of four more kitchen staff around her. They must have gotten reinforcements, Sal realized. Liam came up behind Grace, his face twisted in fury. "Maybe now you will learn that you do *your* fucking job and let Grace do *hers*. Get in there and shut this down; it's getting way out of control."

He definitely did not look like the gentle guy that Sal had spent a passionate night with, but she also found this kind of passion admirable. Most of his rage was directed toward Asanti, as he took the archivist's elbow. "Menchú is waiting at the other end of the alley. You're done here." He pushed her gently toward Menchú and let go of her.

Asanti smoothed her clothes and touched a cut on her head, frowning with annoyance when it came back bloody. She exchanged looks with Sal before she left. "You'll take care of it?" she asked.

Sal nodded. "Promise."

Grace went to open the kitchen door that had closed in the scuffle. She said something in Chinese that Sal would have guessed was not very nice. Sal stepped up beside her and said something in English that she guessed was an approximate translation.

Liam, looking over their heads, just said, "Fucking hell."

The kitchen, at first glance, looked as if it were made of meat. At second glance, she was sure. Made of meat. The countertops looked solid and white like bone, while the floors, walls, and ceiling were red flesh.

It was meat, and it wasn't, Sal thought wildly. You didn't call living tissue "meat," and yet a chef was at one wall, blood up to her elbows, slicing into it and carving out a piece to throw into a frying pan. Sal's stomach did a slow forward roll.

"There," Liam said, pointing to the far wall. He was indicating a book that looked nailed to the wall above a whiteboard that seemed quite out of place in this room of gore. The book was hardbound and open, with a glowing red nail through its spine holding it to the wall. Sal's target, Asanti's bizarre inheritance, and the cause of all of this mess.

The problem was that they had to move past the demon in the middle of the room to get to the book.

Mary Alice Hunter had changed once she entered the meat kitchen. Her uniform had taken on a look of flames, and her had skin burned black. Wings made of skinless meat and tissue had erupted from her back and had unfurled as she looked at the open door with rage-filled eyes.

Through the burned skin on her face, human eyes glinted, begging for help. But the mouth opened and howled, showing sharp, wicked teeth.

"The kitchen changes her?" Sal wondered aloud.

"Mine," Grace said, and ran forward. Sal had never been happier to let someone else go first. Liam was right, this was Grace's job. Sal's job was to figure stuff—and people—out. She reminded herself to buy Grace a drink.

Unlike her dexterous companion, Sal stepped forward into the kitchen and slid on the bloody floor. She swallowed heavily, reminding herself sternly that she had seen much worse while working with the Society, and she would probably see worse again before her time was done, and made her way gingerly around the kitchen.

The chefs and staff, bizarrely, looked at Grace lunging for their head chef, but didn't stop cooking. They shouted instructions at each other, chopped, seared, and fried. The dishwashers were shoving the dirty dishes into the washers and then carefully removing the clean ones so the walls didn't bleed on them. Sal watched, fascinated, as a drop of blood splattered from the ceiling onto a plate, and the dishwasher swore and moved it to the dirty pile again.

The hostess came into the kitchen and yelled that Chef Hunter was in the weeds and needed backup. Then she returned to the front of the house.

In this case, "in the weeds" meant "being beaten up by Grace." The woman was making a show of exciting fighting, more ostentatious than Sal had seen before. She realized Grace was trying to draw the attention of all the kitchen staff—the mostly mindless drones—to her, while giving Sal a chance to deal with the book. But once the hostess had yelled that Chef Hunter needed help, they woke up and moved to assist.

Grace was clever, allowing the demon to bat her aside and purposefully slamming into the sous chefs at the stove, which looked less like a health-department-approved gas stove and more like a stone sacrificial altar strewn with bones. The chefs took up the fight, chasing Grace as she ran toward the demon again.

The demon herself leaped onto the counter and raised her wings, howling with her head tipped back. Sal winced and covered her ears as each of the kitchen minions followed suit, sending their heads back and joining the call. The crowd outside howled as one.

"Oh good, they're all following crazy demon chef," Sal muttered, and got closer to the whiteboard.

The workers in the kitchen were unlucky—when they paused to join their leader in her bellow, they opened themselves up. With ungodly speed, Grace ran from waiter to busboy to chef, stabbing each of them in the throat with two fingers. They collapsed, one after the other, choking and squeaking their outrage.

The demon was ready for Grace by the time she returned, though. It threw a chef's knife at her, which she sidestepped. The knife sank into the wall with a squelch, sending Sal's stomach roiling again. She lost it at last, retching onto the floor. The sight of her vomit on the pulsing, bloody surface nearly set her off again, but she steeled herself and pressed on.

Unfortunately, the demon heard her getting sick and saw her for the threat she was—not only to her, but to her kitchen. Apparently blood and tissue on the floor—making the floor—was fine, but a bit of sick was out of the question. *The health department might get angry,* Sal thought hysterically. She blinked, dizzy, when the demon leaped from the counter and landed in front of her, a cleaver clutched in a clawed hand. Sal ducked the swing and slid underneath the demon's arm. The demon righted herself and swung again, and again Sal dodged.

The foul floor wouldn't let her be so nimble every time, but the demon was quickly distracted by Grace, who had thrown the knife back at her, sending it straight into her neck.

Sal knew a simple stabbing wouldn't stop a demon. They all knew that. But that didn't hide the fact that it was horrifying seeing the demon turn to face Grace with a bloody knife sticking from its neck.

I've got to shut this down, Sal thought, her mind racing. She had reached the whiteboard, which had the specials of the day listed in oddly mundane English, but with runes running around the outside of the board.

First, Sal tried to grab the book, but it wouldn't budge. "It's never that easy," she admonished herself aloud, but she knew to always try the most obvious move first. She may as well have tried to pull a closed door off its hinges. She looked in desperation around the kitchen. Grace grappled with the demon, taking her to the ground and not seeming to care a bit about the gore covering her face, hair, and white blouse. Elsewhere, the kitchen minions were rising to their feet, slowly in some cases, but definitely rallying. They would be a problem again soon.

Despite the living meatiness of the kitchen, Sal noted that it worked the way a kitchen was supposed to work. Before becoming a cop, she'd known some metaphorically demonic chefs; little separated some of them from Chef Hunter besides a lack of magic and a living kitchen. She had loved the hostess job that winter in Vermont, and it had taken some serious thinking to decide that police work was her future, not food. She made her decision one night while trying to help out in the kitchen: She burned the soup—literally burned it. She went back to hostessing and left food service when she entered the academy. She missed it sometimes, and found herself oddly nostalgic now, albeit nauseated and frightened and angry as well. Her nostalgia was for the chaotic order that was a kitchen.

And when a kitchen ran out of a dish, they would eighty-six it and let all waitstaff and chefs know.

Sal picked up the red dry-erase pen and crossed out the first item on the list, salmon cakes.

"Eighty-six salmon cakes!" she yelled to no one in particular.

The entire kitchen automatically echoed her. "Eighty-six salmon cakes!"

The runes drawn around the menu glowed bright for a moment, then dimmed.

She struck out with the pen again. "Eighty-six black pudding!"

Again, the kitchen echoed her, the runes flared, and then dimmed.

"Whatever you're doing, keep doing it!" shouted Grace from underneath the demon. While she seemed to be in the vulnerable position, she had her legs wrapped around the demon, which was struggling to free itself. Its face was a mask of pain, and Sal got back to work.

When she had officially canceled all the specials for the day, the nail in the wall stopped glowing, and Sal yanked the book free and slammed it shut.

4.

Liam and Grace waited in the alley while Menchú and Asanti spoke to the shaken and confused kitchen staff. Sal checked the front of the restaurant, where the police were telling the crowd—now bewildered and unsure where they had received their injuries—to go home. The police officers were barely holding it together and looked as if they just wanted to be done with the whole thing. The front-of-house employees looked deflated—sagging and limp. Whatever magic had sustained them had left when the book closed.

Liam had relaxed back on the concrete steps above the garbage bags and watched Grace walk to and fro. Sal returned to the alley and sat next to him at a companionable-but-not-intimate distance.

Grace, covered in pieces of meat and streaks of gore, ranted as she paced, switching from Chinese to English and back again. It was pretty obvious Grace was lecturing her. The snatches of English she could catch were "stupid" and "team" and "trust."

Liam pulled out his phone. "Sal at least left us a clue," he said, holding out his phone to Grace, who ignored it.

"Telling you she was going to Glasgow with Asanti and asking you to google for good restaurant recommendations is hardly a clue," Grace snapped.

"You're just mad you thought I was wrong," Liam said, smiling.

"I'm really glad you got that," Sal said. "I figured if it was nothing, then you wouldn't find anything weird, but if you did think something was weird, you'd know to follow us."

"Why didn't you just tell us?" Grace asked, wheeling and staring Sal in the face. "Leaving little clues is inefficient. Someone could have been hurt, and that would have been a complete waste of my time."

Sal wordlessly pulled a tissue from her pocket and handed it to Grace. The woman took it and wiped some blood off her face.

"Because I'm new. I made sure you all trusted Asanti to do what was right, and when I was satisfied you were happy with her loyalties, I went with her in case she needed backup. And I left a clue to see if you would think she needed backup too. For what it's worth, thanks for showing up. We couldn't have handled this on our own."

"It's worth nothing," snapped Grace. "You put yourself and Asanti in jeopardy. What if we hadn't gotten here in time? And you never consulted with me about her loyalties."

Sal shrugged. "Menchú told me not to bother you during your off hours. I figured you didn't want to see me. What would you have said, anyway? Do you think she's loyal?"

"Of course she's loyal; that much has never been questioned," Grace said. "There is more than loyalty here. There's common sense, and trusting that we have formed this team for a reason. If you had included all of us, then Liam could have done better recon. Did you know you were walking into a gluttony demon's lair when you came here? Liam did."

Sal glanced at Liam, feeling a bit guilty. He grinned at her.

"You clearly couldn't handle yourself in a fight with possessed restaurant workers," Grace continued. "And how do you think you would have fared against that demon on your own? Menchú is in there cleaning up your mess."

"Doesn't he usually do that? And I thought most of the meat had dissolved to ash," Sal said.

"I was not speaking literally," Grace said coldly. "When we work as a team, we work well together. We are efficient. There are fewer injuries. And we do not *waste time*."

Sal sighed and rubbed her sore neck. The adrenaline would wear off soon, and she needed a burger and a beer. Perhaps two. At a restaurant that was loud and dysfunctional and very, very normal.

"You should know that this is nothing compared to the lecture you're going to get from Menchú," Liam said close to her ear.

Sal nodded. "I figured."

Asanti's history with their target changed one more aspect of their trip; despite the battle, they were there for her to say good-bye to her mentor, and so Menchú allowed one more day in Scotland to attend Seamus Hunter's funeral and to assess Chef Hunter to make sure she was unharmed from her ordeal. They got rooms in a hotel and cleaned themselves up.

Sal wasn't surprised to get a call from Menchú after giving her exactly one hour to wash, telling her to meet him in his room.

Considering Liam's warning, Sal had been dreading the lecture.

Grace, now clean and in fresh clothes, opened the door when she knocked, and met her smile with a stony face.

"All righty, then," Sal muttered as she entered the hotel room.

Menchú had gotten a suite with a couch and a kitchenette. Sal was relieved to see Asanti relaxed on the couch, waiting for her. She wasn't going to be alone in this.

Grace began to pace again, but Menchú put a gentle hand on her shoulder and suggested she go back to her room for a rest. She nodded once and left them without a word.

Menchú put his hands behind his back and regarded Sal and Asanti. He sighed and looked at the floor, then back at them.

"I am aware that Grace has already given Sal the gist of my thinking on this little adventure you two have taken," he said. "I have spoken with Asanti as well. Do you understand why you shouldn't have done what you did?"

Sal nodded. "That much was clear to me by the time the riot started," she said.

"We are a team for a reason. Sometimes Liam fights. Sometimes Asanti and Liam do similar information hunts. Sometimes you and I think along the same lines. But we all have our role to play, and the team needs us like a table needs all of its legs."

He took another deep breath and looked at Sal. "This trip did show me that you can be trusted, though. Your text to Liam was perfect—if there were nothing amiss, we wouldn't have followed you. You supported Asanti, and you kept her secrets. We were under the impression you were trustworthy, and now you have proven it."

Sal blinked at the unexpected compliment. "She said it was important. So I treated it like it was important."

"Thank you, Sally," Asanti said in a low voice.

"I hope this has underscored the truth that drives the Society—namely that magic, whether benign or evil, is beyond our understanding, and it is safest when locked away. For as long as Seamus lived, this stolen book"—he emphasized "stolen" and looked at Asanti when he said it—"could be considered benign, since Seamus knew what he was doing. When he died, the true intent of the gluttony demon was able to come through. Asanti, if we all knew what we were doing, it would be one thing. But even when there was a man among us who did know, the moment he didn't have control over the book, everything spiraled downward."

Asanti nodded, her lips pursed. Sal got the feeling she wanted to argue with him, but currently she didn't have anything with which to back up her argument.

The day had ended better than Sal had feared, with no deaths and only minor injuries. The restaurant looked like it would reopen after some major cleaning, renovations, and possibly a visit from a local priest and some holy water.

Deep in thought, Sal left Menchú and Asanti. She thought about Aaron, and the fact that she had kept him secret from the team, and wondered if she should have said something sooner than she had. But her gut still said she had made the right move. Considering that she had walked straight into hell due to trusting her gut, and only a quick text to Liam had saved them, she wondered if she should continue to trust it.

She took the stairs to the floor below, where she and Liam and Grace had rooms. She paused outside Liam's door, hand raised to knock. She clenched her fist and then dropped her hand without knocking. She took a step past the door, but it opened before she could walk away.

Liam looked startled to see her. "Ah, there you are. Asanti wants to meet in the bar for a short wake for Father Hunter. Bit of food, some beer, some stories. And I think Menchú wants an excuse to spend a little more time to make sure the chef is all right. Do you want to come down with me?"

"Yes. In a little bit," Sal said, and stepped past him into his dark room.

He didn't object and closed the door behind them, pausing only to place the privacy sign on the doorknob.

EPISODE 5

THE MARKET ARCANUM

MARGARET DUNLAP

PROLOGUE

TWO WEEKS—AND ONE GLUTTONY DEMON—AGO.

Father Menchú had passed the point in his life when long nights did not inevitably lead to longer mornings. He had been awakened by a call from Sal and Liam, which had led to the dead body of Katie, ship's steward of the *Fair Weather*, who had been executed by Team One without so much as a consultation with Team Three. *That* revelation had led to a lengthy and dissatisfying confrontation with Monsignor Angiuli, followed by an even lengthier conference between Menchú and Asanti as the two of them tried to determine—not for the first time—if taking their displeasure directly to the cardinal was a moral necessity, or if it would only result in Team Three and its operations being subjected to increased scrutiny and oversight. As it so frequently did, pragmatism had won out over principle.

The familiar creak of old leather and loosening wooden pegs in Menchú's office chair echoed in his own joints. Not for the first time, he wondered if this sort of deep politicking was really what God had intended when he called Menchú to his vocation. *Or,* whispered the tiny voice of doubt, *did you join the Church merely as a way to embrace your politics?*

Menchú had never shied away from politics. He had entered the priesthood with seemingly boundless energy for his calling, shunning sleep for days at a time, going from mass to the homes of his parishioners to late-night meetings with like-minded individuals—inside the clergy and out of it—committed to creating a government and a country worthy of the Guatemalan people. Of course, even in those days, he had eventually succumbed to exhaustion—once, memorably, as he had knelt before the altar celebrating mass.

Decades later, sitting in his corner of the Archives, waiting for his tea to cool enough to allow him a satisfying slug of much-needed caffeine, Menchú thought of the unavenged body of a young Australian woman and wondered if her fate had been a result of letting his ideals interfere with his calling or of failing to pursue his ideals energetically enough.

Fortunately, after a few days, even bad nights receded into memory, edges softened by the sands of time. Until Sal came to revive the events of the *Fair Weather* with a knock at Menchú's office doorway.

"Do you have a minute?" she asked.

Even if Menchú had been inclined to send her away, Sal's expression told him that whatever was on her mind couldn't wait.

"Come in," he said.

Not that there was strictly an "in" involved. Menchú's office was merely a niche among the shelves of the Archives, its "doorway" an accident of the main room's idiosyncratic layout. Still, it gave the illusion of privacy, which was usually enough. Menchú waited as Sal sat down on one of the large piles of reference books that served for most of his furniture. He let her take her time, years of experience telling him that he didn't need to push. She had come this far because she wanted to talk. Eventually, she would.

"There's something I didn't tell you about the *Fair Weather*."

Menchú waited.

"There was a tour guide. Well, I thought he was a tour guide, but that was before—"

Menchú put up a hand. "Take a breath."

Sal did. A little shaky at first, but it firmed up on the exhale.

"Whatever it is, it's all right. Just begin at the beginning."

Sal took another breath. And then, she told him.

The pit of Menchú's stomach pooled with dread as Sal came to the end of her story.

"I know it's crazy," Sal said. "But I think Aaron might be an angel."

Yes, he'd been afraid that was where this confession was heading. Menchú leaned forward, took Sal's hand.

"I assure you. Whatever you encountered, it was not an angel."

Sal shook her head. "Maybe not an *angel* angel. But in the same way that we call the evil things that come out of the books *demons*, isn't it possible that some of these supernatural creatures are trying to help—"

"No!"

Sal jumped as Menchú's empty mug hit the scarred surface of his desk with a near-shattering crack. He noticed her flinch and made an effort to rein in his tone.

"If the man you met was truly a divine messenger, carrying the will of God to his people on earth, why could he only give you vague hints and whispers?"

"I don't know."

"Demons that wear evil on their faces, like the Hand, are easy to identify and combat. In New York, was there ever any doubt in your mind that your brother had been taken by a sinister force?"

Sal shook her head.

"The clever demons are more subtle. They force you to fight your-self, your own doubts, before you can fight them. That is why you must always be on your guard."

Slowly, Sal nodded. "Have you ever seen an angel?"

"Never. Nor do I expect to until after I have departed this world for the next."

When Sal left, Menchú noticed that his hands were shaking. It took some effort to still them.

TWO WEEKS—AND A TRIP TO SCOTLAND—LATER.

Asanti snagged Menchú as he passed her desk by holding up a thick, cream-colored envelope addressed in perfect copperplate handwriting. Menchú recognized the signs of its sender and didn't bother to hide his distaste.

"I guess it's that time again. Are you going to take Liam?" he asked.

Asanti shook her head. "You're taking Sal."

Menchú froze. "In light of recent events, I don't think that's a good idea. . . ."

"From what you've told me about recent events, she's already in up to her neck. Better that she knows what she's swimming in. Besides, don't you wish you'd gone into this with *your* eyes wide open?"

Menchú sighed. Asanti, of course, was right. It was time for Sal to learn about the Market.

1.

NOW.

Sal had come to the gym to lift weights, put in some treadmill time, and take out a little pent-up aggression on the heavy bag. All of those plans, however, flew right out the window when she found Liam with his shirt off, taping his hands and showing off both his physique and tattoos to very good advantage. Not that she wasn't intimately acquainted with his ink already. Still, just because a girl was familiar with the scenery didn't mean that she couldn't appreciate the view.

He caught her looking and smirked.

"You come to work out, or just window-shopping?"

"I can't do both?"

"I'd hate for you to get hurt because you were distracted."

Well, she couldn't just let that pass, could she?

Despite being in a genuine roped-off ring, their sparring was more mixed unarmed combat than straight-out boxing. (Liam was scandalized to learn that New York police did not generally engage in recreational fisticuffs, at least, not since handlebar mustaches had gone out of fashion.) But they both had enough training to make for an interesting bout, and if one or the other of them periodically wound up flat on their back against the canvas, Sal wasn't complaining. From the press of his body against hers, Liam didn't object either.

Liam was helping her to her feet, and Sal was just about to suggest that they hit the showers and then continue their conversation in a less public setting when she was cut off by Father Menchú clearing his throat behind them.

Caught engaging in sparring-as-foreplay by a priest. There was an effective mood-killer for you.

Sal covered her blush by scrubbing her face with a towel.

"Father," said Liam, his form of address betraying the depth of his discomfort. There was one advantage to being a lapsed Presbyterian who just happened to work at the Vatican: Sal might not be familiar with Catholic politics and hierarchy, but at least she didn't have to fight years of childhood conditioning every time her boss walked in. Most of the time, Liam did pretty well at ignoring the fact that Menchú was a priest. This, apparently, was the line.

Menchú nodded to Liam in acknowledgment, then turned to Sal. "I need you to go home and pack a bag. We've got an assignment. Our train leaves in two hours."

Sal snapped into ready mode, tossing aside her embarrassment along with her used towel. "I've got a go bag here. We can leave now."

Menchú raised an eyebrow. "We could, but the train still leaves in two hours, and you need something you can wear in upscale company for the next three days."

Sal wasn't sure she had anything in Rome that she could wear in upscale company. Depending on how upscale he meant, she wasn't sure she owned anything appropriate at all. "What's the assignment?"

"I can't say."

That apparently caused something to click for Liam. "Is it Beltane already?"

Menchú gave him a quelling glance.

"What's going on?" Sal demanded.

Menchú shook his head. "Can't say."

"Can't? Won't? Or aren't allowed to?"

"Does it matter?"

Well, when he put it that way, Sal didn't suppose it did.

The train took them to Zurich. Once there, Menchú rented an economy car, and they drove north through the mountains. Through it all, he wouldn't say a word about where they were going, what they would be doing there, or why they were the only members of the team involved. Although Sal had come to accept that answering questions was not the Society's forte, it was troubling that Menchú didn't want to talk about anything else, either.

Finally, after hours of silence and crossing the border into Liechtenstein—of all places—Sal asked, "Are you mad at me?"

Menchú glanced at her in surprise. "No. Why would I be mad at you?"

"I don't know, but I'm starting to feel like the cat you're planning to abandon three states away, hoping that I won't be able to find my way home."

Menchú looked pained. "I'm sorry, Sal. I've been a bit distracted."

"No shit."

He glanced at a passing kilometer marker and came to a decision. "All right. We're close enough now. Let me tell you about the Black Market."

Somehow Sal had a feeling he wasn't talking about tax-free booze and cigarettes.

"It's properly known as the Market Arcanum, or more commonly, the Market. The Society was first invited in the fifteenth century, thanks to the connections of certain members of the Order of the Dragon. From what we can tell, however, the Market dates back at least another half millennium before that. In any event, every year at Beltane, covert practitioners of magic gather for a three-night conclave. It's part auction, part high-level diplomatic conference for every power player who uses magic to rig the game."

"Wait," said Sal. "There's an annual clearinghouse where people buy, sell, and trade the objects that we're supposed to be hunting down and destroying?"

"Yes."

"And Team One hasn't nuked it from orbit?"

Menchú gave her a sardonic look. "I'm sure you've noticed that individuals within our organization do not always agree on matters of policy."

Sal thought of Katie. "Yeah, but this time you've managed to *stop* Team Trigger-Happy. How?"

"The Society leaves the Market alone for two reasons. First, it was pointed out by one of Asanti's long-ago predecessors that even if we could destroy the Market, it wouldn't eliminate magic from the world. At least this way, we can keep an eye on things."

"That seems surprisingly sensible," said Sal. "What's the second reason?"

"In an open assault against the Market, the Society isn't sure they'd win."

"There are going to be people at this thing who could take Team One?"

"It's highly possible that there are people at the Market who could take Team One without breaking a sweat."

Sal wasn't sure she wanted to contemplate that. "Who are these people? World leaders? Guys who go to Davos? The Illuminati?"

"The members are . . . rather eclectic," Menchú said. "The backbone is made up of representatives from the old noble European families. Though there's been an influx of new money and technologists in the last hundred years, much to the disgust of the old guard. You'll also see practitioners from Africa, Asia, and the New World, but we believe most of them have core gatherings in their own regions."

"I'm sure the Society would love to have invites to those."

"The Society would like to be able to send more than two representatives to this one, but wanting and getting are two very different things."

"Not that I'm complaining, but why isn't this a Team Two job? Aren't they the diplomats?"

Menchú snorted. "They are, but objects and texts are our jurisdiction. Also, the members of the Order of the Dragon who secured the original invitation were part of Team Three, and so, by tradition, we're the ones who go."

Sal had a sudden suspicion. "Are you a member of this Order of the Dragon?"

Menchú actually rolled his eyes. "The Order of the Dragon was founded hundreds of years ago to protect Christendom from encroachment by the Ottoman Turks."

"That is not a denial," Sal pointed out.

Menchú quirked his lips, but said nothing.

They rode in silence the rest of the way to Balzers, a town tucked into a valley in the middle of the mountains, which—as far as Sal could tell—was a fair description of most of Liechtenstein. Spring came late to the Alps, but the hills behind the small B&B where Menchú had booked their rooms were definitely greening up, and Sal took a minute—after she had changed out of her travel clothes into the black pants, black button-down shirt, and black jacket that were as formal as she had managed—to appreciate the smell of clear air and growing things. She was getting used to Rome, but even after all her years in New York, Sal wasn't a city girl at heart.

The Market Arcanum was to be held in Gutenberg Castle. Compared to the Papal Palace it seemed like more of a big stone house than a castle, but Sal supposed that if you ran a country, you could call your buildings whatever you wanted. It was outside the town proper, and she and Menchú walked together up the hill from their inn.

"The Market is run by a woman known as the Maîtresse," Menchú explained. "She sets the rules, and for the next three nights, her word is law."

"What are the rules?"

"The Market is considered neutral territory, which means that no member is allowed to offer violence against another."

"What constitutes violence?" asked Sal. "Harsh words? Assault? Murder?"

"During the Market, violence is whatever the Maîtresse and her Guardians say it is."

"Ah. Gotcha."

"Any bargain struck at one Market must be fulfilled before the beginning of the next. If not, the owed party can demand a forfeit of their choosing."

Sal could only imagine what powerful magic-wielding people could come up with for a forfeit.

"Lastly, anyone violating the secrecy of the Market will be permanently banned, along with their cadre."

The penny dropped. "That's why you couldn't give me any information earlier?"

"Yes."

Sal considered. "So if I piss someone off badly enough, I could get the entire Catholic Church banned?"

"In theory, yes."

"I'm not gonna lie. That's just a little tempting."

Sal wasn't sure, but she could have sworn she heard Menchú mutter, "You have no idea."

2.

The sun was only a finger-width above the horizon when Sal and Menchú reached the castle. The Maîtresse waited at the gates, flanked by two immense statues of armored men carrying stone swords. If the Maîtresse had been anyone else, Sal would have pegged her age as somewhere between her forties and her sixties, an indeterminate maturity where experience, strength, and sex appeal came together, and women with the standing to back it up could wear their power without even a whisper of apology. Something about her bearing, however, made Sal suspect that this woman had not apologized for her authority for a very, very long time.

"Maîtresse," said Menchú with the barest nod of respect. "Thank you for inviting us to the Market once again."

The woman did not return the courtesy. "Bookburner." Her eyes flicked to Sal. "And this is?"

Menchú blinked, but took the hint. "Our newest member, Sally Brooks."

The Maîtresse swept Sal with a penetrating stare. "Is she, now? How lovely for you."

Sal took Menchú's lead and nodded. "Ma'am."

The Maîtresse's gaze lingered for another moment, and then, to Sal's relief, transferred back to Menchú. "Do you claim a debt outstanding from the last Market?"

"We do not."

"Very well." At her gesture, the two statues stepped forward and away from the doors. Apparently, the Maîtresse had figured out how to use magic without being consumed by madness, supernatural backlash, or a demon she sought to control. Which was . . . not a reassuring thought, actually.

The artificial men reached out and opened the huge wooden doors leading into the courtyard of the castle proper.

The Maîtresse's smile was anything but welcoming. "Welcome to the Market Arcanum."

The courtyard was lit by sconces along the walls and illuminated orbs that floated overhead, unconnected to any visible tethers or power sources. Among the crowd already gathered, Sal could pick out at least half a dozen different languages being spoken and guessed there were probably that many more that she couldn't distinguish from the general murmuring.

"Does the Market supply translators?" Sal whispered.

Menchú grimaced. "This is just opening night posturing. Everyone keeping to their own group and proving how esoteric and mysterious they are. Once the Market officially opens, everyone switches over to a lingua franca."

"Please tell me that's pretentious-speak for 'English.'"

"These days, yes. It used to be Latin, then French, and some of the old families who insist on doing business 'traditionally' will use those for official documents and transactions, but English is the world's second language, even here."

"Oh. Good.'

Putting aside for the moment the part of her brain that kept trying to *understand* all of the words floating around her, Sal concentrated on what her eyes were telling her instead. Now that Menchú had pointed it out, she could see that all the people in the courtyard kept to small clusters of four or five. Apparently, not every group was limited to the Society's two invites.

One group of men wearing wolf pelts draped over their shoulders like hoods looked like they had hiked in out of the Alps. The pelts had heads still attached, artificial eyes staring glassily from above their wearers' own faces. It was disconcerting. Especially when Sal saw one of the wolves blink.

On the opposite side of the yard, a group of men and women in jeans and black T-shirts had apparently not gotten Menchú's dress-for-company memo and were all busily bent over some piece of equipment. Support staff? As Sal tried to get a glimpse of just what they were working on, one of the men looked up and met her gaze. Sal felt suddenly cold. Then he looked away, turning back to his work, and she wondered if she had imagined it.

"Who are they?" she asked Menchú.

"Techno-cultists." Sal wasn't sure she had ever heard him sound so disgusted. "They believe that magic, like information, 'wants to be free.' And that by combining human technology with the super-natural, they can bring about the singularity, not just of artificial intelligence, but of all human knowledge."

"What does that even mean?"

"That they're a bunch of anarchists who have no respect for the power they're playing with."

Sal's stomach clenched. "Are these the people Perry was mixed up with?"

"Philosophically, maybe, but we never had evidence that your brother and his friends were working with anyone except themselves."

Before Sal could pursue the subject any further, the loud bang of a wooden bar falling across the entry doors reverberated through the courtyard. The assembly fell silent, and in that pause, the Maîtresse stepped out onto a balcony overlooking the Market.

"Tonight begins the Market Arcanum. For three nights, from sunset to sunrise, all debts and grudges are to be set aside within these walls. In the outside world we are friends, rivals, enemies. Here we are equals."

The Maîtresse clapped her hands once, and the air throughout the castle vibrated, as though they stood inside a giant bell. On the stone wall above her, a clock face appeared. It had only a single hand, creeping from sunset on the far left edge of the circle toward dawn marked opposite.

The courtyard instantly erupted in conversation once again.

The Market had begun.

One of the men with the wolf pelts examined the contents of a lacquered wooden box held by a woman wearing an elegant evening gown, but whose exposed skin was completely covered in tattoos. The techno-cultists went back to their equipment. And a tall man wearing a suit that probably cost more than Sal earned in a year was striding toward her and Menchú.

When he arrived, his voice dripped with false cordiality. "Excellent. I had hoped that the Bookburners would deign to make an appearance."

Sal wondered if everyone at this gathering hated them, or if they just kept running into the ones who did.

"We don't burn books," Menchú said gently.

"Of course not. You take them. Even when they don't belong to you."

Sal frowned and glanced at Menchú. Did he have any idea who this man was or what he was talking about?

Menchú's expression was impossible to read. "There are no debts or grudges within these walls. If you have a problem with the Society, I suggest that you take your quarrel elsewhere, Mr. . . . ?"

The man smiled. "The name is Mr. Norse."

Mr. Norse. Owner of the *Fair Weather*. Sal was mildly impressed that he was more upset about the book than his burned yacht, but maybe he didn't know Team One had been behind that. Maybe his yachts spontaneously caught fire all the time. With hobbies like his, it had to be a risk.

"Since you took something of mine," Mr. Norse continued, "now I'm going to take something of yours." He was practically leering. On instinct, Sal placed herself between the two men.

"You heard the lady on the balcony. This is neutral territory. But if you want to step outside, I'd be happy to kick your ass three nights from now."

Mr. Norse only smiled. "I've already stepped outside, Ms. Brooks."

He laid a particular emphasis on her name, rolling it on his tongue.

Sal felt her phone vibrate against her thigh. Incoming call. She ignored it.

"Congratulations, you know my name. Am I supposed to find that intimidating?"

"You'll want to get that," said Mr. Norse.

Behind her, Father Menchú's hand slid toward his own ringing phone.

"Why?"

"It's the part you're supposed to find intimidating."

Sal pulled out her phone and glanced at the caller ID. Liam.

Liam and Asanti stood at the center of a maelstrom. A fierce wind roared through the Archives, picking up books and sending them flying off their shelves, hurtling through the air like mad birds.

"What's going on?" Liam shouted.

Above them, the towering shelves swayed, metal creaking like an old barn in a storm. Liam wondered just how many tons of paper loomed above their heads, and how long it would take to dig out their bodies if it all came tumbling down.

And then something was falling toward them: Grace. No, she wasn't falling. She had slipped through the lattice surrounding the central stairs and was skittering down the supports like they were a giant, swaying jungle gym. She landed lightly on her feet, not even out of breath.

"Are you insane?" Liam asked.

She shrugged. "Faster than walking."

"Did you find the monsignor?" Asanti asked.

Grace shook her head. "Couldn't get out."

"We're sealed in?"

It wasn't really a question, but Grace nodded. Liam reached for his phone.

"I tried," said Grace. "No signal."

Liam didn't look up. "I've got some boosters built into mine. I might be able to get through whatever's causing this so we can warn the other teams."

Asanti grabbed Liam's shoulder to get his attention. "Try Sal and Menchú first." Even though she was shouting directly into Liam's ear, he had trouble hearing her over the creak of shelves and the thumps of falling books.

"Why?"

"Because the Market began tonight, and whatever this is, it started at sunset."

Once Sal had hung up with Liam, Menchú calmly returned his attention to Mr. Norse. "All right. You've shown that you can attack my people. Now stop."

The other man smiled. "No."

"I will report you to the Guardians. It is against the rules of the Market—"

"The rules of the Market forbid any member to offer violence against another within these walls. I have not lifted a hand against you or your companion. But you killed three of my people. Return my book," said Mr. Norse, "or the attacks will escalate every night until the rest of your team is just as dead as mine."

3.

al and Menchú left the castle the instant the doors were unbarred at sunrise. Their landlady gave them a look as they arrived for breakfast through the outside door, but Sal was too strung out to care. As soon as they could, they adjourned to Menchú's room and called Asanti.

"The maelstrom stopped briefly at dawn," she reported, "but it keeps picking up again, randomly and without warning. Which is almost worse."

"Is everyone okay?" Sal asked.

"A bit battered, but so far, yes."

Well, that was something, at least. "Could Mr. Norse be bluffing?" Sal asked.

Menchú shook his head. "Unfortunately, I think we have to assume that whatever Mr. Norse is doing will escalate to more lethal levels until he makes good on his threat." Then he added, to Asanti, "We should be there with you."

"As much as I'd appreciate your company and assistance, I think you can do more good working on Mr. Norse where you are. Besides, we're locked in."

Menchú said something in Spanish that Sal suspected he wouldn't be willing to translate. She decided to get back to the matter at hand.

"Okay, so if you're stuck in there, what can we do from Liechtenstein to make sure that you don't, you know, die? I mean, besides give Mr. Norse a book leaking demonic goo that wants to drown the world."

"It depends on what he actually wants," said Asanti.

"He sounded pretty clear about wanting all of you dead," said Sal.

"If Norse wanted to kill us, there are a lot of faster, easier, and more deniable ways to go about it," said Asanti.

Menchú grimaced. "Which means that this is just the opening of negotiations."

Mr. Norse responded immediately and favorably to their request for a meeting, which Sal had to admit lent a certain degree of credibility to Asanti's theory. They arranged to meet before sunset, in a small room that was normally part of the castle's museum.

Mr. Norse seated himself on a tapestried stool that must have been at least four hundred years old as though he sat on Renaissance furniture every day. Maybe he did. Menchú and Sal remained standing.

"Thank you for agreeing to meet with us," Menchú began.

"Do you have my book?"

"We do. Locked in our archives."

"Then I suggest you unlock it," Mr. Norse remarked drily. "If transport is a problem, I have an envoy in Rome who will accept delivery on my behalf." He took a card out of his jacket pocket and held it out to Menchú. Menchú ignored it.

"The book is both damaged and highly dangerous. We cannot hand it over."

Mr. Norse raised a brow. "I thought Catholics believed in the value of human life."

"We are aware that you purchased the volume, and are prepared to compensate you for your loss of property."

"My demands for compensation are very simple. I want my book. Since I suspect you will not provide it, I will kill your team. And then, I want you to live with the knowledge of the deaths you caused with your obstinacy." His smile was flat and cold. "Unless you can offer me something better than that, I think our discussions are concluded."

So much for negotiations, Sal thought.

"Time?" asked Liam.

"One minute to sunset," came Grace's calm reply. As though they weren't anticipating all unholy hell breaking loose in the next sixty seconds.

Liam had faith in Menchú and his powers of persuasion. He believed that God would protect those committed to his work on earth. Liam had also been taught that the Lord helped those who helped themselves—and so that was what he and the rest of the team had spent the day doing. Now Liam's entire body felt like one huge bruise, and his ears rang from stress, hunger, and lack of sleep. But this time, they would be prepared.

"Are you ready?" Asanti asked.

"Gimme five seconds."

"Thirty seconds to sunset," said Grace.

Liam took hold of two heavy iron maces—originally part of some forgotten order's regalia, now wrapped in wire stripped from every reading lamp in the Archive—and lifted his arms to their greatest extension, one on either side of his body. "Do it."

Grace and Asanti both jammed spliced electrical plugs into outlets on opposite walls, one for each mace. It hadn't been easy to create electromagnets with things stashed around the Archives, but pain and annoyance were powerful motivators, and Liam had plenty of both to egg him on. Now he just needed this harebrained scheme to work.

"Grace, a little more on your side."

Liam heard a scrape as she pushed a set of iron shelves through the books covering the floor. He fancied he could see Asanti wince out of the corner of his eye, but she didn't say anything. First, save themselves. Worry about the damage later.

The pressure on his left arm eased, as the magnetized mace wavered, torn between the pull of the magnet in his other hand and the huge hunk of iron Grace was moving toward it. The pull was easing, nearly neutral. . . .

"There!"

Grace froze. Liam held his breath. Slowly, carefully, he let go of the maces, trying not to jostle their positions in the air. Then he stepped away. The two weapons hung, perfectly balanced between the attractive force of the iron shelves, the central stairway, and each other.

Liam let out a long, slow breath. No one moved.

"Time?"

"Four seconds to sunset."

Three. Two. One.

The Archives remained silent. No winds. No flying books.

Grace looked at Liam, impressed. "Field is holding. Nice work." Then she frowned. "Do you hear that?"

"Hear what?"

"High-pitched sound. Like a fluorescent bulb that's slightly off cycle."

Liam shook his head. "No, but my high frequencies aren't great."

"Too much time with your headphones on," said Asanti.

Liam shrugged. "Probably." Then a sound tickled at the edge of his hearing. "Wait. Is it kind of . . . ?"

The high-pitched noise exploded in his head like someone was driving an ice pick through his eardrums. Liam gasped in pain. He heard Asanti shout. And Grace . . .

Grace, who could take a fist to the face without blinking, whom Liam had seen head-butt armored demons twice her size and not even bruise, crumpled to the floor, unconscious.

From the instant Menchú and Sal stepped into the courtyard at sunset, it was obvious that everyone at the Market knew what was going on. Not that Mr. Norse had been at all subtle with his threats the night before, but Menchú couldn't help but notice how every whispered conversation paused as they passed and then resumed as soon as they were out of earshot. He wished that Asanti were there with them. Actually, he wished that Asanti were there *instead* of him. Menchú had learned over the years to take people as they came. His easy manner with all sorts was one of the reasons he had been recruited into Team Three. But the Market, with its casual magic use and even more casual classism, made his teeth crawl.

He did his best to shake off his annoyance. It wouldn't help, and railing against the good fortune of people who did evil over those who did good was bush-league theology of the first order.

As if she could read his mind, Sal let out a sigh. "It's not fair."

"What isn't?"

"We probably have the largest collection of magical books and artifacts in the world in the Archives." She gestured to the crowd around them. "We could be sitting on something that could not only stop Mr. Norse, but also make his balls fall off the next time he even thinks about going after our people, but it doesn't do us any good because we never *use* any of the artifacts we find."

Quickly Menchú drew Sal off to the side where they could speak without being disturbed. That kind of thinking had to be nipped in the bud. "We are fighting this, Sal," he assured her, "and we are going to win. Liam, Grace, and Asanti are going to be fine."

"You don't know that. We can't give Mr. Norse the book because he would use it to destroy the world; I get that. But look around us; this place is full of people who use magic every day. It doesn't seem to be driving them insane."

"You don't know them very well yet."

Sal shook her head. "I just don't understand why you won't even consider—"

"Because I know what happens when people try to use forces they don't understand."

Sal was clearly still in the mood to argue, and Menchú realized they would be at it all night if he didn't give her something productive to do. "Why don't you call and check in with the others? Let them know what's going on and make sure that they're still all right."

"And what are you going to do?"

Menchú couldn't stop the grimace. "Look for allies."

Sal's conversation with Liam had not gone well. A burst of static exploded from the phone the instant he picked up. She tried to tell him what had happened with Mr. Norse but wasn't sure that he could hear anything over the bad connection. From what she'd been able to make out, the situation in the Archives had only gotten worse, and there was still jack-all that she could do about it from goddamned Liechtenstein.

When Sal hung up, the techno-cultist who had been staring at her the night before was standing at her elbow. She jerked in surprise, and her phone went flying from her fingers.

The techno-cultist's hand darted out, picked her falling phone out of the air, and handed it to her. All without ever once breaking eye contact. He worked his mouth for a moment, as though he had to remember how to talk. Finally, he said, "You're Perry's sister, aren't you?"

Sal felt her heart lurch in her chest. She checked the courtyard. Menchú was nowhere to be seen. "Yes. Who are you?"

"You can call me Opus93."

"How about I call you by your real name?"

He shrugged. "What makes Opus93 less real than the name I was born with?"

Because Opus93 is a stupid-ass name, Sal didn't say. "What do your friends call you?"

"Opus93."

Sigh. "What do you know about my brother, Opie?"

"Word is he got his hands on something real, but he brought it to his sister the cop. He goes nova, puts out a huge spew of phantom data, then goes dark. And now Cop Sister is a Bookburner, and no one's heard from Perry since."

"What are you implying?"

"Implications are imprecise. Facts are what's needed."

Sal didn't know whether to roll her eyes or fight back tears. It was too much like talking to Perry when he got into one of his esoteric fugues.

"Fine. Are you offering facts? Or just fishing for them?"

"Information wants to be free, doesn't come without a price. You want help with your little billionaire problem, you need to ask the Index."

The Index. Even Sal could hear the capital letter. She looked around again for Menchú. Still no sign of him. She swallowed. "Tell me more."

Either the small room the techno-cultists had reserved for their use during the Market was not normally part of the castle's museum, or it had been lovingly restored to its original purpose of storing dirt. Though dirt wouldn't have required the window the cultists were using to vent the portable generator they had brought. That was the only familiar piece of equipment in the room.

Through a shared childhood with Perry, Sal had become passably familiar with circuit boards, resistors, and the various shells that computers and their innards came in. Not that she could do anything with them, but at least she knew what they were supposed to look like.

These computers—and Sal used the term loosely—had probably started their lives as standard PCs. What had happened to them next . . . One laptop looked like it had been repurposed as a planter, the keyboard replaced with a bed of moss ringed by yellow flowers. Above, a screen glowed with life. As Sal watched, Opie brushed a hand over the moss, and the blinking cursor and command line vanished, replaced by scrolling code that flew by faster than her eyes could follow. Another half-open desktop was filled with boards where glowing crystals grew among the circuits, absorbing the machine into their structure. A screen on the opposite wall connected to a large aquarium, complete with a herd of tiny sea horses milling in the purple-hued water.

Opie caught her staring. "Biocomputer. Only working example in the world." He walked over to the aquarium and pulled a keyboard off a nearby shelf. A few keystrokes later, the blank screen above the tank changed to display a video of a baby panda. "Panda cam in the Beijing Zoo. It's closed circuit. Not publicly accessible."

Sal was more disturbed by the sea horses. As soon as Opie picked up the keyboard, they fell into formation, then scattered. They were currently swimming in a very intricate pattern through the tank. Except that every few seconds, all of the sea horses would suddenly freeze in place, like a buffering video. The baby panda, meanwhile, rolled on its back happily, and a hand reached in from off-screen to rub its belly.

"I thought biocomputers were still theoretical."

"In the rest of the world, yes. But if you have a little bit of magic to help you . . ." He gestured to the rest of the room. "All things are possible."

"Is that the Index?"

"The Index makes this look like a Commodore 64."

"So why are you wasting my time? I have friends in trouble. Can you help me or not?"

Opie gave her a smug look. "I can help you. But the Index contains the sum of all human knowledge. Like I said, you don't get to access that for free."

Sal scoffed and held up her cell phone. "I already have access to the sum of all human knowledge. Costs me sixty-five dollars a month."

Opie snorted. "We both know that if that was enough, you wouldn't have followed me, Cop Sister. The Internet is merely the totality of human knowledge that's been written down and put on online. The Index is a repository of everything known by any human who has ever interfaced with it."

"And that includes Mr. Norse?"

Opie nodded. "Ask your question, and know what he knows about what's happening to your friends."

"What's the catch?" asked Sal, torn between being fascinated by the possibilities and really disturbed by the implications of what Opie was saying.

"For every question you ask, the Index takes one piece of knowledge from your mind, and you can never know it again."

4.

Sal had found Menchú when they both returned to their B&B after sunrise. Predictably, he had not been enthusiastic when Sal told him about her encounter with Opie and his offer.

"I don't like the idea of losing a chunk of my memory any more than you do, but I don't think we have a choice," she said, trying to keep the impatience out of her voice. Sal couldn't imagine that getting snippy with Menchú would help matters, and it wasn't like any of this was his fault.

"We always have a choice," said Menchú. "And we only have the word of one techno-cultist that this so-called Index won't wipe your entire memory. We don't know that it even works at all."

"I'm pretty sure that mind-wiping someone would be considered both breaking a deal *and* offering violence against another member of the Market. Do you really think they'd risk getting evicted?"

"I'm sure their expulsion will be a great comfort to you after your mind has been destroyed by their infernal machine."

"That's the other thing. If this is all a ploy, what's in my mind that they're so interested in? Out of everyone here, why target me?"

"Your brother."

"You know more about what's going on with Perry than I do. Plus more secrets of the Society besides. Why haven't they been eye-fucking you this whole time?"

Menchú didn't even crack a smile. "Because if they'd approached me, I would have said no, and we wouldn't be having this discussion."

"You think they targeted me because I'm the weak link."

"I think they know what you want, and now they're offering it to you. It's what demons do—find your weakness and turn it against you."

"You think Opie is a demon? Seriously?"

"I think something is powering the Index, and it isn't love and light." If possible, Menchú's expression turned even more serious. "You haven't been with us for long, but even so, these people would be foolish to pass up the opportunity to suck you dry of every drop of information you know about the Archives and the Society. You remember how Liam was possessed?"

Sal nodded.

"This wouldn't be the first time techno-cultists tried to use the residue of a demon to access our secrets. And once they've touched you . . . Demons leave scars just like physical wounds. Break a bone once, you're more likely to break it again in the same place."

"So where are you broken?" Sal asked.

Menchú froze. "What do you mean?"

"You recruited me after I fought off a demon possessing my brother. Liam was taken over by something out of his computer, lost two years of his life, and now lives to fight the kinds of things that stole that time from him. I'm willing to bet that Asanti had some brush with the arcane that got her so curious about magic, and for some reason, Grace isn't afraid of getting shot. So what happened to you?"

The silence sat heavily between them.

"Does it have to do with an angel?"

Menchú's head shot up. "What did Asanti tell you?"

"Nothing. But you just did."

Menchú seemed to deflate before her very eyes. Shrinking somehow, as though the clerical collar was just a costume, and he wasn't a crusader saving the world from magic, demons, and things that lurk in the night, but merely a middle-aged man who was suddenly very, very tired.

Sal expected him to tell her that the discussion was over. Or that his past was none of her business. Or even to send her back to Rome. Instead, he said, "It was a long time ago. When I was still a parish priest in Guatemala."

The parish consisted of a single village, tucked into a valley surrounded by as much farmland as the residents could cultivate before the terrain became too steep to support anything but virgin forest. The United States had been telling the world that Guatemala was a democracy for at least ten years, although what evidence it had to support that claim beyond a nominally elected government was dubious. Were mass executions and disappearances the hallmarks of a democracy? Menchú was pretty sure they weren't. And he was dead certain that they *shouldn't* be.

Still, there were a few signs that things were changing for the better, and maybe that was why he had not seen the disaster coming. Unknowing, perhaps he let his guard down. Whatever the reason, the first Menchú knew of the impending disaster was a small fist banging on the door of his residence in the middle of the night.

Menchú had not been asleep and was at the door almost immediately. It was one of the boys from the village, an altar server no more than seven years old, fist already raised to knock again. "Father," he said, "come quickly."

Menchú read his expression in an instant. "What's happened?" he asked, even though he was certain he knew the answer. Still, *What's happened?* was a kinder question than *Who died?*

"The army. They've surrounded us."

Menchú did not ask further questions.

He followed the boy outside into the square. Soldiers were roaring into town now, making no attempt at stealth. Menchú couldn't fathom how he hadn't heard them coming. There was too much noise to pick out what individual men were saying, but their intent was clear. Every resident—about sixty men, women, and children—had been rousted from their beds and corralled into the main square. The man with captain's braid on his shoulders paced back and forth. Behind him, a dozen men stood, their rifles still slung over their shoulders. For the moment.

Menchú didn't fool himself that they were going to stay that way.

"Father," a low voice called. Menchú turned, and his heart sank even further. Apparently the rebels hadn't all made it back to their hidden camps in the mountains in time. And now here they were, guns at the ready, hiding in the shadows by the church.

Menchú paused, and Sal watched him with open concern. "The army just showed up to kill everyone, just like that?"

He shook his head. "There was an excuse. There always was. Harboring rebels who had refused to disarm. But effectively . . . yes. They showed up to kill everyone."

"Why?"

"To prove that they still could."

"And then the rebels found out, and surrounded the army?"

Menchú shrugged. "There weren't enough of them for that. But it was enough for an effective ambush. With the element of surprise, they probably could have killed most of the soldiers. And then the government would have sent more to retaliate. Concentric circles of death all the way down."

Sal wasn't sure what to say. "I'm sorry" seemed inadequate, but it was all she had.

"For years, I wondered if it was because of me. I had distinguished myself within the Church during the civil war. Conflict is fertile ground for demons, and I had made it clear that I would protect both sides from their influence, banishing them back where they came from as soon as they dared show themselves in my presence. I wondered if maybe . . . If someone high enough in the chain of command decided to take exception to that policy of neutrality, they might have made an example of my village in order to send a message."

"The rebels couldn't have been too happy that you were helping the army."

"Not really. But they were more at risk from the demons than the government forces were. Doesn't matter, anyway. Eventually, I realized that trying to blame myself was just a form of self-aggrandizement. There was no way I made enough of a difference for either side to take me down so spectacularly."

"You must have saved lives."

"From demons, yes. But I couldn't stop people from killing each other. And that's what it looked like was going to happen again."

They sat together in silence, until Sal asked, "What happened instead?"

Menchú sighed. "I stopped the massacre."

Father Menchú steeled himself for the strong possibility of death. He wasn't naive enough to believe that his collar would somehow protect him when the bullets started flying. For every man holding a gun who might hesitate to shoot a priest, there was another who would want to be sure that no official representative of the Church survived to tell the world what had happened in a small mountain village.

His only hope was to somehow convince the two armed groups bent on killing each other not to kill a cluster of innocent civilians in the process.

And then a hand caught his sleeve.

The boy was still standing beside him. Only now his eyes were featureless white, his skin glowed with an unearthly radiance, and his hair fluttered by his face, fanned by a breeze even though the air was perfectly still. He was the most beautiful thing Menchú had ever seen.

"What are you?" Menchú asked.

"If you try to talk to them, they'll kill you."

"Maybe not," he said, and then repeated, "What are you?"

"You know what I am."

He did. At least, he hoped that he did. Menchú fell back a step, still cautious, but—for the first time that night—hopeful. "Can you stop this?"

The child nodded.

"Then why don't you?"

"You have to ask."

A part of Menchú's mind, some deep instinct, told him to say no. It warned that there was a trap before him, and the only way to avoid it was to walk away. But hope was too strong. The hope that no one, including him, would have to die that night.

Menchú asked.

God help him. He asked.

"And?"

Menchú looked up from his clasped hands and realized he had been staring silently at them for some minutes.

"I asked the . . . thing . . . to protect the villagers from the army and from the rebels."

"And?"

"It did."

It was as though a madness swept through both armed groups simultaneously. Suddenly the army seemed able to see the rebels wherever they were hiding and fired unerringly into the alleyways. The rebels fired back. The sound of gunfire and screams filled the air.

Instinctively, Menchú threw himself over the child-thing, shielding its tiny body with his own, covering his head and trying not to be noticed or caught in the crossfire. Only when the square once again fell silent did he finally dare to rise.

All around, the buildings were studded with bullet holes, and under the straining glow of the streetlights, the cobblestones ran slick with blood. But in the center of it all, not a single villager had been touched. In shock, Menchú looked down at the child. Its unearthly appearance was unchanged. But then it smiled, and Menchú's blood ran cold. It was not the smile of the boy he knew, or of any child on earth. It was . . . wrong.

"Why are you smiling?" Menchú asked. Was this how God wrought his miracles?

The child's smile grew. "Because what comes next is fun."

Menchú stood there for the rest of the night. He found himself unable to move, speak, or intervene in any way as the demon who had possessed the boy tortured and killed every man, woman, and child in the village, there in the square in front of the church. At dawn it turned to Menchú and slit its host's throat.

Its last words were: "Let this be a lesson to you, Father."

Sal flinched as Menchú gripped both of her hands in his. "I couldn't protect them, but I will protect you. I won't let you be brought down by the temptation of your hopes like I was."

"But what about the rest of our people? How do we protect them?"

Menchú didn't have an answer.

5.

On the floor of the Archives, Grace shuddered and convulsed. Asanti held the other woman's head, making sure she didn't choke on the bile she occasionally dredged up from her empty stomach.

Liam was doing the best of the three of them, and even he had emptied his stomach hours ago. Worse, the tone had grown so loud that it was impossible to hear one another, even if they shouted at the top of their lungs.

Liam left his computer where he had been trying and failing to find a way to block whatever was causing the effect and carried a pad of paper over to Asanti.

No good, he wrote.

Asanti sagged.

He flipped the page. *Your turn. I'll sit with her.*

Asanti yielded her place on the floor beside Grace to Liam and stumbled off, rubbing her forehead with one hand. Liam hoped that the stacks would have more answers than his electronic resources. Given how his search had gone, that was a low bar. He really should find his tablet. That way he could work while he watched Grace. Why hadn't he thought to do that earlier? Noise, lack of sleep, lack of food. It was making him stupid. *Can't afford that. Have to stay sharp.* . . .

With a mental wrench, Liam pulled himself out of his downward spiral. *No time for self-flagellation.* He could get his tablet in a minute. *Just going to rest here for a bit first.* Grace's head was pillowed against his thigh. The fact that she would never have allowed such intimacy had she possessed even a shred of consciousness somehow made the whole situation even worse. She had always guarded her privacy, and Liam had respected that. Seeing her now, he wondered if he should have asked more questions. Then maybe he wouldn't feel so helpless.

Just a minute more. Then he would get the tablet and come right back.

Just one more minute.

As soon as his head stopped spinning.

With the relentless noise and the pain it caused, Liam wouldn't have thought sleep was possible, but he must have lost consciousness, because suddenly Asanti was shaking him awake.

The whine was gone. The wind was back. Grace was still unconscious. But Asanti positively glowed with a smile that lit her entire face.

"What happened?"

"When I found you passed out, I killed the magnetic field, hoping that it might stop the tone, even if the wind came back."

"Congratulations. You're two for two."

"That's not the best part."

A flying book knocked Liam in the back of his head and sent his chin driving down into his chest. "Are you sure about that? Because this is just brilliant."

"Liam." Asanti's eyes danced with triumph. "Look around

you. The wind isn't just picking up books at random."

Blinking past the new pain in the back of his head, Liam tried to concentrate on the spinning storm around him. Asanti picked up a book that had fallen to the floor and another from a shelf.

"This is a seventeenth-century grimoire," she said, gesturing to the book she'd lifted from the floor. "Only copy known to exist. This"—she gestured to the one she'd taken from its place on the shelf—"is a first edition Francis Bacon. Rare but not unique." Then she took both books and flung them into the air.

Liam started. While he had been passed out, Asanti had clearly gone insane. "Did you just—?"

"Watch."

Both books tumbled, pages fluttering, until they finally landed, open, on their backs.

"What am I watching?"

"The pages!"

Liam blinked, still not seeing it. The Bacon lay there, unmoving. The pages of the grimoire continued to flip in the wind.

"These books are the same size, with similar binding and weight paper. The wind is everywhere. *Why aren't the pages of the Bacon still moving?*"

And now that she had said it, Liam saw it. "The wind only affects books that are unique to the Archives."

Asanti nodded. "Yes. Now, if we can just figure out what that *means*—"

But Liam already knew. "What it means," he said, speaking carefully, but with growing certainty, "is we're being hacked."

Finally, something he could work with.

✦ ✦ ✦

At sunset on the third night of the Market, Sal arrived alone at Gutenberg Castle, where she was greeted by the disapproving frown of the Maîtresse.

"Where is the priest?" she asked. "I hope he hasn't decided to depart prematurely."

Sal shook her head, fighting the feeling that she ought to bow or curtsy or something else that would probably just end up looking stupid. "He had an errand to run in town and was unavoidably detained. I'm expecting him soon."

The Maîtresse gave Sal a penetrating look that went a step beyond a standard disapproving-superior glare and straight to look-right-into-your-head territory. Sal fought to keep her expression bland and concentrated on repeating an internal mantra of *I'm not lying to you. I'm not lying to you. I'm not . . .*

Almost as though she really could read Sal's thoughts, the Maîtresse's lips quirked upward.

"Very well, Bookburner. I hope you find what you're looking for."

Sal nodded to the Maîtresse and proceeded to beat a retreat across the courtyard as quickly as she could without looking like she was fleeing for her life. She wasn't sure she managed it. But she hadn't lied. Menchú was running an errand in town. She was expecting him soon. She just had something to do before he got back.

The first night of the Market was for posturing. The second was for negotiations. The third was for deals. Over Sal's head, but low enough that it couldn't be seen outside the castle's walls, a firework in the shape of a red dragon exploded silently. Sal didn't give it a second glance. She had an appointment with the Index.

❖   ❖   ❖

Opie grinned as she approached, noting that she was alone. "Baby Bookburner breaking the rules. Are you going to have to go to confession later?"

"Not a Catholic. Let's get on with this."

Opie opened the door and ushered her through with a mock bow. Sal stepped past him into the room full of fantastical computers, heartened to see that her suspicions were correct: Bowing when you didn't know what you were doing did look stupid. He seemed amused at her impatience as she waited for him to follow her inside.

"You're awfully eager to give up a piece of your mind."

Sal held his gaze, waiting for him to blink first. "I've seen some things since I took this job that I wouldn't mind forgetting."

Opie made a small, negating gesture. "The Index takes what the Index wants. We can't control—"

"Cut the crap."

Opie's jaw snapped shut with an audible click.

"You were trying to stare through me from the first night of the Market. I think you found out that Mr. Norse had a grudge against the Society and offered to let him use the Index to find a weak spot in the Archives. Then, when everyone arrives at the Market and he attacks us—oh look—you just so happen to have the solution to our little problem, for the low, low price of a peek inside my head."

Opie scoffed. "Which makes perfect sense, if everything we do somehow revolves around you."

Sal shrugged. "Maybe you get the benefit of a happy coincidence, then. Bottom line, there's something in my head that you want, and you're not going to trust to random chance that this Index of yours is going to pull what you're interested in."

"And what would you know that would be that valuable to us?"

"I know what happened to my brother."

In the silence that followed, Sal could hear the faint hum of computers, the ripple of the sea horses' aquarium, and the rustle of night moths pollinating the flowers blooming on the moss computer's keyboard.

"You have information I want; I have information you want. Let's make a trade."

Opie blinked. "How very . . . pragmatic."

"I'm a practical person. Hell, we can dispense with this whole Index bullshit for all I care. You tell me; I tell you; we both go our separate ways."

The obnoxious smile was back. "No deal. How would we know you weren't lying?"

"How do I know your Index knows anything useful?"

"Given that I'm not the one with the friends under threat of death, I guess that's a risk you'll have to take."

Sal made a show of scowling. "Fine. Let's do this."

"Temper temper, Baby Bookburner."

"Friends dying. I didn't sleep well last night. PMS. Take your pick. Plus, I think we both want this business concluded before Father Menchú gets back from his errand in Balzers."

That, at least, got Opie moving. He walked over to a large black packing case, opened it, and removed a wooden box just large enough to hold a pair of shoes. He closed the case immediately after removing the box, and Sal caught a glimpse of flames, skittering legs, and a brief moaning sound. *Oh yeah, this is a great idea.*

The box remained connected to the packing case by glowing filaments wrapped in sinewlike tendrils that gave off a faint smell of burning meat. Remembering Scotland, Sal's stomach gave a lurch, and she swallowed bile.

"That's the Index?"

Opie nodded. "The box is the interface, the case is the processor, the server is . . . elsewhere."

He clearly wanted her to ask where "elsewhere" might be, and so Sal declined to do so. It would only bring back the insufferable smirk. Also, she didn't really care. Her job was finding the weird stuff. How it worked was Liam and Asanti's department. Assuming they all lived that long.

"What do I do?"

Opie handed Sal a slip of paper and pointed to a small table in the corner where a stack of paper, a quill, and an inkwell sat waiting. "Write your question on the paper. Hold the paper in your fist, and put your hand in the box." He paused, then added, smirk back in place, "Don't be afraid. Fear is the mind killer."

Sal raised an eyebrow. "Okay?"

Opie made a disgusted sound and muttered something under his breath before gesturing to the table. "Just write it down."

Sal hesitated. "Does the Index read intent?"

"Huh?"

"How literal minded is it? Can the Index figure out what I mean, or do I need to be careful not to make one of my wishes 'Genie, make me a sandwich'?"

Opie shrugged. "The more specific your question, the more specific the answer."

Well, that was helpful. With a sigh, Sal picked up the paper and quill. "This might take a minute."

The smirk was back. "No hurry. No hurry at all."

Ten minutes and a lot of blotting later, Sal clutched a folded piece of paper tightly in her clenched fist. Opie opened the box with a brass key that hung around his neck and held it out for her. "Ready when you are."

Sal hesitated. The wood looked old, but she wasn't enough of an expert to tell whether it meant that the box itself was ancient, or that it had been made from repurposed boards. *Repurposed from what? Charon's rowboat? The Ark of the Covenant? Lumber planed from a section of the True Cross?* Perry had been into woodworking for a while in Boy Scouts. Maybe he would have been able to tell by looking at the joinery.

Yes, think about Perry. And hope you're still able to think about him after this is over.

Opie, for all his professed patience as she'd crafted her question, made a small get-on-with-it gesture. There was a notch cut into one of the short sides of the box for her wrist. Once Sal put her hand in and Opie locked the lid, she'd be stuck until he decided to let her out. Or until she wrenched the box from him, ripped out the connection that tied it to the packing case, and went running through the Black Market with a magical wooden box permanently grafted to her arm. Sal eyed Opie, sizing him up. She could take him. Even one-handed.

Sal placed her hand in the box.

Opie slammed the lid shut. Sal's hand felt cold, then hot, then like it was being stuck with a hundred needles. She flinched. Opie locked one hand around her wrist. His grip was surprisingly strong. "Don't. Move."

The pain faded, leaving Sal's skin cool, but not as intensely cold as before. She felt a soft brush of fur across her knuckles. Then something wet and sticky slid across the base of her palm. *Not a tongue. It can't possibly be a tongue.* Was not-a-tongue any better? *No, definitely not.* Sal shuddered, and suddenly the bones of her hand were on fire. She tried to open her hand, but her muscles weren't listening to her commands, nerves too busy transmitting a constant stream of *Pain! Pain! Pain!* to carry any other instructions. Sal gritted her teeth, closed her eyes, and concentrated.

Sal was back in her past, in a self-storage facility in New Jersey. Perry, or Perry plus a demon, floated in midair, surrounded by a pile of books, pages flipping madly. But it wasn't the same. Because the Index was there too. Breathing down the back of her neck, breath hot and moist, like a wolf ready to snap its jaws through her spine. And when it did, it would take this moment from her forever. This was what the Index wanted. And it was hungry.

Trapped in her own memory, Sal reached for the *Book of the Hand*. Bare fingers inches from the cover. A hairsbreadth away. She could feel the jaws closing, teeth piercing the skin of her neck, and with every force of her will that remained, Sal wrenched her mind to another memory. One much more recent.

She was in her room at the B&B with Menchú, on the phone with Liam. "They're hacking the Archive," he said. "Not the computers. The books. I'm sending a file to your phone. You need to memorize it."

As the wolf's teeth sank into her neck, Sal called up the file to her mind. It was a complex mathematical function represented as a single abstract image. Sal hadn't slept at all, committing every twist and overlap to memory. It was amazing what you could do, if the incentive for success was strong enough.

According to Liam, the Index shouldn't read the image as a threat. Because to Sal, it was only an image. She didn't understand the math behind it, or the program behind the math. She was just carrying the candy coating, to trick the Index into swallowing the whole thing down.

Because even if Sal didn't understand the meaning, it was there. Hidden and coded in every twist and turn and recursive loop. A tiny seed, planted in fertile ground.

Sal could hear shouting. Opie and others. She felt a pain like someone tearing the flesh from her hand, and then a sharper one as something hit her in the head. She inhaled to shout and choked on a lungful of smoke.

Sal coughed for moments, hours, years, until she managed to open her eyes. Apparently the thing that had hit her head was the floor, and she took in the room from her new low and cockeyed angle. Smoke poured from the crate that housed the Index. Her phone, tucked in her pocket, buzzed frantically. Sal crawled to a corner, completely ignored by the frantic techno-cultists who had flooded into the room since she'd closed her eyes.

Sal finally got her hands—hey, she had both hands again—around her buzzing phone. "It worked?"

Liam's voice sounded more tired than she had ever heard it, but also relieved. "It worked."

"Good." Sal hung up. The Guardians were pouring in along with the Maîtresse. And there was Mr. Norse, followed by Father Menchú, whose errand in town had been to keep the billionaire distracted until it was too late for him to stop Sal's plan. A fact that Mr. Norse had realized too late. Sal decided that Menchú could handle him. And the Maîtresse. And the Guardians. He was good with people. It was his job.

✦ ✦ ✦

The Market Arcanum concluded without further incident. When dawn broke over the Alps, Sal watched the men in wolf skins walk out of the castle and right back into the woods. The women in evening gowns pulled on cloaks and veils to hide their tattoos before alighting into their limousines. The techno-cultists had packed their computers into a white panel van and left as soon as it became clear that the Maîtresse did not view the destruction of the Index as sufficient cause to evict Menchú and Sal from the Market. Mr. Norse departed rather more gracefully, although his last words were not exactly a comfort.

"Until next time, Bookburners."

A shadow fell across Sal's path as she and Menchú carried their bags to the rental car, and Sal looked up to see the Maîtresse herself waiting for them. Even in daylight, and without her flanking Guardians, she radiated authority.

"It's been quite an eventful few days for you." Her eyes flicked to Sal. "I hope you're able to get your house back in order after this unfortunate . . . disruption."

"Repairs to the Archives are already underway," said Menchú.

The Maîtresse smiled. "That too."

And without waiting for a reply, she turned and walked away, back up the road to the castle. Sal and Menchú stood together in silence, watching her go, until her steps carried her around a bend and out of sight.

Menchú broke their tableau first, heaving his case into the trunk of the car. "Come on, let's go home." Sal followed suit and slid into the front passenger seat beside him. For the hundredth time, she slid her hand into her pocket, fingers seeking the reassurance of the folded piece of paper she had put there, the only physical evidence that remained of her encounter with the techno-cultists.

It was the paper where she had written her question for the Index: *What is Mr. Norse looking for?*

It now bore only two words: *Codex Umbra.*

Hours later, when Sal and Menchú reached Rome, the Archives still looked like a bomb had hit it. A nonfiery, book-oriented bomb, sure, but a bomb nonetheless.

Asanti took a break from picking up the pieces of her library to hug them both. Sal felt a surge of relief as her arms went around the archivist. Sometimes you just had to touch someone to prove to yourself that they were still alive.

"Liam is glued to his computer," Asanti told Sal when she asked about the others. "Grace went home to sleep."

It had been a long three days for everyone, Sal supposed. Between being up all night for the Market, plus staying up for most of the days between, Sal felt like she hadn't slept in a week. She'd dozed for a few hours on the train, but her sleep had been filled with dreams of wandering the corridors between compartments, looking for something. She certainly didn't feel rested. Then again, she never had slept well away from her own bed.

Bed.

Liam.

Sal excused herself and went in search of their beleaguered tech expert. Time to prove to herself that he was still alive too.

She found him, as promised, hunched over his laptop, and lingered in the doorway, waiting for him to notice her. When he didn't, she cleared her throat. Liam looked up.

"You saved the day," said Sal. "Nice work."

Liam shrugged off the compliment. "Not quick enough. Who knows what those techno-bastards found while they were flipping through the Archives? Or what they left behind."

"Did you find any reference to the *Codex Umbra*?"

"Not even a description of what it might be. Which is what worries me."

Sal sighed. "Take the win, then. We've got a hell of a mess to clean up, but at least we're all okay, right?" She slid up behind him, letting her thumbs dig into the tense muscles of his shoulders. "Thanks to you."

He shrugged her off. "Unless Mr. Norse managed to find and erase the information he was looking for. With all of the books the hack disturbed, it could take us centuries to find out what damage he did."

Liam turned back to his computer. Sal blocked him by plopping down in his lap. "If it will take centuries anyway, it can wait until morning."

"Sal, I'm too tired—" he began.

"And so am I. But I've spent the last three days afraid you were going to die, and I don't want to be alone tonight. Besides, you look like hell. You're going to have to sleep sometime; it might as well be with me."

Liam gently put his hands on her waist and lifted her to her feet. "Okay," he said. "But go ahead. I'll let myself in later."

Sal wanted to protest, but she was too tired. "Fine. Whatever you want."

That night Sal dreamed of wandering the streets of Rome, looking for that same thing she could not name. When she finally woke, hours past dawn, the other side of the bed was undisturbed.

CODA

Menchú stayed in the Archives late into the night. The niche he had previously designated as his office had been completely destroyed by Mr. Norse's hacking. His poor, long-suffering chair had lost a leg at some point, snapped off just below the seat. Menchú located the missing piece and was contemplating repairs when he felt Asanti staring at him.

"Did you tell her?"

"Yes."

"And?"

"Now she knows. But I don't know that it's made her a more cautious swimmer."

Asanti made a noncommittal *hmm* noise.

Menchú quirked an eyebrow at her. "What?"

"Did you ever consider that you learned the wrong lesson from your experience with the angel in Guatemala?"

"It tortured and murdered an entire village. It wasn't an angel."

Asanti shrugged. "You've read the Bible. God kills people all the time. Violence, disease, apocalyptic flood. Even Jesus had a temper."

Menchú felt his own temper rising and made an effort to keep it in check. Asanti continued.

"You'd dealt with demons before. If you'd realized what the boy was immediately and banished him, or refused to make a deal, would the massacre still have happened?"

"If you're trying to say that what I did didn't make a difference, I assure you—"

"I'm saying that you knew demons were evil before that night. If that was the lesson you were supposed to learn, someone was being very redundant with your education."

Menchú let out a long breath. He was too tired to have this discussion now. Possibly ever. "What's your point, Asanti?"

"Demon, angel, or something else, from what you've told me, making a deal with that thing was the only possible way you could have prevented a massacre that night."

Menchú gritted his teeth. "But I did, and it didn't."

"But what if that was the lesson?" Asanti gripped his sleeve, begging him with her eyes to listen and understand. "Next time, make a better deal."

Menchú turned away. Asanti let go of his arm, and he heard her footsteps fading away, quickly muffled by the destruction around them. Her words lingered long after she had disappeared among the stacks.

Next time.

EPISODE
6

BIG SKY

BRIAN FRANCIS SLATTERY

1.

"All right," Cardinal Varano says. "Tell me what happened."

Sal is seated in the wood-lined hearing room of the Societas Librorum Occultorum. Menchú showed her this room once, when she first arrived. She'd thought it looked like a courtroom then. It looks even more like a courtroom now. There is the cardinal, seated at the head of the room behind what looks for all the world like a judge's bench. There is an expanse of floor between him and the rest of the people in the room, the kind of space lawyers should be stalking, though there are no lawyers here, and for the first time in Sal's life, that makes it worse.

Someone needs to witness this, she thinks.

The rest of them are seated behind a long wooden table. The monsignors of all three teams of the Society: Fox for Team One, Usher for Team Two, Angiuli for Team Three. There is Archivist Asanti, and a few of each of the teams' members. They're at a hearing. "Inquest" is the official word. To determine cause of death. But Sal feels more like they're at a tribunal. Maybe they're at a kangaroo court.

"Let's begin with you, Team Three," Cardinal Varano says.

Monsignor Angiuli turns to Sal with helpless eyes. Sal's never spoken to him before today. She's learned some things about him from Menchú, but so far their conversation right before the hearing is the only contact she's had with him. He's a kindly old man not prone to oversight, and he's given Menchú a very long leash in the past few years. He's barely read any of the reports Menchú has filed with him.

Sal looks at the cardinal.

"I've never done one of these before," she says. "Should I stand?"

Varano frowns. "If you want to." Sal may or may not have detected a vague note of disappointment, like a mean grandfather would have. She's messed up, she thinks, either because she wasn't standing already or because she admitted she didn't know the rules, or maybe both—and three other things she doesn't even know about yet.

She puts it out of her mind and stays in her chair. Before she speaks, she looks up at the stained-glass ceiling high above. She wants more light, but it's a cloudy day, and the light won't come.

Cardinal Varano talks slowly, making it plain that he's condescending to speak to her in English.

"You are aware," he says, "that these types of proceedings are highly unusual. They are generally unnecessary. But given the many ways this particular case almost escaped us, and the way it led to such destruction, injury, and loss of life among our own personnel, it is very important that we understand what went wrong, and what it means for Society operations in the future."

Without Sal's permission, a few bad memories flit across her brain. Grace knocked through the air, through the wall of a building. The look on Menchú's face just before the dust cloud overtook him. Someone impaled on a long tooth. Someone else diving into the ground, and the earth closing around him.

A mother and son, crying.

"I understand," Sal says.

The cardinal gives a very hoarse laugh, devoid of any mirth whatsoever.

The sky was enormous. Team Three had just gotten off the interstate, and the van was now speeding down a county road, just a straight shot across the flattest land Sal had ever seen. The tallest things for miles were the telephone poles, in a jagged line running next to the road. In the van, Sal craned her neck to look out the window. She thought she would feel some sense of freedom, of exhilaration. The open road, the open sky, like in a bad country song. But she didn't feel any of that. She just felt exposed. Vulnerable.

"Jesus," Liam said. "There is *nothing* out here."

"You said that already," Grace said. "Four times."

"There's still nothing here," Liam said.

The Orb, Asanti had told them, had gone off in a flash, like something had exploded inside it, before it clacked out the coordinates. It was unusual. Unusually intense. *What does that mean?* Menchú had asked. Asanti shrugged. *I don't know,* she had responded. *Tell me when you find out.*

Then it had been a nineteen-hour trip from Rome, with layovers in London and Dallas. By the time they were on the final leg to Tulsa, even Liam had run out of things to talk about. They got into the van without saying more than three words to one another. And now here they were. The road was loud under the van's tires. The wind battered the windshield.

"There really is—" Liam said.

"Don't," Grace said. "Just don't."

They pulled into the town of Tanner City twenty minutes later. Or what was left of it. Twenty-two hours before, Liam told them, at about one in the morning, a tornado had touched down in a farmer's field a mile away. It grew to be almost half a mile wide and cut a ragged slash through the town. There was little warning, and thirty-three people died. The next morning, some parts of town were filled with debris from other parts of town. One house had been speared by a tree that the twister had uprooted, stripped of its branches, and then thrown back down to earth. Other blocks weren't touched at all. And then there were the blocks that looked as if they'd never been built; there was nothing but the streets, sidewalks, driveways, and the concrete slabs that the houses had once stood on. That was all.

The county road turned into Main Street, and they drove into the middle of town, where Main Street crossed a bigger road. The intersection was clean and tidy; it had been spared. On one corner there was a musical instrument shop; on another, a gas station. They could see a little hardware store, a pharmacy, a restaurant with the specials on a sign taped to the window.

"Is it weird that there's no one here?" Liam asked.

"I was thinking the same thing," said Grace.

"Sal, you're the American here," Liam said. "Is this weird?"

"I . . . don't know," Sal said. "I'm an East Coast girl."

Grace parked the van, and they got out. The stoplight at the intersection changed from green to yellow to red and back again. Still not a single other car.

"Where is everyone?" Menchú asked.

Grace let out a little, impatient sigh. She went to the door of the nearest shop, a liquor store, and tried it. It was locked, and the place was dark inside. She rapped on the glass.

"Anyone home?" she said.

She waited three seconds, then moved to the pharmacy next to the liquor store and did the same thing. Then the jewelry store next to that and the clothing store next to that. Each time, she rapped a little louder, raised her voice a little more. She was moving to the next one when a door opened across the street.

"*Hey!*" a voice said.

Sal turned. It was coming from the instrument shop. There was a man with a neat beard standing in the entrance. He'd opened the door just a little.

"Quiet down!" he said. "Quiet down *now* or they'll find you."

"Who?" Grace said, without quieting down.

"The Tornado Eaters," the man said.

"The what?" Liam said.

"The—" the man began. But he was interrupted. From somewhere, maybe a block over, maybe from the sky, there came a long, high, echoing wail that pitched up at the end.

"Get inside!" the man said.

"I think you have the wrong idea about us," Grace said. She locked her fingers together and stretched out her arms. Another wail began from another direction; this one dove into a low, rumbling moan. It was answered by the first one. They both sounded like they were coming closer.

Menchú walked into the middle of the street.

"Everyone to me," he said.

They came in close to one another. Sal, standing next to Grace, could swear she could see the energy coiled in Grace's muscles, dying to be set free.

"Wait," Menchú said.

The first thing they saw was a foot. It was like a hoof, but with three skinny toes protruding from it. The leg it was attached to was spindly and hairy, bent at a strange angle—part horse, part spider.

Then the whole creature lurched into the intersection.

It had three legs that zigzagged up from the ground to a bulbous, fur-covered body about eight feet off the ground. Somehow stuck on the end of that body was its head, with a face almost like a baby's, but with a gigantic mouth that hung open, flapping, as if it didn't have a jaw. It saw Team Three and its eyes narrowed. It let out a low, guttural, mournful cry. There was another answering wail, and the second creature stepped under the stoplight. *It looks almost like an ostrich,* Sal thought. It didn't have wings; it had one leg and two long arms that reached to the ground, ending in enormous, seven-fingered hands. But it did have the long neck, the head with beady eyes, a squat beak. If it stood up all the way, Sal thought, it would hit its head on the stoplight. But it carried itself hunched over instead. It opened its beak and let out something between a bark and a chirp. Again. Again.

For a moment the creatures just stood there, sizing up the humans in the street. A string of drool fell from the first creature's mouth and smacked onto the pavement.

"If they move, you move," Menchú said to Grace.

"Got it," Grace said.

The creatures shifted. For a moment it looked like they were going to sit down. But they didn't.

They sprang forward, howling and hooting.

Grace went after the ostrich one. She dodged a swipe from its left arm, grabbed on to its right, and vaulted herself up onto the thing's back. She reached forward, got a firm hold on its neck, and snapped it. The head bucked upward and wobbled, and the whole animal pitched forward and collapsed in the street. Grace leaped off and landed on her feet.

The baby-faced creature was still galloping toward the rest of them.

"Sal—" Menchú said.

"Already on it," Sal said. She pulled out her Glock and emptied it into the creature's face. It staggered back, twitched with every shot, and then seemed to slide over sideways. It panted six times, each exhalation more laborious than the last, and then stopped.

The rest of the team looked at Sal.

"What?" Sal said. "We're back in America. Yippie-ki-yay, right?"

"Yippie . . . ki . . . ?" Grace said.

"Forget it," said Sal.

"How did you . . . ," Liam said.

"She's a cop, right?" Menchú said. "I made some arrangements."

"Remember in the airport when I said I needed to go to the bathroom?" Sal said.

"You didn't need to go," Liam said.

She mimed a handoff. Liam shook his head. They passed each other a glance.

Then they all looked back toward the music shop. The man at the door had seen the whole thing. He looked more terrified than ever.

"Relax," said Menchú. "We're not here to hurt you. We've dealt with this sort of thing before."

"You don't have the first idea what you're dealing with," the man said.

"I don't know," Liam said, motioning toward the bodies in the street. "I'd say we did all right."

"Those are just the little ones," the man said.

Sal wanted to ask what he meant. She didn't have time.

A groan rumbled through the earth beneath their feet. A shadow fell across the entire block, and there was another of them, the Tornado Eaters, rising up over the buildings down the block. A monumental body atop three thick legs. A huge, distended belly, like a pregnancy gone too long. A triangular, frowning head. No arms. Sal's eye couldn't put it to scale. It was either too big, or too close, or both.

Definitely both.

A scream filled the enormous sky, filled the air around them. It felt like being electrocuted.

Sal looked up. It was impossible to say how she hadn't seen it coming. It was as though she'd forgotten the sky existed, that the sun was out, that the only clouds were far away.

A new creature was above them, far above them, like an aircraft in flight. She couldn't even tell what shape it was. The five legs descended from it to the ground somewhere—in town, outside town. It was impossible to say. One of the legs moved, and its end, a foot shaped like the head of a hammer, reared up and crashed down into the intersection in front of them. From far overhead, the monster screamed again.

And two monstrous voices answered. One from the triangular head. The other from somewhere else. They couldn't even place it.

"Good God," Menchú said.

The monsters were even closer now. Within striking distance.

"Grace," Menchú said, "give Liam the keys."

Grace shot Liam a glance and tossed the keys to him. He caught them almost without looking.

"Liam," Menchú said, "get far away from here and call Team One."

Grace eyed the giant at the end of the block.

"Don't, Grace," Menchú said.

Liam was already behind the wheel of the van. He started the engine. The giant at the end of the block unleashed a roar and charged.

"Sal," Menchú said. "Take care of the people here, okay?"

The next thirty seconds were hard for Sal to remember later. Somehow a billowing wall of dust raced out in front of the giant as its feet cracked the pavement beneath them. Maybe it was taking off pieces of the buildings around it as it crashed down the block. Maybe it was something it could just do, like summoning the elements. She remembered Grace leaping forward toward that giant, arms out, hands clenched into fists. If she was going to go out, she was going out fighting. Sal sprinted for the music store. The man was still there, behind the glass door. Sal gave him the most pleading look she could muster, and the man opened the door. She glanced toward the intersection, where their van was careening toward the gigantic foot, trying to get around it. The foot gave just a little twist as the van passed, knocking it up onto two wheels. Sal didn't have time to see if it landed again, if Liam got out. She dove through the open doorway, and the man slammed it shut behind her. The last thing she saw, before the street was choked in dust and roars, was Father Menchú, still standing in the middle of the street, watching Grace, watching Liam, as a father watches his children, horrified and proud. Then there was a rumble that turned to a roar, and everything in the street went dark.

"This way!" the man said. He led her to an interior office with no outside windows, and they waited in the howling gloom while the walls shuddered around them. It seemed to go on forever. Then at last it was over.

Sal ran to the glass door.

"Don't open it," said the man. "Please don't."

"I won't," she said.

The street was littered with bricks and dust, broken timbers and glass. The buildings on both sides of the block were wrecked, as if another tornado had come. The traffic light that had hung over the intersection now lay on top of the rubble. The monsters were gone. No sign of Grace or Menchú. The sky was clear again, as big as ever.

"I'm so sorry about your friends," the man said.

"Don't say that," Sal said. It was welling up inside her. She fought it back down.

"I'm Raymond," the man said. "Ray." He extended his hand.

"Sal," she said. She took it and they shook.

"What are you doing here?" Ray said.

"I can't tell you," Sal said.

"I saw what you did," he said, "before the big ones came. You're here to fight them?"

"You could say that," Sal said.

"Are any more of you coming?"

Sal looked out through the glass door again. It was cracked. There was no trace of the van. Maybe Liam had made it. Maybe he had been swept up into the sky.

"I don't know," she said.

"How will they handle those things?"

That was when Sal found a way back.

Investigate, her brain said. *Do what you're good at. Do what Menchú put you on the team to do.*

"Those things," she said. "You called them Tornado Eaters?"

"Yes."

"Do you know where they came from, Ray?"

"Yes," he said. "But it's better if the person who brought them here tells you himself."

"Someone brought them here on purpose?"

"Yeah. The idea was to protect the town."

"Some protection," Sal said.

Ray didn't say anything, but looked stung. She'd crossed a line.

"Sorry."

"It's okay," Ray said. "Let me take you to the person you want to talk to."

2.

Sal looks at Cardinal Varano again. It occurs to her that, sitting there behind the bench, he reminds her of the first giant Tornado Eater they saw, the one with the frowning, triangular head. As far as she knows, Varano doesn't have any arms either. It's impossible to tell under his robes.

"You have amazing recall," he says. It doesn't sound like a compliment.

"I'm a cop," she says. "What do you expect?"

The cardinal's eyebrows rise, and she can read on his brow the disdain he has for cops. Sal decides right then that she hates him.

"And that was the last you saw of Father Menchú or Grace in Oklahoma?"

"Yes," she says. It hurts to say it.

"It's very lucky that you emerged without more than a scratch," he says.

"Yes, it is," she says. She knows he's implying something. That she ducked and ran. That she's not going to tell him everything. But she's not nibbling on that bait. If he's trying to catch her out, he's going to have to try harder than that.

"Go on," he says.

They waited until dark. Ray led Sal to the back of the store, to the door to the parking lot.

"Across the lot," he said, "you'll see a little brick house. It's maybe seventy yards away."

"Ex-football player?" Sal said.

Ray smiled. "Yeah. But we're not running those yards. They'll hear us if we do, and we don't stand a chance at night."

"So what do we do?"

"Walk. Very slowly. Without a word. No matter what. Got me?"

Sal nodded.

"Okay," Ray said. "Let's go."

He opened the door.

The lot behind the store was empty and ended at the next street. Across the street was a brick house, just like Ray had said. The stars were out all over the wide, clear sky, the moon three-quarters full. Ray started across the lot in a slow, quiet walk. Sal followed.

A breeze kicked up, small but insistent. Sal watched it move through the trees near the brick house. Then she realized it wasn't moving through them. It seemed more to be pushing them, as though a giant hand were pressing against the branches.

Ray looked back at her. She could see that he was nervous. Sal looked back up at the moon, and it was wavering, as if through smoke or water. Something was passing in between them, up in the sky, and it was smearing all the light from the moon and stars. Though near the horizon the stars were clear again, all around them. It was then that Sal understood that a monster was walking over them, something even bigger than the monsters they'd seen during the day, and some part of it, a hand, a foot, a finger, was reaching down, feeling its way close to the ground.

The big trees on the other side of the street near the brick house all bowed over at once, groaning, as if they were caught in a hurricane.

We have to stop, Sal thought.

Her step must have changed, because Ray looked back at her, without breaking his stride, and shook his head. She kept moving.

The trees snapped back, popping, and shook it off. But the moon was still wavering.

How can something so gigantic be so close to us without us seeing it? Sal thought. *How have these things not shown up on radar? How have they not been spotted by satellite? Forget Team One; why isn't the National Guard here right now? Why haven't they declared a national emergency? Where are the helicopters and tanks? Where are the fighter planes?*

For a moment it occurred to her that maybe a national emergency *had* been declared. Maybe the area around Tanner City had been cordoned off for miles, and the world was watching. Everyone knew what was happening except the people it was happening to.

But then she would have at least seen a helicopter.

No, the truth was that, somehow, everything in Tanner City seemed normal to the outside world. Nobody had seen anything unusual. It was impossible, but it was true. Which, Sal realized, was her newest and most miserable definition of magic. Because it meant that the few of them left in this town were on their own.

Liam, she thought. *Grace. Menchú. Where are you?*

They reached the steps to the house. The front door opened for them. They hadn't needed to knock on the door. Someone in the house had seen them coming. Someone in there was always watching.

The people inside the brick house had put blankets up over the windows and kept most of the lights out. Word had apparently gotten around the house that Ray had brought in a stranger and everyone came downstairs. They had a lot of questions for Sal but stopped asking when they realized she didn't have many answers. She counted nineteen of them—three families, a married couple, and a handful of others. Ray was one of the others, and one of the few who risked going outside at all.

They had maybe a week's worth of food and water in the house. There were bags of groceries everywhere and packages of non-perishables stacked behind the couch. It looked like a lot of food, but Sal knew nineteen people ate a lot. They were washing their clothes by hand and hanging them up to dry all over the place. There was a clothesline strung across the living room, a short row of drying racks in the dining room. A damp blouse hanging from a doorknob, even though the house had a washing machine and dryer. They were afraid the noise, or the exhaust from the dryer, would bring the Tornado Eaters. They didn't really know why Ray and the others who were willing to go out weren't snatched up right away, given the havoc the monsters had wrought when they first came to town. But Ray and the others had gone out and come back—slowly, quietly—many times now and were still all right. Ray thought maybe the Tornado Eaters just had bad eyesight. Great hearing, incredible sense of touch. But half-blind all the same.

"They don't need to see," he said, "for what they were made to do."

"And who made them?" Sal said.

Ray pointed at a kid, about fifteen years old. "His great-grandpa did," he said.

"My grandpa," said the kid's mother. She looked to be in her mid-forties. "I'm Sharon. This is my son, Jacob."

"It's good to meet you both," Sal said. She was remembering her manners. Realizing, too, just how much being on Team Three had made her forget them.

"This is Sal," Ray said. "I watched her kill one of the Tornado Eaters herself, with a pistol."

"So the rest of the world knows now?" Sharon asked. "And they're coming to help us?"

"I'm not sure," Sal said. "But if you tell me what you know about these things, maybe I can do something."

Sharon took a deep breath.

"How much trouble are we in?" she said.

"You're not in any trouble with me," Sal said.

Sharon nodded. "All right," she said. "My grandpa . . . was a magician. A real magician, do you understand?"

"Yes," Sal said.

Sharon looked at Ray. He nodded. She still hesitated. A look came over her face that Sal had seen dozens of times before, on people about to confess a secret they'd been carrying a long time, now that it didn't matter anymore. The secret was out, anyway. But it still hurt to be letting go of it.

"All right," she said. "He came out here when he was a little boy, just before World War One. There wasn't much of anything around here, then. Oklahoma had only been a state for a few years. They hadn't discovered the zinc in the ground around Tanner City yet. There were already some big farms, but my grandpa told me he still remembered parts of it were just grassland. An ocean of grass. Like it must have looked before any humans ever laid eyes on it, he used to say. But they did have tornadoes."

Sharon paused for a second. "You're from where, again?" she said.

"New York," Sal said. "Before that, South Carolina."

"Ever seen a tornado?"

"No."

"Until last week, me neither. Most of us, even here or up in Kansas, go our whole lives without seeing a single one. But you hear about them. When my grandpa was a boy, he said, his parents had a friend who worked for the Indian mission schools, and my grandpa had the misfortune of hearing a family acquaintance tell the story of what had happened in Vireton in 1917."

"Which was . . . ?" Sal said.

"A tornado hit a mission schoolhouse full of kids, something like twenty of them and their teacher, and only a couple of them survived. That family acquaintance got into some details, I guess. And after that, my grandpa could hardly sleep. Evening after evening, as the sun went down, he'd look toward the horizon for tornadoes coming. After it was dark, he'd lie in bed listening for them until he fell asleep, and then he had nightmares. This went on for a couple weeks, he said, at which point he finally decided to do something about it. And he did. He made the Tornado Eaters."

"He made them?"

Sharon nodded. "When he was a kid. Named them too. Why else would the name be so ridiculous?"

Sal smiled.

"How did he make them?"

"I asked him the same question once," Sharon said. "You know what he told me? *Out of thin air. Same stuff that tornadoes are made of.* Then he patted me on the head."

"That doesn't make any sense," Sal said.

"You're telling me," Sharon said. "I've been trying to make things happen out of thin air for years, and it hasn't worked for me yet. I've just had to get them the old-fashioned way."

"Did he ever do any other magic?" Sal asked.

"People said he did it all the time, but they never caught him at it. So either they were making things up, or he was just really good at it," Sharon said. "The only magic anyone saw for sure were the Tornado Eaters."

"When?" Sal asked.

"Nineteen twenty-one," Sharon said. "Grandpa said he'd had them for a couple years by then. A couple years of good sleep, I hope. But he still kept a lookout for the day he might need them. And then that day came. A storm came rolling up on Tanner City one June evening, just after supper. Sky turned green. Wind picked up. A bunch of people went out in the streets. They knew the warning signs. So they all saw it. Little by little, just outside town, the clouds were spinning into a funnel, and they all watched as it let down a finger to touch the ground. It got wider and wider, and headed for town. Which was when Grandpa let the Tornado Eaters out."

Sal thought of Menchú, his village in Guatemala. *There's no way this ends well,* she thought.

"What happened?"

"No one who saw it really ever knew how to describe what they saw. But Grandpa said they did just what he asked them to do. They jumped out of the box he'd put them in, grew up into the sky, raced out to the field, and . . . well, *ate* it. Then back they went into the box. You'll never even find a record that the tornado happened. Because, well, it didn't."

"You said they went back in a box?"

"Yes."

"Where is it?" Sal asked.

"Here," Jacob said.

Sal hadn't even noticed he was holding anything. It was a just a little green wooden box, and it fit in the palm of his hand.

"This is it?"

Jacob nodded.

"Speak when you're spoken to, Jacob," Sharon said.

"Yes," he said.

"So who let them out this time?" Sal asked.

"I did," Jacob said.

"He didn't know—" Sharon started to say.

"I knew, Mom," Jacob said. "I knew." He looked straight at Sal. *He's going to speak when he's spoken to,* Sal thought. *He's going to do better than that. His mom's going to be so proud, and so scared all at once.*

"Everyone around this town knows the Tornado Eaters story," Jacob said, "but they all thought it was just a folktale. How could it be true, right? And my family never let on that we still had the box Great-Grandpa had made for them. Nobody'd ever tried to use it. Great-Grandpa was a magician, and nobody after him was. Until me. Because I have Great-Grandpa's gift," Jacob said.

Sharon moved closer to her son, as if to protect him. He inched away.

"Mom, she said we're not in any trouble."

"I know," Sharon said.

Jacob turned back to look at Sal.

"I almost never used my gift, and then only in the smallest ways. Only when I knew that I could make a difference by moving something an inch to the left, and not more than that. Never more than that."

Which is why the Society didn't find out about you years ago, Sal thought.

Jacob smiled. "But I saved a friend from being hit by a car that way once. Sometimes an inch is all it takes."

Sal smiled back. "You're a good kid, Jacob."

"But then, after the tornado came, I realized I'd made a mistake. I'd gotten so good at doing small things, not letting anyone know, that I'd forgotten to do what Great-Grandpa did. I forgot to do big things when I needed to. And I decided not to let it happen again. I knew what to do when I opened the box. I knew how to get the Tornado Eaters out of it and keep them waiting for my orders. Just like Great-Grandpa must have."

"You were worried about another tornado coming?" Sal asked.

Jacob nodded.

"Isn't it a little unusual for tornadoes to hit the same place twice?"

Sharon shook her head. "We certainly wish that were true," she said.

"Okay," Sal said. "So what happened?"

"I gave them the wrong orders," Jacob said. "I wasn't as careful as I should have been. It's like Mom said: The Tornado Eaters do just what you ask them to. And I asked them to do the wrong thing. *Protect this place from all threats,* I told them. I imagined them just up there in the sky, or at the edge of town, standing guard and ready. But I think I should have said "town" instead of "place." Because the Tornado Eaters have been in that box a long time, and it's been over a hundred years since they've seen the place. And I hadn't looked at it like this, but in the last hundred years, we haven't been very good to this place."

"So the threat to the place is you," Sal said. "Us."

"I think so," Jacob said.

"And there's no way you can just order them back in the box."

"I live here," said Jacob. "We all do. We're part of the threat."

"But someone from outside of town might not be," Sal said. "Someone who knew what they were doing with magic." *As long as they don't come in here shouting and fighting and guns blazing,* she thought. *Like we did.*

Jacob nodded again. "Yes. I suppose that's right."

There's an opening here, Sal thought. *A way out of this.* There was someone in the Society who knew how to fix this; Sal was sure of it. All she needed was a way to communicate with them, with Asanti, and the Society could send someone in who could put the Tornado Eaters back in their box.

She just had to get out of town, away from the magic, and use her phone.

"Jacob?" she said. "One more question. How many Tornado Eaters did you let out?"

"Five," he said.

"And the biggest one is the one in the sky?"

"No," he said. "The biggest one is underground."

"All right," she said. "I'll take my chances."

"You're going?" Ray said.

"Yeah," Sal said. "Frankly, I don't understand why you haven't tried yet yourselves."

Ray just looked at her. "We're home already," he said. "We don't want to leave."

The walk would have been relaxing, romantic even, if Sal hadn't been so scared. Tanner City was a pretty little town. The moon was setting, and the sky was flooding with stars. The brick and wood houses in the middle eventually gave way to newer places with vinyl siding and wider lawns. There were bikes in the yards. A basketball hoop hung over a garage door. On a mailbox close to the street, someone had hung a sign advertising a tailoring and embroidery business.

It was all so recognizable to Sal. She didn't have a general theory about people—she'd seen a little too much for that—but if someone had forced her to give one, it would have been that most people don't ask that much from their lives. They want a roof over their heads, a job that isn't too terrible, a couple of days off to relax now and again. If they have kids, they want to do okay by them. That's about it.

The world she lived in as a cop, where people did crazy and horrible things to one another and themselves, was abnormal. The world of politics she saw in the news, where people actually wanted to run states and countries, seemed to her to be full of ambitious sociopaths. This—Tanner City—was full of people Sal thought of as like most people. They had crummy but tolerable jobs, friends, and families, and they didn't ask much more than that. They didn't ask for tornadoes and monsters. And right about then, it didn't seem all that fair to Sal that they'd gotten them, though of course fairness had nothing to do with it.

She felt a push in the air and looked up.

The stars were wavering, as if through smoke, or old glass. There was something right above her. How far up, she couldn't tell. But it was right there.

She froze for what felt like hours, until the stars were clear again.

At last she was on the outside of town, and she kept walking for another mile. She went by a billboard that offered farm refinancing on one side and eternal salvation if you accepted Jesus on the other. She looked back.

There was Tanner City. A little cluster of lights on the plain, clinging to both sides of the road into town. No sign at all of the creatures in the sky.

Completely normal.

She took out her phone and turned it on. It was working. She called Asanti.

3.

ardinal Varano frowns.

"I want to thank you," he says, "for exposing the presence of a working magician to the Society. We are in your debt for that."

"Sir?" Sal says.

"You may address me as *Cardinal*," Varano says.

She keeps herself from rolling her eyes. *You can kiss ass when you need to, Sal,* she reminds herself. *This is one of those times.*

"Cardinal," she says, "may I ask what happened to Jacob?"

"What do you mean?" he says. "You know what happened to him."

"No. I mean what we did with him."

"Miss Brooks," he says. "He and his family are safe and sound, where they belong."

Where they belong. She doesn't like the sound of that at all. She looks over at Balloon and Stretch, those two weirdos she'd run into with Menchú when she'd first gone to visit Perry, back when she first got here. They are sitting with their monsignor and Hilary Sansone, another member of Team Two. Balloon and Stretch are both looking back at Sal, as if they've been watching her the whole time. They each give her a huge grin.

"Please proceed," the cardinal said.

Sal's left something out of her testimony, the part where Jacob defended what he did. *You understand why I did it, don't you?* he'd said. *I just love this place so much, and I don't want to leave it. None of us do. Do you understand?*

Sal had looked at everyone in the brick house, and they all nodded. She believed them. The tornado that destroyed half of Tanner City couldn't make them go. The creatures that were destroying what was left couldn't make them leave either. They were the survivors, the people hanging on. The state could unincorporate the town around them, turn off the power, stop delivering the mail, stop fixing the roads, and they'd probably still be out there. And when anyone asked them where they were from, where they lived, they'd still say the same thing: Tanner City. Full stop.

So what did Team Two do?

"Sal," Asanti said. "It is very good to hear your voice." Her own voice sounded strained, anxious.

"Is everyone else okay?" Sal said.

"We heard from Liam. Liam is all right."

Sal felt a weight leave her heart. She hadn't realized she'd been feeling it until it was gone.

"What about Grace and Menchú?"

"No word," Asanti said.

And the weight returned. Sal put it away, the way her job, her life, had trained her to do.

"What's going on?"

"Team One is on its way," Asanti said. "They're probably almost to you now. No more than a few hours off."

"Asanti," Sal said, "I think I may have found a way to fix this without Team One. The Tornado Eaters—"

"The what?" Asanti said.

"That's what they call the monsters around here."

"Who?"

"The people in town."

"There are people in town?" Asanti said. "And they have a name for the monsters?"

Sal told Asanti everything.

"Asanti, is there any way of calling off Team One?" Sal said when she was finished with the story.

There was a long pause on the other end.

"Team One," Asanti said, "is more like the military than the police. Once the gears are in motion, they turn. Team Two is following them in. From what Liam described to us, and now from what you're telling us about the people in town, it sounds like they'll be necessary."

Balloon and Stretch, Sal thought. The cold looks they'd given her. She pictured Balloon and Stretch talking to Sharon and Jacob— doing more than talking—and shuddered.

She suddenly regretted having told Asanti anything. It was what she was supposed to do, but she was wondering if she should have.

Then Asanti said, "Call Liam. You should be together when Team One arrives, at least so you're easier to account for. And Liam will be thrilled to know that you're alive."

"I'll do it," Sal said.

"Sal?" Asanti said. "Please be careful."

"I'll report back when Liam and I have joined up."

She called Liam. He was as relieved as Asanti said he would be, as Sal expected him to be. They figured out they were less than a mile apart. Within a half hour she was approaching the intersection of two local roads, not much more than dirt tracks crossing at the corners of a couple of farms. In the light gathering before dawn she could see that Liam was already there, a shadow standing in the dust. When he saw Sal, he ran to her and gave her a crushing hug, big enough to lift her feet off the ground.

"You have no idea how good it is to see you," he said.

They told each other what they'd done to get there. There wasn't much more to say after that. So they waited for Team One. They were just glad to be there.

In the quiet of the fields at dawn, Sal and Liam could hear Team One rolling down the county road for a good minute before they actually got there. They were in a small line of Humvees that pulled to the side of the road in unison, the first one stopping less than a foot from Liam's shin.

Christophe Bouchard, Team One's leader, got out of the passenger side of the head vehicle.

"Doyle," he said, giving him a smile. "So here we are."

"Yes," Liam said. "I'm glad to see you." He pointed toward Tanner City.

"The monsters there are invisible right now. They won't be when they attack. That's our experience so far."

"We've seen that sort of thing before," Bouchard said. "How many of them are there?"

"At least two," Liam said.

"Three," Sal said.

Bouchard looked at her. "You're sure?"

"Yes. I talked to the person who let them out."

Bouchard's eyebrows rose.

"He didn't mean it," Sal said. "At least not . . . this."

Bouchard nodded. "So many of them always seem to have the best intentions. Good thing managing the general populace isn't my department." He cleared his throat. "How big are they?"

"The tallest one we saw has legs that are possibly a quarter mile high," Liam said.

"That big?" Bouchard said.

"Possibly. Maybe bigger."

"And that's not the biggest one," Sal said. "Not according to the person who let them out."

Liam and Bouchard both looked at her.

"The biggest one is underground," she said. "We haven't seen it yet."

Bouchard pursed his lips. "Okay, then," he said. "Tell me what else you know about these things."

Sal and Liam did. Sal protected Sharon and Jacob whenever she had a chance. Then Bouchard paced over to the lead vehicle and made a gesture. In less than a minute the other members of Team One had gotten out and were standing in tight formation.

"Soldiers," Bouchard began. He walked them through the details of what Liam and Sal had related and waited for a response. There was none.

"We will need everything we have," he finished. "Conventional and unconventional. Suit up."

Out came an assortment of metal pieces that looked like something between medieval armor and an industrial exoskeleton. A crate of oddly shaped weapons. Two pairs of wings, one made of sharp metal feathers, the other almost transparent, like the wings of a giant dragonfly. A pair of claws.

Team One suited up. Two of them took the wings and strapped them to their backs, and the wings softened and fluttered. Another soldier pulled the claws over her own hands, and they seemed to bond to her arms. They donned their armor as if they'd each only found pieces of a full suit. One of them had an arm sheathed in a coppery metal. With that arm, he hoisted a machine gun Sal was sure should be mounted on the front of a helicopter. Another slid into a set of trousers and, testing them, jumped over the van in a single leap and landed crouching on her feet. A third soldier draped a cloak over his shoulders, closed his eyes, disappeared, and reappeared ten feet down the road.

What is all this stuff? Sal thought. And what about the swords, axes, and vials that hung from Team One's belts?

How much magic was involved here?

"All right," Bouchard said. "Let's go in noisy so we can see what we're up against." He turned to Sal and Liam.

"Can you guys drive these?" He motioned to the Humvees.

Sal and Liam nodded.

"You round up the civilians you mentioned and get them out of town, okay?" Bouchard said.

"All right," Sal said. She turned to Liam. "Follow me."

Sal took the lead vehicle. Team One stood in the road in front of her, again in tight formation. Bouchard's arm was raised. He dropped it like the blade of a guillotine.

Team One took off. One soldier grabbed the hand of the one with the cloak, and both vanished. One jumped onto the back of the soldier with the trousers, and they sprinted off down the road, almost flying. The ones with wings began flapping them, rising to hover in the air. They grabbed the final two earthbound soldiers under their arms and flew toward Tanner City. Bouchard himself took off at a run, too fast for humans to go without some kind of help.

Sal hit the gas and careened into town behind them. She looked in her rearview mirror. Liam was right behind her, teeth gritted.

Just after Sal hit the edge of town, she took a sharp left onto a side street, backtracking. She passed the sign on the house where the woman did embroidery. The basketball hoop. The bikes in the yard. The vinyl siding gave way to wood and brick. She was almost back in the center of the town. For a split second she didn't recognize the brick house where Ray, Sharon, Jacob, and the others were. It looked different during the day, from the back. Then she saw the tree, the tree that had bent sideways, as though in a storm, as she and Ray had walked through the parking lot. She pulled into the lot without losing speed and shrieked to a halt.

She looked up, expecting to see the monsters appear in a wink, right out of the clear blue sky. But the monsters were already there. They had seen Team One. The first one was just a block away, towering over the roofs, its triangular head pointed toward the sky. The other one was still there too, its legs arcing down from the clouds, its body way above. Was it only a quarter mile? Was it more? It was impossible to say.

And where was the biggest one?

As Sal watched, the soldier from Team One with the metal wings, carrying another soldier, dived straight toward the monster. The creature's mouth opened into a roar. The wings tucked, and the two team members gained speed. The soldier being carried pulled out a blade that grew in his hand to the size of a lance. More blades sprang from his arms, his legs, until he was covered in razors. He put his bladed arms out in front of him. Before the monster even had a chance to stop roaring, the coupled soldiers started spinning like arrows, flew straight into the monster's mouth, and burst out of the back of its head in a blossom of black blood and torn-up flesh. The blades on the suits retracted and out came the wings, and the two team members sped away in the air, in time to clear a fireball that started in the creature's neck, right below its head, and ballooned outward from there. The Tornado Eater started to let out a horrific cry that was choked off at once as the head separated from the rest of the body and tilted downward to fall into the street.

The two team members paused in midair and looked like they were exchanging jokes with each other. One of them, Sal thought, must have dropped a bomb down the Tornado Eater's throat as they were passing through. Like they'd done this drill a hundred times.

She ran to the door of the brick house and smacked on it with her palm until someone opened it. It was Ray.

"Get everyone out," Sal said. "We're getting you out of town. It's not safe to be here right now."

"We just saw," Ray said, "through the window."

"Then you know," Sal said. "Come on."

All nineteen of them made a break for the Humvees in the lot.

"Don't look up," Sal told them. They all did.

They could see tracer bullets rising from the street toward the legs of the Tornado Eater suspended in the sky. The shots must have been coming from the street. Then the firing stopped, and as they watched, five soldiers came into view, one climbing each leg, until they reached the spot where, against nature, the legs started getting thinner. The Tornado Eater started thrashing, trying to kick them off, but they held on tight; Sal realized they'd each spiked something—a knife, a spear—into the flesh and were hanging on to that. They weren't coming off.

"Get in, get in!" Sal yelled. Everyone did, and they drove a few blocks away, until Sal was sure they were safe. She turned the Humvee around so she could see.

The two team members who could fly shot up toward the body until they were far enough away that no one on the ground could see them. Then some signal must have been given. High above them, the body of the Tornado Eater erupted in flame. At the same time, the team members on each leg drew weapons—swords, axes, some circular bladed weapon that Sal didn't recognize—that grew to seemingly four times the soldiers' height. They flashed in the sun like giant scissors. That they could wield them at all seemed like an impossibility, but there it was. They brandished them in near synchronicity, then together they cut through all the legs at once and scrambled back down. The body started to fall from the sky.

The air darkened, reddened.

It was a mist of blood. Sal turned on the windshield wipers and waited until it cleared.

Outside it was quiet.

"Are we safe?" Sal asked. She looked back at the people in the van.

"No," said a voice. "Not at all." Jacob.

"Tell me," Sal said.

"The last one," Jacob said, "will eat the town before it lets you have it."

"How do you stop it?" Sal asked.

"You don't."

Sal turned the Humvee around and drove frantically to the edge of town. She screamed at everyone to get out, turned back around, and headed straight into town again. Back to the intersection where they'd first pulled into Tanner City.

The street was filled with hunks of flesh, car-size pieces that looked like fatty lobster. The pavement was slick with something clear and viscous. And there was all of Team One, in tight formation, waiting for that third Tornado Eater to show up.

"Sal," Bouchard called. "Please tell me you have endangered your life because you have intel."

"Yes," Sal said. "The last one won't attack until you think you've won."

"Look around," Bouchard said. "I think we just did."

He smiled. Not cocky. Just ready.

But he wasn't.

A long, thin, curved tooth, a row of them, erupted from under the asphalt, one of them right between Bouchard's feet. It speared upward and through him, slid out of his back in between his shoulder blades. He slid down it until something inside him caught on it; then he was borne upward, like a puppet, and died without another word.

The rest of Team One had a chance to jump back and draw their weapons. They watched the row of teeth rise in front of them, and turning around, saw another set rising through the street at the next corner.

The mouth was as big as the block and was about to swallow it.

Which is when Sal saw what Team One could really do.

They ran to the middle of the block, into the middle of the mouth. Three of them chanted something, and the right hands of their suits grew. They curled them into fists, until they looked like wrecking balls. They swung them down on the pavement, again and again, faster and faster, until the hands were blurs and the pavement yielded to dirt. Then the hands opened and started digging, with the same blurry speed. They were drilling through the earth, down to the underground creature's throat.

The teeth were still rising, and the broken earth rolled off them and gave way to dark gums, the edge of a long, dark, hairy lip, caked with dust and rocks. Sal swore she could see all the buildings on the block lifting and shuddering, their foundations cracking. Windows shattered in their frames as the wood around them shifted and closed in.

Then Team One hit bottom and broke through, made a hole to the last Tornado Eater's open throat. They didn't even have to talk about it. As Sal watched in awe, the smallest of them collected a handful of vials of something from the others, gave a quick salute, and jumped in. The rest of them ran, leaped over the teeth, leaped past Bouchard's impaled corpse. One of them picked up Sal like she was nothing and kept running.

They didn't so much hear the explosion as feel it, a rumbling jolt through the ground. It knocked all of them down. The man from Team One who had picked Sal up fell on top of her to shield her. But there was no need.

There was a smell like burning, rotten seafood.

They looked back.

The windows had stopped breaking. The teeth had stopped rising. They just stood in a row across the street like a fence. Bouchard was still there, hanging like a doll. The other soldier, whose name Sal didn't even know, lay buried below the street.

"Two men down," one of them said.

Three of the soldiers slid Bouchard off the tooth and lay him in the street. They all saluted where they stood. No one shed a tear.

The National Guard found Menchú and Grace in the wreckage of the buildings in the middle of town. Menchú had a broken arm and a broken leg. Grace had two broken legs. They'd both been trapped in the debris, like earthquake survivors. They'd lost some blood.

They were dehydrated and starving. Neither of them was entirely sure how they had gotten there. They both remembered ear-splitting noise, a rushing dust cloud under the bright sun. They both must have lost consciousness for a while, and then found themselves pinned under parts of the ceiling that used to be above them. Paramedics got them into an ambulance and to the county hospital before Sal or Liam had a chance to tell them how glad they were to see them alive.

"It's a miracle," Liam said.

Team Two's Hilary Sansone had mastered the blank, friendly face of a career diplomat. There she was, standing amid the rubble in the main intersection in Tanner City, in a work jacket that she somehow managed to make fashionable. She announced herself as being from Catholic Relief Services, called in by Tanner City's parish priest and now helping to coordinate services for the victims. Somehow she had made herself point person for the authorities coming into town now who wanted to find out what had happened. The event of a few days ago, she said, according to eyewitnesses, had been another tornado. The weather service personnel interviewed on the news were unsure of that. There hadn't been any evidence of a storm in the area, they said, and shrugged their shoulders. But the guys in the National Guard called in to clean up the wreckage didn't need any convincing. *Looks like a tornado to me,* they said.

"It's not an airtight story," Sansone told Sal even then, when they had a quiet moment. "There will always be questions, loose ends, things that don't add up about what happened here. If conspiracy theorists ever get ahold of it, they'll blame it on UFOs or the mining companies—you know, because of what happened in Picher—or they'll say it was some weapon the government was testing. Who knows what they'll come up with? Those people can be so imaginative.

The only thing that matters from our perspective is that they don't come up with the truth."

"But the people who live here know," Sal said. "They all do."

"It's easier than you think to get them to cooperate," Sansone said. She gave Sal a thin smile, as if to suggest that she was getting a little tired of talking about it. That maybe Sal was overstepping her bounds.

Sal thought of Ray and Sharon and Jacob.

"Did you pay them off?" Sal asked.

"We like to think of it as donating to reconstruction efforts."

"And they all agreed."

That was when Sansone did . . . something. Sal couldn't say for sure what it was. Maybe she looked away slightly, or hesitated a little too long when she answered. Maybe her breathing changed. It was hard to say. Whatever it was, though, Sal picked up on it, and she was sure then that Sansone was lying.

"Yes," Sansone said.

Then what are Balloon and Stretch doing here? Sal wanted to ask. She had seen them, talking to a few of the people in town. To Ray. To Sharon. To Jacob. She had seen them take each of the residents aside, put an arm around each of them. Confidential. Protective. Maybe abusive. And she had seen Sharon crying, seen Jacob looking stunned and pale. As though he'd seen something horrible, or maybe something terrible had been done to him. She'd wanted to see them afterward, to make sure they were all right. But when they saw her coming, they just shook their heads. *Get away from us.*

"I'm sorry for what happened to your team on this mission. And to Team One," Sansone said. What she meant was: *You're done here.*

"Me too," Sal said.

4.

For the first time, Cardinal Varano gives Sal a smile. The next words come out of his mouth with an audible sense of relief.

"Thank you," he says. "You've been very forthcoming."

He nods to the clerk next to him, who's taking notes. Making the official story. He then turns to the monsignor for Team Two.

"Monsignor Usher, please report," he says.

The monsignor turns to Hilary Sansone, who has the same blank, friendly face on that she had for the Red Cross, the National Guard, the state police. It projects cool competence, a sense of command of the situation without allowing any misconceptions about how in control anyone can be. She gives Usher a small, questioning look, and he gives her a nod. *Proceed.*

"First of all," she says, "Team One did a remarkable job of disposing of the remains of the magical creatures. By the time secular authorities arrived, there were indications of the fires that Team One had set to dispose of the remains, but no indication of the remains themselves."

Monsignor Fox gives a small, grateful smile.

"We were lucky," a member of Team One says. "They turned out to be all soft tissue, somehow, and the fires we set consumed them quickly."

"And we are told by Team One's personnel," says Sansone, "that it was intel from Team Three, gathered by Miss Brooks, that allowed Team One to be ready for the final creature's attack. They lost two of their men that day. According to Team One's personnel, however, they could easily have lost more if they had been less aware of the details of the situation. So we are all grateful for that."

There is a small round of applause for Sal. It feels perfunctory. The cardinal doesn't clap.

"And the cover story?" Varano says. "Is it holding?"

"As I discussed with Miss Brooks at the time," Sansone says, giving Sal a nod, "it is holding to the extent any of our cover stories do. There is, of course, still no meteorological data to back up our claim of a second tornado, which is problematic. But a second tornado remains the most plausible explanation to secular authorities. Competing theories from government officials and scientists still fall under the realm of natural disasters. Someone is examining the possibility of an earthquake. Someone else is poring over the data looking for the chance of a windstorm of some sort, not a tornado but still strong enough to do a lot of damage, particularly to buildings already buffeted by the tornado they do have evidence of. A particularly dogged scientist is building a theory that Tanner City was the victim of a simultaneous earthquake and windstorm."

"Sounds unlikely to stand," Varano says. "It makes Tanner City the most unlucky town in the world."

"But it does explain the destruction with the evidence they have. The theory hasn't been dismissed altogether yet. My guess," says

Sansone, "is that the inquiries will end up being vaguely conclusive. Maddening to a few people, but plausible enough to everyone else that they just move on to the next problem they can't solve."

Sansone takes a breath.

"Forgive me if this sounds callous," she says, "but I think in the end we are very fortunate that a calamity of this scale—one that taxed the Society perhaps to the limits of what it can contain—occurred in a place with very few civilians, and that almost no one outside the town's limits has paid much attention to. If this had been Tulsa, or Oklahoma City, to say nothing of any major metropolitan area on either coast of the United States, we would have a great deal more work to do. As it is, the only people requiring any kind of real focus from us are the few who were left in Tanner City after the tornado. And some of them didn't even see anything."

"But some of them did," Cardinal Varano says.

Sansone looks at Sal again.

"Yes," she says, "some did. Again, fortunately for us, it turns out that our relocation program, and some substantial financial remuneration, is solving the problem. Almost all the families are moving out of Tanner City, starting new lives in other towns, other cities. In some cases other states. To put it crudely, we have bought their silence. But to take a larger view, as the people of Tanner City rebuild their lives, their self-interests and our self-interests converge. They know that no one will believe them if they ever tell the truth. And the social costs will be extraordinarily high if they persist. They stand to lose their jobs, their new friends, everything. So in a sense, we're helping them realize what their futures entail a little faster, and with less drama. Yes, they'll have to spend the rest of their lives knowing something huge about the world that almost no one else knows. But we're all used to that by now, aren't we?"

An appreciative chuckle ripples across the room. Sal feels a little ill.

"What about Jacob?" she says. "What about Sharon?" She blurts it out almost before she knows what she's saying.

"Miss Brooks," the cardinal says. "This is, technically speaking, an inquest to document and explain the deaths on Team One."

"So the people in Tanner City don't matter?"

"That's not what I'm implying," Varano says. "Only that we have procedures to follow."

"I want to know what happened to them," Sal says. "You all just told me what a great job I did. Can you answer my question?"

Sal catches the smallest glare from Sansone.

"Some always prove harder to convince," Sansone said. "But they came around."

"As the box is safe in the Archive now, can we consider this matter closed?" Cardinal Varano says. He sounds a little impatient.

"I would," the monsignor from Team Two says. The other monsignors give their assent.

"Let the record state that the inquest into the fatalities that the Society suffered in Tanner City is declared closed," Varano says. "It is the greatest challenge the Society has faced in some time. But we have held the line. There are, perhaps, tactical changes to consider within Team One and Team Two. But the core of the mission held strong, and all personnel performed with the utmost ethical consideration."

Sal remembers the looks on Jacob's and Sharon's faces after Balloon and Stretch were done with them. *What did they do?*

"Thank you, everyone, for your time," the cardinal says. "And thank you again to Miss Brooks, for your exemplary work."

The room begins to empty.

"Monsignor," Sal says. "Permission to be blunt?"

Monsignor Angiuli's eyebrows rise. "You're asking for permission now?"

"I know I've overstepped my bounds here," Sal says. "But I can't think of any other way to ask it."

"Ask."

"This whole thing was just a CYA boondoggle?" Sal says.

"CYA?"

"Cover your ass. As in, we're here just to cover our collective asses?"

The monsignor gives her a long sigh. As if to say, *You expected something else?*

"It's been a long day," Angiuli says. He leaves.

But Sal can't let it go.

She sees Balloon and Stretch heading down the hall in the opposite direction from everyone else. She follows them. Recalls their names, though she likes her nicknames better.

"Desmet. De Vos," she says. "Hold up, you two."

Balloon and Stretch turn.

"What did you do to Jacob and Sharon?"

"Who?" Balloon asks.

"You know who they are."

She's coming on as strong as she can without actually threatening them. But Balloon and Stretch don't seem threatened at all.

"I think you have some idea what we did," Stretch says.

"Stop fucking around," Sal says.

"Profanity! So quickly!" Balloon says. "I like this one."

"Yes," says Stretch. "Very promising. You would enjoy working with us on Team Two."

"Don't be so sure," Sal says.

"But then you would already know what happened to those

two little rednecks you seem to care so much about," Stretch says.

"Just so you know, they're still alive," Balloon says.

"But you're right that they didn't want to leave. And money was not going to be enough to get Jacob to stop practicing magic," Stretch says.

"So we divided and conquered," Balloon says.

"He took the boy," Stretch says. "I took the woman."

The way Stretch says the word "took" makes Sal's stomach flip.

"We didn't really have to touch them," Balloon says.

"We just had to talk to them," Stretch says. "It was easy. I told the mother the kinds of things I was willing to do to her boy if we ever heard that they spoke a word."

"And I did the same to the boy, about his mother," Balloon says.

"Now and again we'll stop by when we happen to be in their new neighborhood, just to make sure that they still believe us," Stretch says.

"And it will work, too," Balloon says. "All we'll have to do is stand outside their house now and again, and smile and wave when we catch them looking."

Stretch assumes an almost philosophical tone. "It is amazing," he says, "the kind of violence you can inflict with words alone. After all, your body doesn't remember physical pain. It remembers the ghost of it. It remembers what it was like. When you recall a time you were physically hurt, you don't feel it all again. Not like you did then. Words, though—spoken words—are different. You think back to those times someone said something truly awful to you, and you can hear it in your head, can't you? Just like you did the first time. If you're not careful, and most people aren't, your mind can even make the memory worse. Those voices from the past can sound even crueler. You can put words in those memories' mouths to make them say even worse things than were said, so the memory matches the pain you felt, every time. For our line of work, it's a beautiful mechanism."

"Truth be told, though," Balloon says, "we don't mind getting dirty, either. When the job demands it."

"Do you understand?" Stretch says.

"Perfectly," Sal says.

"So we're done here?" Stretch says.

She turns to go. She's not even sure how to get out of the building in the direction she's headed. But it doesn't matter. She can't look at either of them.

"Be seeing you," she hears Stretch say.

It takes even Grace a few weeks to heal. She is not happy about it. Angry, in fact. More angry than Sal's seen her, even when she's in danger, even when she's fighting someone trying to kill her.

What is with her? Sal wonders.

They're reconvening for the first time as a full team since Oklahoma. The Orb has been mercifully quiet. Menchú is out of the hospital at last, though he's on crutches. Grace had to carry him down the long spiraling stairs into the library. He's insisting now on standing, though he's still a little wobbly.

"How are we all?" Menchú says.

They talk about Tanner City. About their fears when they were separated. About how relieved they were to see one another again. Asanti asks if they all got the pastries she made them. They did.

"I'm so glad you're all right," Menchú says to the rest of them.

"Thanks," Sal says, "but I'm not sure I'm all right."

"Well, tell us about it," Asanti says.

"I don't know if I should."

"Our lives depend on being able to talk to each other," Asanti says.

Sal hasn't talked about Balloon and Stretch to anyone. She decides she can't keep it in any longer. She tells her teammates everything. They are the only people she feels she can trust. She's expecting them to be outraged. She's expecting a gasp here, an *Oh God* there. Something to let her know that they're as repulsed as she is.

But it doesn't happen. Sal finishes, and there's nothing but a long, uncomfortable pause.

"Huh," Sal says. "I guess I was expecting you to be more surprised."

"Sal . . . ," Menchú says.

"So when you just said that we need to be able to tell each other anything, you meant I should always tell you everything," Sal says. "And in return, you just keep letting me figure out things you already know on my own."

"That's not what I meant," Asanti says.

"Well, it sure feels like it," Sal says. She looks at each of them in turn—Grace, Menchú, Asanti, Liam.

"I understood that Team Two was kind of like the Society's State Department," Sal says. "When were you going to tell me that it was the CIA, too?"

Menchú and Asanti look at each other, as if Sal's stumbled into a conversation they've been having with each other for years. But neither of them says anything.

"Frankly," Grace says, "I'm a little surprised that you thought we didn't have one. You've seen what we do. You've seen how dangerous it gets."

"And Team Two isn't a hit squad," Liam says. "Most of what they do is, well, pretty boring, to be honest. It's phone calls and meetings and paperwork. You think anyone at the National Oceanic and Atmospheric Administration needed to be coerced into anything?

They just need e-mails. Phone calls. Lots of them. But that's it. And no one is hurt. They're kept in the dark, sure. But you're police. You of all people should know that most people don't want to know what we deal with. They don't want to know that anything we see on our jobs even happens. So we just need to make sure we do the due diligence and then get on with our work."

"How many people has Team Two killed?" Sal says. "Just because they know something they shouldn't and are unwilling to be quiet about it."

The silence after Sal's question is way too long for her.

"None," Liam says. "That I'm aware of."

"You know what?" Sal says. "Right now that is not nearly good enough."

She stands up.

"Where are you going?" Menchú says.

"Home. Away from this place."

Liam moves to intercept her. Menchú stops him with a glance. They all watch as Sal takes the stairs back to the surface, two at a time.

That night, Sal gets a text from Liam.

Can I come in? it reads. *I'm outside.*

She lets him in.

The visit starts off all right. He gives her a long hug. He commiserates about how crappy the job can be sometimes. He tells her he's there for her. He thinks Sal's let it go. She hasn't.

"You know those guys on Team Two offed someone," Sal says.

Sal sees Liam wince a little.

"I don't know that for sure," he says. "There's nothing in the official records that says so. I checked before I came over here."

He was expecting it to be comforting, she thinks, and suddenly knows it's the opposite.

"Of course there isn't an official record of it," Sal says. "It is in no one's interest that it ever gets recorded. Which means people could just be dropping off the face of the Earth, thanks to them. Whenever they think it's good for the Society."

"Killing innocent people would never be good for the Society," Liam says.

"Then why does the Society keep two people like that around?" Sal says. Her voice is rising.

"Because they're good at their jobs!" Liam's voice is rising too.

"Yeah, they're fucking great at them," Sal says. "Just as long as they don't leave a trail of blood and no one ever asks how they do what they do."

Sal feels at once like she's standing on the edge of a cliff. She was standing on it before in Oklahoma. She was standing on it again all through the inquest. And she was standing on it in the Black Archives. She decided not to jump off it then. But now, in her apartment, she decides to jump.

"You know what repulses me so much about this?" Sal says. "It's not that the Society condones what it does. And God knows it's not that the Church does. The Church can condone whatever the hell it wants. It's that *you* do. You and Grace and Asanti and Menchú. God, Menchú of all people, after what he grew up with. But you, too. You've all let this job turn you into monsters."

Sal knows she's said too much now. She sees anger flash across Liam's face. He lets it stay there, lighting him up. She braces herself. He's going to hit her where it hurts.

"And you're not?" Liam says. "Who are you now, Serpico?"

"Nice reference," Sal says. "Thanks for speaking my language."

"Get on out of that," he says. "You're just as complicit as the rest of us. I don't know whether you've been willfully ignorant or just stupid—you know, like every cop who thinks he's one of the good cops, so everything's fine—but you didn't have to play along. You didn't have to sign up. You didn't have to tell us everything in the field. You didn't have to say everything you said at the inquest. If you wanted to protect that little family in Tanner City, you could have, but you didn't, and you got your commendation for it. Team Two does what it does. But you pointed them in the right direction. Live with that."

"I swear," Sal says, "the day my brother either dies or wakes up, I'm out of here."

She knows there's more keeping her here than that. But it feels good to lay it on the table. Just to hear what he says.

"Good," Liam says. "Truth be told, I don't think you're cut out for it, anyway."

What the hell, she thinks. *Let's go for broke. If we're going to get to the bottom of something, let's really hit bottom.*

"And when I'm out, I'm telling the world what's going on here."

"Great," Liam says. "I hope you do."

He's as angry as she's ever seen him, but she knows him well enough to see the look of surprise on his face. He's said what he's said because he's trying to be nasty, she knows that. They both are.

But the last thing he's just said is different. She can tell. A part of him actually does hope for that, does want it. To pry the lid off the whole thing and let all the worms out. To let everything out into the light.

They both want it, the same thing.

For a second they stare at each other, glaring. Then his face softens, and he reaches for her.

"Don't even think about it," she says.

He lets his arm drop, conciliatory. Trying to patch things up a little. "You all right?"

"I will be," Sal says. "Just not now."

"Call if you need me," he says.

"I don't," she says.

"I suppose I deserved that," he says. "Good night, Sal."

He turns and walks out. She locks the door behind him and looks out the window at the sky over Rome. It looks smaller than ever.

EPISODE
7

NOW AND THEN

MAX GLADSTONE

1.

SHANGHAI. THEN.

Chen Juan decided she did not like the Russian.

He smelled of rendered fat and wore a black suit he must have stolen from a funeral. He leaned against the stone rail, facing out over the Huangpu River, away from Shanghai. He wanted her to think he was watching the marshes and warehouses of Pudong across the boat-studded black, but every few seconds, when he thought she wasn't looking, he glanced at Chen out of the corner of his eye. She noticed, and ignored him.

The Bund curved north, bounded to the east by the river and to the west by the alien, yellowed-marble facades of traders' clubs and banks and, far away, the embassies, British and American and French. Nineteen twenty-eight had not been a good year, but good or bad the Bund endured, and served itself, as always. Few Nationalist flags flew here.

Chen had dressed for a party: heels, a long high-collared black dress slit past the knee, a fox-fur stole, silver earrings, gray silk opera gloves with silver trim, and—underneath all that—a tasteful cross. She had not dressed to be ogled on the Bund by some threadbare knife-faced foreign ghost.

She drew a long breath through her cigarette and pondered the exigencies of her profession.

Tallow-stink and uneven footsteps heralded the Russian's approach. When she looked right, he leaned against the rail beside her. His coat was too tight, or there was too much muscle underneath: His head perched between mounds of shoulder.

She tipped ash and straightened to leave.

"Stay," he said in bad Chinese, tones broken, vowels slurred. "I tell you a story."

She responded in the same language, spoken better: "You don't know any story I want to hear."

He caught her by the upper arm as she turned away—his fingers and palm were rough, his grip hard enough to bruise. "I think I do," he said. She stopped. "In the stone den," he continued, pronunciation almost perfect now but singsong, learned but not understood, "there lived a poet." His eyes glittered like ice covered with alcohol and set on fire.

She frowned. "Your boss knows this is the world's worst pass phrase, right? Any child would know the next part. If this was England, would you use 'ring a ring o' roses'?"

"We're not in England. Say it."

She sharpened her voice and wished her consonants could cut him. "He was a lion addict, resolved to eat ten lions."

"What's your name, dear?"

"Grace," she said. For some reason foreigners liked people to have foreign names. Any foreign name would do, didn't have to be Russian or German or whatever. All their languages sounded the same, anyway. Maybe even they couldn't tell the difference.

He let her go and smiled a crooked smile with crooked teeth. "I'm sorry, my dear. I don't make the rules. But it is a pleasure to meet you. Do you have the envelope?"

She snapped open her pearled pocketbook and withdrew a red envelope sealed with white wax and stamped with a winged lion. "Here."

"You open it."

"Don't you have hands?"

"I do. I have yours."

They were alone, despite the lights and crowds. Farther up the Bund, couples strolled. A black car idled near the sidewalk.

She slid her thumb beneath the envelope's flap and tugged once. The seal popped. She withdrew and unfolded the note inside. "There's nothing written here. Just red paper."

"It's not a letter," he said. "It's a packing label."

And his arm was around her neck, his other hand pressing a wadded wet cloth to her mouth and nose.

She let out a muffled cry, stopped breathing, and sagged into him.

Behind them, the car's engine roared to life.

He grunted under her weight, shifted his grip from her neck to her shoulder so he'd seem to be supporting a drunken girlfriend home, and turned them both away from the river. The cloth left Chen Juan's mouth.

She snaked her arm around his, twisted her hip, dropped her weight, and broke his shoulder. He screamed higher than she expected.

Dark spots swam through her vision. The chloroform, or ether, or whatever, slowed her a little. The Russian tripped and fell, and tried to rise even through the pain. She straddled his back, took his neck in the crook of her elbow, and squeezed. His gasps reminded her of a carp she'd landed when she was six. He twitched under her. "Here's a story," she hissed into his ear. "On the mountain was a monk, and the monk said, 'Master, tell me a story,' and this was the story he told—"

She let the Russian go when he passed out.

Car doors slammed up the road and heavy voices, foreign voices, cried: "Stop!" She dove to the ground and rolled. Shots split the night—but the shooter wasn't aiming at Chen. The Russian's friends dove for cover. A second black car pulled to the curb, its door flew open, and Wujing dove out. He ran toward Chen Juan, a black blur, while Ahsan covered them both with his pistol from the passenger seat. Wujing got his arm under the Russian's, lifted from his side while Chen Juan lifted from hers, and together they pulled him into the car's spacious backseat. Wujing climbed back behind the wheel and gunned the engine. Chen Juan cuffed the Russian's hands behind him, shackled his legs together, and tied the handcuffs to the leg irons before he woke up.

He thrashed and roared, as she expected. Up front, Ahsan traded fire with pursuing Russians. Wujing turned a hard left and a harder right.

"What's your name?" Chen's Russian wasn't much better than his Chinese, but it would pass.

"Fuck you!"

She hit him in the broken shoulder, and he screamed.

"Name."

"Vasily," he said, and repeated it, like a charm.

"Let's trade stories, Vasily. You told me one; I told you one. Now it's your turn again."

"I can't."

Wujing yanked the car through a 270-degree hairpin. Chen Juan removed her right glove and placed her bare hand on Vasily's shoulder. "Where are the girls, Vasily? Where's the Professor? Tell me now, and you'll wake up somewhere better than this and never see me again. Hold out, and I'll introduce you to my other friends.

I don't think you would like them very much, Vasily. I don't like them very much, to be honest. But they ask good questions, the kind people just can't help answering."

"No," he said.

"The girls. The Professor."

Ahsan leaned out the window and fired again. The pursuing car swerved and crashed through a cabbage stand.

Vasily slumped.

"They're in Pudong," he said, and gave an address.

"Thank you, Vasily. Turns out you did know a story I wanted to hear." Chen took the chloroform rag from the seat beside her, pressed it over his mouth and nose, and waited for him to still. "We've got it!" she shouted up to Wujing and Ahsan. "Now we just swoop in and save the girls before the Professor can move."

Wujing laughed. "Like it's that easy."

"It's worked so far."

"You think luck is the same as a good plan."

"You have my back," she said, and grinned when she caught his eye in the rearview mirror, "and I have yours. That's better than luck."

Vasily groaned. Chen Juan decided she liked him better this way.

VATICAN CITY. NOW.

"I have never seen such irresponsible, corner-cutting operational behavior in my entire life as I have since you joined up."

A QUIET, PLEASE sign hung on the wall in the Black Archives beneath the Vatican, receiving even less respect than usual. Though, for a change, Grace was the one shouting.

Sal was shouting back. "Excuse me for saving lives!" she said.

"You wanted us to let those tourists die. I saw a chance and took it." She was covered in ash and cuts and bruises, just like Grace—though, Sal noted bitterly, the other woman's cuts and bruises seemed shallower. The rest of the team, Liam and Menchú and Asanti, studiously ignored the argument. "And it worked out. So I don't see the problem."

"I, for one," Liam said, consulting his cell phone, "could murder a pizza."

"You don't see the problem?" Grace seemed to have a less figurative sort of murder on her mind. She brandished her copy of *Middlemarch* the way Sal had seen drunks brandish barstools. "That's exactly the problem. You *don't* see. You're good at patterns, you're good at streets, and you ask all the right questions except the ones that matter, the ones about risk, about death. You and Asanti went off to Glasgow without backup. You plug yourself into a magical computer because oh, *why not*; you endanger us all trying to save civilians from Team One; and now you run into hive-infested tunnels to rescue some dumb tourists who should have listened to the goddamned cave-in warning we put out expressly to keep them from being eaten by giant bugs."

Father Menchú coughed and opened his mouth as if to speak, but Grace wheeled on him and he decided against it. Asanti opened her suitcase and began extracting leather-bound tomes.

"I'm thinking pepperoni and anchovies?" Liam said hopefully.

Sal spread her arms. Ash rained from her clothes. "We protect people. That's the point. That's *my* point, anyway. That's why I'm here."

"We don't just protect people." Grace stormed toward Sal. *Middlemarch*'s spine stopped just short of Sal's sternum. Grace's fingers left smudge prints on the gold-stamped Modern Library binding. "We protect everyone. We protect them from monsters, we protect them from people like Norse who think they can *use* the monsters, and we protect them from Team One, who has to clean up if we fail. And there are, in case you hadn't noticed, five of us. So we protect each other. Which means we don't take crazy risks. We close ranks. We work together. We listen to one another. We take care of one another."

"You want our ranks so close nothing can get through. Hell, you want our ranks so close even I don't know what's going on half the time. If you'd open up a little, maybe I would have known about the pheromones in the first place!"

"Our world's *dangerous*. This isn't a game; this isn't a, what, a campfire circle. I keep telling you, and you don't listen. People. Get. Hurt."

"I don't need to be told that."

"It looks to me like you do."

"My brother," Sal said, slowly, "is in a fucking *coma*, okay? What do you know about getting hurt?"

Grace's face closed like a door. Her nostrils flared. Sal had seen her look calmer while strangling a demon. A muscle at the corner of her jaw twitched. She smelled of sweat, ash, and fury.

Sal wondered, in a distant, academic way, what she would do if Grace decided to hit her.

Grace slammed her book down on the table, turned, and marched out of the Archives.

"Pizza for four, then." Liam thumbed speed dial.

Sal looked from him to Menchú to Asanti, but found no answers. So she left.

2.

HUANGPU RIVER. THEN.

Wujing led the briefing on the barge. The strike team lounged on benches, drinking tea, smoking. The barge creaked around them. Outside, the motor churned. Chen Juan sat in the back; she'd changed at the dock into more comfortable grays—boots and slacks and a long-sleeved blouse. She drank over-steeped tea and wished it would dull the aftertaste of chloroform.

The projector screen showed a pale, dark-haired man in late middle age, high cheekbones, broad eyes, mustachioed, with a touch of beard at his chin. A strangler's humor curved his generous lips. "This," Wujing said for members of the strike team who didn't already know, "is Professor Yuri Antopov, a White Russian émigré and former advisor to von Ungern-Sternberg, the Blood Count of Mongolia." The slouchers straightened. They knew the stories; none had seen him in person, of course. The agents they sent north returned in pieces. The Blood Count had sent a suit made from one's skin, complete with a tanned face mask and an invitation to a masquerade ball in Ulaanbaatar.

"Antopov fled south after von Ungern-Sternberg fell. For years he operated with Green Gang protection in Shanghai's French Concession under the name Alexandrov, concocting new opium additives. He has been, in some ways, a model citizen. We did not know of the connection between Antopov and Alexandrov until an intelligence transfer from the Concession's GRU—coordinated by Officer Chen." He raised a hand to her, and she saluted back like she'd seen Americans do in movies; the strike team laughed. "Antopov used his Green Gang contacts to rebuild his Mongolian workshop. We believe his research is directed toward, ah . . ." Wujing trailed off and looked at the floor. He'd seen the evidence with his own eyes, time and again, but sometimes Chen Juan doubted he would ever truly believe their work.

"He's a Bathorist," she said, to spare him the embarrassment. "He's buying people to render alive for tallow. He believes this will help him achieve immortality, or something like it. And now we know the location of his workshop." Chen Juan finished her tea. "Unfortunately, he knows that we know—so he'll step up his plans, and kill his hostages soon. We have to move fast."

"We'll go in from the waterfront," Wujing said. "The rendering operation takes a great deal of space. It's most likely in the central stockroom, here." The projectionist changed slides, replacing Antopov's sneer with the warehouse floor plan. "We'll secure the dock first, and storm through these loading doors."

Chen Juan nodded. "I'll go in from the second floor before the assault."

"Impossible."

"I don't think so. If I jump from the building next door—"

"That's not what I mean."

The strike team turned sideways on their benches so they could watch Chen Juan and Wujing at the same time. Ahsan chuckled. "We have to get the hostages out," Chen said. "We don't know what he'll do after we attack, except that he's a monster, and monsters don't like to lose. Give me twenty minutes to save lives."

Wujing crossed his arms. "Fine. But I don't want to risk your being caught in the cross fire. Once you have the hostages out, leave—unless we've given the all clear."

"You don't want me riding to your rescue?"

"I want you safe."

"There's no such thing as safe," she said. "But I'll take care."

VATICAN CITY. NOW.

Saint Peter's Square was as good a place as any to stomp and sulk. Sal, hands in pockets, shoulders slumped under her jacket, dodged tourists and stomped through posed photographs with muttered apologies. The basilica dome towered. Crosses were everywhere. Best architecture in the Western world, or at least the showiest. "There is the pope's balcony," a passing tour guide said in Spanish. Or had she said, "There is the pope's hat?"

At least there wasn't an appearance scheduled today. Back home, Sal had checked the weather every morning before getting dressed. Here, she checked the papal schedule. But you couldn't dress for tourists—only suffer them, or not.

"Sal!"

Menchú's voice.

She considered storming on; a large Japanese family was lining up for a group shot with the basilica in the background, and if she timed it just right she could ruin the photo. If she was having a bad day, shouldn't everyone?

She stopped beside a pillar and waited for the priest.

"I don't ask for much," she said while he caught his breath. "I know you all keep telling me to be patient. But I have been. I've learned the rules, and kept them, and I can't catch a break with her."

Menchú took a handkerchief from his inside pocket and mopped his brow. It was cool for a Roman afternoon, but with Roman weather the modifying phrase mattered.

"I mean, I don't even want to talk about it," Sal continued. "Grace is a private person, sure—you've all told me that at one time or another. And we're in this together, five against the world. So we do need to give one another space."

Menchú folded his handkerchief and replaced it in his pocket.

The Japanese family's toddler son escaped his mother and sprinted toward the camera, arms extended. Mom handed the baby to Dad and ran to bring the toddler back; he wouldn't let go of the cameraman's—his uncle's?—arm.

"Why?" Sal asked when she couldn't stand Menchú's silence any longer.

"Why what?" Menchú replied.

"We should be elite, shouldn't we? The best in the world. Asanti is, sure. And Grace, I guess. I've never seen anyone who can take or give a beating like that woman. But Liam should be what's-his-face from that *Hackers* movie, the blond one, and you should be I don't know, Father Teresa and I should be Sam Spade with better clothes, and we should all of us speak thirty languages and know kung fu."

"It would make some missions easier," Menchú allowed. "Do you know anyone like that?"

"No."

"Neither do I." The toddler started crying. Mom lifted him. "People are strange. You never know how they'll respond to what we do until they meet the other world for the first time. Many people break. Some forget. Some become enchanted—they chase after the monsters. Some fight back. You've met all kinds since you started working with us. No way to know who will do what in advance. We've always recruited from survivors."

"Is that how you found Grace?"

Mom sang, and the toddler stopped crying. She blotted his cheeks with her sleeve, then led him back to the family.

"Let Grace be Grace," Menchú said. "She'll be fine. So will you. She just needs time."

"Something's been off between us ever since we met," Sal said. "I want to fix it. This kind of tension between squadmates is dangerous. I've seen it go bad before."

"Grace would never endanger the mission, or any of us. Trust me."

"We need to get this sorted before it's a problem. I should . . . talk to her, I guess. Where does she live?"

"I can't say."

"Seriously?"

Mom took the baby from Dad, who knelt and offered the toddler a chocolate wrapped in foil. Mom scowled.

"She's a private person," Menchú said. "Talk to her on the next mission."

"When we're on a mission, she's either reading and doesn't want to be disturbed, or she's hitting rotting-meat monsters in the face with large rocks, in which case I'd rather not bother her."

"You're still new."

"I've been here six months."

"That's new for Grace. She's a lifer. She'll come to you when she's ready."

"Or the mountain could go to Muhammad."

"Grace's quarters," Menchú said, "are a secret. If you pursue this, you might attract the Church's attention—and I can only protect you so much."

The toddler opened the foil, stuffed the chocolate in his mouth, and smiled with dirty teeth. Uncle, still kneeling, aimed the camera.

Snap.

PUDONG. THEN.

Chen Juan landed so lightly on the warehouse roof that she didn't startle the roosting pigeons. They shifted their wings and glared at her with evil eyes. Around her, under her, Pudong sweltered and stank through the summer night, Shanghai's ugly cast-off skin, lit by red lanterns and the moon. Back west across the river, the Bund squatted, smug as a city on fire. Someday someone would burn it down. Even marble would burn, if the fires were stoked hot enough.

She spidered over rooftop tiles to a latched-shut window and peered through. Empty hallway ten feet below. A row of closed doors, each with a flap in the base. The rooftop windows that should have looked into the closed rooms had been painted black from the inside.

Spread-eagled, Chen Juan poked her head over the roof's edge. By mutual agreement, an oil lamp pretended to light the alley, and a single guard pretended to watch the shadows it cast.

He smoked—just tobacco, she thought, but she couldn't smell for sure from this distance.

The second hand of her watch ticked round the face. She didn't have time for more reconnaissance. No way through but in.

She slipped the latch on the first window, lowered herself into the hall, dropped to a crouch, and listened. Behind each padlocked door she heard shallow breathing. Were the captives asleep? Not drugged, she hoped. Doors blocked both ends of the hall—the first bolted and locked, the second merely latched. She listened at the second door, and when she heard nothing, edged it open. Straight shot through shadows down a stairwell to the back door where the guard waited, smoking. Perfect.

She returned to the first cell door. Antopov must have spent the Green Gang's money on mystical paraphernalia, muscle, and human beings; he certainly hadn't spent any on locks. Chen Juan's mother had taught her to open locks like these when she could barely hold a pick: tension lever, exhale, hook pins and rake and twist. The latch popped. Behind the door, the breathing stopped. Limbs scrambled on straw: the person inside drawing back into the corner, like a scared rat.

Chen Juan wanted to be sick. She'd never felt the way the person trapped here felt. She could imagine, though.

She opened the door.

The girl—the woman—wore a sackcloth dress and had large green eyes and skeletal limbs that had been slender once. She huddled in the corner on straw, knees under her chin, hands curled to claws. She was paler than she would have been if she had been outside recently. When she saw Chen Juan, her mouth slacked, and confusion colored the fear in her eyes. *"Chto?"*

"Menya zavoot, Grace," she said. The woman, thank small

mercies, looked whole: hands battered from pounding the door, wan about the face, bruised on the cheek, but not cut, not burned, not yet. "I'm here to rescue you. But you need to be quiet. Can you walk?"

The woman nodded.

"How long have you been here?"

"Days. Weeks?"

"Do you know how many of them there are?"

"No."

"Wait," Chen said. "I'll get the others."

The next cell held a Fujianese girl who was worse off. She'd fought harder. When Chen Juan opened her door, she pounced. The girl was strong, but she wasn't fast, and Chen wrestled her down with little trouble. "I'm here to help you." She knew the look in the girl's eyes: trust waiting for an excuse to turn vengeful.

Altogether there were eleven prisoners; several rooms held two. Mostly girls from Fujian and Jiangsu, and a few White Russians, taxi dancers who'd made the wrong enemy. Chen supposed she herself would have been the twelfth, with Antopov, conducting the ritual, being its thirteenth participant. Foreigners seemed to like thirteens for some reason. One round of the stars plus one. Two minutes left, said her watch.

Gunfire erupted from the waterfront. She swore. Wujing must have started early.

"Come on," she said to the prisoners.

The stairwell remained empty. The women followed her down. Behind the doors to the main stockroom, guns fired, men screamed, and a high, reedy voice laughed.

Ground floor.

The door opened as she reached for it. The smoking guard

paused, shocked, hand halfway to his pistol. Chen Juan hit him in the knee and in the throat, and he fell back and did not rise. The alley was still. Gunfire didn't raise alarms in Pudong after dark.

And there was gunfire—pistols and automatic weapons. She listened. Cries in Chinese. Those could be Antopov's men or hers. She thought she heard Wujing's voice. The hostages hesitated in the shelter of the warehouse.

She should lead them to safety. That was the plan. Get them to the motor launch and rendezvous with Wujing back at Central.

But someone had started the attack early, and after four minutes Wujing still hadn't given the all clear.

Dammit.

You have my back, and I have yours.

"Go," she told the hostages. "Down to that streetlamp. Turn left. Run straight for the docks. There's a motor launch waiting. Give them this." She reached beneath the collar of her jacket and produced her cross. "They'll know it's from me." The girl who'd tackled Chen Juan upstairs seemed the most calm, so Chen handed her the cross. "I have to help my friends. Go."

They went. Chen relieved the fallen sentry of his gun. She hadn't brought a weapon herself: They were unwieldy for second-story work. Best use what you found to hand.

She heard another scream from the stockroom.

She counted breaths until the hostages disappeared around the corner. *Four. Five.*

She crept down the hall and edged open the stockroom door.

Light dazzled her. She smelled hot wax and burned hair. Antopov she recognized from photographs, though none of the photos had shown him hovering a foot off the ground and cackling. Three goons took cover behind an enormous lidded iron pot, the purpose of which Chen tried not to ponder, and they fired at Wujing's team.

The team, for their part, did not seem concerned by the goons. They were too busy wrestling with sculptures made of wax.

The wax things bubbled up from a trough at Antopov's feet and took shape as they advanced: eight-legged first, then four, then apelike, galloping toward Wujing's commandos with wax mouths open in silent screams. They left bubbling puddles in their wake.

"Come to me," Antopov said in Russian, and laughed. Chen Juan had heard that laugh before in similar scenarios, most recently in Harbin. Normal people, in her experience, did not laugh that way. Sanity tended to mellow the tenor register.

She edged into the stockroom. Antopov hovered, she saw now, before an enormous carved-bone candlestick, upon which rested a candle as thick as Chen's own thigh, lit. When Antopov gestured with his long-nailed hands, the flame leaped and the wax monsters moved. "You come to me, in my house, as if I were a common criminal. My blood is noble, and I have burned in secret fires. I have summoned you, and I will melt you."

A wax gorilla tackled Ahsan, and they rolled together. Ahsan was strong and broad, but when he punched the pasty creature, melting wax clung to his hands. The gorilla dripped onto him, into his eyes, into his mouth, and he screamed. Wujing ran from his cover to kick the gorilla in the face. One of Antopov's goons took aim.

Chen Juan dropped him with two shots to the back and one to the head.

Before the others could turn, she shifted aim to Antopov and fired three more times. Two for the center of mass, and one to the head just in case.

Wax fountained from Antopov's trough and snatched the bullets from midair. The hovering Russian turned to her, roaring with fury. His goons took aim. Wujing saw Chen Juan in trouble, raised his own sidearm, fired. One goon fell, the second turned—and a wax tiger pounced, tumbled Wujing to the ground, and caught his face in its jaws.

Wujing screamed.

So did Chen Juan. She ran for Antopov, gun still in hand, and leaped toward him, shielding her face with her arms.

She was heavier than a bullet. A curtain of hot wax covered her skin, her clothes. It burned, but did not stop her. In an instant she was through and fell into Antopov, hands around the man's legs, dragging him to earth against the obscene weightlessness of his magic.

The Russian cried out as he fell and hit the floor. Chen climbed onto him, ignoring the pain from her burned skin, the stink of her singed hair, and the sickening foreign taste of wax in her mouth.

He twisted serpentlike beneath her, bent 180 degrees from the waist, and lunged to strike the bridge of her nose with his forehead. She fell back, and he was on her—fast, too fast, the candle flame behind him towering into a column of light, licking the rafters. She clawed his face and tore him, but instead of skin, long strips of wax came away beneath her nails, baring more wax beneath, the color of blood.

"Too late," Antopov said, cackling. His teeth were yellow, and his tongue was pink. "The will is the flame and the flesh is the wax. The mind is the mold and the meat is the clay."

His hand grew large and heavy, and he struck her face. His fingers puddled against her cheek, wax smearing to block her nose and mouth. His other hand became a snake, twining around her arm. His limbs pulled like melted sugar when she recoiled, but they did not let her go. The rafters were aflame. Wax ran and bubbled over her skin. Wujing struggled to his feet, head still caught in the tiger's jaws, fighting as he suffocated. Ahsan lay still.

Chen Juan clawed at her mouth but could not breathe. Black spots danced between her and the world, and those black spots had faces in them, and the faces all laughed with Antopov's inhuman cadence. She stumbled, regained her feet, fell against the candlestick. Her hand came away wet with melted wax—a quarter of the massive candle had melted since she had entered the stockroom.

The will is the flame and the flesh is the wax.

Wujing fired twice into the tiger's stomach, and fell.

Chen Juan closed her grip around the candle's wick.

The flame died.

She heard a scream that might have been a laugh, and then was still.

3.

ROME. NOW.

Manhunts, in Sal's experience, resembled wrestling matches: You circled your target and sought openings. Does she shop? Does she stay on the move? Is she a homebody? Any family? Sexual partners? What do you know about her, really?

That said, Sal imagined any wrestling match she might start with Grace would end in a few painful seconds. Sal had seen gangland bruisers on PCP drop easier than that woman. So maybe the analogy broke down. Though, to be fair, she wasn't having much more luck tracking Grace than she would have had wrestling her.

Start with facts: Grace likes books. She speaks more languages than anyone should. She fights. She's on time everywhere, and throws shade when other people aren't. Which might suggest a military background but didn't answer the question of where she lived, and anyway, if you relied too much on guesswork, you fell into the old Sherlock Holmes signal-to-noise trap. Did the mailman forget to shave because he was stressed, or because he lost his razor, or because the razor broke? That mud on the bartender's trouser cuff—really from East London, where it rained at four p.m.? Or maybe the hose out back of the bar was leaking, and he walked through a puddle while taking out the trash.

Grace rode an orange Vespa. Fine, so did half of Rome. She dressed well, understated clean-line fashion sans visible labels. Simple haircut. She never drank as far as Sal saw, but then they'd been on mission most of the time they'd spent together—no sense hunting AA meetings in the Rome metro area.

The brawling was a lead, at least. Grace trained with Liam sometimes, before and after missions, but Liam, when Sal asked him on the sly, didn't know if Grace had other sparring partners. Grace's style wasn't exactly a style at all—hard strikes and bone breaks, throwing her whole weight to snap a joint or sweep a limb, more ferocity than technique. It looked like a hot, vicious mess, with Grace playing the part of *vicious* and the other guy in the leading role of *mess*. Sal spent a week sweeping MMA and boxing gyms, playing innocent. "I'm trying to get my brother's girlfriend a birthday present, like lessons or a free month or something, and I know she trains, but I don't know if she trains here. Chinese woman, about so tall, sharp jaw, dark hair, bob cut, fights angry?" Half the gym attendants segued immediately into hitting on Sal before confessing ignorance; the other half just shook their heads and shrugged. A woman at a boxing gym said she knew most of the fighters in the area, and unless Sal meant Sandy Huang, who was a six-foot heavyweight with a shaved head, the description didn't sound familiar.

Thanks, but no such luck.

Sal visited the clinic where her brother lay comatose and sat beside Perry's bed for hours, watching him, until the attending nurse left to check on a file he hadn't received. She slid into the man's chair—his screen saver wasn't even password protected; Liam would have had a fit—and keyed as best she could through nasty yellow-black DOSesque prompts until she found a search function. "Chen" produced a few hundred hits. "Chen, Grace": zero. Did she use her Chinese name on records? Sal checked her own history—records of treatment and a tag masking her as a part of Team Three. Searching for Team Three members yielded a list of twenty names, most marked dead or retired. Menchú. Liam. Asanti. Sal. No Grace. No Chens on the entire list.

Somehow, in spite of all the getting hurt she did, Grace had never been patched up. Or if she had, there was no record of it here. Was there a separate Vatican clinic for people whose job boiled down to hitting demons very hard in the face? But no—Sal had seen Team One heavies lined up in this very waiting room after a mission. Could Grace's file be sealed? Maybe, but sealed against clinic personnel? And if Grace's history *were* sealed, why wouldn't Sal's be too? They took all the same missions together. Unless Grace was some sort of secret Vatican assassin or something—but if so, why would she be with Team Three? And wouldn't there have been at least one mission where Grace couldn't come? Three seemed to be her permanent assignment.

The nurse cleared his throat, and Sal closed the search. "I'm so sorry; I couldn't get any reception down here, and I'm waiting on an e-mail." She showed him her phone.

"You can maybe switch from airplane mode."

"Oh. Jesus. I mean, God, ah, this is pretty embarrassing."

So: no gym, no medical record. Grace had to be paid somehow, but the Vatican wouldn't just hand Sal its payroll data. She walked back the long way to the Archives, over marble tile and under ceilings painted by Renaissance masters who probably expected the people passing beneath them would have more elevated thoughts than how they could break into their coworker's apartment.

Sorry, Michelangelo.

Then again, she'd read Machiavelli. What was it Asanti kept saying? *Plus, the mum chose?*

"*Plus ça change, plus c'est la même chose,*" Asanti offered when she asked. Sal slumped in Liam's desk chair and stared up into the Archives' vaulted ceiling. Asanti adjusted her jeweler's lamp and the metal armature that held the magnifying glass above the papyrus on her desk. "May I ask why?"

"It was on my mind," Sal said.

Asanti touched a button on the lamp. The light turned ultraviolet, and her nails fluoresced. "Have you ever wondered," she asked, "if there might be more than one history of the world?"

"Not exactly." Sal kicked her legs up on the desk, leaned back, and examined the detritus of Liam's past. "I mean, I guess there are lots of history books."

"Not what I meant," Asanti said. "The conceptual apparatus we deploy to construct world history from the texts to which we have access, and I use that term loosely, of course . . ."

"Of course."

". . . assumes that present conditions also applied in the past. You can see traces of this throughout Shakespeare: Romans throw caps in the air and discuss their hose, as if they wore seventeenth-century English fashion rather than togas."

"But we know they didn't." Sal excavated the desk: interlaced pop-science magazines, an Italian *Maxim*, a printout of *2600*. "Don't we?"

"Certainly. But given what else *we* know"—Asanti adjusted the magnifying glass—"about magic and the occult, it seems likely that the mystical water level, to use Father Menchú's delightful analogy, has risen and fallen before our time. Events once commonplace are impossible these days. But the human mind does not, as we've seen, admit of discontinuities. Kant understood: For experience to function, we require an unbroken and uniform stream of time, even if the noumenal world remains beyond our grasp."

"Uh-huh." Liam had dog-eared his *2600* printout; Sal flipped through but couldn't make sense of the circuit diagrams or the politics.

"So when the water level sinks, we paper over Camelot and the Yellow Emperor, Prester John and Shambhala and Ravana's kingdom in Sri Lanka."

Sal pushed the magazines to one side and saw, soot-stained and golden, Grace's copy of *Middlemarch*. "Does it matter?"

"If nothing else, it lends some sense to *Buffy*. All those eons of demon kings in Giles's books, the monster empires nobody else knows about, which never manifest in the archaeological record: We papered them over."

"I meant does it matter for our work?"

"Obviously the theory has practical applications as well," Asanti said. "But criticism is its own reward."

Sal raised *Middlemarch* like a surrender flag. "Grace left her book."

"She'll pick it up before the next mission. She doesn't read, save on assignment."

"She reads fast, then."

"Poor girl would save a great deal of money if she just checked them out of the library. It's not as though we don't have the best-stocked collection in the world."

"Maybe Grace doesn't like—" Sal pointed to Asanti's papyrus.

"Fifth-dynasty scorpion-charmers' manual. Egyptian."

"Sounds like a page-turner."

"It's a scroll. It doesn't have pages."

"You know what I mean."

"We have a complete edition of *The Mystery of Edwin Drood* in subsection A, if you want a thriller."

Sal frowned. "Where does Grace get the books, then?"

"Buys them."

"She doesn't strike me as the type to browse."

"Why do you ask?"

"Curious, I guess." Sal took her feet off Liam's desk, shook the mouse, and logged in as RIVAL DOG. Grace used a flip phone; she scorned e-mail. Impossible as it seemed, Sal doubted the woman owned a computer. And Liam had set his machine up for guests before Sal joined the team. In which case, who was using it?

Browser history. Scroll down. Bookseller website. Free delivery. Login. Sal typed *G*, waited. Nothing. Delete. *C* instead. Told herself not to hold her breath.

Autocomplete, ever helpful, supplied *chen-dot-grace-at*, with a line of bullets for the password. Nice. Order history. Shipping address.

Print.

Two hours later Sal stood on a street corner staring up at Saint Catherine's Convent. Gargoyles on the corners, heavy drapes on the windows, a guard at the gate, and friendly-looking German shepherds pacing the yard. And there, on the fourth floor, Grace's room.

At least this wouldn't be easy. Sal hated easy.

SOMEWHERE. THEN.

Chen Juan woke on a bed of straw, tasting dust and wax. She sat up sharply, with a cry; her body curled into a ball, knees near her chin, arms raised. The skin of her arms looked like skin. She wasn't burned. She could breathe. She *was*—but there had been a span of time where she wasn't.

Sunlight streamed through a narrow window. She stood. What she'd taken for a bed was in fact a crate, packed with straw, now open. She wore a shirt and slacks of loose cotton. Her feet were bare, and the floor beneath them stone.

Outside the window, tile roofs rose and fell like the surface of the sea in high wind, each roof's corner capped by a dragon. The window faced south and was high enough that she could see over the thick red walls to the gate across Tiananmen Square.

She stood in the former Imperial Palace. Central had called her home.

"Welcome back," said a familiar voice behind her. "Would you like some tea? You must be thirsty."

She turned quickly, already smiling. "Wujing!"

He sat beside a low table and looked thinner than she remembered—his face drawn, but less grievously injured than she had feared. Burn scars rippled his cheeks and forehead, but they had healed well. Aside from those he looked the same as ever. No, she decided. Not the same. He seemed more himself.

"I'm glad to see you." He sounded tired.

Four men in army uniforms stood behind him. She didn't know them, but they weren't important. Beside Wujing stood a thick candle in a bone holder. She tensed when she saw it, but the fire burned low.

"Why is that candle lit?"

"Chen Juan," he said. "Sit down, please."

"We got him?"

"We got him. Have some tea."

She sat and drank. The army men did not move. They might have been carvings. "I don't understand."

"You were hurt," he said.

She read his face. "Hurt badly, I suppose."

"Yes."

"Burned?"

"There were burns, but they've healed."

"How's Ahsan?"

"Fine," he said. "Blind in one eye now. We brought you back to Central, and the scholars have been working on you ever since."

The tea tasted of smoke and time. "Why did you bring the candle? It seems ghoulish."

"The candle." He tasted the word. "The candle is part of the problem, and the solution."

"What do you mean?"

"Chen Juan," he said, and leaned forward. Candlelight and sun glinted off the gray at his temples, which had not been there yesterday. "Please, listen to me."

"No." But she did not move. She sat as still as the army men stood.

"Antopov's notes show that he thought his immortality would be conferred by a baptism of fire. You ran into his circle. You drank the wax. And then you seized his fire and finished the ritual."

She shook her head. She wanted to say something, but she had no words.

"When you snuffed the candle out, the wax stopped moving, as if the flame was all that kept it liquid. Antopov fell, like a statue. And you just stood there."

"How long?" she said. The words were hollow. They must have been hollow: He didn't seem to have heard them.

"We thought it was the wax. We scraped it off, but you didn't wake. Your wounds healed. Your skin was still skin—not like his. But you held still. The scholars think he brought a supply of the final product when he fled Mongolia, an imperfect mixture. He used it to make the candle. It kept him young, while it burned. If he finished the ritual, if he melted those girls, maybe the candle wax wouldn't run, or maybe there would just be more candle. We don't know. But you took the flame from him. The candle's yours now. When we light it, you start to breathe. And you wake up. So do the wax things, of course, but you're the keystone."

Her hand shook. She set down the teacup before she dropped it. "How long?" He wilted beneath her gaze.

He passed her his newspaper. The date on the front page read 1933.

"Five years."

He nodded.

"You kept me under for five years."

She stood. The army men started forward. She glared at them, and they stopped. Fire flowed through her heart instead of blood, bloomed in her lungs instead of breath.

Wujing's eyes were wet. "I'm sorry," he said. "I didn't want to risk it. To risk you. Each drop from that candle is a day you won't get back."

"Every day is one we won't get back."

"But yours are more limited than most," he said. "We've tried to save you, all these years. But we haven't learned how."

"You should have asked me."

"Perhaps." He reclaimed the newspaper and folded it. "Perhaps I couldn't bear to."

Nineteen thirty-three. "What did I miss?"

"Too much. The Japanese invaded. Their monsters came with them. The Bureau of Official Secrets has been busy. I've barely slept in months."

"I can help," she said. "Now that I'm awake again."

He set down the newspaper. "That's not why we're talking."

She should not have listened. She did not want to listen.

"The Japanese threaten to invade Beiping. To protect the Palace Museum, we will evacuate it south, by rail. That's the cover story. In fact, we're moving the entire Bureau collection. For the next few years our efforts will be dedicated to the war, to preventing outbreaks and the fall of cities. I've been commanded"— a word he twisted sour—"to halt research and development efforts not directly tied to the war effort. I wanted to wake you and tell you. It may be a long time before we speak again."

"How long?" Strange that her voice could sound so level. The candle flame jumped beside him. "Five more years? Ten? You'll leave me in a damn crate until everyone I know is old and dead, just to give me a chance?"

He flinched, but did not look away. She wondered if she could have done the same, if their situations were reversed. "As long as it takes," he said. "We won't give up."

She ran.

Four soldiers stood between Chen Juan and the door, but they weren't ready. They must have expected her to bolt earlier; her initial confusion had calmed them. So when she vaulted over the table and kicked the largest soldier in the throat, the others seemed to move in slow motion.

She hit one in the face before he could raise his arm to block. She had never moved this fast; she had never been this strong. She kicked his knee. Arms slipped around her from behind, began to tighten, but she ducked and slammed her elbow into the crotch of the man who'd tried to grapple her.

The room filled with brilliant light: the candle flame a foot high now and blazing as wax rolled down its sides. Wujing revolved, slowly as a planet, and raised the newspaper. Before she could reach him, he swatted out the flame.

She was not strong enough to move her arms. She was not fierce enough to move her feet. She stood like a diorama figure. Color ebbed from the world's edges, and the drain proceeded in. Wujing raised his hand. The army men lifted her like a statue. They straightened her arms and legs. They placed her, gently, on the straw. One of them bled from his mouth and from the nose she'd broken.

"I'm sorry," Wujing said.

She fought to open her eyes, but he closed them. She heard a lid settle against the crate, and then a hammer fell, and time became a stretch of not.

4.

ROME. NOW.

Night in Rome is never quiet, nor precisely dark, but there are shadows. At nine thirty, the front-gate guard of Saint Catherine's changed. The newcomer started her shift with a walk through the garden by flashlight, then released the dogs and returned to the watchhouse to read a romance novel thin enough that she could hide it under a newspaper if anyone came by.

The German shepherds prowled among trailing vines and between rose bushes. The larger of the pair pissed decorously on the lawn.

A dark missile arced over the fence, landed with a thud, and lay still. The larger dog advanced, curious. Whatever this was, it smelled delicious. Tasted delicious too—chewy, good texture, nice marbling of fat. The smaller dog approached; Dog the First growled, less viciously than she intended. In fact, she felt less driven to do much of anything, save sleep.

The second dog finished the steak before he noticed the first was lying down. He didn't think much as a rule, especially when steak was involved. He certainly didn't think much for an hour after this particular meal.

When both dogs lay dreaming, a gray-clad figure climbed the fence in three pulls, vaulted over, landed bent-kneed on the grass, and ran toward the convent's back door. The shadow knelt behind a bush, and when she stood a few minutes later, she wore a black robe and a rumpled wimple.

One advantage of working in the Vatican, Sal considered, was that nuns' habits weren't difficult to find. She reached for the lockpicks in her pocket, then decided to try the door first. It was unlocked.

Inside, the convent didn't look much different from any other building: narrow halls, yellowed walls, arched brick ceiling. She brushed down the hall at a dignified but swift pace until she reached the stairs.

Sal saw nobody on the first floor, nobody on the second. Maybe there was some sort of curfew? Was she supposed to be praying somewhere? Should she worry about cameras? But four nuns lingered in a sitting room on the third floor, talking quietly in Italian and drinking wine. As Sal climbed, she heard an old woman laugh.

The fourth floor was empty again; even the hallway lights were dim. Sal treaded lightly, counting apartment numbers: 416, 417. Behind her, a door opened, then closed again.

Sal forced her heart to beat. She wasn't cut out for breaking and entering. Her career had focused more on the other side of the crime.

She tried Grace's door.

Locked, of course.

Use for the lockpicks after all. Not that she could afford to be seen kneeling in front of Grace's door, raking pins. But she'd come this far. She'd already violated Grace's privacy, not to mention a number of laws—all for nothing if she left now.

Sunk-cost fallacy, Perry would have called that. But if you'd sunk your costs already, you might as well dive to get them.

Sal knelt. She'd learned this from Perry too. He used to test himself against locks in the backyard, asked her to time him. He never offered to let her try; it didn't even occur to him to challenge her, so of course she learned. Beat him half the time, once she got good enough, at which point he stopped testing her. But she still practiced.

Click.

Sal wrapped her hand in the robe, opened the door, and stepped inside.

In a room Sal had never seen, a small red light began to blink.

SOMEWHERE ELSE. THEN.

Thick, stifling, humid air filled Chen Juan's nose and mouth and throat and lungs. She inhaled dust, coughed, shook. Her forehead struck wood. Darkness and straw pressed close around her. She lay alone in black. She could not move. She screamed. The sound she produced was a croak, a roar, not at all the sound a human voice might make.

Somewhere, a man cursed.

Nightmares wormed in her head, enormous gulfs of time filled with humiliating teeth and shredded skin, reflection after reflection after reflection of flame. She cried out again with her broken voice.

The man replied—or spoke, anyway—beyond the dark that was Chen Juan's bounded world. There was an outside. She wasn't buried. She wasn't trapped. She was hot, so deathly hot, and the air lay heavy on her so she could hardly breathe. When she did breathe, she tasted straw and funk and mold.

But there was an outside. The man waited there. Her jailer. Wujing's minion. Wujing who had visited her in darkness—or had he? Had she only imagined him? Wujing whose voice and whose touch on her eyelids had grown roots in her sleep.

She struck the crate lid with her forehead.

Dust and splinters rained onto her face. Blood trickled down her nose.

She could not hit hard enough, bound like this. Gravity told her stories: She lay in a long crate, tilted back. Too shallow for her to generate much power. But there was room enough to slide her arms over her body—her shirt tore even at such light contact—so both palms pressed against the lid.

Drawing breath hurt in this heat. She felt like she was swimming in herself. But she pressed. She growled. She roared, and her roar echoed tinnily. She remembered Wujing, and the casual flick with which he'd swatted out her flame.

She was awake again, so someone must have broken the spell, or lit the candle. If they knew what she was, they would have snuffed the flame already. So they did not know. Which meant—what? Japanese, maybe? Had the train from the museum been captured, leaving the Bureau's precious collection in strangers' hands? Wujing's collection, in which she took central billing? Goddamned girl in the goddamned crate?

Not again. Not anymore.

She pressed.

Fire flickered beneath her skin, like a ghost's touch. She remembered that feeling from the moment of her betrayal.

Let the candle burn. Let it burn me free.

Nails cracked. Rotten timbers gave. And there was light such as she had not seen in . . . *How long?*

She didn't know, didn't care. She stepped barefoot from the crate. Dust covered her. Ragged, rotten clothes hung from her body.

She stood on a hot metal floor covered with broken wood. The room was not a room at all, but a long, corrugated metal box, about nine feet tall and nine feet wide, cluttered with crates and junk. Light entered through a ragged gash in the box's roof, and cast columns in dust-laden air. Above, she saw all the greens of a jade carver's workshop and more, bright and emerald and pastel, green so deep it turned blue, green sharp as knives, featherlight green, green that fell heavy as an anvil on the eye. Behind all that, the sun shone.

"¿Qué?"

The man. She had not imagined him. She lowered her gaze from the hole in the roof.

There was a narrow hall down the center of the metal box, and he stood at the far end, eyes wide, one hand out as if to ward off a blow. He wore a sweat-stained black shirt and a Catholic priest's collar; his skin was dark and his cheekbones high and he was not Japanese. Mexican, maybe? And he was beautiful.

The candle burned between them, on its stand of bone.

She had never learned Spanish. "Hello," she tried in Chinese. She stepped forward. Her feet held. He did not run for the candle. He did not seem to understand. She tried a different Chinese dialect, then Japanese. Russian. He looked confused. "Hello," she tried again, in English.

That, he got. "Hello." He licked his lips. "Who are you?"

"Grace." She continued her slow advance, and he his retreat. She reached the candle and placed a hand on the wax to steady herself. "What's your name?"

"I am Arturo," he said. His tongue darted pink between his lips. She'd seen that expression before. She knew how it felt on her own face. This was a man out of his depth, groping for some procedure to apply. "Father Arturo Menchú."

"Father." She laughed. He was her age, maybe younger. "Did Wujing send you?"

He shook his head. "I do not know that name. The Societas Librorum Occultorum sent me."

Chen blinked. "The Catholic Bureau. You people aren't allowed in China."

"You're not in China," he said. "This is Guatemala. We traced the shipping container from its last port of call in Puerto Vallarta."

Wujing had sent her across an ocean. How bad had the war gone, anyway?

She knew she had not yet asked the only important question. She had let the moment carry her: the young priest, the hole, the layers of dancing green, the sunlight on her skin, the weight of the air worse even than August in Guangzhou, like breathing through blankets last used to dry a hairy, smelly dog after a swim in a muddy river. She did not want to ask the only important question, because once she did, the answer would never be anything but what it was.

"What year is it?"

"I don't understand."

He did. He just wasn't letting himself know he understood. "The year. The date. What is it?" She tried not to speak too tensely. She did not want to scare him.

"July fourteenth," he said, "1985."

She doubled over.

She hadn't thought this could happen in real life: the shortness of breath, the sickness of realization. It did in books, of course, and actors faked it on the stage. But her lungs would not fill. She could not think. The world narrowed to a point.

"Grace," the priest said. "Are you okay?"

No, she thought. If not for her grip on the candle she would have fallen. She looked at him through the strands of hair that fell across her face. *I am not okay. I will never be okay again.*

Fortunately, at that moment, the crates behind Arturo exploded, and a wax lion tackled him, and for a few seconds her world returned to normal.

ROME. NOW.

Sal entered Grace's small apartment and closed the door behind her. The lights were out. She didn't turn them on. She slipped off habit and wimple and hung them on the coatrack by the door, by the jacket Grace had worn to Spain. Right room, at least. She recognized most of the shoes in the shoe rack, too.

There was a small kitchenette to the right of the entrance, just large enough to turn around in and so neatly kept Sal doubted Grace used it much. She had only seen kitchens that clean in movies.

Past the kitchenette, a narrow, sparsely furnished sitting room overlooked the street. An Escher print hung on the wall; aside from that, the only decoration Sal noticed was a photo calendar, each month featuring a new photo of a kitten in mortal danger. Sal had heard people describe this sort of thing as motivational. Maybe it was supposed to motivate you to keep kittens away from calendar designers. This month, Grace had marked off three days. The month previous, two.

Other than that, the room held a single plush chair and a nearly empty bookcase—far too empty for someone who read as much as Grace. Maybe she donated the books when she was done. Sal slid Grace's *Middlemarch* out of her jacket pocket, pondered shelving it and leaving, but decided that would be too creepy.

Every instinct she'd ever possessed, and some she hadn't, screamed: *Go*. She had come to talk with Grace, but the gulf between showing up at a troubled coworker's doorstep unannounced with an apology and breaking into said coworker's apartment to root through her personal effects was—to put it mildly—broad. It was the kind of gap into which people fell screaming.

So of course she opened the bedroom door.

And, because she was so assiduously suppressing her other instincts, Sal also squashed the urge to curse.

Grace lay on her bed.

She wore green pajamas and slept with arms crossed over her chest like Dracula in movies when he was dead.

Sal froze. Running would make more noise than simply backing up, turning around, and leaving. So long as she hadn't woken Grace already. So she waited.

Grace didn't move.

That was good, Sal thought at first.

Grace didn't move some more.

Nor did she breathe.

No one was that heavy a sleeper.

"Grace?" Sal whispered. After that yielded no response, she tried again: "Grace?"

Nothing.

Was she—no, that wasn't possible. People died, sure, all the time—Sal had seen it—people in good health, people who hit the gym, people with eight-pack abs who could bench 430: Blood vessels just burst in their brain at three in the morning and so much for the muscle man. But they didn't go peacefully. They screamed. Their faces twisted. They curled around their stomach in pain as their appendix split. And after they died, they stank. Bowels emptied as muscles slacked.

They didn't arrange their arms in the goddamned Dracula position.

She walked to Grace's bedside. Took her arm. Shook her. "Grace. Dammit, come on, Grace, wake up." Her skin was—not cold, not exactly, but cool to the touch, and more stiff than skin should be. Sal tapped Grace's cheek with the palm of her hand. It was smooth and round, and like the skin of the other woman's wrist it yielded less than Sal thought it should. "Grace? Jesus Christ, Grace, are you there?"

No answer.

Magic. Someone must have gotten to Grace somehow. On the last mission, maybe? A bit of delayed vengeance, courtesy of the Hand? One more Perry for the clinic beds?

No. Grace—there, around her neck, she wore a silver cross without a trace of tarnish. It felt hot to Sal's touch, electric like silver always felt these days, but there weren't any demons at work. She thought. Unless they could get around the silver somehow. Which perhaps they could.

Fuck.

She glanced around the room. All the decoration that wasn't in the sitting room was here: photos covered the wall, pictures of Team Three, large framed shots of a Chinese city Sal didn't recognize, more of an ambiguously European waterfront. Prints of paintings of sunflowers. A Turkish tapestry tumbled down one wall, all geometry and gold thread. Sculptures lounged on shelves.

And beside Grace's bed hung a small sign printed on thick paper in the woman's blocky hand: IN CASE OF EMERGENCY, LIGHT CANDLE.

Beneath the sign stood a thick white candle on a stand made of what looked like a yellowed, fine-grained wood. A matchbook rested on the bedside table.

If Grace had been attacked, this certainly qualified as an

emergency. But what could lighting the candle do? Summon Menchú? Grace scorned magic. Maybe the candle had a special smell, or something, that would wake her?

Don't think too much. Thinking too much was how you got shot. Grace was out. This wasn't natural sleep. It wasn't meditation or anything like that. She didn't have a pulse, for Christ's sake. *In case of emergency—*

Sal struck a match and lit the candle. The curled black wick took flame grudgingly. Sal cradled the ember so a draft wouldn't blow it out. Brightening, the flame warmed her hand. It seemed to have a presence beyond the heat, as if she held a small bird. She shook out the match.

Nothing happened. Of course. That's what came of spending your days dealing with freaky magic. You started to think the world was full of freaky magic, when in fact it was mostly candles.

She licked her fingers and reached to pinch off the flame.

At which point something struck her fast and hard in the face.

GUATEMALA. THEN.

When the fires died, Chen Juan and the priest lay on the ground outside the smoldering wreckage of the container, with the candle upright between them. Rivers of wax ran from the wrecked metal box. Trees towered overhead. Sun through layers of green laid layers of shadow on the earth, and on their bodies.

Chen Juan laughed so hard tears came to her eyes.

"I can't believe," Arturo said. "I can't— I mean. They almost had me. There were so many of them."

"Just like Wujing," she said. "Ship all the wax things in one box to make the bookkeeping easier. He never did like . . . ," she said when she stopped laughing, before she started again. "He never did like filling out forms."

Arturo rolled over on his side to face her. His eyes were deep and liquid brown. A wax burn ran down his temple to his cheek.

"You should have a doctor look at that," she said.

"You're not wax."

"I'm not," she said. "I am not a thing, either. But the candle flame is my life. As long as it burns, I'm awake. And when it stops—" She snapped her fingers.

"When did you go to sleep? Where?"

She liked him for that: *sleep*. Not, *When did they put you in that box?* "China. In 1933."

"I'm so sorry."

"I should go," she said, and rolled to her feet and lifted the candle. Antopov couldn't have come up with a more portable means of eternal life, of course. This must have been the old man's compromise position. Left to his own devices he likely would have built something enormous with a dome on top.

"Don't."

"I have to get back."

"Where?" he asked. She didn't have an answer. "China's changed a lot in fifty years," he said. "The place you left isn't there anymore." He sat up, stood up, reached for her.

"I can't." She recoiled, clutching the candle. "No. If they're gone, then I'll do—something. This candle could last years, if I don't push it. I won't be the first person in the world who died young."

"We can help you. What you did in there—I've never seen anyone move like that before. You could work with the Society. We have resources. We could take care of you while you look for a cure."

"Study me, you mean, like a rat in a maze. The last time I heard that was from the man who put me in that crate."

"No!" That word's violence convinced her: the violence, and his sweat, and his fear. She'd seen men fake sincerity before. When faking, they did not look so afraid. "Grace, no. Look. All the Society does is search for things. One of those things might free you. And if we don't find what we're looking for—at least you can help. You saved my life. You could save the world."

A bird sang high up in the shaggy-barked trees, taller and thicker than any trees she'd seen before. She was far from home.

"You're fooling yourself," she said. "I know how they made this candle. We can't make another. There's no hope."

"There always is."

"You'll have to believe for both of us," she said.

"I will."

ROME. NOW.

Sal's skull bounced off Grace's bedroom wall. Something struck her in the stomach at high velocity, and she doubled over, breathing black. *Knee,* she thought, in the second before her legs swept out from under her and she struck the carpet heavy and limp as a sandbag. A hand, a human hand, thank Whoever for small favors, grabbed her throat, and even as Sal tried to raise her guard, her eyes focused through the stars on a familiar-looking fist—and beside that fist, on an even more familiar face fixed in an equally familiar expression of rage.

"Grace," she gasped with the last of her breath. "Hi."

The other woman's face glowed in firelight: The candle had

flared when she moved, and now it crouched again. *"Nǐ zài zhèlǐ gànshénme ne?"*

The tension around Sal's neck relaxed to let her inhale. "I'm sorry." Sal pointed to the carpet, to the fallen, soot-stained *Middlemarch.* "I don't speak . . . I mean. I brought your book."

"What the *hell* are you doing here? Did Arturo send you?"

"No. I came on my own."

"You had no right."

"I wanted to apologize. Face to face." It sounded so shallow. "I fucked up."

"Yes." Grace's fist opened. She sat back on her thighs, on Sal's stomach, then stood. "I almost hurt you."

"Almost?" Sal rubbed the back of her head. Grace didn't offer her a hand. She rose slowly, with the aid of the wall.

The candle flame danced, twinned, in Grace's eyes. "Get out of here."

And then Sal understood, with the old detective's trick. The problem opened in her mind like a lock at the turning of its key. The calendar, only a few days crossed off each month. The books on assignment, and none at home. No food in the kitchen. No time outside work. No gym, no social life. The photo she'd seen in Menchú's apartment, the father looking young and Grace looking just the same. "It's you," she said. "You're in the candle, somehow." Behind her, on the bedroom wall, all those Society photos: year after year, and Grace unchanged.

"I told you to leave. Do it. Don't tell anyone about this. And we'll both forget you were ever here."

Sal stared at her. *You can't hide this,* she wanted to say, to scream. *Tell me everything. I want to know.*

And that was the heart of it, laid bare. She hadn't come here for Grace, or for the team. She'd come here for herself, not caring what damage she might cause.

"I'm sorry," she said, and meant it this time. The night pressed against the window. "I was selfish. Back with the bugs, and for a long time now. I didn't want to let those people die, so I endangered all of us, and the mission. And here—I didn't have a right to see any of this. I betrayed you because I was hurting, and because I didn't think. Maybe I'll earn your trust someday. For now, I'll go."

She walked past Grace into the barren sitting room and headed for the door.

"You asked what I knew about getting hurt," Grace said. Sal stopped moving. "There's your answer. My friends dead. My life stolen. No escape. And I got out light, by most standards. I only lost everything."

A Vespa sped past on the street outside and far below.

"I didn't know," Sal said.

"Of course not. Everything's about you, in the end." Her voice was a wire garrote, sharp and tight. But when she spoke again, it softened. "We all think it is, most of the time."

"I'm so sorry."

"You should be."

"I'll leave."

"You shouldn't have come. But you might as well stay." She sounded raw. "Better to tell it all at once."

"When did all this happen?" Sal asked.

"A long time ago."

5.

They built a system that worked.

It was easier than Grace expected. She slept most of the time. She learned to think of it as sleeping. He woke her every week without fail, and most of the time she snuffed the fire out again. When the sphere glowed, when duty called, she went. They learned. She fought. They brought what they discovered home.

Father Hunter studied the books and artifacts they found. They collected spent wax and recast it, but those candles did not wake Grace. They carved, at her insistence, a piece of wax from the candle itself and reshaped it into a new, smaller candle—that one would wake her, but it burned faster. The magic did not admit bargains or tricks. No matter how Father Hunter searched, a cure remained outside his grasp.

And when Father Hunter aged, and left, and Asanti became archivist, she tried too, and charted more dead ends.

Grace killed monsters whose gazes drove men mad. Grace tossed a demon over Niagara Falls, and followed it down. Grace wrestled with an angel—or something that claimed to be one. She healed fast, and if she made the candle burn brighter she could move at speeds no human being could match. She ran down a car once, because she had to. When he saw how much of the candle that burned, Arturo asked her to promise never to do it again. That was the first time they fought.

She saved the world.

And every time she woke, the world was older.

The young priest grew scars and a mustache to cover them. Gray colonized his hair, and pain those beautiful eyes.

The missions came more often. In the eighties they needed her once every few months at most. She took vacations, then. Now the missions came month by month. Week by week, sometimes.

And then they met Sal.

NOW.

"Christ," Sal said, when she finished the story.

"Language, please," Grace replied, with a little smile that was still more than Sal had ever seen her offer—easier, and more sad. "I'm an old-fashioned lady." The teakettle screamed, and she poured two cups.

"No one told me."

"Of course not. Even Liam doesn't know. I grew tired of explaining to each new teammate—of being everyone's problem."

"I'm so sorry."

"You said that already," Grace answered. "Can we leave it? I have a condition. Many people do. I manage mine." Steam rose off the tea. "Talking about it makes things hard. People want to fix me. Save me. It doesn't help. Better to be alone."

Sal took the tea and sipped and hissed as the water scalded her tongue. "I've been running around here thinking it was all just me—that I was the one on the outside of everything, of my old life and my new one." She laughed into the steam. "'Always on the outside of whatever side there was.' You ever hear that Dylan song?"

"No."

"You should."

"I'll make time," Grace said.

"I guess what I'm trying to say is, if you ever need someone to be alone with, I'm here. We could, like, go to a movie sometime."

Grace laughed—another first.

"Stupid idea, I guess." Sal set *Middlemarch* down on the counter. "I'm sorry I woke you."

Grace caught Sal's hand before she could withdraw. Her grip was firm and warm. "I'm not."

Footsteps ran down the hall outside. Grace froze.

A key rasped in the lock. The door burst open, revealing Father Menchú. "Grace!"

Sweat shone on his brow. His chest heaved. Sal had never seen him quite so scared before—or, as he processed the scene, so confused. "Sal. Did you do this? You have to get out of here. There's a security team on the way—"

"Don't worry about it, Arturo," Grace said. "I called them off. Sal's here as my guest."

Menchú closed his mouth, but his brow didn't smooth.

Grace waved *Middlemarch* at him. "She came to return my book."

The father looked skeptical.

"She knows, Arturo. And I'm glad. I've been in a dark place. In the end, that's just another sort of wasting time." She finished her tea. "Go. I don't mind a party, but I need my rest."

Sal walked downstairs with Menchú in silence and sat beside him as he drove through a labyrinth of Roman roads.

"You've known her thirty years," Sal said, after they'd been silent in the car for too long.

"And she's known me three," he replied. "You, she's known a handful of weeks. Trust takes time."

They passed beneath a high arch. The wall to Sal's left was built of ruined ages: crumbled marble palaces, medieval plaster, and stolen columns.

"Are you doing this for her?" she asked. "To heal her?"

He signaled right, then turned. "Are you doing this for Perry?"

She remembered the candle and the small new smile and the laugh and the warmth of Grace's hand. She didn't have to say anything. She said: "Not just for Perry."

And then the night was roads, and Rome.

EPISODE
8

UNDER MY SKIN

MUR LAFFERTY

1.

Sal had seen Liam's tattoos many times, but before sex she usually had other things on her mind, and afterward they either dozed off in the dark or one or the other of them left. This particular encounter, starting with apologies and ending up in bed, took place in the afternoon, without other demands on their time. A thread of sunlight snaked over his torso, and Sal got up to open the curtains.

Liam shielded his face and winced. "What are you doing?"

Sal flopped onto the bed and propped herself on her elbows to study his ink, lit in delicious detail by the afternoon sun, like smoke signals from someone trapped deep within him.

She traced her finger along his ribs, making him twitch. Wispy smoke trailed up Liam's flank from a brassy lamp tattooed on his hip. "Why do you have Aladdin's lamp down here when the rest of you's covered in . . . Catholic stuff?"

"That's a thurible. An incense burner."

Sal frowned, tracing the smoke over his ribs and chest, keeping her finger on him even as he squirmed. "But all your other ink's religious."

Liam caught her hand in his and kissed her fingers. "That tickles," he said, pressing her palm against his chest. She could feel his heart beating. "Hang on. You work at the Vatican, but you don't know what a thurible is?"

"Have you ever seen me at mass? I'm still very much not Catholic, in case you forgot." She freed her hand and poked him in the thurible. "So what is it? I'm guessing a genie doesn't live there."

"The priest burns incense in the thing, swings it around, and makes the sign of the cross. It's used in blessings, consecrations, and the like."

"Oh," Sal said. "And I guess that's a rosary?" The beads tattooed on his neck and chest were red and black and grouped in irregular numbers. At the end, a detailed crucifix was inked over his sternum.

"I got that one after a job where it would have been useful to have a rosary along, and I didn't. Now I'm never without one."

"Did you get Menchú to bless the tattoo gun or something?" Sal asked, laughing.

Liam looked very serious. "Every time. It's like holy water, but for ink." He touched the backs of his hands, first the left and then the right. Tiny crude crosses occupied the knuckles where many tattoo enthusiasts put letters. The back of his left hand sported a more detailed cross, while the right had three spirals bundled together. "Except for these. I got these before joining the Society."

Sal examined his other tattoos, from the lamb on his left bicep and the lion on his right to the Greek character on his forearm. More and more Christian imagery. "Why so many? You ink your faith all over you, but you don't seem the devout type day-to-day." She tweaked his nipple.

Liam sat up, removing her hand from his chest. He examined his own tattoos as if he hadn't looked at them in a while. "They're reminders. Protection."

"You think God will protect you more with seven tattoos than six?"

"Leave it," Liam said, looking away.

"Why?"

"These are important to me, and you're laughing at them."

"I just wondered if the number mattered," Sal said. "I didn't realize you took it so seriously."

"Sure, I cover myself with ink on a dare," he snapped.

"And then you have dirty premarital sex with a colleague."

Liam's eyes narrowed. "Are you calling me a hypocrite?"

"I just don't understand. The Church isn't really into this sort of thing." She waved her hands, encompassing his room in general and their naked, postcoital state in particular. "As far as I know. You have all this holy ink, like you're armoring yourself, and yet you're fine fucking me. We're not married; we're not even in love. How does that work?"

He looked at her sharply, as if stung. "This is why I don't discuss my faith with you. You don't ask—you've already made up your mind."

"Liam, I don't assume. I don't care, really. I'm just curious. I want to learn more about you, so—" She faltered.

"So what?" he asked, leaning toward her, challenging her. "So we can start 'dating' in between saving the world from demons? So we can fall in love and maybe get to have a tragic moment as one of us dies in the other's arms? How about we plan a wedding and have it interrupted by the Orb telling us Satan's about to take a piss on Buckingham Palace?"

"That's a little over the top—" Sal began, but he didn't let up.

"When Menchú found me, I was *damned*," he said. "I had been corrupted, body and soul. When he saved me, I opened my eyes and saw God's hand in the world. I pledged myself to do his work."

Sal pursed her lips. She hadn't heard him talk like this before, like someone from a fundamentalist documentary. *I've opened a door I shouldn't have.*

"What you don't get," he continued, "is that we aren't normal people who can afford to have normal lives. We're always on call, with a duty more important than any friend or lover or spouse. Since we can't be normal, I let myself peek through the window at real life from time to time. That's why I'm fine with this." He waved his hand at her. They now stood, nude, the bed between them.

The room throbbed with an electricity only sex or a furious exit could ground—and Sal was too angry for sex.

She grabbed her shirt from the chair and looked around for her pants. "Jesus Christ," she said, purposefully swearing. "Like I don't know the stakes. I'm a cop, Liam. I know what it is to wonder if you're going to live to see tomorrow, to know people depend on you. I lived like that for years. Lots of people do, and they fall in love and get married all the time." She paused in the middle of pulling on her shirt. "It's stressful. We deal with life and death. And magic makes our work scarier. But you grab happiness when you can. If you're determined to be unhappy, that's on you, not the job."

She left before he could reply.

She didn't make it to her apartment. She had stopped in her favorite pastry shop to pick up some comfort cannoli when her phone buzzed. She considered ignoring it, not wanting to talk to Liam, but checked it, anyway.

"Hey, Asanti," she said, the knot in her chest loosening.

"Enjoying your day off?"

Sal wondered again whether Asanti knew what was going on with Liam. The archivist had a keen eye—but then, she rarely hinted when she could say something outright. "Just buying some cannoli. What's up?"

"We have some activity that might interest you. In the United States again."

Working with the Society was the first job to give Sal the full-on roller-coaster thrill/dread cocktail. A trip to the United States meant home, burgers and pizza—American pizza, the stuff she grew up eating, with the chewy crust and the molten cheese—and English spoken all the time. And these days it meant Tornado Eaters and demons and demon worshipers. Oh my.

"More storm-eating monsters?" she asked, paying for the cannoli. The woman behind the counter raised an eyebrow, overhearing her. "Creative writing student," Sal said, covering the phone with her hand.

"Not quite," Asanti said. "I'm still looking into the details. But it's definitely coming from Las Vegas."

Sal had never been to Vegas. She put the pastry bag into her purse and pushed the door open. "Sin City? I'd love to see Grace play poker. That woman has no tells."

"I'll tell her you said so," Asanti said, sounding amused. "Go home and get a good night's rest. We're leaving tomorrow. I'll brief you when I have more information."

"You don't need me to come by the Archives or anything?" Sal asked, frowning.

"Not right now. We won't leave you in the dark, Sal; we just need more information. Trust me." She hung up, leaving Sal glaring at her phone in the middle of the sidewalk.

"I'm getting a burger this time, dammit," Sal muttered, and headed home.

2.

al was hanging clothes on the line when she heard a knock on her door.

Liam stood there, smiling awkwardly, wearing a black T-shirt, his leather jacket, and his backpack. He carried a grocery bag under one arm.

"Time to go already?" Sal asked, not moving out of the way to invite him in. "I thought Asanti didn't need us till tomorrow."

"Not quite. I'm here for both work and pleasure."

Sal opened her mouth to say she wasn't in the mood for pleasure, but Liam raised his free hand to stop her.

"Not that kind of pleasure. Asanti wants us to do some research for our trip. And I thought I could cook dinner while we research."

"Because you're hungry," Sal said.

"Because I want to apologize," Liam said patiently.

Sal stepped aside, feeling small for trying to bait him. "What're we having?"

"Bolognese," he said grandly, leading her to the kitchen.

"Really? Not bangers and mushy peas and blood pudding?" Sal asked, following him.

"You can't get good mushy peas this far south. I think it has to do with the climate," he said with a grin. "We work with what we have."

Sal poured wine while he puttered around her kitchen. "I didn't know you cooked," she said, handing him a glass of Shiraz.

"There's a lot you don't know about me," he said. "I started cooking after I woke up."

Sal nodded. "You can trust food you cook yourself."

Liam looked surprised, but nodded. "Exactly."

Sal sat down in a chair to watch him cook. "What do we know about this job?"

Liam judged Sal's kitchen knives one by one, found them all unsatisfactory, produced his own knife from his backpack, and began chopping onions. "You'll love this," he said, focusing on the chopping. "The strange activity is coming from a tattoo parlor in Las Vegas."

Sal took a long drink of wine. "Of course it is."

"It gets weirder," he continued, wiping his eyes with his shirt-sleeve. "Half the problem is recorded and online—or rather, the lead-up is. Turns out our monster's on a tattoo reality show."

Sal held up her hand. "Wait. We have research that doesn't involve dusty books or listening to Menchú and Asanti fight? We can prep with wine and trashy reality TV?" she asked in wonder.

"Exactly," Liam said, reaching into his bag to pull out another bottle of wine and three wrapped butcher packages.

"Good," Sal said. "We're going to need more wine."

"That's for the sauce," Liam said, reaching into the bag again. He handed her a second bottle. "That's for us."

The last thing he pulled from the bag was a loaf of bread. "Freshly baked, but we'll want to warm it up for dinner." He reached for the oven handle, but Sal placed her hand over his and held it there.

"Oven's broken," she said absently. "I'm sure the bread is fine as is."

"Living without an oven is barbaric, Sal," he said, winking at her.

Sal smiled, feeling the tension finally crack. "We all have our struggles. Now let's get watching."

Sal stirred the Bolognese, and Liam set the laptop on the kitchen table and plugged it in. "I downloaded the four episodes that aired before the show was canceled."

Sal fought to unstick some meat from the bottom of the pot. "Do you think the demon's the reason it was canceled?"

"Oh, definitely," he said, and pulled up the first episode full-screen on his laptop. "Luckily, I found some more footage. Hollywood's really clueless about network security. Keep stirring." He uncorked the sauce wine and poured it into the pan, where it hissed and spat. He took over stirring, pausing to add more wine and then a small carton of milk. He turned the heat down, dumped in a zip-top bag of dried herbs, and put the lid on. "Now we wait," he said.

Sal poured more wine and joined him at the kitchen table.

The show was called *Ink Stainz: Vegas*, with tacky hearts and thorns and dripping blood surrounding the show's logo.

"Classy," Sal said. Liam snorted.

The first episode introduced the artists, twelve heavily tattooed people of different races and genders, all looking as tough as they could for the camera. One of the men had a locust tattooed on his Adam's apple, and Liam pointed to him. "That kind of tattoo will make you throw up. That guy, man. Watch him."

Five of the people interested Sal. The man with the locust, who went by the very original name of Hannibal, was thin and small with full sleeve tattoos and bright red flames peeking out from the collar of his white T-shirt. A bald Latina who went by the name Sugar Skull had black lines tracing her skull bones, with brightly colored flowers sprinkled around. A very tall, large black man had full sleeves on his arms, normal enough, but his hands were inked entirely black, like a pair of gloves. Including his palms. His name was Charles.

By now, Sal was wincing. "These people have got to be addicted to pain," she said.

"The endorphin rush is amazing," Liam admitted. "But it takes a special kind of person to get that much ink."

The last two were the most interesting. One was a white woman almost as large as Charles, about fifty years old, with horrible illustrations of children's heads up and down her arms, complete with dates underneath them. She looked like a frequent canvas, not an artist herself. But she called herself Mama Tat.

"And if you call me Mama (*bleep*), we're going to have a problem," she said to the camera during her interview.

The camera then cut to Sugar Skull, who looked impressed. "That is a woman who has run out of (*bleep*)s to give," she said. "Maybe she once cared what people thought of her, but not anymore."

"I thought they were supposed to all hate each other on sight," Sal said. "No one's even said they're not here to make friends yet."

The final person introduced was a small man with light brown skin and large eyes. He wore a long-sleeved shirt and khakis, with no visible ink. His name was Gardener.

"This guy must have wandered in off the street, looking for a martini bar," Sugar Skull said when they cut back to her. Seemed like Sugar Skull was the go-to for opinions about the others. "He just don't fit in."

The interview camera went to Charles then. "What's that little (*bleep*) doing in here? He doesn't have any (*bleep*)ing ink! You gotta pay your dues in an industry like this." He held his ink-covered hands to the camera.

They cut to another contestant, a woman with a long blond braid and a leather vest over a white tee. Her tattoos were all cursive words written down her arms, over her hands, and one word going up her neck. Sal couldn't read any of it. "A guy like that is the kind of (*bleep*) you get drunk and make him get some ink," she said. She flexed her right arm, and the word on her bicep was censored, so Sal assumed it was a swear word. "This was my first tattoo. My rite of passage."

"They have more footage of people talking about Gardener than of him talking about himself," Liam said.

Sal shushed him and leaned forward. "He's back on," she said.

Gardener had limp black hair that looked unwashed. It hung in his eyes. "I have a parlor on the Strip," he said. "I specialize in anything with plants. Mostly flowers, but I can also do seeds, vines, insects. Leaves. I'll do whatever the customer asks, of course," he added. "But I love inking plants."

Cut back to Sugar Skull. "Plants," she said in a deadpan.

Back to Gardener. "I have no tattoos of my own," he said, looking sad, as if he were talking about children.

"Yeah, that guy needs watching," Sal said. "I know they edit these shows to make us like or dislike certain people, but a clean-skinned tattoo artist is like a tan hacker or a dental hygienist with bad teeth."

Liam had returned to the sauce. He poured in a can of tomatoes and added a bay leaf. "I've never seen someone who works with ink not have their own," he agreed.

The first challenge came up, to do a cover-up job on botched or crappy existing tattoos. Two customers wanted exes' names eradicated; one embarrassed guy wanted to remove a tattoo he'd decided, while drunk, belonged on his butt; and an older man in a suit wanted a youthful indiscretion (a dog urinating on the German flag) removed from his arm. The artists each managed to cover their client's tattoo, with talking-head interviews interrupting the tattooing scenes. Charles's interview was so laden with profanity that it was more *bleep* than anything, but Sal got the distinct impression that he didn't approve of his client, a small blond man who needed his ex-girlfriend's name removed before his current girlfriend would agree to marry him. Charles had given him a detailed train covering the name, complete with it going into a tunnel at the top of his shoulder.

"You know, like when he (*bleep*)s his new wife." He talked slowly, as if everyone around him was stupid. "The train is his (*bleep*) and the tunnel is her (*bleep*). It's metaphorical. I don't know why he got so (*bleep*)ing bent out of shape," he said.

Cut to Sugar Skull, laughing too hard to say anything.

Mama Tat had a man who wanted to remove a small pink flower on his forearm. He mumbled something about a drunken night, not looking into the camera. Mama Tat had given him a bigger, pinker flower.

"The guy is closeted, and needs to (*bleep*)ing embrace his true nature," she said simply.

Cut to Gardener, who looked coldly at the camera. "I should have gotten the flower."

Sal was convinced the client would be super pissed. "Tat's going home," she guessed.

But no, Charles with his metaphorical sex tattoo went home, along with three others. The shocker was that Mama Tat had been absolutely right about the man, who had a tearful confession, coming out during his exit interview, cradling his forearm as if he had just won a trophy.

Cut to Mama Tat, looking pleased with herself. "I got an eye for little boys not knowing their true selves," she said simply.

Gardener had the man in the suit as his customer. He turned the rude image into a full-sleeve giant redwood, with rich browns and reds and greens growing up the man's arms, roots wrapping around his wrist, and leaves covering his shoulder. It was a huge tattoo to do in one sitting, the narrator claimed, and the client was sweating and shaking by the end of it.

"I thought he just wanted a cover up so he could go golfing. That thing is huge!" Sal said.

That customer also cried during his exit interview, expressing extreme happiness at his ink and saying he would definitely be back for more from Gardener in the future.

Gardener won the challenge, making Mama Tat say some choice expletives during her talking-head interview.

"It's fun to watch," Sal said, shoveling pasta into her mouth. Liam definitely could cook. "But I don't get the weird part. What's the threat here?"

Liam pulled a tablet from his backpack and began searching online. "The threat is the reason they canceled the show," he said, his eyes widening. "Every client we just saw is now dead."

The other episodes were as entertaining as the first, only overshadowed by the fact that Sal knew everyone under the tattoo gun would die.

"Why did they even air the show if people started dying?" Sal asked.

"They didn't start dying until after the show aired," Liam said, reading from Menchú's e-mail. "It began four months after people got their tattoos. This show aired faster than most, so they were two episodes in before the deaths began. After four episodes the producers put things together and canceled the show before anyone else figured it out."

Sal thought for a moment. "Las Vegas is a tourist city. Most of these clients got their tattoos and went home, so they have only one connection. How many episodes did they film?"

"Twelve," he said.

"And people kept dying after they pulled it." It wasn't a question.

"Yeah. This week would have been episode six."

Sal ran her hand through her hair. "So people continue to die every week or so, everyone who got ink on the show. Not just under certain artists?"

"All of them. Menchú thinks it has something to do with the ink itself—ink is easy to bless or curse. But the curse had to come from somewhere. Find the spell, remove the curse, the remaining ink should go dormant." Liam considered his own hands again. "But if whichever tattoo artist is doing this got sent home, it should stop, right? We just track who went home when and when people stop dying we can figure out who did it."

"Sure, if you want to wait and see when people stop dying," Sal said, exasperated. "What if whoever did it ended up winning?"

"That's a good point," Liam said, frowning at the bottle of wine— the second one was half drained. "I think it's time to put this away and pay closer attention. Who do you suspect?"

"Mama Tat convinced a guy to come out on national television. He was wearing a wedding ring, Liam. That says magic to me."

"Or she's just very convincing," Liam said. "What about Charles? He could have been out for revenge. He got voted off first, and the tattoo was quite good, if lewd."

"Gardener is just creepy," Sal said. "Another guy whose customer acted in a way we really didn't expect."

They added Sugar Skull to the list just because she didn't act like a normal reality show contestant, being impressed, amused by, or otherwise friendly toward her fellow contestants.

"Let's keep watching," Sal said, opening the bag of cannoli and offering one to Liam.

The third aired show cut Hannibal, who turned out not to be hard-core at all despite his locust, and two other artists who hadn't really impressed Sal and Liam. Nothing strange happened, except that Gardener's customers were always 100 percent satisfied with their work, which was consistently plant based. Sugar Skull showed her skill as an artist and was also the only person to give the customers a lot of TLC regarding the pain.

Mama Tat showed loud, expletive-laden maternal love for her customers, not all of whom appreciated it, but it seemed to help her in the challenges.

After the last aired episode, Sal threw down her pen in frustration. "Nothing. No clues."

Liam stretched. The wine had worn off, and they had both switched to water. "We're narrowing it down, at least. Now we start on the raw footage."

He sat down next to her and draped an arm across her shoulders. She let him.

3.

A gainst everything Sal would have expected, Grace was the one most visibly excited about Las Vegas. She sat in her seat clutching *The Remains of the Day*, bookmarked nearly at the end, and stared out the window, drumming her fingers. Sal, in the seat beside her, was trying to use the plane's Wi-Fi to look up all the tattoo shops in Vegas, while Liam sifted through records of how each of the victims died.

"Las Vegas has some great bookstores, I've heard," Grace said. "I hope we'll have time to visit Amber Unicorn Books."

"Are you a collector?" Sal asked. "The ones I've seen you reading have been pretty new."

"I'm looking for rare books," Grace said. "Online shopping is fine, but nothing beats a good used bookstore. I'm looking for Mary Shelley's lesser known books."

Menchú and Liam were talking about the job. "What did you and Sal find last night?" Menchú asked.

"The unaired footage, the dailies—they showed some pretty weird stuff," Liam said. "Dull as hell to wade through and find the weird stuff, though."

"I wouldn't want to have to edit those shows," Sal said, leaning over their seats. "Tattooing is pretty damn boring. And they ask these horrible leading questions during the interviews. The producers have in their heads who they want to show as the slightly crazy one, who's the darling, who's the asshole. They ask questions to bring that out. They could make Grace sound like a party girl and Liam like a tweed-elbowed egghead if they tried. It's a shame they canceled it; it would have made for some ratings gold."

"Did you find out who won?" Menchú asked.

Liam shook his head.

The footage was raw and lacked selective editing and talking heads to narrate the action, but the challenges continued, with Mama Tat and Gardener taking top place most often. They grew to hate each other, and dormitory footage showed that their midchallenge arguments often continued when they returned to their rooms. Sal and Liam reviewed as many hours as they could, but there was more footage than they could watch in one night. They skipped around to find the winners and learned that Mama Tat and Gardener reached the finals together, but not who had won.

They did find out that the final challenge had been to tattoo each other.

"So I thought we could just find out who was doing all of this by waiting to see which one dies," Liam said. "But Sal was against that idea."

"It would be efficient," said Grace. "If time-consuming."

"But we're not Team One. We want to stop these deaths," Sal said.

"Sal," Menchú said, disapproving. "Team One doesn't kill indiscriminately."

Sal nodded. "And the government and the Church have our best interests at heart; I know, Father."

He sighed and turned back to Liam. "Any word on causes of death?"

"It's not the tattoos themselves, at least not obviously. We had one heart attack, one car accident, one fall from a ladder, one from a fast-growing cancer. One man from the first episode had a stroke on a golf course."

"The redwood guy? I liked him," Sal said. "What about the guy who came out on the show?"

"Tripped over his dog and hit his head. Died instantly," Liam read from his computer.

"One interesting thing," he continued, "was that each victim was pale and emaciated at the time of their death, even those who didn't die of sickness. As if they had been drained." He looked at Menchú. "Does that sound familiar?"

Menchú nodded and pulled a heavy book from under his seat. "Tattoos come from all over the world," he said, settling into his lecture mode. "They can indicate anything from the places a traveler has been to whether a woman has reached marriageable age. Some use them to channel spirit animals, some for protection against magic. Some tattoos even indicate the specific skills of the wearer. Did anyone you saw last night look like their tattoos had any rituals associated with them?"

Liam nodded. "A couple of guys with prison or gang tattoos. One Asian businessman had some interesting tattoos on his back."

Grace leaned forward with interest. "Was he from Cambodia?"

Liam shrugged. "I can look him up."

"I've got it," Sal said, looking at her notebook. "Kang Keo; yeah, Cambodian. He was heavily inked on his back. A lot of circles with spikes, and animals. Two tigers."

"When was he on the show?" Grace asked.

"Sixth episode. He was part of the history-of-tattoo challenge, where the tattoo artists had to give ink from a culture they weren't familiar with," Liam said, pulling up the footage and passing his laptop back to Grace.

"I remember him. He had a bunch of tattoos, and talked like he would throw a fit if they disrespected his culture," Sal said. "It made me wonder why he was taking a chance on a reality tattoo show."

Mama Tat won the round by giving Kang Keo a tattoo of nine spikes on the back of his neck. The client seemed happy. Sugar Skull left the show for going to her tattoo design book for a Japanese kanji that was supposed to mean "peace" but actually meant "rat."

Menchú flipped through his book, leaning close to the fine print. "If he was tattooed in the sixth episode, he shouldn't be dead yet, right?"

Sal turned to the page in her notebook with the list she and Liam had made of the remaining clients and their projected death dates. "The clients from the fifth episode would have died six days ago. They took a week off before the sixth episode, and so we have one day to stop the next batch from dying."

"It sounds like Mama Tat and Gardener are our two main suspects. So when we touch down, I want Grace and Sal to go to the tattoo shops. Liam will search to see if any clients from the sixth show are still in Vegas," Menchú said.

"How many of the clients were tourists?" asked Sal. "Those would all be back home by now, wouldn't they?"

"Kang Keo was in Vegas for a lengthy business trip," said Liam. "Probably still there."

Grace leaned her seat back. "Are any of these tattoo shops near a bookstore?"

* * *

After the eighteen-hour flight, Menchú gave them an hour to get situated in their hotel before they got to work. Once freshened up and somewhat alert, Sal and Grace headed out to scout for food, books, and tattoo joints.

Mama Tat's tattoo parlor was called Baby Face, and it was a short walk from Amber Unicorn Books, in which Grace spent eleven minutes and forty-five seconds finding two Mary Shelley books. They dropped by a casino for a burger and to plan their next move.

"How are you going to fight a tattoo artist?" Sal asked through a mouthful of Angus beef. Twenty-seven dollars seemed a lot for a burger, but the Vatican could afford it.

Grace considered. "Same way I fight anything else. I find a place that hurts, and I punch it. It's easier than you'd think."

"But haven't you gone up against, I don't know, a ghost or anything? Something insubstantial?"

"Ghosts always have a physical anchor, like a book or a bed or a candle. Ghosts are easy."

The waitress, a woman with bottle-red hair, wearing far too little and looking even more tired than Sal felt, came by to check on them.

Sal spied a tattoo on the swell of the waitress's right breast. It was a hummingbird sipping at a delicate yellow flower. She pointed to it. "Beautiful ink. Did you get it in town?"

The woman smiled and stuck her chest out farther. "I call it my tip magnet, on account of my tips doubling since I got it. Take my word for it, ladies. Men like boobs with the ink."

Sal coughed, and Grace stared at the woman. "Thanks for the advice," Sal said when she recovered. "Where did you get it?"

"Little joint on the Strip. Butler's Tray, it was called. Odd place. It closed down a few weeks ago, in fact."

"Why's that?" Sal asked.

"Too much competition. If you're not on a reality show now, you don't get the business. At least that's how it seems," she said, and left to check on other customers.

"Even if nothing was weird here, why would someone think only twelve tattoo joints could service a city as big as Vegas?" Sal asked. "There has to be something else going on."

Grace shook her head. "I can't see why someone would waste time and energy marking their skin on purpose."

Sal thought about Liam with his ink and smiled. "They have their place."

Grace looked at her strangely. "Have you done it?"

Sal snapped back to reality. "Gotten tattooed? No, never. I'm not against it, just never found something I wanted to put on my body forever."

Grace nodded. "Since forever is an even longer situation for me, I agree."

Sal searched for the location of Butler's Tray on the Strip, and for other tattoo places. Baby Face was close, in fact, and open all hours.

"Who would want to get a tattoo at three in the morning?" Grace asked as they left the casino.

"Jet-lagged businessmen. Drunk tourists. Jet-lagged drunk tourist businessmen," Sal said.

Grace checked her watch. "How are we going to find this Mama Tat person? With her fame, I expect she will be too busy for chatting."

"I thought about getting an appointment, but I figured she would be booked because of the TV show. So I'll just flash my badge," Sal said, moving aside her jacket and pointing to the badge on her belt.

"You mean the badge that says NYPD on it," Grace said flatly.

"No one ever looks at the badge too closely. I had a buddy who got backstage at a concert with a school safety badge." Sal laughed, remembering. "She got in trouble for that, big time. And she found out the guys from Maroon 5 really don't party much. Bunch of yoga mats and fruit juice."

Grace didn't smile, and Sal wondered if she kept up with pop music. Probably not. "We can try the walk-in method first, then the badge, and if all else fails, we break in through the back door."

Grace nodded at last. "Sounds like fun."

"Let's try the carrot before the stick, Grace," Sal said, checking her phone again for the address to Mama Tat's.

The front window of Mama Tat's Baby Face was decorated like a lot of tattoo parlors: neon signs, roses, jesters, and the face of a baby Sal remembered from Mama Tat's many baby tattoos. Inside, blue polyester couches and gaudy framed pictures of half-naked women and men furnished a waiting room full of impatient tattooed customers.

Behind the red counter stood a woman with blond hair swept into a bun, blue hipster glasses, and a pink business suit. She looked closely at a clipboard, ticking something off a list. "Penelope Yancy, you're next," she called in a drawl Sal recognized as Georgian.

A young white woman with blue hair, several facial piercings, and a white tank top that showed off her many tattoos pulled herself off a couch. "My name's Black Mamba," she complained.

"I take your name from your ID, honey. Your friends can call you whatever they like," the receptionist said without looking up.

Black Mamba flipped her the bird halfheartedly as she slouched through a door, following a heavyset black man. Sal blinked and realized the man was Charles, from the show.

"I'm almost willing to let you assume she's the demon—just go ahead and punch her," Sal said, nodding toward the receptionist, who clearly didn't fit.

"There's nothing demonic about this place," Grace said. "Get your info, but whatever it is, it's not here."

"All right," Sal sighed, and walked up to the counter. "We'd like to see Mama Tat, please."

The woman looked at them over her glasses. "Do you have an appointment? The question is rhetorical because all of her appointments are already here. What I mean to say is anyone who thinks they can walk in and just get Mama Tat is deranged or drunk. And we don't service drunkards. They bleed too much."

"You don't seem—" Sal began, but the woman interrupted her with a wave of her hand.

"Like I should work at a tattoo parlor?" She rolled her eyes. "After the show started, they realized that they had to stop hiring their tattooed buddies to hold down the front desk and get a real administrative professional. Look at what I have to deal with, though—they don't even have a computer here, though Mama Tat could afford a server farm at this point."

"Is it usually like this?" Sal asked, gesturing to the waiting room. She let her Southern drawl creep into her voice.

"Every hour of the day," the admin said.

"Impressive. And what's the wait for a tattoo from Mama herself?"

"Three months."

"Cost?"

"Fifteen hundred an hour."

Sal choked back a laugh. "Is she that good?"

"She's famous," the admin said. "That's all she needs. Now, is there anything I can do for you ladies that doesn't involve Mama Tat?

Perhaps an appointment three months out? Or you can see one of our other artists in two weeks."

"You can tell me if there have been any complaints from the customers," Sal said carefully, not wanting to say "deaths" right away.

"None. Mama Tat has satisfied customers or she touches up for free," the admin said. "Are you from the health department? You're required to show me ID if you are."

"Not the health department," Sal said. She moved her jacket aside so her badge peeked out. "But I do have some questions for her."

"Let me see that," the admin said, gesturing. Sal groaned inwardly and passed the badge over. "En, Why, Pee, Dee," the admin said carefully. She glanced back up at Sal. "And I'da pegged you as Southern."

"South Carolina, originally," Sal said.

The admin's eyes narrowed. "Clemson?"

"My daddy went to Georgia Tech," Sal lied smoothly.

The admin relaxed. While not a fan herself, Sal could speak the language of college rivalries.

"Is Mama Tat in some kind of trouble?" the admin asked.

"No. We're asking questions regarding the TV show she was on, but she isn't in trouble," Sal said, silently adding, *Not yet, anyway*.

The woman nodded smartly. "Since you're a Southern gal, I'll tell you this. Mama Tat takes her after-work drink at Caesar's. She gets off around eleven."

"Thanks, hon," Sal said.

4.

enchú and Liam exited the taxi in front of Sunrise Hospital
and Medical Center on South Maryland Parkway, Menchú in
his usual priest's garb, Liam in the black deacon's shirt he
wore if he needed to visit a place where priests were more welcome
than brawlers.

Menchú squinted up at the hospital. "What did you say was Keo's
room number?"

"He's still in the ER, according to their database," said Liam,
checking the cached info on his laptop.

"He can't stay there," Menchú said. "He's a risk to the other patients."

"I can move him up in the queue," Liam said. "I just need an
Internet connection. This is America—there must be a Starbucks
around here."

"Do it," Menchú said. "That diner across the street says free Wi-Fi."

They sat over coffee and watched the triage program as Keo moved
up in the queue, then was taken to an ER station and diagnosed with
a "cardiac incident." By their third cup of coffee, he'd been admitted,
room 350.

"Let's go," Menchú said, leaving money on the table.

Menchú signed himself and Liam into the hospital registry, showing his Vatican ID to an impressed receptionist who seemed embarrassed to tell them she was a Baptist (but she told them, anyway). They found room 350 and peeked in.

A nurse was settling Keo, who looked to be about fifty, in with his monitors. She turned when they entered.

"Visiting hours are over, Father," she said. "I don't think anyone called for you. He'll be fine." She gave a friendly smile to the man in bed, who looked drawn and afraid.

"I'm with the Vatican, and I need to ask Mr. Keo some questions of importance to the Church," Menchú said. The nurse looked startled but, after a quick check of a list, nodded and left the room.

Menchú made the sign of the cross and sat down next to the bed. Liam took up a post at the door.

"Mr. Keo, I'm Father Menchú of the Vatican. That's Brother Liam."

"Why are you here? I am not Catholic," Keo said, his voice faint.

"That doesn't mean you're not in danger," Menchú said.

Keo lifted a hand with an IV in it, and dropped it weakly back to the bed. "Do not minister to me. I have seen enough of your meddling in my own country."

"I'm not here for ministry," Menchú said. "We believe you are sick because of a tattoo you received on the *Ink Stainz* reality show."

"Impossible," said the man. "That was months ago. And this isn't a skin infection; it's my heart. Too much fried food."

"Father," Liam said softly. He had opened his laptop and was staring at the screen. "Police reports are coming in that the other clients from episode six are dying. A heart attack. A dog mauling. Drug overdose."

Menchú looked at Keo's heart monitor. It beat regularly at seventy beats per minute.

"How are you feeling now?" Menchú asked.

"Better than I was, actually. They gave me nitroglycerin. What is this about?"

"What tattoo did you get on the show?" Menchú asked. He knew the answer, but didn't want to disturb the man.

Keo sat up with little effort and gestured with his non-IV hand to the back of his neck.

Menchú opened the hospital gown. The tattoo looked as it had on the television footage Liam had showed him, except now it was bright red instead of black.

"What does the tattoo mean?" he asked, gesturing for Liam to come and see. The Irishman swore softly.

"It's an old symbol, protection against evil spirits," Keo said. "Is something wrong?"

"What color did you ink it? All of your other tattoos are black."

"Yes, black," Keo said, frowning. "They're all black."

Liam stepped back as the tattoo glowed brighter.

Mr. Keo twitched, looking over his shoulder. "What's the matter? It's starting to burn. What do you see?"

"I wish Grace were here," Liam said.

"Call Sal," Menchú said.

Sal and Grace were sipping sodas at a bar in the grand sprawl of Caesar's Palace when Sal's cell vibrated. It was Liam.

Get here ASAP. Sunrise Hospital. Rm 350. Bring G.

"Shit," she said. "Something's going down at the hospital."

It was only ten o'clock; they had an hour to wait for Mama Tat. Too long. Sal paid the tab, and they ran for a taxi.

Late night on the Strip was not the time to get anywhere quickly, but after a ten-dollar tip to the driver they were whizzing down side streets; they reached the hospital five minutes after Liam's text.

The hospital receptionist paid much less attention to Sal's badge than the admin at Baby Face, and Sal and Grace took the steps to the third floor.

Clambering up the stairs, they passed a night nurse having a hushed, tense conversation on her cell phone. She barely paid them any attention.

Sal's cell buzzed as they opened the door to the third floor: Liam, one word. *Scalpel.*

Sal stopped short. She didn't think hospitals kept scalpels just sitting out for anyone to grab. The night nurse had been careless to leave her post for the phone call, but hadn't left any sharp instruments out.

"Do you have a knife?" she asked Grace.

"Of course," Grace said.

They got to room 350, which was the only door closed on the floor. They opened it to chaos.

Liam was sitting astride a man who lay facedown on the bed, screaming into a pillow. Menchú was praying while pressing on the man's back with both hands.

His pressing didn't seem to help. Something black ballooned from the man's skin like a huge bubble about to burst. It thrashed, swelling around Menchú's hand, relaxing, and pulsing back with more force.

"Did you bring something sharp?" called Liam. Grace ran forward with the knife.

"Cut it out carefully, before it kills him!" Menchú leaned away, his hands still on the man's back.

"Cut what out?" Sal said. "Shouldn't we know—"

Before she could finish, Grace slid her knife along the membrane, and something burst out, spraying black goo.

It flailed on the floor, a childlike horror made of ink. It reminded Sal of a monkey crossed with an octopus, throwing tentacles about that tried to wrap around the chair leg, Menchú's cassock, and Sal's ankle. Its grip was weak, and it called plaintively, its mouth full of sharp teeth, its eyes red.

Grace impaled it on her knife and then cut its head off.

"Everyone all right?" Grace asked, and they all murmured some level of agreement.

Liam, Grace, and Menchú relaxed, panting. Sal kicked the limp tentacle off her foot, shuddering. The man on the bed ceased struggling and relaxed, his eyes closing. The wound on his back, a cut rather than the ragged hole that likely would have been there had they not arrived to give the demon an assisted birth, ran black threaded through with red traces, until finally the discharge looked like regular blood.

Menchú shifted Kang Keo's head to the side so he wouldn't suffocate and reattached the heart rate monitor. His pulse was swift, but slowing, and his breathing settled into something like sleep.

Menchú opened a drawer in the bedside table, found gauze, and pressed it on the wound. Without being prompted, Liam brought him a wet washcloth from the bathroom. Menchú cleaned away the blood and black goo.

"The tattoo is gone," said Liam.

"It served its purpose," Menchú said grimly. "The others won't have been so lucky."

"What the hell happened?" asked Sal as they tried to clean up. The black goo that had splattered them was thin and odorless, but it stained their clothes.

"It's ink," Liam said, rubbing his fingers together.

"The time came for the sixth-episode people to die," Menchú said, continuing to clean Keo. "But this man received an ancient protection tattoo on the show, and that saved him. From the looks of it, a demon was implanted in the tattoo—but unlike with the other victims, it was not allowed to fester and rot and consume the life force from within. It stayed in the tattoo, finally trying to escape the only way it could."

Sal toed the body on the floor, which was already melting. She was reminded of the movie *Gremlins*. "What was it?"

Menchú knelt beside it, taking a picture with an old-fashioned, film-loaded camera. "I don't know. I've not seen anything like this before. I'll send a picture to Asanti."

"If you can find somewhere that develops film," Liam said, snorting.

They cleaned up most of the ink before the night nurse burst in on them, face flaming with what Sal suspected was shame as well as rage.

"Mr. Keo's heart monitor was interrupted. What—what happened here?" she asked, eyes going wide as she rushed to Mr. Keo's side, checking his vitals.

Sal flashed her badge, and Menchú and Liam showed their collars. "We needed to ask Mr. Keo some time-sensitive questions. But, dammit, my fountain pen exploded when I was trying to get his statement. I use the old kind, with a bottle of ink. Used to think it was quaint. We are so sorry for the mess. We tried to clean up as much as we could."

After she had determined that Mr. Keo was fine, albeit ink stained, the nurse glared at them. "I am going to get the janitor. I want you gone when I get back, or I'm calling security." She glanced at Menchú. "Even on you, Father."

Menchú nodded graciously. "We'll be but a moment longer."

Mr. Keo was stirring now and watching them all with bleary eyes. He remembered very little, even as Menchú talked him through his experience.

"Do you remember anything from your tattooing process?" Menchú asked. "Anything at all about your tattoo artist or the show runners? Anyone?"

"I found the show atmosphere very strange, but I had meant to get a nine-spire before I left Cambodia, and got too busy. I get a new protective tattoo every time I travel. It was a spur-of-the-moment decision to get it on the show," Keo said. "Why did you ask about the color?"

Menchú wrote Liam's cell phone number down on the notepad by the bed. "Your tattoo is gone, Mr. Keo. I believe it did its job admirably, protecting you exactly as it was meant to do. You're a lucky, lucky man. If you have any more problems with your tattoos, call this number; Brother Liam will be happy to hear from you."

Liam didn't look happy at all, but Mr. Keo wasn't looking at him.

"You believe in my tattoos? Aren't you going to lecture to me about my blasphemous ways?" Mr. Keo said, his voice tired.

Menchú smiled his priestly, calm smile. Sal knew by now how many emotions that smile could hide. "I have seen enough in my life to know that God works in various ways."

"You believe your god made my tattoos protective?" Keo said.

"It doesn't matter what I believe, Mr. Keo. You are alive, and I hope you stay that way for many years. Go forth, be kind to others, and God will sort us all out when we're done with this mortal world." Menchú rose and made the sign of the cross by the bed. Liam and Grace crossed themselves automatically.

Keo touched his neck. "It's gone?"

Menchú unbuttoned the top of Keo's hospital gown. The cut had healed, and the skin where the tattoo had rested was white and smooth.

"It left a memory behind. Get well soon, Mr. Keo." And Menchú gestured to the others to leave.

The group went to the Denny's across from the hospital. They took a booth, Liam and Menchú facing away from the door and Sal and Grace on the other side.

Menchú sighed and ran his hand through his graying hair. "We saved one of, what, six?" He looked at Liam, who nodded. "How long before the next group?"

"Two days," Sal said, checking her notebook. It had, she noticed, soaked up a lot of the demon blood/ink. She made a face. Grace's copy of *The Remains of the Day* was also ruined. She fanned the pages and dabbed at it with a napkin. She'd left her new books in the taxi, she had been dismayed to realize after the excitement at the hospital.

The waitress came to the table with her notepad ready. Menchú ordered coffees all around.

"I've had enough caffeine—" Sal began, but stopped when the door to Denny's opened. Her eyes grew wide. "Never mind. Coffee, yeah."

Menchú looked up. "What's going on?"

But by then the very large woman had reached the table. "All right. What do you want with Mama Tat?"

"I've had my share of stalkers," Mama Tat said, leaning back in the chair the waitress had added to their booth. "Comes with the reality show territory."

In person, she was bigger than she looked on the show, tall and broad and muscular, her arms featuring those creepy baby tattoos. She grinned at them, completely unthreatened by the dirty, exhausted strangers in front of her.

"I finally decided to turn the tables and stalk them back," she continued. "My admin tells them where I'll be so I can get a look. I tailed you when you left the parlor, but we wondered why you left early for the hospital."

"I *thought* it was too easy to meet up with you," Sal said.

"When we followed you to the hospital, we saw you were visiting that nice Mr. Keo. So I just wanted to straight-up ask you . . ." Mama Tat leaned forward, staring at Sal. "What do you want with Mama Tat?"

Sal glanced at Menchú, who nodded. She took a deep breath. "Every person who has gotten a tattoo from your show, up to episode six, has died. They all died in different ways, and many died at home, so only a few people have connected the accidents to the show."

The color drained from Mama Tat's face. "All of them? How do you know?"

"We have spiders crawling databases to find connections between people," Liam offered. People usually backed down when offered answers of a technological nature they didn't understand, and Mama Tat seemed satisfied with the lie.

"And who are *we*, exactly?" she asked.

"We are a group of people affiliated with law enforcement and the Catholic Church, investigating strange coincidences," Menchú said. "We acquired the data from the unaired show and noticed that you had given Mr. Keo a protective tattoo."

Mama Tat nodded, looking both stricken and wary. "I did," she said. "Listen, do I need my lawyer?"

Sal held up her badge. "NYPD. I have no jurisdiction here; we're just looking for information. And we are pretty sure that you saved him with that protective tattoo. He's the only one from the sixth episode to survive."

Menchú leaned forward. "Do you know of anyone on the show who would have had reason to do this? Or the capability?"

Mama Tat snorted. "Didn't you notice that squirrely little bastard, Gardener? He was on my back from day one. I'm sure he has something to do with it."

"What was his difficulty?" Menchú said. "You don't seem very unlikable."

Mama Tat grimaced. "He didn't approve of me. Something about me was supposed to be revealed in episode seven. This wasn't my first reality show."

Sal glanced around the table. "I'm the only American here, Mama, and I don't watch a lot of TV. You'll have to help us out."

Mama Tat took a deep breath. "About seven years ago, I was on the second season of *Acceptance*. The queer reality show, like *Queer Eye for the Straight Guy*, only reality style."

Sal remembered the show. "Season two was the transgender-focused season. So Gardener wanted to out you?" she asked.

Mama Tat laughed. "Not quite. The show was going to out me; they figured it would bring in some old *Acceptance* fans when we had a midseason slump. I won the whole thing, see, and made a new life for myself with the winnings. Changed my name and came out here to Vegas. I started getting inked with all my babies. Didn't want to let them think I had forgotten them, even though they forgot about me." She smiled sadly and touched the head on her shoulder that was labeled with *Bryan*. "After about three tats, I was hooked and wanted to learn the craft."

Grace, Menchú, and Liam all looked stunned. Liam opened

his mouth, and Sal kicked him sharply. "So what does this have to do with Gardener?"

"He didn't like that I had an edge, that I would have a new, massive fan following come midseason. And he didn't approve. He's one of those religious assholes who think people like me are an 'abomination.'" She raised large hands for air quotes. She glanced at Father Menchú. "No offense meant, Father, if you're not one of those assholes."

Menchú nodded once. "None taken."

Mama Tat took a long drink of coffee and poured herself another cup, adding whiskey from a flask she carried in her purse. "I offended his orderly view of the world, he said. Said he didn't believe in me. Like I was Santa Claus or something. So I got him back."

"You threatened him?" Sal asked.

"I don't threaten," Mama Tat said. "One night after the third episode, I sat on his back and tattooed a gadfly on his forearm. He left me alone after that. Did you know he didn't have any tattoos before the one I gave him? What kind of freak is that?" She took another sip of coffee and sighed. "Anyway, for the last show we had to tattoo each other, and as a peace offering I turned the fly into a rose, considering the little bastard likes plants so much."

"So he has an orderly view of the world, and might be putting something evil into the ink. Why did he need to be on television?" Sal asked.

Mama Tat snorted. "Money and fame, honey. Why else do it?"

Menchú sighed. "Of course. The bigger he got, the more people he could tattoo and infect. It's all about quantity."

"What tattoo did he give you?" Grace asked, leaning forward.

Sal went cold. Mama Tat was likely on the same clock as everyone else on the show. She tried not to show her anxiety.

Mama Tat pulled her tank top strap down and showed them her

shoulder. "Asshole gave me a snail. Male and female parts, you know. Thought he was being clever."

It was a work of art, with blues and greens and small hints of pink in the shell. The snail glistened, if not attractively, at least realistically with slime, and it sat atop a purple mushroom that resembled a parasol.

"So what's this about people dying?" Mama Tat asked. Her voice was light, but Sal could hear the tension underneath.

"People are dying four months after their tattoo," Sal said. "The people from episode six are dying right now. We were able to help Mr. Keo, but the others are tourists, all of them back home already. We're trying to figure this out before any more die."

"Including me," Mama Tat said. "In two weeks. They filmed the last few episodes days apart."

"Probably you," Sal said. "There's a chance you're safe, because we assume if Gardener was polluting the ink, he would have wanted to protect himself. But we can't be sure. We'll stop him tonight, one way or the other."

"Then I had better get my drink in while I can," Mama Tat said, rising to leave. "Thanks for being the most interesting stalkers I've ever had."

"Mama Tat," Sal asked. "Who won the show?"

"I can't tell you that," she said, winking. "Even though the show was canceled. You should see those contracts they make us sign. Maybe that ink was cursed as well."

Sal thanked Mama Tat and picked up the tab for her coffee. Mama Tat laid a business card on the table as she got up to leave. "You ever need any ink, you show that to Miss Priss at the front desk. She'll get you in to see me that night. And if you need to ask me anything else, or tell me you've taken that little bastard in for something, just call that number."

"One moment, Mama Tat," Menchú said, holding his hand up to stop her from leaving. "You seem to be taking this all in stride. Even the part about your tattoo saving this man's life. Most people we discuss our work with call us insane at best."

Mama Tat avoided his gaze. "I knew about some of the deaths. I knew about my clients, and Gardener's. I kept in touch with a few of them, and after three died, I started getting scared. I just didn't know it was everyone. Also, I don't have to go far to believe this shit is magical." Her hand went to the snail on her shoulder. "You folks go on and stop that little asshole, okay? I'd really hate to stop living right now. There's so much out there to live for." She winked again at Sal and then ambled away.

Sal did a quick image search on her phone. She found what she was looking for. "That mushroom the snail was on, it's deadly. Causes liver failure in a few weeks. That guy is all about the symbolism," Sal said.

"And Mama Tat is a man," Liam said.

"She's a woman," Sal said. "And that isn't important except as it pertains to why Gardener hates her."

Liam shrugged, still looking uncomfortable.

"Oh get over it, Liam," Sal said, sighing.

"Let's focus on the problem at hand," Menchú said mildly. "We find Gardener tonight, and stop these deaths."

"Or get Mama Tat to ink that spire thing on everyone who's left," Sal suggested.

"It's too late for protection," Grace said, a touch of flat bitterness in her voice. "The damage has already been done."

"Right," Sal said. "So let's find Gardener, and undo it."

❖   ❖   ❖

If Mama Tat's Baby Face had looked like a tattoo parlor and nightclub, Gardener's shop, Ink Seeds, resembled a morgue. A freestanding building on the outskirts of town, with no windows and very little signage. And yet the parking lot was full.

"This place is messed up," Sal said as they exited the cab.

Liam stepped ahead of Sal. "Let me take point on this one. I have an idea how these things work," he said.

Sal shrugged and stepped back.

The door was locked. Liam knocked, and the door opened a crack. "Got an appointment?" The accent sounded Mexican and male.

"No, mate," Liam said. "I have a message from Mama Tat."

The door opened wider. A man with black vines tattooed all over his face looked out. "What is the message?"

Liam crossed his thick arms, making all of his ink noticeable. "That's for Gardener only. She says it's about the gadfly."

The door slammed. Liam held up a finger to the rest of them, and a minute later, the door opened.

The interior looked nothing like Mama Tat's place either. Sal wondered if it really had been a morgue once, or a funeral parlor. The walls and furniture were drab and understated, as if the whole building mourned something lost. The customers looked like they were in a waiting room for an STD clinic, jumpy and scared. Many of them had what looked like fresh tattoos on their arms, necks, and faces. Those with newer tattoos had an unnatural pallor to their skin, ranging from stark white to ashy gray, and they sat listless on their vinyl chairs. There was no front desk, no cash register, and no health inspection placard on the wall.

"Creepy place," Sal muttered to Liam.

"This isn't normal," he said.

The vine man bowed mockingly and led them through a door. "Gardener will see you immediately," he said.

"Does it feel demonic here?" Sal asked Grace, her voice low. Grace nodded once, a sharp movement of her head.

Fists clenched, Grace followed the man down the dimly lit hallway.

He led them to a small room with a chair, a sink, several tubes of black ink (no other color), and blank walls. Gardener sat on a rolling stool, latex gloves on, tattooing a woman's forearm. Every few seconds he would dip the gun into a bucket of viscous ink at his feet. He didn't look up when they entered.

"Welcome," Gardener said. "What are you looking for tonight? A rose? A forest? A seedling just breaking through the soil? I hear you're walk-ins, but you come from a friend, so you are of course welcome."

He wiped away the ink on the woman's arm, a demonic face peeking out from underneath the skin, and told her to take a break. She obediently went to the wall, slid down it to sit on the floor, and began to weep.

He was smaller than he had looked on television, with the same type of long-sleeved shirt and slacks. His hair was slicked back, and he looked as if he had just come home from dress-down Friday at an accounting firm.

"Mr. Gardener, we are looking into the deaths of people on the show *Ink Stainz*," Menchú began.

Gardener looked up and took them in, still stained with the demon's ink. His nostrils flared, and he sprang to his feet, dropping the tattoo gun. "I can smell it. I can *see* it on you. My beautiful baby's ink—it died tonight; it *died*. I planted its seed, and it failed to grow because of that unnatural *bitch*." He took a step forward, his hands curling into claws. "I felt it die. I didn't think its murderers would deliver themselves."

Grace stepped in front of Menchú, shielding him.

"We just want to talk," said Sal, stepping forward, but then Gardener attacked.

Before, Sal would have said that Gardener was so slight a stiff breeze could stop him. But of course she didn't take into account whatever was possessing him, nor what was apparently secreted away under his skin.

His perfectly pressed shirt ripped away as inky black wings burst from his back, changing quickly to tentacles that struck Grace aside. She went crashing into the tubes of ink, spilling one. When it hit the floor, it began to bubble and stream out, seeking something.

Grace swore and held her arm. The skin was red and blistered where the tentacle had touched her. "Don't touch the ink," she said, and was on her feet again.

"Liam, let's get that client out of here," Menchú said. "Sal, shut this down."

He and Liam picked up the woman and ran toward the hall, Liam yelling as a tentacle lashed his back, leaving a smoky black wound.

Grace had her knife out, and Gardener picked up the tattoo gun, which whirred to life. Sal's eyes darted around the room, looking for the source, the book, whatever drove this possession. The tentacles struck out again; Grace avoided one, but another wrapped around her forearm. It picked her up, and she writhed in pain.

Sal threw the rolling stool into Gardener's face. He stumbled back, and dropped Grace. She was on her feet in an instant, running for the man.

Gardener's nose bled black fluid, like the abomination from

Keo's back. Sal searched the room frantically and saw a cabinet with drawers. One drawer was open. She ran for it.

Inside lay a book.

Behind her, Grace and Gardener fought, his acid scouring her arms and face even as she struck at him, batting aside the tendrils that sprung from his back. She turned at a shout—Liam had returned to help and was yelling to distract Gardener.

"Find it in a hurry, Sal; Grace needs some help!" he said, then stumbled over the bucket of ink, tipping it toward Gardener.

The ink splashed up with much more energy than any normal liquid would have done, splattering both Gardener and Grace. Immediately, tendrils began burrowing into their skin, smoke rising from their bodies. This was not the ink Gardener had used on the show, Sal realized. This stuff was much, much worse.

Liam regained his balance, horrified, to wrest Grace away from Gardener. She kicked Gardener, who fell backward and released her. Liam pulled her to the side, said something to her, then ran back to face Gardener. Grace stood, panting for a moment, and then joined him.

"Dammit, Grace, I said I could handle this!" he shouted, his attention divided, and Gardener struck.

The tattoo gun slid across Liam's shoulder, a line of black cutting into his skin. He screamed. Sal knew she had to figure out how to close the book, and fast.

She pulled the book out easily, but closing it did nothing. She flipped the heavy pages with the tips of her fingers, and saw that the ink glistened wetly on each page as if new, and the pages varied from light peach to deep brown. Human skin.

The words started to speak to her, encouraging her to read the book aloud, to unlock what was inside. A tap at her calf distracted her, and she looked down, breaking the hold of the words. The tattoo gun's cord was bumping against her leg as Gardener fought with it.

"Well, hell, that's easy," Sal muttered, and yanked the cord to grab the gun from Gardener.

He didn't expect a pull on his weapon, and dropped it. Grace punched him, hard, and then kicked him in the face when he went down. He didn't move again. Sal took the moment to pick up the tattoo gun and begin slashing through the skin pages, cutting the words with ink until they became illegible.

Screams erupted from the waiting room, and the tentacles on Gardener's back rose high, agitated, and crashed down in a torrent of ink. His scream sounded as if it came from something other than the man himself, something higher or older or weirder. Ink leaked from his eyes and mouth and nose.

When Sal was done with the book, he had bled out, ink was everywhere, and the floor had stopped hissing.

She closed the book and unplugged the tattoo gun.

Sal hadn't seen Liam since they'd returned to Rome. He'd been silent on the trip back, mostly sleeping or brooding. She had texted him a few times without an answer. Sal finally figured she would ask Menchú if Liam was all right.

Sal heard voices from the priest's office. She stood flat against the wall.

She heard weeping.

Menchú said something in Latin that sounded like a prayer. Then, "Liam, child of God, you are forgiven your sins and are free of Gardener's taint. The book holds no more power."

"I'm broken, Father. I have been since you found me, and Las

Vegas just made it worse. I won't ever be free of this *fear*," he said, his voice thick. "I am a sinner. I summoned a demon—"

"And then we saved you, and you found Christ, repented, and were forgiven," Menchú interrupted patiently. "Your years since then have changed you."

"I lost two years, Father. I woke up when you found me in that closet, tangled in wires and chanting. What if whatever did that to me is still here? What if that damned tattoo artist put something else inside me?"

Sal peered around a bookcase into the priest's office.

Liam knelt, shirtless, at Menchú's feet. The ink from Gardener's attack had drained out after Sal had destroyed the book, leaving a small white scar. Liam's skin was red and irritated. Long scratches crossed the white mark, as if he'd tried to tear it from his skin with his own fingernails.

"I can't, Father; I can't have another one in me. I'm not strong enough," he said, slumping against Menchú's bed.

"And you don't, Liam. You weren't carrying a demon when we found you; you were its tool, not its vessel. And now we've confirmed that Gardener's death, and the confiscation of his weapon, freed everyone he infected—including you. You belong to yourself, and to God. You are a warrior of Christ. You'll be fine. Go and get some sleep."

Sal had heard enough. She left them talking and went to help Grace remove the bandages that had covered her burns.

"Did you tell Mama Tat she's safe now?" Grace asked as Sal tended her wounds.

"Yeah," Sal said. "She offered me a free tattoo, but I didn't really feel like one after all that. I kept her card, though."

"What do you think will make you change your mind?" Grace asked.

"Who knows? I've changed my mind on a lot of things, just in the past week." She tossed the last bandages into the trash, stretched, and yawned. "I'm heading home before Menchú can find another crisis. I need some sleep. I'll see you later."

When Liam called Sal later and asked her to come over, she wasn't surprised. "You were right," he said flatly when she reached his apartment. "I can't do this anymore."

Sal crossed her arms. She wanted to argue, but she couldn't do that to him now. "So that's it?"

"I am a weak man, Sal, weaker than you deserve. I have to find out who I am before I give myself to someone else."

It hurt more than she expected. "And you have to do this alone? No help along the way?"

"No," he said. "What happened in Nevada . . ." He raised his right hand as if about to pull back his sleeve and show her—then dropped it again. "I can't."

"'It's not you; it's me,'" Sal said. She stood. "If working with this team has taught me anything, Liam, it's that we all need someone to cover our backs. If you want to figure out this 'weak man' crap alone, fine, but your team would be here, your friends would be here." She wanted to go further, but she didn't know what to call herself. Finally she said, "I would be here. If you asked."

He closed his eyes and shook his head. Sal got her coat and left.

Liam wasn't only damning himself to solitude, she realized. He had been her closest friend on this continent. Now she was alone too.

Again.

EPISODE
9

ANCIENT WONDERS

MARGARET DUNLAP

1.

INSIDE A SMALL MONASTERY, SOMEWHERE NEAR BOURG-EN-BRESSE, FRANCE.

The village, two miles from the crumbling farmhouse and out-buildings (home to two monks, a donkey, and a truly staggering amount of cheese), had a name. But given Sal's circumstances—back-to-back with Liam, fighting off shuffling, undead monks—she couldn't be bothered to remember such an unimportant detail. Hell, she barely had breath to share important tactical updates with her comrades in the field. Vital information like:

"Zombies? Seriously?!"

Liam answered her between punches. "Animated remains, not zombies."

"What are you talking about?" Sal swung a long broom handle like it was a baseball bat and knocked out the knees of the decayed *thing* coming up on her. It fell to the floor and kept crawling forward on its hands and stumps. Sal turned the push broom around and clubbed it on the head. The undead monk collapsed and went still. "They rose from the graveyard and only go down from a head shot. They're zombies."

"Duck," said Liam. Sal did, and Liam's fist went flying over her head, right into the skull of a shambler. The cemetery near the monastery hadn't been used in recent centuries, and the brittle bones of the long-dead monk caved in around Liam's fist, sending up a plume of moldy dust. The remains crumpled at Sal's feet. "If these were zombies, do you think I'd be dumb enough to hit them with my bare hands?"

"I don't know. Apparently, I don't know you as well as I thought."

"Maybe if you had waited before you jumped my—"

"Do not put your Catholic guilt on me—"

A blast from the doorway left Sal's ears ringing. A shotgun was really not designed to be used anywhere near enclosed spaces. On the other hand, it was an efficient zombie deterrent. Sal wondered where Grace had found it.

"Work out your personal issues on your own time," said Grace, leveling them both with a withering stare. "We've got another six incoming."

Unfortunately, lack of personal time was exactly the problem. Even the most amicable breakup required a certain amount of emotional negotiating, and Team Three had been lucky to put together twenty hours at a stretch between calls for the last two weeks. Mr. Norse had stepped up his search for the *Codex Umbra*, and the Orb was going nuts. Which meant Sal and Liam had been spending their scant downtime eating, sleeping, tending to their wounds, and *not* working out their "personal issues." If they'd had the time, they totally would have been acting like mature adults about the fact that they were no longer sleeping together, and not busily finding other ways to avoid each other. Totally.

But since Sal and Liam were definitely not using work as a way to back-burner their feelings, the only silver lining to their current schedule was that the constant magical flare-ups probably meant that they were still on the trail of Mr. Norse and his goons in their pursuit of the *Codex Umbra*. Unfortunately, every lead Team Three had followed from the Orb so far had been a dead end. Or, rather, a previously pillaged end. And more often than not, the elusive billionaire had left behind a little surprise to keep them occupied while he moved another step closer to the mysterious *Codex*. Asanti still wasn't sure what exactly the book did, but it seemed a safe bet that anything a man like Mr. Norse wanted that badly wasn't something he should be allowed to have.

Which was why Sal, Liam, and Grace were currently holding the line against a horde of zombies/animated remains in an anteroom outside the monastery's small archive of medieval manuscripts while, inside the archive, Asanti and Father Menchú searched for clues as to the location of the *Codex*. Sal's ears had just stopped ringing when the second blast from Grace's shotgun went off, taking Sal's hearing and another two zombies with it. Out of ammo, Grace shifted her grip and commenced using the rifle stock as a club.

Sal risked a glance behind her. There weren't that many documents in the small archive. How much time did Menchú and Asanti need?

"Is it a good sign that they're still in there?" she asked no one in particular.

"Probably not. If they'd found something, they'd be back," said Liam.

"Maybe they found more than they were expecting," said Sal before she could stop herself. Disagreeing with Liam felt like a spinal reflex lately. "Or Asanti is milking it because she wants to stay in the field."

Grace and Liam both scoffed at that suggestion, which, Sal had to admit, was probably deserved. It wasn't that Asanti wasn't allowed to do field work. In terms of actual hierarchy, she was the head of Team Three, outranking even Menchú, and could go on any mission she pleased; she just usually chose to do her research under less hectic conditions. Unfortunately, she was the only one of them who could read Latin and Old French quickly enough to be useful when under assault from the undead.

As though summoned by Sal's question, Asanti and Menchú came barreling out of the archive into the small anteroom, empty-handed and followed by a cloud of smoke.

"It's on fire?!"

This time, Sal's question had been honestly rhetorical, but Menchú answered it, anyway.

"Incendiary booby trap set on a locked chest; blew as soon as we got it open."

Taking a second glance, Sal noticed that Menchú's beard was a bit shorter than it had been that morning, and smoking faintly. Both he and Asanti had burns on their hands.

Asanti cursed. "Another present from Mr. Norse. I *knew* that chest looked more Flemish than French, but the period was right . . . right enough. Should have known it was bait . . ."

Grace swung the shotgun around and clubbed a zombie as Liam brought his fist crunching down on a final crumbling skull. "Time to leave?" Grace asked.

Sal checked the monastery's archive room. Old paper and older wood burned quickly, and flames were already licking at the back of the door as she hastily slammed it shut. "Past time," she said.

✦ ✦ ✦

Later, the team stood in the monastery's farmyard, joined by the two monks and the donkey. All of them watched the outbuilding burn to the ground.

"What happened?" asked one of the monks.

Menchú's expression was grave. "Unfortunately, there was a catastrophic reaction between underground cave gases and some of the mold from your cheese. You'll have to go elsewhere until we can verify that the danger has passed."

The monk frowned. "But we thought we saw movement from the cemetery. . . ." A black van pulled up the drive toward them. Sal recognized Balloon and Stretch through the windshield.

"These gentlemen will take care of you," said Menchú. And with those words, their flimsy cover story was officially someone else's problem. Sal might have worried about that, having seen Team Two's methods in action before, but she was too damn tired. Less than an hour later, they were on a high-speed train, heading southwest toward the Italian border.

TEAM THREE HEADQUARTERS, INSIDE VATICAN CITY.

Too few hours of sleep later, Sal and the rest of the team gathered at Asanti's desk, summoned by Monsignor Angiuli, their immediate overseer at the Vatican.

"Another dead end?" he asked. He sounded frustrated.

What does he have to be frustrated about? We're the ones running all over Europe on a snipe hunt, thought Sal.

"We did put down a magical manifestation and keep it from spreading, so not a total waste of time," said Grace, expression blank.

The monsignor gave her an annoyed look. "Shouldn't you be resting?"

Menchú spoke before Grace could answer, or kick the monsignor in the head. "If this is a strategy meeting, we will need the insights of our entire team."

"Besides, something might need hitting," Grace added.

"Grace . . ." Asanti gave her a quelling look.

To the monsignor she said, "I thought you believed in a hands-off management style."

"I let you run your department as you see fit because you get results," said the monsignor. "But you've been out on more calls in the last fortnight than you used to cover in a year."

"That's not our fault," said Menchú.

"I know that, but it's not only your team involved in this. When you call in support from One and Two, the other monsignors notice, and then Cardinal Varano notices. Soon, he's going to ask questions, and when he does, I need to have answers." He paused. "This isn't just an effect of the rising magical tide, is it?"

"No," said Asanti.

"Have you at least found out what this *Codex Umbra* does?"

A heavy silence fell over the room.

Monsignor Angiuli shook his head and sighed. "I'll cover for you as long as I can. But if you don't want a ton of cardinal landing on your heads, I suggest you get answers. Soon."

Sal waited until she heard the main door of the Archives close behind the monsignor before she asked, "How soon is soon?"

Menchú and Asanti had a brief, silent conversation with their eyes, then Menchú answered, "If he sees fit to warn us about it, very soon."

"So what do we do?" asked Grace.

Liam shrugged. "It's not like we've been *trying* to hit every dead end on the continent. If we had better leads, we'd be on those instead."

"I'm not sure what we can do," said Asanti. "Except keep working at it, and hope we can eventually get ahead of Mr. Norse."

"You do realize that repeating the same exercise while expecting different results is the definition of insanity," said Sal.

"If you don't have anything useful to contribute—" Liam began, but Father Menchú cut him off.

"No, Sal's right. We've been playing defense for weeks, following hot spots indicated by the Orb or clues that we pick up from locations that we found *while* following the Orb. We can't get ahead of Norse if we keep following in his footsteps. It's time to try something new."

"Like what?" asked Grace.

Menchú took a deep breath. "Talk to the Pythia."

Sal was evidently the only one in the room who had no idea what that meant. From the explosion of verbal disbelief that followed Menchú's announcement, her best guess was talking to the Pythia involved some kind of human sacrifice. The babble was so intense that Sal could catch only disconnected snatches:

"The Pythia? As in *the* Pythia?"

"You know how to reach her? And you never thought to mention this, over all these years?"

"You want us to use *magic* to defeat Mr. Norse?"

Menchú eventually waved everyone down. "Please. I will answer all of your questions. Just . . . one at a time."

Before anyone else could jump in, Sal raised her hand. Menchú looked at her, openly relieved.

"Yes, Sal."

"What's the Pythia?"

"Not what," said Grace. "Who."

Sal rolled her eyes at this oh-so-helpful clarification. "Okay. Fine. Who is—"

Liam answered before she could repeat herself. "The Pythia, also known as the Oracle at Delphi. One of the most ancient channelers of magic on the planet. Very dangerous. And completely mad."

Sal whirled to look to Menchú. "Is that true?"

He sighed. "The Oracle herself isn't technically ancient. The high priestess of Apollo at Delphi has the gift of sight, not immortality, and I haven't ever met her in person, so I can't say for sure, but yes, according to most reports, sanity is an optional job requirement. However," he continued, "she can see both the future and the past, and knows more about things that the world has forgotten than anyone else alive."

Sal took this all in. "Well, that could be useful."

"If you don't mind consorting with witches," muttered Liam.

Menchú caught Liam's eye. "I don't like this any more than you do."

Liam glared. "The Pythia voluntarily allows herself to be possessed by what is either a demon or a pagan god. If we go to her, we might as well admit that all our talk about holding the line against magic doesn't matter the minute we think a little woo-woo can get us through a tough spot."

Menchú didn't blink. "Do you have another suggestion?"

"Yeah, let Norse find the *Codex* first, and then send in Team One with the napalm as soon as the Orb spikes over it."

"How many people die in the time it takes Team One to arrive? Or what if Mr. Norse's plan isn't something that can be solved by the copious application of high explosives?"

"Napalm isn't a high explosive," said Liam.

"How many people, Liam?"

"How many people die following *your* plan?" Liam asked.

As the silence stretched, Asanti cleared her throat. "I, for one, am more curious to know why, if you have a way of gaining access to the Oracle, we are only hearing about it now."

"I don't have access to the Oracle."

"Then why are we even having this debate?" Liam burst out.

Menchú's expression turned grim. "I have a friend who owes me a favor."

BORG EL ARAB AIRPORT, FORTY KILOMETERS OUTSIDE ALEXANDRIA, EIGHT HOURS LATER.

The flight landed at a gleaming glass-and-steel terminal that reminded Sal of connecting through Charlotte when she visited her parents, except that the proportion of Egyptians was rather higher than in North Carolina. Once the team was through customs and passport control, a man about Menchú's age waved them over from the curb. He waited next to a van that read ALEXANDRIA TOURS UNLIMITED on the door.

Although, as they got closer, Sal couldn't help notice that he didn't exactly seem overjoyed to see them.

The man greeted Menchú with a nod. "Arturo."

"Youssef."

And that was the end of the polite chitchat.

The man opened the door to the van. Menchú entered. The rest of the team, perforce, followed.

After driving in silence for several minutes, Menchú asked, almost casually, "How are Catherine and the kids?"

The man did not soften. "They're very well. Thank you."

"Good to hear."

Half an hour later the van pulled into an office park that, except for the Arabic script on the signage, possessed all the exoticism of suburban New Jersey.

Asanti blinked. "Wait a second. Is this—?"

"Yes," said Menchú.

Sal looked at Grace and Liam, who looked as confused as she felt. She waited, but neither of them asked the obvious follow-up. *Once again, the new girl falls on the dumb-question grenade.* "And 'this' is what, exactly?" she asked.

Menchú took pity on her. "My friend Youssef works as an archivist at the Library of Alexandria."

"The one that burned down thousands of years ago?"

"It was a series of fires over many years," said Youssef. "After the first one, we took precautions and moved to an alternate site." If smug could radiate, Youssef was putting it out in waves. He turned to Menchú. "Considering how many popes ordered the later fires, I should call us even merely showing you the parking lot."

Menchú shrugged. "But imagine how much you're going to enjoy holding a favor over my head for a change."

"Which is why I still take your calls." And without another word, Youssef led the group across the parking lot and into one of the office buildings.

Once inside the airy, greenery-filled atrium, they stopped at a security desk where a guard issued them visitor passes and swiped them through to a private elevator that required security codes from both Youssef and the guard before the doors would open. Inside the elevator, Sal noticed that it took Youssef swiping his identity card and entering yet another security code before they actually began to descend.

"So," said Sal, as they fell into silence *yet again*, "how did you two meet?"

Youssef shrugged. "My wife is Catholic. I am a Copt. Arturo performed our wedding."

Liam shot Menchú a look. "You're allowed to do that?"

The priest shrugged. "They met at an interfaith conference in Cairo. Demons broke out; I got called to the scene. We were all locked in a room together, and I was pretty sure we were going to die. It seemed like the right thing to do."

"And when we did not die, and the Coptic Church refused to recognize our marriage, Arturo insisted on personally smoothing things over with the patriarch." Youssef sounded oddly bitter about this for a happily married man.

Menchú shrugged again. "Still seemed like the right thing to do."

"And my wife is eternally grateful, and will now not even consider converting."

"She was never going to convert."

"She would have."

"You could always embrace Catholicism."

"We could both convert to Islam. We could allow our daughter to bleach her hair and dye it pink. We could do many things. That doesn't mean that any of them are actually going to happen."

Menchú shrugged yet again. Youssef rolled his eyes. Perhaps it was just as well that the elevator chose that moment to arrive. The doors opened with a soft *ding*, and the team got their first look inside the fabled Library of Alexandria.

Sal's primary impression as she stepped out of the elevator was of overwhelming *light*. She knew from her ears' reaction to the elevator ride that they must be deep underground, and she couldn't see a window anywhere, yet the entire room was bathed in what felt like natural sunlight. Sal craned her neck, looking for the source. She caught a glimpse of bright latticework somewhere high above them, but before she could get a better look, Youssef hurried them forward.

They passed row upon row of shelves, but unlike the Society's Archives, these were further divided into square cubbyholes, each holding one or more tightly furled scrolls. Asanti watched the collection flow past their hurried steps with undisguised longing.

Sal fell into step beside Menchú. "You really think he's going to help us?"

He nodded. "Of course. We've been friends for years."

Sal blinked. "How does he treat people he doesn't like?" she asked.

"I certainly don't invite them inside the most extensive collection of ancient texts in the world," said Youssef.

Sal startled. She thought she had kept her voice low enough to avoid eavesdroppers. Still, if Youssef took offense at her question, he at least didn't seem any more offended than he had been before.

Presently, they passed through the stacks into a smaller corridor that led to Youssef's private office, a cramped room with walls covered in children's drawings and a small icon of Saint Mark.

"If the Greek civil or ecclesiastical authorities confront you as to your purpose in their country, I will deny that we have ever met," said Youssef.

"If the authorities give us any trouble, I'll assume that you were the one who called them," said Menchú.

Youssef seated himself behind his gray steel desk and drew out a sheaf of bright white paper. Taking the top sheet off the stack, he removed a fountain pen from a stand beside his blotter and quickly wrote a few lines before turning the paper and pushing it across the desk toward the team.

He pulled a second cap off the back of the pen, revealing a sharp point at the tip of a slender tube. "Prick your thumb and sign."

Menchú reached for the pen, but Grace put out a hand to stop him. "What are we signing?"

"Your pledge that you will abide by the rules of the Oracle, and that you understand that this invitation can be revoked at any time."

Grace didn't move. "We're supposed to take your word for that?"

"No," said Asanti. "I read Greek. That's what it says." Stepping around Grace, Asanti took the pen from Youssef's outstretched fingers. As she pricked her thumb, the blood from the wound was drawn into the pen through the tube. Asanti signed as though she wrote her name in blood every day.

The rest of the team followed her example, Liam going last and most reluctantly.

Youssef took his pen back, pricked his own finger, and signed his name at the bottom of the page. Then he capped both ends of the pen and returned it to its stand. After folding the invitation, he produced a lighter and sealing wax from another drawer. Sal flinched when, instead of using a signet ring or seal, he pressed his thumb directly into the hot wax before presenting the paper to Menchú.

"This will allow you in to see the Pythia. However, if you want a prophecy, you'll each need to bring a sacrifice."

"What kind of sacrifice?" asked Asanti.

"Magic adheres to the laws of cause and effect, and works through the principles of correspondence. Reflection: like attracts like. Participation: links the practitioner to the ritual, and to the result. And sacrifice: because for something to be created, even by magic, something of equal value must be destroyed. There is no specific recipe, no ritual by rote, but the nature of what you choose to sacrifice will determine the direction, potency, and accuracy of the Pythia's visions. I suggest you choose wisely."

"You have our blood already," said Liam. "What more do you want?"

"If what you sought could be summoned by a few drops of blood, I seriously doubt you would have made this journey."

Menchú sighed. "I fear you're right." He offered Youssef a small bow. "Thank you."

Youssef accepted this, and then said, in an unexpectedly conversational tone: "Do you have time to come to the house? I'm sure Catherine would very much like to see you." Sal blinked.

Menchú took this abrupt change in tone and topic in stride. "Unfortunately, not. And with the trouble that's been following us recently, I'm not sure that you'd want us in your home."

Youssef regarded Menchú with solemnity. "That is a debt you will have to settle with her, then."

"Please give her my regrets."

"Of course. I'll see you out."

Sal's first and last view of the pyramids was from the window of their plane as they sped north, back to Europe. *Travel the world, meet exotic and unusual people . . . and try to save them from demons.* Still, in contrast to the last two weeks, at least this trip had been free of zombies, locusts, and unexpected incendiaries. That was probably a good sign.

2.

al groped for her phone buzzing by her ear, but by the time she could convince her fingers to listen to her brain, the call had already gone to voice mail. She blinked blearily at the display: six missed calls from the rest of the team. How had she slept through six calls? She hadn't meant to sleep at all. She'd gone back to her apartment to grab a few things before meeting the others for an early morning flight to Athens. She must have been more tired than she thought. But in spite of her accidental nap, she still didn't feel rested.

Her phone was buzzing again. This time Sal answered it.

"Sal? Where the hell are you?" It was Menchú. She'd never heard him swear before. Not in English, anyway.

Sal looked around. She was in the Archives. Except that didn't make any sense. The last thing she remembered was going home. . . .

"I'm . . . ," Sal began.

"We've been calling you. Why didn't you answer your phone?"

Belatedly, Sal checked the time. Their flight to Greece was due to depart in less than an hour.

"Sal?" Menchú's voice shifted from anger to concern. She had paused too long. "Are you okay?"

"I'm . . ." Sal swallowed what she had been about to say. Now was not the time to confess that she was delusional with exhaustion. They were on a mission. She glanced over to her workspace. Her go bag was right where it should have been. A quick check showed it was packed with clean clothes, restocked, and ready. *When did I do that?* "I'm on my way."

Sal grabbed her bag and sprinted up the iron stairs two at a time. It was early enough that Roman traffic would still be on the light side. If she got a taxi driver who was just the right kind of crazy, she might still make the flight.

Sal made it onto the plane seconds before the crew closed the door, and slid into her seat beside Liam as they pushed away from the jet bridge.

Menchú's expression was a silent censure, and Sal felt herself flush. "Sorry. Got delayed."

Luckily, Menchú seemed inclined to let it go at that. Asanti didn't look up from her work, and Grace was already buried in a book, completely ignoring the in-flight safety briefing.

It was Liam who muttered, "Hope it was worth it."

"Piss off." If Menchú wanted to take her to task, she could live with it. She had been late, and he was her boss. But Liam? She'd made the flight. He could get over himself.

"Be a professional and I will."

"Stop taking the fact that you hate this mission out on me, and I'll listen to your opinion on professionalism."

Grace glared at them both over her battered copy of *Moment in Peking.*

Sal closed her eyes. She could feel Liam staring at her, wanting to continue the fight. He could go right on wanting. She wasn't going to play. Eventually, he let out a small huff, and she felt his weight shift in the too-narrow seat. A short time later, she could hear the familiar clicks of his laptop keyboard under the drone of the plane's engines.

While Sal pretended to sleep, her mind raced. Ever since her visit to the Market Arcanum, she'd had recurring dreams of wandering, looking for something she could never remember on waking. Often they left her feeling even more exhausted than she'd been when she went to bed. But they were only dreams. They had to be. She tried to remember if she had been dreaming when the phone woke her.

She tried, but she couldn't be sure.

No, she was being paranoid. It was a common result of exhaustion. Sal hadn't had a good night's sleep since long before the trip to Alexandria. She had come home, repacked her go bag, and then— instead of trying to grab a nap like a sane person—she'd pushed herself too hard. Gone back to the Archives to work. There, her fatigue had finally caught up with her, and she'd succumbed to exhaustion.

That was all.

A calm fell over Sal as the pieces of the explanation fell into place in her mind. Surely that was what had happened. *Yes.*

Sal's breathing deepened, and she slipped into unfeigned sleep.

THE RUINS AT DELPHI, AN ANNOYING NUMBER OF HOURS LATER.

Unfortunately, getting to Delphi wasn't as simple as catching a connecting flight from Athens. Even with Grace behind the wheel of their rental van, it had taken nearly three hours on winding mountain roads before they reached the Oracle's home. It was as if the ancient Greeks hadn't wanted anyone and everyone showing up at Apollo's sacred temple demanding to know what the Fates had in store for them.

As they drove, Asanti grew more eager. Grace grew more annoyed with Greek drivers, and Liam's scowl reached epic proportions. Sal concentrated on the view out the window and on not snapping at Liam. She'd been listening to his low-grade grumbling since the jolt of their plane landing had jerked her out of a sound sleep. Which was about the least attractive part of him to wake up to. If the flight had been six hours longer, she might have gotten enough sleep to muster the mental resources to deal with his attitude. As it was, she was hoarding her meager reserves for whatever the Oracle decided to throw at them.

For ruins that were both (a) thousands of years old and (b) a tourist draw, the scene the team found upon exiting the van was remarkably serene. Even so, it was mid-July, and milling tourists covered the site like ants on a picnic blanket.

Grace put Sal's exact thoughts into words when she said, "There's an oracle? Here?"

Menchú nodded.

"Where?"

This time it was Asanti who answered. "If *anyone* could see it, we wouldn't need an invitation."

Menchú looked startled. "Have you been researching the Oracle?"

"The site at Delphi has been continuously active for thousands of years. It's proof that magic can interact with the material world without being destructive. I wrote a dissertation on it. Why do you think I was so upset you hadn't mentioned that you had an in?"

Menchú shrugged, allowing her point.

"You have a PhD?" asked Sal.

"Several."

Liam rolled his eyes. "If we're doing this, can we get it over with?"

Menchú cleared his throat. "Indeed." He gestured to Asanti. "Since you're the expert, would you care to do the honors?"

Following at the back of their little group, Sal had to admit the site offered commanding views. Asanti took them past the ruins of the Temple of Apollo to a path labeled CASTALIAN SPRING. Following it, they continued up the mountain under dappled shade—a welcome relief from the hot summer sun—until the trail ended at a sign labeled clearly in half a dozen languages: ACCESS FORBIDDEN: FALLING ROCKS. Asanti stepped around this barrier without slowing down and led them toward the smaller and more crumbling of two stone huts beyond.

The hut was just big enough for the team to stand comfortably inside a ring of stone benches surrounding a marble basin in the center of the space. In the basin, water bubbled lightly.

Asanti looked at Father Menchú. "The invitation?"

Menchú produced the paper, still folded and sealed, from his coat pocket and handed it to her. "You're sure this is the place?"

Asanti seemed vaguely insulted. "Of course. The source of the Oracle has always been the spring, not the temple. Some scholars have actually posited that ethylene gas, percolating into the water from volcanic vents, was responsible for the Pythia's divine gifts, but hallucinogens in the water don't explain—"

"What are you doing in here?" a man's voice barked.

Sal whirled to find a man in casual business clothes, collar open against the summer heat, staring at them from the hut's doorway.

"Visitors aren't allowed—"

As Menchú moved to placate the man, Asanti broke the seal

on the invitation, opened the paper, and plunged it into the water until her arm was submerged nearly to the elbow.

As she did so, the room was filled with a roaring sound like a waterfall, and the man vanished.

Sal gasped in the sudden silence, the sound of her own breath and heartbeat the only things reassuring her that she hadn't gone deaf. The team hadn't moved, but something in the air had changed, and Sal suspected that it was they, and not the man, who had vanished.

Slowly, Asanti withdrew her arm from the pool. She still held the paper, but the ink—and the blood—were completely gone.

"What happened?" asked Liam, if anything even more on edge than he had been for the last two days.

Menchú looked around. "Perhaps we should go outside and investigate." No one seemed to have a better idea, and so they filed back into the dappled shade.

Outside, they found not an angry administrator, but a woman in a white draped garment with laurel leaves twisted through her dark, curling hair. She smiled, as though she had been waiting for them.

She said, "Welcome to Delphi."

3.

THE CASTALIAN SPRING, NEAR DELPHI [APPARENTLY].

In spite of her own supernatural preservation, Grace had never been particularly sensitive to magical phenomena, much to her relief and Asanti's disappointment. However, at the moment of transition from *there* to *here*—wherever here was—she had felt a faint tremor in her bones. A resonance. A *sympathy*.

She examined the woman in white, who looked like she could have stepped off the side of a painted amphora, and she knew what bound them together. "This is a place out of time."

The woman nodded. "Yes."

"Where are we?" asked Sal.

"I told you," said the woman. "This is Delphi."

"But we were in Delphi—"

Asanti cut off Sal's objection. "We were in the Delphi of the world. This is the Delphi of legend."

The woman in white nodded.

"Is this how the Pythia sees the future?" Asanti asked. "By existing in all times at once?"

The woman held up a hand. "You have come with a question," she said, "but not, I think, that one."

"Do you know what information we seek?" This time the question came from Menchú.

"No, but we were told to expect you."

"By whom?" asked Grace.

"By the Pythia, naturally."

In retrospect, Grace supposed she should have seen that answer coming.

Liam grumbled to himself as the woman in white led the group back down the path, away from the spring. "*Naturally*, the Pythia said to expect us." Liam had never met an oracle before, but so far the Pythia was exactly as annoying as he had anticipated.

He glanced at Sal, his normal go-to for an appreciative audience of mildly witty snark, but she was walking with Menchú. It was like she'd been purposefully avoiding him since the breakup. Which was stupid. They had to work together. They could be friends, even if they had given up the benefits. But apparently Sal didn't see things that way. The suspicion that their friction was not entirely Sal's fault did nothing to help his mood.

Liam was so engrossed in his own spiraling grumpiness, he didn't notice when they had left the woods until suddenly the whole of the valley was spread before them, and the group could see the slopes of Mount Parnassus.

It had been a holy site since pre-Hellenic times, consecrated to Apollo and then also to his brother, Dionysus. Temples had been destroyed and rebuilt, destroyed again, and rebuilt again, until ultimately passing into ruination by a combination of the rise of Christianity, natural disasters, and the march of time.

Until now.

The team froze in their tracks. The Temple of Apollo was once again—*still?*—all gleaming columns on a pristine marble foundation. Where there had once been a village, there was now a shining city.

Where there had once been tourists, there was now not a single living soul.

"What happened to everyone?" Liam asked.

The woman in white shrugged. "We used to have many supplicants, and all who sought us came in good faith. Now the Pythia must be more selective about whom she lets inside her doors."

"We're honored to be here," said Asanti.

"Γνῶθι σεαυτόν," said the woman, chiding, and resumed walking. The rest of the team hurried to catch up.

Γνῶθι σεαυτόν. Although Asanti could read ancient and modern Greek fluently, she had to admit that her grasp of the spoken language was a bit rusty. Still, a little historical context made the meaning of the woman's phrase clear enough: "Know thyself." It was the phrase (or perhaps one of three, depending on your source) engraved on the Pythia's temple in ancient times. But what had the woman meant by it?

Asanti had merely spoken the truth. She was honored to be here. Of course, that wasn't what she had said, was it? But surely her colleagues must appreciate the sheer awe, the simple wonder of being here, in spite of their personal prejudices and misgivings?

She glanced back at her companions. Perhaps not. She wondered if she should have come alone. But no, they needed one another, and Menchú would never have allowed it. In any event, it was far too late to worry about that now.

As she followed the woman in white, Asanti let herself picture all the travelers who had come before them. A trader from Athens, a mother from Crete, a senator from Rome. All had been part of the same pilgrimage over the millennia, changed in details, but not in spirit.

The first step in obtaining a divination from the Pythia was determining that an omen was needed and then making the journey to Delphi. Done. The second step was ritual purification in the Castalian Spring. As if reading her mind, the woman in white led the group to a place outside the temple where the spring flowed into a deep pool, and directed them to wash. Asanti knelt at the edge without hesitation.

"Is this really necessary?" asked Liam.

The woman in white replied evenly, "Only if your question is important to you."

Menchú tried to reassure Liam. "Ritual cleaning is an important part of most religious practices, even our own."

"I've been baptized once already, thanks."

Asanti ignored them, plunging her hands into the spring and bringing up an armful of cold water to splash over her face and hair. Menchú and Grace followed suit. Sal didn't seem much more thrilled with the procedure than Liam was, but pressed ahead—Asanti suspected—so that it wouldn't look like they were in agreement. *What happened between those two?* she wondered.

The water slid down Asanti's back with a slight tingle, like carbonation fizzing against her flesh. When it passed, she felt strangely refreshed, as though the last few weeks of constant stress and travel had washed away.

Rising to her feet, Asanti reached up to squeeze her hair and was shocked to realize that it, along with her hands and her clothes, was completely dry.

"Oh, weird . . ." From Sal's reaction, Asanti was not the only one to notice this phenomenon. Once everyone had washed and observed that they were both cleaner and just as dry as they had been before, the woman in white gestured them forward into the temple.

In his life both before and after entering the priesthood, Menchú had had cause to visit sites considered holy by many different peoples: churches of all denominations, mosques, synagogues, Buddhist and Hindu temples, ancient groves, and standing stones. He wouldn't go so far as to say they all felt the same; that was both a gross oversimplification and the kind of platitude that had always annoyed him. But he was willing to allow that when a place was imbued with divine significance by the people within, there was a . . . quality . . . that was common to all. Different in flavor and degree, perhaps, but which spoke to a union of all divinity that had been part of his faith from childhood and had never left him. The Temple of Apollo at Delphi had that quality, but with an added . . . something.

Shadows of Doric columns fell slanting across Menchú's steps as he followed behind his team, led in turn by the woman in white. *Wouldn't we all feel stupid if it turns out we haven't reached the Pythia, after all?* For all that this mission had been Menchú's own suggestion, it would have been a lie to say that he was completely at peace with asking the Oracle for help. Liam's words pricked at him. *Is this the only way? Or is it merely the only way we can see? If we had persevered in our pursuit of Mr. Norse, would God have opened up another path? Or is this the doorway he has provided?* Menchú was forcibly and uncomfortably reminded of a joke an American colleague had told him where the punch line was God telling a drowned man who had turned down repeated rescues during a flood because he was so sure he would be saved by divine intervention: "Didn't we send two boats and a helicopter?"

Menchú hoped that whatever they learned was worth it. And then they were descending a short flight of stairs into the presence of the Oracle.

Sal wasn't sure what she had been expecting the Pythia to look like. Ethereal? Ancient? Infused with the divine? She definitely hadn't been expecting to see a woman her own age, sitting in a small room on a stone bench beside a pool of water, flipping through a glossy magazine.

Given Asanti's expression, her extensive research hadn't covered that little detail either. The woman in white bowed, murmuring, "The pilgrims you were expecting," and then stepped forward to take the magazine. The Pythia handed it over with only a trace of reluctance. Those formalities complete, the woman in white turned to the team. "This is the Pythia."

The Pythia apparently didn't get a name, which hadn't seemed strange to Sal until she had seen her flipping through a copy of *Vogue*. *People who read* Vogue *should have names,* she thought. As the woman in white withdrew, Sal glanced at the magazine, and blinked. The text had been completely whited out, leaving only the pictures. The Pythia answered her unspoken question.

"The role of the Pythia is to foretell the future and divine the past. Being too bogged down in the present is deemed . . . distracting."

Deemed by whom?

"By Apollo, of course."

"Stop doing that," said Sal, aloud this time.

The other members of the team turned to stare. Grace had already moved her weight forward to the balls of her feet, ready to act if this woman turned out to be not a seer, but a threat.

"She's answering questions that I'm thinking, not asking," said Sal, feeling a little silly.

"Sal," said Asanti, "she hasn't said a word."

"You didn't hear that? About how Apollo doesn't want her to read the articles in *Vogue*?"

Grace blinked. "People read the articles in *Vogue*?"

"Not the point," said Sal.

The Pythia looked apologetic. "You can see why avoiding distractions is important. My apologies."

Sal thought that maybe inadvertent mind reading and forgetting to talk so that everyone in the room could hear you were arguments for having a few more distractions in your life, but what did she know about being a prophetic priestess of Apollo? What she said was: "It's okay." Then added, "But please stop reading my mind."

The Pythia shrugged. "I wouldn't if your thoughts weren't so loud. Is that why you're here?" she asked.

"No," said Asanti. "We come seeking information."

"What kind of information?"

"We need to know about the *Codex Umbra*."

The Pythia considered this. "And what will you sacrifice for that knowledge?" she asked.

Sal's stomach went cold. A sacrifice. She'd been so distracted after she'd nearly slept through their flight she had completely forgotten she needed one. *What had the others brought? The Pythia must accept small offerings. No one else seems to have anything huge with them . . . unless Menchú has been hiding a baby goat under his jacket this whole time.*

Sal tried to be subtle as she slipped her hands into her pockets. It was probably futile to try to fool a demonstrated mind reader, but maybe she could manage to avoid letting the rest of her team know what a flake she was. And then . . . beside her keys and a handful of loose euros, her fingers closed around a folded square of paper. *A receipt? Old grocery list?* Sal squeezed the packet. It gave slightly, as if it was folded around something. *What the hell?*

One by one, the others brought out their offerings: Grace's copy of *Moment in Peking*, the first novel she had read in English; Menchú's Bible, given to him by a parishioner before he left Guatemala. Asanti had brought letters from her dead mentor. Liam, breaking the written material trend, produced a fighter's knife, which he placed on the table before the Pythia without offering any explanation. At least, not aloud. Then it was Sal's turn. She took a deep breath, drew out the folded paper, and hoped like hell she wasn't about to offer the Oracle a piece of old gum.

Slowly, she opened the packet, revealing a tidy bundle of mousy brown hair. Sal's mind raced. *Hair? Where did I get—* And then she knew. With absolute certainty. She *knew*. Sal swallowed. It was her brother's hair. *That's what I was doing in the Archives. But how—*

The Pythia's voice in her head cut off Sal's mental spiral. *An interesting choice. We accept your sacrifice.*

Then she stepped forward, took the paper and lock of hair from Sal's hand and placed them next to the other sacrifices before seating herself behind them on a small three-legged stool. "Your sacrifices are all fitting." She dipped a hand into the pool at her feet, brought a mouthful of water to her lips, and drank.

For a moment, nothing happened.

And then the Pythia spoke again, but her voice had changed— though maybe it was only that Sal was hearing it differently. The

Oracle's words filled every corner of the room, and yet she spoke so softly, Sal found herself straining to hear.

"The *Codex Umbra*: a prison of demons, the worst placed together, to be more easily guarded by the followers of the cross. Until the *Codex* became too dangerous to be safely held. Even the jailers could not be trusted to the temptations of the prisoners."

"This book was created by the Church?" asked Menchú.

"Assembled, not created. A compilation, pieced from fabrics ready-made, not woven as virgin cloth."

"Dear God," whispered Asanti.

Sal caught her breath as she began to understand. The Black Archive's books were dangerous. The Pythia's words implied that someone had decided to take the most dangerous sections of the most dangerous books and put them all together in one place, a supermax for demons. Sal shuddered. "Dear God" was right.

"Where is it?" asked Liam.

"The wounded knights knew it must be hidden, so they found a place where no—"

The Pythia's voice ceased abruptly. Her face grew red, then dusky purple. *Is that normal?* The woman in white screamed and rushed forward. *No, definitely not.*

"She can't breathe," said Liam. For once, Sal was relieved that someone was cynical enough about this whole excursion to keep their wits about them. Liam rushed to the Pythia's side, working with the woman in white to ease the Oracle to the ground. He tipped her head back, checking her airway. Something about the familiar emergency procedures caused Sal's training to kick in, and she unfroze, moving to join them.

The Pythia was still conscious, and Sal grabbed her hand. "Can you hear me? Blink if you can."

The Pythia blinked.

"We're going to help you out, okay?"

From up close, it wasn't hard to tell what the problem was. The golden necklace the Pythia wore around her neck had sprouted thorns that had dug their way into her flesh.

"Are those going through to her airway?" Sal asked Liam.

He shook his head. "More likely it's the delivery system for some kind of toxin, and her throat is closing down as a reaction. Either way, her throat's almost completely blocked."

"Don't suppose anyone here carries an EpiPen?" Sal asked.

The woman in white clutched the Pythia's other hand. Menchú and Asanti shook their heads.

Sal turned back to Liam. "Should we try to get it off?"

"I don't see how it could make things worse."

"Famous last words," Sal muttered.

But Liam was already lifting the Pythia's head, gently so as not to bend her already compromised trachea. "I can see the clasp."

Sal reached forward, but just as her fingers touched the metal of the fastener, Grace's hand slid in under her hers, grasped the clasp, and wrenched it open. As it sprang free, the necklace flew through the air, landing with a soft clink against the hard floor.

The instant the necklace was gone, the Pythia convulsed in Liam's arms, her eyes rolling back and bloody foam bubbling up through her lips. She kept writhing as Liam set her down. Menchú slid his folded jacket under her head to protect her skull from banging against the stones, and Sal turned the Pythia's head so that she wouldn't choke as she began to vomit. First bile and then blood.

Sal watched the struggling woman's pulse pound in her neck. Saw her diaphragm strain to pull air past her blocked throat. She had already coughed up so much blood that the additional stream when Liam cut a hole for a field tracheotomy barely made a difference. But mostly Sal watched her heartbeat, proof that she was still fighting to live with everything she had. She kept fighting through it all.

In the end, it wasn't enough.

4.

CHAMBER OF THE ORACLE, A SHORT TIME LATER.

The woman in white was so obviously upset, Asanti drew her into her arms like she was a child, absorbing her grief at the loss of the Pythia against her shoulder. Eventually the woman in white pulled herself together, extracted herself from Asanti's arms, and turned to face the truth of her oracle lying dead upon the stones. Asanti rose to join her.

"I'm so sorry," she said.

The woman nodded. "Thank you."

"Do you know where she got the necklace? Who might have wanted to harm her?"

"It was a tribute from a supplicant, in thanks for a prophecy fulfilled."

"Do you know this supplicant's name?" Asanti asked.

The woman in white turned and looked Asanti in the eye for the first time since the Pythia had fallen. "It does not matter. The assassin's aims have been achieved." Then, "You and your friends should go."

"Ms. Brooks is a trained investigator. We can help you—"

"Now."

As she spoke, a peal of thunder echoed across the clear sky. Clouds soon followed, accompanied by a distant pounding noise. Rain or footsteps. Many, many footsteps.

"Surely you don't think we are responsible," said Asanti.

"It does not matter," the woman in white repeated. "The Pythia is gone. We must mourn, and bury her. And then find and anoint her successor. You are no longer welcome here."

"But we need to know—"

"What you need is no longer relevant. Return to the fountain house, it will bring you back to your own place and time. Go!"

The thunder cracked again, and the stone floor shook beneath their feet. Asanti turned to the others. "I think we should listen to her."

Asanti thought she heard Liam mutter, "Finally."

Together, they ran.

THE FOUNTAIN HOUSE, IN DELPHI OF THE WORLD.

"What happened back there?" Grace asked as soon as they were once again in the dappled world of modern Delphi and had enough breath for asking questions.

"Besides someone killing the Pythia?" asked Liam.

Grace leveled her best do-not-mess-with-me stare. "Allow me to rephrase: *How* did that happen back there?"

Menchú shook his head. "Aside from ourselves, the only person present at her death was the woman in white. And I know none of *us* killed the Pythia."

"Verbal trigger," said Asanti.

Liam blinked. "Excuse me?"

"It strangled her, cutting off her voice, as she was about to tell us where we could find the *Codex*. That can't be a coincidence. Whoever gave her that necklace—"

"And by *whoever*, you mean Norse," said Sal.

"*Whoever* gave her that necklace clearly meant it as a trap. She starts divulging information they don't want to get out? No more Pythia."

"The Pythia will be replaced," said Grace. "And she won't be stupid enough to wear the necklace that killed her predecessor."

"Maybe that doesn't matter," said Sal. "I'm guessing that anointing a new Pythia isn't a quick process. Most likely, it'll be weeks before they reopen the shrine. Norse left us alone for nearly a month after the Market Arcanum. Now, suddenly, we can't go twenty minutes without the Orb triggering. Norse is on a timetable, and my bet is that by the time we can ask the new Oracle where to find the *Codex*, he'll already have his hands on his very own *Norton Anthology of Evil*," said Sal.

Three pairs of eyes blinked at her in silence.

"If any of you had gone to an American high school, that would have been a very clever reference," said Sal.

Liam crossed his arms. "We know what a Norton Anthology is," he said. "Norton is a British publisher, but unless your American high school taught you where to find evil books sought by madmen, we're back where we started. Only lighter by five sacrifices and heavier by one dead Pythia." He glared at Menchú. "So glad using magic was worth it."

Sal couldn't quite believe that Liam had basically told his boss (a priest, no less), *I told you so*. On the other hand, Liam wasn't wrong.

"Actually," said Asanti, "we aren't exactly back to square one."

"How so?" asked Menchú.

"At the Library of Alexandria, Youssef told us about the nature of magic, the special rules of cause and effect that apply. And before she died, the Pythia showed us how to access the power of the Castalian Spring."

Liam stared at Asanti, mouth agape. "No." He turned to Menchú. "She can't. You can't let her."

"Technically, she outranks me," Menchú pointed out.

"I don't care," said Liam.

"You don't even know what I'm suggesting," said Asanti.

"You're suggesting that we try to channel the magic of the spring ourselves. And I'm saying that it's a terrible idea."

"I'm inclined to agree," said Menchú.

To everyone's surprise, Grace spoke up. "We should do it."

"What?!"

"If we do nothing, Norse gets the book. We don't know what his aims are, but he still wanted the last book back *after* he knew it was leaking demon ooze. If we let Asanti try to use the spring, it might go horribly wrong. She might die. We might all die. But if it doesn't, the rest of the world will have a fighting chance."

Liam shook his head. "There has to be another way."

"How long will it take you to prepare?" Menchú asked Asanti. "And I mean *properly* prepare. Taking every precaution."

Asanti considered. "Two hours."

Menchú turned to Liam. "If you can use what we've learned so far to find a solid lead on the location of the *Codex Umbra* in three hours, we'll follow it. Otherwise, I'm going to let her try. Grace, Sal, help with whatever either one of them needs in the meantime." And with that, Menchú began picking his way down the path.

"What are you going to do?" Sal called after him.

Menchú didn't look back. "Pray."

Since all Liam needed was the fastest Internet connection available in Delphi (surprisingly fast for a place that was so hard to get to, but Liam just muttered something about tourist traps and credit card processing and buried himself in his computer), Sal and Grace got a list of supplies from Asanti and then left her to meditate and cleanse herself pre-ritual while they went into the town.

Having learned that Grace wasn't one for idle banter, Sal was prepared to spend the walk in companionable silence. Grace had other ideas, however.

"What's Liam so pissed about?" she asked.

Sal's step hitched, and she hoped Grace hadn't noticed. "He was once possessed by a demon, and now he's touchy about even brushing up against magic?"

"That's been his problem for years. This is new."

"What makes you think I'd know?"

"You want me to open up to you? That goes both ways. If we're going to be friends now, then we're going to be friends. So. Share. Liam has a problem with you. Is it because you're sleeping together?"

Sal nearly choked on her own spit. "I thought we were being discreet."

Grace gave her a look. "My life is made up of patches of coherence surrounded by long stretches of unconsciousness. People don't always think to summarize what I've missed. I've learned to observe details and get up to speed quickly."

"Oh."

"One reason I don't tell people about my condition, by the way, is that when I do, they tend to give me looks like that."

"Sorry," Sal said. "I just . . . Sorry."

"What happened?"

"Well, mostly, we aren't sleeping together anymore."

This time it was Grace's turn to say, "Oh." And, a hesitation later: "Sorry."

They walked together for a few more minutes until Sal realized that Grace was content to leave the topic there. And it wasn't that she had been looking forward to the third degree. But . . .

"So you're not going to give me the don't-shit-where-you-eat speech?" Sal asked.

Grace raised an eyebrow. "Was your relationship the equivalent of a pile of dung in the dining room?"

"Well, no."

"Was he trying to hurt you?"

"No."

"Did you enter the relationship wanting to hurt him?"

"Of course not."

Grace shrugged. "Then if you loved him, why shouldn't you have pursued it?"

Sal wasn't sure "love" was exactly the right word for what had been between the two of them, but maybe it wasn't exactly the wrong one either. "But isn't it messing up team dynamics now or something?"

Grace shrugged. "If this didn't, something else would have. I've been around awhile. Trust me."

They had reached the town's main street, and Sal was left to consider Grace's words as they set about finding the items on Asanti's wish list: a lighter, cigarettes, a wooden bowl, and a large box of salt. That last item made Sal think of the *Fair Weather*, and Katie, and she boggled at how many things had followed from a collapsed bookshop.

As they started back up the path toward the spring, Sal returned to their earlier topic of conversation. "What you were saying before, about Liam and me and pursuing chances?"

Grace nodded.

"If we're friends now . . . were you speaking from personal experience?"

Wind rustled dry grass. They walked for a long time in silence. Then Grace spoke: "When I met Arturo Menchú, I had been alive for more than sixty years, and we looked like we were the same age.

"He worries about my candle. I've been watching his burn down for thirty years."

A SECLUDED CLEARING NEXT TO THE CASTALIAN STREAM, THREE HOURS LATER.

Asanti knew that Liam, and even Menchú, thought she was too cavalier about magic. But lack of care for the dangers magic presented wasn't the reason why she consistently pushed for the Society to take a less abolitionist stance against the rising tide of the supernatural into the world. If the theories of the Society were right—and every part of her research and that of her predecessors indicated that they were—the question wasn't *if* magic would break through into the world, but *when*. The time to learn how to harness, control, and manipulate those forces was now, not when they were all awash in the flood. The Mr. Norses of the world would be ready. The Society had to be as well.

Which was why Asanti had been studying the manipulation of magic and demons for most of her professional life. Still, even as she laid out her preparations, she searched her mind for an alternative to putting her theoretical studies into practice. If Liam came up with a lead, she would yield to him in a heartbeat.

In the end, she was glad that Menchú had allotted her three hours instead of the two she had requested. Magic was a lot like cooking, the *mise en place* always took longer than you expected. She was finishing when she heard Menchú's footsteps approaching through the woods, alone.

"Are you sure about this?" he asked.

Asanti shook her head. "Of course I'm not sure. But unless Liam found something, I think we should try."

"We don't have to."

"When the consequences of inaction outweigh the risks of action, the only possible course is to act."

"Mandela?" Menchú guessed.

"My mother. When asked why she gave up a comfortable life as an expatriate to return home and fight for an end to colonial rule. I've taken every precaution I know. This is as safe as I can make it."

"And if those precautions aren't enough?"

Asanti raised an eyebrow. "Does Sal have her gun with her?"

"She's still not cleared to carry in EU countries."

"Then tell Grace to snap my neck quickly. If a demon tries to use me as a beachhead, killing me should send it back where it came from as surely as closing a book."

Menchú gave her a solemn nod. "I'll get the others."

And with that, the time for doubts was over. Soon the rest of the team stood in a circle around her, one at each of the four compass points, centering them in a geographical system of mapping the world.

Correspondence. The map and the territory. The idea of the thing, and where it could be found.

A circle to create a border: magic within, mundane without. Making the circle out of salt wasn't necessary, but it had historical precedent. Also, it was the substance that bound earth and sea. Air was present in abundance. For fire, Asanti lit a cigarette from the pack Grace and Sal had bought and left it on a flat rock to smolder.

Finally, Asanti ordered her thoughts. She called to mind everything they knew about the *Codex Umbra*. It wasn't much, but she made the most complete mental picture she could, turning it over and over in her head. Finally, she dipped her hands into the stream, brought the cool water to her lips, and drank.

As soon as Asanti drank the water from the spring, Sal felt a charge hit the air. As though the space was suddenly . . . filled . . . with something weightless and invisible but that gave the atmosphere a substance that it hadn't had before. Like the feeling of a summer afternoon before a thunderstorm.

Then Asanti spoke. "The *Codex Umbra*: What you seek cannot be found, although you can reach its hiding place. Go to where dawn first lights this land, where a Titan once stood watch. The *Codex* lives in shadow. To protect the world, the wounded knights locked its prison, which can only be opened on the lightest of days."

Asanti fell silent. Blinked. "I think that's it."

Sal caught Liam's eye from where he stood around the circle to her left. He looked relieved, but quickly masked his expression when he saw her watching. "I suppose coordinates would have been too much to ask for?" he grumbled.

Sal couldn't stop the smile twisting at her lips. He smiled back. *Maybe we'll be okay, after all,* she thought. Inside the circle, Asanti reached forward to stub out the cigarette, but as her fingers closed around the filter, the smoldering end flared into a jet of flame.

"Asanti!" shouted Menchú.

Her eyes gone completely white, Asanti didn't answer.

"She's going to set the trees on fire," said Grace, her tone as calm as if she was commenting on the weather.

Sal looked at the stream. At least there was a source of water. She turned for their gear, looking for something she could use as a bucket. That movement saved her life.

An instant after she turned away from Asanti, a blast of heat struck Sal's left shoulder, and her hair begin to burn.

5.

STILL BY THE STREAM, THREE SECONDS LATER.

Asanti wasn't responding. Liam stood transfixed. Sal was on fire.

Grace leaped into action. She had her complaints about what her encounter with a crazed magician in Shanghai had done to her life, tying her existence and consciousness to a magic-infused candle. But having a body essentially impervious to physical harm was not one of them.

She barreled straight into Sal, tangential to the circle, sending the other woman stumbling toward the stream, then dug in her heels, planting herself right in the center of the flame a tranced-out Asanti was launching from her cigarette. At least, that was the plan.

Grace felt the wash of fire distantly, as a pleasant warmth that told her the flames were there, even if they weren't doing her any harm. And then the heat was gone. Asanti—or whatever was controlling Asanti—wasn't mindlessly attacking. It had shifted its aim. Pursuing Sal. *That's not good.*

❖ ❖ ❖

Liam froze. *If anyone should have been prepared for disaster, you should have been,* he reproached himself. And yet when his worst fear came to life, when he saw the humanity in Asanti overwhelmed by the sheer power she had tried to bend to her will, he froze. He wanted to run to Sal. Stop this disaster before it could spread. But he stood rooted to the spot, heart pounding in his ears. He didn't know what he had done or where he had been during his missing years. But that feeling in the air, the smell of fire different from any fire on earth. He could not remember having seen, or felt, or smelled those things before. But they were familiar nonetheless, and that terrified him to his core.

He closed his eyes. *You're clean. The Church says so. The Society says so. Menchú says so. This isn't you. You're clean—*

"Liam!"

Menchú's voice jolted Liam out of his reverie.

"Get in here and help me with her!"

Menchú had stepped into the circle with Asanti, trying to wrest control of the cigarette with one hand while wielding a bottle of holy water in the other.

Menchú's voice cracked against Liam's hesitation: "Now!"

Liam jerked into action. One foot in front of the other, and in two strides he was next to Asanti. Years ago, she had helped him find his way back to himself. Now was his chance to help her do the same. He pulled her body against his, her back to his front so that he could use his right hand to grip her right wrist, pushing it, forcing the flaming cigarette down. Farther, farther, until he jammed the tip against a large, flat rock. The flame sputtered and died. The dry leaves next to the rock began throwing off smoke, and he moved to stomp them with his boot.

"Let Grace handle that." Menchú again. "Hold Asanti still."

Exorcisms were not designed to be conducted in the middle of the woods, only a few hundred yards from a notable tourist site, and without weeks of extensive preparation. Good thing Menchú wasn't planning an exorcism.

He was, however, praying for divine assistance. "Oh Lord, from the beginning, your act of creation was rooted in separation: light from darkness, heaven from earth, the waters above from the waters below. Help us now. Separate your earthly daughter from the foreign force that seeks to use her to breach this world, as the root does the wall that upholds the foundations of your Church and your creation. We ask this in your name, amen."

He distantly heard Liam echo his "amen" under Asanti's wordless scream.

"Hold on, friend," said Menchú, and he tipped the vial of holy water in his hand into Asanti's mouth. She sputtered, choked. For a second of heart-stopping terror, Menchú feared he was about to see Asanti die like the Pythia. But then Liam was bending Asanti forward, and she was heaving up a stream of clear water from her throat. Much more than the vial of holy water had contained. And not a trace of food or bile.

"It's from the spring," said Liam.

As the last drops hit the dry earth, the heaviness in the air lifted.

"Are you all right?" Menchú asked Asanti.

She nodded. Her eyes met his. Her eyes that were once again a familiar dark brown. She cleared her throat. "Thanks for finding a way to do that without killing me."

"Anytime."

Cautiously, Liam let her go.

"Do you remember what you said?" asked Menchú.

"Yes. Sorry to be so cryptic." Her eye fell on a very damp—but no longer burning—Sal. "And about that."

"That wasn't you," said Sal.

"And as for the cryptic," Liam added, "I've got some ideas."

Menchú looked at his team. The cop. The haunted programmer. The indestructible woman out of her time who would probably out-live them all. The archivist who held them all together.

"Come on," he said. "Let's go home."

EPILOGUE

R hodes." Liam looked up from his computer. "The *Codex Umbra* is at Rhodes."

"You're sure?" asked Menchú.

Liam nodded. "Farthest east of the major Greek islands, that's 'where dawn first lights this land' if you're in Delphi. Also, formerly home of a colossus that was one of the wonders of the ancient world."

"'Where a Titan once stood watch,'" quoted Asanti.

"That still leaves us a lot of ground to cover," said Sal. "Well, maybe not in absolute terms, but I'm guessing a major Greek island has more than one place to hide an evil book."

"Well," mused Menchú, "if the book is at Rhodes, the wounded knights must be the Knights of Saint John. Checking their records might give us a place to start looking."

"And the lightest of all days?" asked Sal.

"The summer solstice," said Grace.

"Which is fourteen days from now," said Liam.

"So," said Menchú, "that leaves us two weeks to discover

462

the secret vault of the Knights of Saint John, and come up with a means of keeping the *Codex* away from Mr. Norse."

Liam looked over at Asanti. "It's still more information than we used to have."

Asanti nodded, accepting the implied apology. "I have some books that might be useful."

Menchú looked at the team. They'd been running ragged for nearly a month. At the moment they were feeling the surge of energy that came with new discovery, but he knew from experience that it wouldn't last. "First," he said, "everyone go home. Eat real food. Get real sleep. And if I see any of you in here before noon tomorrow, I'm going to force you to take *two* days off."

Sal grinned. Menchú didn't. "Ask the others if you think I'm kidding." For a bunch of dedicated workaholics, it was an effective threat. Menchú didn't threaten frequently. He kept that one in his arsenal for emergencies.

Sal's expression sobered.

It was a sign of how exhausted they all were that no one actually fought back. Even Asanti didn't seem inclined to linger. And then Menchú and Grace were alone in the Archives.

"I hope that noon rule applies to you as well," said Grace.

Menchú chuckled. "Yes, ma'am." She poked him with her elbow. "Anything else?" he asked.

"Actually, yes."

"Name it."

"I need a break. We've been running from crisis to crisis too long. I'm rested, but I'm not getting any mental downtime."

Menchú nodded, catching her meaning. "Are you sure?"

Grace nodded. "I want my day off, and this seems like a good time for it." She looked to him, suddenly seeming unsure.

"I can take noon to noon, though, if you want to sleep in."

"No, I can wake up. I know how much you like your mornings."

Grace smiled. After all these years, Menchú still loved the way it lit her face. "See you in the morning, then," she said.

He watched her go.

As the door closed behind her, he said, "See you in the morning."

EPISODE 10

SHORE LEAVE

MUR LAFFERTY

PROLOGUE

MAESTRI DEL TEMPO, ALWAYS.

Nothing felt as right as a clock. Nothing was so perfect, and so taken for granted, as the little wheels and springs that measure that master of us all—time.

Bella screams as she takes her first breath, cupped in a midwife's hands, trying to focus on a pair of smiling brown eyes behind a mask.

Her nephew Matteo had said that the new games on expensive phones, apps, made pleasure centers fire in people's brains, which led to addiction. While Bella Ferrara disapproved of the time Matteo—so handsome if you saw him from the angle that didn't show the scar on his right cheek—spent with his phone, a small, secret part of her understood completely. She felt that way whenever she could make the gears fit, make the ticking happen, make a clock live again. Every tick was dopamine to her.

She hides from bullies in an old clock shop, and as she watches the old clockmaker's hands work, so deft and so precise, her fear fades, and her own world snaps into place.

Matteo understood. He was her protégé, her lousy brother's third child, ignored by all except his aunt. He didn't have the skill, but he had the passion.

Mother laments that Bella will never find a husband, never knowing that Antonio left for the war, carrying her heart, and never brought it back home to her.

Her hands were old now, the knuckles swelling and the movements painful and slow, as if she had just dragged them from an ice bath. Her days as a clockmaker were numbered, she knew, and none of her nieces or nephews wanted the shop that would be their inheritance.

Golden streams of time, snarled and tangled like yarn and smoke and veins of silver. Time is everywhere and everything.

"Zia Bella, why don't you just retire? You deserve it!" Matteo would say. "Sell the shop, buy a cottage by the sea, and live out the rest of your life relaxing."

Antonio touches her, lights fires within her, and time slows.

Matteo had the passion, but his hands were large and bulky, the hands of a sailor or a construction worker. If she had willed the business to him, he would have had to bring in another clockmaker, and that wouldn't do. No one else in her family wanted the business. She was sad they didn't love it as she did, but someone who didn't love this business had no right being in it. Clockmakers are called.

Her father dies in a stinking hot room, and time stops. But only for a second.

At night she would dream of time, golden streams of it, how they crossed, some going faster than others, and all she had to do was pick a stream to place a boat upon, and go anywhen. During the day, her shop sang to her, the little ticks and clicks marking her life. Every hour the song reached a crescendo, and then subsided. Going home was always a disappointment. Removing her hands from her work broke her heart a little each day.

She receives riches, as more and more wealthy customers seek her, as

Rolex hires her to consult, as she becomes known as the finest clockmaker in Italy, but never leaves her tiny shop.

Matteo's love for his *zia* and his impressive business skills (something to do with computer chips, things with even smaller working parts than ladies' watches) led him to scour the antique shops when he traveled on business, and he brought her wonderful treasures: clocks to fix, clocks to clean, antique tools even older than her own. The latest find had been glorious. He would tell her nothing about where he got it from, except to say that the seller's name was Norse.

She buys the clock shop from her old master, the man who unknowingly rescued her, body and soul, the day she ducked through his door. She pays in cash she has saved for decades.

It was a rounding-up tool made of brass. It was clearly old, but had no sign of wear on it anywhere. She knew it was old because these tools simply weren't made anymore. It sang in her hands, like her clocks did. The wheel spun silently, and everything seemed to slow as she worked on her clocks. She had never been happier.

She dies, bleeding and broken in the corner, thinking it is somehow fitting that she dies among her clocks, and she wonders if any of them will stop when she does.

Everything happens at once, and it takes forever.

1.

SAL'S APARTMENT, 5:47:39 A.M.

Cleaning house.

Buzz.

Time to clean the house. Get the gloves and the bucket and—

Buzz.

Like a towrope pulling her from deep water, the buzzing phone led Sal from her dream into reality. She blinked, then swore.

Buzz.

She stood in her bedroom, her hands flat on her dresser. Nothing was amiss beyond this—her modest jewelry box still sat in the middle of the dresser, and on the left side was the stack of clean laundry she was too lazy to put away.

She looked up into the mirror and met her own eyes, seized by a sense of vertigo. "Why are you standing here"—she checked her bedside clock—"before six?" she asked her reflection.

It didn't answer.

"At least I'm not in the Archives this time," she muttered, rubbing her face.

The phone buzzed again from its place next to her clock, and

472

Sal finally was able to unlock her joints and walk on shaky legs to retrieve it.

It was a text from Grace. The Orb must be active. Menchú had said they'd earned a day off, especially Grace. But if duty called . . .

"Time to make the donuts," Sal grumbled, and pulled up the text. *"Knock, knock, Neo."*

The phrase stuck in her head, but she couldn't place the memory. She blinked and was about to text back, but a knock came at her door.

Right. *The Matrix.* She sighed and went to answer the door.

Grace stood there, a backpack slung over one shoulder, grinning widely. Sal stared at her, sure that something had to be wrong. "What's going on?" she asked. "Is it the Orb?"

Grace pushed past her with no invitation. "Of course not," she said. "It's my day off. Remember?"

"Why does your day off mean I get dragged from my bed at ass o'clock?" Sal asked.

"Because you're coming with me," Grace said. "Arturo approved it. Insisted on it, really. We're going to have some fun, and nothing is going to interrupt us."

Sal raised her hand. "Okay. My brain is going about five miles an hour. I'm gonna make some coffee, and you're gonna tell me what exactly you're talking about."

Grace frowned briefly in irritation, but then relaxed into her grin again. "Usually, when a mission's done, Liam goes to surf the Internet. Arturo returns to his church duties and his studies. Sometimes, he tells me, he sees a movie. You come here and do . . . whatever the hell it is you do." Grace waved her hand to encompass Sal's apartment. "You know what I do?"

Sal paused from scooping coffee into her coffeemaker. "I know you can't afford to burn your candle on relaxation," she said softly.

"Exactly. When I relax, it's usually while traveling to and from a mission. Even then Arturo had to fight the big guns to not keep the candle snuffed until the team needs me."

Big guns. Sal had never thought of the priests and cardinals as big guns.

Sal winced at the idea of carting Grace around like a vampire in a coffin, waking her up only to fight. She wondered who was in charge of deciding when to light Grace's candle, but saved that question for another time.

"A few years ago, I demanded a day off, twenty-four hours just for me," Grace said. She sat down in a kitchen chair and leaned back, smiling. "No demons, no travel, no demands. So they gave me one a year."

Sal got two mugs from the dishwasher and filled both with coffee. She put a bottle of cream on the table and handed Grace one of the cups. Sal sat to join her, sipping her black coffee. "Not that you don't deserve it, but I find it hard to believe they agreed to not having you on call at least. That's what bugs Liam: We're not like normal cops because we're always on call."

"Liam gets downtime. I don't," Grace said.

"Hey, what was with the *Matrix* quote, anyway?" Sal asked.

Grace's eyes gleamed. "A while back I watched a marathon of all three of the Matrix movies. I loved them."

"*All* of them?" Sal asked suspiciously. "Years after they came out?"

Grace nodded.

"You really are sheltered from pop culture," Sal said.

"I catch up as much as I can on days off. Sometimes travel. Now finish your coffee. I have a full day planned."

✦ ✦ ✦

A spin class. Grace wanted to go to a spin class. They bought a trial membership to a local gym and made it in time for the seven a.m. session.

"Why are we doing this again, exactly?" Sal asked.

"All of my workouts consist of sparring with Liam and doing . . . our job," Grace said, glancing at the people around them as she watered down their day-to-day duties. "I never, ever, get to exercise just for the fun of it."

"We could go for a run, hike near some of the ruins outside the city, take a swim . . ." Sal trailed off as music began thumping and a tightly muscled woman with short, white-blond hair began talking into a headset.

"Oh, we'll do those things too, if you want," Grace said, "but I've seen these classes on TV, and I've always wanted to try them." She turned the tension up on her bike and began to pedal furiously.

As she climbed onto the bike next to Grace's, Sal found herself hoping to be called away to fight demons. It would likely be more fun. As soon as she started pedaling, her phone buzzed, and she gratefully searched her pocket for it. Asanti was texting. *Oh, thank God.* She glanced at Grace. "Asanti," she said, waving the phone.

Grace didn't take her eyes off the class leader. "Answer her if you like. I'm not going back until this day is over."

Sal slowed her pedaling and focused on her phone, avoiding the irritated looks of the men and women pedaling to the video of the Italian countryside that was playing behind the leader.

Did Grace drag you out of bed? Asanti texted.

Yep. We're at a freaking spin class. Everything okay there?

Things are fine here, u 2 have fun. Likely be the last fun you have b4 summer spotless.

Will try. Would rather not be spinning tho. Sal sent the final text and put the phone back in the slot on her handlebars made for those who couldn't be away from their precious devices.

She picked up her pace to rejoin the fake ride through the countryside (when the real countryside was just a few miles away), but the class leader pointed her out.

"If you do not respect the class, you are given the mud bike!" she called in heavily accented English. She pointed to a bike near the back, far from Grace. Sal paused to see if she was serious—the woman had stopped pedaling and kept pointing.

Sal groaned and grabbed her phone, then went to the bike and climbed aboard, noticing that it didn't have a tension knob. The pedals were very heavy. It had been locked on the tightest position. Like she was biking through mud. Clever.

Sal shot an irritated look at Grace, who grinned at her and shrugged.

I'm doing this for her.

It was going to be a long hour.

THE BLACK ARCHIVES, 7:04:43 A.M.

"Damn autocorrect," Asanti said after she reread her last text. She put the phone in her pocket, then glared at Liam. "Can I help you, Liam? Or do you want to watch the next text I send as well?"

"'Things are fine here'?" he asked, pointing at the glowing Orb, its transcription apparatus chattering quietly as it delivered information. "Does that look 'fine' to you? Why did you lie to her? We might need them."

Asanti glanced at the notes the Orb had spat out thus far. "I don't think so. It doesn't seem like a big deal. Local. Something has awakened. We can handle it with the people we have."

"Just the two of us?" Liam asked, nodding toward Menchú, who sat at Asanti's desk.

"Of course not," Asanti said, finishing her notes. "I'm going with you."

Liam rolled his eyes and stomped off, mumbling something about breakfast.

After he had gone, Asanti looked at Menchú. "At least this looks like minor activity."

"Don't discount minor activity. It can turn major in a short time. The Glasgow incident started minor, didn't it?" He looked at her, unblinking.

She met his gaze. She knew he was waiting on her to show some sort of guilt for the Glasgow trip, but she regretted nothing. They had learned a lot about Sal on that trip, and the group enjoyed their one-day vacation in Glasgow. Yes, the vacation had been largely spent at a wake and funeral, but a change of pace was nice.

"We'll be fine," she repeated. "And if you don't trust me on this—"

"Don't say that, Asanti, not again," he said, interrupting her and standing up. "I trust you to do the right thing, always. I just don't trust you to judge the danger of a situation as quickly as the others. They see a lion, while you see a fascinating bone and muscle structure of yellow purring fluff you'd like to study more closely."

"Then I'm not sure about the wisdom of having Sal exempt from duties, as Grace is."

"Sal will come if we need her," Menchú said, watching the Orb. "And Grace has never let us down."

Liam returned clutching a bag of breakfast sandwiches, which he dropped on Asanti's desk. He rummaged around in the bag and grabbed a sandwich. "What I don't understand," he said, as if he had never left, "is why Sal gets a day pass. Grace deserves one; she doesn't take a lot of time off, it seems. But the new bird comes in and suddenly gets the same treatment."

He shrugged, winced, then stretched. Asanti watched in sympathy. They needed more than one night's sleep to recover after the Delphi trip, but the Orb had to be heeded.

"With what we've been dealing with, everyone needs time off. You get tomorrow," Menchú said.

Liam pulled a chair to Asanti's desk and tore into his sandwich as if it had offended him.

"I think someone is a bit jealous," Asanti said. The Irishman flushed. "It's tough being the odd person out. But they're not consciously excluding you."

Liam choked. "That's not the issue."

Asanti noted how he avoided her gaze and began to guess the real reason behind his discomfort. "Does this have something to do with you and—"

"Goddammit, Asanti," Liam said. "Mind your own business. I'm fine."

Asanti watched him carefully. She would have to broach the subject with him later, without Menchú around. Liam needed to talk something out, that was clear.

The Orb glowed again, and Asanti examined the new data. "We have the location now. A clock shop a few kilometers north of here. Looks like an artifact, not a book. Thank goodness."

"An artifact in a clock shop?" Liam asked. "How much do you want to bet it messes with time? How are we supposed to deal with that?"

"Carefully," Menchú said. "Find out who owns the shop."

Liam frowned and went to his backpack to get his laptop. Asanti glanced at Menchú and noticed him typing on his phone, his back to them.

Asanti wasn't worried. If he was texting Grace, she'd ignore him today. Unless maybe Menchú was in trouble.

2.

H ave a Bellini," Grace said grandly, passing one of the tall bubbling flutes to Sal. "It will calm your muscle spasms."

"It will?" Sal asked, raising an eyebrow. Her legs had been shaky and unpredictable after the spin class. Add that on top of the aches and pains she had from the previous day's trip to Delphi, and she felt about a hundred years old.

She'd not been allowed to get off the "mud bike" for the entire class. She almost left, but the look on Grace's face—pleading—stopped her.

Not that Grace was pleading now. She lounged across the table at perfect ease, in a tie-waist floral print dress and a panama hat cocked back at an angle. The woman didn't even have the decency to look flushed.

Sal accepted the glass and sipped the Bellini. She didn't understand why one would ruin sparkling wine with peach puree, but guessed adding the fruit made it okay to booze it up in the morning.

"Maybe. I don't know," Grace said, flipping a hand, careless. "Alcohol relaxes you. Doesn't it?"

Sal looked at the menu. The prices were shocking, but Grace had said she didn't have a lot to spend her income on, especially with the Vatican covering her lodging at the convent. Sal thought about all the gold that was rumored to be inside the Vatican and figured they could spring for expensive pastries and a few more Bellinis. They ordered, and then relaxed back into their seats.

Sal wasn't used to drinking in the morning, and the wine hit her hard. She studied her friend. "One day off a year. How do you not lose your mind?"

Grace frowned. "What do you mean?"

"I've seen a lot of cops get PTSD from dealing with shit much less scary than what we fight. They need rest with friends and family and, sometimes, a therapist. But you have terrifying fights, go down, and wake up to more terrifying fights. It doesn't seem mentally healthy."

Grace focused past Sal, thinking. "Arturo helps me. He wakes me every week for a short talk to let me know what day it is and what has been going on." She took a sip of her drink and smiled at Sal. "Lately we've had so much activity that he doesn't need to do that, but it helps when things are slow."

"You two have been through a lot together," Sal said, putting down her empty glass. Another Bellini appeared at her elbow.

"Yes. For me, it's only been a few years' time. For him, decades." Grace focused again behind Sal, toward the windows of the café. "Imagine it. You've been here a few months. What if everyone else had aged forty years by now, and you stayed the same?"

Sal shook her head. "I couldn't handle it. And we come back to my original question: How do you deal with this without going crazy? I mean, you could outlive us all if you burn your candle right. Have you ever thought about leaving the Vatican and taking your candle along?"

Grace drained her second flute. "All the time. But I can't live alone. I would need someone I can trust to relight the candle, or I just let it burn, and my life would last—not long."

"Or forever," Sal offered, to break the uncomfortable silence. "If you blow it out and no one relights it."

"Right."

"So you trust Menchú," Sal said.

"I trust all of you," Grace said, bringing her focus back to the conversation. "Although Liam doesn't know yet. I'd probably trust him to do the right thing if he had to."

"'Probably'?" Sal asked.

Grace nodded. "Liam knows something is different about me. We don't talk about it. But he . . ." She frowned, looking for the words. "He has a bad history with magic. Very bad. The truth would hurt him. As it stands, he knows there's something wrong with me, but he is good at compartmentalizing."

"Yeah, but he'd deal if you came clean," Sal said, waving her hand in an attempt to sound eloquent. "Your candle isn't just another spell that can go wrong, like Delphi."

"There's more to magic than *harmful* and *harmless*," Grace said. "It's complicated. Liam knows that, and fears what he doesn't understand."

Sal thought of their last real conversation and felt a twinge in her chest.

"I know you care for him. Or cared for him," Grace said. "But he's damaged."

"We all are," Sal reminded her. "So much for Liam. And everyone who knows your secret is on Team Three?"

"A few higher-ups know, but I don't trust them. I'd never leave the team—not while Arturo is alive, anyway. I'm in his debt; he saved me from eternity in a box."

"The debt thing comes in a lot, I guess," Sal said, thinking of Perry, and of Liam waking up among the wires, missing two years of his life.

"It's a powerful motivator, if you have any sense of honor," Grace said.

"How many times have you saved Menchú's life?" Sal asked. "I know I've seen a couple."

"Three hundred and forty-seven," Grace said.

Sal blinked. "I was being rhetorical. I didn't know you kept score."

"Numbers and precision come naturally to me," Grace said, shrugging. "I don't expect payback. I just keep track of things. I know how many times I've genuinely feared for my life, for example." Another Bellini arrived, and she looked thoughtfully at the bubbles breaking on the orange surface. "And I know how many minutes I have left."

Sal's head snapped up. "You do? How many?"

Grace took a long drink and then looked at Sal with a level gaze. "I'll tell you when you tell me how many minutes you have left in your life." Then she laughed. "I'm just joking. I don't really know for sure. But the look on your face was great."

Sal laughed, unsure whether Grace was really joking after all. "Have you ever taken these days off with anyone else? Menchú?"

"I'd rather not talk about him anymore."

"I thought you were doing math tricks," Sal said. "Were we talking about him?"

Grace stared at her row of empty champagne flutes. "I was. But I'm done now."

Shit. Grace was going morose. She had to get Grace sober and cheered up. Their food arrived, and Sal asked the waiter to bring Grace a big glass of water, and to keep that coming instead of the champagne.

"So what are we doing next?" she asked. "I kinda feel like drunk-texting Liam, but I'm betting that'll piss him off."

"He's fun to poke," Grace allowed. "More fun to hit."

Sal laughed. "Not sure I'm up for sparring with him. At least not until the breakup is a bit more in the past. That could get ugly."

Her pocket buzzed, and she fumbled for her phone. "Speak of the devil," she said, then regretted the idiom. "Text from Liam."

"What's he say?" Grace asked around a mouthful of cheese pastry.

The text said: *Local shit going down. Thinking some sort of time artifact,* followed by an address.

Sal wiped her mouth and half rose from the table. Her head spun, and she sat back down again. Grace raised an eyebrow, seeming to have regained her usual self-control. "How is Liam?"

"He says there's some magic going down nearby," Sal said.

"He'll be fine," Grace said.

Sal opened her mouth to argue but reread the text. It sounded like every other text he'd sent about Team Three: matter-of-fact, calm, and informative. There was no sense that the world was about to end, no sense that he was frightened. No sense that he even needed her. *Them,* she reminded herself. Her and Grace. Liam wasn't blaming her for not being there. She rubbed her head to try to shake the buzz. This was an it's-time-to-go-to-work message, nothing more.

And Menchú had ordered her to take the day off.

She slipped the phone back into her pocket. "So, you're Liam's sparring partner," she prompted. Grace nodded, grinning, and began to tell a story about the time Liam broke her nose.

A fourth Bellini arrived, and another platter of pastry. So much for sobering up. Sal finally began to relax.

THE ALLEY OUTSIDE MAESTRI DEL TEMPO, 10:28:02 A.M.

For the fourth time, Liam pulled his phone out to check for texts. Nothing from Sal. He swore and dropped it into his backpack.

He stood with Menchú and Asanti in an alley outside a dilapidated shop. The building was clearly more than a hundred years old, with cloudy windows that hadn't been cleaned in ages and ancient wood that had never been replaced.

Liam tried to get more information about the shop and clockmaker online. He found one Google review of the shop (three stars, the clock was fixed but the owner was rude) and nothing else. "This woman isn't even on the grid," he said to the others. "It's like she doesn't exist in the new millennium."

"Yes, because e-mail is all that makes you whole in the eyes of God," Menchú said over his shoulder.

"You want me to do my job or not?" Liam asked sourly. "I got some information about time artifacts. Surprise, they alter time. Either slow it down or speed it up."

"Anything that helps someone walk through time?" Asanti asked.

"No one has invented a time machine yet," Liam said. "Not to say that a few cultists in Arizona aren't trying." He glanced away from his laptop. "Hey, why aren't you going in? Is the owner in the shop?"

"She's there," Menchú said, peering through the dirty window. "So is a younger man with a scarred face. They're not moving."

"What, are they dead?" Liam asked, closing his laptop and putting it into his backpack.

"No, she's sitting upright at her table with all her tools and clocks,"

Menchú said. "He's next to her, looking like he's about to hug her. They're just not moving."

Liam joined them and squinted through the window. The woman was indeed sitting at her table, working on a clock, but she looked like a mannequin, or a paused television show. She focused intently on her job; she just didn't move. The clock she worked on was brass and gold. Liam couldn't see the face, as it had been removed so that the clockmaker could get at the guts of the thing, but it looked fancy and expensive.

But the man . . . "That's not a hug," Liam said. "He's attacking her."

"You're right," said Asanti. "We have to do something."

"Do you think the clock is the artifact?"

"No. Look at the tool she's using." Asanti pointed. Beside the clock sat a tool made of what looked like gold. It had a large wheel attached to many smaller parts, reminding Liam of an old film projector. But there was no film here, just gears and an unearthly glow that pulsed slowly, like a heartbeat.

Menchú sighed. "I hate artifacts," he said.

"At least it doesn't look violent," Asanti said. "Not Grace-level violence, anyway."

"I really miss Sal's deductive skills right now," Menchú said, but when Asanti put her hands on her hips, he added, "but we'll make do without. Liam, do we have anything to go on yet?"

Liam rolled his eyes and got his laptop out again. "Nothing. Let me see what my mates in antiques have to say."

After another half hour, no one had thought of anything, and the people inside still hadn't moved. Menchú stood. "I'm going in."

Liam closed his laptop and looked at his mentor. "It's a bad idea, but I don't have a better one. Godspeed you, black emperor."

"What?"

"Don't worry about it. Do you want backup?"

Menchú nodded. "You follow me in. Asanti, keep watch out here. Text Sal if things get dicey."

Asanti nodded, and Liam stashed his backpack in the van. Menchú took hold of the door handle, pushed, stepped inside the shop, then stopped.

"What's wrong?" Asanti asked him.

Menchú didn't answer or even move. He seemed frozen entirely. Liam reached in to touch him, but Asanti slapped his hand away. "It's caught him. Let's not have it catch you, too."

"Is he frozen?"

"No." Asanti pointed above Menchú's head where the bell hung, knocked aside by the door. Where it should have been swinging and ringing to announce Menchú's entrance, it hung nearly on its side, midswing, the clapper almost reaching the side of the bell but not quite. "Listen," Asanti whispered. If they watched very closely, they could see the clapper move, millimeter by millimeter, toward the edge of the bell. When it struck, it made a muffled ring that lasted much longer than a normal bell ringing should have. "He's moving, just . . . slowly. How long will it take him to reach the artifact at this rate?"

Liam did some calculations on his phone. "He's doing about a millimeter a second," he said. "So if the effect is constant, he'll reach the clockmaker in . . . around five days. We may want to do something before then."

"At least Grace would be free."

"What do you want her to do?" Liam asked. "Punch really slowly?"

"Fair point. Our options are: Return to the library and do research, but I don't like leaving them alone. We could call Sal and get her take. We could call in Team One—"

"Team One? I'm not sure shooting very slow bullets will do much good," Liam said. "We have no idea what effect they'll have on the artifact. Could just make matters worse."

"What do you suggest?"

"We could pull him out."

Asanti paused. "That's . . . direct."

"Can you think of any reason not to?"

"You could get caught in the same time field."

Liam waved his hand dismissively. "Nah. Here." He motioned for Asanti to join him. Together they reached for Menchú's arm, still close to the doorframe, and yanked. Menchú was heavier than he had any right to be, but he did ease out, and the more of him that emerged from the store, the faster he came, until he stumbled out entirely and went sprawling on top of Liam.

"What did you do that for?" he asked, rubbing his hip where he had landed.

"You don't remember?" Asanti asked, who had neatly avoided the falling men.

"Remember what? I walked in and you yanked me back out."

"Check your watch," said Liam, and then pulled his phone from his pocket. "I'll bet it's a few minutes behind ours." So that they might stay on top of Grace's anal-retentive timetable, everyone on the team had perfectly synchronized clocks and watches.

Liam pointed to his phone's clock, which said 11:45 a.m. Menchú's watch said 11:41. "See?"

"So time slows inside," Menchú said thoughtfully.

Asanti squinted at the sky, and then looked at the shadows in the alley. "Nearly noon? In midsummer? The light's wrong."

Liam went to his bag and pulled out his laptop. It said 2:31 p.m. "Shit. The Internet's three hours ahead of us. The shop's inside a bubble. And it's growing."

"I'm calling this an emergency," Menchú said. "Bring in Sal."

3.

STARSI DISCOUNT THEATER, 12:00:08 P.M.

There was a local theater that specialized in cheap blockbusters a couple of months old, and Grace wanted to spend some of her day off on a kung-fu flick.

Sal was looking down at the ticket as she walked forward and bumped into Grace's back right outside the movie doors.

"What's up?" she asked, regaining her balance.

Grace didn't turn around, but she stood, rigid. "We are being followed."

Damn champagne. Sal should have known they shouldn't have relaxed. "Who?"

"Vatican," Grace said, her jaw clenched. "They're keeping tabs on their asset."

"Okay. Let's go inside and—" Sal wasn't able to continue, as Grace had turned and dashed away.

"Damn," Sal said. She turned and followed Grace.

Grace turned out to be right, if running away while being chased meant that you were guilty of something, because someone was definitely running from Grace. Yes, he moved calmly, as if the whole thing were his idea, but he was still running away. Sal swore and ran faster.

He wasn't from the Vatican.

Grace saw as much when she chased him down an alley and tackled him, trapping his arms behind his back and pushing his face into the asphalt. She grabbed his hair and pulled his head back.

"Wait, who the hell is this?" she asked. "Did the Vatican hire you?"

Sal stared stonily at Grace's captive. Even trapped on the ground, arms and head pulled in painful angles, he still managed to look serene. So annoyingly comfortable in any position.

Aaron.

"They did not hire me, Grace," he said. "I needed to talk to Sal. Business."

Grace dropped him back to the ground and stood up. "This piece of garbage is for you? What the hell did he interrupt my day off for?"

"I have no idea," Sal said. She put her hands on her hips. "But I think we should hear him out."

Grace walked past Sal without a glance. "You hear him out. I have a movie to watch. If you want to enjoy your day off, tell the bastard to come back tomorrow. You want to be a slave to work, then listen to him now." With that, she was gone.

Sal glared at Aaron. "What the hell do you think you're doing?"

Aaron gestured toward a delivery box that sat outside a door in the alley. He offered the cardboard box as a seat as if he were guiding Sal to a velvet couch. "Thank you for coming. We need to talk."

Sal stayed where she was. He sat on the box instead and faced her.

"Your phone is broken?" she asked.

He raised one perfect eyebrow. "I'm sorry?"

"Clearly you know about Grace's day off. So you're following us for some reason instead of using a more human means of communication. Stalking and goading women into attacking you is your way of sending a message? I thought you were supposed to be one of the good guys."

"While it's fine to cyberstalk her and then break into her room to uncover her secret?" he asked, smiling.

"Shit, is there anything you don't know?" Sal asked, collapsing against a wall and crossing her arms.

He didn't answer that. He simply smiled. She waited, and finally he said, "I had to speak with you today. And you're a hard woman to contact."

Sal waved her phone at him. "You know what this is, right? You've used it before."

"I have texted you several times," Aaron said. His patience infuriated her. "I have tried to call your apartment. Your cell phone. I can't get through. Why do you think that is?"

Sal threw her hands up in frustration. "I don't know, shitty Italian cell service?"

"Possibly," he said. "I wanted to talk to you. If I had contacted you when you were working, you wouldn't have left a job and put the team in jeopardy to come meet me. If I had tried to call you today during Grace's day off, you wouldn't have met me, out of respect for her."

"How did you know Grace would leave us alone?" Sal asked. "She could have stayed and made this difficult for you."

Aaron raised an eyebrow. "She's not that hard to figure out. She holds two things sacred in life. One of them is this day."

"You are a deeply creepy individual. And you have fifteen minutes before I leave."

He nodded once and started to speak.

Since Grace wasn't around to scold her, Sal texted Asanti and Liam before she entered the theater. She put the phone on vibrate and went into the theater to join Grace.

The matinee was relatively empty. Grace sat in the center of the theater, a super-expensive tub of popcorn, a box of candy, and a vat of soda within reach. Sal noticed identical snacks sat on the seat beside Grace, waiting for her.

She'd only missed the previews and credits. She picked up her snacks and slid in next to Grace.

"Sorry about that," she whispered.

"Shh," Grace said, looking at the screen. "Quiet."

"Do you want to know what he wanted?" Sal asked.

"Not even a little bit. Tell me tomorrow if you have to."

Sal opened her mouth again, but Grace shushed her before she could speak. Impressive, as her friend hadn't looked at her. She sighed and tried to enjoy the movie and not think about Aaron. Or the fact that Asanti and Liam hadn't gotten back to her.

They finished the movie, Grace breaking her own speaking embargo with eager commentary about the historical accuracy and her derision of the flashy martial arts moves.

"Just punch him! So much can be done with just a freaking punch!" she yelled at the screen. Sal stifled a laugh.

When it was done, Grace's soda was gone, and she was in desperate need of a trip to the bathroom. Sal joined her and checked her phone as Grace was washing up.

"Shit," she said.

"I know that 'shit,'" Grace said. "That's a Liam shit."

"A 'Liam shit'?" Sal asked, confused.

"Sure. That's how you react when he texts you. Lately, anyway. So are you going to mess up my day off again?" She faced Sal, her face impassive.

"That's not fair. It's not my fault that people followed us, or that Liam needs us."

Grace snatched Sal's phone from her hand and read the texts, ignoring Sal's outrage. "Yeah, and he didn't say he needed you until you asked him specifically if he did. That's not what a friend does when she's dedicated to a day off."

Sal grabbed her phone back and pocketed it. "Fine. Sue me for being concerned about the other members of our team, who are off dealing with danger while we're here drinking heart-palpitation levels of caffeinated soda. Grace, you guys are the only people I know in Rome, my only friends. I'm sorry if I tend to be concerned about some people who are in danger. This team is all I have right now."

She stormed out of the bathroom and stopped in the lobby to read the text again. The team was in trouble; they needed her. Liam had laid out the details in the text.

Trust your mind, Sal, Aaron had said in the alley. *Own it.* The light from his hand shone brightly for a moment in her memory.

Now Sal closed her eyes, concentrating on the details. Liam and the others were handling an artifact that messed with time. What was it that was niggling at her about that? It felt familiar somehow, like . . . like she'd been thinking about it a lot lately. *Grace.*

The light that Aaron had shone in her eyes flared. Would Grace's own ensnarement in a time spell protect her from a different one? Would her candle cocoon her from the shock everyone else would suffer from this type of magic?

Big logical jump there, Sal. But Aaron had told her to trust herself. She didn't—not exactly. He'd helped her before, though. They'd never have found the *Fair Weather* without his guidance. And if she'd trusted him once, then . . .

The problem was, she was alone, and Grace was left in the women's room, unwilling to abandon her day off. She paused and considered going back but honestly didn't know what kind of argument would make Grace follow her. If she was so convinced the others could handle things alone, Sal wouldn't be able to change her mind.

The restroom door slammed open behind her, and Grace stormed out, grabbing Sal's arm as she passed. "One perfect day. That's all I ever ask," she said through her teeth.

"Is it perfect when your family is in danger without you?" Sal asked, catching her stride.

"Where are we going?"

Sal told her. As Grace pulled her along, she thought about how Grace's real curse wasn't the candle, but the fact that she was tied so tightly to the team's fates—as well as her own.

BORGO SANTO SPIRITO, 2:28:58 P.M.

Sal, still half running down Borgo Santo Spirito to keep up with Grace, considered reminding her that Liam had not strictly asked for Grace to come. They at least tried to respect Grace's day off. But maybe what Grace needed was a good fight, where she could just let loose. The kind of fight she got during a job. Maybe she needed their "work."

Sal put on a burst of speed and grabbed Grace's arm to slow her down. "At least you'll get something to hit today, to make up for not hitting that guy in the alley earlier," she said.

Grace stopped suddenly. "Do you think I'm that simple? That

hitting something—anything—is enough to make things better? I'm like an indentured servant to the Church, Sal, while my life burns away and everyone I know ages around me. When I die, I'll have spent my life fighting, without a real chance to rest or enjoy myself or even just take a nap. Will hitting something make me forget all that?"

"No," Sal said quietly. "But you were mad before the movie, and now you're madder. This will give you something to do with that adrenaline, and when you're done, maybe you'll be able to think more clearly. Enjoy the rest of the day." She paused, then added, "Arturo needs you."

Grace's dark eyes focused sharply on Sal, a spark of fear in them. Sal had never used Menchú's first name before.

"Where do we go? And what do I punch?"

Sal worried that there wouldn't be anything to punch, really. Liam had said a time artifact was messing with them, and his phone time stamp was eleven forty-five a.m. Why had the text taken almost three hours to reach her? She knew sometimes phones delayed message delivery, but this was worse than usual. You couldn't punch time.

But Sal knew, gut-knew, that Grace was the only one who could save them. Aaron had told her to trust that. Grace herself wasn't magical, at least, not as Sal understood it, but Sal's theory rested on the fact that two time curses would counter each other, making Grace at least immune to whatever they were up against.

They arrived at the clockmaker's street and looked down the dark alley where the shingle hung above the door, identifying the shop as Maestri del Tempo. The sign itself looked a hundred years old.

The rest of Team Three stood outside the door. Well, Asanti stood.

Liam and Menchú were sprawled on the ground, unmoving. Liam held his phone and stared intently at it.

Grace surveyed the scene, arms crossed. She pointed to Liam's backpack, where the corner of the magic-dampening shroud peeked out. "Liam's got the shroud," she said to Sal.

"Great, get it from him and go get the artifact. I'm going to stay back here, but I think you'll be okay to deal with this magic."

Grace smiled wryly. "I thought you said I got to hit something."

"We don't know what's in that clock shop, Grace. It could just be one little artifact, but I find it difficult to believe it's creating some sort of time-slowing bubble all on its own. These things typically need a driver at the wheel, don't they?"

"I might get caught in the time bubble too."

"You won't."

And with a trust that made Sal feel vaguely guilty, Grace ran into the alley, where she promptly disappeared.

MAESTRI DEL TEMPO, 2:32:06 P.M.

Grace knew pain. It had become almost an afterthought, as accepted a part of her new career as menstrual cramps had been in her teens. The night the candle changed her life. The bullet holes and knife slashes, acid and claws from demons, broken legs from Tornado Eaters. Pain was a way of life.

Exhilaration, though. That was new. The moment she crossed the invisible border of the time bubble, the world around her slowed to a stop, but she remained herself. She could sense the conflicting time magic around her, like she had felt in Delphi. This artifact would feel her as an irritating grain of sand in its slow, uniform takeover of the city: Grace's curse, which locked her to every second. For one of the few times in her life, the magic she encountered didn't frighten her into action; this magic had handed her wings.

Grace would not be Icarus, though. She jogged up to her team and waved a hand in front of Arturo's face. "Hello? Can you hear me?" she asked.

He lay on the ground, looking pained and annoyed. She felt a tiny ache in her heart as she looked at the gray that streaked his previously glossy black hair. She considered reaching out to pick him up, but if he was super slowed, or she was super sped up, she could break his bones by simply touching him. She stepped carefully around him, pulled the shroud out of Liam's backpack, and, with one more glance at her frozen team, entered the clock shop.

It would have been a dump, or perhaps a nest, a cozy and dirty place of clock parts and tools and myriad timepieces on the walls. Small cubbies and drawers were set along the sides, some open, some tagged with order numbers. It would have been a dingy place if the air wasn't broken by golden streams of light rippling like a gymnast's ribbon on the air. Some of these streamed quickly, some moved slowly. They all came from one area: the artifact, the watchmaker's tool attached to a worktable with a vise.

Grace realized with a shock that she had been here before, to have her watch serviced. She owned a Rolex, a gift from a Swiss watchmaker who had been grateful for her saving his livelihood from a gear-eating demon. The Swiss man had tried to tell her something about clock pieces and nightmares, but Grace had let him explain to Arturo so she could focus on her part of the job.

She knew this woman. Bella. The woman lay slumped on the table. Her eyes were open, and they glistened with tears. Blood ran from the woman's ears and nose, and from the mess, Grace could tell that something very strong had broken her back. She still lived, or was in the second between living and dying, as she watched the time streams flow around her.

The thing that had broken her was a man, younger than Bella, but bulky, like a former athlete. His large hands turned the crank on the wheel of the artifact, the only thing besides Grace that didn't move incredibly slowly. His eyes rose to hers, and they were brimming with bright, golden tears, dripping down his face like molten streams. He opened his mouth, and instead of a tongue, more molten time flowed out. His body convulsed, and he jerked, but his hand continued to turn the crank on the device.

This host was dead; whatever was inside had taken over completely. Grace regretted this, but part of her was delighted. Finally, something to punch. She picked up a clock and threw it with all her strength. The host's body stopped convulsing, and its free hand reached up and batted the clock away. She heard bones break in the host's hand and arm, but it didn't flinch.

She ran toward the host, but was caught unaware when it opened its mouth again and howled. A golden river washed over her.

She tried to dodge but saw the inevitable coming for her. Grace tensed, ready for pain, ready for the searing heat she'd felt falling through the wax. But instead of burning, she was—

Watching. Always watching. Grace is a child named Chen Juan, a slip of a twelve-year-old girl who watches daily at the window while the big boys in her village chase her brother, laughing at him because of his limp. She sometimes cries when they catch him. Fai never cries, though. He is so brave.

Gritting her teeth, Grace stood up, feeling the magics within her and without her fighting even harder. Her fingers ached from the strength of her grip on the windowsill as she watched Fai get punched and kicked.

She ran at the creature again and was ready when it opened its mouth. She launched herself off a stool and leaped over the worktable, hitting the demon in the chest, feet first. He howled as she collapsed his chest, and more time flooded over her, catching her full force now.

The books. She steals her father's anatomy books and studies them, learning about pressure points and the soft parts and the weakest joints. Eyes, throat, fingers, belly, groin. No kwoon will take a girl to train in kung fu, and her parents wouldn't let her go, anyway. So she teaches herself. At the next attack, Chen Juan runs out to help her brother. The bullies are no longer boys: They are necks and fingers and scrotums and knees. One of them is only an eye. It is easy, despite one of the boys landing a punch in her face.

Night falls in 1989, and she cannot find Arturo. The darkness swallows Leningrad in June, when there should be twenty hours of daylight. A sorcerer has enshrouded the city in darkness so that he can bring forth his dark child, sleeping under the Hermitage Museum. He makes a mistake then, cracking a crude joke about the priest and his geisha. Red replaces the black in her eyes, and she finds him effortlessly, remembering the soft parts, the weak parts. Arturo is safe.

Grace blinked. Her eye was swelling up from the boy's punch; she had red welts on her hands and wrists from the sorcerer's whip.

"Enough," she said, and snapped the golden creature's neck.

The wheel on the clockmaker's device began to spin with no hand on it, the golden streams moving faster instead of dissipating. Grace staggered to her feet and threw the shroud over it, trying to catch the handle as it tangled in the fabric.

Her death. A bed. Someone she doesn't recognize reads a newspaper to her. She turns her head from the date. She doesn't want to know. Her last breath bubbles in her chest—

The device stopped. Grace leaned over it, panting, watching the golden ribbons in the air begin to fade. She quickly unscrewed the vise that kept the artifact on the worktable and headed for the door . . .

. . . which was halfway to exploding.

Time had begun to catch up with itself, and Grace realized the force with which she had hit the shop door was akin to a bullet hitting it, and once it struck the wall, that door began to splinter. She watched in fascination as it separated into pieces and those pieces began to split apart in midair. Time to get going.

She tucked the shroud tighter around the time artifact and placed it neatly beside Arturo, then jogged back to Sal.

MAESTRI DEL TEMPO, 2:32:08 P.M.

Liam hit send on the text to Sal and glanced at Menchú, who was starting to rise to his feet.

They were both tossed back by a massive wind, flattening them and blowing the door open.

"Shit," Liam said, and looked up. The door had exploded, leaving a rough memory of wood hanging from the hinges. Asanti leaned on the wall as if she had been pushed against it. Liam scrambled to his feet and ran to the door, skirting the edges of the stronger part of the time bubble. He blinked at the carnage inside, then drew back. "How long was I in there just now?"

"Only a moment," Menchú said, brushing himself off. "It appears the problem has solved itself." He frowned at the enshrouded package next to him, which was the same size as the large wheel that had previously been attached to the clockmaker's table.

"There are two bodies inside," Liam said. "And the artifact isn't on the table anymore."

Asanti crouched next to Menchú, peering at the package without touching it. "That's because it's right here."

"What the hell happened?" Liam asked. "Did someone with another time artifact come in and save us?"

"Or someone who has spells or abilities that stand outside of time," Menchú said thoughtfully.

"Or curses," whispered Asanti, looking at Menchú. His eyes went wide momentarily, but he said nothing.

Liam sighed audibly and stomped past the shattered door into the clock shop. The woman on the floor—dead. Looked as if it was blunt-force trauma. The man on the floor—also dead. He appeared deflated; the blood that leaked from his nose and ears was tinged with streaks of gold. He had no eyes, and his open mouth showed no tongue, only charred holes.

Liam felt the man's pockets for identification, not realizing until it was too late that his finger had trailed through some of the gold-tinted blood on the man's shirt. He quickly wiped it off, expecting it to burn.

She stretches out beneath him. "Show me the vastness, Liam." He is vaguely gratified she isn't making a bad sexual pun. There is ecstasy, and then a buzzing high, and then the wires, and then there is nothing but vastness for such a long time—

Liam wiped his fingers on his jeans hastily, his mind reeling with the memory of his ensnarement. He stood. "They're both dead. Looks like the man messed with the artifact and probably killed the woman."

Asanti and Menchú didn't answer. They were too busy conferring on the street. Liam crossed his arms and surveyed the ruin of the shop. If this had been a computer game, he would have been able to take his pick of the contents, but people tended to frown on grave robbers in real life. Shame, too. There were some nice clocks on the wall.

"Liam, we're calling the police. It's time to go," Menchú said through the door. "We're done here."

"Better call the cleanup crew first," Liam said, wiping his fingers on his jeans once more. He felt tainted. "It's not completely cleared in here yet."

Menchú nodded and began to dial the special crime-scene cleanup crew that commonly worked with Team One.

Liam rubbed his fingers together unconsciously, trying to rid himself of the heady feeling of the memory, sexual and terrifying. He didn't need to go back to those times.

Back in the Black Archives, Liam scrubbed his hands under hot water until they were red before meeting Asanti and Menchú for debriefing.

"I don't know why you didn't want to stay there longer," he said. "That wind we felt was definitely not human. Don't you want to know what it was?"

"I have Asanti doing some research on that. What I'd like you to do is find out what you can about this." Menchú produced the artifact, careful to touch it only with the shroud. "I have a bad feeling about it."

"Beyond the fact that it just killed two people?"

"Yes. Far beyond that."

4.

RED JADE, 3:32:10 P.M.

S econds after she had left, Grace reappeared in a gust of strong wind behind Sal. Her face was swollen, and her hands and forearms were red.

"You look like hell," Sal said.

Grace smiled. "You were right. I needed that."

"You want to tell me what happened?"

Grace motioned to her. "I'm starving. Let's go and I'll tell you along the way."

Grace took Sal to her favorite restaurant, Red Jade. Inside, the owner, an ancient Chinese woman, greeted them joyfully and came to embrace Grace. They spoke in Chinese briefly, and then Grace introduced her to Sal. The woman led them to a corner booth and said to order what they liked.

"I didn't know you had friends outside the team," Sal said as they sat down.

"Zhen is an old friend. I saved her restaurant in 1984," Grace said, calmly accepting an ice pack delivered by an earnest young waiter and putting it on her face.

"From what? Demon?" Sal asked.

Grace shook her head. "Mafia. Arturo and I were having dinner when they got visited. I didn't like them. Before we went back home I convinced them to leave her alone."

"And she hasn't noticed that you haven't aged in the past thirty years?" Sal asked.

Grace smiled. "She knows I helped her. Doesn't much care about the rest."

They ordered and then settled back. Grace lowered the ice pack, her face already healing. "We had better not tell Asanti that we secretly did some work today."

Sal grinned, relieved that she had been right about the time magics working against each other. "If only we could slow everything down whenever we need you to punch something."

Grace shook her head. "It's too dangerous. I'll destroy anything I touch when I'm that fast. That door is sawdust by now, and if I had touched Liam or Asanti, I could have killed them."

"And that bruise on your face, really from a fifteen-year-old boy in 1920?"

Grace shrugged. Their food arrived, and she snagged a chicken foot from a platter. "It's the only explanation, I didn't just remember what had happened; I was there. The same with the Soviet sorcerer in eighty-nine."

"Intense. I'm sorry you had to deal with that alone," Sal said.

"It's okay. I enjoyed it," Grace said. "You were right. I needed something to clear my mind. So are you going to tell me about the tour guide who was following us?"

Sal grew cold. She had hoped Grace hadn't recognized Aaron.

She thought up a lie, and then sighed. Grace didn't deserve that.

"He had some information about Norse," Sal said. "He gave me a clue about the time magic."

Grace frowned as she sucked on the chicken foot. "How did he know?"

Sal shrugged. She honestly had no idea. "He said I didn't answer the phone, so he came looking."

Grace raised an eyebrow. "In all of Rome."

"I don't know," Sal said, not looking at her. "I was more concerned with what he was telling me rather than why."

"You need to tell Menchú," Grace said. "What did he say about Norse?"

"Just that he was up to something today. And told me to look into not just what the artifact was, but why. What's the purpose of it?" Sal asked. "Why stop time?"

"It didn't stop all time," Grace said. "It may have eventually, but it was just holding that shop and the alley where it was. Why would someone want to stop that particular shop?"

Aaron's advice. The light. A sense of focus. "Norse wanted to delay us. Again," Sal said slowly.

"You're thinking this was sabotage?" Grace said, frowning with skepticism.

"It makes sense. Without you, I don't know how we could have fixed it. Norse doesn't know about you, so he didn't know you could just cut through that magic like a hot knife through butter. It makes sense." Sal was talking faster and faster, getting excited.

"That . . . does make sense," Grace said thoughtfully. "But this means we have to tell Arturo, and he's going to know we worked on my day off."

Sal grinned. "We'll tell him you needed to blow off some steam, and you ran across a possessed dude who needed punching."

SAL'S APARTMENT, 7:03:41 P.M.

After their midafternoon meal, Grace didn't want to stop. She'd fought a demon, but she was determined to live the fullest day she could. They hiked the city, looked at ruins (something, admittedly, Sal had not paused to do since she had arrived), shopped for shoes—or, rather, Grace shopped, ending up with a pair of heels with a price tag Sal tried very hard not to think about—and finished off the day at a mug-painting café where they had suboptimal coffee and painted mugs in hideous colors. They were supposed to pick up the final product the following week, and Sal idly wondered if they would ever return for their art.

Finally, Grace agreed to some downtime involving sweatpants, movies, and ice cream in Sal's apartment. They even stopped to buy Grace some sweatpants for the occasion. She had not participated in such a ritual before, never having taken her day off with a companion.

"How is this better than a movie theater?" she asked, frowning at Sal's television. "The screen is so small."

Sal started counting off on her fingers. "One, sweatpants. Two, we pause the movie anytime we need to pee. Three, snacks cost about a tenth of what we pay in the theater. Four, we can watch whatever we want, my DVD collection and Internet streaming permitting. And five, sweatpants."

Grace perked up. "Can we watch the Matrix trilogy?"

Sal made a show of looking at her clock. "We have time for the first one," she said, inwardly wincing at the thought of all three movies at once.

Keanu Reeves was waking up in a vat of goo, attached to many cables, when Grace fell asleep. They were on the couch, sharing a blanket, and Grace was relaxed back, her face soft, her breathing deep.

"When was the last time you just took a nap?" Sal wondered quietly. She turned the volume down on the television a bit, tucked Grace in with the blanket, and went to the kitchen to make some tea. While the water was heating up, she called Asanti.

"I'm sorry to bug you at night," Sal said. "I wanted to let you know that we're okay. I'll make sure she gets back to her room in an hour or so."

"That's fine; I appreciate your telling me," Asanti said. Sal could hear a television in the background. "Although I'm fairly sure Grace can handle the trip home by herself."

"Someone has to wake her up first. Has that woman ever napped just for the pleasure of it?"

Asanti laughed. "You know, I have no idea. How did the day off go?"

"Fun, except for that spin class. Exciting at times. We got bothered by that guy, though, the one who warned me about the yacht."

"What happened?"

"I think he wanted to make sure we were going to help you, since we were the only ones who could. Well, Grace was. I was just there to watch. Don't tell Grace I told you. I think she doesn't want Menchú to know she worked on her day off."

"Well, we had already figured out it was you two. Thanks for that, by the way. I'm more troubled by this Aaron fellow showing up again."

"I'll tell Menchú about it tomorrow, but I'm pretty sure it was benign. He told us to have your backs," Sal said, hoping Asanti wouldn't hear the lie of omission.

"I should warn you," Asanti said. "Liam and I are taking our day off tomorrow."

Sal grinned. "I'll try to leave you guys alone."

"I think Liam would have rather had his day off today," Asanti said, a strange edge to her voice.

"You couldn't do without three of us, though, right?" Sal asked.

"That's not what I'm getting at. He didn't like you two having a day off together, and I think I know why."

"Oh, so you know about that," Sal said, feeling tired all of a sudden.

"Not until you just confirmed it. You two hid it well. But it's over; that much is obvious," Asanti said. "It's probably for the best, actually."

"Easy for you to say," Sal said, and in an instant she found herself spilling everything to Asanti: her feelings of isolation and loneliness, how she and Liam had connected early and passionately, and how they had flamed out as fast. Asanti listened patiently and didn't interrupt.

When she was done, Asanti said, "Liam has a strong need for control. Especially self-control."

"Tell me something I don't know," Sal said, laughing bitterly.

"He must have had strong feelings for you, to pull back so abruptly," Asanti said. "It's got to be hard to see you spending time with someone else, someone he himself has tried to befriend. He and Grace are sparring partners, but they're not what one would call close."

"It's probably got to do with the secret. He knows she has one even if he doesn't know what it is," Sal said. "When do you think he's going to find out the whole truth about her? He needs to be told. It's not fair to him."

"That is Grace's decision," Asanti said.

Sal sighed. "All right."

"There's something you should know," Asanti said. "The artifact we recovered today: Liam traced it back to a Cambridge archive purchased by a Mr. Norse and immediately sold to another buyer."

"Norse again. We figured the same."

"Luckily you and Grace saved us."

Sal laughed. "Grace, really. How did you figure it out, anyway?"

"There is only one person we know who could resist the time magic *and* would leave the artifact with us. And you were the only person who would have figured out that Grace would be unaffected. The one thing we couldn't figure out is how you got her to work on her day off."

"She needed something to hit. I think she forgot for a moment that she actually enjoys her job. She lost her temper and you guys said you were caught in a time spell, so I put two and two together and set Grace on the artifact. She said a guy had been corrupted by the artifact and was . . . swimming in time or something." Sal shrugged, remembering Asanti couldn't see her. "But it all worked out, so long as you guys are okay."

"We are, thank you. Get some rest tonight. You sound tired, which is not what a day off is supposed to do to you."

"I'm on it. I'll wake Grace and send her home."

She hung up, and then checked to see if Grace was still dozing on the couch. She was.

Sal went to the mirror in her bedroom and looked at herself, standing where she had been when she had woken up that morning. She met her own eyes and felt a frightening sense of vertigo. Then she remembered the white light.

"I wanted to check on you," Aaron had said.

"You don't automatically know everything in the world? My underwear size? My menstrual cycle? My favorite cake flavor?" Her hands were starting to flail. She had to calm down. She took a deep breath and forcibly relaxed her shoulders.

He smiled, annoying her further. "I could know those things if I wanted to, but in this case, perhaps I should say I wanted you to know I was checking on you. I wanted to know how you think you are doing."

Sal choked out a laugh. "Oh, I'm great. Shot a Tornado Eater in the face. Probably caused irrevocable emotional damage to a young boy. Thought about getting a tattoo. Fought meat. Among other things."

"Are you sleeping well? Are you feeling confident in your self-control?"

Sal had stopped her rant and looked at him closely. "Why?"

"Do you wake up in places other than your own bed, Sal?" His voice was soft.

"Why?" she asked again, her voice breaking.

"Do you ever meditate? It does wonders to still the mind. Helps one know oneself."

"Stop saying 'one.' You're talking about me; don't mince words."

He continued as if she hadn't interrupted. "I think your mind is full of tumultuous waters that could use some stilling. Do you meditate?"

"I . . . don't. No."

"You should. Sit." He had gotten off the box and faced her as she took his place. He raised his hand, palm out to her, and it glowed with a white light. "Now watch my hand, and clear your mind."

Sal looked instead at his eyes. "This sounds more like hypnotism than meditation, and I don't trust you that much."

"The light is there to give you a focal point for your meditation."

"You went through all this trouble to teach me to meditate?"

"No one else was doing it," he said. "Oh. And the next time Liam contacts you, pay attention."

Then there was light. And then there was nothing.

Now, in her bedroom, Sal took a deep breath and pictured the light again, and the sense of vertigo fled. Frustration bubbled up inside her, a foreign feeling, and she tore her eyes from the mirror.

She looked down and noticed one thing was wrong with her dresser. A strange memory poked at her, and she flipped up the lid of her small jewelry box, the one that held, among other things, the tarnished silver cross she had received when she had rescued Perry. The box was empty.

She looked into the mirror again. "What did I do?"

EPISODE

11

CODEX UMBRA

MAX GLADSTONE

1.

Alex hated the Somerset house. Rooms full of shadow rambled and transformed when he wasn't looking. His parents liked to tell the story of their first visit, fresh from Hong Kong in linen and silk, winding up the long narrow drive: *Dear Alex was so excited to see his grandmama's estate for the first time that he climbed up front beside Jonathan and pressed his nose against the windshield—but when we rounded the hill he fell back, screaming!* Which, told with the proper arch and timing, yielded laughs around dinner tables in Singapore, Fiji, Sri Lanka, and Grand Cayman, and the clinking of champagne flutes. Alex himself laughed with the other guests, aping their sophistication, projecting charm he did not recognize as charm: a child of eight so far above his more childish self of four.

His parents waited for the laugh to finish before continuing the story: *Of course, when he met his grandmama, when she introduced him to the house and it got to know him, all fear vanished. He ran down the upstairs halls and jumped on the beds and curled himself in nooks, reading. Our brave little Alex.* And sometimes, if Mother felt particularly cruel, she'd pinch his cheek there and turn on him the private smile that always scared him in company. Private things, he already knew, were best kept private. Sharing that smile where others could see—the smile she used to banish nightmares and soothe him to sleep in hurricane winds—sapped its strength. One day he would need that smile and find its power gone.

Their friends, at dinner parties on islands around the world, did not understand. They were warm-weather people, though they professed allegiance to a chill, wet, distant home. Not even his mother understood: She had not known Soldown Manor as a child. She had come to it as a grown woman, in Father's company.

She did not know how it felt to see that crumbling, vine-shrouded expanse, that elegant ruin like some toy or tool God had abandoned, small beneath the boiling gray sky, yet so much bigger than Alex Norse, age four. Soldown Manor, the beast of his family, crouched at the end of the road and watched their approach with rows of enormous black glass eyes. Waiting, it breathed through gated mouths. Long dark runnels discolored the stone where ivy did not grow: the beast stained by its own ichor. There was no end to the thing. If he let it draw him in, he would remain whole, embedded in its belly.

On that first trip he did run down the upstairs halls, in part to flee the skin-wrapped bone sculpture with fierce glittering eyes his parents introduced as Grandmama, but also in part because he thought, *Now that I'm inside, I must find some escape. If I can map Soldown Manor, I can—if not master it—at least conjure it to devour someone else, and spare me.* He jumped on beds to chase out dead souls. He curled in nooks because nothing could sneak up behind him there except the walls, and he read because, buried in a book, he could ignore the featherlike, fingerlike shapes moving at the edge of his vision. He held the books as close as masks.

Mother did not know. Father told the story too. But he did not laugh. Father had been the last Norse raised in Soldown Manor, and there were reasons he made his fortune in Hong Kong.

They spent Alex's twelfth Christmas at Soldown. In years past, Father said, servants lit lanterns to fill the manor with light. For one night, no shadows lingered on the estate. But this year's only guests were Grandmama's manservant and her live-in nurse, the only music the sound of ventilators and heart monitors and a distant drip of water. Father watched his mother on the bed and worked his hands as if washing them. Mother held his arm. He did not seem to notice her.

But Alex could not wait in that firelit room where Grandmama lay. In her eyes, darting beneath thin, stretched lids, in the unconscious grasping of fingers like once-taut gloves pulled over a wire frame, in the regular rasp of her machine-forced breath, he found something he feared more than the breathing manor's hunger.

He did not run from the firelit room. He climbed the stairs he'd charted in his panic long ago, round and round and up and up, until he reached the long halls down which he'd fled, age four. They seemed narrower now, and shorter. Whispers drew him on.

In the drawing room where he'd curled in the corner, he looked up. One of the ceiling panels was hinged. He had never noticed it before.

He stacked books on a chair, climbed from the desk to the stack, strained (teetering atop the books) with a broom handle, and pressed the panel's edge. With a click, the panel slid back and then down. A ladder unfolded from it like a mantis's arm extending. Soft creaks spoke to long disuse. The ladder's brass feet settled softly into light depressions in the drawing room carpet.

Alex climbed, either out of Soldown Manor, or farther in.

The cramped, low-ceilinged room above was dark. Narrow

triangular windows would have admitted sun, but the sun had set long since. By the light from the open trap door Alex saw shelves on the three windowless walls, all dust-covered. One shelf held calipers and needles and knives. One shelf held books—older, larger, rougher than the books in the drawing room or parlor or any of the libraries. One shelf held skulls: rodent, cow and ram, lizard and monkey and horse and man.

Many boys Alex's age would have screamed, but Alex had spent more than half his life hating the manor, and fearing it. He was too tired to scream. If anything, he felt gratitude: On this dark, starless night, the house confirmed his fears and showed itself to him.

Against the fourth wall, beneath the triangular windows, stood a desk, empty save for a book. And the book breathed.

Here lay the secret heart of the hated house, as small and unassuming as any book with covers closed. He could turn away, retreat, shut the panel, and know he had faced the house's brutal core, he had swum to the bait on the lure and found it wanting. Soldown's hold over him would break. Leaving this room, he need never return to it again.

But leaving, where could he go? Save down and down and round and round to the firelit room and his father washing his hands in air.

Alex opened the book.

He read it by the darkness beyond the window: The night lay on the pages like candle flame, and the words caught and burned with viscous, wet radiance.

Alex touched the book, and the burning words clung to his fingers, sticky and golden and sweet as syrup. He felt warm. He felt strong. And though there were no servants, and though there were no lanterns, and though there were no guests, still Soldown House filled with light.

＊　＊　＊

Two nights until the solstice.

Alexander Norse, age *enough*, as he'd say now, danced a flame from fingertip to fingertip and regarded the enormous tent, lit from within to nighttime-roadwork brilliance, that towered over the farmland in this dry stretch of Rhodes. Far away, a mountain stood. Far above, stars watched. They'd watched him his whole life. He'd soon give them a proper show.

Footsteps approached. He hid his light from the world. "Sir," his servant said: a wind chime chorus, a fist clenching around broken glass. Others would hear the voice as a human woman's, but he knew, and could see, the truth. It was his business to know such things. "Mr. Alhadeffs to see you."

"I am wanting," said the old man by the servant's side, "for you to explain what you have done."

Alhadeffs was a bent figure of olive and copper, with fierce black eyes and a fierce, curling, gray-thorned beard. Norse's servant herself was brass and silver, with springs of steel, her face a sculptor's suggestion over a metal skull. Her fingers were knives, her heart a spring, and the only words in her brain were words he'd put there. To the farmer Alhadeffs, and to Norse's own security team, she seemed a normal human woman, brusque and strong and well armed. The mind closed to cover a wound, and she was a walking wound.

"I am sorry if we've offended," Norse said. "We have a permit for this dig, and you will be handsomely compensated for the damage my expedition inflicts on your land—though we are of course working to minimize such impact."

"Your men chopped down the olive trees in the eastern field."

A regrettable necessity. Ritual ingredients had an unfortunate tendency to resemble a deranged hermit's shopping list. He required a mirror like the one that hung in the old purification chamber, with a frame made from local wood of sufficient age. "I am sorry. We will pay you whatever you need."

The man flushed. "Four hundred years, those trees have been in my family. What payment can you offer? Those olives were not mine. They were my daughters' and my sons'."

"And I will pay you enough, Mr. Alhadeffs, that they will praise your memory when what's left comes down to them." He extended a hand. Alhadeffs did not take it.

"You have not dug beneath my olives," he said. "You cut them down. You do not dig in my land. You build atop it. You spill poisons into the soil. I will report you to the police, to the government."

"Please, Mr. Alhadeffs." Norse set his arm around the man's shoulders. "We'll be finished in two days—that's all. You'll be rich, your farm will recover, and you'll be all the happier, despite this unfortunate disagreement. Look. Come with me. Let me show you the progress we've made, so you understand why I can't afford to interrupt our work at this critical moment."

He tried to guide Alhadeffs toward the tent, but the man pulled away. Norse's hand grazed his neck. "No," the old farmer said. "I will not work with you," he tried to say next, but could not—fingers of skin knit across his lips.

The new-grown flesh muffled his scream. He doubled over, clawing at his mouth, but more skin sealed over his fingernails, wrapped his fingers together. Skin climbed up his throat, covered his beard and his hair, pinched shut his nostrils. He fell. His eyes glittered with terror and fury before the skin covered them, too, leaving him to writhe beneath a hardening caul of flesh.

Norse knelt beside Alhadeffs and stroked the new skin. It

breathed softly; Alhadeffs mewed inside, then settled as the skin sang him to sleep. Good. Norse's world felt gray and saturated at once: as if something else, from somewhere else, replaced his normal vision. In better days he would have talked the man down, would have charmed him with a smile and a wink and a glass or three of ouzo. Not magic. Never magic.

The recent strain was wearing on him.

Let it wear. He'd be a god soon enough.

"Bring him," he told his servant. "We have work."

Sal did not vomit after watching the farmer get sealed inside his own skin. Which was progress, of a sort, she supposed. Hooray.

"Jesus," Liam said in the Rhodes Hilton, staring at the grainy night-vision-camera image on the television screen. The tent flap swung shut behind Norse and the smudge that followed him, carrying the other smudge that had once been the farmer. Magic played havoc with cameras at the best of times; Sal wished it had played a little more havoc, earlier. "Have you ever seen anything like that?"

"Once or twice," Grace said, from her perch on the desk by the wall. She had a thumb in *Ulysses*.

"Of fucking course."

"What's that supposed to mean?"

Liam said nothing.

Father Menchú sat on the bed beside Liam, his hands crossed, watching the television image. "At least we know we're in the right place. Norse is here. The way he's behaving—spending money, power, influence, using magic—he thinks the *Codex Umbra* is too. I doubt he'd put so much on the line if he didn't think there was a real chance he'd get the—what did Sal call it? The *Norton Anthology of Evil?*—in exchange."

Asanti had turned away from the television when the man began to change. Not, Sal thought to judge from her face, out of disgust or revulsion: She'd known what was about to happen and decided not to watch. "We knew that already. The Oracle doesn't lie."

"You've had better experience with oracles than I have," Menchú said. He volleyed the conversation back to Liam: "What are our chances?"

"In my professional opinion?" Liam tapped an incantation on his laptop; the television blanked, then displayed a satellite photograph. "We're right fucked. Here's the site from two weeks ago: Notice all the nothing here, where Norse's tent stands now. The camp's on the grid, but they have portable generators, too, and if they have a network, it's so hardened I can't even knock on the front door."

"Physical security," Grace added, "may not be airtight, but it's strong. He's working with local talent for the most part. They're good. Barbed wire around the base, motion detectors, bright lights, guard rotations. We're not sneaking in."

"What about Team One?" Sal asked. They all turned to look at her. "I don't like the guns-blazing routine any more than the rest of you, but you have to admit: secret base, top security, evil magic . . . This is more their bailiwick. I'd rather deal with this on our own, but why shouldn't we call in the big guns? Or the, you know, any guns?"

Menchú looked tired. "I tried them already."

Sal blinked.

"You're right. It makes sense. But Corporal Shah—she's in charge of Team One now, after Bouchard was eaten—doesn't want to risk the chance that Norse could put up a magical fight. The island's full of tourists, and there's some sort of financial conference under-way. Society diplomats can only hush up so much."

"It'll be worse if Norse gets ahold of that book, is all I'm saying."

"I made that point. If it comes to that, they're prepared to step in. Until he has the book, we're on our own."

"If he gets the book, they might not be able to stop him."

"Nonetheless," Menchú said, "that's where matters stand. Corporal Shah does not want to start a bloodbath without cause."

"Of all the times for Team One to grow a conscience."

Nobody spoke for a long, silent minute. Finally, Asanti turned back to the television. "We could use magic."

"No," Menchú said.

"I think he wants to enter the Knights' old archives: They used to stand on that hill, but they vanished just before the Ottoman invasion. Not burned—they were sent away. The Knights couldn't escape with the *Codex*, but couldn't let anyone else have it either, so they just—shoved it off, into magic. He's trying to find it again; we could do the same. The ritual's mostly benign."

"After Glasgow, Oklahoma, and the Oracle, I don't think we're likely to survive another mostly benign ritual."

"You were the one who suggested the Oracle."

"And it almost killed us, again." He shook his head. "No magic."

Grace set down her book. "Do we have another choice?"

"We might have," Liam said, "if someone hadn't taken a day off to go to the movies."

Sal closed her eyes as the argument continued: The nearer they drew to the *Codex Umbra*, the more anxiously they circled the same old fights. There must be an option they hadn't yet considered, something outside their usual approach, something Norse would never expect a room full of law-minded Bookburners to try.

"Oh," she said, and opened her eyes.

The others were looking at her again, with a different, more hopeful expression.

"What if we steal our way in?"

No one spoke, still, but the silence sounded . . . receptive, at least.

"Father, you said there was a financial conference this week. Liam, is there a list of attendees? Maybe Norse is there, in some capacity?"

Liam cracked his knuckles and plied the keyboard. Real computer work involved a lot more humming and waiting than rapid-fire typing and animated displays, but before long Liam leaned back on his elbows, smirking. "You know, this job's pretty tough, with all the secret organizations and the magic. I sometimes forget how good I am."

"Give it to us," Menchú said.

"I've been building my known alias file on Norse, see, and—"

"The point, please."

"He's not technically attending the conference, but he's on the guest list of a billionaires-only sort of party being held by one Emma LaCroix on her yacht—"

Grace groaned; Liam ignored her.

"Can you score us invitations?" Sal asked.

"Done and done." Liam glanced up from the keyboard. "Wait. Why?"

"We'll get to that. Now you just need to rent yourself a tux."

2.

ow this," Sal said, "is how I like my yachts."

Whoever Emma LaCroix was, she threw a hell of a party. Hanging crystals reflected firelight, and space heaters cast warm shadows on a deck swarming with the great and good—or at least the great—of fifty nations. Light-capped waves rolled off toward the jewel that was Rhodes. The ocean breeze cooled Sal's skin.

"Covered with infuriating, garish displays of wealth?" Menchú wore a black suit, black shirt, and white collar; Asanti, something heartbreaking in cream; and Sal herself, black and spangles. Asanti (thanks to the Vatican Amex) had financed their expedition to procure fancy dress, but Grace had stepped up as fashion team leader, navigating boutiques, selecting cut and color, negotiating prices, and generally surprising the crap out of Sal.

"Not possessed by demons," Sal replied. She snagged a champagne flute off a passing tray and toasted the others. "As long as we're here, why not enjoy ourselves?"

"What is there to enjoy?" Menchú glowered at a man laughing by a roulette wheel.

Asanti grabbed his hand. "Come on, you old Marxist. Let's get to work." She took point, leading them through the crowd.

Roulette wheels and baccarat tables crowded the first deck, and dancers the second. On the third, the highest and least populous level, two massive and mostly naked men pummeled each other in a roped-off ring while an audience drank, watched, and sometimes spoke around the edges. Groans and the pop of flesh striking flesh added a complementary rhythm to the big-band music from below.

A bell sounded the round's end. The taller, thinner fighter staggered back to his corner, half his face curtained with blood.

Norse stood near the bloody fighter's corner, nodding approval. Two broad-shouldered men accompanied him, sensibly far back, wearing earpieces and—Sal judged from the poor fit of their jackets—armed.

Sal cut through the crowd toward Norse; the mooks shifted but did not try to stop her. Maybe they had standing orders against interfering when a woman in a cocktail dress approached their boss. "Enjoying the fight?"

She had hoped for at least an instant's surprise, but Norse turned from the blood with an easy grin. "It's just grown more interesting, Detective Brooks. You look well."

"No thanks to you."

"Oh, come. I know you're new to our game, but certainly you don't hold a grudge for that minor lapse of mental privacy you experienced at the Black Market? Or for the invigorating chase I've led you on around the world?"

"You killed people. You used me."

"And you caused me to incur the Maîtresse's disfavor. I assure you, you have no idea how much of an inconvenience that presents in my line of work. Good evening to your comrades as well," he added as Menchú and Asanti joined them. "Madame Asanti! Unexpected and transcendent." He bowed. "Your presence honors me. You really should get out more."

"You," Father Menchú said, "are a monster."

The mooks tensed, but Norse raised one hand and they relaxed. "I want power," he said, "and knowledge, for mankind. Your church has spent millennia hoarding magic for no purpose but to scorn it, like a dragon using a mound of gold as a litter box." He raised a glass and drank. "Which sounds more monstrous to you?"

Menchú's knuckles cracked. Sal set a hand on his arm.

"I did not expect a warm reception, Mr. Norse," Asanti said. "You haven't exactly been a model of bonhomie."

The next round's bell disturbed the music, and the bleeding fighter staggered to meet his opponent. Around the deck, glittering men and women turned back from rails and sea to watch the blood sport. "Call me Alex, please." Fist met face. "And, though we work on different sides, do know that I hold you in the highest respect."

"I'm waiting for the evidence," she said.

"For evidence—God, how about my being here, engaging in this conversation, rather than fobbing you off on security when I know none of you have a legitimate invitation? We're not allies, madame, far from it. I have tried to check you and your friends at every turn, as you know." The bloody fighter raised his arms to absorb a rain of punches. "But we have a common cause. We want to understand this strange new world so we may use it, and build a civilization on the breast of the rising tide."

"You invaded my library," Asanti said.

"And you'd no doubt happily return the favor." The fighter fell back, one eye swollen shut now, rolling with body blows, ducking away from jabs. His sweat glittered. A woman in a short skirt laughed at something the man beside her said. "You and I, Archivist, want to protect the world from its changes. I feel magic should bow to man. In the *Codex Umbra*, we have a vital tool: demons, collected and collated, name by name, with their secret needs and words of power, so each may be called or loosed on the world at the wielder's whim. We could use that power to prepare ourselves."

"Enrich ourselves, you mean," Menchú said.

"Prepare. We've all seen the signs. Magic is seeping back into the world, whatever the cause. Outbreaks grow common. Children perform feats of magic the most learned practitioners of our art would have believed impossible ten years back. Your team's staffed for magic the way it used to be, not the way it is, or for what it will become—your organizational goals are outmoded, your objective incoherent."

"And yet we win."

"You never win, Father. You postpone. Madame Asanti knows this. I bet she's told you as much, and you've laughed it off."

Asanti raised her chin. "We do the best we can with the materials on hand."

"As do I. But I have more materials, and greater freedom to use them."

"Like a child left alone in surgery has freedom to play with the tools."

"Yes—and, if such a child's careful, he can learn. I have. Ask yourself this, Archivist: When the world breaks and magic returns—not these pale shadows you've fought and contained for so long but real magic, golden and true—would you have rather spent your decades in a terrified, vain attempt to fight the future, or preparing yourself to rule the wave?"

"You can't rule a wave," Asanti said. "We can ride waves, yes. Channel them. But waves laugh at scepters. Some powers are beyond our reach."

"That's what people said of lightning. When the walls fall down, I'll be Alexander Norse, tamer of demons, and your backward church will stand, as ever, on the wrong side of history. But I'm no genius—I just have vision. You have the languages, the mind, the discipline. Work with me. We could achieve wonders."

"That's enough," Menchú said. "We're leaving."

"How about it, Asanti? Or you, Detective Brooks? You have hidden depths; I can teach you how to use them."

Sal looked away. "I'm good, thanks."

"The father's too hidebound, but if either of you want to be on the winning side, well . . . I'm always hiring. And I have a very comfortable benefits package."

Menchú's wet, dark eyes glistened. "You won't win," he said. Asanti put out one hand to stop him, but he ignored her. "I've seen a hundred like you before: You talk revolution, but you want power for yourself. You sicken me."

Norse retreated a step, his forehead wrinkling in perplexed innocence.

"Excuse me," a deep voice said. "I'm afraid I'll have to ask you three to leave."

There were four of them, all built to a size Sal didn't know people were still made. Shoulders that broad should have gone out of style with Hercules. "It's all right," she said. "We were going, anyway."

In the ring, the bleeding boxer ducked around a punch and struck his opponent three times in the face. A fourth punch, to the body, doubled the man over, then back to the head, cross after cross. The opponent fell, to a light rain of applause.

❖   ❖   ❖

"That went better than I expected," Menchú said after the security launch deposited them on the dock.

"You did great, Father."

"I thought you laid it on a bit thick, myself," Asanti said. "I could have handled him without trouble."

Sal leaned against a stanchion, slipped off her left shoe, and rolled her ankle until it popped. "The plan wasn't to handle him. We wanted him angry—or we wanted someone angry, at least."

"Arturo does have some anger issues to work out, it's true."

"I," Father Menchú said, staring off at the retreating launch, "do not have anger issues. I'm just passionate."

"Of course you are, dear."

They found a small dockside restaurant, open late, and ate stuffed grape leaves and small fried balls of dough and octopus until Grace and Liam returned. "How did it go with the guards?" Sal asked when they sat down. "We tried to keep Norse distracted; I hope we gave you enough time to work."

"Time wasn't a factor." Grace polished off the last of the fried dough. "I baited the hook, but neither guard was biting."

"Damn," Sal said. "I guess it's plan B, then."

"I didn't say that."

Sal blinked. "What?"

Grace's eyes darted right to Liam, who'd taken a brief respite to consult the calorie tracker on his phone. He locked the phone, halved a stuffed grape leaf with his knife, and popped one of the halves into his mouth. Lines of muscle rolled across his jaw as he chewed. When he swallowed, he grinned.

"Oh," Sal said.

He dried his fingers, then withdrew a folded cocktail napkin from his tux. "I got a number. And we're in luck—he and his roommate go on shift tomorrow at sundown. I'll drop by early. He says he can get his roommate out of the hotel. I'll take the guy, Grace will jump his roommate, and we'll relieve the gate guards. Easy."

"Won't the team be worried if they don't recognize the relief?"

"If this were a regular outfit," Grace said, "yes. But they're stitched-together contractors. Nobody knows anyone else. A lot of the security personnel were only hired for tomorrow night, anyway—Norse expects something big."

"Because of the solstice," Asanti said, after a mouthful of beer. "The stars are right for the ritual after sundown."

"But Grace and Liam only go on shift at sunset. We won't be able to get in the camp fast enough to stop him." Sal frowned. "We need more time."

Liam pondered the second half of the grape leaf and then shrugged and ate it, too. "I think I can slow them down a tick."

3.

Norse almost missed the camp in the predawn mist. He frowned: He should have seen the searchlights from the road. "Go back," he told his servant. "Turn here."

By the time they reached the gate, the sun had burned off all but a few wisps of clinging fog. Guards stood at attention, rifles slung, dark circles under their eyes. "Sir."

Norse descended from the jeep. Mud squelched beneath his patent leather shoes. "Why are the lights off? What happened?"

"Power died at midnight," the guard replied. "We ran off generator fuel until we were down to the reserves. After that, we killed the lights and doubled patrols. No one's entered or left the camp since the outage."

They should have called him—but he'd left orders not to be disturbed, so long as the tent was not compromised. He'd needed sleep last night, and meditation, incense burned on rooftops, charms chanted to prepare. They scratched inside his skull, burned his eyes. "The power's still down?"

"The utility office doesn't open until eight. We called their emergency number. No response."

"Fine," Norse said, though it wasn't. He detected the Bookburners' hands at play. "You left the fuel reserves?"

"Yes, sir."

So they'd have power to open the way and keep it open all night. Good. He clasped his hands behind his back, looked down, looked up. "Get on the phone to the utility. Send a team to buy extra fuel. One way or the other, I want power to the camp before dark."

"Yes, sir."

He returned to the jeep and swore, fluently, while waiting for the gate to open.

"Trouble?" his servant asked in a voice like hanging knives struck together.

"Not yet—but something that could become trouble if we aren't careful." The jeep jostled over the dirt road his men had carved through Alhadeffs's field. He wished the servant could offer suggestions of her own, could plan in ways that surprised him. He wished Asanti had accepted his offer. He'd walked a long and lonely path from Soldown Manor to the isle of Rhodes, and left too many people behind on the way, lying in their own firelit rooms. "Without power, I'll have to perform the final incantations manually. Watch the tent. Guard the camp."

She parked the vehicle and said, "Yes."

The tent, in morning light, looked gray. Dew clung to the thick fabric and wet his hand as he parted the flap.

Coils and wires, Jacob's ladders and silver tubes running with a supercooled mixture of antifreeze and blood—all the accoutrements of magic—clustered around the tent's edge, leaving a patch of bare earth in the middle, crisscrossed by more wires terminating in a silver circle. The circle, in turn, surrounded a mirror.

All the devices and systems save the mirror were standard, insofar as standards existed for this work: They'd been tested, and those who performed the tests had not died yet. The devices amplified and accentuated power. Only fools trusted objects that worked magic on their own, but amplifiers made business sense. Back in the old days whole monasteries of cultists might have gathered to chant the same spell, lending their voices and their blood. Hardly tenable in the modern age. Industrialization spelled the end of all the old guilds and cults, even the mystic ones.

But the mirror was different—was necessary.

The most basic of all laws of magic was the principle of correspondence: Like calls to like. Magic, at its root, was a form of con artistry: Talk fast enough, in the proper languages, and you might convince the world two similar objects were the same.

The Knights of Saint John left few records of the old library that once stood where Alhadeffs's farm lay now. They did not want the Vatican to learn the depth of their betrayal, however well-intentioned. Nor could they take the *Codex Umbra* with them when they fled Rhodes: The demons within the book railed against imprisonment, and there would be too many chances for them to break free on the long flight west. So the Knights used what power they'd gleaned from the book's pages and made the library swallow itself: Unmoored it from this or any world.

That much he'd learned from darkness and divination. But he'd found the key in an otherwise-inoffensive English monk's diary, describing the rituals of entry. *We pass through the antechamber. We regard ourselves in the blessed mirror, carved from olive wood of this isle, blown from glass of this isle, finished with consecrated silver. In its light our impurities stand revealed. And through the mirror we enter the sanctum of the book.*

A mirror was easily made. The olive wood he'd cut from Alhadeffs's groves. Nor was consecrated silver hard to find, in these fallen days.

The mirror glittered, ugly, misshapen, in the center of the tent. It cast bubbling and imprecise reflections. But when night came, it would serve.

His tools were useless without electricity, but while he waited, he could prepare in the old-fashioned way.

Alhadeffs lay before the mirror, entombed in his own skin. Norse watered him with a can; the hide-caul drank hungrily. The man within writhed.

"Don't worry," Norse said. "We're almost done."

He drew a knife. Then he drew Alhadeffs's blood.

There were screams, of course, but muffled, and easily ignored.

The jeep Norse's camp sent to town for fuel blew a tire on the way. The man in the passenger seat stepped out, knelt to check the tire, and growled, "Where the hell did you learn to drive?"

No response from the cab. The man, formerly of the passenger seat, sighed. That was the problem with civilian security: Everyone always wanted to play hard bastard of the week. If you were lucky, you worked with men or women you'd served beside. You had nothing to prove to them, and they had nothing to prove to you. If you were unlucky, you got a job like this. And then came a pharaoh who knew not Joseph, Exodus read.

"I'll get the spare."

No answer. At least the money was good. He shouldered his rifle, walked around to the trunk, and began to unscrew the spare.

An arm wrapped around his neck and squeezed. He tried to speak, but breath wouldn't come, tried to bowl his assailant to the ground, but his limbs were heavy. His world went dark.

Grace settled the merc to the ground, estimated his body weight with her eyes, drew a syringe, and pinched it into his neck. She tossed the merc into the trunk, then dragged the driver around from where he sat, as unconscious as his comrade. She changed the tire and added the wrecked one to the trunk with the unconscious men. A dust-colored bird sang in the tree overhead.

"Three seconds shy of your previous gank-two-berks-and-a-tire-change record," Liam said over her earpiece as she kicked the jeep into drive. "But it's early yet, and you may not want to overexert yourself."

"You did a good job with the power. Can you do that sort of thing anytime, anywhere?"

"God, I hope not. The local utility was running an old SCADA system, a few update cycles behind. Once they find out what I've done, they'll patch it."

"So they made a mistake."

"I would have found a way. You and Sal aren't the only competent ones around here."

She turned onto a side road toward the shed where they'd chosen to store the unconscious mercenaries. "You sound defensive. What's up?"

Static and silence over the line. "Why are you and Sal such good friends all of a sudden?"

She parked the jeep, entered the shed, and returned with burlap sacks and a coil of paracord. Good stuff, paracord—durable, cheap, knotted well, cut without fraying, and even if it did fray, you could melt the ends solid with a pocket lighter. Most technological development since what Grace preferred to call the good old days, back in Shanghai in the twenties, she regarded with suspicion at best, but paracord could stay. She measured out the cord in coils around her arm. "Friction between coworkers wastes time." *And I don't have much to waste,* she didn't say. Somewhere, liquid wax ran down a candlestick—that was her life, burning off with each waking instant. She'd worked beside Liam for years, from his perspective, but he respected her privacy and hadn't yet learned about her candle or her curse. Sal she'd known for months; the woman was infuriating, refused to respect tradition or precedence or Grace's own boundaries. And yet, when Sal found Grace in her solitude, she'd reached out. Why to her, not him?

She cut the measured rope.

"You didn't give me the time of day for three years after I joined this team," he said. "That's fine. I respect a professional. But now I'm wondering if maybe it was just me. Did I do something to piss you off? Do you not like me?"

"I like you fine." Sacks for the legs and arms, blindfolds, cord around everything, not too tight. She hefted the first unconscious man over her shoulder. "Maybe Sal just has a winning personality."

Wandering down the medieval backstreets of central Rhodes with Asanti, Sal couldn't think of anything to say other than, "So, you and Norse, huh?"

The archivist waved derisively with the back of her hand, as if shooing away a small dog. "He should be so lucky. Even if he were not—I believe the English expression is—'an insufferable prick'? He is younger than my middle son." They'd left Menchú in the hotel, reviewing and blessing their equipment before the attack tonight. Nobody, so far as Sal knew, had conclusive proof blessings helped; that said, nobody had conclusive proof they didn't.

Sal considered letting that one drop but didn't. "You got started young."

"I started everything young." Asanti looked up at the stone walls closing out the sky. "This is not the road to the Palace of the Grand Master."

"I know," Sal said. "I wanted to see what else was out this way. We don't have much chance to sightsee on these trips."

Asanti laughed. "It reminds me of my old days in the academy. Travel to scenic destinations around the world, only to spend your whole stay in a convention center that looks no different from any other."

The narrow street opened onto a cobblestone square beside the city wall. "It's amazing these are still standing."

"They built fortifications to last in the old days," Asanti said. "The Knights of Saint John spent centuries defending themselves against invasion, or, from a more accurate perspective, centuries defending their invasion from counterattack—and they accumulated fortunes of plunder. They clung to this island like an eagle to a tortoise. In the end, though, Suleiman the Magnificent was too much for them." Asanti blinked herself back from the reverie of ages past. "I find no appeal in Mr. Norse."

"If you say so." Sal's gaze descended from the ramparts to a squat stone building, a watchhouse or gatehouse, maybe. "What's that?" Without waiting for an answer, she jogged across the street, New Yorkering past an onrushing Audi.

"He is, I'll admit," Asanti said when she caught up, "a compelling adversary. I wish the Society would give me nearly so free a hand as he enjoys."

Halfway up the stairs, Sal turned back. "You want to kill people and raise zombies?" Two locals glanced over, confused. Sal grinned and waved, and they moved along, hopefully thinking they'd misheard the English.

Asanti bought a basket of cherries from a fruit vendor and followed Sal up the stairs. "Of course not, though were such activities moral, there are a few people I'd joyfully terrify." She chewed a cherry, swallowed, and spit the pit over the staircase's edge. Sal wondered how many of Asanti's victims would belong to the Society. "His freedom to explore magic does interest me. We stand on the brink of many possible futures: Topias, u- and dys-, jockey for position. Norse is right, in a way. The Society, and organizations like it, can only protect the status quo so long. If the current rash of mystical intrusions is not a storm season or even a tide, but a rise in sea level, we may not have decades to acquire the knowledge we need. We may not have years."

"Jesus."

"That would certainly be one possible outcome of an influx of magic," Asanti said, contemplating the cherries and the square. "Some elements in the Society no doubt believe, or would like to believe, that our traumas herald a second coming, or similar messianic event."

"Seriously?"

"Not so many as you would find in some Protestant circles in your country, but I've heard people make this argument. In some ways this is a hopeful read on the situation—that the hierarchy believes everything is proceeding according to plan. There was, if you'll remember, a film in the 1990s asserting that global warming was the result of an alien plot. The alternative—that my reports are being read, and then ignored, because systematic change is difficult and the current, let's dignify it with the term 'solution,' seems to work—is . . ." She searched the sky for the right word. ". . . unsettling. Norse's freedom attracts me. His wealth lets him study as he wills without consequence, save, of course, the generally lethal aftereffects of dabbling in magic, which he seems to have avoided so far. Some people have all the luck."

"Why not work outside the system?"

Asanti turned to Sal, head cocked, one eyebrow raised.

"I'm not suggesting you go over to the dark side. Just—I bet you have your reasons, and they're better than 'because I'd get in trouble.'"

"It's a complicated subject. Cherry?" She offered Sal one, and she ate. It tasted more sweet than tart, rich and fresh and full. "Cherries come from around here. Just up the coast, through the Hellespont past Troy, on an island smaller than this one."

"Cool," Sal said, chewing.

"I could have been lying just then, you know."

"Were you?"

"You trust me. But here's the funny thing: I trust myself too. I'm smart. I think deeply, and for the most part well. I've been right often in the past, though not always. So how can I tell if I am lying to myself? If I believe a certain moral corner must be cut, certain risks must be taken, how do I know whether I'm right, or whether I'm listening to a demon's voice in my ear? Reason models its own progress poorly. But you, and Arturo, and Grace, and Liam—I care about you all. I would not hurt you. If I find myself forgetting that, if you become acceptable losses, I know I've strayed."

"Like Liam's trip wires. His possession tests."

"Similar," Asanti allowed. "I'm in danger on my own. If I'm to be part of this secret world, I need to stand beside friends. Some days, to be honest, I wish none of this was real—that I was assembling occult knowledge in some research library for pure curiosity's sake."

"You could try this place." Sal pointed over her shoulder with her thumb to the open door at the top of the stairs. "Rhodes Public Library. Says here the building goes back to the Knights."

"I'll consider it." Asanti chose two cherries, ate one, passed the second to Sal. "Come on. Let's see what trouble Arturo's made for himself."

"I," Liam said as he climbed the hotel stairs, "have a fantastic personality."

"Seriously?" Grace's voice crackled in his ear. "You're still on about this?"

"I am a witty, charming, intelligent man who stands by his friends."

"And among your many fine qualities, you are great at letting things go."

He consulted the room number on the cocktail napkin for a third time and counted down doors to 314. "I'm just trying to understand what I've done wrong in your eyes. So I can mend my erring ways."

No one up or down the hall. He checked his smile in his cell phone reflection. Looking, if not good, then at least inoffensive. Cell phone back in pocket, crack the neck, roll the shoulders, game face on. Check the seal on the champagne. He rapped shave-and-a-haircut on the door. When Tariq opened it, Liam grinned and tried not to feel bad.

"Hi."

"If you want the truth," Grace said over the earpiece, "how about: Your morose self-pity, self-defeating mockery, and crushing attacks of guilt make me uncomfortable?"

He kept his smile broad. Tariq's roommate bowed out quickly and left the pair of them alone. *Game face,* Liam told himself as the man took his arm. He poured champagne; they clinked glasses. Tariq drained his. He looked happy. Then his features went slack, and the rest of him followed. Liam set down his own undrunk glass.

His lips tingled, numb, where they'd touched the drugged liquid. Should wear off in a few minutes. "Sorry, Tariq." He laid the man out on his bed, checked the vitals: all good. He hated drugging people.

"See what I mean? Guilt."

"What church do you think we work for again? The Northern Vermont Provincial Church of Fluffy Rabbits and Joyful Acoustic Guitar?"

"I don't think Vermont's a province."

"You know what I mean."

"Hold on." He heard a series of grunts and short, sharp impacts of flesh and bone on bone and flesh.

"As if you have room to complain about personality conflicts, oh dame sans mercy." A growl on the other end of the line; metal clanged off concrete. Liam found Tariq's fatigues in the closet and his boots, shined. The fatigues were roughly his size; he'd have to fake the boots. "This may be the most honest conversation we've had in all the years we've worked together, and we're only having it now because I'm fed up."

"I have reasons," she said; the mic picked up a swoosh of something heavy passing nearby, then a man's voice, cursing in maybe Turkish. "For a long time now I've thought talking about myself was—"

"A waste of time, I know." He poured the rest of the champagne down the sink, wiped the bottle with a rag, and let himself out with a brief apologetic salute to the unconscious Tariq. "God himself knows I have my secrets. We all do. I understand you and Sal have a connection we don't share, wherever it comes from. I'm just asking you to consider how that might make me feel."

"Come down here," Grace said, "and get in the car."

Infiltrations were Grace's least favorite part of covert ops. They almost never worked against a prepared enemy. She liked shadows and sneaking up from behind. Failing all those, fair fights had their charm. But to insert yourself into a unit, you couldn't look too suspicious, couldn't hide. You had to move and act like you belonged there, when of course you didn't.

Norse, fortunately, lacked a military background and seemed to have been arrogant or hurried enough to have resisted hiring an on-site advisor. When they drove Tariq's car to the camp at sunset, the explanation Liam offered—Tariq and his partner are patrolling the woods; they brought us in for the gate—seemed to work. The guards coming off shift told them where to park and retired to the mess tent.

Not for the first time, Grace wondered how many systems were two bad lies away from collapse.

Stars emerged. Behind her, a generator coughed to life. Grace drew a flashlight, aimed it toward the ridgeline, and blinked it three times; she saw a gleam in answer.

Fine. Sal and the others were in place; they'd approach, Grace and Liam would let them through, and with luck they'd reach the central tent before anyone noticed. This crazy idea just might work.

Then she heard a click.

"Drop the flashlight," said a voice of wind chimes and gravel. "And the gun. Or he dies."

Grace's cross chilled and burned at once against her skin.

She let the flashlight fall. Unholstered the gun—slowly—ejected the magazine, and tossed mag and gun away. Small loss. She never liked that gun, anyway. Not that she liked any guns.

"Turn around, slowly."

The thing that held Liam—its fingers like knives against his throat, its gun against his temple—was not even close to human. It had a face like a broken promise. Red lenses clicked and refocused in its eyes, and dark oil trickled between the blades it had in place of teeth. A homunculus. That was why Norse's servant had looked blurry on the hotel room television—she wasn't wearing magic or using magic. She *was* magic.

The soldiers flanking the homunculus, though, they were plenty human and did not seem to notice or care that their companion wasn't. They had their rifles out and level.

Norse must have used a glamour to make the homunculus seem normal to people who weren't wearing silver. Saved having to explain his demons to the hired help.

Grace hated magic.

On even ground she could probably beat this thing. But she couldn't move fast enough to stop it before it cut Liam's throat or put a bullet in his brain.

"Sorry," Liam said.

She raised her hands and did him the favor of not looking in his eyes. "I surrender."

The soldiers cuffed her wrists behind her. The homunculus watched and did not let Liam go until Grace was bound.

"Come," the homunculus said. "He wants to meet you."

Grace knew many languages and swore silently in most of them.

"Fuck," Sal said, and passed Asanti the binoculars.

"They're taking them to the central tent," Asanti said. "The homunculus has Liam hostage."

"Maybe it'll get careless. Maybe Norse doesn't know what Grace can do."

"Unlikely," Menchú said. "Magic calls to magic. That thing won't give Grace a fighting chance." He frowned. "At least it has to deal with them, now, which means it won't be around to stop us. We have the jeep—we could ram the gates, drive toward the tent."

"Come on, Father." Sal shook her head. "Grace said a frontal assault on this place wouldn't work."

Asanti lowered the binoculars. "I see only one option."

"No," Menchú said.

"I understand your negativity, but—"

"Magic has tried to kill us every time we've used it."

"We don't have much choice, unless you want to fight Norse once he has the book. Without Liam. Or Grace."

Menchú paced the roadside in silence until the words came. "Even if we did want to use magic, how? Norse has time on his side. Machines. Tools. Knowledge."

"We're agents of the Church," Asanti said. "Like the Knights. That gives us a head start. We need something connected to the library of the Knights of Saint John—the study in the Palace of the Grand Master, perhaps. An archive or treasure house. Someplace with a mirror."

"You're suggesting we break into a major historical site in the next two hours, without Grace or Liam."

"Do you have any better ideas?"

The silence between the priest and the archivist stretched taut and angry, and Sal had to force herself to say, "I do."

4.

Miss Chen, Mr. Doyle." Norse welcomed them with an offhand wave but did not look up from his console. "Kind of you to join us." He turned a knob, and the chants that filled the room adjusted pitch and speed. "Do get comfortable."

The tent was brightly lit, and empty save for Norse and his machines. Two chairs faced the warped mirror in the wire circle. "Sit," the homunculus said. A trickle of blood ran down Liam's neck and stained his shirt. A claw had slipped, or else he'd breathed too deeply.

Before the mirror lay the farmer trapped inside his sack of skin.

Grace met Liam's eyes and sat. The homunculus walked Liam to the chair beside her. When the knife-fingers left his throat, he tried to rear up and tackle the homunculus, but it struck him across the temple with its gun, and he fell into the chair. The homunculus retreated, gun leveled on Liam, until it was far enough away to watch—and shoot—them both if needed.

Grace waited. Beside her, Liam bled.

The chanting grew. Fluid gurgled down translucent coils at the tent's edges. She did not want to know what kind of fluid it was; she strongly suspected she knew, anyway.

Norse frowned and adjusted other knobs on what Grace assumed was a mixing board. The sound didn't change, but she felt a shift in her bones and blood. "It's amazing what you can do with the Mechanical Turk," Norse said, though no one had asked him. "Magic likes human minds—they're its favored operating platform. Someday we'll have artificial intelligence for this sort of thing, selective brain simulation, and we'll be able to conduct massively parallel incantations. For now, simple human intelligence tasks are best performed by humans compensated—so cheaply!—for the loan of their brains. Like, say, an hour's repetitive chanting over Skype, timing forced via click track." A slider sharpened the treble of the sound. "Lag's an issue, hence the mixing board, and it turns out there are a handful of ancillary effects for which blood and other humors serve as a focus or insulator, hence the machines. Cultists are easier, and more traditional, but their care and feeding has ruined richer men than me. I'll stick with the modern method."

Grace waited. Liam watched Norse and his homunculus, burning with rage Grace understood, but refused to let herself share. The machines burbled.

"No questions? No protestations that I'll never get away with this? I'd hoped for conversation at the very least."

Grace smiled at him.

"Fair enough. I work best on my own."

He fussed over the board for almost an hour, singing softly to the chant now and again, pressing one ear closed with his finger to test his pitch. The words twisted inside her, wriggled through her blood. Liam roared in pain. "Stop it, you bastard—"

Norse flicked a switch.

The chanting stopped.

No. That was wrong. She could still feel the hooks in her heart, the worms beneath her skin, but the chant had transformed, vibrating some medium other than air. She grimaced. Nails scraped the chalkboard of the world. The tent pulsed and bulged like an animal rotted from the inside.

The warped, misshapen mirror in the center of the room was no longer warped or misshapen at all. The once-bubbled glass surface lay smooth as a reflecting pool. The frame stood just and true. Norse took a bow. No one clapped.

He knelt beside the bound man. A knife blade painted a line of red down the center of the flesh that should have been his face. Approaching the mirror, Norse wet his fingers with blood from the knife, and drew a circle on the glass. When the circle closed, the glass disappeared.

Beyond the mirror's frame Grace glimpsed gleaming stone, a checkerboard floor, and light.

She could stop him. Even if the homunculus tagged her with that .45, she was fast enough, probably. If he didn't have other protections in place. If she didn't mind letting Liam die.

She shouldn't mind. Fate of the world at stake: What do you do? Stop the bad guy? Or save your friends?

Norse stepped through the mirror, and Grace watched him go.

Breaking into the Rhodes Public Library turned out to be easier than Sal had expected, at least until the alarms went off. "It's a good thing," Menchú observed as they ran past a circulation desk lit by strobing emergency lights, "that magic doesn't need concentration or silence!" He had to shout to be heard over the sirens.

"Breaking into stuff isn't my job," Sal said. "It's not my fault an evil wizard took our B-and-E team hostage."

"This was your plan," Menchú replied, which she really wished he had not pointed out.

"This way." Asanti led them down a modern staircase; at least here the sirens weren't echoing off bare stone.

"We don't have much time," Sal said. "The cops will arrive soon."

"We're almost there."

"What are we looking for, anyway? Some old artifact?"

"Not exactly," Asanti said, and opened the door to the women's bathroom: Buzzing fluorescent lights illuminated green institutional tile.

Menchú skidded to a stop. "What?"

"The records describe a purification chamber, with a mirror, in a library owned by the Knights of Saint John. This is as close as we will get." Asanti opened her purse and removed a cigarette lighter, a sleeve of needles, a thin paintbrush, and a silver bowl, setting each on the makeup shelf beneath the bathroom mirror. "If I'm right, Norse's work has, let's say, dug a well, bringing our world closer to . . . wherever the Knights sent their archive when they left Rhodes. We don't need his resources to dive into that well alongside him."

She burned the needle's tip black with the lighter, pricked her finger, and squeezed a drop of blood into the bowl. Asanti licked the paintbrush to a fine point, wet it in the blood, and drew a circle and a line of sharp letters—not quite Greek—on the mirror.

Above, Sal heard a battering ram strike the library's front door.

The mirror remained a mirror.

Asanti burned the next two needles and passed them to Sal and Menchú. "The magic needs to know all of us."

Menchú glared at Asanti, at the needle, then stuck his finger.

Sal felt her wound not as pain exactly, too much adrenaline for that, but as a warmth that collected in the red drop she added to Asanti's bowl.

Upstairs, the front door gave, and booted feet stampeded into the circulation area.

Asanti elaborated on her design. The blood trail burned with black flame. It pressed against the mirror as if against a rubber sheet, but still could not break through.

Shouts in Greek from above, clear and sharp. Sal didn't know the language, but she knew the sentiment: search orders.

Asanti frowned, considering.

"What are we missing?" Menchú asked.

"Confession." The word slipped out of Sal's mouth before she realized she'd been about to speak.

Asanti laughed, as if there were not booted feet approaching down the stairs. "Of course!"

"We don't have time for confession," Menchú said.

"An abbreviated form, surely. The magic needs fuel, that's all. Tell it your sin, Father." She leaned toward the mirror and said, "Mine is pride."

The fire leaped, and the mirror flexed inward.

Menchú sighed and leaned in. "Wrath." The glass cracked.

A cop tried the door, which didn't open. Sal wondered who'd locked it. The cop's full weight struck the wood—panels, latch, and hinges all held. Sal joined them at the mirror. She meant to say "lust," because it probably counted, but she did not hear the word that actually slipped from her lips before the mirror shattered and pulled them in.

✢   ✢   ✢

Liam, in the tent, glared at the homunculus with the gun.

He'd worked his hands free from the cuffs. That was easy—all he needed was a bobby pin and time. But he couldn't trick his way out from under fire.

Light seeped from the mirror, corrupting, glistening, like spilled oil at sunset. Norse was in there—how long would it take the man to get the book? If they could break the machines, maybe close the mirror off with him on the other side, drowning in whatever monsterland the Knights had used to hide their archive, maybe it wouldn't matter, maybe even with the *Codex* he wouldn't be able to tunnel home. A man could hope.

That was all they had left now.

His fault, all of it. He hadn't heard the homunculus creep up behind him. There must have been signs.

He turned left, to Grace. "I'm sorry."

Grace stared back, then let her eyes slip sideways, toward Norse's abandoned console. He read the message: *Go for it.* In spite of the homunculus with the gun. In spite of certain death. "Could have happened to anyone," she said.

She must have a plan. He didn't know what it could be—she was strong, yes, fast, yes, but not that strong, not that fast. No one was. When her eyes returned to his, he waited for a breath, then blinked, once. *Okay.* He could not say with a blink: *Whatever you're planning, it better be good.* "I trust you," he said.

Grace went loose all over. He recognized that slack, the softening of muscles ready to work. Her shoulders rolled.

Her hands were still bound. He tried not to think about that.

He measured ten slow breaths, then ran.

⟡   ⟡   ⟡

Sal stood on a checkerboard floor in a vaulted stone room. Stone shelves crammed with books covered the walls, but the books were suggestions, memories: They shifted when she wasn't looking. Only one book in the room was still.

She had not expected the *Codex Umbra* to be so small. It rested on a stone lectern behind a towering figure of golden light, whose face was branded with a shadowy cross.

Menchú and Asanti took shape beside her, or else she had just noticed them. And across from them, also facing the *Codex* and its guard, stood Alexander Norse.

Sal tried to run for the book, but she could not move.

A current flowed through her—no, that wasn't quite right. Her muscles were wrong, too solid, too unyielding. She could let herself go, if she tried—flow beyond her skin and become something else. Everything else.

She remembered a carpet of fingers and a door of hair, remembered a goblin in a small apartment in Madrid, and ignored the temptation. She focused on her bones and skin. She existed. She stayed human. For now.

"You have come for the book," the light said. "There is no other purpose here. Why do you seek its power?"

The light did not move, but Sal felt its attention rake across her skin. Something deep within her chest, some secret guilt or shame, curled into a ball, pressed itself into the shadows of her being, and hid. She tried to speak, but she could not find her tongue.

Norse seemed to have no trouble. "I have come to continue the old masters' work. I call the magic to my service, and the service of mankind."

"He lies." Asanti's voice was deeper and steadier than Norse's. She strode forward, full of command, and the library flexed beneath her feet. "He has abased himself in search of power. He has no order. He has no comrades. And his mind is broken."

The light burned in silence.

Norse's laugh was cold and harsh. "What are you talking about?"

"Haven't you noticed it by now, Alex? You have a demon in you."

Liam dove for the console, flying more than running, a horizontal line above the earth. The gun spoke.

He didn't know what being shot would feel like. Bullet scars on his torso suggested he must have known, several times, but that had been during his possession, and he doubted demons (or humans ridden by them) felt pain the same way as mortals of the unmodified type. But all the stories he had heard suggested he would have felt something.

He didn't. The homunculus fired three times more, but Liam was behind Norse's control panel by then, breathing hard, glancing down, no blood, heart racing, sweating everywhere at once.

God. Grace.

He risked a glance around the panel's edge—she lay on the ground, unmoving, in front of her chair.

No. She couldn't be; she couldn't have. He wouldn't allow it.

But—

Her arms were in front of her. Somehow. And there was something wrong about her shoulders beneath the jacket.

As he watched, they clicked back into their sockets. One of Grace's hands lay in front of her on the bare earth. It was bleeding.

The homunculus' attention drifted toward her. Liam shouted, "Hey! Ugly!"

Two more gunshots answered, splintering the panel.

Grace moved.

"A demon? Impossible."

"I wouldn't go that far," Asanti said. "The *Codex* has been hidden for hundreds of years, and yet you hunted this place down, yourself, alone."

"I'm smart. I have money, and magic."

"So do others who want this book. Do you think you are smarter, more powerful, more rich, than the Maîtresse?"

Norse wavered. His outlines smudged, and while he did not lose balance, his form shifted from side to side, as if he were a painting on a flag blown in a high wind. Asanti stepped forward. "I'm more ruthless," Norse said. "More aggressive. Tradition binds the others, blinds them."

"While your eyes were open. Because something opened them for you. You stayed one step ahead of us this entire hunt."

"I started before you."

"You knew where to go. You found the one book in an archive that might have helped you; you killed the Pythia just before we could ask her how to beat you. The world's full of strange coincidences, but they do stack up."

"You're grasping at straws. You want to make me doubt myself."

"I want you to doubt yourself," Asanti said, "because there's a monster in your mind, and it's ridden you this far because it wants that book, to call its other monster friends to play."

"I would have seen—"

"No," she said. "You wouldn't. You have your resources, your powers—but what friends would have held you back from the brink? Who would have noticed the demon dig its claws into your mind?"

Grace moved faster than anything Liam had ever seen—blurring to tackle the homunculus, which staggered beneath her. She kicked its leg and the metal bent. He'd seen her fight before, but never like this.

She was not just good. She was unnatural.

Magical.

He'd known, of course. Suspected, but never asked, because if he'd asked he would have had to accept that this person who fought beside him was touched by the same force that had claimed his mind and destroyed his old life.

She was magical. And she'd saved him.

He heard footsteps outside: Soldiers coming. Grace had the homunculus distracted, and he could probably figure out this panel, but she'd be exposed. Fast as she was, he doubted she could outrun fire from automatic weapons.

Dammit.

He edged toward the tent flap and hid behind Norse's burbling blood tanks. A merc stepped through, saw Grace, raised his rifle— and Liam took the rifle from him and hit him in the face.

This, at least, felt right.

Norse blurred again. "I learned the secret ways of power. Demons answer when I call them. Magic obeys my command!"

"Magic commands," she said, "and you obey."

"No!" Desperation shone naked in his eyes.

"Look into your past, Alex. I bet I know how it happened: Some night you were alone, and scared, and a voice whispered to you, offering freedom, offering control. You let that voice lead you, and you've been led ever since. You're being led now. Is it you that wants the book, or the voice? You were scared, and something crept inside your skull and used that fear to rule you. Tell me if I'm wrong."

"I . . ." He tried to walk toward the book and fell to his knees. He tried to speak, but his mouth was an inky smudge, his words a hopeless wail.

Sal wanted to be sick.

Asanti advanced toward the light and the podium. "That book belongs with a person who will not let it rule her."

The cross on the golden figure burned with shadow.

She passed through the light, bowing a little beneath its weight, as if it struck her like falling water. Then she was through, and the light failed.

She touched the *Codex Umbra* and closed her eyes, and when she opened them again the burning light was in her. She wept.

Menchú took the shroud from his shoulder bag and held it out. "Asanti. Give me the book."

She bared her teeth in something that was not quite a smile.

It is, Liam reflected bitterly on occasion, much harder to hit people so they stay down than media suggests. Even Peggy Carter indulged in the old one-punch knockout from time to time. To be fair, Liam did hit the first mercenary with the butt of his own gun and then trip the second without getting shot himself—but while struggling for merc two's gun, of course merc one got up, which divided Liam's attention because he had to break that guy's knee with the rifle, then shift back to head-butt the second, duck out of the way of a rifle blow, oh shit he's going for the knife, okay, hit him in the throat, maybe this time—

At which point he realized he'd kept his eyes off merc number one too long, long enough for the guy to go for his sidearm and—

Merc number one's arm broke at the elbow with a sickening crunch, and Grace stood over him, gun in hand, covered in deep cuts that closed as Liam watched. Grace spun a glorious circle and kicked merc number two on the temple, and he fell.

"You," Liam said. "I mean."

"Can we talk about this later?"

The mirror erupted with light.

"Sure."

She raised the gun and took aim.

The light died.

Menchú, Asanti, and Sal stood in the tent. Menchú held a shroud-wrapped book.

Behind them, the mirror warped back to its initial shape, and shattered.

On the ground, among broken pieces of homunculus, the bundle of skin split and opened like a flower. A man lay within, weeping.

"Sorry we missed the party," Sal said.

Grace ejected the magazine and tossed the gun away. "Took you long enough. Where's Norse?"

Asanti shook her head. "Somewhere else."

5.

They escaped.

There was a tense bit with Grace laying down covering fire while Liam rammed a stolen jeep through a perimeter fence and Menchú performed CPR on Mr. Alhadeffs, while Sal laid down cover fire, but the salient point remained: escape, *Codex Umbra* in hand, wrapped in the shroud, harmless for the moment. They took Alhadeffs to a hospital.

Then it was time for a party.

Liam brought whiskey he'd smuggled in his carry-on bag; Grace changed into clothing that was, at the very least, less bloodstained, and ran out for mixers. Sal DJ'ed for the first hour until Menchú took over. The father's phone turned out to contain zero applications save what came preinstalled, and sixty gigs of soul.

Sal sang; she danced with the archivist. She poured drinks and muddled cherries in them. Why not? They'd won.

"How did you know?" she asked Asanti between dances.

"I didn't," she said. "But neither did he."

"What?"

"We're not so different, Norse and I. I hit him where I knew it would hurt the most—because it would hurt me. It's true, our search has been plagued by coincidences, but as many have helped us as hindered us. Likely Norse was seduced by a demon; I wouldn't put it past him. But 'mere suspicion in that kind will do as if for surety,' as the Bard says." She leaned back against the wall and closed her eyes. "The mind's our strongest tool, Sal. It can take anything in the world apart, including itself."

And Diana Ross still sang.

After a while, Sal couldn't bear it anymore. She stepped out onto the balcony, cradling her cocktail in both hands, staring out over rooftops toward the harbor, and thought about underwater chains.

"Hey." She didn't turn to look. Liam joined her by the railing. "You all right?"

"I'm fine," she said. "You could have died."

"Not really. Grace has my back."

"Even now that you know she's magic?"

"Can't say I'm wild about that, but . . ." He knocked back the last of his whiskey. "Nah. I have a bad history with magic and demons both. I can't blame her for being close with her past, given that. But we have to look out for one another."

"I guess so." Melting ice in her glass clinked and settled into a new formation.

"So, come on. Apocalypse averted. Our biggest coup in—well, since I joined, at least." He offered her his hand. "As friends, okay?"

"Thank you." She took his hand and felt the strength she knew there. "But it's been a long day. I almost got you killed. I need some rest."

"Of course. Fine." He didn't sound as if it were, but he didn't press her either. "Take care of yourself."

They walked back into the party together, but he stayed, and she returned to her room alone.

There is a house, somewhere—not in this world, or at least not in the part of this world you'll ever visit if you're lucky. Can you remember the last time you felt the sun? Can you feel its warmth on your face?

If so, you're probably safe.

But even if you are—trust me. There is a house, somewhere, and in that house is a boy named Alex, and in that house Alex runs, screaming, from a firelit room. He runs toward something. He hasn't reached it yet.

Sal closed her hotel room door. In darkness, she walked to the bathroom and closed that door too. Fluorescent lights carved shadows from her face. Moths fluttered against the open window's screen.

She stared into her own reflection's eyes.

"I know you're in there," she said, cautiously, as if testing whether she could speak the words aloud.

Nothing happened.

"You overplayed it in the library bathroom. But then, I guess you had to—win now, or walk, isn't that right? You couldn't afford to let Norse get your number."

Crickets chirped.

"Like Asanti said: You gave me hunches that always led us almost right. You sent Grace and Liam in to die, knowing the homunculus would catch them—because you wanted them out of the way. You made sure we found the library. You made sure I remembered where to go at the right time. You even helped us work the spell. I wondered, dammit." Her throat choked off her breath. Her eyes burned. A tear rolled down the curve of her cheek. She saw the tear but could not feel it. "I wondered why silver tarnished so fast on me. I wondered why I could close your book with my bare hands."

She was wrong. The mind can take anything apart, even itself. This was stress, and terror, and the afterglow of magic. That was all.

"Give me my brother back, you son of a bitch."

She couldn't finish the words.

Her eyes closed.

When they opened, they were pools of blood, and from her tongueless mouth a voice of fire answered: "No."

EPISODE
12

PUPPETS

BRIAN FRANCIS SLATTERY

1.

A man in a tan jacket, hands in his pockets and mumbling to himself, headed across the courtyard toward the Papal Palace in the early morning light, weaving among the tourists and people idling in the sun. At first there wasn't anything about him that drew the attention of the police or the Swiss Guard. He just walked like he knew where he was going. Then something changed in his step; it was too quick, too deliberate, and getting faster.

A policeman noticed his dark, moving shape in the crowd the way a lifeguard at the beach notices the shadow of a shark in the water. He put his handset to his mouth to tell a couple of other officers. He headed over to investigate.

The man in the tan jacket noticed the policeman, too, and further quickened his pace. He stopped weaving and started to make a straight line for the palace. He jostled a woman trying to take a picture, bumped shoulders with a tourist walking the other way. "Hey," the tourist said. The man in the jacket didn't look back. His pace was even faster now, almost a run.

The policeman moved through the crowd toward the man and

radioed for backup; two other policemen responded. The second officer approached the man in the jacket from behind, the third from the side.

The man broke into a run. A sound came from him, a whine that burst into a roar too big for a human throat. The third policeman reached him first and grabbed one of his arms. The man tried to throw him off, but the policeman wouldn't let go. The man leaped forward, still in the direction of the palace. That was when his skin began to change. It started to shine, to shimmer, until it was almost translucent. Then it tinted a splotchy red. The man kept running.

The first policeman yelled at the crowd to clear the square. Most followed the order. A few whipped out their phones to take videos. The phones didn't work.

The second policeman caught up to the man from behind and tackled him to the ground. The third policeman had one arm. The first policeman ran and pinned the other one down.

"Calm down, sir," the first policeman said.

The man roared again, louder than before. A torrent of words, in a language none of the officers had ever heard before, rushed out of his mouth. They sounded like curses, old and foul.

Then the man blistered all over, in seconds. His skin cracked open, and smoke poured out. Blood burned off before it could flow, and the policemen jumped away as the man self-immolated in front of the Papal Palace, so fast that he left his clothes behind—pants, socks, jacket, and all—singed and smoking but still there.

"What the hell was that?" the third policeman said.

The second policeman just stared, wide-eyed, shaking his head.

"Back!" the first policeman yelled at the crowd, which was starting to move forward, wondering what they had seen. "No pictures, you understand? No pictures!"

Later, the three officers were informed that they had thwarted a terrorist attack. They were given bonuses and a few days off. Hilary Sansone from Team Two made the rounds in the media and gave them the same story. The newspapers and TV shows were satisfied. It was what eyewitnesses thought they saw; it was the best way to explain the memories they had. No one could explain why none of the cameras worked, but there was nothing to be done about that fact. "Something about the bomb he had," someone said, and that was enough.

The Society knew what had happened. It was the third attack they'd faced that week. Team Three had found one small demon on a highway into the city. There had been a car chase for a few kilometers and then a zigzag through back streets before the demon, which didn't know where it was going, hit a dead end. It turned its host into water, there in the driver's seat of the car it had made the man steal, as Grace approached.

Another demon, brawny but stupid, managed to land itself in jail for brawling and hanged its host in the cell. Team Three only knew about that one because of the Orb. The man had no identification. The police buried the body. The demon was still out there, looking for another host, another shot. Team Three was sure of it. So was Team One.

Team Three was all together in the Archives when Team One's new leader arrived. Thavani Shah descended the long spiral staircase fast, with three men in tow, and somehow found her way straight to Asanti's desk. She gave each member of Team Three a courteous smile and a quick nod, but it was hard for Sal to shake the feeling that Shah was here to arrest her.

They know, Sal thought.

No, they don't, the Hand said.

"Father Menchú," Shah said. She turned to each of them. "Grace. Liam. Sal. Asanti. Is it all right if I address you this way? For those of you who haven't met me: I am Thavani Shah, the new head of Team One. I've been reading up on all of you and these archives you oversee, and I want to tell you how much I admire your work."

"Thank you," Menchú said.

"I hear some of you were present when my predecessor died."

"Yes," Sal said.

"I hope I can serve you as well as he did."

I hope you can do better, Sal thought, but kept it to herself.

Shah looked around. "Fascinating place. I'd like to visit someday when I can have time to appreciate it. But we have work to do."

Her eyes focused again on Menchú.

"I know that you have some very capable people, but we are going to strengthen security here." She extended her hand to her left, toward the three men who had followed her in. Two of them were wearing the bright uniforms of the Swiss Guard, a look that Sal was still having trouble taking seriously. One of them was dressed in the loose fatigues the members of Team One liked to wear.

"This is Gardist Schaffner and Gardist Huegin," Shah said. "With them is Joki Vaz, one of our own. I'm going to ask you if I can station them here in the Archives."

"It's a little crowded in here already, don't you think?" Grace said.

Shah turned to Grace. "Agreed. The situation is not ideal. But we're concerned about a visible increase in security outside the Archives, even within the Vatican. We don't want to alarm people unnecessarily."

Grace nodded. "That's fair," she said.

"I'll ask you to brief these men on the important details," Shah said. "Please let me know if I can help you in any other way." She looked back up toward the stairs.

"Thank you, Shah," Menchú said.

Shah left. The three soldiers looked at Team Three. Team Three looked back. There was a tiny—and, to Sal, very uncomfortable—pause.

"Have you ever fought monsters before?" Grace said.

Vaz nodded. The two Swiss Guard soldiers didn't move.

"Good luck," Grace said to them.

"How many . . . ," Schaffner said. "How many monsters are you expecting?"

Asanti shrugged. "It's hard to say," she said. "It's my understanding that the demons have always preferred to stay away from this place. The things we have here may be interesting to us—to people—but they're not as interesting to them. At least, not interesting enough to justify the trouble of getting in here."

"Until now?" said Huegin.

"We seem to have collected something that's suddenly worth the trouble," Liam said.

"The *Codex Umbra*," Vaz said.

"Good," Asanti said. "You did your homework."

"What is so interesting to the demons about this book?" Vaz said.

Asanti shrugged. "I haven't found a good answer to that question."

Sal wanted to ask Asanti the same thing. She wanted to get a couple of steps ahead of the Hand. To let the demon know that she had something on it, some kind of advantage. But she found she couldn't talk. Couldn't move at all.

Let me go, Sal said to the Hand.

Not until you promise to behave, the Hand said.

If you don't let me go, everyone will notice that I'm not moving.

Look around you, dear, the Hand said. *No one notices.*

Why do you want the Codex Umbra? *What does it do?*

Somewhere in the middle of her skull, she could hear the Hand snicker.

All in due time, it said.

Sal grimaced.

Menchú cleared his throat. "Let's hope we don't find out," he said. "I think that we cannot wait for a fourth or fifth attack. If the answer is not here, then it is out there. Somewhere, someone knows." He turned to Liam. "Do you know who we might talk to?" Menchú said.

Liam allowed himself a small smile. "I might have a couple promising leads," he said.

"Your underground people," Grace said.

"I don't think they'd call themselves that, but yes," Liam said.

"When can we see them?" Menchú said.

"Anytime," Liam said. "No time like now, right?"

"Good," Menchú said. "Lead the way. Sal, I'd like you to come with us. Asanti, call us if there's anything more from the Orb."

Liam got up from the couch, already making calls.

Menchú turned to Grace. "Now that we have these soldiers here, let's get you some rest, okay?" he said.

Sal could tell Grace didn't like it. But there was nothing else for her to do.

2.

The café was like a hundred others in Rome. Sal freely admitted that when she had first come to Rome, the romance of it got to her a little bit. In the web of her American associations with all things Roman, those cafés were either for stopping in while on your honeymoon or for hiding in plain sight from Interpol because you were on the lam due to some elite crime, like robbing a casino. She realized, stepping into this one with Liam and Menchú, that she'd spent enough time in Rome for places like this to just become coffee shops. And even though they were bathed in slanting afternoon light, the two men waiting for them at a glass table weren't romantic in the least.

"Liam," one said, nodding. It was unclear how he'd recognized Liam, since the man had dirty white bandages wrapped over his eyes. As though he'd had an operation a month ago and spent the time since then walking around next to a highway.

"Is Liam here already?" the other one said. He wore large circular glasses that made his eyes look even bigger than they were.

"Pardon him," the one with the bandages said. "He doesn't see very well."

"Gentlemen," Liam said. "These are two of my colleagues, Father Menchú and Sal Brooks."

The one with the bandages stood up and extended his hand. "A pleasure," he said. "I am Cosmin Nicolescu. This is Hasan Marangoz."

Marangoz nodded in their general direction. "Good to see you, Liam."

He nodded toward Sal, too, she noticed. As if he recognized her.

The waiter came over with three coffees for them.

"We ordered for you," said Nicolescu. "We thought you could use a little lift."

"You're going to need it," said Marangoz.

"What do you mean?" Menchú said.

Nicolescu and Marangoz looked at each other, then at Liam.

"Is this a setup?" Nicolescu said.

Liam shook his head. "You're safe here."

"We need some reassurance," Marangoz said.

Menchú nodded and handed them each a small stack of bills.

"There," he said. "Now we're complicit. At least for the moment."

Nicolescu looked at Menchú approvingly. "It's best when we all have a skeleton in the closet."

"Yes," Menchú said. "Now, tell us what you know."

Nicolescu took a sip of coffee. "You've become famous."

"I thought we were always famous," Liam said.

Nicolescu gave a dismissive wave of his hand. "Among the likes of us, yes. Among demons themselves, no. I understand that you believe your job is important and that the Church has devoted considerable resources to it for a few centuries. But you have merely been collecting the objects that humans might use to bring magic into the world."

"The truly powerful objects," Marangoz said, "the ones that *demons* would want to use to wield magic—have almost never made it here. Why would they? The demons want them, and they keep them."

"Except for . . . what we have," Menchú said.

Now both Nicolescu and Marangoz smiled.

"You don't have to be vague," Marangoz said. "We know what you have. Everyone is talking about the *Codex Umbra*. And the word is, the demons are too. They say the news has swept across the world already, and a wide variety of supernatural beings are very, very interested in what you have there in the Vatican Library."

"How many are we talking about?" Sal said. Against her will, she realized. She sounded like that poor Swiss Guard in the Archives.

"In the world, or coming for you?"

"Coming for us," Sal said.

Nicolescu looked at the ceiling. "There are at least a dozen in Rome right now."

She heard the Hand snicker again. *I would ask them who specifically, but that would arouse suspicion, wouldn't it?*

Don't gloat, Sal said.

But it's so much fun, the Hand said.

"You should lower your dozen to nine," Liam said.

"We're not counting the ones who have already tried to get it," Nicolescu said.

"Fine. A dozen, then."

"And more are arriving," Nicolescu said. "You can assume they will keep coming until you get rid of it. Which reminds me." He took a sip of coffee and looked at Menchú. "You know, Father, if you were willing to part with it, you could make a great deal of money. Even after our standard commission. Enough that you and your team could retire from this game for good."

"We're not interested," Menchú said.

"I appreciate that," Nicolescu said. "But I should warn you that those three were little ones. Stupid ones. Some of the demons will be bigger. And smarter. Much smarter. And there are a lot of them. No matter how secure you think you can make it; I assume you've— What is the English phrase? Beefed up security? It doesn't matter. One of them will still get in, one of these days. Probably one of these days this week."

Somewhere behind her right ear, Sal could hear the Hand laughing.

If only they knew, it said.

"In other words," Liam said, "you're telling us your offer will stand if we change our minds because we decide we can't handle it."

"Of course," Nicolescu said. "Though the price will drop some— perhaps drastically—when everyone realizes how dangerous the book is. The time to sell is now."

"Nice pitch," Liam said.

Nicolescu shrugged. "It's a living," he said. "But business interests aside, I am trying to tell you that you have only seen the beginning of your problems. To my knowledge you have never had a book like this before. You have avoided, to a large extent, seeing what magic really looks like."

Father Menchú bristled. "We know what magic looks like."

"Begging your pardon, Father," Marangoz said, "but no, you don't. You have only seen its manifestation in our world. You have never seen beyond that. But you will. Soon."

Sooner than you think, said the Hand inside Sal's head.

"You seem to know these demons personally," Menchú said. "Can you tell us anything about them?"

"What can we say?" Marangoz said. "They don't tell us what they're planning, or even what they can do." He stopped and thought for a moment. "Though I can say that some of them seem to be working together, cooperating, forming alliances. So the next attack you see, there will likely be more than one of them at once."

"They're teaming up?" Sal said.

Nicolescu smiled. "It's only fair. You did it first."

3.

The streetlights came on outside the bar where two men and a woman sat at a table near the window. One man had been there all day drinking beer, but he was still sober. The other man had arrived a half hour ago and ordered an *aperitivo*. The woman had just sat down, hadn't even taken her jacket off yet. She ordered a ginger ale.

"Lightweight," the drinker said.

"Gorogor," said the one with the *aperitivo*, "be quiet. Eriath can drink what she wants."

"You be quiet, Resketel," said Gorogor.

"Both of you be quiet," Eriath said. "Don't let your nervousness make you run at the mouth."

"I am not nervous," Gorogor said.

Eriath sighed. "It's like you forget that I can read minds."

"Whatever you are reading, it is not nervousness," Gorogor said.

"Then what is it?" Resketel said.

"Excitement," Gorogor said.

"So do we go over the plan one more time?" Resketel said.

"One moment," Eriath said. She had the woman she was inhabiting close her eyes. It made it easier for her to sweep the minds in the room. She learned that the woman sitting in the corner in the green skirt was about to break up with the man at the bar in the black shirt. The man in the black shirt, meanwhile, was about to ask the woman in the green skirt whether she would consider a threesome. The five people gathered two tables over from them all worked at the same company, Eriath discovered. They were sitting there laughing and talking about nothing. Of the five, four were unaware that the fifth one was about to fire them. At the table right next to them, a woman and a man, both with streaks of gray in their hair, were talking about their favorite movies. They were both divorced and had only met once before at the party of a mutual friend. Both of them were playing it cool. Both of them were crawling out of their skin with lust for each other. Eriath hoped it worked out for them. But from her perspective, the only thing that mattered was that nobody was eavesdropping on them.

"Okay," she said. "Let's talk."

"Let's walk through the plan backward," said Resketel. "When we are in the library, the plan is straightforward. Eriath, you read the librarian's mind to know where the *Codex Umbra* is. You put this information in my mind, and any other information I may need to get there."

"Right," said Eriath.

"Then your job is essentially done," Resketel said.

Eriath made her possessed subject smile.

"Then it's my job to go get the book itself," Resketel said. "Yes?"

"Are you sure you can do it by yourself?" Gorogor said.

"Positive," said Resketel. "As long the obstacles are merely physical, there are no obstacles."

"And Gorogor, you remember your job, right?"

"Excuse me?" Gorogor said. He had taken another long swig of beer and was now staring at the ceiling. "Oh. Yes. My job is to create havoc."

"The important part of this being?" said Resketel, as though they were reciting a catechism.

"That I cannot remain in this human form and still sow chaos," Gorogor said. "I must . . . burst free of it first."

"Right," Resketel said. "Which means?"

"That I must not do this until we have no use for our disguises."

"Correct," Resketel said. "And who decides when we have no use for our disguises?"

"When Eriath detects that someone knows we are . . . not what we seem to be."

Resketel nodded. "Good. You got it."

"I have been studying," Gorogor said with a smile.

"It shows," Resketel said.

"You do not have to be condescending about it," Gorogor said.

"I'm not," Resketel said. "I promise." Resketel's eyes flicked toward Eriath, just to let Eriath know that he knew that she knew he was lying.

"So before that," Eriath said to Gorogor, "all you have to do is be quiet and follow us. Resketel and I will talk our way in. Until we can't anymore."

Gorogor nodded. "Do you think you can do it?" he said.

"Yes," Resketel and Eriath answered together.

"Good," Gorogor said. "Because I do not want to destroy the entire Vatican Library for one book. That would be tiring. But I will do it if I have to."

"You won't have to," Eriath said.

Gorogor fidgeted in his chair.

"Would you like to go home now, Gorogor?" Resketel said.

"Yes," Gorogor said, with relief.

"All right. Tomorrow morning, then. Outside Vatican City."

"Yes," Gorogor said. "Tomorrow morning. I cannot wait to have the book in our possession."

Gorogor got up from the table and gave them a little bow, then headed out the door. They smiled and waited until he was gone.

"So we agree that we don't really care what happens to him?" Eriath said.

"Of course," Resketel said. "I'll make sure he never touches the *Codex*. Once we have it, we'll be able to do away with him in the blink of an eye."

"He wouldn't know what to do with it, anyway," Eriath said.

"Really, we're doing the worlds a service," Resketel said.

Eriath nodded. "I'm looking forward to ruling with you."

"And I you," Resketel said.

Eriath tried to look into Resketel's head but couldn't. She had never been able to. *It must be part of his power as a shape-shifter,* she thought. *He can hide what he looks like, make himself look like something else. Why not hide what he's thinking, too?* Following the logic of that, though, didn't make her feel better. *He'd only hide his thoughts from me if he didn't want me to see them.*

They turned their smiles on each other. They didn't trust each other at all.

4.

Sal unlocked the door to her apartment. She didn't want to be there. At all. She'd tried to resist the Hand. She had fought it, exerted all the will she had to keep it from using her as its puppet. But the Hand was too strong for her. It had made her say that she was tired and needed a few hours' rest in her own bed, even though she wasn't tired at all. It had made her come all the way back to the apartment, take out her keys, turn the lock, and walk in.

What are we doing here? Sal said.

She heard the Hand sigh.

This talking to yourself has become awkward, it said.

Sal felt a tap on her shoulder and turned.

It was Perry, following her inside.

"Hey," Perry said.

"Oh my God," Sal said. "Is it really you?"

"Nope," Perry said. "There is, in fact, no one else here at all. This is just a demonstration of the things I can make you see. The things I can make you feel."

"You asshole," Sal said.

"Suit yourself," Perry said. He melted in front of her, right into the floor. Sal felt a rush of wind behind her, from inside the apartment. She heard two feet alight on the floor. It was her mother.

"Stop fucking around," Sal said.

"Fine," the Hand said in mock exasperation. Her mother reached into her own chest and threw off her skin in one dramatic gesture. It flew into the air behind her and turned to smoke. Underneath that was an almost perfect replica of Sal, except for the eyes, which were like negatives of her own: white pupils, gray irises, floating in little black pools between her eyelids.

"Get it?" the doppelgänger Hand said. "It's like you're talking to yourself."

"Except I'm not talking out loud," Sal said.

"You can sense that?" the Hand said. "That's good. You're strong. I knew I picked the right host."

"Don't be so sure how right I am," Sal said.

The doppelgänger looked around her apartment. "True. Perhaps I should have taken over Father Menchú instead. Then I would already have the *Codex*, instead of having to watch while that sad little priest stuffed it into that . . . magic sack, or whatever it is. On the other hand, that I now simply have to wait until someone unearths it from your archives is a mere question of patience. And from the sound of things, I won't have to wait long at all. Sooner or later—and probably much sooner—some clever creature will do the tricky work of extracting the book from the Archives. And I will be there when it happens."

"Then why did you just make me come home?" Sal said.

"Housekeeping," the doppelgänger said. It walked into the kitchen. "Actually, you should come and see this. It's going to be like the scene in *The Shawshank Redemption* when the warden finally figures out what's going on."

"You've seen *The Shawshank Redemption*?"

"My dear, everyone has. Come on."

"As if I have a choice," Sal said.

"Right now you do. I suppose."

"Don't play mind games with me," Sal said.

"Sal," the doppelgänger said, "your life since I entered it has *all* been a mind game. You don't appreciate just how much I can make you see and do—perhaps because I haven't yet exerted my full authority over you."

The doppelgänger lifted a finger into the air, and with a faint smile, it drew a line downward toward the floor. A slit opened in Sal's vision, or the air, or the world—it was impossible to say which— and the doppelgänger reached in and pulled it open, like a curtain. Through the window in the air were miles of burning fields, towers that had once reached to the sky now crumbling in dust and smoke. Over it all, the shadow of a greasy wing blotted out the sky. The doppelgänger pulled the curtain closed, and it was gone.

"What did you just show me?" Sal said.

"Whatever I wanted. That's just the beginning."

Now Sal found her right hand rising in front of her, turning toward herself. The hand tightened into a fist, then extended the pointer finger, in line with her left eye. Slowly, irresistibly, the tip of that finger pressed closer to her face.

"You wouldn't," Sal said.

"It's just to prove a point. I can probably fix your eye again after you've poked it out. But the pain will teach you a lesson."

The tip of the finger was too close to her eye and getting closer. That was when Sal made a decision.

"I'm not doing this," she said.

"You are very much doing this," the doppelgänger said.

"Like hell I am." *Sorry, Perry,* she thought. *I failed you.*

In a move that must have broken the Hand's concentration for a moment—there was no other way to explain why it worked—Sal ran for the balcony. The door was already open, which she was thankful for. It made what she wanted to do that much easier. She sprang for the railing. The doppelgänger didn't move. Didn't have time to, Sal thought.

Sal grasped the railing with both hands, lifted herself up off the balcony floor like a gymnast, and started swinging her legs over. In less than a second, the momentum of that swing and gravity would send her headfirst toward the street. She wasn't that high up, but she was high enough. She'd seen what happened to people who fell from heights like these. With luck, it wouldn't even hurt.

Except that midway through the swing, she stopped. Every muscle in her body froze, as if paralyzed. No. As if turned to stone. Her legs were suspended over the railing in midair. Her elbows were bent. She was just tilting forward. But her hands, her arms, weren't letting go—they held on with a strength she hadn't quite known she had.

"Nice try," the doppelgänger said. It waved its hand in the air, and Sal collapsed onto the balcony. "Come back inside. I have something to show you."

The doppelgänger was reaching for the handle of the oven.

"You have something in there?"

"Sal," the doppelgänger said. "You really should bake more."

She opened the oven. A mist rose from it that smelled as if something amphibious had died in it. The mist cleared. There was a mortar made of dried lava. A clump of leaves tied in a bundle. A bird's wing. A desiccated finger with a claw at the end of it. All around the oven, bright yellow spiders the size of Sal's hands were spinning a network of webs into what looked like a tunnel. The doppelgänger opened her mouth and moved her lips as though she were speaking, but Sal only heard a few syllables, flitting in and out of silence; it occurred to her that the rest of them were too high, or too low, to hear. The spiders stopped what they were doing and turned to face her. They were talking back. The doppelgänger nodded and closed the oven door.

"Good," it said. "It's ready."

"What is?" Sal said.

"When I have the *Codex*," it giggled, "all I need to do is say the magic words, and a portal will open between wherever I am and here. It's my escape hatch."

"When did you do all this?" Sal said.

"See? I told you it was going to be like *The Shawshank Redemption*," the doppelgänger said. "You've been sleepwalking, night after night, ever since you got to Rome. At first I thought I might find what I wanted at the Archives, but what you had there was, shall we say, not germane to my goals. So then it was just a question of letting you go out, looking for the right book, the right amulet, even the right moment, for me to make my move. I had no idea it would come so soon, or be so promising. The *Codex Umbra*! I couldn't have asked for better."

"To do what?" Sal said.

The doppelgänger looked toward the ceiling, making a show of thinking. "Can you see it yourself?"

Sal could. "No," she said. "Please don't."

"It only looks like hell to you," the doppelgänger said. "To us, it's what this world could look like when I flood it with magic. You may have noticed that the more magic there is, the more I can control it. If I bring enough magic into this world, I can make it mine."

"Why do you want this world so much?" Sal said.

"Let's just say that in my world, there are politics," the doppelgänger said.

"You mean that there are demons back there more powerful than you," Sal said.

"'Demon' is not a word we would use to describe ourselves," the doppelgänger said.

Sal kept a straight face. She'd learned something, even if she wasn't sure how to use it yet.

"Now let's go back to the Archives," the doppelgänger said. "I don't want to miss the show. You can take us there or I can make you take us there."

"I'm going," Sal said. "But just so you know, the second you give me the chance, I'll kill you."

The doppelgänger vanished. The Hand was back in her head, right behind her eyes.

I wouldn't want it any other way, she heard it say.

5.

Vatican City was a little quieter than usual. The news had gotten out that something had happened there, and some of the tourists were staying away. Though not enough of them. The line to enter the Vatican Museums and Library stretched down the block.

"We are not waiting in that," said Gorogor. He gritted his teeth.

"Easy," Eriath said. "Remember what we talked about?"

"Excuse me?" Gorogor said.

"About holding it together and just following us until we're inside."

"Oh. Yes."

"Good," Eriath said. "Come with me."

Eriath, Resketel thought. *You can hear me if I think directly to you, yes? As I can hear you when you think directly to me?*

Yes, Eriath thought back. *Privilege of being a mind reader. I can open a two-way street.*

Good, Resketel thought. *So Gorogor can't hear me talking about him. Why did we pick such a loose cannon?*

You know why, Eriath thought back.

The three of them walked to a little office inside the Porta

Angelica. A good-natured official waited behind the counter.

Do I destroy him? Gorogor thought, loud enough for Eriath to hear.

No! Eriath thought. *We're not even inside yet.*

"Good morning!" Eriath said to the official, who nodded. "We have an appointment."

She pulled a small stack of blank papers out of a satchel and handed them to the official, who looked them over with eyebrows raised. He stamped them and signed them, then looked at the three of them.

"Welcome back to the Vatican, professors," he said. "I trust you know where you are going?"

"We do," Eriath said.

"Please proceed," the official said. The three of them continued on their way, blank pieces of paper in hand.

"What did you make him see?" Resketel said.

"I didn't make him see anything," Eriath said. "I let him see what he wanted to see. I let his brain make us whatever would make his job as easy as possible. The fantasy is more persuasive—and forgettable—that way. To tell the truth, I was expecting him to make us ambassadors, or perhaps police. But apparently visiting professors are the easiest. At least for him."

"Well, professors are so docile," Resketel said.

"And delicious," Gorogor said.

Resketel made a sound of disgust.

"That was a joke," Gorogor said. "I occupy professors. I do not eat them."

They were approaching a courtyard jammed with parked cars. There were three entrances to the building in front of them. A white door to the right.

"That's it," Eriath said, pointing to the door.

"You really do know where you're going," Resketel said.

"It's easy when you can read people's minds."

"So you know where we're going once we get inside?"

"No. We'll just have to find someone else."

A policeman met them with a quizzical look on his face as they entered.

"We are here for research," Eriath said, showing the blank papers again. "If you'd please show us to a librarian, we'd be much obliged."

The policeman scrutinized the pages. Then: "Right this way." He led the trio to a man clutching a small stack of books under his arm.

"Hello again, Massimo," Eriath said. "It's good to see you." She pulled out the blank sheets of paper again and handed them to the librarian.

"Yes! Of course!" Massimo said. "Welcome back."

"Thank you," said Eriath with a small smile. "These are my associates."

"It's his first time here?" Massimo said, pointing to Gorogor, who was staring at the explosions of color on the walls and ceilings. They'd lost him for a moment.

"Yes," said Eriath.

How are you going to do this? Resketel said.

Power of association, Eriath said.

"I hear the renovation of the library went splendidly," Eriath said.

"Oh yes," Massimo said. "We're quite up to speed now. So much more has been digitized since the last time you were here. The Vatican Library is more accessible than ever. It could be the most accessible it has ever been in the entire history of the Church."

"That's wonderful," Eriath said, and leaped into Massimo's brain. "But surely not everything is digitized, even so."

"No," Massimo said. As he spoke, Eriath watched Massimo's

memories light up. There was a stultifying argument Massimo had to sit through, months ago, over whether a folio full of meeting minutes from the eighteenth century should or should not be digitized. Massimo had said nothing for the entire meeting, thanks to his certainty that no one would ever look at them in whatever form the Vatican stored them in. They could hire a skywriting plane to spell out the contents above Rome and still no one would look. In Massimo's memory, the head librarian, whom Massimo thought of as a tool, had gotten very passionate about it and hurled curses at another librarian. *Some things we must still keep to ourselves,* he had said. Massimo, daydreaming, had spent the entire meeting replaying in his head being in bed with his wife two nights before. It had gone on for a while and been particularly satisfying to both of them, and Massimo recalled that he had smiled a little, there at the meeting, feeling pretty sure his coworkers had no idea his sex life was so torrid. The secret made it better.

In the library, Massimo smiled a little. Eriath tried not to laugh.

"Some things, I imagine, can't be digitized," Eriath said.

"That's right," Massimo said. "For all kinds of valid reasons."

Now Massimo's memories were sweeping through the library, the building itself, just like Eriath wanted. She followed his mind's eye out of the splendor of the reading rooms, down the much more quotidian hallways that led to the back offices, and past a wooden door with a seven-pointed star on it. Massimo had never given the door much thought, but he had noticed it just enough to wonder what it was. He'd never asked; it was a question that occurred to him only when he passed the door, but he forgot it a minute later. A few times, the question had reemerged in his mind when he saw a similar shape somewhere else. He thought to ask about the mysterious door, but then was distracted by other things. He also kept seeing the shape in *Game of Thrones*, which he'd become a huge fan of, but he wasn't the kind of person who brought his work home with him, so the question flitted through his mind and left again. It was never in there for long. But it was in there long enough.

And now, just lately, a policeman had been stationed at that door.

Eriath thought to the other two, *Found it.*

Let's go, then, Resketel thought back.

"Well," Eriath said to Massimo. "It was very nice to see you." She headed into the library with Resketel and Gorogor in tow.

"Where are you headed?" Massimo said.

"I'm sorry; I thought the forms I gave you were clear."

"That's a staff area," Massimo said. "I can't let you go there unaccompanied."

Now? Gorogor thought.

Not yet, Eriath thought.

"Fine," Eriath said. "I'll appreciate the help."

They walked through the library, opening a small door into one of the back hallways. They passed a middle-aged man with a mop and a bucket, getting ready to clean the floor. Something about him made Eriath jump into his head for a moment. And there: It was just as she thought. This man was a soldier posing as a janitor. There was a gun in a holster beneath his jacket, and he knew how to use it better than anyone on his unit.

He also knew exactly what door it was that he was defending.

We're close, Eriath thought to the others. She picked up her pace, just a little.

"You seem to know where you're going very well," Massimo said.

"You took me here last time," Eriath said, and jumped into Massimo's brain to plant the memory. "Don't you remember?"

"Yes, that's right," Massimo said. "I do remember." But the librarian seemed startled that this was the case. In her haste, Eriath had been sloppy, and something about the memory—Eriath didn't have time to figure out what it was—wasn't sitting right with other memories he had.

We're losing him, Resketel said.

Hold on, Eriath said.

The door they wanted was now just down the hall. There was the policeman, this one in uniform.

"What was it you said you were looking for again?" Massimo said.

"I didn't say," Eriath said.

They were in front of the door now.

"What's their business here?" the policeman said.

"Would you care to tell me what you want?" Massimo said. He finally sounded a little irritated. No: a little worried.

Eriath looked up and down the hall. There was no one else around. She sighed.

"Gorogor," she said. "Do what you came here to do."

Gorogor curled his hands into fists and raised them above his head. For a split second, the fists bulged, as though they were being pumped full of air. Then they popped, in a small firework of blood and tissue. There were purple fists beneath them, nine fingered, with scaly skin and pulsing with veins. The new fists grew until they were as big as Gorogor's head. Bigger. Gorogor brought the fists down onto Massimo's and the policeman's skulls. The policeman cried out and dropped. The librarian let out a small moan and flopped to the floor, as though a switch had been flipped.

"Are they dead?" Resketel said.

"Their brains are," Eriath said.

"Sorry," Gorogor said.

"It was only a matter of time," Eriath said. She nodded toward the door. Gorogor popped an even bigger fist out of his right arm and started punching. The door was thick, the hinges sturdy. It took twelve hits for Gorogor to break it, but he did at last.

An alarm shrieked. From somewhere down the hall, the demons heard voices.

"There goes our cover," Resketel said.

"Then we only have a little more time."

They ran through the broken door and started down the spiral stairs to the Black Archives.

6.

The Orb had given off a faint glow an hour ago. Its numbers spun.

"What does that mean?" Schaffner had asked.

"It tells us where magic is being used," Asanti had said.

"And where does it say that is?" Huegin had said.

"Right here," Asanti had answered.

Team Three had looked around the room, at one another. Sal wondered if somehow the Hand had set it off, but then there was the demon's voice in her head, at the top of her skull, soaked in sarcasm. *You think your Magic 8 Ball's going to find me?*

Schaffner and Huegin fetched their rifles. Vaz, without any indication that anything was out of the ordinary, fastened a vest to his chest and proceeded to hoist aloft a hammer that was far too big for him.

"Please try not to upset the books with that," Asanti said.

Vaz winked. "I'll do my best, madame."

The next couple of times the Orb shone, the light inside got brighter and brighter. The numbers didn't move.

"What is it saying now?" Schaffner said.

"Too close to say," Asanti said.

"I feel like I'm on a sinking ship," Liam said.

"Or sitting on a bomb," Grace said. "This strategy is crazy. Let's go do what we always do. Bag it and tag it."

"In the Vatican?" Menchú said. "I'm not even sure the authorities would allow it." He looked at Vaz.

"It's not advisable," Vaz said. "Our orders are to contain ourselves to the Archives."

"Hilarious," Grace said. "Team One can do whatever the hell it wants in every country in the world except its own."

"Welcome to the Church," said Liam.

"That's a little unfair," Menchú said.

"Is it?" Liam said.

"Gentlemen," Asanti said. "Let's not fight among ourselves, all right? We don't have to make their job any easier for them."

Which is when the Orb flared so bright that, for a second, they were all blind. They heard something crack. There was the smell of burning copper. The Orb fizzled and dimmed, but kept sparking.

Upstairs, it sounded like someone was pounding on the door with a sledgehammer. The alarm screamed on and stayed on.

"Uh-oh," Liam said.

Asanti headed to her desk.

"What are you doing?" Menchú said.

"This is my life's work," Asanti said. "Do you really think I haven't taken some precautions?"

At the top of the stairs, the vault of the ceiling opened all around Eriath, Resketel, and Gorogor. There were the curved walls. There was the city of books below them in the gloom.

The three demons had all heard about the Black Archives at some point in their existences on earth. It was the place where the magic things went after humans got the best of them, after the Society showed up to ruin the demons' fun. It had always been a source of idle speculation as to what the place looked like. Demon society knew the Church was a wealthy, powerful organization, and over the centuries had constructed an elaborate idea of what the vaults were like, what powerful forces the humans could employ to keep the magic locked away. So Eriath, Resketel, and Gorogor imagined encountering wizards, witches, warlocks, shamans, priestesses. Women and men like the ones they used to see, way back when humans used magic all the time, before they swapped it for civilization and ruined the world. Beings of power.

They laid eyes on Sal, Menchú, Liam, Grace, and Asanti, standing in a patch of light near the bottom of the stairs, ready to fight. Another man with a ludicrous hammer. Two men who looked to them like clowns. Behind them, a glass ball in a case was sparking. Something was wrong with it. It was overloaded. Aside from that ball, even the books piled around the humans reeked of mundanity—dead paper without a scrap of magic. They kept their real treasures locked in the vaults, Eriath supposed. She swept through the minds of the humans below her and noted, to her satisfaction, that they were afraid.

"Is this it?" Gorogor said. "This is all it is?"

"This will be easier than we thought," Resketel said. That was when he noticed that Asanti was holding something, a remote control. She twirled a dial and pressed a button. The couple of stairs beneath them, with a strange kind of precision, exploded and began to fall. For Resketel, though, this wasn't much of a concern. Quickly, effortlessly, he shed his host and spread himself out as a net to catch Eriath and Gorogor.

Gorogor grew another arm out of his back.

"Let us fall," he said.

Resketel did. Midair, Gorogor scooped up Resketel and Eriath and held them above his head. He landed on the floor with both feet.

"Gorogor," Eriath said. "It's time."

Gorogor shed the rest of his human skin.

Eriath closed her eyes and invaded Asanti's brain. For the briefest of moments, the smallest possible passage of time, it made her stop, because Asanti's mind was a thing of beauty, vast and organized, less a library than a cathedral of knowledge, of history, of memory. There was Asanti as a young girl in Kinshasa, holding her mother's hand as they walked through the center of a bustling market, filled with the smell of vegetables and dust. Then there she was again, just a couple of years older, in Paris. The sights and the smells were completely different, and her hand had grown; her mother's had gotten a little stiffer, the skin a little thicker, but it still felt the same. There were the births of her grandchildren—it seemed she was there, in the room, for all of them—and she seemed to remember everything, the particular sounds of their cries, some like laughing, some like grieving for loved ones gone, but every one its own song. And then there was just how much she knew, how much she had done. She knew how to weave and spin her own wool. She knew basic carpentry and fly tying. She knew how to blow glass. She had forgotten almost nothing about any of it. Then there were her professional obsessions, her encyclopedic knowledge of the Black Archives. That was where Eriath found what she was looking for. It was a recent memory and therefore fresh, vivid with color, of the particular shelf in the particular vault of the Black Archives where she had decided to keep the *Codex Umbra*.

It was in a metal box, and the box was locked. But it was so close.

Just behind one of those doors. There were two combinations to get through those doors, but Eriath knew them already. What were a few numbers after all she'd sifted through?

Eriath took the memories she needed, jumped out of Asanti's head, and jumped into Resketel's. Gave him Asanti's knowledge. Asanti had felt the whole thing, Eriath knew. If she had more time, she could have been more subtle. But there was no time.

Go, she thought to Resketel. And opened her eyes.

It all took less than a few seconds. Except for Asanti, nobody had even moved yet.

"They know where the *Codex Umbra* is," Asanti said.

Grace looked in their general direction, toward the bottom of the stairs.

"There were three of them, right?" she said.

"Right," Asanti said.

"I can't see them at all," Grace said. "Really wish you didn't have so many books in here right now."

Asanti hit another button. Floodlights fired up on the ceiling.

"Better?" Asanti said.

"Yes," Grace said, "a little."

A dull roar came from the bottom of the stairs. They could all hear the flutter of pages flying and tearing, and then saw a cloud of paper rising above the towers of books, as though they were being mowed, or harvested. Gorogor broke through the final stack of books, just before the edge of Asanti's desk.

He was now a fat, squat thing on five legs, a sixth limb curving out from the middle of his back like a scorpion's stinger, except that it ended in a large, long-fingered hand. His eyes were lost somewhere in the folds of his face, and he had a huge mouth, now full of pulped paper. He spat it out in a wad and snarled.

Schaffner and Huegin yelled and fired their weapons at Gorogor. They put at least twenty holes in him, making him slick with some pinkish substance that oozed out of his wounds. But it didn't slow him down at all. He leaped forward as though he were a cricket, and was on top of them. They stopped yelling, Schaffner because his rib cage was shattered and Huegin because his neck was flattened. A sound came out of Gorogor that must have been pleasure.

Grace shot Vaz a glance.

"You ready?" she said.

"Absolutely," Vaz said.

Vaz leaped in and gave Gorogor a wallop of an uppercut with the hammer, jerking the demon's head around. Grace snarled and jumped onto Gorogor's back, grabbing onto the base of his arm. The hand at the end arched over and in, trying to pluck her off. She reached up and snapped the wrist. Gorogor howled. Grace smiled.

Then Gorogor hopped, much higher and faster than his legs should have been capable of carrying him. With Grace on his back, he bounced from wall to wall, a cannonball of fatty flesh. Vaz jumped in pursuit, careening off the walls, striking blow after blow with the hammer. The three of them plowed into piles of books and laid them low, carving channels through the stacks and towers. Making chaos, just like Gorogor was supposed to. Grace hung on.

The rest of them almost didn't notice Resketel, who had wriggled out of his host and left the remains on the floor by the stairs so he could change shape unencumbered. The rug, the desk, the area Team Three occupied were between him and the door he needed. That didn't matter. He stretched himself out until his limbs were impossibly long and skinny and in two steps had passed over

Team Three. But Resketel made a mistake, brushed against a book that somehow hadn't fallen over yet, and made it plummet to the ground.

Liam looked up.

"Oh no you don't," he said, and jumped for Resketel's passing leg. "Sal, come with me."

Sal didn't move. Menchú shot her a glance, somewhere between confused and angry. But there was no time to question it. He followed Liam.

At the door to the vault, Resketel was putting himself back together. He was, more or less, humanoid, though with features a talented child would make out of wet clay. They worked, but there was no detail. They were put together in haste. He raised an append-age, formed a ball at the end of it, and two fingers out of the ball, enough to spin the combination lock on the door.

Liam reached Resketel first. He had the idea that he would give this thing a full-body tackle and knock it to the floor. But Resketel just stretched out all around him, accommodating him. An image popped into Liam's head of trying to break through a giant condom that was still rolled up. He pushed into the membrane and then started to try to gather it in his hands to move Resketel. Menchú caught up and headed for the appendage that was fiddling with the lock.

Resketel worked fast. The door opened, just a crack. All of Resketel turned to almost liquid, dropped to the floor, and slipped through it.

"Goddammit," Liam said.

"Asanti," Menchú said. "Lock this place down and call the rest of Team One." He pushed the door open with his shoulder, and he and Liam charged in. They were now in a triangular anteroom with a door on each of the other two walls. It was designed to be confusing, to slow anything down that didn't know where it was going and trap it there. But Resketel knew where he was going.

"Sal!" Menchú called. "Help!"

Sal still hadn't moved. She watched as Grace flew around the room on a demon's back, Vaz in pursuit. She spared a look for the two mangled Swiss Guards on the floor, half-covered now in fallen books and torn pages. Liam and Menchú had run after another one. There had been a third. Where was it?

The demon was still leaping through the air. Grace almost flew off it but held on.

Like a rodeo in a library, Sal thought helplessly. *Like a bull in a china shop.*

Inside her head, the Hand was laughing at her. But she could tell she was frustrating it. When it wasn't her own suicide she was contemplating at the same time, it turned out she could keep the Hand at bay. At least for a second. Not for much longer.

Stop resisting me, she heard the Hand say.

Sal was trying to leave, to get the Hand as far away from the Archive as she could. The Hand wouldn't let her. But Sal was putting up enough of a fight that, at least for the next thirty seconds, nothing was moving.

I don't want to have to shatter your ankles in order to move them, the Hand said. *But I will if I have to. I can still make you walk.*

Go ahead, Sal told him.

You don't mean that, the Hand said.

Try me, Sal said.

You're even stronger than I thought, the Hand said. She caught a hint of genuine admiration in its voice. *It will be a pleasure to break you.*

In the air above them, Grace was climbing toward the demon's throat.

As though from far off, Sal felt someone touch her arm. Asanti.

"Sal?" she said. "Are you all right?"

If Sal hadn't been looking at Asanti when she spoke, she wouldn't have understood the words. Her ears were rushing with blood.

"No," she said, with great effort, against the Hand's will. She looked at the tank Asanti held.

"What . . . is that?" Sal asked.

"It's a flamethrower," Asanti said. "For the demons, hopefully. But if they win, maybe for the books. It's better than the demons having them."

"Use it . . . ," Sal said. *Use it on me,* she was trying to say, but the Hand stopped her.

"I plan to," Asanti said. She ran toward the part of the Archives where Liam and Menchú had gone.

You have less than a minute before you fall to me, the Hand said.

It's a minute I can be proud of, Sal said.

Resketel chuckled to himself. He had this.

He was a puddle on the floor of the antechamber. He extended a crude tentacle upward toward the next door he needed to open and spun the combination lock to the vault where the *Codex Umbra* was held.

"What's the call?" Liam said.

"If we can't stop the demon," Menchú said, "maybe we can stop the door."

Liam nodded. Both men charged for the door, stepping into Resketel, who had just finished unlocking it. Resketel formed another tentacle and headed for the handle. Menchú and Liam braced themselves against the door. Resketel tugged at the handle. The door didn't move.

"Ha, you shite piece of Silly Putty," Liam said.

Menchú smiled. Resketel let out a little gurgle.

"That's right," Liam said. "Ready to give up?"

Then Resketel made sure they could tell he was just chortling. He grew four pseudopods out of himself, latched onto the humans' legs, lifted them up and away from the door, and tossed them to the other side of the antechamber. As Liam and Menchú were scrambling back to their feet, Resketel inched the door open and slithered through.

He was in the vault now, a long room with four stories of shelves that vanished to a point somewhere in the middle distance. The shelves were locked down, protected with metal shields that must have been triggered when they broke in. Resketel glanced toward the ends of the shelves and saw that each one could be unlocked with a key. He loved it when safety measures worked in his favor.

He pulled himself up and grew long legs, built for running. He gave himself a fleeting couple of seconds to consider the objects he was flitting by. There was a rope that promised the man who found it he could climb to heaven, then strangled him to death when he tried. By a strange coincidence, Resketel had been there for that. There was a helmet that offered infinite protection to the wearer as long as he didn't mind going insane first. There was a statue of an angel, guarding the vault, and a holy relic, the finger bone of a saint, in a metal glove under glass. A sticker below the case read IN CASE OF EMERGENCY, BREAK GLASS. Resketel smiled to himself. At least this librarian had a sense of humor.

And there were the rows upon rows of books locked away, in

all the languages of this world, several from Resketel's, and more from beyond them both. Some were just blank pages, he knew. Others were illegibly black with ink. The mischief that could be made with it all! But Resketel was smart enough not to be distracted by that. He knew what he'd come for, and thanks to Eriath, knew just where it was.

He found the right shelf, shaped a short appendage into a key, and had it unlocked quickly. The metal shield slid away, and there was the safety box the *Codex* was in. Another lock that needed a key, another finger shape. It was all too easy.

He already had the *Codex* out of the box and was headed toward the door when Liam and Menchú got inside. Resketel grew a head, a face, out of courtesy to them. It allowed him to throw Liam and Menchú a hideous, triumphant smile and emit a shriek of glee. The two men lunged toward him. Resketel admired their pluck. But they were exhausted, and it was a simple thing for Resketel to bend his legs wide and avoid them. Menchú's age seemed to catch up with him all at once. His attempted tackle made him lose his equilibrium, and he hit the floor, hard. Liam was younger, stronger, and doubled back. He sprinted, leaped, and managed to latch himself to what, in Resketel's current form, passed for a torso. Still heading toward the door, Resketel first just elongated the arm holding the book so Liam didn't have a chance of getting it. Then he split himself in two.

It was a trick he liked to save for this point in a job. His adversaries always found it so demoralizing. Liam watched in astonishment as the body he was clutching withered away in his arms and dissipated. He fell to the floor. The legs kept running. Before the upper part of the torso, with head, arms, and the *Codex Umbra* still attached, hit the floor, it had grown legs too. The upper half jumped and joined with the lower half just before Resketel reached the door, and he was out.

He could hear Liam and Menchú calling behind him as they picked themselves up and gave chase, syllables that must have been the names of the other people on their team. He didn't care. The door to the hub of the Black Archives was still open. There was Asanti, standing in the way, smiling.

"Perfect," she said. "I don't even have to burn any of my books."

She let out a sheet of flame from the nozzle of the flame-thrower. Resketel recoiled for a split second. But even this wasn't so bad. He jumped up and spread out over the ceiling. Asanti let out another burst of fire at him, though by then he was already racing down the walls, a liquid in a fast flood, except for one hand still clutching the book. He channeled the rest of himself into the seam between the wall and the floor. To Asanti it looked like the book itself had grown invisible wheels. It raced along the edge of the floor and then between her legs. Resketel regrouped behind her and burst through the doorway, into the library.

It was snowing shredded paper. Gorogor lay on a slope of books that had fallen into a pile, as if for a bonfire. His head was at an odd angle, and the humans who had fought with him stood over him, panting; they must have gotten the better of him.

Eriath was already halfway up the stairs that remained, rickety from Asanti's explosion, but still there.

Gorogor's dead, she thought in Resketel's head.

Good, Resketel said. *They've done our work for us.*

Yes, they have, said Eriath. Right about then was when Resketel was glad he could hide his thoughts from his partner. It saved him the awkward conversation they would have to have when Eriath understood that Resketel was already figuring out how to kill her, and have the *Codex* for his own. Eriath was the one who wanted to use the book to take over this earthly realm. For someone so smart, Resketel thought, she was incredibly naive. Sure, the taking over part would be fun. But running it afterward, managing the slaves and minions, not to mention overseeing the vast bureaucratic infrastructure to torture the doomed and the damned—that, Resketel had decided, would be his own personal hell. Besides, Resketel liked this world fine just the way it was. He even found much of it beautiful, more beautiful, in its small, subtle way, than anything his own world had offered to his sight.

He just wanted to have the money to live in it well. Sure, he could have just inhabited a rich person, but he wanted to make his own money. He liked the challenge. This codex tucked under his arm, though, was just the way to get his payday in one shot. He'd make sure to sell it to someone who was interested in using it on some other plane of existence. *I'm definitely saving this one,* he thought, *for myself.* All he had to do was kill Eriath as soon as possible—maybe before he even left this room—and the dream would be his. He had his eyes on a house on the coast of Kyushu. He could already see it in his mind.

Which was when he felt the pressure around his torso and found that he couldn't get free.

Sal was still fighting the Hand when the liquid demon reappeared with the *Codex* and started sprinting across the wasteland of paper for the stairs. She had seen the flames light the antechamber to the Archives, seen Resketel jump from the door, followed by Asanti, Menchú, and Liam, trailing smoke from Asanti's fire. It had been two minutes since the demons had arrived and demolished the library. She hadn't moved an inch.

Somewhere near the base of her skull, the Hand purred.

Fire. Good idea, it said to Sal.

She felt a heat inside her, a growing fireball, just under her heart. It coursed through her limbs, broke through her skin. She screamed.

Don't kill me, she pleaded. *Please don't.*

I have no such plans, the Hand said.

The flames cauterized as they cracked through her, and the pain gave way to something else.

For the rest of Team Three, it was as though a torch had been lit. Sal was still Sal. Except that she was wreathed in purple fire.

She raised her right hand as Resketel passed, and a million bits of shredded paper and splinters of bookcases kicked into the air in his wake.

Resketel changed. He split in two. But this time it wasn't his idea. As the conscious half of him looked back in surprise, the other half had formed into the hand that now captured him. He had lost control of himself.

"I do not at all appreciate you attempting to steal what's mine," the Hand said. Smoke poured from Sal's throat as it spoke.

Resketel looked down at the human form that held him captive.

"My lord," he said. "If I'd had any idea you were here, I would never have done what I did."

The Hand's voice curdled. "Give me the book."

Resketel dropped the *Codex Umbra*. It fell toward the floor and stopped in midair, then floated over to Sal's outstretched left hand.

"Excellent," said the Hand. "For your compliance, I offer you a quick death."

As Resketel howled, the Hand pulled another hand, bigger than the first, from Resketel's own body and wrapped its fingers around his head. Both giant hands tightened their grips, twisted Resketel four times over as though wringing out a wet dishrag, and then pulled him apart. A dark orange liquid burst from him as from a water balloon. The hands fluttered and disintegrated in the air, and Resketel's thin, empty skin dropped to the floor.

The Hand made Sal take a deep breath.

"And you," he said to Eriath, who was in a frenzy trying to get to the top of the stairs. "You who sought to use the book to usurp me. Come back here."

The Hand made Sal open the *Codex* and pulled power from it like a battery. Sal's fingers made seven quick flicking motions, and the top seven stairs, above the gap Asanti's explosion had left, popped out and bounced off the stone walls of the Archives, just before Eriath could escape. Now Sal made a motion with her hands as if opening a book, and the protective cage around the stairs opened to expose the terrified demon. Eriath shouted and flailed. Then, at once, she wasn't moving at all, or making a sound.

"And you call yourself more than human," the Hand said. "My host has more strength than you do."

With a languid, beckoning gesture, the Hand caused Eriath to float from the stairs, through the air, down to the floor in front of it. Eriath's face was frozen in the shriek she had been making.

The Hand put both hands on Eriath's head. The demon's body shuddered and cracked, and then, in a sudden series of crackles, imploded up into her skull. Circling Sal's fingers across Eriath's scalp as if polishing it, the Hand worked the demon's head—its host's head—making it smaller and smaller, until it was big enough to fit in the palm of Sal's right hand.

Then the Hand made Sal eat it. She turned to her teammates.

"And to think that creature is still alive after all that," she said, sending a new trail of smoke toward the ceiling. "That must be painful."

Grace leaped at the Hand, fast. But not fast enough. The demon pushed air toward her and knocked her to her knees.

"Anyone else want a shot?"

Liam and Asanti just stood there, anger and terror passing across their faces.

Behind Sal, Menchú was murmuring to himself.

"Is that the Litany of the Saints I hear?" the Hand said. "An exorcism prayer? Save your breath, Father. We're long past that. There are no books to help you understand what I am about to unleash upon this world. And you will have no words for description when you see it. There are none. Not in human tongues."

The Hand brought the book to Sal's breast.

"See you soon," the demon said out loud.

Are you ready? the Hand said to Sal, inside.

For what? Sal asked.

You'll see, the Hand said. A flood of feeling poured through her. More pain. A lot more fear. But underneath it, something else, growing stronger and stronger, an emotion intense enough that it took Sal a moment to recognize what it was, and then be horrified for feeling it: exhilaration. Ecstasy.

Wrapped in flames, Sal's face broke into an expression of pure bliss. She heard her own voice intoning words she didn't understand. She pointed upward with one finger, and a door opened in the air above her. A wind picked up, and the millions of scraps of paper strewn about the Archives lifted into the air like luminous feathers. Sal was swept into the door. It closed behind her. In the Archives, the paper settled. And just like that, she was gone, and the *Codex* with her.

The alarm still blared away. Team Three could hear voices above them, from Team One. They'd arrived. Just too late.

Grace stood up.

"What's our next move?" she said. "We can't let Sal just be taken like that."

Asanti and Liam both looked toward Menchú. He stood there, unmoving.

"Do we even have a choice?" he said. "We have to go find her. Get rid of the *Codex* at last." He looked at Liam. "And figure out how this happened."

EPISODE
13

KEEPING FRIENDS CLOSE

MUR LAFFERTY

1.

F alling. Not the wind-whipping-through-your-hair falling, but the stomach-precedes-you-by-about-fifty-feet falling. The feeling of being completely out of control, and knowing that when the thrill stops, there's going to be nothing but pain.

Sal had stopped trying to wrest control of her body from the Hand. She mentally let go, not wanting to see what it was doing to Team Three's library with her body. She didn't want to feel the pains— little burns and cuts, but enough—the Hand's spells inflicted on her. She didn't want to see the looks on Grace's, Liam's, Asanti's, and Menchú's faces.

Once she let go, she fell into the maelstrom of the Hand.

As a child, she had visited Niagara Falls with her family, and she remembered being disappointed. She had wanted to see a waterfall, but she only saw a big cliff, and then a lot of mist. She wished she could have seen through the mist to the waterfall, never mind that the waterfall and the mist were the same.

Now she felt as though she would be able to see the Hand, understand it, if only the chaos of its power wasn't making it impossible to concentrate. She glimpsed a ruined plain, cracked and smoking, with countless demons of all sizes standing still, waiting. Another vision buffeted her, and she saw herself, startled, but grim and determined. Perry's view, she realized. Her face looking into the mirror, slack and lifeless except for the eyes, and then her kitchen, and her oven.

The sudden stop after the Hand's rampage hurt. It hurt more to open her eyes and look at her apartment.

Sal wanted to ask how they got there, but she didn't have to. They stood in her kitchen, the Hand and Sal, and her oven door gaped open, with light streaming out of it.

Close the oven; you're wasting energy, she admonished mentally. She wanted to laugh at the absurdity. The laugh didn't reach her mouth.

"Welcome back. I thought you had maybe checked out for good," the Hand said, using Sal's voice. "You missed the fun."

Missed. Funny word. Sal pushed momentarily at the barrier the Hand had raised between her and her actual motor functions, and it didn't give. *So you have what you wanted. What are we going to do now?*

"'We'?" Her voice sounded odd to her ears. "You make it sound like we're partners in crime. Or that I want you along."

You need a body, so perhaps wanting and needing are the same thing. Was it time to devolve into 1970s soft-rock references? Probably not. *And the whole of the Vatican just saw me blow shit up and attack my friends and steal from the library. I think we broke about five commandments and committed five deadly sins right there. They will always suspect me now.* She felt sick—but the sensation didn't make it to her stomach. The Hand apparently controlled involuntary muscles as well.

"No one left to play with," said the Hand, rummaging through her dresser. "You always wear the most boring things. Why can't you look more interesting?"

You have the Codex Umbra, *you have control of a cop's body, and the first thing you're going to do is play dress-up? You're wasting one of your wishes, man!*

The Hand actually laughed. "No, I'm not playing dress-up. Just looking for your spare weapons. You hide them like squirrels hide acorns." Her hand closed around a small gun. She tossed it onto the bed. "But someone who understands fashion might be good to talk to, now that you mention it. I hadn't thought of her . . . yes." It removed her cell phone from her pocket and dialed it.

Cell phone service has been crappy in my apartment, Sal said helpfully.

"No, I've been blocking your reception," the Hand said. "Now hush, I'm on the phone."

Sal realized with horror that the Hand had started to take on her way of speaking. This would be bad if they encountered Team Three again. Her only saving grace was that the Hand was very obviously not Sal, behavior-wise. What if it started acting like her?

She held her mental breath and waited as the Hand spoke into the phone.

2.

If she had hoped to eavesdrop on a conversation between two demons, she was out of luck. The Hand spoke guttural, harsh syllables Sal would have been incapable of making on her own. The voice on the phone was similar, crude and cruel. Sal focused on her body briefly, feeling the burns on her hands, the cuts on her arms, the scrape on her leg. She held on to these little pains as tenuous connections to something she no longer owned.

The Hand ended the call. "You wanted to find out what I'm up to. Come and see," it said as it stashed the *Codex Umbra* under her arm as if it were nothing more than a textbook.

Like I have a choice.

Sal was grateful that they didn't travel by oven again. She suspected it was that moment that she had lost control, when everything around her had gone from using magic to being used by magic. She hadn't considered what the view would be like while teleporting. She had never had reason to wonder. But this time, the Hand left her apartment and walked confidently out into Rome.

"We're going to see an old friend," the Hand told her. "A number of friends, in truth."

You going to kill these demons too?

"Not all of them," the Hand said, with mock hurt in its voice. "You'll like Vogue. She lives at the offices of a leading Italian shoe designer."

Let me guess. A demon of vice? Pride?

"We all own each of the sins to one degree or another. But sometimes one sin can dominate the others, yes. We don't fall into categories, though."

No one around to classify you into the right kingdom, I suppose. Are you vegetable, mineral, or plant?

The Hand didn't answer. Sal concentrated on the feel of her feet on the sidewalk and the scents of the city in summer.

You want to tell me why we aren't taking your magic oven teleporter?

Again, no answer. They continued on toward the corporate offices of Monroe, the premier Italian shoe designer.

Liam watched the people, robed and not robed, scurry about with their accusations and their questions. He didn't care. Other, better people were there for damage control. Grace rushed around busily, cleaning up books under Asanti's direction. There were the damaged books and the undamaged books, stacked near their former shelves. The dangerous books she kept next to her desk. The archivist looked disheveled and defeated. A thin cut on her cheek bled freely, and she ignored it.

Menchú was speaking to some officials, low and quick, trying to undercut their objections, calm their obvious rage. They swept from what was left of the library, with promises to return.

Liam noticed and dismissed all of this. He was helping clear a space for the temporary ladder to get people in and out of the Archives now that the stairs had been blown up. He refused to touch anything associated directly with the library.

As he cleared more rubble, he thought about Bran. Liam had trusted him. He had introduced Liam to the group that eventually plugged him into the vast expanse.

Jenna, with the deep brown hair and dimple on one cheek. Short, curly haired, round face, not the kind of person you'd think was into dark magic. But she'd tricked him, and fucked him, and the trap sprang shut. Metaphorically and physically.

He had trusted Asanti until he had seen her eyes light up at each new magical abomination.

Grace had been odd, but seemed trustworthy, despite keeping her situation from him for so long.

And Sal. How long had she hidden a demon inside her? What influence did it have on their relationship—good or bad? He shuddered, remembering the times they had been intimate: Sal, Liam, and whatever was inside her.

Menchú could still be trusted.

"Liam, you were closest to her. How could you not see this?" Menchú said from across the room.

Liam looked up so sharply that his neck cracked. He winced and rubbed it. "That's where we are, then? Blame? Usually you circle the wagons before you start whipping the children."

"Easy, Liam," Grace said, her voice dangerous.

"And you're the one who just spent an entire day doing God knows what with her," Liam said, waving his hand at Grace. "How come you didn't see anything? You're supposed to be all attuned to this shit."

He turned to Asanti. "And your special 'this-magic-isn't-bad-because-it's-useful' Orb, how come that didn't catch anything, huh?"

"Liam," Menchú said.

"No, don't do that, don't point your self-righteous finger at me. If I'm to blame, we're all to blame. And while we're blaming, has anyone noticed that Sal has the *Codex Umbra*?"

"It's not Sal," Grace said, low and stubborn. "She's a victim here. And we have to help her."

Liam stared at Grace. "Are you serious?"

Menchú gave him a level look. "Sal is in trouble. She's possessed."

"Sal is dead," Liam said. "Demon ate her, took over her body, good-bye stubborn-as-nails cop from New York."

"Shut up, Liam," Grace said, carrying a stack of singed books to where Asanti directed her. "We're going after her."

"The lot of you are crazy! How many people have we actually saved who have been full-on possessed like that? I'll even let you count dear comatose Perry. That's one. Anyone else got another?"

Menchú's tenuous calm broke. "Should I have left you, then? A boy plugged into a server? A tool for a digital cult? I could have let you die. I could have left Grace packed in a crate in Guatemala. Should I have? Sal is a member of our team. She is in trouble. Therefore we help. She would do the same for you."

Liam pressed his lips together. He picked up a book at random. The pages still smoldered. He dropped the book with a wince.

"We're going after her," Menchú said. "Are there any other objections?"

Asanti and Grace were silent.

"Good," he said. He put another book on a scorched pile.

"I have more faith in our ability to separate Sal from the demon than I have in our ability to protect her from them right now," Asanti said. She jabbed her finger at the now-stable ladder by which the men had departed.

Menchú frowned. "We're going to have to stay a few steps ahead of Team One. We don't need another gaping hole to explain."

"I wasn't thinking of One," Asanti said. Even Liam looked up at the seriousness of her voice. "You know what Team Two will do if they find her."

Menchú set his jaw. "So we'll find her before they do. Liam, Grace, you're our search party—but I need to have a word with Liam first. Outside of that, I'll run political interference here. Asanti, see if you can get a fix on Sal with the Orb."

Asanti glanced at the precious artifact on her desk. It had a scorch mark on the right side and looked battered. She rubbed a sleeve across its smooth surface. "I'll do my best."

"Okay, Father. What's the big— Ow!"

Menchú grabbed Liam's ear and dragged him down the hall outside the Archives. Outrage bubbled up in Liam at the treatment, and he almost punched Menchú, but decided against it. The priest pulled him toward a door that said MANUTENZIONE. Liam had always assumed it was a broom closet.

Inside was an asymmetrical architectural afterthought, about a meter and a half wide. It *was* roughly the size of a broom closet, but held no cleaning materials. Instead it was furnished with a wooden bench, a crucifix on the wall, and a stained-glass window high up. As they were still underground, the melancholy light that came through must have come from a recessed lightbulb.

Menchú pushed Liam through the door and he stumbled, coming to sit painfully on the bench under the crucifix. Menchú loomed above him, the blue light on his face giving him a morose aura. But his face was anything but morose.

"What the *hell* is wrong with you?" he snarled.

Liam blinked at him. Father Menchú seldom swore. "Me? I'm the only one with sense around here! We've lost team members before! It's a tragedy, but it's part of the job! Suddenly Sal gets possessed, and you're willing to drop everything to save her?"

"Sal is not gone. I have faith." Menchú's jaw was clenched.

"Why?" Liam asked, utterly baffled.

"Because she has to be all right," Menchú said, his face finally falling. He slumped, and then sat on the bench beside Liam. He rubbed his face with his hands. "This one feels different. I've done this long enough to know at least that much. Either way, the Hand has the *Codex*, and we have to get it back. If we can save Sal in the process, is that so bad?"

Liam gritted his teeth. "Even if we save her, we can never trust her again."

"That's something you'll have to work out yourself," Menchú said, standing. "But don't presume to speak for the rest of the team. You deal with your own demons, Liam. I'm tired of holding your hand. Now go do your damn job."

He left the room, and Liam sat, stunned, in the weak blue light.

3.

Sal always had a sense that fashion companies were probably inher-
ently evil, but she had not expected the walls of this corporate
office to begin bleeding as soon as the Hand entered the room.

"Vogue," it said, and Sal could feel her face smiling.

The blood coalesced into a shape. It wasn't a woman's shape, it
was more like a floating being of fire and blood, like a puffer fish but
without the ridiculous bulging eyes. The spines around it reached
out and licked at her, and she winced inwardly at the pain that
shot up her arms as the demon investigated her and the Hand.

"You're back," she said. "I like this form."

"I am," the Hand said. "And we're finally ready to open a door."

The shape laughed. The spines contracted a bit as she chuckled.
"You've been saying that for centuries. Besides you devouring this
very fine body, I don't see what's different."

Something welled up inside Sal, and she realized it was gleeful
anticipation on the Hand's part. She groaned inwardly.

"So you won't help me?" it said. Sal could tell the demon was
hoping Vogue would say no.

"No."

The Hand revealed the *Codex Umbra*, and Vogue began to scream.

Sal had read a fantasy book once, *Unlikely Destiny*, in which a peasant became a field medic during a bloody magicians' war. He feared the sight of blood, trembled when sewing up a cut, felt sick amputating a limb, but the alternatives of actually going to war and fighting were much worse than learning this skill on the fly.

It was a terrible book. But Sal remembered it because she had felt for that one cowardly character and the role he *had* to take, whether he liked it or not.

And so she paid attention as the Hand tortured and dismantled Vogue, with a mixture of magic and brute force. Her hands blistered and bled as it tore at the being of blood and fire, breaking her to its will and then, once she submitted to it, tearing off her spines one by one. As it did so, the walls bled more, pooling on the floor but not soaking into the carpet. The demonstuff held together like a gelatin mold, quivering slightly. There was a strange sense of expectancy to the gore.

"That was fun," the Hand said when it was done. "Who's next?"

Between Sal's cell phone, reading passages from the *Codex Umbra* that made her throat bleed, and apparently a sort of demonic rumor network, the Hand had soon filled the office's front foyer—which had grown somehow to accommodate the newcomers—with demons of all kinds. Some looked fearful. Some looked as if they were there against their will. Others looked like Christmas had come after their wealthy, mean grandfather had died.

"More to come," the Hand said, pacing back and forth as the demons from Rome answered its call. It picked two as its deputies, a purple pig-headed demon with snakes for fingers that Sal mentally called Oh-Christ-What-Is-That? and a huge, bulky, chalk-white creature that Sal was strangely relieved to see looked like a normal everyday ugly demon. It left a white residue on anything it touched, including the desk where the *Codex Umbra* lay open.

Chalky and Oh-Christ-What-Is-That? stood on either side of the desk, protecting the *Codex*. Some of the demons, those that had answered the call of the book itself, tried to get closer, but the Hand's command to stay back kept them obedient. Some still got too close for the Hand's liking, and they died messily. Still, many more remained.

It's building an army, Sal thought. *Those it's not killing, anyway.*

Unsurprisingly, the Hand dismantled the ones who were there against their will. The demons may not have wanted to be there, but they obeyed the *Codex*, and they submitted to the Hand even while they screamed as it tore them apart. The quivering piles of demon-stuff grew.

You're taking them apart like LEGO toys, but what are you going to do with the leftovers?

It had been a while since she had talked directly to the Hand, and she wondered if it would reply to her. She didn't have to wait long.

You'll see.

The Hand pulled two more demons forward, relatively human shaped, and gave them instructions. Their language sounded like grunting and screaming. Sal tried to pay attention, but she could feel her sanity slipping. To learn that language would be to lose everything else, she figured, so she retreated inside.

Her body had become a painful vehicle she recognized, but no longer remembered how to drive. She felt like a Roman noble in the time of Caesar who found herself in a Buick instead of a chariot of her time. She relished the pain, and tried small acts of disobedience as the Hand continued its work. She succeeded in blinking once. To make sure it wasn't luck, she tried to curl the toes of her left foot. The toes obeyed.

Sal thought how wonderful it would be to control her body again, and then how it would feel to have control of her body again amid a room full of demons. Waiting was safer.

She retreated further and thought about Aaron's bright white light. The Hand's chanting continued, and the walls kept bleeding.

Asanti stayed at her desk, cataloging the damage and watching the Orb. It lurked silent and sullen by her hand. "Lurking" and "sullen"— the pathetic fallacy at play, her own imagination investing the Orb with consciousness. Probably. Though, considering the volatile nature of most artifacts, it wouldn't be out of the question for the Orb to have emotions. Sometimes, like now, with a team member possessed without anyone's knowledge, she thought the Orb picked and chose what to report. Nothing would surprise her anymore.

Well. Not quite nothing. She had, for example, been quite surprised when Sal turned out to be housing a demon.

Sorrow warred with rage inside her, but she kept her face calm as she reviewed the wreckage of her life's work. No truly valuable (or, as Menchú would have said, dangerous) books seemed to have been seriously hurt, but in Asanti's line of work there was no such thing as an acceptable loss.

Which brought her to the second list, of missing books, which contained only one entry so far: the *Codex Umbra*.

"Can we talk?" Menchú asked in a low voice, pointing at a

chair beside her desk that was piled with charred books.

Asanti nodded and rose to move the books herself. She had to make sure she knew where they all were, so she didn't allow anyone to touch them once they had been counted. She set the stack beside the chair, and dusted some ash off the seat before offering it to Arturo.

"How is Liam?" she asked.

"I'm worried. I think he's becoming unhinged. He's deeply frightened. And he's diving into the grieving process too quickly, as if he's trying to get it over with," Menchú said.

"We don't have time for that," Asanti said flatly. "Normally, yes, but right now Sal really needs help. Liam can't split our focus." She paused, looking around the library until she spotted Grace, still stacking books. "Send Grace after him."

Menchú followed her gaze. "You think?"

"Liam needs some sense knocked into him. Possibly literally. And they have to find Sal."

Menchú checked his watch and grimaced. "I have a meeting shortly. Team Two wants a briefing."

"What are you going to tell them?"

Menchú sighed. "The truth."

"Really?"

He nodded. "The truth is we're on the case and are doing our jobs. When we need them, we'll call them."

"Do you think that'll work?" she asked.

"It's all I've got right now," he said.

Two hours, thirty-seven minutes, and fifteen seconds after Sal had left the Archives in a maelstrom of fire and chaos, Grace punched Liam in the face.

She held back, of course. She didn't want to break anything. But she did punch harder than she usually did while sparring, so he went down, hard.

"Why. THE FUCK. Did you do that?" he asked, lying on his back and cradling his cheek. Rage twisted his face into a snarl.

"Because I knew I'd find you here. I knew you'd be coming down this corridor to sell her out. You are the pettiest man I know."

Liam lay on the rich carpet of the corridor that led to the Team Two offices. The Vatican's labyrinth of halls and rooms usually stayed simple, the flashier displays of wealth either in deep vaults or the public view. But Team Two did not scrimp. The carpets were blue and gold, and showed no sign of wear. Damask wallpaper covered the walls, also blue and gold. Grace found the display offensive.

"You're supposed to be working with me," Grace said. "Menchú is taking care of the higher-ups and the other teams. Do your job, and we can take care of this mess."

Liam stayed down, glaring at the ceiling, which was painted with intricate cherubs and lit with small chandeliers.

"You're as deluded as the rest of them," he muttered.

Grace strode forward and stood above him, one booted foot on each side of his head. "Did you go to Team Two yet? Did you tell them what was going on?"

"No," he said, sliding away from her boots and wincing.

Grace stared at him, and nodded once. "Then let's go after Sal."

"She's gone."

"You don't know that. You weren't."

"Don't you get it, Grace? I don't know that I ever came back."

His voice echoed in the empty hall.

Grace was not a good person. She knew it, because she let him lie there at her feet, at war with himself, for what felt like a long time before she held out her hand. "Come on. Let's do our job."

He did not look at her until they hit the street.

Menchú touched the crucifix around his neck and said a quick prayer for guidance. He promised to not bear false witness, but he gave no promise to say everything he knew.

The crucifix in his hand grew warm as he waited. Perhaps he should simply avoid this meeting. *Hurry,* he thought. *Just go after Sal.*

He paused, and then turned around.

Peter Usher, the monsignor in charge of guiding Team Two, turned down the hallway with a smile, the kind that doesn't reach the eyes, on his face. Behind him trailed Monsignor Angiuli, Team Three's council representative, looking fretful.

Menchú ground his teeth. He prayed for forgiveness and took his hand from his crucifix. "Father, I'm glad to see you. I was about to let you know that cleanup will begin soon on the Archives, but we have a lead on the demons that attacked us. We have to strike now. I will let you know the details when we return."

Usher put up his hand, stopping Menchú with the gesture. "We know what happened, Arturo," he said. "Monsignor Angiuli described the breach. The Archives have been compromised, as well as your team. As of right now, Team Two is taking over this investigation."

Menchú nodded once. "That's for the best. I think that's for the best. Yes. Let me know if we can assist in any way. Any way."

Both monsignors raised eyebrows at his stumbling words, and he cursed silently. "Sorry, I'm rather overwhelmed. Tired. I'll go tell my team they can stand down and wait for debriefing from Team Two, shall I?"

"We have some points to discuss," Monsignor Usher said, gesturing to Angiuli. "About the future of the teams. I'll send someone to get you after we work some things out."

"Good, good," Menchú said.

"You'll need to remove Asanti from the Archives for now, until we figure out what's going to happen with Team Three."

Menchú swallowed the lump of rage in his throat. "Understood." He leaned away from them, eager to leave. He didn't care about the existence of Team Three at this point, he just wanted to get Liam, Grace, and Asanti away from the Vatican.

The inside of the shoe-design office looked like an abattoir. Sal wondered why no security alarms were going off—but if the Hand had blocked her phone communications in her apartment, it wasn't too big a logistical leap to think that it could block cameras and alarms.

If the human race lives through this, there's going to be a huge carpet-cleaning bill.

"Quiet," the Hand snapped. Sal's voice sounded strained.

She was distracting it. Which meant it needed its full attention for the task at hand.

The Hand had slaughtered many of the visiting demons and dismantled them, starting with Vogue. It then laid the bits of smoking flesh on the floor, taking care to put each in the right spot. Making itself a body.

Chalky and Oh-Christ-What-Is-That? were busy cutting various bones free from the dead demons (and a few live ones) and adhering them to the bleeding walls. They were building something that looked like an archway, long leg bones making the sides and cracked ribs forming the arch.

The demons that were neither slaughtered yet nor working directly for the Hand milled around, some of them hanging back in fear, some of them eagerly watching. A few masochists were offering themselves to the Hand to help it achieve its greatness.

The Hand snared one of these, a small, six-legged, catlike demon with black spines instead of fur, and broke it in half. The spines cut Sal's hands, but she barely felt the pain anymore. The Hand muttered some words, glancing at the *Codex* as it chanted, and formed each side of the cat demon into horns it fixed to the forehead of the body on the floor.

Oh, now that was unnecessary. You had to kill that cat-thing just so you could have horns? What's next—kill someone else to make sure your dick is big enough? She wasn't sure why she was defending a demon, but the Hand's actions still seemed pretty shitty.

"Quiet," the Hand said again, louder this time, and the demons around them subsided.

You don't like me in your head bugging you? You're really going to complain about that after the last few months? You're nothing but a hypocrite. Sal was enjoying herself, in a perverse way.

"Soon enough," the Hand panted, "I will be free of you." It took a breath. "And then ending you will be the first thing I do."

The wall inside the bone arch began to shimmer and crack, and blood-red light spilled into the room. The Hand kept reading, and the wall shattered, giving Sal a good look into the world beyond. It was a world she remembered having seen while glimpsing the Hand's memories, and for a moment she was worried the Hand would take her there.

No. It's an exit. And it's not for us.

Demons teemed around the portal, waiting for it to stabilize so they could come through.

The room pulsed with energy, and the demons inside roared and cheered and hissed. The Hand positioned Sal's body between the portal and the piles of gory bits of slaughtered demons.

The portal pulsed again, and Sal's body shook from the pressure of the magic around her. Light shot out from the opening and around Sal, then through her, to fall on the cobbled-together body on the floor. The bits melted to form a more recognizable shape.

It was going to be quite tall. Sal thought the Hand was getting ambitious; it could have built a shorter body and killed fewer demons in the process, but then, people who thought like that probably didn't tend to end up being demons. The body lying in the center of the foyer would be at least eight feet tall, with huge muscular thighs and shoulders, hands that ended in three claws, cloven feet, and horns that had previously been the six-legged cat-thing.

Sal could feel the strain the Hand required to focus the magic into its new body. She looked at the huge, inert form, and thought for the first time that perhaps getting the Hand out of her head wasn't the best idea at this moment.

I miss my team, she thought. *Grace would have a field day in here.*

The body had formed almost completely. The new skin was brown and bumpy and tough. The flesh underneath looked hard as stone, and fangs grew from its gums.

Her ears pricked as she heard a sound far off, beyond the screams of the demons and the pressure the magic had put on her senses. It was a sound like a door being kicked open.

"Soon," her own voice said, but she didn't know whether she or the Hand had spoken.

4.

ecades of fighting demons and dealing with intricate Church politics (not to mention the intimidation and manipulation practiced by Team Two) hadn't scared Menchú as much as that moment in Guatemala with the angel. In one shining moment of beauty and blood, he'd been changed.

Still, he had found it helpful in the years following Guatemala to study body language, both of humans and demons. Humans were easier to read and anticipate.

Keep your body language neutral.

Let them get emotional.

And do not speak first.

The problem was, Hilary Sansone didn't get emotional.

Menchú sat in the understated-yet-expensive office of Team Two, watching Sansone stare right back at him.

The first time Menchú had heard the American phrase "Butter wouldn't melt in her mouth," he'd thought of Sansone. Cold, and dedicated to her work. The few times he had seen her outside the Vatican, in the guise of a civilian enjoying Rome, she had seemed friendly and approachable. But behind that desk, inside that suit, she was Team Two.

Looking directly into her pale blue eyes could make anyone nervous. Stories about Hilary Sansone circulated around the office: People tended to blurt things to her. Once a stranger on the bus confessed, unprompted, that he was cheating on his wife. "I just have one of those faces," she joked. When she joked.

Rumor had it that, years ago, the monsignor of Team Two had asked Sansone if she ever thought about becoming a nun and putting her organizational flair in direct service to God. They would have found it more convenient, she had confided in Menchú during one of their rare encounters outside work, if she were a man so she could take confessions. Since she had no interest in being a nun, and less interest in becoming a man, she remained in her current role.

After a minute, the smallest smile twitched at her lips. She had caught on to the game. She leaned back in her chair, crossed her legs, and regarded Menchú like an interesting insect.

Menchú reviewed the list of the demons he had faced. All of them were scarier and more willing to tear him apart than Sansone. Then he said the Lord's Prayer to himself, in many languages. He mirrored Sansone's body language.

Sansone was flanked by two members of Team Two whom Menchú had seen, but never met. They were large men—*When did Team Two start employing nightclub bouncers?*—and they did not look at either Sansone or Menchú.

Finally, Menchú looked at his watch, quirked an eyebrow at Sansone, and rose from his chair. He was at the door with his hand on the knob when she spoke up.

"Arturo," she said, her voice mild and pleasant. "Where are you off to?"

"I've been here for five minutes," Menchú said. "You clearly have nothing to say to me, and I have responsibilities."

"This won't take a moment. I only need you to tell me: Where is Sal Brooks?" Before Menchú could answer, she added, as if it was an afterthought, "Oh, and how long has she been possessed?"

Menchú looked into Sansone's eyes. "Sal left after the battle. She was injured." *All true, from a certain point of view.*

"And the possession?" Sansone asked, raising her eyebrows.

"We're unsure what happened to Sal. After we settle things, we will make certain she's all right." Menchú's heart began to pound.

"And the possession?" Sansone asked again, softer and slower.

"Hilary, I can't tell you anything I don't know myself. If your people went off after every single suspected possession, then there would be no need for Team Three," he said. "I will let you know when I know something."

That was the first lie. He started making a list for his next confession. *Forgive me, Father.* He broke eye contact and put his hand on the door handle to go.

Sansone wouldn't back down. "Father Menchú, you do realize that when we find her, we will have to remove the demon from Ms. Brooks."

"If she is possessed, of course you will."

"So, you are of the opinion that she is not possessed?"

Menchú's back was still to Sansone, but he heard the smile in her voice. He turned back to face her. "Hilary. Our Archives were attacked. We have injuries. Priceless books were damaged or destroyed. There are numerous, as Team One would say, 'priority one' demands on my attention—among them, learning our teammate's status. When we're sure demons won't attack the Archives again, and that nothing inside the Archives is an immediate threat, we'll be—"

Sansone's voice cut through Menchú's like an ax. "You don't consider Sal Brooks an immediate threat? She has had complete access to the Archives."

"That remains to be seen. We will let you know what we find," Menchú said, and opened the door.

"We're not done, Arturo," Sansone said.

"You may not be done, but I have to lock down the Archives, and I am finished playing games. If you have a genuine complaint with me or my team, take it up with Monsignor Angiuli. Now—I have a job to do." He left.

Before he shut the door, he heard Sansone say, "So do I."

"Give me a challenge, why don't you?" Liam grumbled, fingers stabbing at his laptop. The R kept sticking, which made hacking into "secuity cameas" difficult.

First he accessed the ones outside Sal's apartment building.

"No record of her entering the building," Liam said, scrolling through the archived video of the last hour.

"The demon disappeared," Grace reminded him. "It likely teleported her somewhere— Wait. There she is." She pointed at the screen, where Sal was leaving the building. "But that's not her."

"Of course it is. She's even wearing the same clothes she had on during the fight," Liam said, glancing up at Grace's stony face.

"No, look at the way she's walking. That is not how Sal moves. That's not her. It's still inside her."

"Now maybe Menchú will listen to me," Liam grumbled, and was rewarded with a slap to the back of his head.

"Do you want her to die?" Grace asked.

"I want you to realize she's already dead. The next step will be hard enough." Liam's throat went dry as he watched Sal walk in that very un-Sal-like way.

"When she gets better, Sal will never forgive you. I hope you can live with that," Grace said. Then, as if they hadn't been arguing, she pointed to where Sal had left the camera's view. "She's turned north. Follow her."

For the next few minutes, Grace looked at a map while Liam hacked the security cameras along Sal's route. Most of them caught her, striding purposefully down the sidewalk. She made a call, and kept going.

When she approached the doors to Monroe Shoe Designers, the Monroe security cameras went black. Liam tried to access the other street cameras in the area, but all of the cameras cut out at the same time: when Sal reached the doors.

"Well. Now we know where she is," Liam said. "Nothing makes cameras go dark like considerable magical activity. "

"Let's tell the others," Grace said. She cast a withering eye at Liam as he was closing his laptop. "And by that I mean Asanti and Arturo."

"Lay off me, Grace," Liam said in a low voice. Grace left, and it was clear she expected him to follow. Liam sat down once again and opened his laptop, scrolling through the various surveillance they had found showing Sal. It was her, but it clearly wasn't. He wouldn't let himself hope. She was gone. And now his job was to keep his team safe.

"Where's Liam?" Asanti asked as Grace entered the library.

"Bathroom, maybe? He was right behind me when we got to the Vatican," Grace said, looking back over her shoulder. "But he should be here shortly. We need to move. We found Sal."

"Please tell me she's close," Asanti said.

"Monroe Shoe Designers," Grace said. "A few blocks from her apartment."

Asanti frowned at the Orb, still dark and silent on her desk. "I think Liam and I will have to knock this thing about a bit when all this cools down. It's not telling me anything."

"And then I will fix a computer, because I used Liam's once," Grace said.

Asanti smiled at her. "Fair enough. But the Orb's all we have, and if we don't fix it, we're sitting in the dark." She looked up at the ruined ceiling, where some lights flickered bravely among the shattered bulbs. "Literally."

Menchú entered the room and winced at the destruction, as if he had forgotten its extent. "Please someone tell me something good," he said.

"We found Sal, and she's close," Grace said.

"That will do," Menchú said. "Get Liam and let's get down there."

Asanti nodded at Grace. "Go ahead. I need to gather a few things," she said, and Grace walked toward the ladder.

"No, you have to stay here," Menchú said. "The Archives are compromised. We need someone here we can trust."

Asanti resisted the urge to snap back. "Let me at least give you three some equipment."

"What equipment?" Menchú asked, suspicion in his voice.

Asanti rolled her eyes. "Nothing dangerous. New silver crucifixes. Yours are probably tarnished black by now." She went to a file cabinet that sat beside her desk. It had survived the battle, but only barely. The side had been smashed in, and black soot covered it. She unlocked the top drawer and struggled with the handle. The dent in the side made it impossible to remove.

Grace and Liam returned, Grace's face a mass of storm clouds. "Grace, can you open this for me?" Asanti asked.

Grace trudged over, put one hand on the top of the cabinet and one on the handle. With a yank that looked halfhearted and a screech of metal, the drawer came free. It was full of files, all badly scorched.

"How were *these* damaged?" Asanti asked out loud. Then she reached behind the folders and found a box made of carved cherry wood. She glanced up and saw that Menchú and Grace were badgering poor Liam. The boy didn't deserve this—he was grieving, but couldn't show it. Stupid, but understandable. She opened the box and removed four shiny silver crucifixes with her right hand. One remained in the box. With her left hand, Asanti picked up the small silver knife that lay under the necklaces.

It was about the size of a letter opener, but very sharp. She didn't know where it had come from; she had received it from Seamus before he left the Society. She once kept it on her desk, trying to hide it in plain sight, but its proximity made the Orb malfunction—some might say *made the Orb nervous*—so she hid it with her spare silver.

She had used it once, the last time the Archives were attacked— during the few days between Seamus's handoff to Arturo, when they were short-staffed. The team had brought in a book that wasn't locked down. Asanti had put it on a stack for shelving, but when the team left the Archives, the book popped open and began reading itself with eyes and a mouth drawn on the inside cover. Sticky webs began covering the wall, and Asanti had had no time to alert anyone. She searched through her silver for anything she could use, and she found her knife.

In retrospect, she was relieved that the cabinet hadn't been damaged, because, though the webs covered her skin to wrap her up, she was able to retrieve the knife and slice herself free. The web shriveled where the knife touched, and Asanti slashed her way through the fibers until she found the book, teeming with tiny spiders. She couldn't close it, since the book began chanting even louder, so she stabbed the knife straight into its pages.

The book exploded. She never wanted to feel anything like that again, especially at her age. The knife pierced the open book and the volume on which it rested, mixing the magic inside them and destroying both.

The team found her sitting, dazed, among the ruins of two books. She had told them the books exploded when she tried to move them, and they believed her.

She had asked herself why she didn't put the knife, which didn't tarnish like normal silver, in the Archives with the rest of the artifacts, why she didn't give it to Menchú after she learned to trust him, or even offer it to Grace. She told herself it was because she didn't know how it worked, but Asanti knew it was an excuse. The knife was a gift from Seamus, and she didn't want to have to give it up. They might also take it away from her based on the fact it was a magical artifact she shouldn't have. But Sal was alive, and Seamus was gone, and anyway, the man's other parting gifts hadn't gone so well. Memories were enough.

Asanti handed necklaces to each team member and then pulled Liam aside.

"You going to tell me how selfish I am too?" He pushed his chest out and lifted his chin.

"No, I'm sure you've gotten an earful already," Asanti said. "I wanted to give you this trinket." She handed it to Liam, handle first.

He accepted it. With a glance over his shoulder to see if Grace and Menchú were looking, he shielded the knife with his body and gave it a careful inspection.

"Asanti," he said, his voice sounding more like his old sardonic self, "have you been hiding a magic weapon? That's against the rules."

"Desperate times, Liam," she said, smiling at him. "Careful, it's sharp. The sheath was lost years ago, I'm told. Now listen. I've only used it once, and the results were . . . unexpected. I can't tell you when to use it; I can just tell you it's powerful."

"Might as well give me a flamethrower without telling me which end the fire comes out of," he said, his grip on the knife becoming more tentative. "Why are you giving this to me, not Grace?"

"You want the lie that makes me look good, or the truth that doesn't?" she asked.

Liam actually considered the answer. "The lie first, then the truth."

"Grace can handle herself. She already has magic on her side. It's a curse, but it's magic, and it helps her in these scenarios. You don't have that."

Liam frowned. "That sounds plausible. What's the truth?"

Asanti stopped smiling. "If I give it to Grace, Menchú will know, and he will take it away from me."

"If I use it, he will probably notice," Liam pointed out. "He tends to pay attention when we're fighting."

"It's a chance I'm willing to take," Asanti said. "For Sal. I believe in her. I want you to believe as well."

Liam took a shirt out of his backpack and wrapped the knife in it, then put it in the front pocket of the bag. "I can't promise belief, Asanti. That's impossible. But I can promise I'll do everything I can as if she were still alive."

"That will have to do," she said. She gave his crucifix a little tug. "And don't take this one off, either."

"Wouldn't dream of it," Liam said. Then, suddenly, he bent down and kissed her cheek. "Thanks, Asanti."

She put her palm over the place he had kissed and stared at him. "Miracles do happen, Liam. You're proof of that."

Liam knew the knife was a test of something. He just wasn't sure of what. Was Asanti testing if he would tell Menchú? Or not tell Menchú? Was it a test of his loyalty to Team Three? He could easily tell Team Two about the knife. They'd be interested in Asanti's other secrets too. Was it a test to see if he turned to a crutch in a fight?

The knife made him feel heavier as they barreled through the city streets in a cab. It felt odd, just the three of them—odd already, after only a few months.

He had been magically tied into the Internet, and they'd gotten him out. Grace had been locked in a box for decades, and she'd been rescued. Why was he so reluctant to admit Sal might be saved?

He knew the reason. Like Asanti, he knew the lie he told himself, and the truth underneath. When Sal had changed, when she had become the Hand, he saw a look in her eyes of pleasure and triumph, and he'd seen that look before, when they were in bed together. And that scared him. How long had she been like this, more Hand than Sal? Had he been close to the demon? Had he made love to it? He shuddered.

And if he couldn't tell a demon from Sal, he was in the wrong line of work. Sal's betrayal made him question everything—*everything*—about his own life. No praise from Menchú would help. No confession, no drunken bar fight, no violent video game. No sparring with Grace. He couldn't trust any of them.

Grace and Menchú were reviewing their plans, and Liam stared out the window and thought about the knife in his bag. It was a test. But what kind?

Monroe Shoe Designers' corporate offices were in an older building. It had been spruced up with security cameras, but the door was still locked with an old-fashioned bolt. Menchú ordered Liam to pick the lock, and he set to work. Liam had to put away his computer, which was ready to hack the security code, and get out his seldom-used lockpicks.

As he inserted his tools into the keyhole, he thought again of what a waste of time this was. Dealing with possessions was Team Two's job. What was Grace going to do, anyway? *Not* hit the demon controlling Sal?

The pin inside the lock slipped, and he started again. He expected Grace to get impatient, but she waited a few feet away, giving him space. She and Menchú watched him work.

One more try and the bolt was free, letting them into the offices.

Their ears were attacked first, with the screams of what sounded like hundreds of demons down the hall. The hall carpet was sticky with blood and ichor. "Oh no," he said.

"It may not be Sal's blood," Menchú reminded him, and sprinted down the hall, followed by Grace.

Liam felt dizzy. He fell to his knees, his backpack sliding off his shoulders, screaming inside—*Stop being paranoid, don't feel, just do your job!* The collapse could come later. For now, he had demons to fight. And if one of them was his ex-lover, then so be it.

Hands were on him, strong, small hands. They gripped his shoulders and pulled him up. Grace.

He expected worse abuse than her quick slap on his cheek. Her voice was oddly gentle. "Come on. I know it hurts. But Sal needs us. Can you do it for her?"

Liam nodded mutely. He picked up his bag and ran after her down the hall.

Somewhere in the back of his mind, he noticed that his jeans were filthy with the gore that soaked the carpet, but his backpack was pristine.

5.

The light pushed through Sal as if she were a window, and she felt the Hand's hold on her lessen. The Hand was easing out of her body, into the body that lay before them. Once it animated that monstrosity, who knew what it could do?

The Hand had been clear enough about one thing: Tearing her to pieces would be the first order of business. Weaponless, teamless, and surrounded by demons, how could she fight it? She had to stop wishing for Grace. That wasn't a good use of a wish.

Not that she had any wishes. If she had, she would have prevented this from happening, all the way back to Perry taking up his weird hobbies in high school. If the Hand hadn't possessed Perry, she would have avoided Team Three, numerous flirtations with death, and a very unsuccessful love affair with one of her only friends in a foreign city.

Yes, prevention was better than cure. Good old vaccines. A fence at the top of a cliff instead of an ambulance below. A condom instead of Plan B.

The madness was causing her to retreat into her thoughts. She forced herself to see the world. The Hand was a red mist, creeping from her pores into the body in front of her.

The eyes opened, a purplish red; they looked around and fixed on hers.

Soon.

Grace rapidly took in the scene. A room too large for the building that held it. A portal made of bone, glowing as it slowly opened. An inert demon body on the floor, and scores of demons, most of them so transfixed by the spectacle they didn't realize humans had arrived.

And Sal in the demons' midst, immobile, with demonic light shining straight through her to illuminate the body.

Most of the demons were human-size or smaller, and Grace figured they'd be little trouble to kill, so long as they didn't swarm her. She'd leave the portal to Menchú. Liam would have to deal with Sal.

The demons hadn't noticed her, but Sal, or whatever was in her, did. Her eyes flicked to them and held Grace's. They were desperate and afraid. They were Sal's.

Liam had seen it too. "She's still in there," Liam said from beside Grace. His voice was soft with wonder.

Menchú frowned, his mustache drooping low. "Liam, help her. Grace, keep the demons off us. We have to destroy that portal."

They inched behind the demons along the wall, toward the portal. Grace crouched between the men and demons, ready to spring. One thin head with an incredibly long beak, or maybe it was a stinger, had begun to turn when Sal screamed.

"Go!" Grace said, and they went.

Clever Sal. A diversion, to keep the demons focused.

At least, Grace hoped it was a diversion.

Sal didn't want to enjoy a few moments of freedom just to be devoured. If that was her choice, she'd stay with the Hand a little while longer. But how?

It had been weakening all day, after using most of its power to escape with the *Codex Umbra*. Since then the Hand had used the power of its sacrificed friends, not itself. She could feel its fatigue, its desperation to move into its new body and the strength it offered, to tear open the portal and welcome more demons into the world. Sal could even control her own body now, focus her eyes elsewhere, like on the door opposite the portal, which was sliding open to reveal Liam, Grace, and Menchú.

She looked at them, met their eyes, and saw each of their faces change. Grace looked relieved, Liam anguished, Menchú determined. They began to move.

The Hand was slipping away from her, as if it had gotten its head and shoulders through the birth canal, and now the rest was easy.

"Not that easy," Sal said, determined. And then she laughed. She had control of her mind again. She wanted to keep the attention of the demons, so she screamed as loud as she could, and they moved in eagerly. It was almost feeding time.

A few demons near the back noticed Grace and Liam and Menchú, and bodies began to fly. Menchú and Grace had reached the portal.

The light intensified. It was nearly open, and the Hand was nearly free.

Grace fought the demons with more finesse than Liam had ever seen. He wished they could take a moment to enjoy this, because she truly was a master. She had grabbed a small humanoid demon with a crocodile head by one hand and leg and was swinging it around like a weapon, impaling demons and stabbing them right and left with the spines on its back.

Menchú studied the arch briefly, and then touched Liam's arm. "How do we dismantle it?" he asked.

"Find the keystone," Liam said, his eyes flicking around the gory arch, seeking the bone that held the thing together. "There," he said, pointing at a rib cage at the top. "Bust that up. I'm going to go help Sal."

He had no idea what he was going to do. She didn't seem to be held by anything he could break, not even a magical tentacle.

Something screeched, and Liam looked up to see the crocodile demon fly over his head, then crash straight into the rib-cage keystone. It shattered, and the bones tumbled to the ground. The portal faded. The light went out.

Sal stumbled and sank to her knees. Liam rushed toward her. He put his hand on her shoulder.

"You're okay now, we got it closed," he said.

"No, we're pretty damn far from okay," she said. "It's out."

Liam blinked. "What do you mean?"

The remaining demons around them were staring at them, unmoving. They had even stopped attacking Grace (who hadn't let that stop her from attacking them).

"The Hand. It's not inside me anymore," she said, staring at the bloody carpet.

"That's good, isn't it?"

She raised a shaking hand, dirty and lacerated, and pointed to the body in front of her, which had begun to stir. The demons hadn't been staring at them. They had been staring at the body on the floor—not dead, like Liam had thought. Alive. Animated. Rising.

"It's very, very bad."

That was the Hand—in a fresh body.

Liam saw her, now. One hundred percent Sal. The possession hadn't been her fault, and she'd been fighting this whole time.

He could still trust her. This was his test. If there had been any test at all.

He reached into his bag and grabbed the knife.

The Hand got to its feet, flexing its new limbs. Its eyes still glowed with hatred as it surveyed the damage Team Three had done; then it fixed its eyes on Sal.

"My vessel," it said, its voice so deep that Liam felt it in his chest. "Your time has come."

Liam pushed the knife into Sal's hand. "From Asanti," he said. "I don't know what it does. But I bet you can figure it out."

Her eyes met his, and then she looked at the knife. She smiled. "You're okay, Liam."

The Hand had raised a fist and uncurled its fingers, like a very sharp, very venomous flower. Each claw dripped with ichor, and Liam shouted to Grace and Menchú.

Sal stood up suddenly, pushing the knife into the Hand's belly and up into its chest.

"Not your time yet, asshole!" she shouted.

Usually, at moments like this, the demon's eyes would grow wide, and it would crumple, or shower the humans with blood and goo. Liam had seen enough death that he thought he knew what to expect.

He didn't expect the demon to outright explode.

Sal opened her eyes. A severed demon arm lay in front of her face, and she grimaced and pushed it away. She was covered in demon gore, and hurt all over.

Her mind was full of screaming. A rage unlike any she had ever heard or felt. No words, only emotion. It had worked. Sort of. She had killed the Hand's new body—so it seemed to have gone back into hers. But she was still in control. The Hand had weakened.

Great.

Beyond the screaming, she could hear Grace finishing off the demons. From the looks of it, some had fled, and some had gotten caught in the blast when the Hand exploded.

As for Sal, except for the bruises from where she had hit the wall, she seemed relatively unscathed. The knife was still in her hand, twisted and blackened. The *Codex Umbra*, the book they had nearly died for multiple times, lay to the side, burning with a white-hot fire.

Should have gotten a book sleeve for it, she thought. *Asanti's going to be pissed.*

Liam ran toward her through the demonic mess. "Sal! Are you all right?"

She nodded and tossed the black and twisted knife on top of the *Codex Umbra*. Might as well stack all the ruined magical items together. "We stopped him."

"And that fucker is dead! Piles of demon meat!" Liam grinned.

Sal shook her head. Menchú hurried over to her.

"It's still here," she said. "Back in me, now." She tried to point to the body, then realized it was spread out all around her.

Menchú nodded. "The lesser of two evils," he said, and reached down to help her up. "We'll figure this out together, Sal. Come on, we need to get you somewhere safe."

Sal looked up. "Safe? What do you mean?"

Menchú's mouth compressed into a straight line. "Come on," he said again.

They had almost reached the door when it flew open. Team One soldiers rushed in, training rifles and spears on Sal. Two familiar figures trailed Team One into the room.

"Good job," said Balloon.

"We'll take her from here," said Stretch.

EPISODE
14

AN EXCELLENT DAY FOR AN EXORCISM

BRIAN FRANCIS SLATTERY

1.

Sal woke to a night sky. Stars, traces of cloud. She couldn't move. At first she thought she was still asleep and having an irritating dream. But there was the Hand in her head, talking. *You're awake,* it said. *We're in trouble.*

She lay on something uncomfortable. A wooden board. She tried to take a deep breath. A leather strap across her chest pushed back. There were straps at her wrists, another at her waist, another at her knees. The last one at her ankles. They were all nailed to the board beneath her. As if whoever did it wasn't expecting her to get up again. Four men she didn't recognize ranged around her, two on either side, each of them holding identical little red books. Beyond them, forming a vague perimeter, were guards with machine guns. At her feet, a man she did know: Stretch.

Uh-oh, she thought. "Where am I?" she said aloud.

"A monastery," Balloon said. "Or at least the ruins of one." He was standing at her head, closer than she expected. Way too close for comfort. He had a small, dark red book in his hands, and he wet his lips before speaking again. "This courtyard, I am given to understand, used to be a garden, full of herbs and vegetables. On the land outside the walls, the monks had a vineyard. According to the people in the town nearby, the wine was very good. But this monastery hasn't been used in more than a century."

"Declining enrollment," Stretch said.

"It's just as well, though," Balloon said. "This place has become very convenient for us to conduct rituals of this sort without . . ."

"Overbearing oversight?" Stretch said.

"Thank you, yes," Balloon said.

The four men shifted a little. *They're uncomfortable with this,* Sal thought.

"Junior colleagues," Balloon said. "This is their first exorcism, and we're glad they're seeing this one."

Stretch produced a small bowl of holy water and walked around the circle, blessing each of the men with it. When he got back to his spot at Sal's feet, he flicked the water across her body. It was cooling, a small comfort.

"It is a small mercy to us that you're awake," Balloon continued. "In our experience, an exorcism is more effective when the subject is conscious."

"It lets us know when it's working," Stretch said.

"So what are the men with guns for?"

"In case things get out of hand."

"Get me out of these straps," Sal said.

Stretch smiled.

"You're going to be glad we restrained you," Balloon said. "The demon inside you is very powerful, and there's no telling what it may try to do to you. Or to get you to do to yourself."

"You're not going to be so glad when I get out," Sal said.

"Now, now," Balloon said. "We're on the same side, remember?"

He addressed the four men at Sal's sides. "You may begin."

The men all opened to the same page in their red books and began chanting. Their voices blended in the night air, quickly found the same note, and relaxed into a rhythm that let them all fall together at the end of every phrase, a little sigh that spoke of peace. The music reached the crumbling stone walls around the courtyard; it soaked into the grass; it rose, like thick, sweet smoke, toward the sky. Even Sal could hear that it was beautiful, pure. Like the singers themselves, so full of good intentions.

Stretch produced a thick leather crop with seven long tails on it.

"I thought you said we were on the same team," Sal said.

"We must weaken the demon through the mortification of the flesh," Balloon said.

"But it's my flesh," Sal said.

"The mortification brings you closer to Christ's suffering, which repels the demon."

"I'm not sure I buy that."

"And I can't be sure whether I'm talking to you or the demon. Mortification is one way to find out."

Stretch lifted his arm behind his head and brought the crop down on Sal, hard. She had no idea it would hurt so much. The wounds it left first stung, and then burned. She felt cold wetness creeping down the sides of her rib cage. Stretch whipped her again. A long string of obscenities flew from her mouth. The chanting continued, still serene, but a little more uncertain. Sal made eye contact with one of the men and gave him an imploring look. The man held her gaze. He understood. He was doubting this whole thing; Sal was sure of it. But he didn't look like he was about to speak up.

Stretch lifted his arm a third time.

I can get us out of this, the Hand said, somewhere behind her eyes.

Then do it, Sal said.

She felt a rustling in her mind, the Hand trying to expand. It could take over again if she let it. She gave it a push back, and the rustling subsided. All that business with the *Codex Umbra* must have weakened the Hand. It was healing, gaining strength. Soon enough it would be able to assert control over her. But for now, it was Sal calling the shots. At least in her own skull.

Stretch's arm fell. Both Sal and the Hand had to wait for the wave of pain to pass before speaking again.

You'd rather be whipped to death? the Hand said.

I was willing to throw myself off a balcony instead of living with you, Sal said.

I haven't forgotten, the Hand said. *But I don't want to suffer the indignity of dying at the hands of this clown, and I don't think you do either.*

Better than dying at yours, Sal said.

Humans. Threaten to eat someone once, and they never let you live it down.

At her head, Balloon produced a pair of gloves from his pocket and pulled them on.

"Those aren't magic, are they?" Sal said to him.

Balloon gave her a tiny smile.

"You hypocrite," she said.

He shrugged and passed his hands through the air over her. She could not see the flames sweep across her skin, but she could feel them. She shut her eyes; the pain was so convincing that she believed if she opened them again, she'd look down and see herself as only a mass of seared flesh, her clothes turned to charred scraps.

If you let me, the Hand said, *I can pay him back for that.*

No, Sal said.

Stretch raised his arm to whip Sal again. The four men at her sides kept chanting, though she was sure she could hear their confidence collapsing.

They'll put a stop to this, Sal said.

Not soon enough, the Hand said. *They're too weak. You'll be dead first.*

Menchú will find me, Sal said.

Perhaps, the Hand said. *He is a capable man. But will he work fast enough?*

The whip came down. Balloon's hands passed over her, and the flame closed in. Sal was sure she blacked out, came to again. It was impossible to know how long she had been unconscious.

If these straps were off and I could reach to touch him . . . , the Hand said. *Oh, the things I could do.* It sounded almost nostalgic.

I'm not releasing you, Sal said.

I don't understand why you would be willing to die out of spite, the Hand said. *Meaninglessly. On this table.*

We've been over this before, Sal said. *It'll be worth it to take you with me.*

Even if you don't get to see your brother again?

There was never any chance of that. I see that now.

I can take you to him right this instant, the Hand said.

What? Sal said.

That's right. I've been able to do it all along.

Sal did the math. *If you take me to wherever you've put him, that means I become a vegetable here.*

Possibly, the Hand said. *I'm counting on it seeming that way just long enough for them to take those straps off.*

The chanting continued. Balloon and Stretch were both raising their arms again.

If it doesn't work? Sal said.

Then at least you and your brother will be together, the Hand said.

How do I know you're not just going to go back home and leave me there?

She heard a rustle, somehow, as if the Hand were shifting a little in her brain.

Isn't it obvious? the Hand said. *If I wanted to go back, I would have done it already, before you ever had a chance to join the Society. I'm not done with your world yet.*

And you'll let me see Perry, Sal said.

Yes.

Another wave crested over them, and she blacked out again. Came to.

All right, she said. *All right.*

The Hand gave a small chuckle. Sal felt the rustling, the expanding, in her mind and this time pushed back less, gave it space to move. It seemed as though a dark mist swept over the courtyard. First the outer walls faded into blackness, then the grass around them. The faces of the men chanting at her sides blurred and disappeared. Balloon was swallowed in shadow. At her feet, Stretch was bringing down the crop for another blow, but he and his instrument vanished before the crop struck her, and she didn't feel it. She felt, and saw, nothing. For a few more seconds, she could hear the chanting, the shaky voices trying to be brave. Then they faded into silence.

A pink sun streamed through a large window. Sal sat on a simple bed with yellow sheets under a thin blanket. She was in a small wooden room, a tiny cabin. There were no other furnishings. A man, too tall and too thin to be human, stood in the center of the room.

"Thank you," the man said, in the Hand's voice.

"What just happened?" Sal said. "It felt like dying."

"In a sense it was," the Hand said. "In the monastery, your body is likely going through a series of violent convulsions. Which is just what those sadists want to see. It makes them think the exorcism is working."

"Funny to hear the word 'sadist' coming from you," Sal said.

"My dear," the Hand said in mock offense, "that's unfair. While I admit to a certain satisfaction in my work, I would not describe it as pleasurable."

"Tell that to those demons you dismantled."

It shrugged. "Pain serves a purpose. Which is more than I can say for Stretch's riding crop."

"So you're saying the exorcism is bogus," Sal said.

"Well, not entirely. True exorcisms—as opposed to the vast majority of supposed exorcisms—involve no physical punishments and are more like a very convoluted form of therapy. Your tormenters do succeed in separating, shall we say, guest from host. The guest returns whence he came. But the host almost never survives the ordeal, and when he does, his mind is rarely intact."

"So an exorcism is like a lobotomy," Sal said.

"That's right," the Hand said.

"Like the state you put Perry in."

"Ironic, isn't it?"

"I'm not sure," Sal said.

"I imagine Balloon and Stretch consider that result a success, in any case. And you would have been another one of their successes if you hadn't allowed me this." It spread its arms to indicate the cabin, the sky outside the window flooded with light.

"And what is this, exactly?" Sal said.

"A little something I built just now to ease the transition from your world to mine."

Sal gave herself a few seconds to figure out how to respond to that.

"That sounds too much like dying," she said.

"Can I say that you're perhaps a little preoccupied with your own mortality just now? But you have a point. When you fully enter my world, your body in the monastery will lose whatever consciousness remains to it. You will still be breathing, but your brain will be essentially nonfunctioning."

"So why don't we just wait things out here?"

"The convulsive state you are in right now will not make them stop," the Hand said. "It will only make them think they have more work to do. Only if they believe you to be dead, or nearly dead, will they take those straps off your limbs."

"So your plan is for us to play dead?"

"Well," said the Hand, "it's not exactly playing if those two keep up the, ah, good work. But we don't have to wait long."

"How do we know when the straps are off?" Sal said.

The Hand gave her a questioning look. "You can't still feel them?"

"No," Sal said.

"That's a small mercy. Concentrate and you'll be able to."

Sal did. She pulled into herself, and yes, it was just as the Hand said. There was the leather straining against her wrists, against her ankles. Straining hard against her chest. She heard a distant echo of her own voice, shrieking. There was bile and a little blood in her mouth. She must have bitten her tongue.

"Come back," the Hand said. "Come back here."

She did, gladly.

"When we fully enter my world and the screaming stops," the Hand said, "it'll only be a matter of time before they take the straps off."

Sal nodded. "All right, then. Let's go."

The Hand looked toward the ceiling and closed its eyes. The floor opened beneath them, which was when Sal realized where the cabin was. There was no land at all. Just the sky, above and below and all around them, clouds flooded with pink light.

They began to drop.

2.

'm telling you," Liam said. "I didn't turn her in."

"And why should we believe you?" Grace said.

Team Three was arguing in a room in the catacombs of the Society. The walls were lined with cypress, the floor a ceramic mosaic. A painting on the ceiling depicted the Archangel Michael fighting the dragon. But they were deep underground, and there were no windows, one heavy door, and a private in the Swiss Guard stationed with them. The room was made for protection, but it felt like a cell, too.

Asanti sat in a chair in the corner, shaking her head slowly. Menchú stood near her, his arms crossed. The old colleagues circling the wagons.

"We know how you feel about possession, Liam," Menchú said in a gentle voice. "We understand if you did what you felt you had to do."

"*I* don't," Grace said.

"Grace," Asanti said, "that's not helpful."

"What's not helpful," Liam said, "is the condescension from the two of you in the corner over there. At least

locks to come out and say what she's thinking."

"Tempus fugit, Liam," Grace said.

"Yeah, and my answer's not changing."

"It better soon."

"You want me to lie?" Liam said. "You want I

thing up?"

None of them said a word to that.

"Look," Liam said. "I know what I've said al

wasn't lying, either. But I didn't sell Sal out. I almost

all right? Hell, I think I'm more than half a hypocrit

walk free, most days. Why you all believe in me, I'

if you can believe in me, I can believe in Sal. I tho

all the people in the world, would understand be

I always thought better of you, but now I'm not

to remind you all how much magic has ruined

Father? Or yours, Grace?"

He stared at them hard.

"That was unnecessary," Menchú said.

"Piss off," Liam snapped.

"This is unproductive," Asanti said.

"Finally, one of you says something that m

Liam said.

"All right," Menchú said. He put his hands up

ture. "If you didn't give her up, then how did Tear

the Hand?"

"Hell if I know," Liam said. "I hate those bastar

as I hate what we're locking away. Not sure how I f

Church most of the time these days. The only thi

I feel about is you people. You're driving me cra

I've got your back. Maybe that's just how stupid I am, but it's true. Against the rest of the Society. Against the Church. It's us against the world right now, and I pick us. I don't even care if you'll have me. I pick us."

Grace, Menchú, and Asanti looked at each other.

"Nice speech," Grace said.

"Screw you," Liam said.

"No, I mean it," Grace said. "Well, yes, I was being a little sarcastic, but I mean it." She turned to Asanti and Menchú. "Even if Liam did sell Sal out—"

"Which I didn't," Liam said.

"But even if he did," Grace said, looking at him, then back to the other two, "he's still not crossing lines Team Two crosses all the time."

"Or at least Team Two's less savory members," Asanti said.

"I think we know who we're talking about here," Grace said.

Menchú nodded.

"We don't know how complicated this problem really is," Grace continued. "But I think we know how to simplify it."

Liam smiled. "You're a human Occam's Razor," he said.

"I don't know what that is," she said.

"We should protest Sal's arrest with Cardinal Varano," Asanti said.

"Of course," Menchú said. "But if Team Two is conducting an exorcism, that won't save Sal."

"And besides, Cardinal Varano will be more interested in covering his own ass than getting to the bottom of things," Grace said.

"You sound like Sal right now," Liam said.

Grace shrugged.

"So," Menchú said. "Asanti, you talk to Varano."

"Done," Asanti said. She got up to go. The Swiss Guard stepped in her way. He looked a little sheepish.

"I have orders," he said, "to keep you in this room. For your protection. In light of recent events."

"Orders from whom?" Asanti said.

The guard hesitated.

"Are they directly from Varano?" Asanti said.

"No."

"So we're clear, then?" Asanti said. She was polite, even kind. But there was an unmistakable edge to her voice.

"Yes," the guard said. He stepped aside.

"He's with me," Asanti said to the guard.

"Grace," Menchú said. "Watch—"

Liam glared.

"Wait here with Liam," Menchú said. "Asanti, I'll follow you out. Call me when you have news."

"You too, Father," Asanti said. And they were gone.

Grace looked around the room, then back at Liam.

"Just so you know," she said, "I still don't trust you."

"You will," Liam said. "I'll make sure of it."

"If we learn that you sold Sal out, I'm going to kill you."

"Grace, if I learn that I sold Sal out, it'll mean I've been possessed too. And if that's happened, I'll beat you to the punch."

3.

H ilary Sansone lifted a glass of wine to her lips and drank.

She waited in her apartment in the center of the city, an older place with crown molding and panels on the walls, an intricate hardwood floor—the kinds of details not found in apartments anywhere anymore. She sat down on a plush couch, put her feet up on an ottoman, took in another mouthful of wine, swallowed it, and closed her eyes.

Someone knocked on the hallway door.

"Who is it?" she asked in a nervous voice.

"Father Menchú." She almost couldn't hear his voice through the door. She got up and put her eye to the peephole.

"Let me in, please," she saw him say.

She paused, looked at the floor for a moment, and then undid the chain on her door and opened it.

"You're in a lot of trouble, Father," she said.

"I know," he said.

"It's only because we've seemed to understand each other over the years, at least a little, that I opened the door. How did you even get into the building?"

Menchú pointed at his collar. "It's good for some things."

"I should call the police," she said.

"Thank you for not doing so already."

She went on as if he hadn't spoken. "You know that the last few incidents at the Vatican have been labeled as terrorism. All of you on Team Three are foreigners. The narrative fits. It would be very easy to sell it to both the police and the newspapers."

"I'm hopeful that there is a reason you haven't set this narrative in motion."

Sansone gazed at Menchú in a way that a dumber man would have misread as a sexual invitation.

"Do you drink wine?"

"Not now, thanks," he said.

"That's smart. I shouldn't have started in on this glass."

"You seem completely sober to me."

"It's not working like I want it to," she said. "Have a seat."

He took a chair opposite the couch. She sat to face him.

"I couldn't help but notice your teammate's discomfort during the hearing after Oklahoma," she said.

"You mean Sal," Menchú said.

"Yes."

"She accused us then of being more interested in preserving ourselves than getting at the truth," Menchú said. "To her, that made a lie of the Society's work."

"How did you respond?" Sansone said.

"Professionally, I hope," Menchú said.

"But you agree with her."

"If I did, I would have no business being here," Menchú said. He frowned. "But a small part of me—maybe not such a small part—sees what she sees."

He looked away from Sansone. If she was going to make the leap to agreeing with him, he wanted her to make it herself.

She nodded.

"I see it too, of course," she said. "How could I not? It's my job to prevaricate, to equivocate. To obfuscate. To tell you the truth, it's distasteful, though that doesn't stop me from being good at it. And I believe in the Society's mission enough to exercise my talents on its behalf."

"I feel the same way," Menchú said. "But that belief isn't absolute, is it?"

"No," Sansone. "Only my belief in God is absolute."

"Good answer," Menchú said. "The textbook answer."

"I write the textbooks," Sansone said.

"Yes," Menchú said, "you do." He let a few moments pass, to provide a chance to turn the conversation. "I'm glad you mentioned that you find some of your work distasteful. It's a relief to me when others in the Society feel that way."

"How could they not?"

"Some enjoy themselves."

"On your team?" Sansone said.

Menchú allowed himself a small chuckle. "My team? Sometimes I wonder how the Society lets me have them at all, with the things they think."

"Because they do the job," Sansone said.

"Yes, but so do all the soldiers on Team One, and I think they take a pride in their work that no one on my team does."

"Team One has that privilege, doesn't it?" Sansone said. "They're superheroes, saving the world from magic and us from ourselves. Our work is a little more complicated."

"True," Menchú said. "That's what gets us in trouble." He was beginning to despair. Sansone was throwing up quite a smokescreen and seemed content to stay behind it. He couldn't force anything out of her, couldn't make her tell him what he'd come there to learn, and she knew it.

He shifted his legs in the chair, as if to start to get up.

"I think that's better, though," Sansone said, "than enjoying the work too much."

Thank God, Menchú thought.

"How so?" he said.

She put her glass of wine on the coffee table in front of her and looked straight at Menchú.

"It's one thing to feel distaste at your job in the service of a good cause. It's quite another to feel that some of your colleagues are undermining that good cause," she said.

"Are you talking about anyone in particular?" Menchú said.

"Someone has to come out and say it," she said. "Desmet and De Vos."

"Ah," Menchú said. "Yes. Did you know Sal has nicknames for the two of them? She told me once. She calls them Balloon and Stretch."

"Bal . . . *looon?*" She laughed, short, a little too hard. Took a deep breath and calmed back down. "That's good," she said.

"The names fit," Menchú said.

"They do," Sansone said. "I even knew which name went with which man." She picked up her wine and took a sip. "I can't help but think, sometimes, that the things that I most dislike about my work are the very things they love. I fear we've created—"

"A few bad apples?" Menchú said.

"Thank you," Sansone said. "Yes. A couple of bad apples."

She took another sip.

"I'm horrified and repulsed by what happened to Sal. What she has become. But not as repelled as I am at what I've learned Desmet and De Vos are up to."

That's as good an opening as I'm going to get, Menchú thought.

"Hilary," he said, "do they still have her?"

"They haven't called in yet. So as far as I know, yes."

"Do you know where?"

"For what they're planning, there can only be one place," Sansone said. She told him, then, about the town, the monastery. "It's a beautiful place, really," she said. "Idyllic. Secluded. Far too nice for the horrible things they do there."

She pursed her lips.

"I suppose I'm telling you all this," she continued, "because I feel that, at last, they've gone too far. They've buried too many people in the monastery's vineyard already. Exorcisms gone wrong, they've always said, though I've sometimes had the feeling their own zeal was as much to blame. And now they've turned against one of our own. Someone I believe they have a personal interest in making trouble for. Someone I respect enough to think she doesn't deserve what they're doing to her."

"Thank you," Menchú said.

"I hope you can do something with what I've told you," Sansone said. "If the situation at the monastery got out of hand, and my team were to lose certain of its members, I can't say I would be sorry. And this goes without saying, but: This conversation, this bottle of wine, your visit here—none of these things happened."

"Understood."

"I'll show you out," she said. "Go get Sal back. Don't call me when it's done."

"What are you going to do then?" Menchú said.

"What I do best," Sansone said. "Write the textbook. Put us back where we always were. If I'm lucky, back before I ever laid eyes on Desmet and De Vos."

"I see," Menchú said.

"Yes," she said. "You do. Call your people."

Menchú took out his phone.

4.

al and the Hand fell for eight seconds. They fell for a thousand
years, through the pink light. The space below them darkened,
solidified, for as far as Sal could see, as if they were plummeting toward the surface of another planet. Or maybe the planet was rushing toward them. A voice, two-toned—one low and rumbling, the other pitched like a baby's—rose from the darkness. At first, Sal couldn't understand it. It was a hissing rush and then a cry, pinched off and arcing upward at the end. It repeated itself and got a little clearer. It was a word, a name. *Hand?* it said. *Hand?*

The surface below curled around them. Towers with walls of crushing black ash, like skyscrapers, like stalagmites, like trees dying in a swamp, rose. Some shot far overhead, blotting out the light. Others were as big as houses, others as big as cars. Some were about the same height she was. Sal and the Hand landed among them, touched down on ground that crunched beneath her feet. She looked down. The ground that at first seemed more or less flat was still more towers, some as tall as her finger, some as tall as her fingernail. Some smaller than that. They kept going, she realized. Somewhere maybe there was a tower as big as a universe. Another one tucked inside an electron, if there were electrons here. How many cities could you fit on the head of a pin? She took a step and understood that, possibly, she had obliterated civilizations under her heel. And maybe something much bigger was coming that would do the same to her.

Hand? the voice called again, angry and urgent.

"Who is that?" Sal said.

The Hand sighed. "The Eye," it said.

A globe of smooth skin with nine small arms protruding from it at odd angles, and no other discernible features, flew down from the top of a nearby tower.

"Hand!" it shouted again. "Why have you come back? I thought we had an agreement."

"We do, we still do," the Hand said. "We won't be here long."

The Eye leveled itself with Sal's head. "Your host?" it said.

The Hand nodded. "She can't stay here much longer like this."

"So I see," the Eye said. It seemed reassured.

"So you'll tell the Tooth?" the Hand said.

"I'll tell Tooth only after you're gone," the Eye said. "It will be very upset you were here at all, but by then, of course, there will be nothing it can do about it." A choking stutter emerged from somewhere on the Eye.

"Are you okay?" Sal said.

"I'm laughing," the Eye said. "Don't you know what laughing sounds like?"

"Are we the only ones here?" Sal said. She looked pointedly at the Hand.

"Ah," the Eye said. "Hand didn't tell you he was banished from this place. What you see here is only the outside. Hand is not allowed to go in anymore. Too dangerous."

"For who?" Sal said.

"For everyone. Hand and us. The war is still too fresh in everyone's minds. The things it destroyed. The things it brought to life, that are still alive, that we are still dealing with. Hand has a lot to answer for."

The Hand made a helpless gesture toward Sal.

"Don't try to belittle what you did here," the Eye said.

"This isn't the first time you tried to take over," Sal said.

"It's at least the fifth," the Eye said. "It would have succeeded if not for Tooth."

"And who is Tooth?"

"A demon we made," the Eye said, "that, at last, got the better of Hand, and allowed us to banish it."

The Hand smiled. "So," it said, "now you've met a little bit of the family."

Something shuddered through Sal.

"The convulsions have stopped," she said.

"Time to go back, then," the Hand said.

"You said you'd let me see Perry first," Sal said.

The Eye laughed again, in its way. "The human you left here?"

The Hand nodded.

"He's my brother," Sal said.

"I'm sorry," the Eye said to Sal, "but Hand promised you something it couldn't deliver. Your brother is inside, where Hand can't go. We can't allow it."

"But you can allow me," Sal said.

"You and Hand are connected," the Eye said.

"I can leave it here if I need to."

"You can't," the Hand said.

"Watch me," Sal said. "I'm not going anywhere until I see my brother." She turned to the Eye. "Take me to him if the Hand can't do it."

The Eye bobbed in the air in what seemed like a bow, or a mockery of one. It moved to the edge of the nearest tower, twice as tall as Sal was, and opened a door. Light and sound streamed through the opening.

"Wait here until I get back," Sal said to the Hand. "I won't be long."

"Don't be," the Hand said. "For both our sakes."

"For mine and my brother's," Sal corrected him. "Not yours."

Sal stepped into the tower, descended a flight of steps, and came up out of the ground, as though the world had flipped over while she was walking. She emerged into orange light, a swarm of sound. She was in a mobbed city that had only marginal use for gravity. Buildings floated in the air, connected to the ground and to each other by long chains of ladders that swayed as the buildings moved. The web of edifices stretched into the sky, as far as Sal could see: small islands of houses in the shapes of rough jewels, enormous structures that looked as though they'd been assembled by switching on a huge magnet and letting the pieces fly together. The ground and the air were full of creatures of too many shapes and sizes for her to take it all in. She dodged past a long, sticklike thing ambling along with five legs and tiny vestigial wings; passed through a cloud of hundreds of tiny beings that sang to one another in sixteen-part harmony; ducked under the legs of a mammoth humanoid that seemed to be made of clay; squeezed between two squat individuals, each with three heads and six arms, gorging themselves on succulent fruits and laughing. The Eye stopped her short in front of a thing no taller than a child, with a tiny head and spindly legs.

"Don't move," the Eye said. "Or it will eat you."

"How long do we wait here?"

"Until it loses interest," the Eye said.

They didn't move. Neither did the creature. Without warning, an enormous hand shot down from the building right above them and scooped up the little thing. Sal watched as the hand brought the thing to a mouth in the side of the building, closed a set of rocky teeth around its neck, and pulled off its head.

"That's one way for it to lose interest," the Eye said. "This way." It motioned to a ladder, and Sal began to climb into the sky. Above her, the air was thick with creatures in flight. The smaller ones flitted past each other, landed on the sides of houses, and climbed into windows. The bigger ones lumbered through the air at speeds so slow it seemed they were moving through water instead. A three-limbed being with a long snout was coming down the ladder Sal was climbing up; as they neared, the creature let out a snort and flipped to the underside of the ladder, continuing on its way. Following the Eye, Sal reached a building that looked like a salt crystal blown out of all proportion. She walked along its surface to another ladder, leading to a tiny island spinning slowly in the air. There was a break in the buildings above her, and she looked up. Holes in the sky, tattered at the edges, had light and traffic streaming in and out of them, coming in from elsewhere, heading out.

"Here," the Eye said, and pointed to a window. Sal jumped through it. She landed on a hard, black floor polished to a sheen. There was light at one end, a small room made of glass. And there, imprisoned behind a tangle of black briars, was Perry, sitting cross-legged, his head down, his eyes closed, less like someone meditating and more like a little kid who just got in trouble.

"I told you he was safe," the Eye said.

"No, you didn't," Sal said. She walked up to her brother. "Perry," she said. Perry didn't move. She said his name again. There was still no response. She reached out and put her hand on his shoulder. His eyes snapped open and he screamed, terrified. "Perry!" she said again. "Perry, it's me. Sal."

Perry's breathing slowed. His eyes went from wide, to a squint, to the eyes she knew. The ones that shone when he'd figured out how to cause trouble and pin it on her. The ones belonging to the kid who stole licks of ice cream and jumped off a dock with her one summer. He always jumped first.

"Sal?" he said. "How did you get here?"

"Long story," she said.

"Can I go now?"

Sal looked at the Eye.

"This is Hand's place," the Eye said. "A place it made. Only Hand can unlock it."

"It can't even get *in* here, you said."

Without moving or speaking, the Eye conveyed the distinct impression that this was Sal's problem.

Sal looked back at Perry. "No. Not yet," she said.

"But you're here. Why can't I go?" He seemed drugged.

"You just can't yet, okay?"

"I've been here so long."

"I know," Sal said. "I'm trying. I'm close, I promise."

"I hardly remember who you are. Or Mom or Dad or anyone anymore."

"Perry, stop it."

"It's so hard to hang on to all that here."

"I know," Sal said. "Do you remember when we were kids?"

"No," Perry said.

"I'm not done. We were playing at the school playground with a bunch of other kids, and someone kicked the ball onto the roof. And you said you'd go get it. Do you remember that?"

Perry just looked at her.

"There was a metal ladder attached to the side of the school that led up to the roof. Who knows what it was for. But we'd been told not to climb it and none of us did, because we were too scared. You climbed it all the time, though, and you did then to get that ball."

Perry smiled.

"I remember watching you disappear when you got on the roof. For a minute it seemed like you were gone for good. Then the ball came sailing back down, onto the playground, and all the kids cheered, and you stood on the edge of the roof like Superman, just taking it all in. Do you remember that?"

"I think so."

"Then you'll know what happened next," Sal said.

"I fell," Perry said.

"That's right. You fell off the roof of the school, right onto the pavement. It wasn't that high, but it was high enough. You fell and landed hard and for a second you didn't move. I thought you were dead."

"You did?" Perry said. "You never told me that."

"I did," Sal said. "I remember wondering what on earth I was going to tell Mom and Dad. We gathered around you and you just lay there. Then you coughed a couple times, got up, and threw up against the side of the school."

"I remember that part," Perry said.

"But that was all, Perry. You were alive. No broken bones. No huge cuts. Just a bunch of scrapes and the wind knocked out of you, and you lost your lunch. That's it. Do you remember?"

"Yes," Perry said.

"This is going to be just like that, Perry. Like you fell off the roof and were gone for a minute, but you're going to return from this as if nothing ever happened. Got it?"

"Yeah, got it," Perry said. "Just one question."

"What is it?" Sal asked.

"Why are you crying?"

"I'm not crying."

"Yes, you are."

Sal turned away for a second. Turned back.

"Just know that I'm coming to get you, okay?" She reached her hand through the briars. Perry reached out to her. Their hands met and held.

"I miss you, Sal," Perry said.

"I miss you, too," Sal said.

Very touching, she heard the Hand say, from somewhere above her mouth. *But you have to go. And I'm impressed that you'd lie to your brother like that. You're not getting him back.*

I will, Sal said. *You'll see.*

Far away, if she concentrated on it, she could feel a tugging at her chest and wrists.

"Bye, Perry," she said.

5.

We're too late," Grace said. She sat in the passenger seat as Liam
drove. Menchú was in the backseat. The car bounced along
a road that used to be cobbled but had fallen into disrepair.

"Don't be so sure," Menchú said. "I am heartened by my talk with
Sansone."

"And how did Asanti do with Varano?"

Menchú sighed. "He suggested we let Team Two do its work."

"That's weird," Liam said.

"That's protocol," Menchú said. "Maybe Monsignor Usher has
a little too much sway with him. But still: protocol."

"Ass covering," Grace said.

"Yes," Menchú said.

Liam turned the car onto a winding dirt track.

"This must be it," he said.

"Are you sure?" Grace said.

"It looks right," Menchú said.

"Right?" Liam said. "It looks like a fucking cliché."

The car was heading toward the vineyard's crumbling outer wall.

Up ahead, dark against a night sky set aglow by a half-moon, they could see the outline of the monastery, built on a rise in the land.

"Should we stop here?" Liam asked.

"It doesn't matter now," Grace said. "If they were worried about visitors, I think they would have at least closed the gate."

"They must have thought the seclusion was enough," Menchú said.

"Or didn't want to draw too much attention to the fact they're here," Grace said.

The road ended at a small square paved with cobblestones. There were three vehicles there that looked like moving vans. A man stood near the monastery's entrance with a rifle. He approached the car with a confident swagger but didn't seem wary of them.

"I don't recognize him," Menchú said.

"Good," Grace said. "That probably means he doesn't recognize us."

Liam lowered the window. "Good evening, sir!" he said in Italian.

The guard nodded. "Are you a tourist?"

"My accent gives me away every time," Liam said, and laughed. "Yes. I'm here with my wife and father-in-law visiting the countryside, and we seem to have gotten turned around."

There was no outward physical sign from either Grace or Menchú, but Liam was pretty sure he could feel them wincing. *Did someone say 'cliché'?*

"I'm sorry," the guard said. "This is private property. I can't help you."

"You can't tell me where I am?" Liam said.

"You're on private property," the guard repeated. "Now please go before I call the police."

The guard was standing out of reach.

"I'm not sure I like your tone of voice," Liam said quietly.

"What?" the guard said, and took a step closer.

"I said," Liam said more quietly, "I don't like your tone of voice."

The guard's face, which had been impassive at first, showed his annoyance.

"I *will* call the police," he said.

"I have a better idea," Liam said. "How about *I* call the police? You don't look like any kind of authority I recognize, which means you probably shouldn't have that rifle. They could put you away for that, couldn't they?"

"Listen," the guard said, closing in on Liam to try to intimidate him. "I don't know who you are—"

Liam punched him in the face. He stumbled backward and fell. Liam was out of the car in a flash, on top of the guard. He hit him four more times, fast, and the guard was out.

Liam shook out his hand. "Ow," he said. "I might have just cut open a knuckle."

"On him?" Grace said. She and Menchú were already out of the car too. "You fight monsters every week."

"They're different," Liam said.

"Apparently. We need to train more."

"Yes, we do."

Liam gave Grace an expectant look. *Do you believe me now? That I didn't betray you all? Are we okay?* Grace gave him nothing back.

"Let's go," Menchú said. "It's a miracle no one else was out here to see this."

"Traveling light," Grace said.

Liam searched through the guard's pockets, found a set of keys, unlocked the door, and they were in. They gave their eyes a moment to adjust to the dark. There was just enough light to see by. The monastery really was crumbling. There were small holes in the roof, water stains on the floor. Here and there the rain had gotten the better of the building and a wall had caved in, the floorboards had given way. They passed a row of broken windows and reached a stone staircase that seemed to follow the slope of the hill, leading up and into the building. Somewhere ahead they heard people arguing. Liam pointed in that direction, and Grace and Menchú nodded.

At the top of the stairs they saw sky and the silhouettes of two more guards. Menchú gave them a signal to group together to make a plan, but it was too late. Liam bounded up the stairs, grabbed a head in each hand, and smashed them against each other until both of them fell down. He turned around and motioned for them to come up.

"That was an unnecessary risk," Menchú whispered.

"Worked, didn't it?" Liam whispered back.

The moon was brighter now, the arguing louder. They could tell where the voices were coming from. They knew where to go.

"Sandro, don't touch the straps again," Stretch hissed.

Sal lay unmoving on the board, the straps still restraining her. There was blood and vomit on her shirt, on her face. The four men in Team Two had closed their little red books and stopped chanting. Balloon and Stretch still loomed over her with gloves and crop.

"Pray," Balloon barked at them. "George. Sandro. Marcus. David. Pray."

The guards at the perimeter shifted from foot to foot. Stretch raised the crop again.

"Stop," Sandro said. "The exorcism is not working."

"Not working!" Balloon said. "Look at her. We are nearing the end. We have calmed her."

"I am looking at her," Sandro said. "I think you killed her."

"Is she still breathing?" Marcus said.

Stretch did not check. "Of course she is."

"I'm not so sure," David said.

George gave Balloon a long, hard look, as though he were putting together a longer story. "You seem pretty calm for someone who may have just ended another person's life," he finally said.

Balloon turned to George. "What exactly are you implying?"

"That you have a contingency plan for this. That there's a reason you control a monastery with several acres of unused land."

"George," said Stretch, patting his crop. "You're newer to the team, and this is your first exorcism, so I'm going to allow that your line of questioning is the result of shock brought about by what I understand can be a frightening experience."

"I don't know about that," said George. "It looks to me more like you've overstepped your authority. This isn't how Team Two works."

"Exorcisms are well within our jurisdiction," Balloon said.

"Yes. The kind where priests gather around a victim of possession— without touching her—and help her to get the demon out, through prayer, kindness, and support. Not this."

"The straps are for her own safety," Stretch said.

"And the crop?" George said. "And those gloves, the magic ones? Are those for her own safety too?"

Balloon narrowed his eyes. "It's very brave of you to talk this way after the work has been done. I didn't hear your objections while it was happening."

"I regret that now," George said.

"Regretting your actions doesn't make you less complicit," Stretch said.

"So," Sandro said, "you're saying that we may actually have killed her?"

"Sometimes," Balloon said, "when you separate the demon from its host, the demon takes too much with it for the host to come back."

"How many people have you killed out here?" George said.

"That isn't a question you have the authority to ask me, and as such, it's one I don't need to answer," Balloon said.

"That is not at all reassuring."

"It isn't my job to reassure you," Balloon said. "It's my job to do the will of God, to help protect the world he created from being taken over by the creatures he cast out of heaven. It is not clean work, but it is holy. If I would reassure you of anything, it is that regardless of what I have done that looks ugly through earthly eyes, I sleep soundly at night, knowing that I will surely look upon the face of my Savior when I die. Can you say the same?"

"I think," said George, "that maybe you have been doing this job for far too long."

Balloon looked at Stretch. "How did a man of such little faith come to be on our team?"

"I don't know," said Stretch, "but he won't be for much longer."

"You're damn right I won't," said George. He moved to undo the straps.

"Don't touch her!" Stretch said.

"I'm not," George said. "I'm letting her go. If she's even still alive."

He loosened a strap. Balloon stepped forward to intervene. Sandro intercepted him and held him back.

"Take your hands off me!" Balloon said.

Stretch took a few steps in their direction, raised his arm, and sent the crop across Sandro's back. Sandro let out a short cry but didn't let Balloon go. Now, from the other side of the slab, Marcus and David undid the straps around Sal and pulled them off. Sal still didn't move. Marcus shook her. Nothing. George just took a step back. Balloon stopped struggling, and Sandro dropped to his knees to vomit from the pain.

"She's dead," David said. "She's really dead."

The guards at the perimeter were craning their necks, trying to see.

"What's happened?" one of them shouted.

"Pray for her," Balloon said. "Like I asked you to. Pray for her soul."

"Probably better if you pray for your own," Liam said, stepping into the courtyard. His face fell as he saw Sal, heavy and motionless. Grace was only a couple of steps behind him.

"Is that Sal?" Grace said.

"I'm afraid so," Liam said.

Their fists tightened simultaneously, like they did when they used to spar.

"You want to intimidate us?" Balloon said. "You're just criminals, I hope you understand. We'll turn you over to the police as terrorists."

Menchú stepped up behind Liam and Grace.

"Guards," Balloon continued, "these three have wrought havoc upon the Vatican and the Society. They have destroyed property and caused loss of life. Perhaps most egregiously, they allowed one of their own to be possessed by an unholy spirit for so long that, it appears, we were unable to separate the demon from the host without her death. In the meantime, who knows how many of our secrets the demon learned? Centuries of work undone in weeks. Round them up so they may accept whatever judgment the earthly and heavenly powers see fit to render."

The guards began to move.

"Liam, Grace," Menchú said. "Get it done."

If Liam and Grace exchanged a glance, it was too short to see. They split up. For the guards, the experience of fighting Grace was like being victims in a cruel magic show. The spot where Grace had been, where they had trained the barrels of their guns, was empty. Then their weapons were out of their hands, flying through the air, clattering to the ground. One guard was leveled as though he'd been hit with a cannonball. Another spun around five times where he stood and fell. Yet another was swept off his feet; for a moment his toes were higher than his head. He hit the dirt hard and didn't get back up. In the second and a half the remaining guards had to react, they dropped their guns and started running. The guns didn't connect with the ground before they did.

By that time, Liam had reached the center of the courtyard. The four members of Team Two who'd held their red books and chanted, protesting only too late, dropped to their knees in surrender. Balloon and Stretch did not.

Balloon flexed his fingers inside his gloves. Stretch raised the crop, ready to use it. But Liam was angry, and Liam was faster. Before Stretch could swing the crop around, Liam had buried his fist in Stretch's cheek. Stretch's head snapped back. He pulled it forward again and spat out a tooth. His arm swung around to flail at Liam, but Liam caught it at the wrist and held it there for a second, then twisted it behind Stretch's back. Stretch cried out and dropped the crop.

"Not as easy when your victim can move, is it?" Liam said. He couldn't do anything about Balloon, who was coming up behind him, hands extended, still wearing the gloves. Balloon had his fingers close enough to touch Liam's neck when he was pulled back. He staggered and fell. Grace stood over him. She put her foot on the side of his face, pressing his head into the ground.

"Touch me with those gloves," she hissed, "or any part of you, and I stomp."

"Let me up," Balloon said.

"Promise to behave?" Grace said.

"You bitch," Balloon said.

Grace smiled. "Showing your true colors. Always knew you had it in you. Promise to behave?"

"Yes," Balloon said.

Grace took her foot off his face. All around them the guards were moaning. The four acolytes of Team Two were still on their knees, silent. Balloon scrambled to his feet, but he and Stretch just stood there, like children who had broken something. Which was when Menchú approached Sal.

He laid his hand on her forehead, like a father testing for a fever. Said her name over and over again. And she moved. First just her eyeballs twitched under her closed lids. Then she began to shift, waking up. She opened her eyes.

"Menchú," Sal said.

"Are you all here?" Menchú asked.

"Yes." She sat up, wincing. "Both of us." She looked at Balloon and Stretch. "All this was for nothing. You're frauds."

"The demon remains inside you?" Balloon said.

"Yes," Sal said.

She felt the rustling in her head turn into a rush, a glimmer of ecstasy, of losing herself like she had in the Archives, and started to panic. The Hand was still weak, but so was she. She pushed back, but couldn't keep the Hand all the way down.

Here I come, the Hand said to her.

She got to her feet. The Hand propped her up. It was hard to tell whose decision that had been.

"Careful," Menchú said. "You're hurt."

"Get away from me," Sal said. "For God's sake, get away."

Inside her skull, she heard the Hand laughing.

"Sal?" Liam said. His voice was streaked with worry, even alarm.

Those gloves, the Hand said. *I can do things with them.*

I won't let you, Sal said. She pushed against it, harder.

You don't have to let me do anything, the Hand said.

She felt a sudden shift in her head. If they'd been wrestling, it would have been a flip and a half pin.

She was made to take two steps toward Balloon. Strength and power surged through her. She was filled with a fire that purified and cleansed, but could not hurt her. She reached out to Balloon.

No, Sal said. *I won't let you do this.*

"Sal—" Menchú said.

Sal watched herself take Balloon's hands in her hands. Felt, against her will, a rising pleasure in the confused, then stricken look on his face when he realized that the gloves weren't hurting her, that she was drawing their power into herself.

"You know," the Hand said, "Sal's had nicknames for you two since she first saw you. Stretch"—she nodded toward him—"and Balloon."

Before either of them could respond, the Hand put one of Balloon's hands in Sal's mouth and blew. Balloon inflated. First his hand, under the glove, splitting the fabric. Then his forearm bulged. His elbow burst out of its sleeve, kept expanding. His biceps disappeared into his side. Balloon started to scream as his chest stretched outward, ripping his shirt, the skin shining under the strain. Then the air moved up his neck and cut his screams off.

Sal felt both herself and the Hand flow into him, felt the Hand growing to fill the space. Felt Balloon's bones creak and pop. The Hand was going to kill him. Sal knew it, could see how it would go. For a few more seconds, Balloon's head and thighs inflated at the same time, and he began to float into the air. His head became nearly spherical, his ears like little knots on either side, the shocked, silent expression on his face looking almost drawn on.

Time to pop this balloon, the Hand said. Sal felt them both flowing into Balloon's head. In a second, the top of Balloon's head would tear open from the pressure, and everything would come out at once with a sound like a wet cough. It would be so—*funny.*

That wasn't her. That was the Hand. And as much as she hated Balloon, she wasn't going to let him die. Wasn't going to give the Hand the satisfaction of using her to kill him.

She pushed—for herself, for Balloon, for everyone on Team Three. For Perry. For the past few months and everything she'd had to go through. She pushed.

Balloon was still floating in the air. He gasped.

Why save this horrible man? the Hand said.

Because you don't get to decide when he dies, Sal said. *Got it?*

The Hand hung on. She pushed again.

You'll regret sparing him, the Hand said.

I can live with that, Sal said. *More than I can live with you.*

One more push, and Sal and the Hand were flowing back out of Balloon, out of his head, his chest, his thighs, his arms, his hand, his fingers. Balloon fell to the ground and screamed. He was a different shape, a jumble of a man. But he was alive.

Grace and Liam stood in place with their mouths open. Sandro gagged. The guards who had regained consciousness looked stunned.

"You see," Stretch said. "This is why we need exorcism." He found his full voice. "You will be called to account, and repent for your sins. Do you understand? There are times to follow protocols. To go through the proper procedures. To have hearings. To render judgments. And then there are times to use your authority to make judgments yourself."

He called to the guards. "Shoot them."

The guards looked at Team Three, and at Stretch.

"There is a demon within her, and the others are in league with her!" Stretch yelled. "Do you need more proof?"

None of the guards said anything. One of them lowered his weapon.

"You will all be called to account for your insubordination."

"Good," George said. "I'm out."

"Me too," said Sandro.

The other guards lowered their weapons.

"You ask too much," Marcus said.

Balloon writhed on the ground. "Exert your authority," he said to Stretch. Stretch walked over to one of the guards. It was clear what he was about to do, or try.

"Run," Grace said to Liam and Menchú.

They ran, sweeping Sal up, out of the courtyard, back down the stairs through the dark monastery, to the car. Grace had the engine started. Liam was last in. He closed the door and shot a glance toward the monastery.

"Are those gunshots I hear?" he said.

"Who knows?" Grace said. "Let's go."

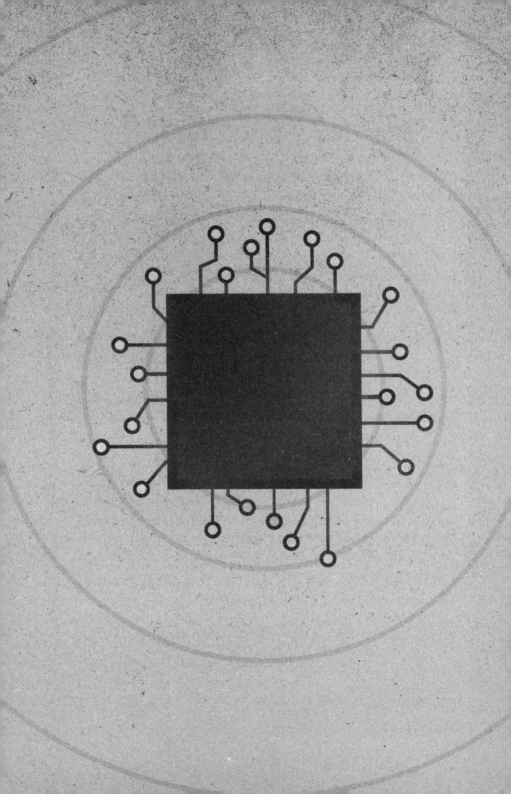

EPISODE
15

THINGS LOST

MARGARET DUNLAP

1.

Asanti rejoined the rest of the team that night. They met her at a deserted bus stop outside Rome, really nothing more than a patch of dirt on the side of the unlit country road, marked by a wooden post that might have once held a sign but now relied on regional memory to carry its message. Grace drove a circuitous route to be sure none of Balloon and Stretch's people were following them, while Menchú gradually guided them toward their destination. Asanti squeezed into the back with Sal and Liam, and Sal could feel her relief to see them all alive and whole. Sal wished she could share the feeling.

"Were you followed?" Menchú asked from the front seat.

Asanti shook her head. "No sign of anyone. And on a road this empty, I would have noticed."

"After what happened in the monastery, Balloon and Stretch will be licking their wounds for a bit," said Liam.

"Not for long," said Menchú. He turned to Grace. "We should get moving." Grace nodded, already putting the car in gear.

"What happened at the monastery?" asked Asanti.

"Long, painful story," said Sal.

"What happened in Rome?" asked Menchú.

Asanti sighed. "I went back to Cardinal Varano, who remains as dedicated as ever to saving himself paperwork. However, I think I was able to convince him that Balloon and Stretch will end up causing him even more paperwork than Sal's possession. Unfortunately, he won't make a move to help us until we have our own house in order."

"Which means getting rid of the monster in my head," said Sal. She was recovering faster from their ordeal than the Hand was, but she could feel it gathering its strength, waiting until it was ready to make its move.

"Yes," said Asanti. "But if we can do that, Sal's testimony should convince Varano to shut down Balloon and Stretch once and for all."

"That's a big if," said Liam.

"About that," said Asanti. "We need tools to force the Hand back to its home dimension. I tried to go back to the Archives after my meeting with the cardinal, to retrieve the *Book of the Hand*, but our entire wing is under lockdown. The new guards were keeping me out of the Archives. *Me.* I don't know who they report to, Arturo, but it wasn't anyone friendly to us. I was looking for Sansone when I got your 'not safe, leave now' message. Three buses later . . . Well, here we are."

The group fell into silence, broken only by the thrum and rattle of the tires against the poorly maintained rural road. Sal looked out the window, but all she could see was black land spread beneath endless blue-black sky. The car's headlights sliced the road ahead of them, a tiny bubble that seemed wholly inadequate to keep the pressing dark at bay.

Their destination proved to be a beautiful stone villa situated on five rural acres outside Rome. The building was more than three hundred years old, set back from the main road behind a low wall more decorative than functional. Behind the main house a fig tree shaded a flagstone patio, and grapes grew over a wooden pergola. Beyond, a small guest house stood between an ancient olive grove and a lake.

The guest house had been originally built as a pump house, then expanded to store olive oil. Now the only signs of its former purposes were wooden casks repurposed as end tables and the old well cover located under a throw rug in the center of the larger bedroom. Asanti, Grace, Liam, and Sal waited as Menchú rolled aside the rug and lifted the heavy cover, revealing the inky blackness of the stone shaft below.

Sal swallowed and asked, "What's down there?"

"Somewhere we can rest."

In the last twenty-four hours Sal had suffered an exorcism, died, then come back to life after a harrowing trip through a demon dimension. The prospect of stopping in safety, even for a little while, was too much to refuse.

Once the well cover was back in place, the blackness inside the shaft was complete. Asanti, clinging to the ladder between Grace below and Sal above, felt a bit of mortar crumble away from the wall and silently counted until she heard a quiet splash. It was a very long way down.

Menchú snapped a chem light and passed it down the line to Grace. "Do you remember how to open the passage?" he asked.

"Yes," said Grace.

"Are you sure? It was twenty years ago."

"Less for me," said Grace. The yellow-green light clipped to her belt descended, and Asanti hurried to keep up.

It wasn't far to climb, really. After ten feet or so—that only felt like they stretched for miles—Grace stopped again. A press and turn of a loose stone and a hidden door swung inward to reveal a gently sloping stone-lined passage, just wide and tall enough for them to walk single file without stooping. Once they were all inside, Menchú took the light and the lead.

After another few hundred feet of twists and turns, the passage joined a cave system that opened into a natural cavern stretching far beyond the reach of their meager light source. With some fumbling, Menchú located an oil lamp, and the sickly green of the chemical illumination was eclipsed by a warm golden glow.

Sal caught her breath. The cave was huge. The ceiling stretched easily twenty feet above their heads, and the far walls were hidden in shadow. What she could see of the space was lined with rows of shelves filled with bedding, emergency supplies, and books. "It's the Archives," she said.

"No," said Asanti. One word held all the sadness of an exile longing for her lost homeland.

"It's a bolt-hole," said Menchú. "This cave system was discovered during World War Two by the Italian resistance. They told a few priests friendly to their cause, but for . . . various reasons . . . its existence was never officially shared with the Vatican."

Asanti made a noise that implied she had clear opinions about what those reasons were.

"It felt appropriate," Menchú continued. "And since I found out about it through another priest, not the Society, there's no reason to think that Team Two knows about it. We should be able to rest here, for a little while."

"As long as we're sure the other teams don't know," said Asanti. "I mean, someone told you all those years ago, and if Balloon and Stretch—"

"If they do," Liam said, "we'll deal with them. But we had to go somewhere, didn't we?"

Asanti made a tired, waving gesture to erase her previous statement. "You're right. Of course. I'm just . . ."

"You're exhausted," said Grace. "You all are."

Grace hadn't included herself in that assessment, but even she seemed worn thin by their last few hours.

Menchú looked over his group. "We'll be safe here. I promise."

Whether because of habit, faith, or desperation, they all believed him.

Menchú set himself the first watch. The others slept, except for Grace, who—when she realized she couldn't convince Menchú to rest—wandered into the back stacks of their hideout's collection looking for something to read. He knew that he should listen to her. They couldn't afford to stop for long, and he should rest while he had the chance.

Menchú pondered his team: They quivered on the edge of fracture. Any jolt could shatter their newly healed alliance. He knew his aura of certainty helped glue them together, but he was running on momentum and adrenaline. If he stopped moving forward, moving anywhere, he wasn't sure he'd be able to start again.

Gradually, the others began to wake, internal clocks telling them that the sun had risen even without any visual cues inside the cave.

As soon as Liam was up, he pulled out his laptop.

"Can you get a signal down here?" Menchú asked.

Liam shrugged. "I've got a repeater set up. We're fine."

Grace emerged from the stacks. "Will they be able to trace us if we go digging into the Society's system?"

Liam gave her a hard look. "I'm not going to log in and check my e-mail," he said. "If I go through a VPN, we can see what's showing up in the public news sources without anyone figuring out who or where we are. The last week has been loud enough that the Society will have had to put out some kind of cover story to explain what's been going on."

"Oh," said Grace. Then, "I didn't mean to imply you—"

"I know," said Liam, cutting short her impending apology.

After that, the room fell silent, save for the tap of Liam's fingers on his keyboard.

Maybe an hour later, Sal woke with a start and joined them, followed by Asanti. "Find anything?" Sal asked. She rubbed at the fatigue etched into her face, but only succeeded in moving it around a little.

Liam grimaced. "Not much. The Vatican put out a press release that there was a threat against the pope, and the palace has been closed to tourists. Other than that, it's all pretty usual."

"That will be Sansone," said Grace.

"Wait," said Menchú. "Click on that story there. Down at the bottom."

It was a small item, easily overlooked next to a cluster of buttons and site navigation links. When Liam pulled it up, Menchú felt his gut go cold.

Sal squinted. "Is that Latin?"

"Yes," said Asanti. Menchú couldn't even bring himself to nod.

"What does it say?"

When Menchú didn't answer, Asanti leaned in closer to read the screen. It was a short missive, only a few hundred words, and it didn't take Asanti long to decipher the message.

"Oh, Arturo. I'm so sorry."

"What is it?" asked Sal. Liam looked equally confused.

"Tell them," said Menchú to Asanti, then turned and walked away. He didn't want to be the one who broke the news. If he said the words, it would only make them real. It was bad enough hearing them in Asanti's soft alto.

"It's an announcement that the Vatican has begun the process of having Father Menchú defrocked."

Menchú closed his ears to the others' sympathy and disbelief. He couldn't cope with them right now. He had reached his limit, and so Arturo Menchú stopped.

2.

Sal's watch told her she'd been in that dark cavern less than a day. It felt like weeks. She was exhausted, but when she tried to sleep she could feel the Hand gathering strength, pushing to get out. When she actually slept, she dreamed agonizing dreams of the exorcism, of her skin on fire, of Perry trapped in a demon fortress.

A demon fortress in a demon dimension. Her brother's spirit was trapped in a hellish prison, tethered to this world by his own body, which Sal had helped to keep alive in a secret Vatican clinic. How much had she forced him to suffer, hoping he would return to her?

What have I left him to now?

She could see Perry suffering, not bound by a demon to some cruel parody of the afterlife, but at the hands of Team Two's less gentle ministers. Balloon and Stretch whispering, "If we can't have you, we'll take him instead."

Sal sat up with a jolt. She must have fallen asleep. She hoped she had fallen asleep. Still, the dream shook her. If Balloon and Stretch realized that her brother was a helpless hostage in the Vatican, they would try to find a way to use him as leverage against her. Would they code their threats into a Vatican press release, like the news about Menchú, to draw them out of hiding? In her heart, Sal knew she wouldn't be able to stop herself from taking that bait.

The voice in the back of her head whispered, *He's your little brother. Keep him safe.*

Except Sal didn't know how to save her brother without falling into Balloon's and Stretch's hands. And she couldn't help Perry if she was dead.

Worse than that, Sal wasn't even sure she could trust her own thoughts. Not with the Hand inside her, still whispering.

Sal was sure of one thing, though: If she didn't get out of this cave and clear her head, she was going to go fucking mental.

Sal looked up at the cloud-covered sky. They were near enough to Rome that she could still see the glow of the city on the horizon, but far enough that—she suspected—on a clearer night she would have been able to see the stars. She picked her way through the shadows of the olive grove, pausing at every unexpected noise.

In retrospect, maybe sneaking out into the dark hadn't been the best plan to settle her nerves. But at least out here she wouldn't fall asleep.

A twig snapped, and Sal froze.

She couldn't see anyone, but that only made the silence more unnerving. *Just because they're out to get you, doesn't mean you can't be paranoid.*

Sal had just about convinced herself she was hearing things when a dark figure detached itself from the shadow of a bent tree trunk. Sal held her breath. It was coming toward her.

Too late to avoid a confrontation now. Whoever this was, they couldn't know where the others were—or they would have been waiting for her to emerge from the guest house. That simplified Sal's priorities. Keep her pursuer from finding the others. Outrun them if she could. If not, well, she'd already died once in the last forty-eight hours. Maybe this time it would be a quicker and more permanent process. Sal waited until the figure slipped into another shadow, then took off running from the guest house as fast as she could. The whip wounds in her side tugged and burned. *Thank you ever so much, Team Two.*

Sal stuck to the trees at first, figuring that the cover was to her advantage, except that it also meant she had no way of telling if she had managed to shake the mysterious figure. She needed a plan beyond "run."

Okay, then. She'd just have to take her pursuer out of the equation. That decision made, Sal looked for her best opportunity.

There. Three steps, two, one . . . Sal leaped to catch an overhanging branch, hoping to pull herself into position for an ambush from above.

A hand snagged her ankle. When had she lost her lead? Her pursuer's grip was monstrously strong. Sal kicked for all she was worth, but couldn't shake free.

A voice below hissed: "Sal! Stop it!"

She kicked harder.

There was a sharp yank on her foot, and Sal was falling.

An instant later, stunned and winded on the ground, Sal felt a weight settle on her back. The voice returned, whispering, "I'm not going to hurt you."

She tried to roll, but was completely pinned. She took a breath to scream when a cold weight settled behind her right ear. Gun. Fuck.

Sal went still.

"I only want to talk. If I let you up, are you going to try to run again?"

The voice was calmer now, and while still soft, the speaker was no longer whispering. In fact, the voice was familiar. It was . . .

"Aaron?"

"Indeed."

Sal rolled onto her back, and this time, Aaron didn't stop her. He even stood up so that she could climb to her feet. The gun, if there had ever been one, was no longer visible.

Sal really, really hated magic.

"What are you doing here?" Sal asked. "Did the Hand summon you to Rome too? I hate to break it to you, but the demon reunion has been canceled."

"I didn't come for the Hand," said Aaron. "I came to see you."

"Why?"

"I can help you. The Vatican has been locked down. You won't be able to get past security—"

"Thanks for the vote of confidence."

"—without my help," Aaron finished.

"What makes you so sure we're going back to the Archives?"

Aaron didn't even blink. "Because you have to."

He was right, of course. The *Book of the Hand* was their only chance to pry the demon out of the corners of her mind—and she had to help Perry.

Menchú had warned Sal: *Demons offer you what you want. But they will always ask for more than you can pay.*

Sal wanted. She wanted more than anything.

She licked suddenly dry lips. "What's the price?"

Before Aaron could answer, a Grace-shaped shadow fell from the trees and knocked him cold.

Sal looked at Grace in utter shock. "Were you following me?"

Grace rose to her feet. "Be glad I was. Next time you decide to do something moronic like take a walk while you're supposed to be in hiding I might not be around to save you from your own stupidity."

Sal frowned. "Why didn't you knock him out earlier?"

"I thought you needed the exercise."

Grace was trying for her usual deadpan, but Sal heard the tension there. She held back a shiver. *If Grace is worried enough to let it show, we are well and truly screwed.* Sal toed Aaron's inert form. "What do we do with him now?" She suspected her own attempt at nonchalance was just as transparent.

Grace bent down and heaved Aaron onto one shoulder. "Don't suppose you brought any rope?"

Asanti had noticed when Grace snuck out, and she expected her to return presently with a penitent Sal in tow. The unconscious man slung between them was rather a surprise, however.

The man, Aaron, seemed less startled than one might expect to wake tied to a chair in the middle of a dimly lit cave.

He blinked, taking in their faces and his surroundings in the dim light. Asanti held out a cup of water, and he nodded. After a few careful sips, only wincing a little, he said, "Well, this saves me convincing Sal to introduce me to the rest of you."

"What are you doing here?" asked Asanti.

"At the moment?" He gestured as well as he could with his hands bound behind him. Grace had tied him, so there wasn't much slack in the ropes, but he still managed to convey a fatigued sense of: *What does it look like I'm doing?*

Asanti glanced back to Menchú, looking for where to go next.

They rarely needed to interrogate people so explicitly, but this was the sort of field activity where Menchú, by rights, should be in the lead. Unfortunately, he didn't seem eager to get up and do his damn job. Asanti was sure Aaron had noticed the shift in her attention. *Well, at least someone is learning something from this exercise,* she thought. If Menchú was out for this round, they were left with the archivist, the hacker, the hitter, or the cop to take point. Asanti nodded to Sal. *Go ahead.*

"Let's start with simple questions: How did you find us?" Sal asked.

Aaron's lips twisted into a smile. "I've always been able to track you," he said. "Thanks to your little passenger. Do you really think we first met by coincidence?"

"You were following the Hand."

"Yes."

"Why?"

"That was the mission I was given."

"By who?"

"Whom."

Asanti had never seen Sal want to slap someone so badly. Training held her back. Grace had no such compunctions. The room felt her hand crack against Aaron's face.

"Answer the question," Grace said.

Aaron didn't flinch from the slap or the tone. He stared Grace down until, unbelievably, she was the one who blinked and withdrew. Only then did Aaron turn back to Sal. "Ask a question that matters, and I'll answer it. Don't waste my time or yours on irrelevant details."

"I'd call your mission and your motivation very relevant," Sal returned.

Aaron sighed. "I am not attempting to track the Hand out of a desire to join a thrall army and release a flood of magic to destroy life on Earth as it is currently known. You want the demon safely contained, as do I. Since my objectives and yours align, I sought you out to propose a collaboration."

"Are you saying you can remove this thing from my head?" asked Sal.

"Not without the book," he said. "If I could do that on my own, I would have done it when we first met, months ago."

"You knew this thing was in my head all along? Why didn't you tell me?"

"I tried. You weren't eager to trust me, and if I'd said it plainly, the Hand would have grown even more cautious—hidden itself so deep you would not have found it until it was too late."

"It's pretty damn late," Sal said. "The bastard almost destroyed the world. I *died* yesterday."

"It would have been worse."

"How?"

"You got better, didn't you?"

"*We* can get it out of my head with the book," said Sal. "What do we need you for?"

"You need me if you want to get back into your archives without being arrested the moment you set foot in Vatican City. Also," he added, "I suspect that the book isn't the only thing you'd like to retrieve once you're there." His gaze took in all of them, but finally settled on Menchú.

Menchú looked up. He bore the weight of Aaron's regard steadily and without fear.

"What," Menchú asked, "do you ask in return for this valuable assistance?"

Aaron's default expression read something close to smug. But he only looked tired as he replied, "Nothing you haven't lost already."

Once it was clear that Aaron didn't plan to say anything more, Sal left him tied to his chair and busied herself taking inventory of their supplies. Aaron probably had other limiting factors in mind when he said they couldn't hide forever, but he wasn't wrong. Although the space was originally intended to shelter dozens, the old Italian MREs didn't have an infinite shelf life, and—after spoilage—Sal estimated they had food and fresh water for a week, two if they stretched it. On the bright side, she also found a box full of tiny airline whiskey bottles which were almost certainly still good, if not exactly part of a complete and balanced breakfast.

Not that she thought the Society would wait to starve them out, but making lists and inventories helped keep Sal's mind off what might be happening to Perry. And the fact that there was a man tied to a chair not fifty feet away who offered at least a chance of saving him.

Aaron had never lied to her, as far as she knew. But Menchú said there was no such thing as angels, or benevolent demons, or whatever Aaron might be, and she did trust Menchú. Maybe Aaron was waiting for the right moment, feeding her the truth until she let her guard down and was swallowed by a lie.

Of course, as the tickle at the back of her mind reminded her, if she did nothing, she would soon be swallowed up by something else entirely.

Grace sank into a crouch across the supplies from Sal. "Are you going to try to make a deal with Aaron so that you can save your brother?"

Whatever Grace's talents were, they did not include telepathy, no matter how much it might seem like it sometimes. "No. Menchú's right; we can't trust—"

Grace cut her off. "You should do it."

"What?"

"But only if you take me with you."

"Why?"

"Beyond the fact that you can't go out for a walk in an olive grove at night without getting ambushed?"

Sal crossed her arms. "Yes."

Grace frowned. "Count the light sources in this room."

"What?"

"Sources of light. In this room. Get your head out of your own problems for two seconds; look around and think about what you aren't seeing."

Sal frowned but obeyed. "There's an oil lamp. A glow stick. What looks like one of Liam's screens . . ." She trailed off. "Your candle isn't here."

"I didn't have a chance to take it when we ran. Sooner or later, our enemies will realize what they have, and when they do . . ." She mimed pinching out a flame. "I have to get it back. I won't let them make me abandon the rest of you. So make the deal with Aaron, and take me along."

Sal pulled out two tiny whiskey bottles and cracked the caps. She offered one to Grace, and after a silent toast, the two women wordlessly downed the drinks. Sal relished the burning rush of alcohol and resolve. Time to move.

"Let's do this, then."

3.

Of course Asanti caught on. No matter how quiet Sal and Grace were, which was pretty damn quiet, they were trying to conduct a whispered negotiation with a supernatural creature while the people they were trying to hide the creature—and, for that matter, their negotiations—from slept nearby. Even if it was a rather large space, in the silence of the cave, voices carried.

But still, when Asanti hissed, "What are you doing?" Sal felt like a teenager caught sneaking out after curfew.

Grace was less easily cowed. "Getting back into the Archives."

Asanti's lips narrowed. "We don't need to make a deal—"

Sal cut her off. "If you, or Menchú, had another plan, we would be on our way to Rome by now, not huddling in the dark. My brother's in there."

"My life is in there," said Grace.

"Menchú is the field leader," Asanti said.

Menchú has been stabbed in the back by the Church he gave his life to, and now he's bleeding out before our eyes, Sal thought. What she said was, "Menchú has a lot on his plate right now."

"Then that leaves me in charge," said Asanti. "We're a team, you can't—"

A soft light fell over the scene, and they all turned to see Menchú standing behind them, holding the oil lantern. He looked tired, but determined. "We're a team," he said. "We need to start acting like one. And that includes me." He cleared his throat. "After all, if we can't stop the Hand, my ecclesiastical career will be the least of our worries."

He turned to Aaron, still tied to the chair, who had been observing this entire exchange with seemingly detached interest. "What do you want?" Menchú asked him.

"I told you," said Aaron. "Nothing that you haven't—"

Menchú cut him off. "I've dealt with your kind before. Pardon me if I insist on the details."

Aaron looked sad again. "The boy in the village wasn't me."

"I know he wasn't. His name was José, and he was nine years old when he slit his own throat. As for the thing inside him, I didn't ask if it was you, and I don't care. If you don't want to set your own terms, this is the deal I offer: You want to help us reach the Archives for purposes of your own. I will allow it on the condition that in your mission and your aid to us you will not cause any living creature harm, or allow them to be harmed by your inaction."

Sal thought she saw Grace hide a smile at that. Why, she had no idea.

Aaron considered the proposal. "That's not a small thing to ask."

"If you don't like it, you're welcome to refuse," said Menchú. "You can wait here, take your chances, see whether we can contain the Hand or if the Society tracks us down first. Whatever happens will certainly be interesting."

"Well, when you put it that way—"

Menchú held up a hand. "There's one more thing," he said.

"One *more* thing?"

"If you make this deal and then betray either the letter or spirit of our agreement, I will end you, even if that task takes all eternity."

Sal blinked.

Menchú didn't move. "What is your decision?"

Aaron nodded. "I will abide by your terms."

"Excellent," said Menchú. "Now that we're all going to hell, let's get this over with. Someone wake Liam."

In spite of everything, Sal couldn't help smiling. She'd already been to hell once this week. Finally, she was on familiar ground.

The team arrived in Rome in their "borrowed" vehicle and parked in an alley near the Vatican, just as dawn washed the city in rosy light.

Liam—not exactly happy about the deal with Aaron but accepting its necessity—quickly got down to the heart of the matter. "Okay, whatever you are, what's the plan?"

"We move, and quickly," said Aaron. "The new guards are in place around the clock, but the fewer other employees we encounter, the better for our chances of secrecy."

Menchú accepted this with a small *of course* gesture. "Our first priority is to get the *Book of the Hand*. I'm sorry, Sal, but if the Hand unleashes a flood of demons into the world—"

"Perry will be screwed, anyway. Understood."

Menchú continued, "Aaron says he can get us into the Archives undetected. Once there, Asanti and I will secure the book."

"While I find more evidence to convince the cardinal that Balloon and Stretch have crossed the line," said Liam. "They can't have hidden their work entirely. A pull of Team Two's internal databases should have everything I need."

"And I assist Sal in seeing to her brother's safety," said Aaron.

Menchú blinked. "I see you've all given this some thought." He turned to Asanti. "Anything to add?"

She shook her head. "The plan makes sense to me."

"Me too," said Sal.

"And while you are doing all that," said Grace, "I'll get my candle."

Menchú shook his head. "I don't want us to split up more than we have to. Your candle is outside the main complex, in a lighter security zone. We can pick it up on our way out."

"Assuming we aren't leaving under hot pursuit," said Grace.

"All the more reason why we need you with us," said Menchú.

"But if we don't control my candle, I can drop at any time—I'll be more of a liability than an asset," Grace pointed out. "Since the candle is still lit, there are two possibilities for what's going on. One is that Balloon and Stretch don't know about the candle, or haven't realized it's important. In which case, it won't be guarded and I can easily get it, then cover you from the outside. The other is that our enemies know exactly what the candle is and why I have to come back for it, so they're using it to bait a trap."

"Which is why you shouldn't go alone," said Asanti.

Grace shook her head. "That's exactly why I *should* go by myself. If our enemies wanted to kill me, they would have destroyed the candle by now. Anything nonlethal they want to throw at me, I can cope with, but not if I have to worry about protecting the rest of you at the same time. Even if they do take me down, I'll be safely comatose until you can destroy the Hand, prove your innocence, and rescue me."

Menchú didn't look happy. "I don't want you becoming a hostage."

Grace leaned in and kissed him lightly on the cheek. "I've always been a hostage. Look on the bright side: If things go horribly wrong on the main raid, I'll still be free and will avenge you all with bloody death that will turn even Balloon's and Stretch's stomachs."

"That's not exactly a comfort," he told her.

"Don't lose hope," Grace said. Then she slipped away down a narrow side street. In seconds, she was gone.

Not being entirely willing to trust Aaron's assessment of the situation on the ground, the team took the time to confirm that security around the Vatican had been locked down to pope-in-peril levels not seen since the assassination attempt against John Paul II.

Menchú looked neither happy nor surprised. "All right," he said. "Aaron, how can you sneak us in?"

"Wait here," Aaron said.

With that, he left the alley where they had been hiding, walked straight up to one of the Vatican guards, and tapped him on the shoulder.

"Shit," Sal breathed. "He's going to sell us out."

In a show of admirable restraint, Liam did not say, *I told you so.*

Menchú held up a hand to keep the others in place. "If he betrays us, regroup in Alexandria. Don't try to return to the villa."

Sal felt the Hand's itch at the back of her brain grow stronger at the thought. If this went south, she wouldn't have time to get to Egypt. She wondered what would happen to the Hand if she simply blew her brains out. Maybe it would pop back to the demon world. Or maybe she'd wind up a possessed, headless corpse. That seemed more in keeping with her recent luck.

The guard Aaron had approached nodded, left his post, and walked straight for them.

"Arturo?" Asanti asked.

Sal was ready to grab the archivist by the collar and force her to run, hoping that Liam would do the same for Menchú, when she noticed Aaron was still standing where he had tapped the guard. Blinking, as though dazzled by a bright light, or confused. After a few seconds he pulled himself together and walked purposefully toward a nearby metro station.

Sal looked at the approaching guard again. Now that he was closer, she could see his face more clearly. There was something about his eyes. They were . . . familiar. "It's Aaron," she said.

Liam blinked. "What?"

Sal remembered how the Hand had prepared to leave her body for another one. There hadn't been an aura when Aaron had touched the guard, but maybe it looked different when *her* body wasn't the host in question.

"He jumped bodies, took over the guard. That's how he's going to sneak us into the Archives. We're just going to walk in the front doors."

Liam looked incredulous. "Like Chewbacca?"

The guard arrived, lips now twisted in an all too familiar smirk. "Ready to go?" he asked. The body was different, the voice unchanged.

"A little warning could have saved us a lot of stress," Menchú said.

Aaron shrugged. Sal couldn't help but notice he seemed to be breathing heavily after the short walk.

"You left me tied to a chair for hours," Aaron said. "I think I'm entitled to a joke or two." He gestured toward the doors that would, eventually, lead to the Archives' hidden entrance, and offered a mocking bow. "If you would come this way . . ."

＊ ＊ ＊

Liam wasn't sure which of his poor life choices had led to him walking into the Vatican under the supposed supervision of a demon-possessed guard—or angel-possessed, to credit Sal's optimism for a tick—but he felt certain God's plan had gone seriously off-course somewhere along the way.

The most obvious choice for "somewhere" would be right around the time he was possessed by a demon himself and lost two years of his life. Liam was a God-fearing man, but if that particular twist of his fucked-up existence had been intended as part of God's larger tapestry, he had grave reservations about the nature of the final design.

At the moment, however, his choices were simple and limited. He could either trust the demon, or run like a coward and leave his teammates in the shit. Put that way, it was hardly a choice at all.

That didn't stop Liam from sweating bullets as Aaron made small talk with one of the new, heavily armed guards. He waited for the man at the door to notice his colleague's voice had changed, or that he had four people following behind him. But the conversation concluded without incident, and they walked quickly past. No one gave the group a second look.

As he passed the guard on the door, Liam risked a glance at his face. The man's expression was impassive, but his eyes were covered by a filmy gray mist. Liam swallowed, and sent up a silent prayer that he was still working for the good guys.

Grace slipped over the rooftops toward her quarters in Saint Catherine's. After years of near invulnerability, she rarely worried about fights anymore, but now, her pulse thrummed and she had the distinct impression she was about to walk the line between near invulnerability and the actual sort.

Grace found she had to consciously slow her breathing. Her muscles were tense, and she felt a sharp pain in her palms. The last seven decades hadn't left her a stranger to fear. She felt it often: the dread when the others were at risk, the sharp pang as she put out her candle and had to trust that Menchú would be back as he had promised—to light it for her again. But she rarely feared for herself. Now, with the others gone, she felt the weight of her enemy's malevolence pointed at her. And this enemy knew how to hit her where it hurt.

Good thing she knew how to hit back.

Grace was alone on a rooftop, heading into an ambush where she would almost certainly be outnumbered and outgunned. For the first time in nearly a century, she was walking into a fair fight, and she couldn't help relishing the prospect.

Aaron paused after he closed the door to the Archives, as if listening for pursuit, but Asanti noticed how he let the wood take his weight, how he closed his eyes for a moment and fought to regain his breath. He was trying to hide it, but the man was exhausted. *How much does shifting from one body to another cost him?* Then he opened his eyes again and caught her watching.

"Hiding four people in plain sight must be a strain," she offered.

Aaron's new lips thinned, but he didn't try to deny it. "A bit."

Then they were descending into the Archives, and Asanti didn't have attention for anything else. She paused on the ladder while she was still high enough to see over most of the shelves. She had still been reassembling the collections after the techno-cultist's whirlwind hacking when the Hand broke out and started eating invading demons. The damage from the latter had eradicated all signs of the former, but as far as silver linings went, that was definitely a thin one.

Still, there were signs that others had been here since Team Three left. For instance, she was sure the Hand hadn't ransacked her desk and filing cabinets. That was Desmet and De Vos, no doubt. And somehow that violation of trust by her erstwhile colleagues felt even worse than the demon's. Asanti descended the ladder's final rungs and stopped in the wreckage of the Archives.

Menchú's hand settled on her shoulder, a comforting weight.

"First, find the *Book of the Hand*," he said.

Asanti nodded. One step at a time. Stop a demon from breaking out of Sal's head and ending the world. Then worry about the damage done to her catalog system.

Liam peeled off to see if any of his computers had survived the Hand and subsequent ransacking. Asanti pulled out her keys and led Menchú back to the third point of the star—the most secure of the Archives' vaults—where they'd stored the *Book of the Hand*.

Menchú continued giving instructions as they crossed the charred floor to the vault. "Sal, watch Aaron and the door. Liam, when you're done, help her. Asanti—"

But his words were lost in the thunderous pounding of blood in Asanti's ears, overwhelming all thought.

The vault door stood open.

And things had been going so well. . . .

The people watching the convent from the café across the street were trying to look nonchalant, but their lack of conversation made them easy to identify, and their fixation on the door made them even easier to evade. A tree growing over the courtyard of the neighboring building provided Grace with both a route to her own roof and a vantage point to check for surveillance above street level.

There wasn't any. Which meant that either their enemies *were* idiots, or this was definitely a trap. And while setting a trap for her was not the smartest idea, Grace was certain that given Desmet and De Vos's treatment of Sal—who was merely possessed—they weren't likely to let her waltz in and reassume control of her own life if they could prevent it.

Better to be prepared. If she was wrong, the job would be easy, and she could be pleasantly surprised. If not, being ready might make the difference between ending up comatose in a box at the end of the mission or not. Win-win.

It was more fun to imagine she was walking into a trap, anyway.

Grace cautiously let herself down to the roof's peaked ridgeline from the tree. No alarms. A quick look showed no activity from the watchers at the café. She picked her way over to where the chimney blocked most views of the gutter and swung down. Her toe just found purchase on the window ledge of the nuns' communal bathroom. At this hour, the sisters would all be at morning prayers, and unless someone was ill or playing hooky, she should have the place to herself.

Grace's luck held. All of the good nuns were where they were supposed to be, and once she had squeezed herself onto the ledge above the sinks, she slipped to the floor unobserved. She didn't even knock over anyone's toothbrush, which she imagined the sisters would appreciate if they knew. Once she found her feet, Grace slowly cracked the door to the hallway. Her rooms were at the far end of the corridor, close to the stairs and the linen closet. Outside her door sat a woman in a habit. *It would have to be a woman. The only man allowed into the residential areas would be a priest, and someone would ask questions if a member of the clergy just sat around all day.* Grace was also certain that "woman in a habit" was a more accurate description of the person she was looking at than "nun." Sisters possessed many skills. Hand-to-hand fighting wasn't generally one of them. And this particular individual had swollen knuckles and a nose that knew how it felt to break.

Good. This ought to be interesting.

Liam wasn't surprised that the *Book of the Hand* was missing. *Would have been too easy to just leave it for us to find.* On the other hand, storing such a dangerous artifact anywhere other than the Archives' vault smacked of the kind of moronic decision-making that generally required either a dedicated committee or a truly clueless superior. Possibly both.

He let Asanti and Menchú worry about the book. He plugged into the network, let his programs loose on Team Two's intranet—always felt a nice bit of guilty pleasure breaking out the black hat—and turned to his main objective. He hadn't sold Sal out, but they'd learned somehow. Liam didn't think any of the others would have let the information slip even by accident. Which left one possibility: They had all told Balloon and Stretch about Sal's little problem, because Balloon and Stretch were listening to their private conversations. *We don't have a leak problem. We have a bug problem.*

In the convent's shower room, there was a small wooden hatch that allowed access to the pipes, drains, and emergency shutoff valves.

These centuries-old buildings didn't have central heat or air conditioning, so convenient and illogically load-bearing air ducts connecting every room of the convent would have been too much to hope for, but a person who didn't mind a tight squeeze could force their way from the drain access up to a storage space below the roof-ridge that extended down the entire wing—a storage area wider than the corridor below it. Grace counted steps to the room at the end of the hall. Then, she pressed down as close to the eaves as she could, and with a swift kick, broke a hole through the ceiling of her bedroom.

Now was not the time for subtlety. If Grace was lucky, the woman in the hallway would pause for a moment to summon help before going inside to investigate the cause of the noise in what was supposed to be an empty room. If she wasn't lucky, there would be another guard inside. In either case, her best chance was to grab her candle quickly and take any resistance by surprise.

First piece of luck: no one in the bedroom. Second: Her candle was still burning on her bedside table where she had left it . . . how long ago? Grace forced herself not to notice how far it had burned since they'd gone on the run. She reached for a glass chimney to protect the flame. . . .

The door from her sitting room burst in, revealing three men in ill-fitting clerical collars. Grace grabbed the book sitting beside her bed and threw it into the face of the first man through the door, which granted her an extra moment to slam the hurricane chimney over her candle, pick it up, and launch herself at him. The man blocked the door—his buddies couldn't get through, and the three-to-one matchup turned head to head.

Even one-handed, it was hardly a fair fight.

Grace knocked the first man cold and sent him tumbling into

the second just as the "sister" from the hallway burst in on the scene. The third man had a knife, and a gun he didn't have time to aim before Grace kicked it from his grip. The second man was still trying to throw off the unconscious first, which Grace judged would keep him busy long enough for her to knock out the one with the knife. If she was fast, she could then deal with the woman, followed by the last man, and be back on the roof with her candle and on her way before the couple at the café could cross the street or summon reinforcements. If they had reinforcements. Balloon and Stretch were supposed to be a faction within Team Two, not the whole damn team—how many goons could they field?

The man with the knife fell to a quick kick to the temple, underestimating how far she could reach while holding a lit candle in one hand. Grace used her momentum to whip around and face the woman from the hall—who was carrying a fire extinguisher.

"Try me," she told Grace. "Let's see who goes down first."

"We can talk about this . . . ," Grace began, and then—while the woman hesitated—flung her candle in its glass lamp straight up into the air. The ceiling was just high enough that she'd have a few seconds to disarm the false nun and still have time to catch the candle on the way down.

The woman gaped, fishlike, as Grace hurled herself at her. With both hands free it was a simple matter for Grace to yank the false nun's robes over her face, tangling her in her unaccustomed habit.

Grace turned back, reaching out for the candle that was now falling, just where she wanted it, right into her waiting hand . . .

. . . not *her* waiting hand. The last man had freed himself faster than Grace had anticipated. He plucked the candle from the air, jerking it from her reach even as her fingers brushed against the protective glass of the chimney. A swing of his arm and the lamp shattered against the wall.

Grace could still reach the candle. She hadn't lost yet.

The man's eyes met hers as he pinched out the flame.

Grace was gone before her body, or the candle, hit the floor.

Liam's first guess was that Balloon and Stretch had compromised one of Team Three's computers. Not his—after getting sucker-punched and possessed through his laptop, Liam was more than a little obsessive about security—but the older Vatican machines weren't such hard targets. An e-mail link, a keylogger— Then again, out of the rest of his teammates, Sal was the only one who regularly used technology more advanced than a flip phone, and she didn't have her own machine in the office.

If I were a bug in the Archives, where would I be? In the center of the room probably, near Asanti's desk, where they gathered whenever they had anything important to discuss. Except that was out, because anything tech-based would be fried by its proximity to the Orb. (Liam had learned that the hard way, having lost more than one piece of scanning equipment trying to figure out how the damn glowy Magic 8 Ball worked.)

Across the room, he heard Sal ask, "How long before Grace assumes we've all been taken and starts on plan B: bloody vengeance?"

Menchú pulled out his pocket watch. "About ten more minutes."

Sal looked at Aaron, still leaning against the stair railing.

"Can you get us out?" Sal asked him.

Aaron nodded.

"We can't leave without the *Book of the Hand*." Menchú slipped the watch back into his pocket. It was an antique, encased in silver, which—as far as Liam could tell—was the only reason it was still working. Because by rights, nothing that complex should still keep accurate time when surrounded by the amount of magical backwash the team was exposed to on a regular basis.

And then Liam's eye fell on the antique pen case resting in its usual spot on Asanti's desk. His own desk had been thoroughly tossed, Menchú's too. So had Asanti's files and cabinets. So why was her pen case still there? Completely undisturbed. *Or, perhaps, returned.* Because Team Two, for all of their confidence, would want to hedge their bets in case Team Three found a way to sneak back into the Archives. *And if we did, we might just say something worth hearing.*

A new voice sounded from the top of the stairs, and Liam knew he had come to this conclusion just a moment too late.

Cardinal Varano looked down at them like God the Father. "You won't be leaving at all."

4.

Your Eminence," Menchú said, though the term seemed out of place addressed to a man flanked by machine-gun-wielding toughs. "I can explain."

"I'm not here for explanations, Arturo." The man in the red robes sounded sad more than angry. "I warned Asanti there was nothing I could do until you dealt with the problem of Ms. Brooks. And your response to that was to break into the Vatican. Looking for this, I expect." The cardinal gestured, and one of the guards opened a leather case to reveal the *Book of the Hand*.

It was still wrapped in a protective shroud, and seeing it, Menchú muttered, "Thank God."

"If I were in your position, Arturo," said the cardinal, "I would pray for mercy and forgiveness, not in thanks."

"Your Eminence, we need that book to free Sal."

"An exorcism? But those are quite beyond your bailiwick, Arturo. They're Team Two's responsibility. And you attacked Team Two's operatives, with magic, no less, to free her. De Vos, or Desmet—I can never remember which is which—anyway, he's been grievously injured. Surely you understand the predicament you've left me."

"Desmet and De Vos are *killing people*." Menchú's voice shook with rage. "They're torturers and thugs."

"And they are efficient," the cardinal said. Which was when Menchú started to worry.

Sal trusted her teammates, but she'd never felt altogether comfortable around the Society higher-ups—so as soon as Varano entered with the machine guns, she jumped straight to: *Holy fuck, the cardinal's selling us out.*

But she hadn't gotten much further when she felt Aaron's hand at her elbow. "Don't talk," he whispered. "Just follow me. And whatever you do, be very, very quiet."

And bail on the others? Fuck that noise.

Sal set her heels as Aaron tried to guide her backward. His grip on her arm, although shaking, was surprisingly strong.

"I can get us all out of this, but you have to come with me. Now," he hissed.

Sal risked a glance at the cardinal. He wasn't even glancing in Sal's direction. Neither were his guards. And sure, Aaron was quiet, but someone should have noticed him moving around, right?

Magic. Dammit.

"We have to help them," Sal said.

"We have to save your brother first. We'll come back, but only if we survive—which will only happen if you shut up and walk."

Sal weighed her options. Go with a demon (or angel) who had helped them so far, versus stay in the machine-gun sights, then get herself thrown into a cell subject to the tender mercies of Balloon and Stretch. Somehow she didn't think the maiming the Hand had inflicted on Balloon would put him in a kind mood. Aaron pulled at her arm again, and this time, Sal followed.

Aaron guided her backward at first, taking tiny steps into the ruined stacks. Once they were out of the cardinal's direct line of sight, they turned, and—locking her hand in his—he towed her out of the Archives through a back door, up a narrow hallway, all the way to . . .

Perry's room.

Sal froze as they crossed the threshold, and Aaron released her hand. Even in the short time since her last visit, Perry had visibly deteriorated: skin pale and slack, cheeks hollow. A forest of machines surrounded him. He was breathing on his own, but the sound had a broken, rasping quality.

"Did they do this?" Sal asked. No need to elaborate on who "they" were.

"No, this is the Hand's work."

Sal poked at the buzzing at the back of her brain. *Did it do something to Perry while I was possessed?* "When? He was fine . . . not fine*"*—Sal foundered for words—"but he was stable." Sal reached for her brother's hand, felt his skin, dry and soft like paper. "What changed?" she asked, not caring if she got an answer from the demon inside, or the one by her brother's bed.

"I don't know," Aaron said. "But I have a theory. Possession is a swap, of sorts—a soul dragged into the other world for a soul forced into this. But the Hand's larger than Perry, or you—most of its being remains in the other world. It merely . . . extended itself into this domain, through Perry, and through you. But when the Hand broke free, its use of power taxed this vessel—like electricity through a filament."

"Then why wasn't I hurt?"

"My best guess is that the Hand wanted you mobile; Perry, not so much. But you should have both been hurt when it began to use its power. Why you're fine and Perry's not—well, it's not important now."

As Aaron continued to talk, Sal felt the itch of the Hand in her mind, and her eyes slid, unbidden, up to Perry's left ear. Something was different about it. But what? And then it hit her: She could see Perry's ear . . . because the lock of hair that normally covered it had been cut off. A lock of hair, folded into a scrap of paper, and given to the Oracle at Delphi, who had demanded a sacrifice.

Interesting choice, the Pythia had said.

Oh God, what had she done?

Aaron leaned forward, demanding Sal's attention again. "This is what I need from you. Why I brought all of you here. I can save him. But I need your permission."

"Why would you need my permission to save my brother?"

"Menchú made me promise not to harm anyone living."

"He's alive, then?" *Perry's soul, hunched in a demon dimension in a cell of glass and briars.* "He's not gone?" *I haven't lost him.*

"He is not . . . entirely gone. But the man you knew as your brother will not fit in a body so used as this. The Hand has scoured him clean." Aaron gestured to the bed, to her brother. "But if I take his body, I can give him life."

"You said 'harm.'"

"I'll have to make a little more room for myself." Aaron faltered. "And rewire him from the inside, somewhat, which might be construed as . . . It— He won't work quite like a human anymore. But he will leave this place."

The buzzing at the back of Sal's skull throbbed and pulsed. Sal asked the only question that mattered.

"Why?"

Aaron did not speak until she met his eyes. "Because I can.

THINGS LOST 733

He is one life, and each life is everything." He pressed both hands against the edge of Perry's bed, and Sal realized he was using it to support his weight. "I am careful. I do not vandalize the bodies I visit. The man you know as a tour guide will return to his life none the worse for wear, and without knowledge or memory of his time with me. But if I stay in one body for too long, I cannot help doing irreparable harm, as the Hand has done here. I shift back and forth as I must, to save my hosts. But with each shift I lose a piece of myself. Your brother has been . . . hollowed. Hallowed, you might say. There is space for me in the empty places within him, until the one who owns my service finally calls me home."

Sal shook her head. "I can't make that decision for him."

Aaron lifted Perry's other hand, holding it carefully so as not to disturb the tubes and wires that gave him a semblance of life. "There is no one else who can."

"Have you ever wondered," the cardinal continued, "how this whole edifice functions? We have operatives on all continents; we protect the world from threats no one else admits exist. We all have to be on the same page. We need efficiency, and loyalty."

"Desmet and De Vos are not efficient. They're not loyal."

"Judged by what standard, Arturo? They have their messes, yes, but they clean them up. They've been honest with me about the situation, and I've repaid their honesty with trust. Killing the possessed—"

"Or those they claim to be possessed."

The cardinal shrugged. "You have to admit, it's clean. Compare that to your team—chasing all over the world after magic, trying to save everyone, generating headlines and expense reports and *paperwork*. It's a sickness. You try to save the unsavable—right down to Ms. Brooks, who is literally possessed by a demon."

"That's our mission," Menchú said. "Our calling."

"Your *job* is to protect the Society and keep the monsters contained! Instead you've gone around . . . *recruiting* them. It's a nightmare. The other teams see what you get away with, and grow bolder. The mission of the Society is to keep *order*. You've made your entire division an anathema."

"You're honestly saying we should let people die."

"A small town in the southern United States disappears—nice and neat. The authorities there deal with that sort of thing all the time. Certainly to be preferred over calling in a strike team and costing us a team leader. We searched high and low but could not find a better replacement for Bouchard than Thavani Shah, who I'm sure you'd agree is hardly an ideal candidate—"

"I don't know," Menchú said, voice tight and vicious, "what you're implying."

"It's a question of . . . cultural fit. Anyway, if I were in your position, Arturo—"

Menchú did not look away from the book as he said, "If you were in my position, Your Excellency, how many hundreds more would be dead?"

His words were greeted by thunderous silence.

Finally, the cardinal rasped: "How *dare* you? You've disobeyed orders. You've stolen into the Vatican by who knows what black arts. You've broken faith, Arturo."

Menchú raised his eyes to meet Cardinal Varano's.

"I have never broken faith with the Church. But if the Church wishes to break faith with me, I will protect myself, and my people."

The cardinal's face had darkened to a red so deep it was nearly purple. He closed his eyes and breathed deeply until he paled again. "You're a sickness at our heart, Arturo. A cancer, building a team of cancers." Varano's gesture took in Asanti and Liam as well. "The weak and the possessed, squawking about virtue. Once I've made an example of you, the other teams will fall in line. It won't even be difficult to turn them against you. Your people are barely even human!"

At this cue, a guard at the back shoved Grace forward to fall at Cardinal Varano's feet. She crumpled, careless and limp, like a puppet with cut strings. Menchú felt his heart stop. The cardinal noticed his flinch.

"Fortunately, De Vos and Desmet kept me informed of your illicit activities. You have given me trouble for years, but that ends now. Surrender, and cooperate. Confess what you are told to confess and affirm what you are told to affirm." He held up Grace's unlit candle. "And I will not have this—thing—destroyed."

Menchú swallowed. "Would you let her live?"

The cardinal smiled, sensing he had found his point of leverage. "She will be safe. Maybe someday she will even be found again, once all of this is safely behind us."

Once everyone in this room is dead, Menchú translated. He hoped that someone else on the team had a plan. Because other than stall for time by keeping the cardinal talking, he was fresh out of ideas.

Menchú took a breath to do just that—and smelled smoke. Surely Varano wouldn't try to burn them out when he was inside the Archives. But no, it wasn't bonfire smoke—just enough to stain the air. As though someone had put out a match.

The cardinal's eyebrows knit. "Is something burning?" he asked the guard at his left.

The guard shook his head.

A wisp of smoke caught Menchú's eye. He traced it back along its curving path to its source.

The wick of Grace's candle was smoldering. Menchú was certain it hadn't been before. And then, before his very eyes and without visible cause, it caught fire.

For the first time since that bloody night in Guatemala, Menchú believed in miracles.

After that, things happened very quickly.

The cardinal noticed the flame, and his eyes widened—but before he could react, Grace caught the candle in one hand and his wrist in another. She yanked the cardinal's arm down; their skulls collided with a *thunk*, and Varano slumped to the floor, blood streaming from his nose.

Liam jumped over Asanti's desk into the fray, and Asanti threw books at whoever came into range. But most of the fight was Grace, moving like a whirlwind of poetic destruction: kicking and choking until the cardinal and his entire complement of guards lay unconscious at her feet. She surveyed the room, burning candle still clutched in one hand, and turned to Menchú.

"Where's Sal?" she asked.

Sal? Sal was right there, where she'd been standing this whole time. . . . Except she wasn't. "I don't—"

"I'm here," said Sal, behind him, as she emerged from the fallen stacks. She was walking slowly, and her arm was around . . . her brother? Who was clearly very weak, but—just as clearly—conscious. *When did that happen?*

Sal helped Perry sit, and he leaned forward against his knees, exhausted.

"Sorry," said Sal. "He isn't moving very well. I think lighting Grace's candle from across the room really took it out of him."

Menchú's heart sank in his chest. *Not a miracle.* "Sal," he asked. "What happened to Aaron?"

Sal gestured to Perry. "Everyone, meet my brother, Perry. Sort of."

Menchú looked at the young man he'd first seen months ago in New York, playing host to a demon once again. He prayed that Sal had made a better deal than he had all those years ago.

Perry managed, with difficulty, to pull his head off his knees. "Charmed." He spoke with Aaron's voice.

Asanti blinked. "Oh, Sal . . ."

Sal looked nearly as tired as Aaron. "Please, can we talk about this later? When we aren't surrounded by people who want to kill us?"

Somewhere above them, muffled by the closed door, a Klaxon sounded. The alarm was followed by the heavy pounding of booted feet above their heads.

"Good plan," said Liam.

Asanti nodded to Perry's exhausted body. "He can't get us out the way he got us in. He can barely walk."

Aaron struggled to his feet, and Menchú watched as Sal held a steadying hand under his elbow. Was she responding to her brother's body, or the thing within? He wished he could say for sure. "Fortunately, I happen to know an alternate route."

"What is it?" demanded Asanti, bristling like a mother hen.

"Did you know," said Aaron, "that the original Roman water system connects to most cave systems in central Italy?"

5.

I t was a very long, very dark walk back. But, as promised, all sewers, then catacombs, then caves led away from Rome, and following Perry's—or, Sal reminded herself, Aaron's—directions, they reached the hidden cavern they had snuck out from the night before. Between the length of the journey and Menchú and Asanti's confusion, she decided to believe Aaron's assurances that no one else knew of the route they had taken. She didn't ask how he knew about it. The Hand was pressing at the back of her mind, growing in strength and insistence, and she decided that she had other things to worry about.

Once they were back, Liam, who in spite of his antipathy for demon artifacts had insisted on carrying the shroud-wrapped *Book of the Hand* the entire trip, lifted one corner of the wrappings and pulled out Asanti's silver pen case, which had been tucked inside.

"What on earth?" asked Asanti.

Liam gestured for silence, and pulling out a multi-tool, carefully cracked open the casing to reveal a tiny chip and transmitter. He pulled the chip off the battery and let out a slow breath.

Taking in the team's confusion, he explained. "*This* is how Balloon and Stretch found out about Sal. They bugged the Archives, and we all told them everything they wanted to know."

"And you brought it back here?" said Grace. "They might be able to trace us with it. We should smash—"

Liam pulled the bug hastily out of reach. "It's too small to transmit over any kind of range," he said, only a little defensive. "Let alone through this much rock."

"Yes," said Menchú. "But why not leave it where it was?"

Liam's grin turned positively wolfish. "Give me twenty minutes and I'll show you."

A short time later, Liam had hooked the bug's central chip up to his computer, and they were all listening to a recording of the cardinal's unhinged rant about their team—crypto-racism, threats against Grace, and all, culminating in his plan to force them into coerced confession.

Menchú shuddered. None of that had been easy to hear the first time.

"Can you put that on the Internet?" Sal asked.

"Sure," said Liam.

Menchú shook his head. "You can't."

"But . . . ," said Sal.

Menchú cut her off. "According to the rest of the world, magic doesn't exist. Our team, the Society, doesn't exist. Keeping that secret is the most important part of our job. I will not forsake my duty."

Asanti put a hand on his shoulder. "Then we don't tell the world. We just find the people who can help us stop Cardinal Varano and his coconspirators, and tell them."

"And who would that be?" asked Grace.

Liam had stopped the playback from the bug when their

discussion started, but without warning, the speakers on his laptop crackled back to life.

A woman's voice spoke, highly distorted but unmistakably that of Thavani Shah. "Team Three. You are in rebellion against the Society and the Church. We have you surrounded. Surrender yourselves now, and receive what mercy you may."

"I thought you said it couldn't transmit!"

Liam glared at Grace. "It shouldn't be able to! Maybe they found this place in church records. Or maybe they traced us some other way. They're the ones with the magic."

"Either way," Sal muttered, "it's not exactly an appealing offer."

"If you do not respond within twenty minutes, we will be forced to act. We do not wish to harm you, but we will if you do not surrender."

Liam was typing furiously, and with a quick series of keystrokes broke into the feed. "Why don't you surrender? Traitor!" he shouted back into the computer's mic.

There was a short pause. "Oh good, you *can* hear us."

Grace let out a small groan.

"Surrender yourselves," the voice from the computer said calmly. "If you don't, my entire team is standing by, and I'd hate to make them go home without using any of the lovely toys they've brought."

EPISODE
16

SIEGE

MAX GLADSTONE

1.

Father Menchú paced the ill-lit shadows of Team Three's hideout. Sal watched him. The strain of the last few days was showing: Menchú had never expected to shelter here from his own. Yes, no one in Team Three ever, exactly, disclosed the hideout's existence to the Vatican, but that had been more tradition than treason. Menchú maintained the bolt-hole, but Sal doubted he had ever planned to use it.

"We don't have time for this," Menchú said.

"Make time," Asanti shot back, as she chalked a silver circle on the stone floor. "The rest of us are working as fast as we can."

"Team One is waiting upstairs. The Vatican wants us to give ourselves up. We have to run. Back through the tunnels, maybe— there must be some other exit between here and Rome."

"They'll follow us," Asanti said. "Even if we make it out of the country, where would we hide? And we have the evidence we need: Liam's pulling the cardinal's confession off the bug and processing the Team Two database—"

"But it'll take a while," Liam said from his workbench. "Devilish little bastard, no mistake. At least I've stopped it transmitting. Give me—" Sparks fountained when he placed a lead. "Fuck!"

Asanti continued as if he hadn't spoken. "Sal won't last long. We need her to testify, but the Hand's regaining power. If we don't banish it first, we might as well give her back to the exorcists."

Sal crouched beside the circle. When she brushed the chalk lines, her fingers tingled, and a coiled thing in her chest shifted in uneasy sleep. The demon inside her did not like silver mixed into the chalk. She'd worked with Team Three for months, and the whole time she thought she'd felt irritated by the touch of silver because the metal was protecting her from evil. If she'd realized earlier that the silver was trying to protect her from herself, she would have spared them all a lot of trouble. "What's the play?"

"You lie down in the circle with the book," Asanti said. "We light the candles. Liam starts the pendulum. I chant. The words and cadence set up a harmonic resonance in your mind. That builds— if our world's on a beach, and magic's the ocean, we're digging down until we reach water. The pendulum keeps time. When it stops, the ritual's over. Ordinarily we could never do this with so few people, since the pendulum would stop before we got anywhere but—" She adjusted a coil of wire on the table. "Magnets really *are* useful, you know."

Sal drew back from the circle. "That works? We can just . . . cheat?"

"We have no idea what we can do," the archivist replied. "Or what we can't. If we had ever studied this formally, I'd know. But for the moment I have to rely on inside information." She nodded toward the shadows beyond the circle of lamplight, to a figure Sal wished she did not have to see.

Aaron did not quite fit in her brother's body. Sal did not know what she expected an angel (spirit? Monster?) to look like, occupying a comatose man's flesh, but Aaron still got it wrong. Not in any obvious way—her brother's eyes did not glow, there were no wings over his shoulders—but she knew Perry, and this was not him. She watched her brother's hands chalk diagrams on the chamber floor, but they didn't move in the jagged motions she remembered. She'd made the deal, she'd let Aaron into Perry's body, but she didn't have to like it. "We get through," Aaron said with a voice that was not Perry's, but sounded so close, a voice lightly shaded with Sal's brother, "and then we close the book."

"It's closed already."

"That's what we thought." Asanti paged forward in her notes. "When we met the Hand in New York, Sal closed its book, which should have cut off its influence on Earth. Yet it remained. Sal saw Perry's soul imprisoned when she visited the demon world. Perry's a sort of spiritual doorstop—the bond between his soul and his body holds the *Book of the Hand* open."

"So we free my brother," Sal said, "and suck the Hand back into the demon world. Free me before Team One bursts in."

"Exactly."

"I'm game."

Father Menchú's frown deepened. "Since Sal joined us, we've used magic three times, and each time we've failed, or something horrible has happened. We can't risk that. We have to run."

Asanti waved him off and turned a page. "Rhodes was under pressure, and that turned out well enough."

"Only because the Hand wanted the *Codex Umbra* as much as we did."

"What about the Oracle, then?"

"You tried to kill Sal after you drank from the spring."

"Because she had a demon inside her."

"She still does!"

"Father," Sal said. Menchú stopped pacing. The words Sal wanted to say were too hot to hold in her mouth. "The Hand won't go back to the Vatican without a fight. That gives you two options."

Liam reached for her, but she pulled away. If she stopped now, there'd be no starting again.

She took a knife from Asanti's bag and held it toward Menchú, hilt first. "You kill me now, and maybe the demon goes with me. If we're lucky. Or you buy me enough time to go through that portal and bring my brother back." The priest stared at the knife as if she'd offered him a corpse. In a way, she supposed, she had. "I know what I'd rather do."

He didn't move. Neither did Grace, leaning against the wall behind him. Grace could cross the room and snatch the blade from Sal's hand. Would she stop Menchú, if he took the knife? Would she take it herself?

Menchú closed his eyes. A year passed.

"Get ready," he said.

He left the cave, and Grace detached from the shadows, deadly quiet, to follow him.

Thavani Shah waited, smoking alone, by the villa's front gate. She wore khaki trousers, a khaki shirt, and combat boots; she bore a side-arm and no insignia whatsoever. Streaks of iron gray shot through her hair; she wore it braided up and back from her face. Cigarette flame lit the blacks of her eyes.

The priest emerged from the villa and walked the long path toward her. He kept his hands in his pockets, and his head down.

The path lights glinted off his crucifix, and he still wore his collar. She counted footsteps on the gravel. At twenty-three, he stopped, ten feet from her. He had, she thought, a fine mustache. "Corporal Shah," the priest said. "I don't see your legions."

"You wouldn't, Mr. Menchú," she replied. "That collar isn't yours to wear anymore."

"This is bigger than you know, Corporal. The cardinal's not the man you think he is. He's covering for murderers in Team Two. Give me time, and I can prove it."

"I offered you a chance to surrender. That was a personal favor." She flicked ash from her cigarette. "My orders are to bring your team in. I'd rather do this peacefully."

"You're being played."

"You'll get your hearing when you're in custody. In the meantime, I have my orders. Ms. Brooks is possessed. Your team stopped an exorcism to free her—and broke into the Vatican to retrieve your books and tools. You've gone rogue. You know what happens next. They call me."

"Desmet and De Vos," Menchú said, "are traitors, and torturers, and the cardinal's working with them. Your squad is a weapon in their hands."

She dropped her cigarette and crushed its ember with her heel, then hooked her thumb through her belt. Her hand was not on her sidearm, but it was near. "Way above my pay grade, Arturo. I should bring you in right now, then root out the others."

"Are you sure you can?"

The priest had not spoken.

Wind whispered through the uncut grass.

"Evening, Grace," Shah said, without looking. She knew that even if she had looked, she would have seen nothing.

"Evening, Thavani."

Shah didn't bother trying to pinpoint the voice.

"I can prove my case," Menchú said. "I have log files. Blackmail material. Eyewitness testimony. I just need a few hours."

Shah stared at him, through him. "I'll give you one."

"An hour?" Sal had never heard Asanti's voice rise quite that high. "Impossible. I need at least three. One's barely enough to get Sal *into* the demon world, let alone for her to do anything once she's there."

"Shah's giving us what she can," Grace said.

Sal sat in the silver circle, holding the shroud-wrapped book. The ancient fabric scratched her palms when she tensed her grip. The book wriggled underneath, echoing the Hand's movement inside her, two malevolences burrowing toward one another through paper and flesh. "Send me through. Worst-case scenario, when they break in, I'm stuck on the other side, with the book. They won't have any evidence that you helped me."

"Like evidence matters," Liam said. "They'll just burn us all."

"You mean, like, in the spy sense, right?"

No one answered her, which was not reassuring.

Menchú pinched the bridge of his nose. "What do they have, Grace?"

"The squad's gathered. Their conventional response team is gearing up. I didn't see the reliquary yet. They scrambled to encircle us as soon as they had our location. The relics will come, though. The cardinal will be all too happy to authorize their use against us."

Liam cracked his knuckles, then his neck. "They'll send the conventional team in first. Standard protocol. Don't use magic if men with guns will do the trick. And women," he added. "I can buy us time.

The convies use GPS, electronic compasses, comms, telemetry—I can monkey with those."

"How?"

"Well." He ran a hand over his scalp. "I, um . . . I've been coming out here in my spare time, you know. I stashed surprises through the tunnels, in case of just such an emergency."

"You planned," Menchú said, his voice somewhere between awed and furious, "to fight Team One?"

"Or the cops, or the military, or fuckin' zombies, right? Man needs a hobby. I can hold off Shah's boys until they bring out the big guns. Not much I can do against magic, though."

"Don't kill anyone."

"They'll be fine," he said, and Sal heard the "probably" there.

Grace stepped into the light. Sal had seen her like this before: kindness, arch humor, and all the other human bits scoured down to underlying iron. "Once the relics come out, I'll do what I can."

Menchú raised his hands, then let them fall. "These people have trained with you. They know what you can do."

"No. They really don't."

"All of this is touching," Asanti said behind her podium, "and I love you all, but a few extra minutes won't matter. I won't send Sal through just to leave her trapped on the other side."

"I can help," said a voice Sal almost mistook for her brother's.

"No," Menchú said automatically.

"Are you crazy?" Liam said.

"I," Grace put in, "will cut you."

Asanti said nothing.

"You have the right approach," Aaron said. "But you don't have the power. I do. It's the least I can offer, after what you've done for me."

Sal watched the angel. "I thought you couldn't go home again."

"We're not going anywhere near my home. As far from it as possible, in fact."

Liam frowned. Grace held a knife—and she did not put it away. Menchú stared at Aaron, at Perry, in horror. Asanti, though—Asanti was still running the math, and she seemed to like the answers she found.

"What are you waiting for?" Sal said to Aaron. "Get in the damn circle."

2.

Sal held her brother's hand, and did not. Back when the thing beside her lived within a tour guide's body, a cut-rate mysterious figure in jeans and a company logo T-shirt, she'd wondered how Father Menchú could claim angels were terrifying. Aaron wasn't terrifying, though he sometimes showed her terrifying things. But what was Aaron, anyway? He lived as a whisper, a dance of spirit in a tour guide's blanked-out brain, and then jumped from the guide to a Swiss Guard, then into her brother's body, and each time stayed the same and each time changed. He hadn't betrayed her yet, but the *yet* mattered.

Though this touch, hand in hand in the magic circle, was a betrayal all its own, because when she held his hand, years of childhood memory screamed to her she held her brother's.

And yet her brother was not here.

Asanti chanted. Sal tried to grasp the divisions between one word and the next, but the sounds slipped from her mind like small, smooth rocks through her fingers. The cavern walls throbbed with rhythm, or candle flame, or both. Resonant frequencies, the archivist had said.

Beyond the circle, Liam reviewed his defenses from his laptop, activating hidden cameras and pressure plates. Beyond the circle, Grace prepared herself for battle. Beyond the circle, Menchú fetched equipment and adjusted dials as Asanti called instructions. They were fighting, she realized, for her, as much as for themselves. Even now, with the evidence they'd gathered, they could turn themselves in, and fight the cardinal in council chambers. Maybe they'd have less chance of succeeding without her, but not so much less. They put themselves in danger for her.

The words that spilled from Asanti's mouth, the shadows licking the cavern walls, the staring audience of skulls—these lived; these breathed; these pierced the skin of language and small time into a part of the world that bled. The archivist's voice did not change rhythm, but Sal did—the metronome in her mind sped up. Her muscles were cello strings, and the chant bowed her.

"Ready?" Aaron said, with a calm assurance she'd never heard in Perry's voice.

She could not speak. When she opened her mouth, solid sound rolled in. But she could nod, and did, and then she fell into the heart of God.

Shah was reviewing her troops when the Team Two emissaries arrived. She'd grudgingly judged her own soldiers adequate—boots shined, weapons cleaned and cleared, crosses in place, they hewed to their catechism like schoolchildren with a nun watching. As well they might. Shah had one hell of a ruler.

The mismatched pair from Team Two did not belong. The tall one picked his way uncomfortably through her mobile command post, wheeling the round one in a chair. The round one sat, hands nested atop a wool blanket that concealed a stomach-turning tangle of legs. She'd worked with Desmet and De Vos for years and still lost track of who was who. Presumably, they knew. Then again, with Team Two, you never could tell. In recent months she'd heard them called Balloon and Stretch, though never to their faces, and the names fit. "Gentlemen."

"Corporal," the tall one said, and tipped his hat, as if Shah were some sort of lady. She didn't dignify that with a response. "Good evening. Looks like you're all set to go."

"Soon as the timer runs out."

"About that," the short one said. His voice bubbled wetly, and he laughed, though no one had made a joke. Shah recognized the dullness of painkillers. Balloon took an envelope from his inside pocket and offered it to her. "New orders from the cardinal."

"This isn't the cardinal's operation, gentlemen."

"The cardinal," Stretch said, "wouldn't dream of micromanaging. But this is a strategic matter. He wants you to go in now."

Shah nodded to the clock. "They have thirty minutes, and the reliquary isn't here."

"They have a demon-possessed woman down there, and a critical artifact. If you give them as much as an hour, they'll use both against you. Team Three has no intention of surrendering. Our path is clear." Stretch stroked her chart table, checked his gloves for dust, and then leaned back against the table. They wore black suits and white shirts. If one of Shah's old instructors had asked her to describe the worst possible camouflage for a night battlefield, she might have settled on that uniform. "Go in now."

"I spoke with Menchú," she said. "He seemed in control of his own faculties. And he had some very interesting things to say about your group—and the cardinal."

Balloon's mouth crinkled up at the corners. "Did you listen?" he asked dreamily.

"No."

"Good," he said. "Demons have a strong influence on the mind. They make people see things, say things. Believe things. Menchú might not be possessed himself, but the demon's warped him with its lies. That's why these people are dangerous. They're strong in faith, and they have a monster in their midst, but . . ."

Stretch picked up as Balloon trailed off. "Fortunately, we've just put the finishing touches on a new, better tool." She wondered if they rehearsed, or they'd simply worked together so long that they lived in each other's heads as much as in their own. She'd had a partner like that once, who died. Stretch reached into his jacket, asked her permission with his eyebrows. She did not shoot him, which he seemed to take as an endorsement. From his inside coat pocket, he produced a black metal cylinder with three needles at one end, and a red gem at the other. "The mark one demon detector. Be careful with that."

The gizmo weighed more than she expected. She held the gem to the light.

"Press it to a suspect's heart," Stretch continued. "If the crystal lights up, she's possessed. Liquidate, with all possible speed. If it doesn't, you're in the clear. One shot, so don't test it. Uses a saint's knucklebone for a filament, and we don't have enough of those lying around."

"Enough that we're sure are real," Balloon corrected. "Plenty of knucklebones in general, but few of 'em are authentic. We're not making new saints fast enough to go wasting the ones we've got."

Shah frowned. "Why am I just hearing about this now? We could use it in the field."

"Mark one, like I said." Only Balloon hadn't been the one to say it, she realized. "Experimental technology. This is as close as we've come to a production model. This is an important case, Corporal. We're pulling out all the stops on our end. Do your job."

Shah would have cursed if she thought it would make any difference. The two men waited and didn't even have the dignity to look expectant. She supposed they were used to waiting.

She left her post. "Move up the clock," she called to her aide-de-camp, and then, to the troops still checking their equipment: "Point team goes in five, people. Get it together."

Even in Shah's few clockwork missions, the last couple minutes had been a scramble; so much more, then, when she was forced to speed up her timetable. No wonder, in the swarm of uniforms and buzz of gear, that she missed a brief exchange between Balloon and Stretch, left alone in the command post.

"Saint's knucklebone. Really."

"I thought it sounded better than 'a battery and an LED.'"

"Amazing what you can do on the cheap these days."

"Yeah, 3-D printers are wonderful things."

"We'll have to remember this trick."

"Oh, trust me. I think it has a lot of potential."

Let's orient.

That great, unblinking, billion-pupiled eye—hurts to meet its gaze—pierces your soul and spreads like a surgeon's calipers until you, staring into it, feel yourself naked and known, until you quake and weep and scream all your secret shames because it's better to cry them out loud where anyone can hear than to let that gaze pull them from you—why not call that the sun, and the rippling skin in which it's set, colorless and tense, name that sky. Oh, yes, the folly of it bends the knees, the joke's in vomit-worthy poor taste, because the existence of those *things* you don't want to call sky and sun makes you want to curse, to scream, to spit into that eye and plunge your fingers into its blue sclera and claw and claw until the jelly runs out, and by thinking that way, by pulling concepts like *sky* and *sun* over those horrors, you're in some way kneeling beneath it, allowing it, surrendering to it—but what choice do you have?

Don't stare into the sun.

You can't fight something that large.

Yet, Sal added, and thinking that, was once again herself, at least in general outline. She tore her mind from false sun and false sky. She lay on hard barren ground that wasn't ground. She heard a heartbeat somewhere far beneath the cracked dry surface, and a periodic rush as of running water, and rejected all the other terms that suggested themselves for the thing like ground on which she sprawled.

She tried to sit up. Ropes of grass had grown over her in the timelessness as she stared into that eye, and the teeth of its edges bit her when she pulled against it. The grass-blades' tips, she saw, were forked, like tongues. They wriggled. Wind hissed through the dry field—she hoped that was wind.

With a roar, she pulled herself upright. Tightening grass cut, but was not strong enough to stop her—she popped it free of the soil and ignored the blood that dropped from its translucent roots. She still held the *Book of the Hand* to her chest, good, she could move, yes, and Aaron—Perry—

She almost couldn't see him, because he was so bright. He burned, here, like an overexposed film elf, or a moth Icarused aflame. Things not entirely unlike wings sprouted from his shoulders and writhed against the ground; the grass that crisscrossed him seemed grown from ink. He let out an incoherent groan and sank deeper into the not-really-soil.

Sal swept the *Book of the Hand* through the grass. Inky strands parted. Aaron dampened back into Perry's body, tore himself from the soil, and scrambled to his feet, sweat covered, scared, and cursing. She caught him in her arms and held him until he stopped shaking, and dammit, that whole time he felt exactly like her brother.

After a while, he recovered enough to draw back from her. He still stumbled when he tried to walk alone. "Thank you," he said. "I could not."

Apparently the list of things he could not do included finishing that sentence.

Sal laughed at the thought. This wasn't the place or time for levity, but what other weapon did she have against this enormity but humor? "We're fine" felt like an even worse joke—or was that irony?

"We have to find Perry," she said. "Somehow. Any ideas?"

"We could follow that," he said, and pointed, shakily, toward her chest.

Sal looked down.

She hadn't, yet.

She didn't think she'd been avoiding it on purpose, but—

Worms of fire filled her. Beneath her parchment skin they writhed and twisted and wove into a hand around her heart. More worms roped her to the book beneath her arm and wound from the book out behind her over rolling mounds of something—not skin, not flesh, not a *body*, because no body could possibly be this large—to a tower of broken bone.

Hello there, the Hand said.

And then Sal realized the fire inside her hurt.

She screamed, and fell toward waiting tongues of grass.

Perry caught her—no. Aaron. Aaron caught her. Held her.

"We can do this," he said. "You can."

His tone turned a key in her spine. Her molars ground. She shoved him back. "Of course I can. Let's end this."

Shah's advance squad did everything by the book. Despite an apparent lack of external defenses, they crept across the lawn, shadows rolling from cover to cover past a sculpture garden and the lake until they reached the villa. Entry occurred from the front and rear doors simultaneously, as well as through the garden window. They cleared the house in thirty seconds. Flashlights swept dark rooms. HUD maps worked perfectly, comms clear, thermals good to go.

Flanked by two soldiers offering covering fire, the point man advanced to the double bookcase in the villa's parlor and examined the bookcase for a few silent minutes. He removed the *Divine Comedy* translation on the third shelf top left, adjusted a crucifix on the middle shelf, right, and swapped the positions of *L'Aiguille Creuse* and *The Quantum Thief.*

Then he collapsed, the floor beneath his feet having become briefly but intensely electrified.

"I thought you said no casualties," Menchú said in the caves below. He watched the camera feed on Liam's monitor, so he did not have to watch Aaron and Sal in the center of the circle. They were not precisely hovering, but they were not precisely lying on the ground, either.

"He'll be fine once he wakes up," Liam said. "I can control the voltage from here. And then there were nine."

The advance team killed the power to the house and tried again.

"And then there were eight," Liam said. "Really, did they think I'd run my toys off the main grid?"

"Don't get cocky."

"Nothing wrong with a little joy in the Lord's work, I'd think, Father."

The advance team got smarter—tore up the floorboards, found the power cables connected to the hidden door, and clipped them. Without power, of course, they had to pry the bookcases apart by hand, straining against hydraulics. They propped the doors with a couch and descended the winding stair two by two, three turns round into the labyrinth.

They consulted the maps on their wrist displays, turned left, then right, then left again. Comms fuzzed out. Annoying, but not dangerous—visual contact maintained. Straight for a hundred steps, until a shaped charge collapsed a section of tunnel, trapping half the group on one side, half on the other.

"And then there were—hmm, two groups of four? Doesn't sound right."

The hindmost group consulted their maps: "There's a longer way around. We'll link up at the seventh junction." No one noticed that their maps had changed in the confusion of the collapse. There were many tunnels under the villa. And when the hindmost team turned one particular corner, a stone wall slid into place behind them, and their maps blinked off and on again.

"And then there were four."

Menchú shook his head. "When did you install *that*?"

"Hobbies, like I said."

The final four were harder. They noticed the trip wires. Liam caught one with a tranq dart to the neck. "Lucky shot," he admitted. "But I'll take it." Grace rolled her eyes.

But the last three avoided the trapdoor and noticed the next time Liam changed their maps. He killed their lights and electronics, but they kept coming, feeling their way down tunnels in the dark. "Persistent bastards." He blew the tunnel in front of them, at last, and they stopped moving. "As well they should. Can't see, can't speak, can't trust the floor, can't retrace their steps. They'll hold tight for now. And then there were none."

"Not bad," Grace said.

"Not bad? *Not bad*, you say—ten of Team One's finest out of commission without a drop of blood shed, just me at my keyboard, and *not bad* is the thanks I get. Why do you hate genius, Grace? Why not recognize a master in his own time?"

"Celebrate," Menchú said, "when we get out of here." He tapped the top left screen, the grounds surveillance. "Looks like the reliquary's arrived."

"Well." Liam closed his eyes and drew a deep breath. "Fuck."

Sally, Sally, Sally, said the Hand as Sal and Aaron staggered toward the bone tower—staggered, because with every step the grass grew over their feet and twined up their ankles, and with every step they ripped it free. The uprooted blades trailed red fluid Sal didn't let herself call blood. *You don't want this.*

"Pretty sure I do," she said under her breath, hoping Aaron wouldn't hear. He glanced at her, concerned—but without Perry's edge of surprise.

We make a good team, I think. We could work together. There's room in this body for the two of us. Sort of.

The tower of broken bone jutted from the flesh plane. Slit windows marred its surface high overhead, and red light burned beyond them. From within, she heard screams that sounded almost human. The cord of fire ran from her chest, through the book, and beyond, through the bone tower's enormous closed double doors. "The Hand showed me Perry's prison—and this doesn't look anything like it."

"Our world doesn't work like yours," Aaron said. "You don't have the right concepts for it. Each time you approach, your mind stitches the pieces it can grasp into a new fabric. The reality doesn't change, but you can never see the reality, just images."

"How can I change anything, then, if I can't see?"

"How do you change anything in your world?"

"There, I know what's real."

"You don't. You make models and approximations all the time. You think surfaces exist—they don't. You think geometry's real—it isn't. You believe the person who went to sleep last night is the same as the person who wakes up in the morning."

"None of that changes how I live," she said. "Geometry won't help me save my brother."

Neither will he.

"Trust what you see here, as much as you trust your senses back in your world."

"I hate philosophy."

Aaron shrugged, and Sal resisted the urge to punch him. She marched to the doors instead, and knocked three times. "This is Detective Sal Brooks of the New York City Police Department. I'm looking for my brother. Open up, or I'll open you."

Nothing happened, except another scream from within.

Dammit. Trust your senses, huh? She glared at the fiery cord passing through a gap between the doors. She touched the cord, felt around its burning edges. She forced her hand into the hole, braced her legs against the ground and tugged. No use. The doors remained stubborn and still.

Her fingers slipped, and she fell against one of the doors. Behind her, the not-blood trail had vanished. She liked that even less.

Another scream. Perry's voice, in pain.

Maybe if you set the book down. Pull with both hands.

She nearly did it, too—she was that angry, scared, desperate, and the thought had been perfectly pitched so it almost seemed her own. But she stopped herself.

Can't blame a guy for trying.

She could, but didn't want to waste the time. "Help me," she told Aaron, and guided Perry's hand to the gap. He pulled, and she pulled, but the doors stood firm as cliffs. Her arm quivered, her back strained, her feet tore red furrows in the ground, and at last the doors sheared open.

She almost fell. Shadowgrass reached out for her, and she swatted it away with the book.

Red light rolled out, and bore them in like the tide.

Thavani Shah watched her advance team feeds go dark one by one. She winced at the electric floor. She cursed when she found her voice did not reach the team's ears. Doyle, no doubt—and she wondered if he did not know about the video feeds, which her predecessor, may the poor man rest in peace, had added to the standard kit shortly before his death. Then again, maybe Doyle did know, and wanted her to see him take her team apart. "Clever," she said after the map switch. The final darkness was a letdown, but she did recognize and appreciate—however grudgingly—that Doyle had not actually hurt anyone. He even shied away from tricks that *might* have killed them—no deadfalls that might have left a soldier bleeding out from a broken femur.

He showed mercy. Or he was afraid. He knew how far Shah would chase him if he killed her people, how little forgiveness would follow. Or maybe, remembering Menchú's plea, he meant to send a message: We're all on the same side here. We should not be fighting. Who are your real friends, and who your enemies?

She ordered her divers to the lake.

Stretch watched, arms crossed, over her shoulder. She glowered back at him. "Can you not do that?" But he feigned confusion as to what she'd meant. Balloon cleaned his cuticles with the tip of a nail file. Shah did not even try to remember the last person she'd seen use a nail file.

"There's no water access to the caves," Stretch said.

Shah nodded. "I know."

"I understand your reluctance, Corporal. Team Three is a hard group to beat, but no one wants to use the devil's own tools against him."

"Still, we can't help but notice that the reliquary has arrived."

"And we doubt Doyle's preparations can account for . . . extraordinary matériel."

The video feed died, finally. Shah stared into static snow. "I'm still waiting for clearance from the cardinal."

"Did we forget to say?"

"I suppose we did." Balloon drew a piece of rolled parchment from his jacket and handed it to Shah. She didn't need to open it. She recognized the seal and the texture. "Apologies. You seemed intent on handling matters your way."

Or they'd hoped the Team Three defenses would push too far, that one of her advance team might die—and when her knights went down into the labyrinth, they'd be seeking vengeance.

Her orderly returned, and he, too, recognized the document she held. "Tell the heavies to suit up," she said.

His hand shook as he snapped his salute, but she didn't mention it, or blame him.

3.

F ive knights marched toward the abandoned villa. Armored from head to foot, no two looked alike: One wore a mask of thorns, one a curved mirrored plate where her face should have been. One wore mail, one a fluttering multicolored coat bright with gems, one flowing robes that flapped and floated in the light breeze yet left deep gouges where they brushed the ground, as if the hem was a blade and the fabric weighed ten thousand pounds.

They entered the villa. The lead knight stepped on a pressure plate, and electricity arced through her, high voltage, furious. It danced along her skin and gathered into a small fluttering sphere in her palm. She let the sphere go; it discharged into the walls. The woman with the mirror mask pinched salt from a pouch on her belt and tossed it into the living room. The room died. Silence fell. Small noises ceased, barely audible hums and whirs of air-conditioning, water heater, hidden motors and security systems—all failed.

Soundless, they descended into the labyrinth.

The lead knight's glove glowed dimly as she neared certain turns, and those turns, she took. The others followed her. Ground opened beneath their feet, but none fell. The lead knight dug her fingers into the wall; the second vaulted catlike over the drop; the third did not break stride, her sandals as steady on empty air as they would have been on a battlefield. The fourth followed—his robes darting out like spider legs to span the gap and dig pits into the walls. No one saw the fifth cross.

Darkness did not trouble the knights. None of them needed light to see.

Behind her thorn mask, the lead knight prayed. She did not like the relics she used. Guns she understood, and knives, rockets, bombs. But the relics scared her. She trained with them; it was an honor to be so trusted, and the relics themselves had been studied, scoured by generations of archivists. They did not taint the soul. They did not tempt, or taunt. No one ever claimed they did. There were not even barracks stories about relics whispering to the unwary. No matter how well told, the joke would hit too close to home.

The relics kept her safe. She confessed each time she used them, subjected herself to the most rigorous observation afterward.

Still, she prayed.

The tunnel collapsed on top of them. The second knight swung her net and swept the falling rocks away.

Near the labyrinth's end, they found the way blocked by stone. The fifth knight grasped the rock and pulled it like taffy to make a door.

So close, now.

The leader strained, like a hound, for the prize, and hoped it was really her straining.

The armor moved about her like a second skin.

When the fifth knight finished reshaping the stone wall, she led them through.

There, in a damp round chamber lined with sarcophagi, stood Grace Chen.

Echoed chanting filled the room. Water dripped from budding stalactites.

They moved.

Sal found Perry pinned open in the center of the bone tower.

When the tide of light had dragged Sal and Aaron in, at first she'd thought to follow the screams—but she could not follow them, because they came from everywhere. Bone walls echoed cries of pain. Sal thought, feverish, following the fiery cord through the maze, that she might be screaming herself.

Turn and turn and turn through the bone tower. She wondered how she'd ever find her way out again. After a long time she risked a glance back, thinking Lot's wife, thinking towers of salt, thinking Orpheus. Behind her, the high-ceilinged hall ran straight a hundred feet to the open doors and the skin-field beyond.

They found Perry soon after.

Someone had opened him from collarbone to groin, and shucked half the skin and muscle of his chest and stomach, pinning it like a butterfly's wing to the table on which he lay. Silver pins held his arms to the table, and his feet. Another long, thin pin pierced his neck. His chest rose and fell. His heart, she could *see* it beat.

He was not dead.

She ran to him. Open eyes darted and rolled, staring at nothing or everything at once—then locked on her face. Pupils tightened. She wanted to be sick. She would not let herself be sick, would not let this place do that to her.

Aaron swore. His native language sounded like cut flowers.

"Perry," she said. "Come on. Let's get you out of here."

She forced her gorge down and touched the pin through his neck.

—*held to the blacktop, choking on his own blood, with the other boy on top of him as the fists came down and he can't breathe and he can't breathe and he can't—*

She pulled her hand back.

"Sal," Aaron said. Not her brother. This was her brother on the table, if she could just get him out. "Sal."

None of this is physical. Remember that. Perry wouldn't have survived this long, pulled open like this, in the physical world. Your mind's grasping for categories, shuffling stuff that doesn't make sense into shape.

When she'd found Perry in the demon world before, he'd had so few memories—because his memories were being used to bind him here.

"Sal!"

Her eyes burned, and she couldn't breathe. She wiped her eyes on her sleeve. Bubbling shapes had risen from the skin fields outside the tower, viscous and ruby red, lurching forward on splashing pseudopods. Well. She'd wondered what had happened to the trail of blood.

"I can free him," she said. "But I need time."

Bloodshapes bubbled into the hall. They burbled and roared.

"I'll see what I can do," Aaron said, and her brother's shoulders sprouted wings.

Sal turned back to the body—no, to the soul—on the table. Speared through with silver needles in vital organs, which she was sure meant, in this dumb crazy sideways spirit logic, that he was locked by moments he could not let go. Behind her, Aaron joined battle. The sounds made no sense—searing screams, noises that were colors, impacts that washed over her like heat and made the walls ripple and flex. She ignored it all and grabbed the silver needle.

—blood in his mouth, he couldn't breathe, raised his hand to ward off the falling fists—

Her gritted teeth widened into a smile. This one was easy. She wouldn't even have to lie.

—and then he's free, and the bigger kid's beside him on the blacktop, staring up, bleeding from his mouth, and a pigtailed seraph's standing over them both, with a rock in her hand and a look on her face like: Yeah, just you fucking dare get up—

The pin slipped from her brother's throat. She remembered how the rock had felt, striking Bobby Gunnel's head. She'd been grounded for a month after and had to sit through a long lecture about proportionate response, but the moment of impact? Worth it. Seraph, huh?

Perry always had a flair for the dramatic.

She tossed the pin behind her and did not hear it land.

The walls stopped screaming.

"Sal?"

Goddammit, she was crying. *Okay. Keep it together; keep it cool.* "I'm here, Perry."

"Sal, it hurts."

"I know." She kissed him on the cheek, on the forehead. When she drew back, her shirtfront was bloody. "Come on. Let me help."

You're not, you know, the Hand said. *Helping.*

She ignored it and reached for the next pin.

Grace let herself go.

Fights have their own math, a slow balancing of strengths,

weaknesses, reach, speed, risk tolerance, intent. *What's my motivation?* matters almost as much in combat as on the stage. A fencer five points up plays with a different tempo than her opponent, rejoicing in the space to improvise, locking down on defense and trying the odd edge case attack because there's room; a fighter recovering ground sifts chaff for the true golden opening. Situation awareness is more than physical pathfinding. It's deeper than vantage points and ambushes. The internal landscape harbors as many traps and pitfalls as the outside world. Step wrong and you'll collapse.

Grace did not like the magic Asanti worked behind her. She did not like the angel, or whatever, in Sal's brother's skin. There had been so many bad decisions in the last few days, so many mistakes. They'd slipped, time and again, from handholds over a precipice, and still they fell.

But she could stand between her friends and the sword.

Team One's knights trained with their tools. They used relics collected over centuries, tested and purified. They were surgeons of surpassing skill, wielding blades fine and sharp as whispers—but they were still people holding weapons.

And Grace was herself a weapon.

She rushed the first knight, ducked her gauntlet—wreathed in fire and so strong a grazing blow could shatter steel—dislocated the woman's arm from the shoulder, kicked out her knee, and moved on to the robed figure even now clearing the hole they'd opened in Liam's barricade. She caught her about the waist and twisted her whole body—she flew, but her robes splayed and dug into the stone, turned her round, darted tendrils toward Grace. She danced between them and hit the woman in the throat, then jumped back toward the door to deal with the third. The first knight was still falling.

She couldn't keep this up for long. She only had so much candle—only so much life. But that was true for everyone, really. At least she could choose how to spend it.

Sal pulled the needle from her brother's peeled-back chest and tossed it over her shoulder with the others. It fell, soundless. One left—through the breastplate into Perry's heart. His hands had fallen limp when she unbound them, his legs the same. With each needle removed the beast within her chest tightened, and the cord of fire strained thin and taut as a rubber band about to snap.

Sal Brooks, goddammit, think about what you're doing here.

Behind her, the fight continued. Aaron cried out in a voice like Perry's but deeper, mixed with drums or an eagle's cry or a horn or all of the above. She did not look back. The bone tower changed around her as she unpinned her brother's soul. Was this whole place her brother's body? If so—

She forced the thought away and reached for the pin.

Do you really want to kill him?

"I'm freeing him," she said. "From you."

Oh, yes, the Hand replied. *Freedom. Where do you think he'll go, when you pull out that pin?*

She hesitated.

What body's left to him?

"His own," she said, knowing she was wrong.

The body your angel friend's riding now? The one he can't let go?

"They'll share."

Your friend's not the sharing type. Even if he was, there's no room in that body for two. You and me, we get along just fine, because most of me's out here, beyond your world. *I just need to burn out a space in you to fit my . . . hand. So to speak.* It laughed at that. *But your buddy, he's all in.*

"You're lying."

I would, the Hand admitted. *For fun, or to mess with you and yours. But you know I'm not. You pull that pin, and dear darling Perry pops free, out into the world you love to call real, finds his body full, then . . . Well. What do you think happens to people when they die, Detective Brooks? Really die, I mean. He'll find out.*

Fucker. Trying to shake her, dull her edge, break her nerve. No way it was telling the truth.

But she didn't reach for the pin.

The Hand lied. *Had* lied. It'd lie now to save itself, to protect its investment—in her, in her world—or just to hurt her. But its voice in her head had a self-assured and vicious edge. This wasn't a poker player daring her to call. It was showing an ace-high straight.

"Aaron," she said.

"A bit busy now." His voice heavier and thicker and older than her brother's.

She turned around.

An Escher confusion of blood and light twisted and twisted in her head, like one of those Magic Eye illusions only all screwy, shapes locking in, manifesting, shifting, breaking apart again. "Aaron, is the Hand right? Perry dies when I set him free?"

"You'd rather he live here? Suffering like this?"

"Answer my fucking question. Does he die?"

"Sal, we can't let the Hand loose. It's evil. It's immortal. It's incredibly powerful."

She wanted to kill someone. She didn't care who. "Is it telling the truth?"

The confusion of blood and wings said, "Yes."

4.

When the last knight fell, Grace slowed down, and heard applause. Behind her, two knights who'd been flying or falling through jellied air struck the ground in quick succession and did not rise; the first knight, whose neck Grace held in the crook of her elbow, flailed one final time and passed out.

She let the knight fall and looked up at Thavani Shah. The woman stood just outside the cave entrance, and she bore no relics that Grace could see.

"You're good," Shah said. "I think you've kept from us exactly *how* good."

"Under-promise and over-deliver, right?"

"That's the idea." Shah laughed. "I'm giving you a last chance to stand down."

"I won't give up my friends."

"I don't want to have to stop you."

"You can't."

Shah shrugged. And—

Grace saw a twitch in the other woman's forearm—the arm

leaning against the wall, out of sight. She thought, *Remote control*, and burned, and moved—

She was fast, but not faster than the shock wave. Rocks fell, and water behind the rocks, as the lake overhead emptied into the cave. Grace dove for Shah, but the waterfall pressed her down, tossed her up, turned her in a whirlpool slurry, and she gasped for breath that did not come.

Shah didn't have to wait long for the water to drain. She'd done her homework—no sense drowning her objectives, or her own team, for that matter. Romans had built these tunnels; they understood drainage. The shock wave and surprise mattered more than the actual flood. Grace was fast. Maneuverable. But so were flies—which was why people invented the flyswatter.

She waded through the sludge, drew a syringe from her shirt pocket, and injected Grace with a sedative. Inelegant, but she didn't care. She checked her knights: alive, barely. Waterlogged. Ngo would not walk again for a while. Possibly not ever without a limp.

The rest of the team joined her, followed, at last, by Stretch, who wheeled his partner through the water, walking tenderly as if he hoped to spare the shine on his shoes. She wondered how he'd convinced her men to help him carry his partner through pits and deadfalls. She weighed the demon detector in her hand. "Come on. Let's end this."

"No," Sal said. "I didn't do all this just to watch him die."

"Sal." The more he spoke, the more she could see him in the center of that Escher whirl. "I can't give up this body."

"You lied to me."

"I didn't. I just—"

"Find another way. Let him in."

"There is no other way."

"Make one."

The fire that coursed through her was only partially her own. The Hand laughed. She ignored it.

"There's not enough room in this body for both of us."

"Then make yourself smaller. Or get the hell out. Or else I'm not pulling this pin."

"Then your friends die. And you die. And the Hand wins."

"The Hand stays right here with Perry and me. And you. I bet you have something you want to do back on Earth, don't you? Something you want really badly. Or else you wouldn't have needed us. So—you get him back, or we all stay right the fuck here, with the Hand. Should be fun. Maybe the demons will pin us all to those tables side by side."

"I—" His voice broke. "There's a way. But it's not—we can't both fit in here together. Not like we are. But we can combine. I can let him into me. Not two people, not a host and a rider like you and the Hand. One person."

"Fuck," Sal said.

"I can't leave this body without killing it. That's done. But this way you get a part of your brother back, at least."

She wanted to murder him. She wanted to say no. She wanted to stay here and fight this out, set this whole impossible place on fire until some other solution presented itself. And let Grace and Asanti and Liam and Menchú die.

No.

She did not want that.

Goddamn.

"Do I have your word?" she said.

"Yes."

She was crying. She did not care.

She seized the final pin.

—*and he's run from colleagues and friends and Bookburners and criminals to land here, in his sister's living room, with the* Book of the Hand *on the coffee table before him, upon a nest of T-shirts. Blood clouds warp and mist on the cover's pale leather surface. No. He knows what human skin looks like, by now. He's learned that, as he's learned too many things he wishes he could forget.*

Voices at the door. Sal's there, trying to protect him. "Sir, I'm a police officer, and I'm armed." She doesn't know these people, what they'll do to him, what they might do to her. He'd hoped he could escape them, but he wasn't fast enough, wasn't strong enough, wasn't smart enough. He never has been.

But you could be, *the book whispers.*

He's frozen, and someone pounds against the door, but time slows and sound reaches his ears warped. The book has plenty of time to talk.

You can hear me, *it says,* stronger now. You know what I can do. You've wanted this, in your every moment of weakness. Power without fear. Strength and independence. Accept me, and I'll save you, and save her, too.

He knows how the next part goes. He touches the book. Opens it. His tongueless mouth gapes, and he weeps blood tears. He is power. He is pain.

He is power and pain forever.

But Sal—

Sal's not fighting. She walks toward him, ignoring the Bookburners, lowering her gun. "Perry. You don't need him."

No, she doesn't understand, he has to save her for once, to save them both, and without the book he's weak, so weak, he knows what they do to people, everyone knows. The book's the answer, the book's the truth, he knows it is because it tells him so in a language only they can speak, they understand each other, the book and him.

And Sal continues to refuse the script.

"I'm here for you. We can do this. Together."

Her hand drifts toward him. His hesitates over the book cover. Red mists shape in anticipation of his touch.

He ignores them, and reaches for her.

Somewhere, a scream—

5.

Sal woke, free.

For months she'd borne the Hand, its fingers slithering around her heart and weaving through her brain stem, unawares—for months ignoring its hooked gentle whispers in her ear. She felt fiercely light, and she heard a ringing silence. Sal was Sal again, and joyous.

Then memory caught up with her.

She woke, free, yes, in a chalk circle, to the pound of booted running feet. Her first attempt at speech produced a hacking cough before her lungs remembered how to fill. Someone shouted words she did not recognize. She couldn't even place the voice. Grace, maybe? Half-conscious, she reeled to her feet, staggered across the silver circle, and blinked her eyes into focus.

"I said, freeze!"

That, Sal understood.

Also, the guns.

Team One troops ringed the far wall of the chamber, crouched, aiming. Laser sights danced over Liam's computer, over his chest.

A dot rested on Father Menchú's collar. Three darted across Asanti's face. The archivist seemed more annoyed than unnerved. Sal looked down. Five dots burned on her own bloodied shirtfront.

She understood, then, how Asanti felt.

Corporal Shah stood at the room's entrance, behind her troops, and beside *her* stood Stretch, wheeling the wreck of Balloon in a chair. Sal's guts seized at the sight of them. She filled with anger, or was that fear? They tasted about the same. She remembered a wooden table and stars overhead.

"Back for more?" Sal said. "Convincing Corporal Shah to do your dirty work?"

"You escaped custody," Balloon replied.

"You're possessed by a demon."

"You misled your teammates."

"There's no end to your lies and wickedness."

Sal wanted to argue, wanted to strangle each of them in turn, but didn't spare either Balloon or Stretch a glance. Shah watched her with the patience of a guillotine. "Corporal. These men tortured me. They've killed others. They, and the cardinal, have been spying on all of us and conspiring to cover up their crimes. Liam's computer has the proof: a recorded confession."

"Recordings can be faked," Stretch said.

And Balloon continued: "So can eyewitness testimony."

"If a demon is involved."

"As one is, in this case."

"The demon's gone," she said. "I kicked him out. That's what all this is—real exorcism, not torture. No one has to die today." She hoped. God, she hoped. Perry lay in the circle behind her, unmoving. She wanted so badly to check on him, but those gun sights pinned her with coherent light. "Don't you see? We won."

"She's telling you what you want to hear."

"The enemy's lies know no bounds."

"The enemy will stop at nothing."

"Sal," Menchú said, "is telling the truth."

Asanti nodded. "We all heard the cardinal's confession."

"And even if we hadn't," Liam said, "I have the recording right here."

"The demon's turned them all."

The firing team crouched. Sal could not see faces beneath or behind those plastic visors. "Where's Grace?"

"Safe," Shah said. "Unconscious, but well. Better than I can say for the soldiers she tried to stop from reaching this chamber. You inspire a particular loyalty, Ms. Brooks."

"Take us back," Sal said. "Put us on trial. We'll tell everyone what we know." If the case ever came to trial. If they did not disappear into some cell somewhere. And how much work would Balloon and Stretch need to do before any of them would confess to anything?

"And give your team more opportunities to escape, and the demon inside you another opportunity to strike at the Vatican."

"You're being used. This isn't what you were meant for. We have a duty to protect people, and you've been drawn into their sick power games instead. Once they have their claws in you, they'll never let go."

"Fortunately," Shah said, "we have another option." Shah removed a tube of black metal from her pocket. Three needle-sharp prongs capped one end, a ruby the other. Sal did not at all like the expression on Balloon's face when Shah produced the device. "You've just volunteered, Ms. Brooks, to be the first field test subject of Team Two's demon detector."

"Demon detector?" Asanti scoffed. "We've tried for centuries to build one, without success."

"Team Two claims to have solved the problem. This is, they

say, a working prototype. Gem lights up, you're corrupted."

"They're lying. Do you have any proof it works?"

"Frankly, Archivist, I don't think you and your team are in much of a position to accuse anyone who hasn't broken into the Vatican of anything. Ms. Brooks, you understand what I'm offering."

Sal did. Pass the test, and Team Three goes free, evidence believed, all debts paid. But she wouldn't pass. There was no such thing as a demon detector. If they had the technology, they would have used it on her. What, then?

Say she failed. Say that gem glowed from within. Say she launched herself at Shah, tried to kill her. Say she went down, shit, in a hail of bullets while resisting arrest. Her guilt would be clear; the others could claim the demon controlled them. Beg off. Survive. Maybe.

Slim odds, but better than the odds they faced now.

"Do it," Sal said.

Menchú shouted, "No!" but when he began to move, more lasers swung to his chest. Asanti's hand settled on his shoulder.

"Come on." Sal glared at the corporal. "Let's get this over with."

The firing team parted before Shah's advance. She marched forward, grim and inevitable. "Kneel."

Sal glared pure hatred into her, but Shah didn't seem to notice. Sal knelt.

The corporal drew her sidearm, and leveled it at Sal's head. She set the detector on the floor between them, and circled counterclockwise. Her first shot would take Sal through the temple.

"Place the needles over your heart. When you're ready."

The demon detector was lighter than Sal expected. She positioned the needles. She tried to plan what she would do when the gem glowed, but now there was so little time left, she could not quite fit everything she wanted to do inside it. Perry was back, at least, or a part of him. The team would be safe. And the world.

That counted for something.

She plunged the needles into her chest, and waited for the killing light.

But the jewel stayed dark.

"Interesting," Shah said, and shifted aim. "Mr. Desmet. Mr. De Vos. Please do not move. I would not enjoy shooting you." Sal heard an unvoiced "much" in that sentence.

Sal forced herself to stop staring at the gem and look up. The firing team had swung their rifles round to Balloon and Stretch.

"Insane."

"Preposterous."

"You really think—"

"I think," Shah said, over and through their protests, "your own device seems to have exonerated Ms. Brooks. Which lends new weight to her team's accusations. Don't you agree?"

Sweat ran down Balloon's cheek.

Stretch tried, for whatever mad reason, to run. Shah's gun spoke once. Stretch fell and screamed.

"He'll be fine," Shah said, and offered Sal a hand up. "Come on."

"What . . ." was all the question Sal's numbed mind could frame.

"They couldn't even rig a decent fake." Shah drew a nine-volt battery from her pocket, tossed it up into the air, and caught it. "A weapon in their hands indeed. We have brains, you know." The battery vanished into her pocket. "Let's get you cleaned up. Oversight has questions, and you owe them answers. And me."

"Thank you," Sal said to Shah's retreating back.

Behind her, in the circle, Perry groaned, and sat up. "Sal? I dreamed—"

Before he could finish, she was there.

EPILOGUE

S al found Asanti swearing in the Archives.

"Can you believe this mess?" The demon invasion and their own break-in had left the orderly maze of piled manuscripts a swamp. Sal waded through leather-bound tomes and tried not to step on any scrolls. They might snap. "And you haven't even seen inside the secure vaults. I can't believe those morons didn't let me back in earlier."

"They hadn't formally decided we weren't evil yet."

"Evil or not, this is damned inefficient." Asanti strained to lift a book with a snarling face embossed into the cover and deposited it with a thud on Liam's desk, which had ended up miraculously clean after the chaos, all its loose papers knocked to the floor. "We need every second to reassemble the collection. Looks like my grand-nephew's bedroom in here, only with less Kleenex everywhere." She blew dust off the book's cover. The growling face twitched, wrinkled its nose, sneezed, then resumed its mute snarl. Asanti stroked its forehead. "Not to mention tracking down what's lost. The vaults were unsupervised for seventy-two hours; I don't even know what's missing from the deep catalog yet. Now Arturo's on parole, I hope he understands that top priority for us, in the near future, will be to track down the absent volumes. Five hundred years of archivists thinking of this as a black box—I barely even know what we *had*, let alone what's gone. And the farther I get into deep storage, the more vaults I find. If my predecessor knew how much was down here, he didn't tell me." One of her braids had come loose; she tossed it over her shoulder. "Not your problem, though, I expect."

"What do you mean?"

"You joined to save your brother, and you got him back. The Society hasn't exactly treated you like family—or, if they have, I'd rather not know the details of their family lives. Why stay?"

"The cardinal's gone," Sal said. "Balloon and Stretch, too. Court-martialed, disciplined, exiled, imprisoned, whatever. We won, in case you hadn't noticed."

"Still."

"And Sansone's cleaning house in Team Two. I don't buy the a-few-bad-apples story any more than you do, but the council's given her a big broom, and she's using it. She's one of the good guys, or she would never have helped you rescue me. I don't know if I'll ever be comfortable here, but this is as clean as the Society's likely to get."

"Balloon and Stretch imprisoned you. Tortured you. Would have killed you. Did kill others. They didn't do that on their own." Asanti reached for a book, which snapped at her fingers. She caught its covers closed and bound them with a leather strap. "If I were you, I might see myself elsewhere."

"And miss all the fun?" Sal shook her head. "What would you do without me?"

Asanti set down the book. "You really are staying." She covered her smile almost as quickly as it appeared. "Good. I'll need a stronger back than mine to open the lower vaults."

"I wondered," Sal said, "if you had any books about angels."

Somewhere, a young boy runs screaming down the hallway of an enormous mansion. He does not remember what he's running from. He cannot bear to turn his head and look. But whispers catch his ears like thorns—slight, sharp whispers in tongues he does not know—and those whispers and those tongues build nests beneath his terror. He does not understand their promises.

The boy does not know that all hallways end.

The boy does not realize that the smartest monsters know where you'll run, and wait.

The boy will learn.

A man carries a book into a pub in the Seven Dials in London. He meets a woman there. They talk, over drinks; she touches his arm, flirting.

When last call comes, the bartender decides to wake the man sleeping at the corner table. He is not asleep. The book is gone. So is the woman. The coroner, later, finds five white dots on the man's arm—positioned correctly for a human hand, but printless and unbruised.

In a dark, dry room, someone lights a candle.

✦ ✦ ✦

Sal made it home by sunset, hip-checked the door closed, and dumped her keys into the bowl. "Perry, you'll never believe what I found." Just saying those words out loud, and knowing she could expect an answer, felt warm.

"Decent pizza?"

She set the stack of books down on the kitchenette counter. Perry sat on her couch, backlit by setting sunlight. Comatose months had left him pale and shrunken even compared to his pasty, skinny baseline, but he looked better, if not exactly *good*. "We had pizza last night."

"Doesn't taste like back home."

"What, like Domino's? This is the good stuff. Keep an open mind. I asked Asanti about angels—we're still not sure *what* Aaron is, was, but she had a few books that might shed a little more light on the situation."

"Yeah," Perry said, apologetic. "Sal, I wanted to talk to you about that."

"What's up?" She circled around the counter and sat on the couch. He didn't look like he wanted to be touched—drawn into himself, wound tight. Hands together, long fingers interlaced.

"I keep having these dreams, you know?"

"Angel dreams."

He nodded. "I think Aaron, he— I—I think there was some crazy shit going on with him. Some reason he needed a body, some stuff he wanted to finish, stuff he would have, might have finished if you hadn't . . . forced him to let me back in. I'm thinking, maybe I should look into that. It's only fair, right?"

She gripped her own wrist. "I'd be careful, if I were you. There's a lot more to magic and demons than you think, even now. We're only just starting to learn what's out there. Now our names are clear, Menchú's argued us a wider mandate. Maybe we can look into some of these . . . angel dreams of yours."

"Yeah." His head bobbed on his neck. "I figured you might say that. It makes a lot of sense. I'm not sure why I need to do this alone. I just feel it somehow, you know? Deep down?"

"Hey," she said. "Stick with me. I busted you out of hell. There's nothing we can't do so long as we're together."

She tried to set her hand on his shoulder, but her fingers passed right through.

When he looked up at her, his eyes were clear and pale as ice.

"I'm sorry," he said.

And he was gone.

ACKNOWLEDGMENTS

No book is an island, and that goes double for madcap serial story-telling adventures. Together, we'd all like to thank Julian Yap, Molly Barton, Leah Withers, and the rest of the Serial Box team for their spirit, support, and ideas, in particular Mark Weaver and Jeffrey Veregge for the chilling episode covers, and of course Marco Palmieri and Noa Wheeler for brilliant editing and copyediting.

BRIAN would like to thank Julian Yap for believing that he could write like this, and Margaret, Max, and Mur for teaching him how. Thanks to New Haven, Connecticut, for being the kind of town where, as a local musician put it, people play Frisbee over a mass grave. Finally, thanks to his agent, Cameron McClure, and to the coffee bean.

MARGARET would like to thank Max, Mur, and Brian, who welcomed her into the tribe with open arms, and especially to Julian, who was a very good sport about the number of note cards a writers' room requires. Additional thanks to all the Shamers for their unflagging support and community carbs. And finally, to her manager, Joe Riley, who never hinted that he'd rather she write another pilot instead.

MAX would like to thank Brian, Margaret, and Mur for joining up into crazy storytelling Voltron and making something cool, and for being patient while he learned to outline. He'd also like to thank Jessie, Danny, Emily, and the city of Montreal, Canada, without whom none of this might have happened. Margaret, thanks for the note cards. And, Steph, thanks for all the usual stuff, which is to say, everything.

MUR would like to thank Margaret, Max, Brian, and Julian for being wonderful to work with and teaching her so much. Especially about the note cards. Thanks to her ever-patient agent, Jennifer Udden, and her even-more-patient family for keeping her sane from project to project. Thanks to the listeners of her podcasts, without whom her career would be nothing. Special thanks to Max and Steph for hospitality during writing meetings and blizzards.

THANKS ALSO and always to the great team at Saga Press for the volume you hold in your presumably hot whatever-size-they-are hands—to Navah Wolfe, editor most intrepid; to Jeannie Ng and Brian Luster, for copyedits; to designer Michael McCartney and jacket artist Marko Manev for making us all look so damn good; and to Faye Bi at Vorpal Publicist +5.

And finally—thanks to all our readers, for coming along for the ride. See you next season!